D1261890

MIKE MIGNOLA'S
B.P.R.D.
HELL ON EARTH
VOLUME 4

THE DEVIL'S WINGS
STORY BY **MIKE MIGNOLA** AND **JOHN ARCUDI**
ART BY **LAURENCE CAMPBELL**

THE BROKEN EQUATION
STORY BY **MIKE MIGNOLA** AND **JOHN ARCUDI**
ART BY **JOE QUERIO**

GRIND
STORY BY **MIKE MIGNOLA** AND **JOHN ARCUDI**
ART BY **TYLER CROOK**

FLESH AND STONE
STORY BY **MIKE MIGNOLA** AND **JOHN ARCUDI**
ART BY **JAMES HARREN**

EXORCISM
STORY BY **MIKE MIGNOLA** AND **CAMERON STEWART**
ART BY **CAMERON STEWART**

THE EXORCIST
STORY BY **MIKE MIGNOLA**, **CAMERON STEWART**, AND **CHRIS ROBERSON**
ART BY **MIKE NORTON**

COLORS BY **DAVE STEWART**
LETTERS BY **CLEM ROBINS**
COVER ART BY **LAURENCE CAMPBELL** WITH **DAVE STEWART**
CHAPTER BREAK ART BY **LAURENCE CAMPBELL** WITH **DAVE STEWART**,
VICTOR KALVACHEV, AND **DUNCAN FIGREDO** WITH **DAVE STEWART**

PUBLISHER **MIKE RICHARDSON**
EDITORS **SCOTT ALLIE** AND **KATII O'BRIEN**
ASSOCIATE EDITORS **DANIEL CHABON** AND **SHANTEL LaROCQUE**
ASSISTANT EDITOR **JENNY BLENK**
COLLECTION DESIGNER **PATRICK SATTERFIELD**
T TECHNICIANS **CHRISTINA McKENZIE** AND **CHRISTIANNE GILLENARDO-GOUDREAU**

DARK HORSE BOOKS

Neil Hankerson EXECUTIVE VICE PRESIDENT • Tom Weddle CHIEF FINANCIAL
Randy Stradley VICE PRESIDENT OF PUBLISHING • Nick McWhorter CHIEF B
DEVELOPMENT OFFICER • Matt Parkinson VICE PRESIDENT OF MARKETI
LaFountain VICE PRESIDENT OF INFORMATION TECHNOLOGY • Cara Ni
PRESIDENT OF PRODUCTION AND SCHEDULING • Mark Bernardi VICE PR
OF BOOK TRADE AND DIGITAL SALES • Ken Lizzi GENERAL COUNSEL • Dav
EDITOR IN CHIEF • Davey Estrada EDITORIAL DIRECTOR • Chris Warner
BOOKS EDITOR • Cary Grazzini DIRECTOR OF SPECIALTY PROJECTS • Lia
ART DIRECTOR • Vanessa Todd-Holmes DIRECTOR OF PRINT PURCHASIN
Dryer DIRECTOR OF DIGITAL ART AND PREPRESS • Michael Gombos DIRE
INTERNATIONAL PUBLISHING AND LICENSING • Kari Yadro DIRECTOR OF
PROGRAMS • Kari Torson DIRECTOR OF INTERNATIONAL LICENSING

Published by Dark Horse Books
a division of Dark Horse Comics, Inc.
10956 SE Main Street
Milwaukie, OR 97222

DarkHorse.com
Advertising Sales: 503-905-2315
Comic Shop Locator Service: comicsho

First edition: December 2018
ISBN 978-1-50670-654-2

10 9 8 7 6 5 4 3 2 1
Printed in China

Library of Congress Cataloging-in-Publication Data

Names: Mignola, Michael, author. | Arcudi, John, author. | Davis, Guy, 1966-
  artist. | Crook, Tyler, artist. | Fegredo, Duncan, artist. | Stewart,
  Dave, colourist. | Robins, Clem, 1955- letterer. | Campbell, Laurence,
  1969- artist. | Sook, Ryan, artist.
Title: B.P.R.D. Hell on Earth / story by Mike Mignola and John Arcudi.
Description: First edition. | Milwaukie, OR : Dark Horse Books, 2018- | v. 1.
  New World, Seattle, and Gods art by Guy Davis ; Monsters and Russia art
  by Tyler Crook ; An Unmarked Grave art by Duncan Fegredo ; colors by Dave
  Stewart ; letters by Clem Robins ; cover art by Laurence Campbell with
  Dave Stewart ; chapter break art by Guy Davis, Ryan Sook, Dave Johnson,
  Duncan Fegredo, and Dave Stewart.
Identifiers: LCCN 2017035913 | ISBN 9781506703602 (v. 1 : hardback)
Subjects: LCSH: Comic books, strips, etc. | BISAC: COMICS & GRAPHIC NOVELS /
  Horror. | COMICS & GRAPHIC NOVELS / Fantasy. | FICTION / Occult &
  Supernatural.
Classification: LCC PN6727.M53 B24 2018 | DDC 741.5/973--dc23
LC record available at https://lccn.loc.gov/2017035913

This book collects B.P.R.D. Hell on Earth volumes 10, 11, and 14.

By now our monsters have terrorized mankind long enough it's status quo, but John Arcudi always finds ways to make it very new and very human.

It's never been more human than in "Grind," a story that demonstrates the collaboration so special to *B.P.R.D.* We'd brought Tyler Crook on to be the main *Hell on Earth* artist, but the story had evolved in a direction that didn't suit him—we all knew the giant monsters and the military action weren't really Tyler's bag. But we wanted him to stay in the mix, so Mike came up with "Grind." When he told me the story, I said, "That's a perfect Arcudi story!" There was a pause on the other end of the phone, and I imagined Mike thinking, *You know I just came up with this, right?* John made it his own, with the kind of "sad monster" Tyler had acknowledged as his specialty. Tyler planned to follow this up with another *Witchfinder* book, but instead focused on *Harrow County*. We were glad he could leave *B.P.R.D.* on such a high note.

James Harren's *B.P.R.D.* swan song "Flesh and Stone" also plays to his strengths, returning to the prehistoric world he first drew in "Abyss of Time," while the Black Flame—which no one drew better than James—terrorizes New York, and Varvara terrorizes Iosif. If Howards wasn't already a favorite among readers, this story made him one. It also shows a key aspect of John's genius—his ability to build up the epic threads crucial to the finale, while keeping things grounded in a way other grand-scale comics often forget to do.

Eschewing subtlety for a minute, John brought in Joe Querio for a rare foray to the far east, pitting an Ogdru Hem against a kaiju, leaving nothing standing in a lesser-known Japanese metropolis. Joe wasn't the only new face working on the book this time around, though.

While this series is dominated by Lovecraftian themes Mike introduced in *Seed of Destruction*, he and I always sought to balance that with a classical take on the supernatural, so this volume is bookended with some biblical demons from Hell (which is where Hellboy is by this time).

In "The Devil's Wings," Kate Corrigan, current leader of the B.P.R.D., unearths a mystery that brings demons right into headquarters. Meanwhile, Agent Ashley Strode, who Kate sent on a throwaway mission, trains as an exorcist, setting her up for a crucial role later. . .

I'd gotten Cameron Stewart into the Mignolaverse by giving him fairly free rein. He wanted to establish a new female character, and picked Ashley, a young agent impressed by Liz Sherman in an Arcudi-written story in *Plague of Frogs* Volume 3. Cameron gave her the last name Strode in honor of Jamie Lee Curtis in *Halloween*. Mike coached him on the exorcism material—the traditional Catholic stuff, and cross-cultural influences per Ota Benga, a character Mike and Josh Dysart introduced in *B.P.R.D. 1946*. Cameron's first story came out in 2012, whereas most of the stories in this book came out 2014-2015. After that I kept asking Cameron to round out a trade paperback of Ashley stories, but he got too busy with *Fight Club 2* to do it. Chris Roberson—whom I'd recruited for *Witchfinder: City of the Dead* before asking him to replace Arcudi as our main *B.P.R.D.* writer—scripted Cameron's plot (including an abandoned central Oregon house Cameron and I had explored), joined by Mike Norton for his 2016 Mignolaverse debut.

Another major debut around this time was Katii O'Brien, who came on as Assistant Editor in May 2015. Katii interned at Marvel Comics and Candlewick Press before Lauren Sankovitch (then of Marvel, now with Milkfed Criminal Masterminds) recommended her. Katii quickly became a crucial member of the team, like the assistants before her, but her passion for the horror genre, great eye for story, and devotion to the creators—as well as hailing from the same swamplands of Massachusetts I came from—made her an ideal successor to the job I'd loved for so long. I hope she gets a couple good decades out of it.

Scott Allie

CONTENTS

THE DEVIL'S WINGS

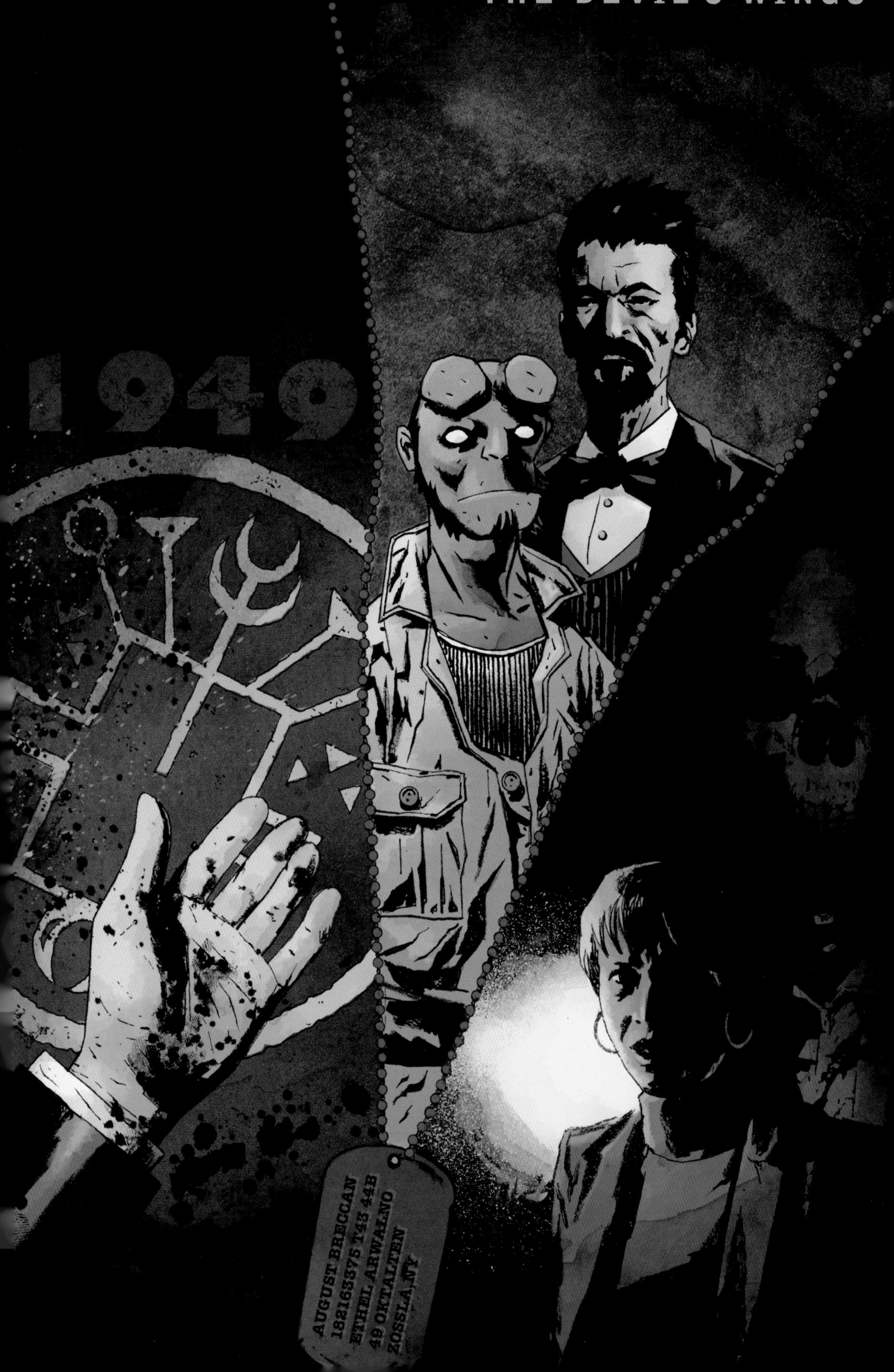
1949
AUGUST BRECCAN
18216337S T43 44B
ETHEL ARWALNO
49 OKTALTEN
ZOSSLA, NY

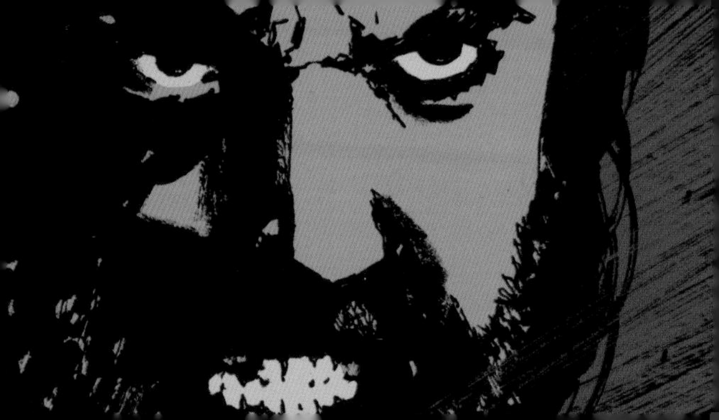

B.P.R.D. HEADQUARTERS IN COLORADO.

EXCUSE ME.

EXCUSE ME. WHAT'S HAPPENING HERE?

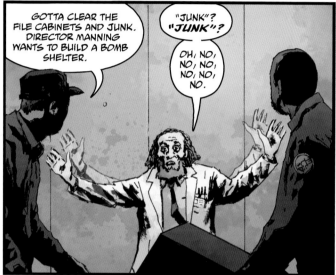

GOTTA CLEAR THE FILE CABINETS AND JUNK. DIRECTOR MANNING WANTS TO BUILD A BOMB SHELTER.

"JUNK"? *"JUNK"?*

OH, NO, NO, NO, NO, NO, NO.

NO, NO, NO, NO, NO, NO, NO.

I'VE BEEN DIGITIZING THESE FILES.

I'LL TELL YOU WHAT YOU DO. YOU BRING ALL OF THEM UP TO MY QUARTERS, YES? YOU'LL DO THAT?

UHH, YOU'RE THE BOSS.

11

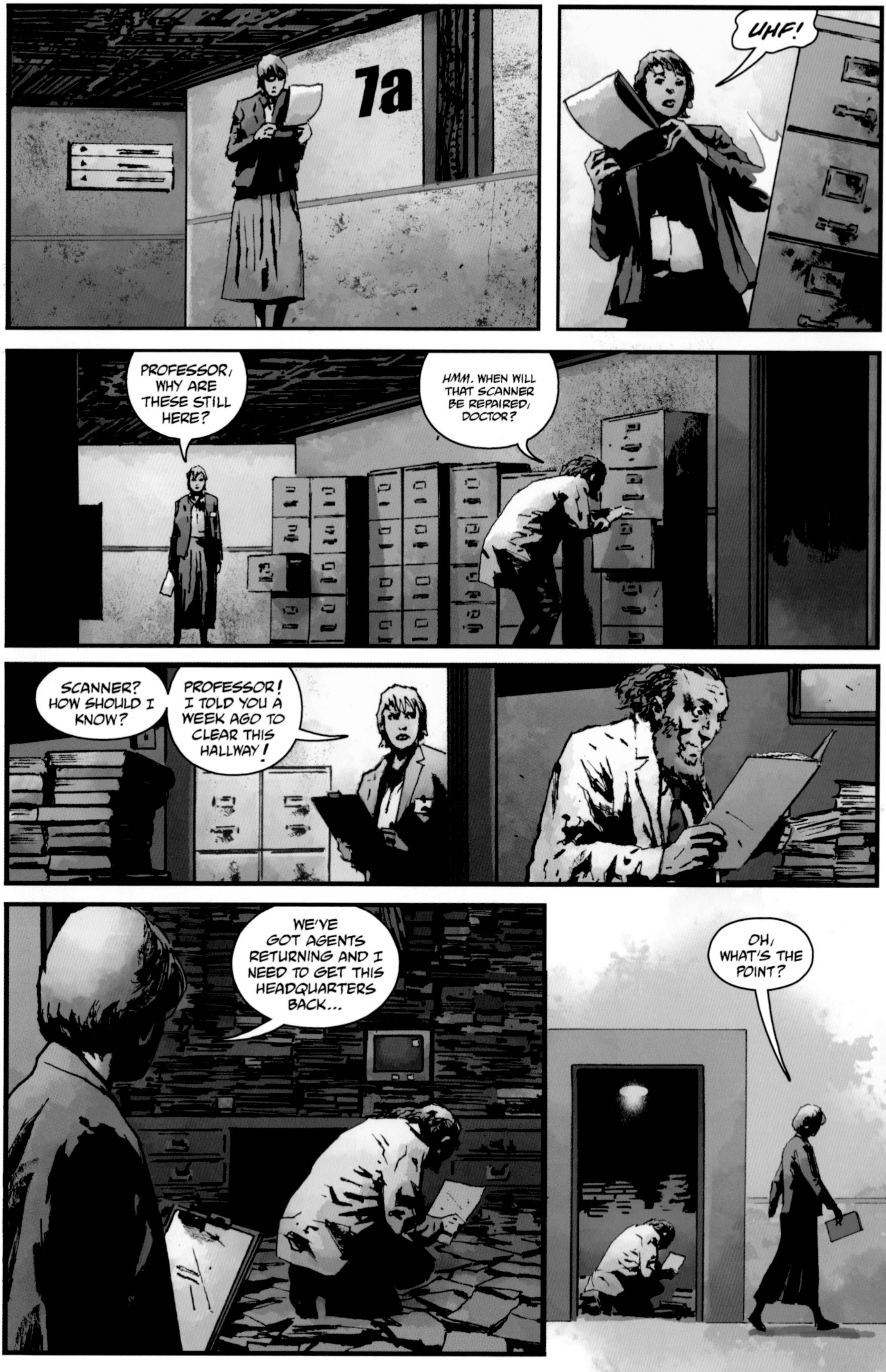
7a
UHF!
PROFESSOR, WHY ARE THESE STILL HERE?
HMM. WHEN WILL THAT SCANNER BE REPAIRED, DOCTOR?
SCANNER? HOW SHOULD I KNOW?
PROFESSOR! I TOLD YOU A WEEK AGO TO CLEAR THIS HALLWAY!
WE'VE GOT AGENTS RETURNING AND I NEED TO GET THIS HEADQUARTERS BACK...
OH, WHAT'S THE POINT?

AH, GOOD DAY, KATHERINE. ELIZABETH, CARLA, AND FENIX AREN'T IN YET, IF THAT'S WHY YOU'RE HERE.

I JUST HOPE LIZ ISN'T IN A WHEELCHAIR ANYMORE. SHE'LL NEVER GET THROUGH THOSE HALLS.

WHAT'S THIS? DOESN'T LOOK LIKE A NEWS FEED.

JOHANN HAS ENLISTED A NEWS TEAM IN JAPAN TO TRANSMIT DIRECTLY TO US.

I DON'T EVEN WANT TO KNOW HOW ALL THAT WAS MANAGED.

TO BE FAIR, IT'S A GENUINELY GOOD IDEA-- IN THEORY, ANY-WAY. SO FAR, IT HASN'T QUITE--

HELLO? I THINK THEY'VE SAID YOU SHOULD BE RECEIVING ME.

OH!

YES, JOHANN. WE ARE. WE HAVE VIDEO, ALSO.

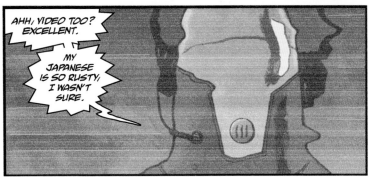

AHH, VIDEO TOO? EXCELLENT.

MY JAPANESE IS SO RUSTY, I WASN'T SURE.

...DIGITAL RECORDING... TEDIOUS...TEDIOUS-- AH, HERE IS A FILE ON AIR FORCE CAPTAIN AUGUST BRECCAN.

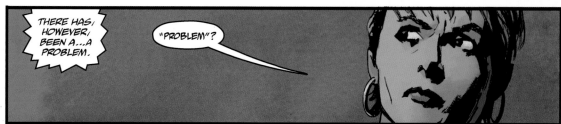

THERE HAS, HOWEVER, BEEN A...A PROBLEM.

"PROBLEM"?

AH, *THIS* IS RARE! THE CAPTAIN'S DOG TAGS ARE INCLUDED IN THE FILE.

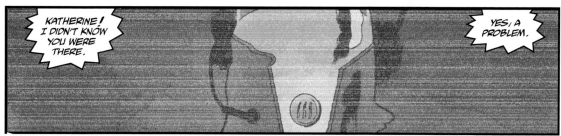

KATHERINE! I DIDN'T KNOW YOU WERE THERE.

YES, A PROBLEM.

--182163375 T43 44B, ETHEL ARWALNO--

G. FAUX, LT. U

...ure of Summary ...

...NG AUTHORITY

...RAVATED ASSAULT, INSUBORDINA...

...CT, ABSENCE WITHOUT LEAVE AN...

...T UNBECOMING AN OFFICER

request re...

...MANDI... OFFICER

...t to submit w...
...quest for clem...
...General.

AUGUST BRECCAN
182163375 T43 44B
ETHEL ARWALNO
49 OKTALTEN
ZOSSLA, NY

...MBER 1949

...Da...

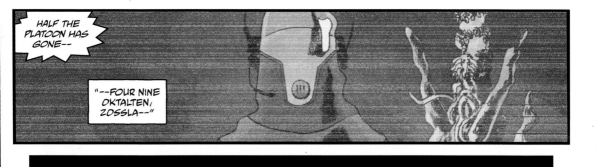

HALF THE PLATOON HAS GONE--

"--FOUR NINE OKTALTEN, ZOSSLA--"

ZEENK

SON OF A...

ANOTHER DAMN POWER OUTAGE?! REALLY?

PANYA, DO WE STILL HAVE RADIO CONTACT WITH MAINTENANCE?

PANYA?

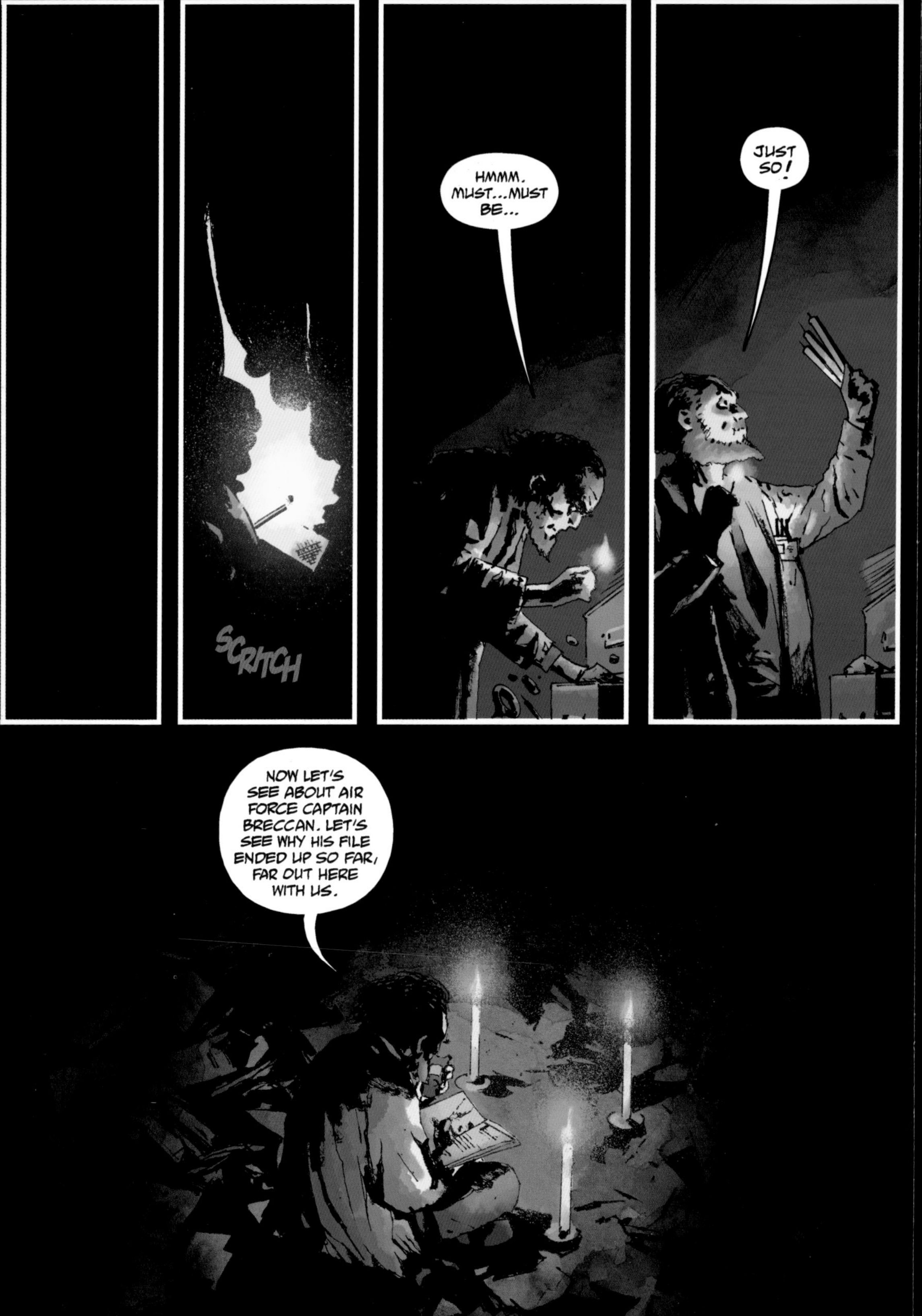
SCRITCH
HMMM. MUST...MUST BE...
JUST SO!
NOW LET'S SEE ABOUT AIR FORCE CAPTAIN BRECCAN. LET'S SEE WHY HIS FILE ENDED UP SO FAR, FAR OUT HERE WITH US.

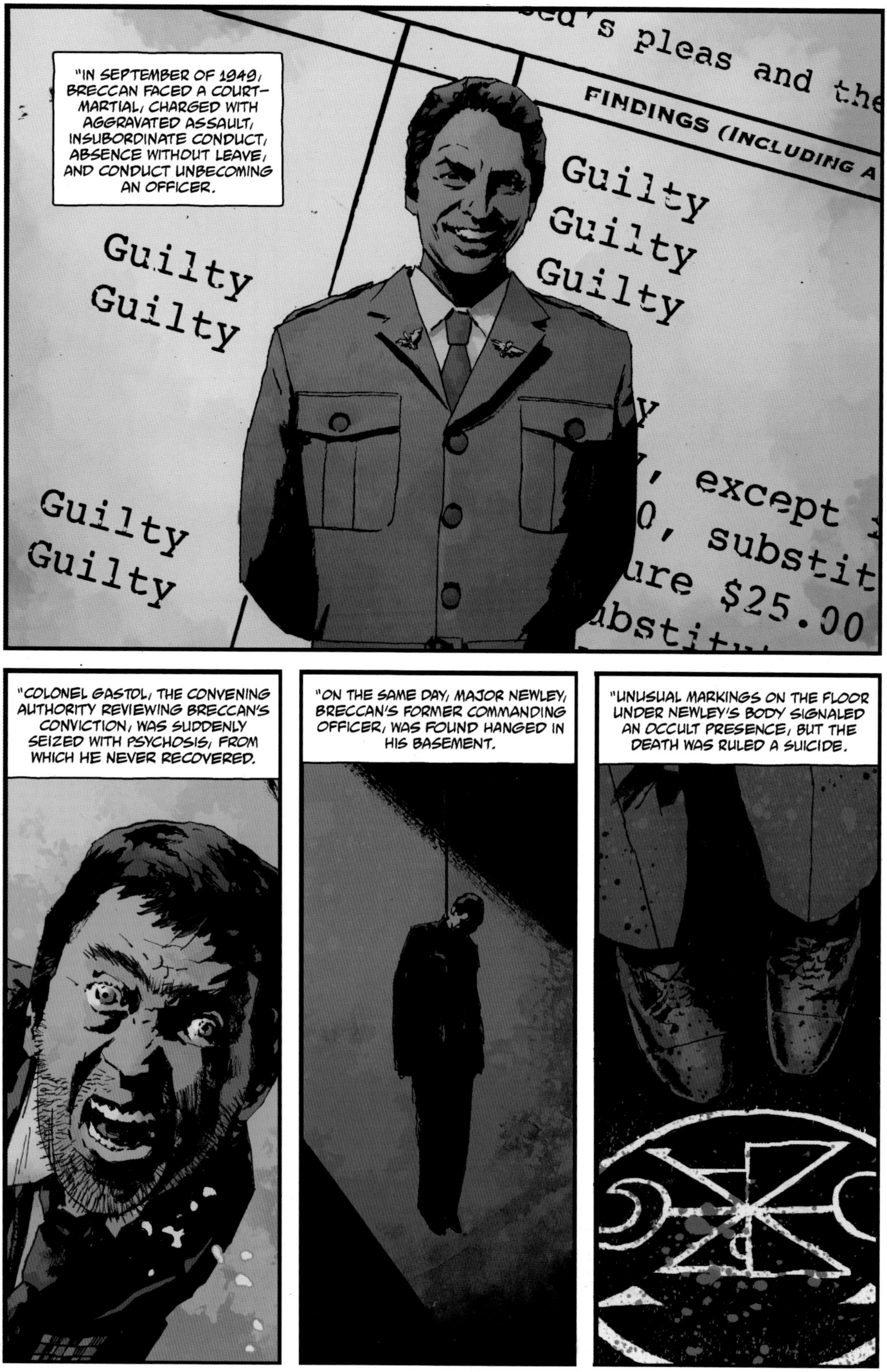

"IN SEPTEMBER OF 1949, BRECCAN FACED A COURT-MARTIAL, CHARGED WITH AGGRAVATED ASSAULT, INSUBORDINATE CONDUCT, ABSENCE WITHOUT LEAVE, AND CONDUCT UNBECOMING AN OFFICER.
's pleas and the
FINDINGS (INCLUDING A
Guilty
Guilty
Guilty
Guilty
Guilty
Guilty
Guilty
, except
, substit
ure $25.00
"COLONEL GASTOL, THE CONVENING AUTHORITY REVIEWING BRECCAN'S CONVICTION, WAS SUDDENLY SEIZED WITH PSYCHOSIS, FROM WHICH HE NEVER RECOVERED.
"ON THE SAME DAY, MAJOR NEWLEY, BRECCAN'S FORMER COMMANDING OFFICER, WAS FOUND HANGED IN HIS BASEMENT.
"UNUSUAL MARKINGS ON THE FLOOR UNDER NEWLEY'S BODY SIGNALED AN OCCULT PRESENCE, BUT THE DEATH WAS RULED A SUICIDE.

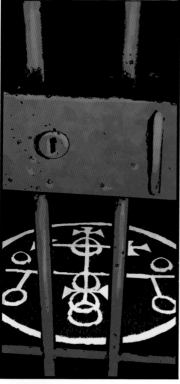

"CAPTAIN BRECCAN'S MIRACULOUS ESCAPE, HOWEVER, RAISED CONCERNS AIR FORCE OFFICIALS COULD NOT IGNORE.

"SECRETARY OF DEFENSE JOHNSON SUGGESTED A CONSULTATION WITH THE BUREAU FOR PARANORMAL RESEARCH AND DEFENSE.

"THE AIR FORCE'S SKEPTICISM WAS BRUSHED ASIDE BY JOHNSON, WHO, DURING THE WAR, HAD BEFRIENDED THE BUREAU'S DIRECTOR--

"--PROFESSOR TREVOR BRUTTENHOLM."

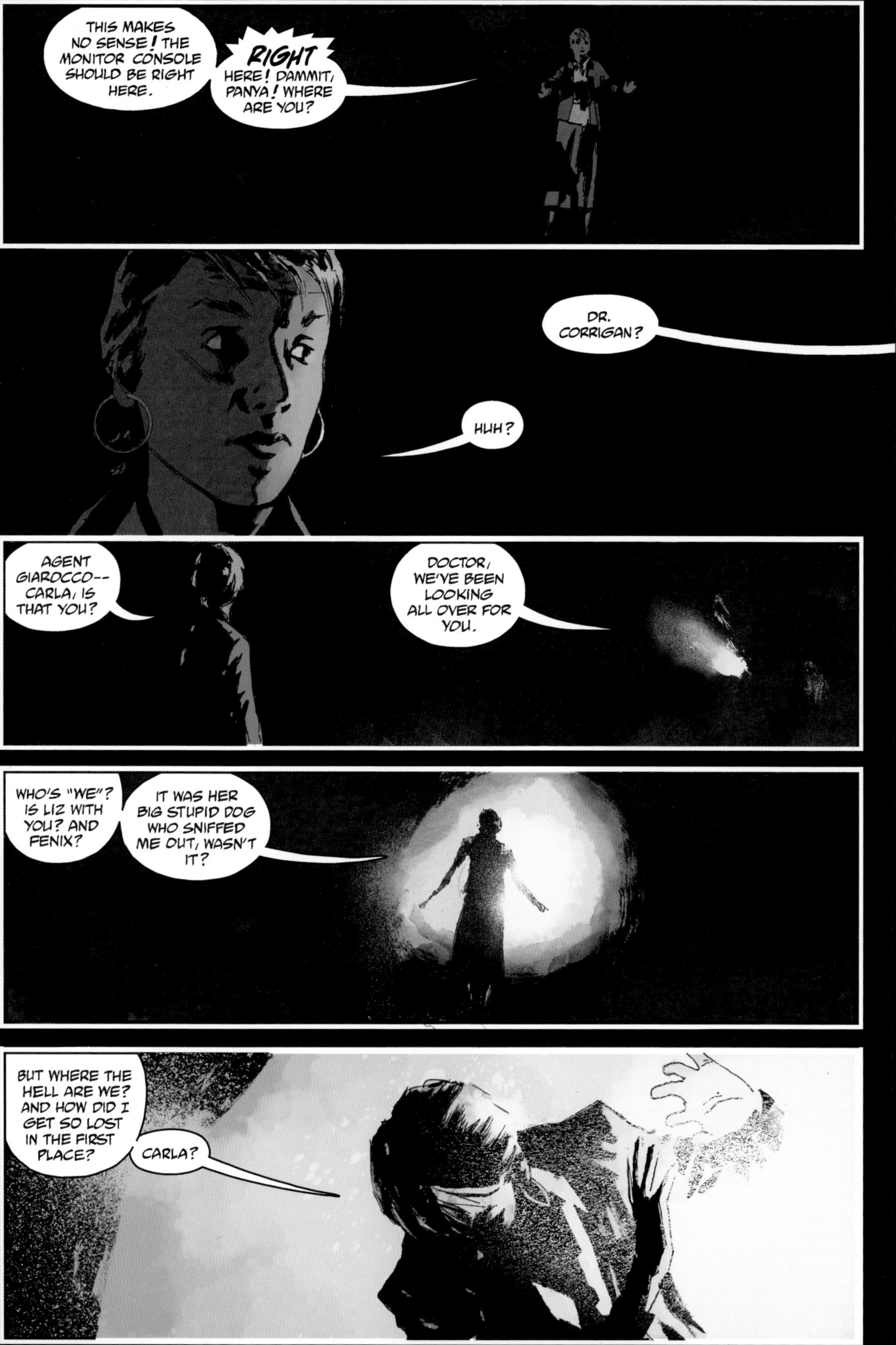
THIS MAKES NO SENSE! THE MONITOR CONSOLE SHOULD BE RIGHT HERE.
RIGHT HERE! DAMMIT, PANYA! WHERE ARE YOU?
DR. CORRIGAN?
HUH?
AGENT GIAROCCO-- CARLA, IS THAT YOU?
DOCTOR, WE'VE BEEN LOOKING ALL OVER FOR YOU.
WHO'S "WE"? IS LIZ WITH YOU? AND FENIX?
IT WAS HER BIG STUPID DOG WHO SNIFFED ME OUT, WASN'T IT?
BUT WHERE THE HELL ARE WE? AND HOW DID I GET SO LOST IN THE FIRST PLACE?
CARLA?

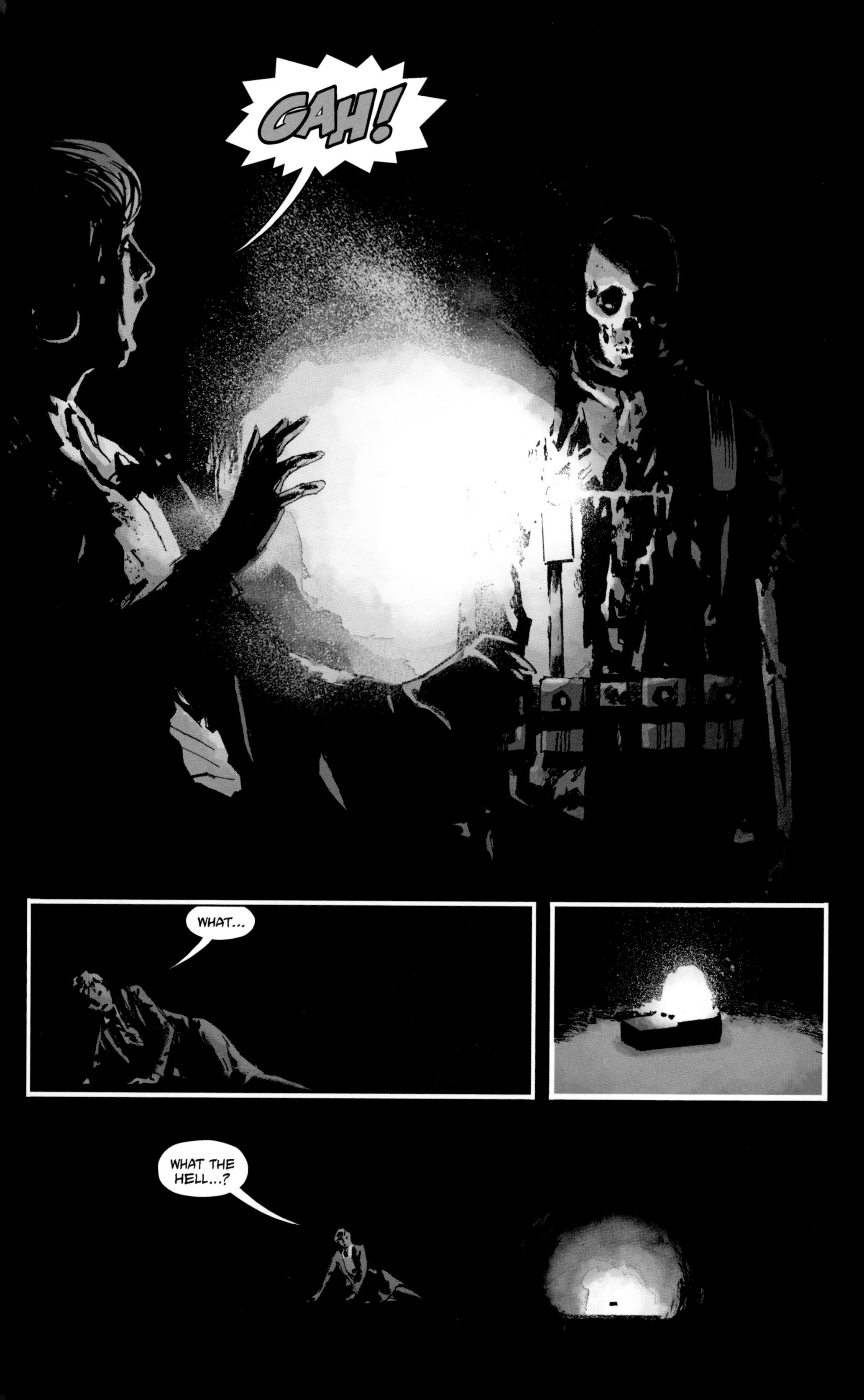
GAH!
WHAT...
WHAT THE HELL...?

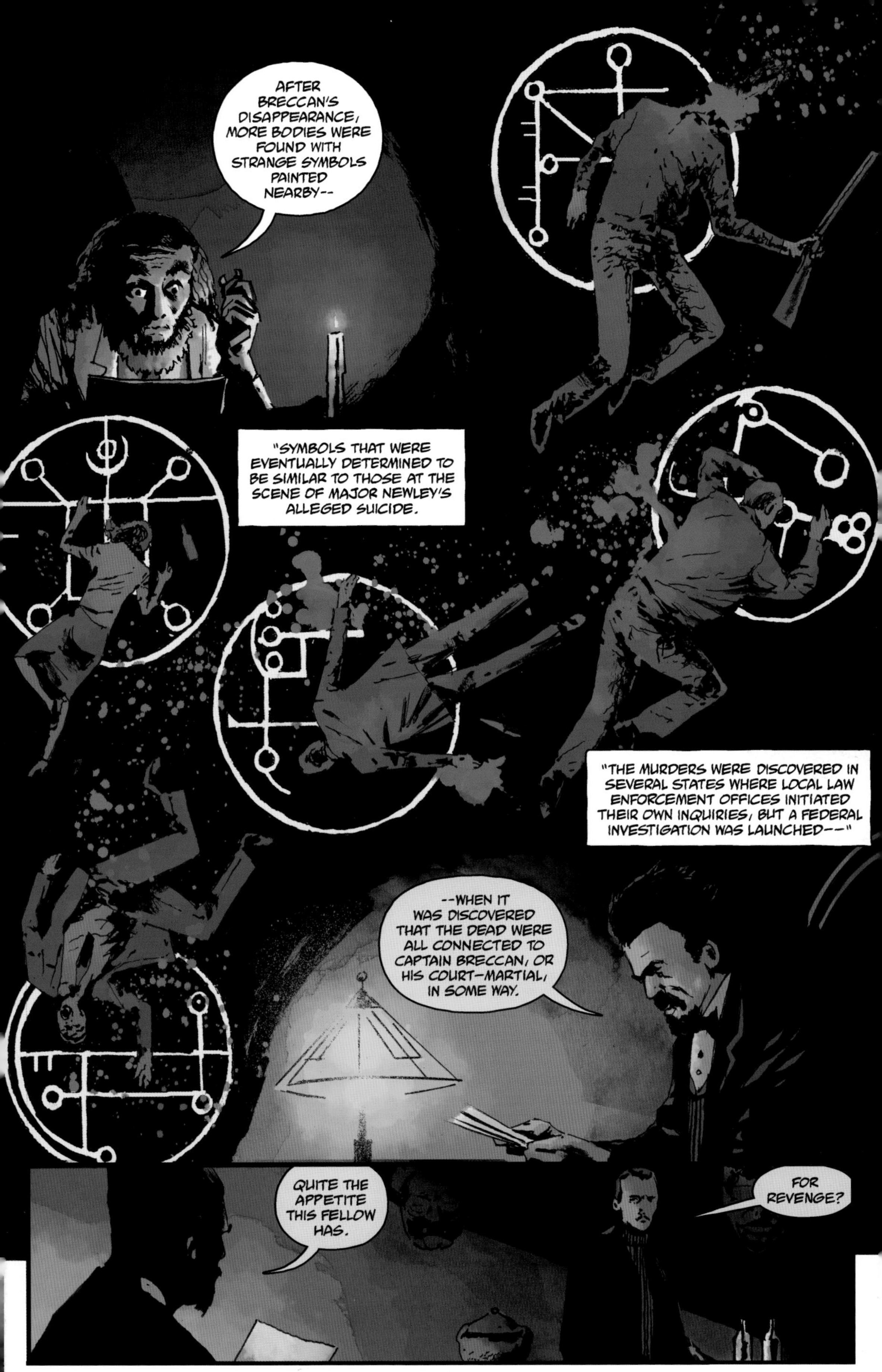
AFTER BRECCAN'S DISAPPEARANCE, MORE BODIES WERE FOUND WITH STRANGE SYMBOLS PAINTED NEARBY--
"SYMBOLS THAT WERE EVENTUALLY DETERMINED TO BE SIMILAR TO THOSE AT THE SCENE OF MAJOR NEWLEY'S ALLEGED SUICIDE.
"THE MURDERS WERE DISCOVERED IN SEVERAL STATES WHERE LOCAL LAW ENFORCEMENT OFFICES INITIATED THEIR OWN INQUIRIES, BUT A FEDERAL INVESTIGATION WAS LAUNCHED--"
--WHEN IT WAS DISCOVERED THAT THE DEAD WERE ALL CONNECTED TO CAPTAIN BRECCAN, OR HIS COURT-MARTIAL, IN SOME WAY.
QUITE THE APPETITE THIS FELLOW HAS.
FOR REVENGE?

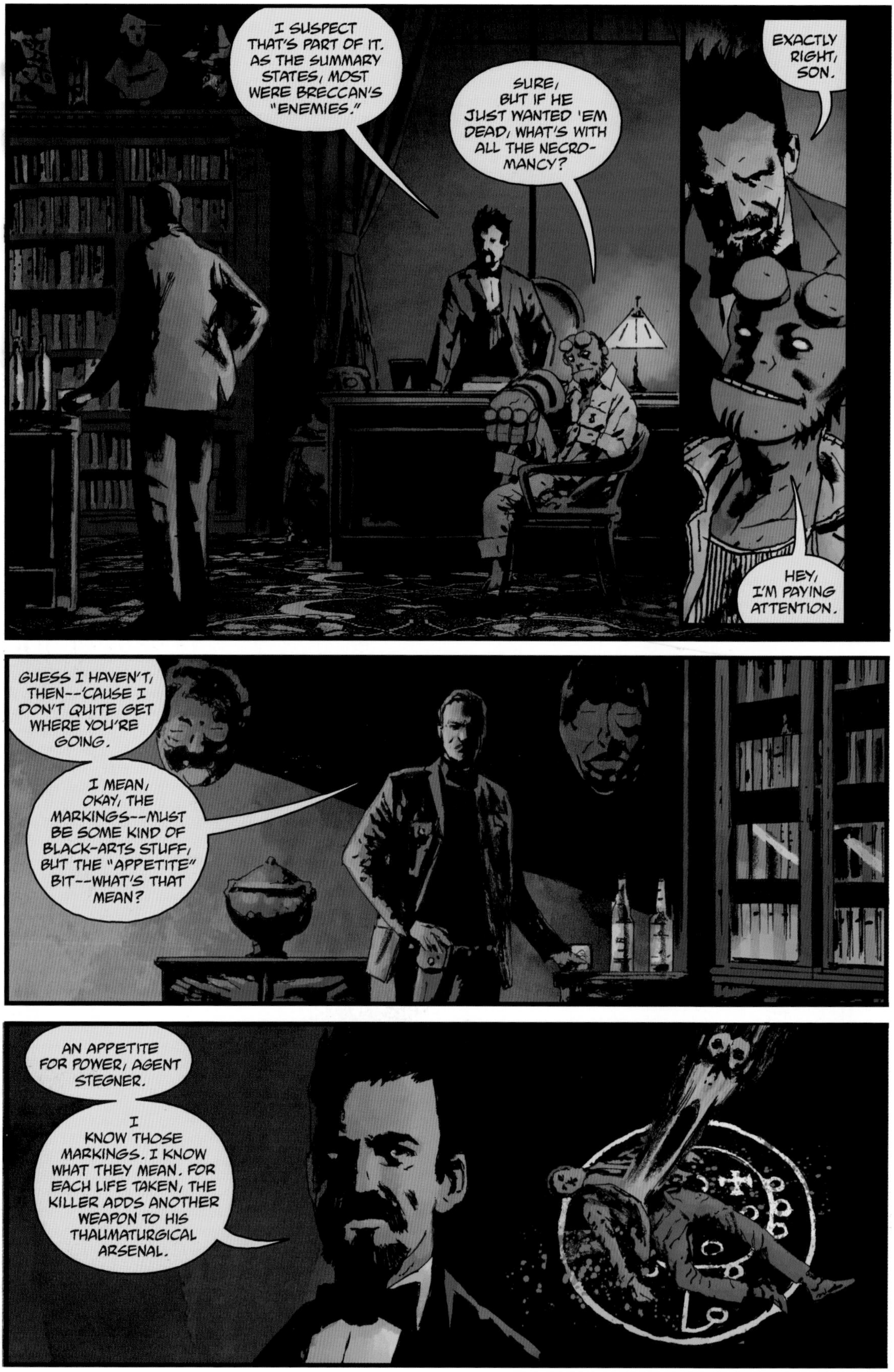
I SUSPECT THAT'S PART OF IT. AS THE SUMMARY STATES, MOST WERE BRECCAN'S "ENEMIES."
SURE, BUT IF HE JUST WANTED 'EM DEAD, WHAT'S WITH ALL THE NECRO-MANCY?
EXACTLY RIGHT, SON.
HEY, I'M PAYING ATTENTION.
GUESS I HAVEN'T, THEN--'CAUSE I DON'T QUITE GET WHERE YOU'RE GOING.
I MEAN, OKAY, THE MARKINGS--MUST BE SOME KIND OF BLACK-ARTS STUFF, BUT THE "APPETITE" BIT--WHAT'S THAT MEAN?
AN APPETITE FOR POWER, AGENT STEGNER.
I KNOW THOSE MARKINGS. I KNOW WHAT THEY MEAN. FOR EACH LIFE TAKEN, THE KILLER ADDS ANOTHER WEAPON TO HIS THAUMATURGICAL ARSENAL.

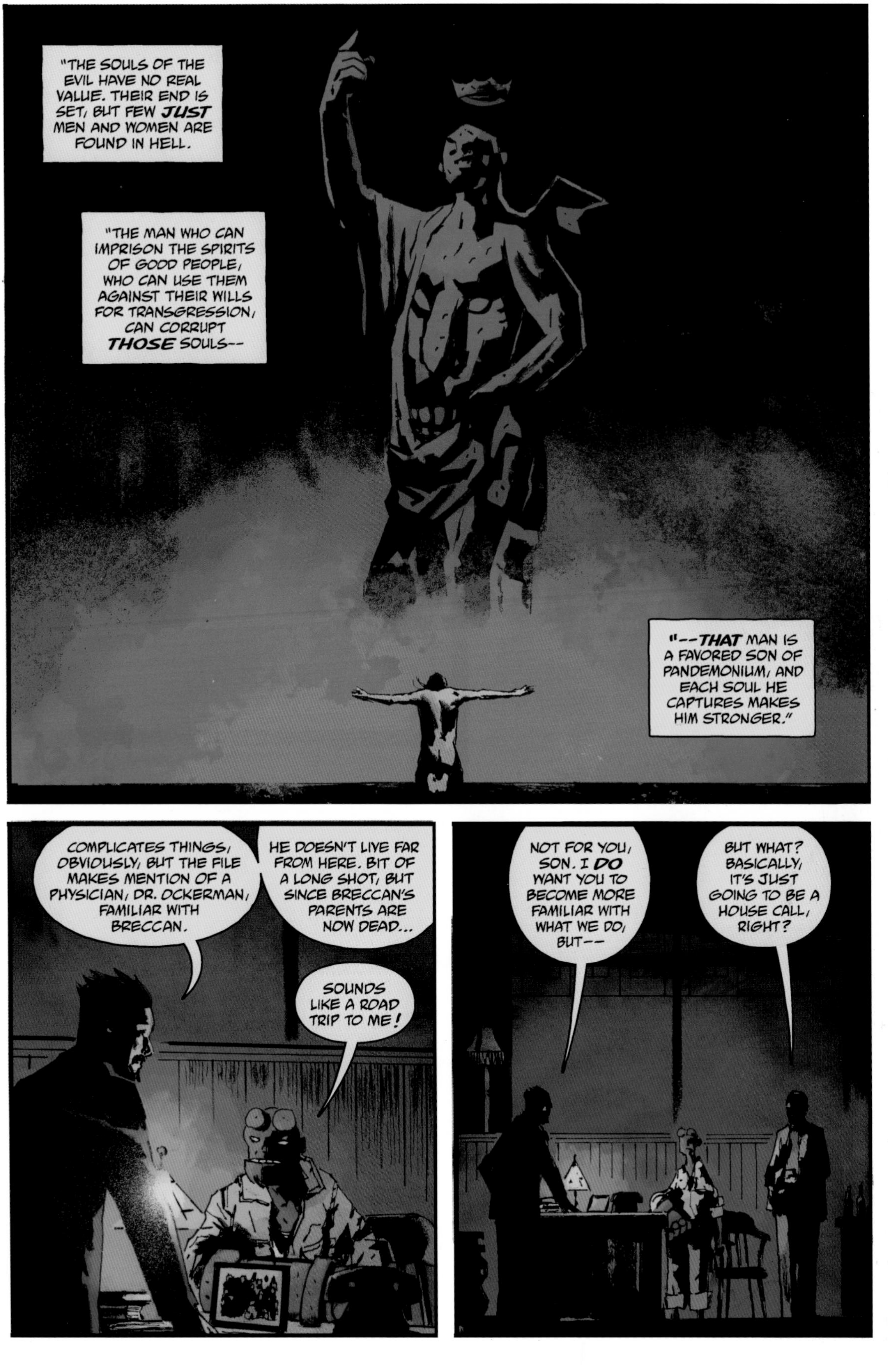
"THE SOULS OF THE EVIL HAVE NO REAL VALUE. THEIR END IS SET, BUT FEW JUST MEN AND WOMEN ARE FOUND IN HELL.
"THE MAN WHO CAN IMPRISON THE SPIRITS OF GOOD PEOPLE, WHO CAN USE THEM AGAINST THEIR WILLS FOR TRANSGRESSION, CAN CORRUPT THOSE SOULS--
"--THAT MAN IS A FAVORED SON OF PANDEMONIUM, AND EACH SOUL HE CAPTURES MAKES HIM STRONGER."
COMPLICATES THINGS, OBVIOUSLY, BUT THE FILE MAKES MENTION OF A PHYSICIAN, DR. OCKERMAN, FAMILIAR WITH BRECCAN.
HE DOESN'T LIVE FAR FROM HERE. BIT OF A LONG SHOT, BUT SINCE BRECCAN'S PARENTS ARE NOW DEAD...
SOUNDS LIKE A ROAD TRIP TO ME!
NOT FOR YOU, SON. I DO WANT YOU TO BECOME MORE FAMILIAR WITH WHAT WE DO, BUT--
BUT WHAT? BASICALLY, IT'S JUST GOING TO BE A HOUSE CALL, RIGHT?

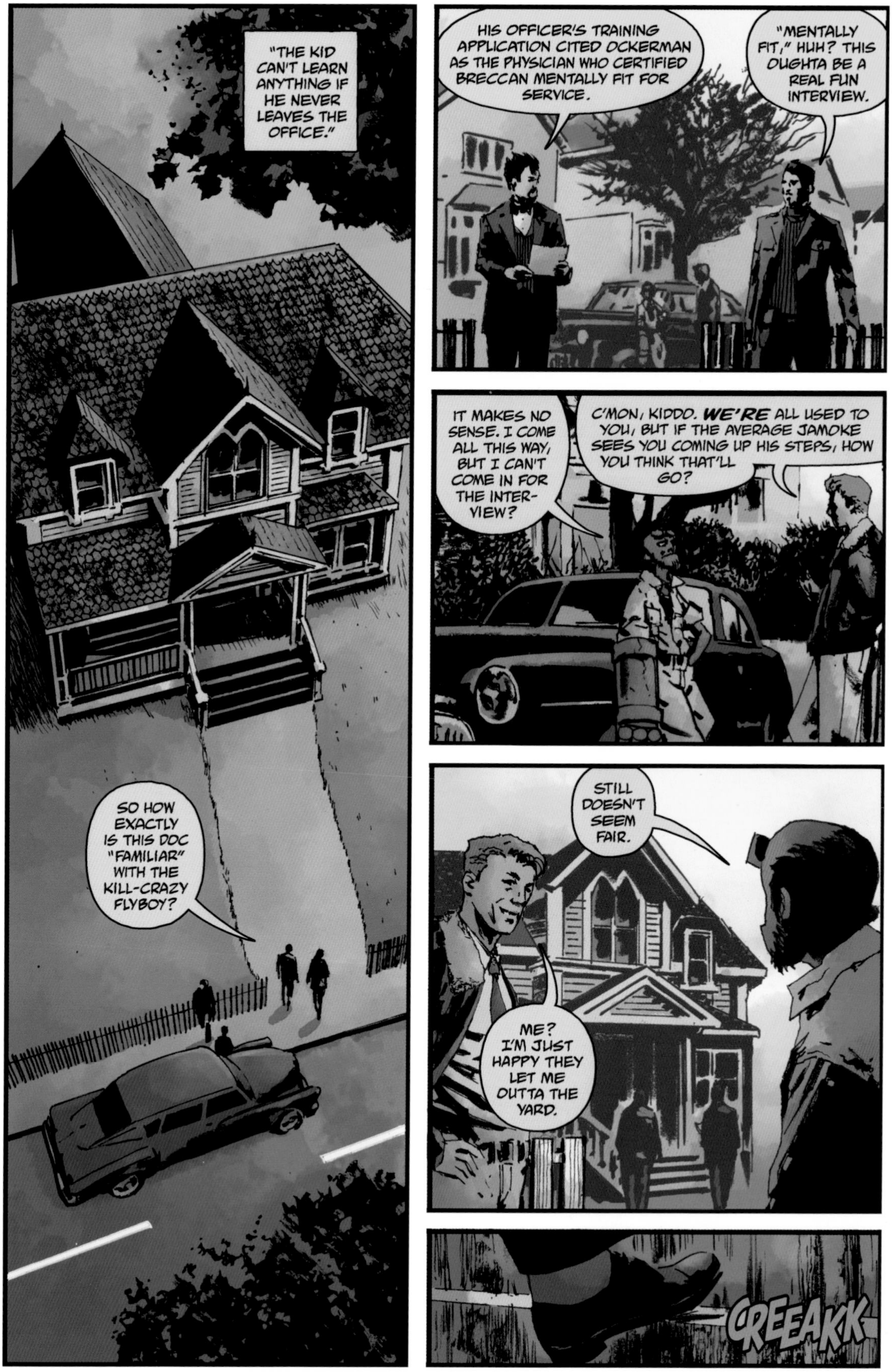
"THE KID CAN'T LEARN ANYTHING IF HE NEVER LEAVES THE OFFICE."
SO HOW EXACTLY IS THIS DOC "FAMILIAR" WITH THE KILL-CRAZY FLYBOY?
HIS OFFICER'S TRAINING APPLICATION CITED OCKERMAN AS THE PHYSICIAN WHO CERTIFIED BRECCAN MENTALLY FIT FOR SERVICE.
"MENTALLY FIT," HUH? THIS OUGHTA BE A REAL FUN INTERVIEW.
IT MAKES NO SENSE. I COME ALL THIS WAY, BUT I CAN'T COME IN FOR THE INTER-VIEW?
C'MON, KIDDO. **WE'RE** ALL USED TO YOU, BUT IF THE AVERAGE JAMOKE SEES YOU COMING UP HIS STEPS, HOW YOU THINK THAT'LL GO?
STILL DOESN'T SEEM FAIR.
ME? I'M JUST HAPPY THEY LET ME OUTTA THE YARD.
CREEAKK

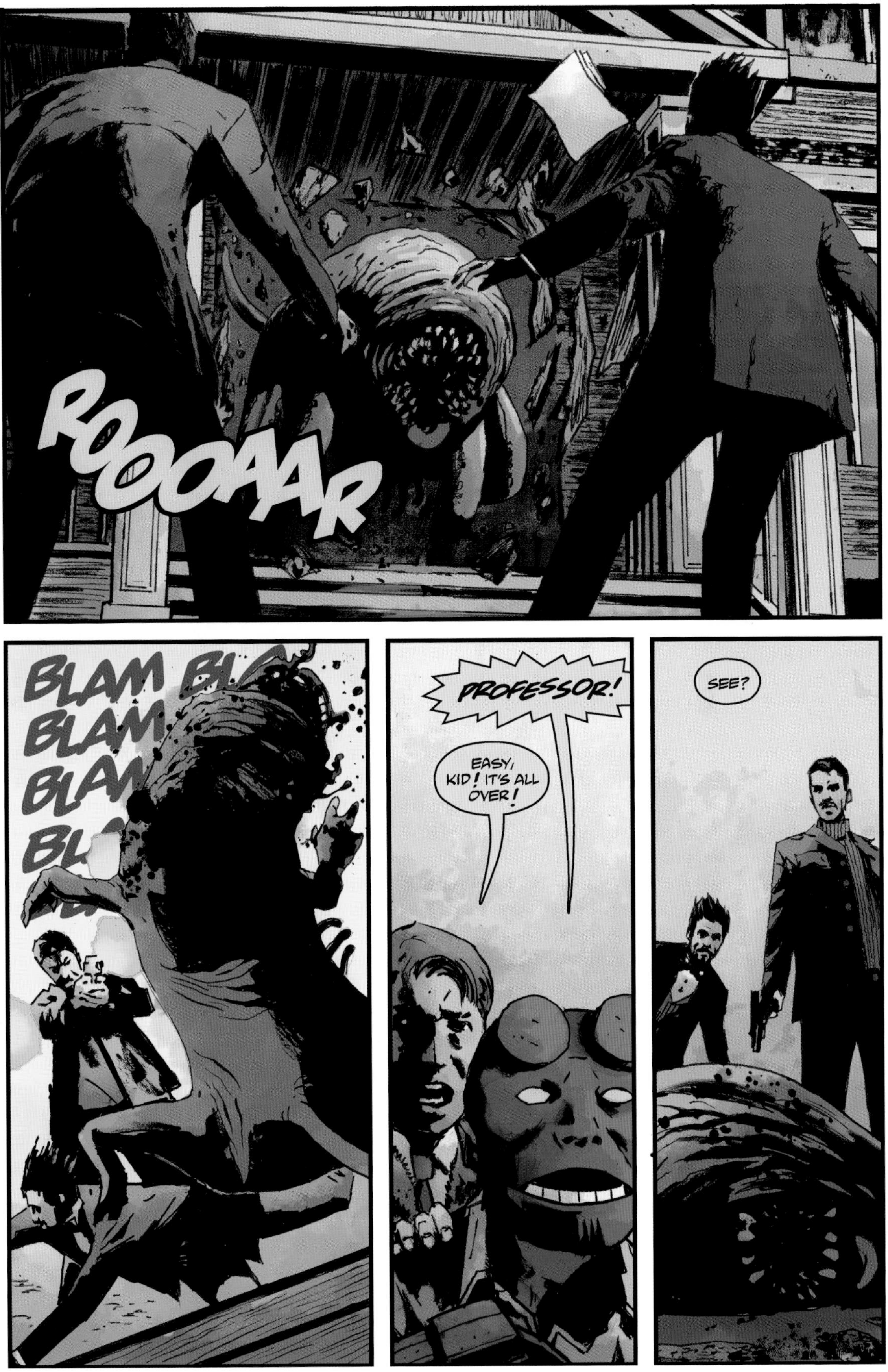
ROOOAAR
BLAM BL
BLAM
BLAM
PROFESSOR!
EASY, KID! IT'S ALL OVER!
SEE?

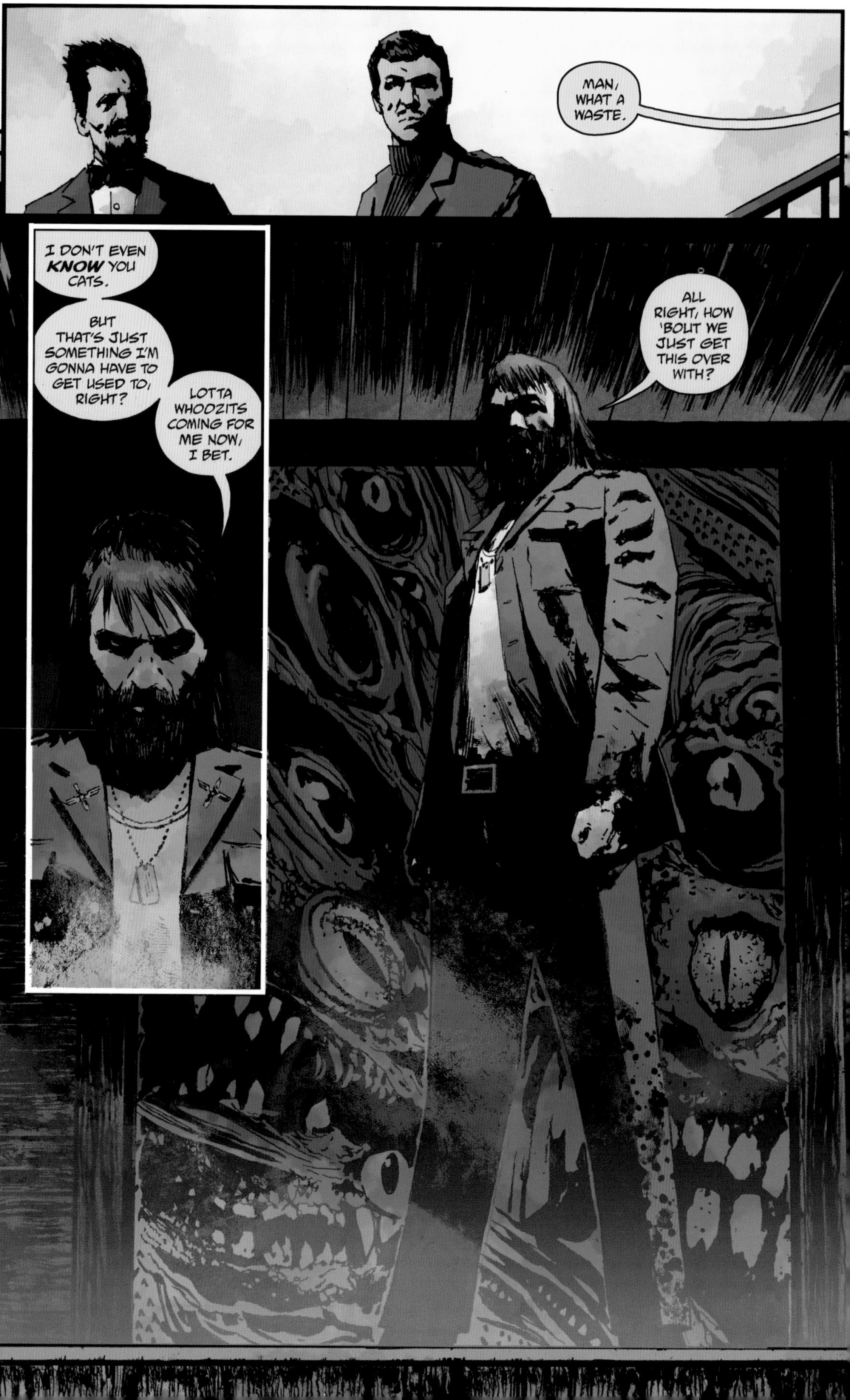
MAN, WHAT A WASTE.
I DON'T EVEN KNOW YOU CATS.
BUT THAT'S JUST SOMETHING I'M GONNA HAVE TO GET USED TO, RIGHT?
LOTTA WHOODZITS COMING FOR ME NOW, I BET.
ALL RIGHT, HOW 'BOUT WE JUST GET THIS OVER WITH?

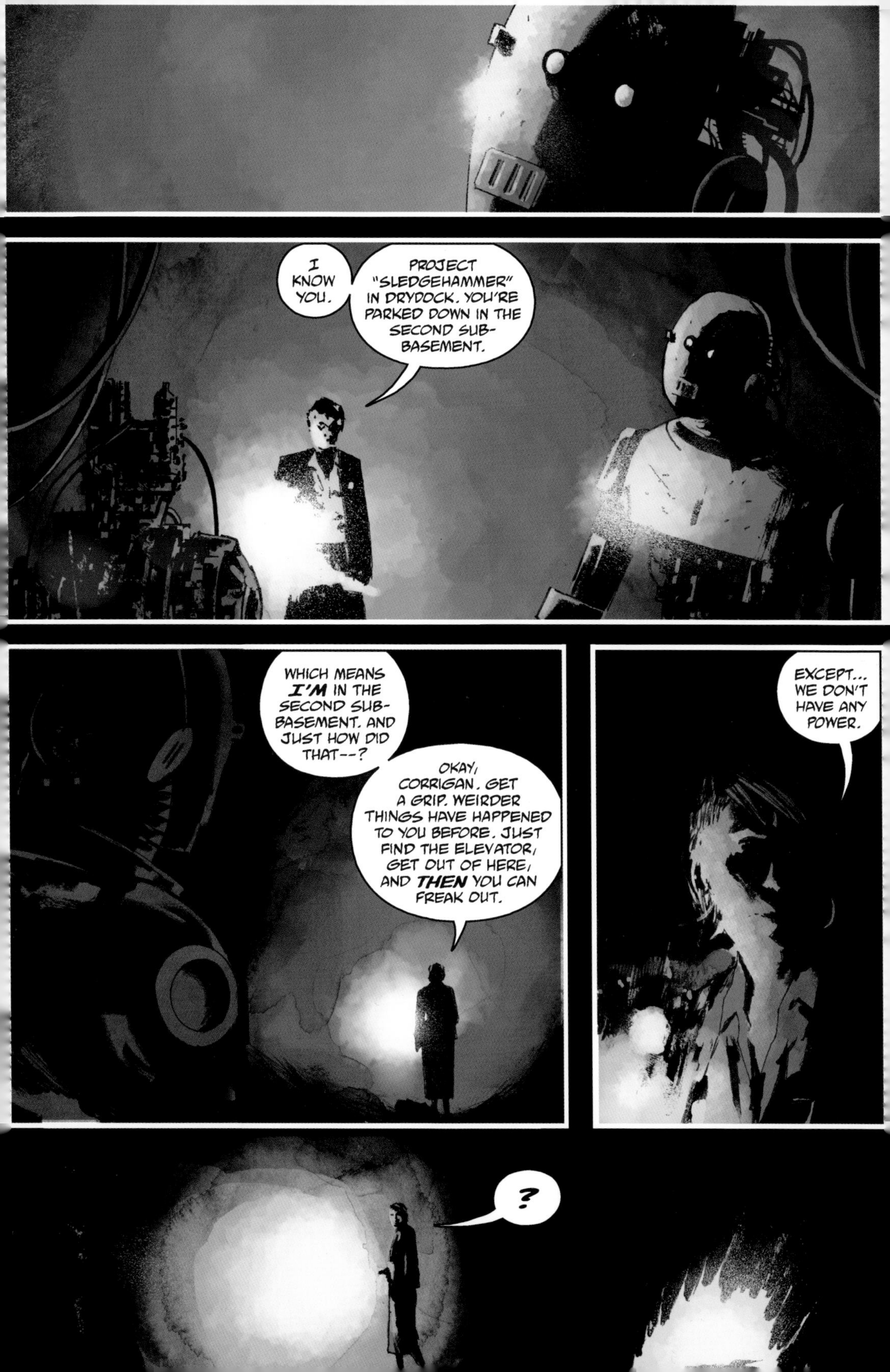
I KNOW YOU.
PROJECT "SLEDGEHAMMER" IN DRYDOCK. YOU'RE PARKED DOWN IN THE SECOND SUB-BASEMENT.
WHICH MEANS *I'M* IN THE SECOND SUB-BASEMENT. AND JUST HOW DID THAT--?
OKAY, CORRIGAN. GET A GRIP. WEIRDER THINGS HAVE HAPPENED TO YOU BEFORE. JUST FIND THE ELEVATOR, GET OUT OF HERE, AND *THEN* YOU CAN FREAK OUT.
EXCEPT... WE DON'T HAVE ANY POWER.
?

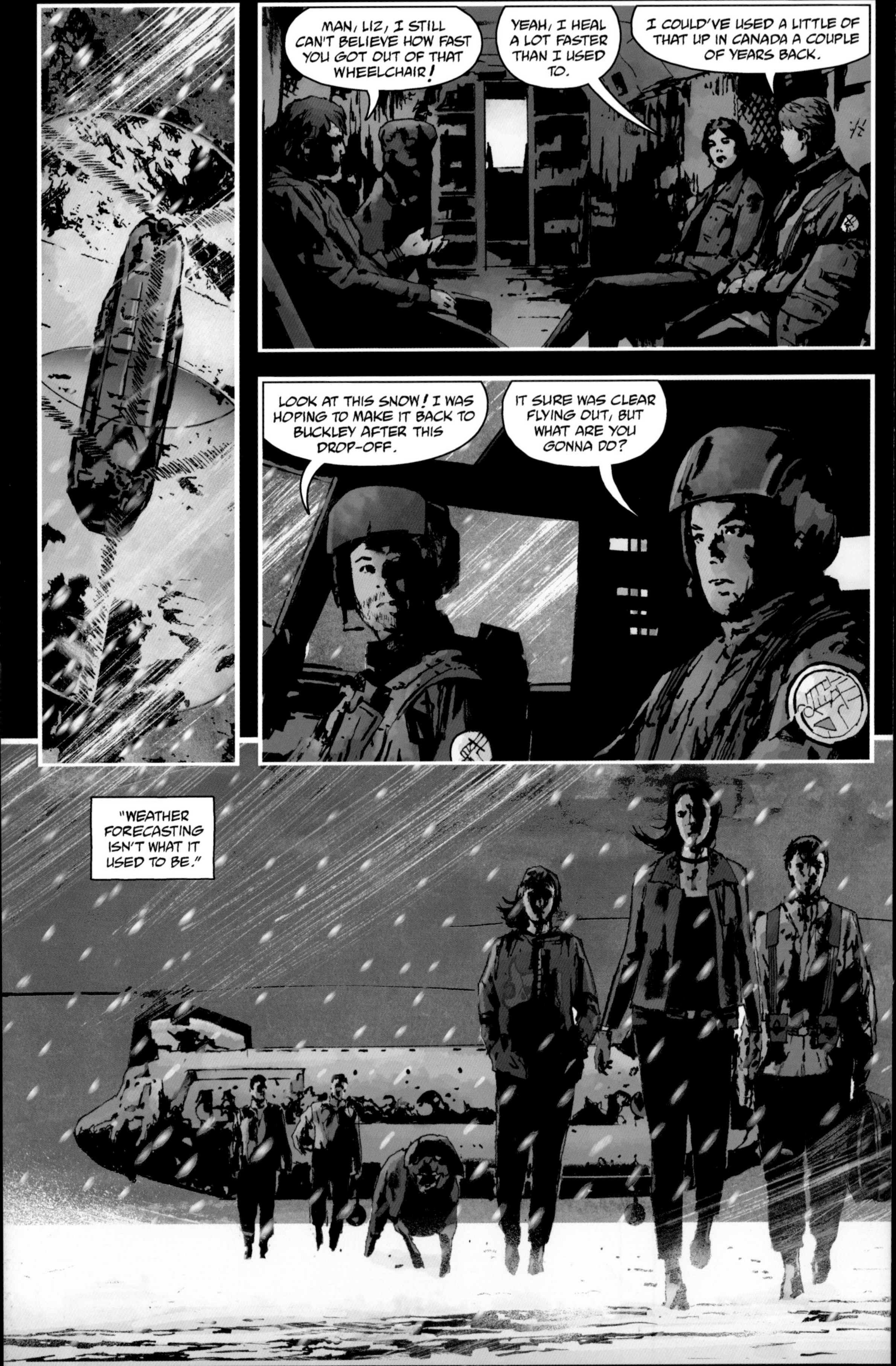

MAN, LIZ, I STILL CAN'T BELIEVE HOW FAST YOU GOT OUT OF THAT WHEELCHAIR!
YEAH, I HEAL A LOT FASTER THAN I USED TO.
I COULD'VE USED A LITTLE OF THAT UP IN CANADA A COUPLE OF YEARS BACK.
LOOK AT THIS SNOW! I WAS HOPING TO MAKE IT BACK TO BUCKLEY AFTER THIS DROP-OFF.
IT SURE WAS CLEAR FLYING OUT, BUT WHAT ARE YOU GONNA DO?
"WEATHER FORECASTING ISN'T WHAT IT USED TO BE."

HUH, WON'T OPEN.

THINK THE HYDRAULICS ARE FROZEN?

CHECK IT. LOOKS LIKE POWER'S OUT.

GENCY XIT

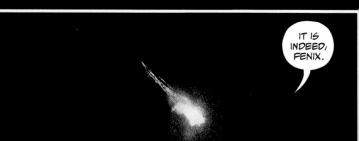

IT IS INDEED, FENIX.

GENCY XIT

HAPPENS FROM TIME TO TIME, AS I THINK AGENT GIAROCCO KNOWS, BUT THIS GO- 'ROUND...

THIS FEELS DIFFERENT.

DIFFERENT HOW?

AND WHERE'S KATE?

THAT, MY LOVES, IS AN EXCELLENT QUESTION.

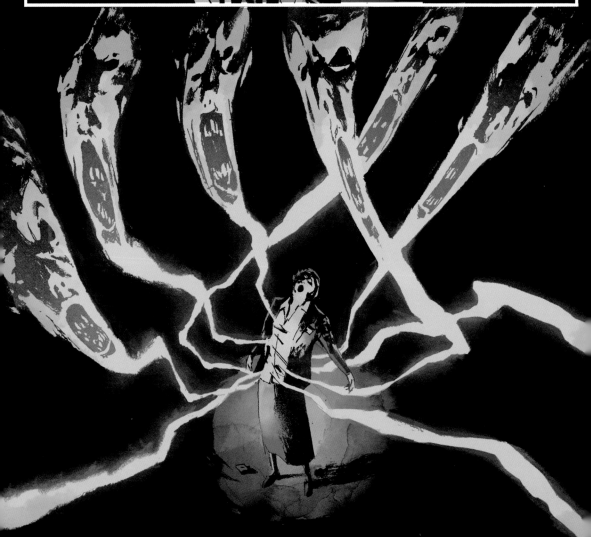

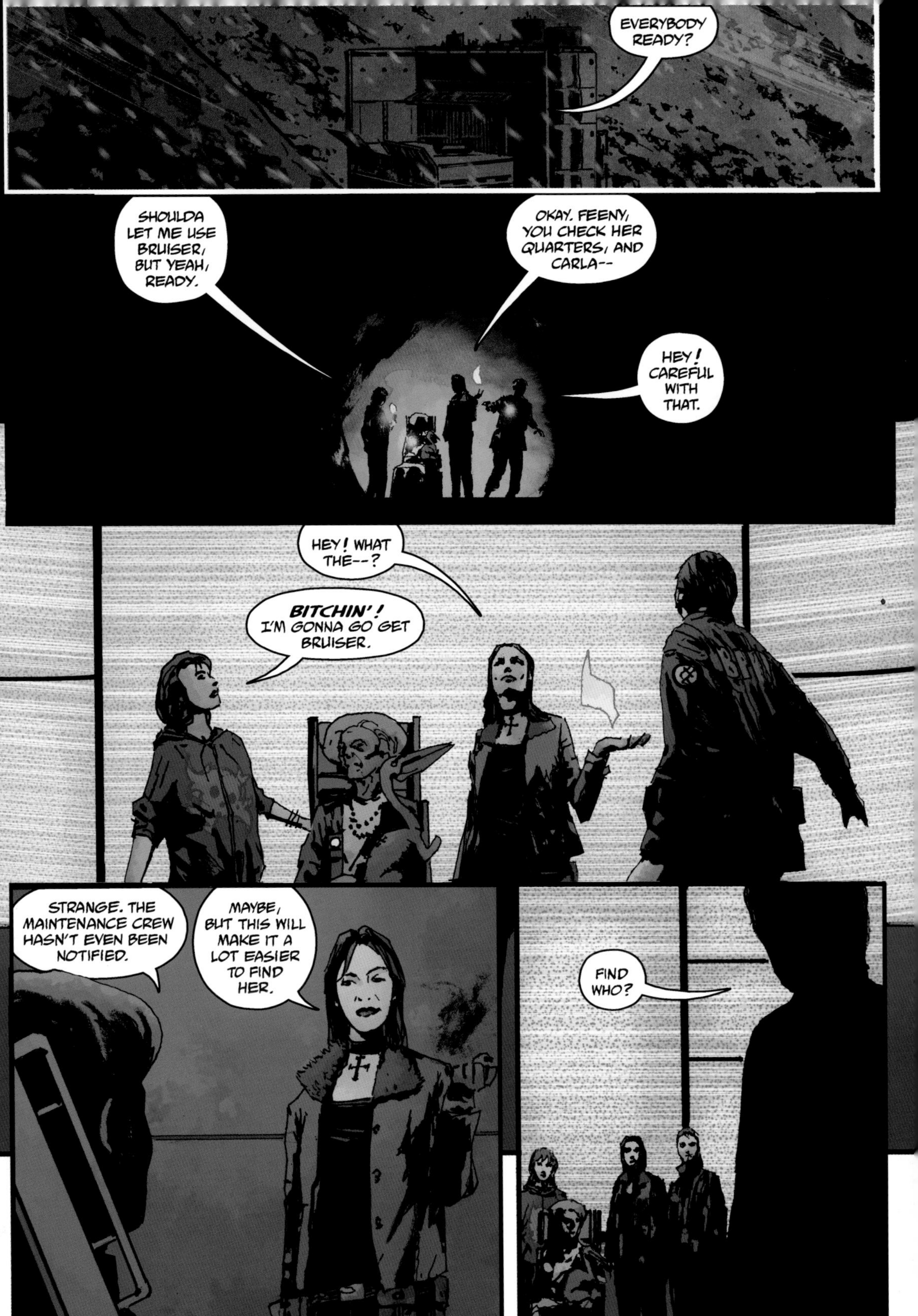
EVERYBODY READY?
SHOULDA LET ME USE BRUISER, BUT YEAH, READY.
OKAY. FEENY, YOU CHECK HER QUARTERS, AND CARLA--
HEY! CAREFUL WITH THAT.
HEY! WHAT THE--?
BITCHIN'! I'M GONNA GO GET BRUISER.
STRANGE. THE MAINTENANCE CREW HASN'T EVEN BEEN NOTIFIED.
MAYBE, BUT THIS WILL MAKE IT A LOT EASIER TO FIND HER.
FIND WHO?

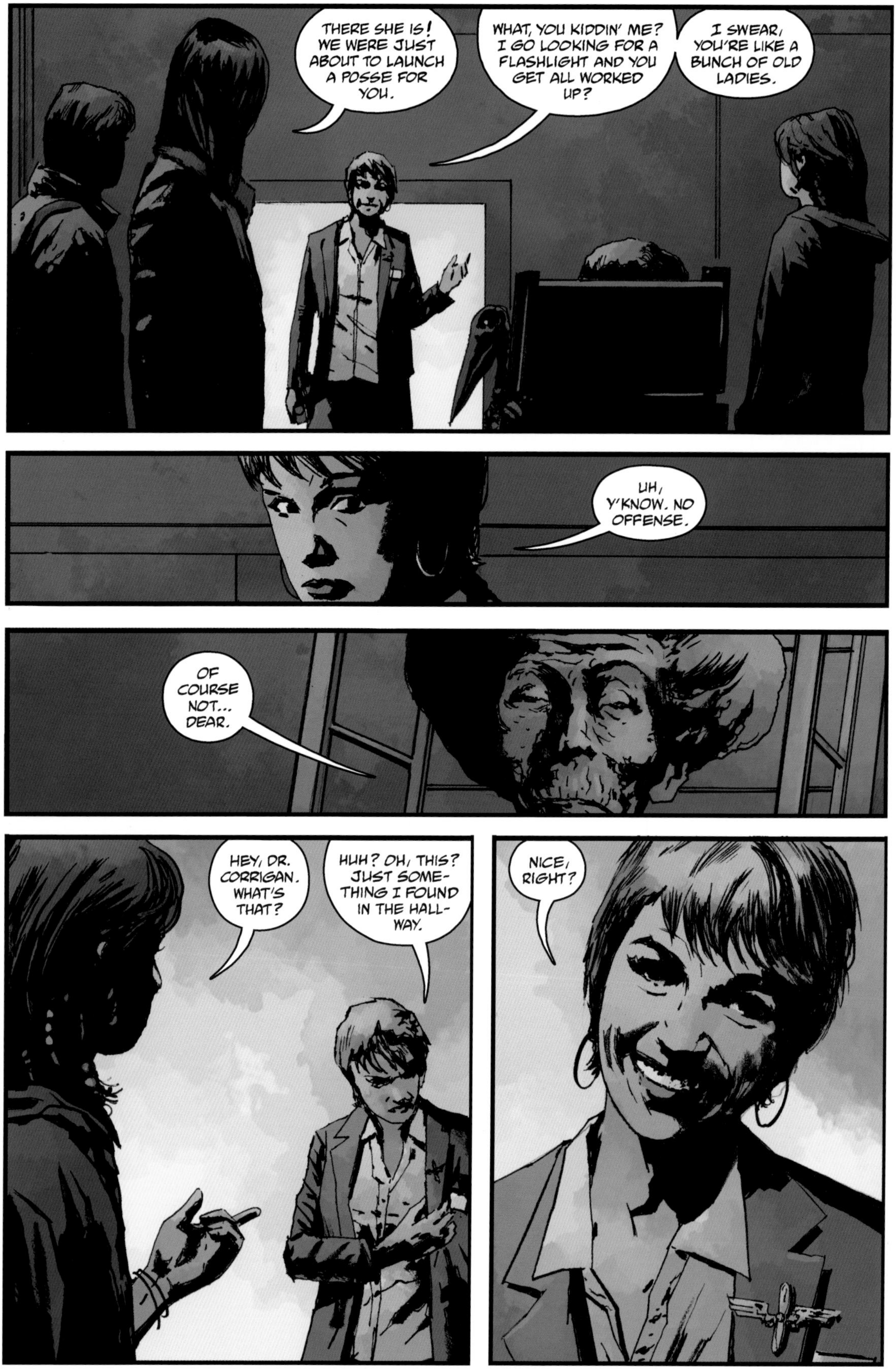
THERE SHE IS! WE WERE JUST ABOUT TO LAUNCH A POSSE FOR YOU.
WHAT, YOU KIDDIN' ME? I GO LOOKING FOR A FLASHLIGHT AND YOU GET ALL WORKED UP?
I SWEAR, YOU'RE LIKE A BUNCH OF OLD LADIES.
UH, Y'KNOW. NO OFFENSE.
OF COURSE NOT... DEAR.
HEY, DR. CORRIGAN. WHAT'S THAT?
HUH? OH, THIS? JUST SOME-THING I FOUND IN THE HALL-WAY.
NICE, RIGHT?

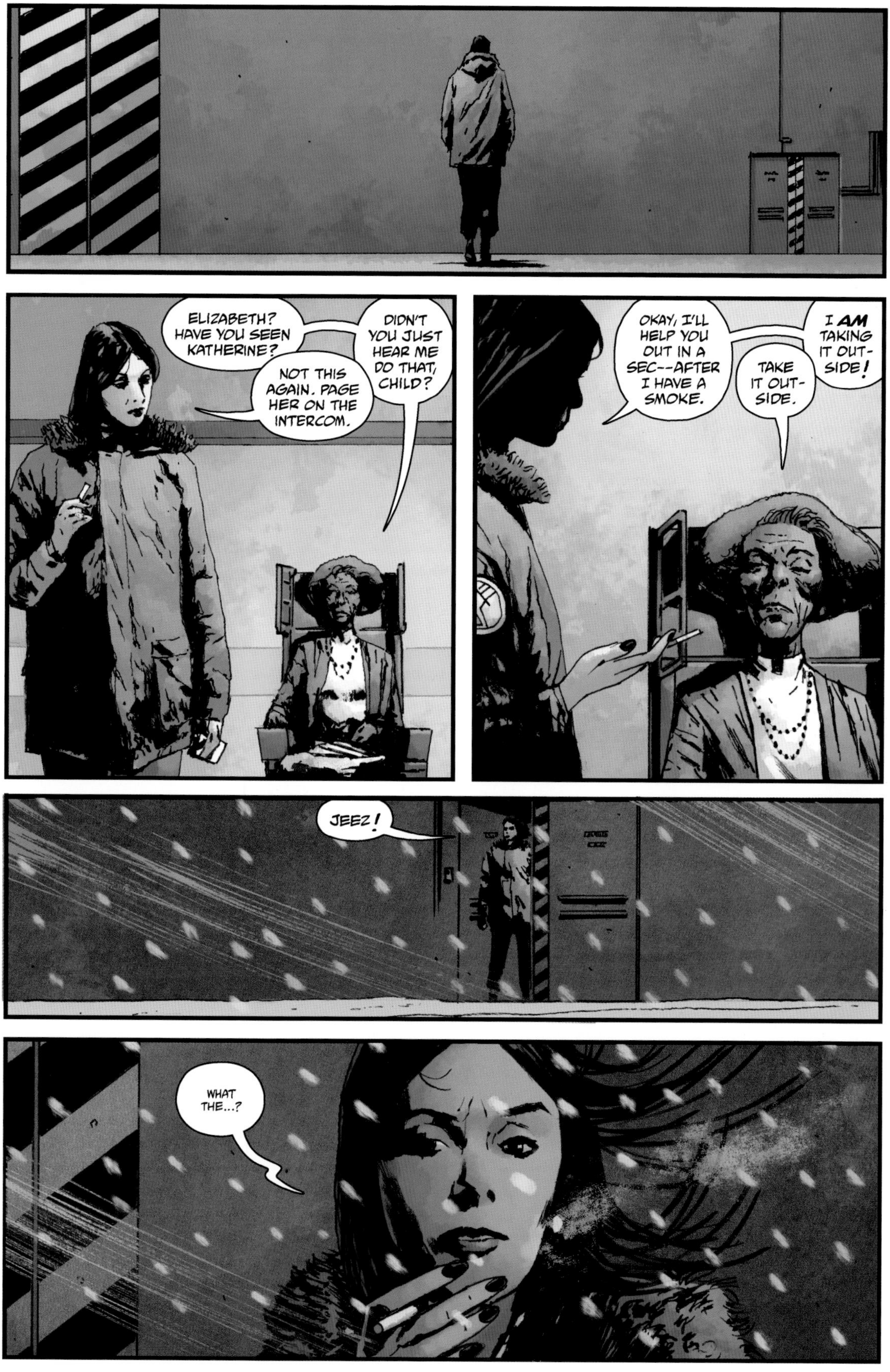
ELIZABETH? HAVE YOU SEEN KATHERINE?
NOT THIS AGAIN. PAGE HER ON THE INTERCOM.
DIDN'T YOU JUST HEAR ME DO THAT, CHILD?
OKAY, I'LL HELP YOU OUT IN A SEC--AFTER I HAVE A SMOKE.
TAKE IT OUT-SIDE.
I AM TAKING IT OUT-SIDE!
JEEZ!
WHAT THE...?

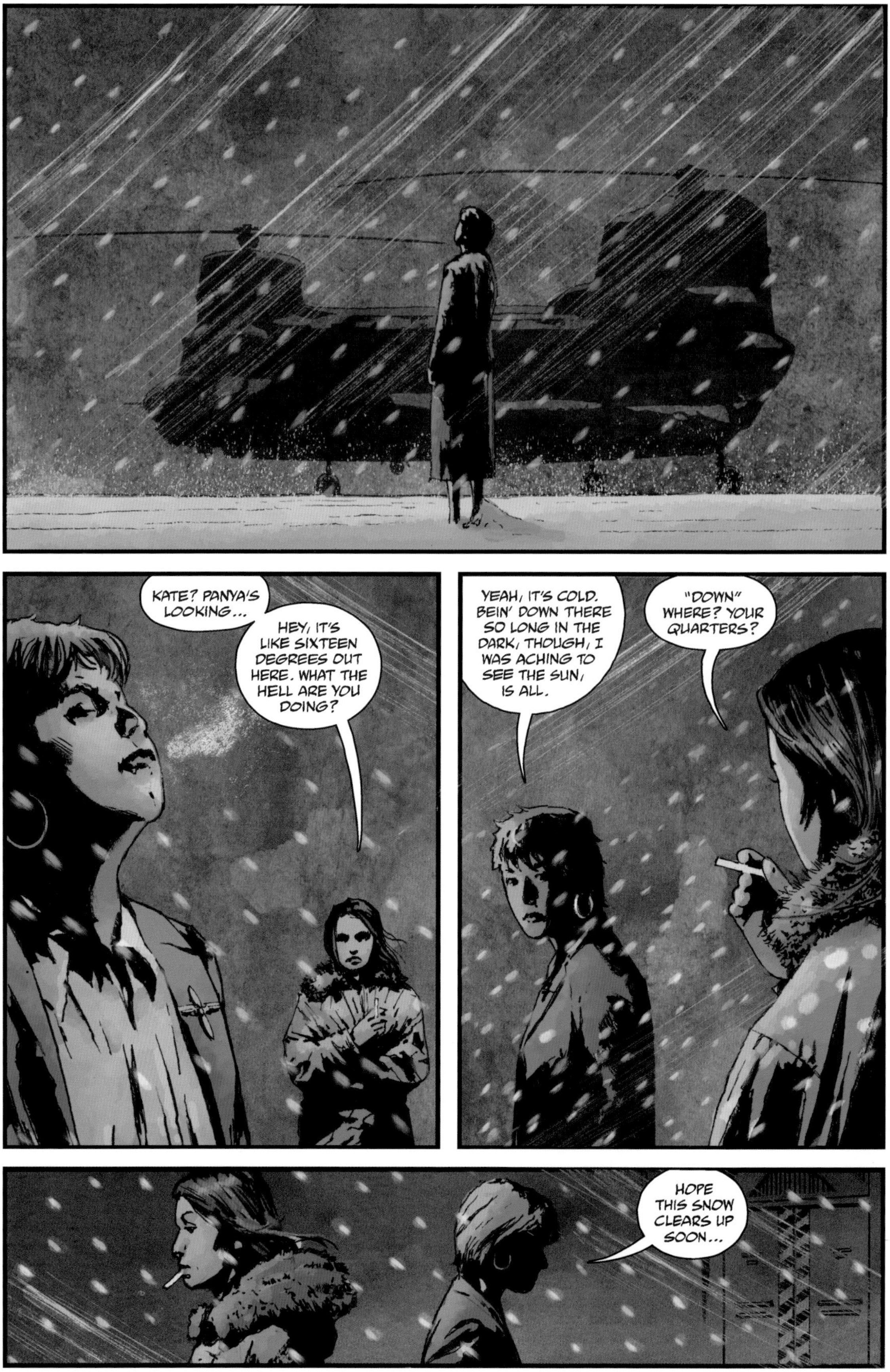
KATE? PANYA'S LOOKING...
HEY, IT'S LIKE SIXTEEN DEGREES OUT HERE. WHAT THE HELL ARE YOU DOING?
YEAH, IT'S COLD. BEIN' DOWN THERE SO LONG IN THE DARK, THOUGH, I WAS ACHING TO SEE THE SUN, IS ALL.
"DOWN" WHERE? YOUR QUARTERS?
HOPE THIS SNOW CLEARS UP SOON...

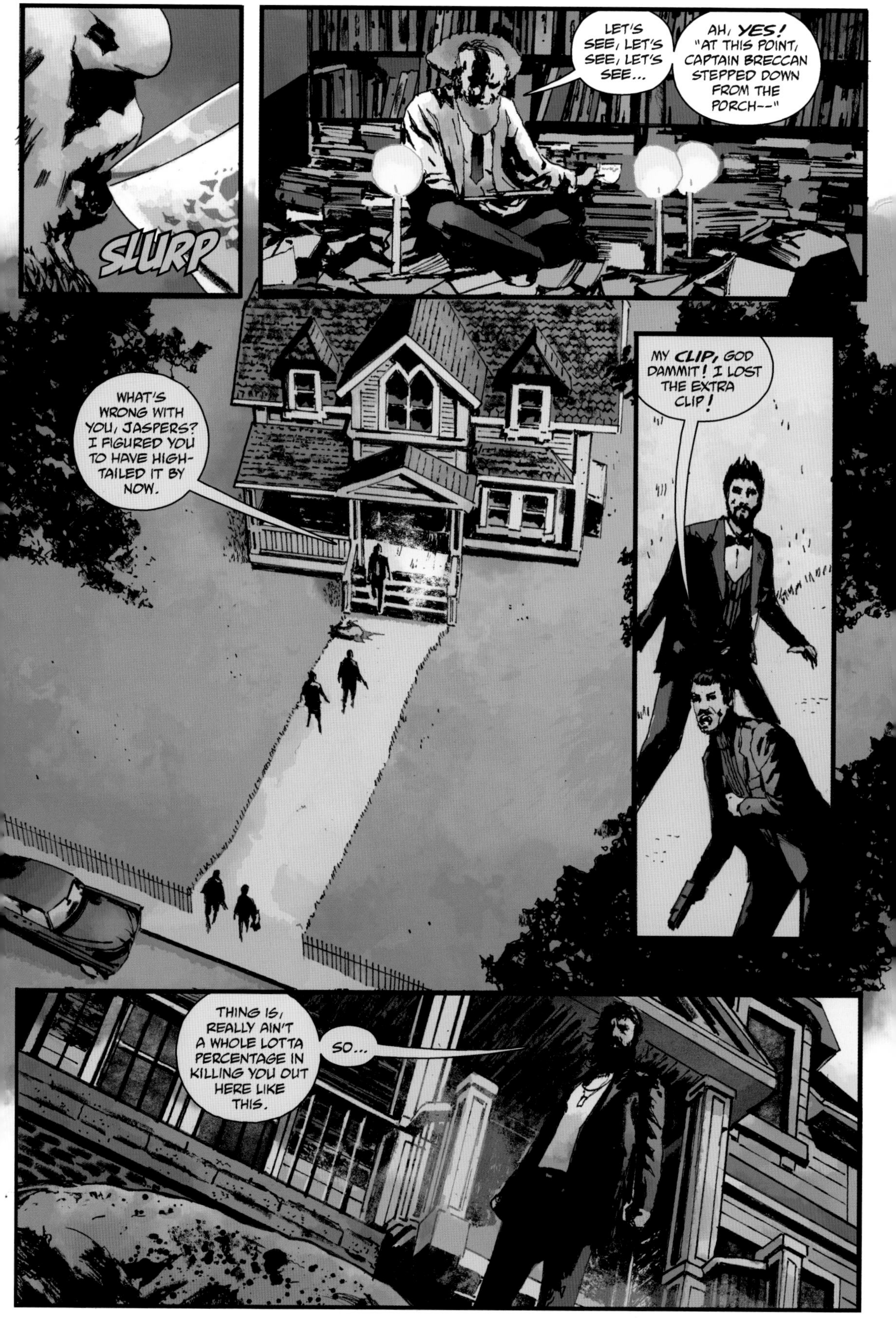
SLURP
LET'S SEE, LET'S SEE, LET'S SEE...
AH, YES! "AT THIS POINT, CAPTAIN BRECCAN STEPPED DOWN FROM THE PORCH--"
WHAT'S WRONG WITH YOU, JASPERS? I FIGURED YOU TO HAVE HIGH-TAILED IT BY NOW.
MY CLIP, GOD DAMMIT! I LOST THE EXTRA CLIP!
THING IS, REALLY AIN'T A WHOLE LOTTA PERCENTAGE IN KILLING YOU OUT HERE LIKE THIS.
SO...

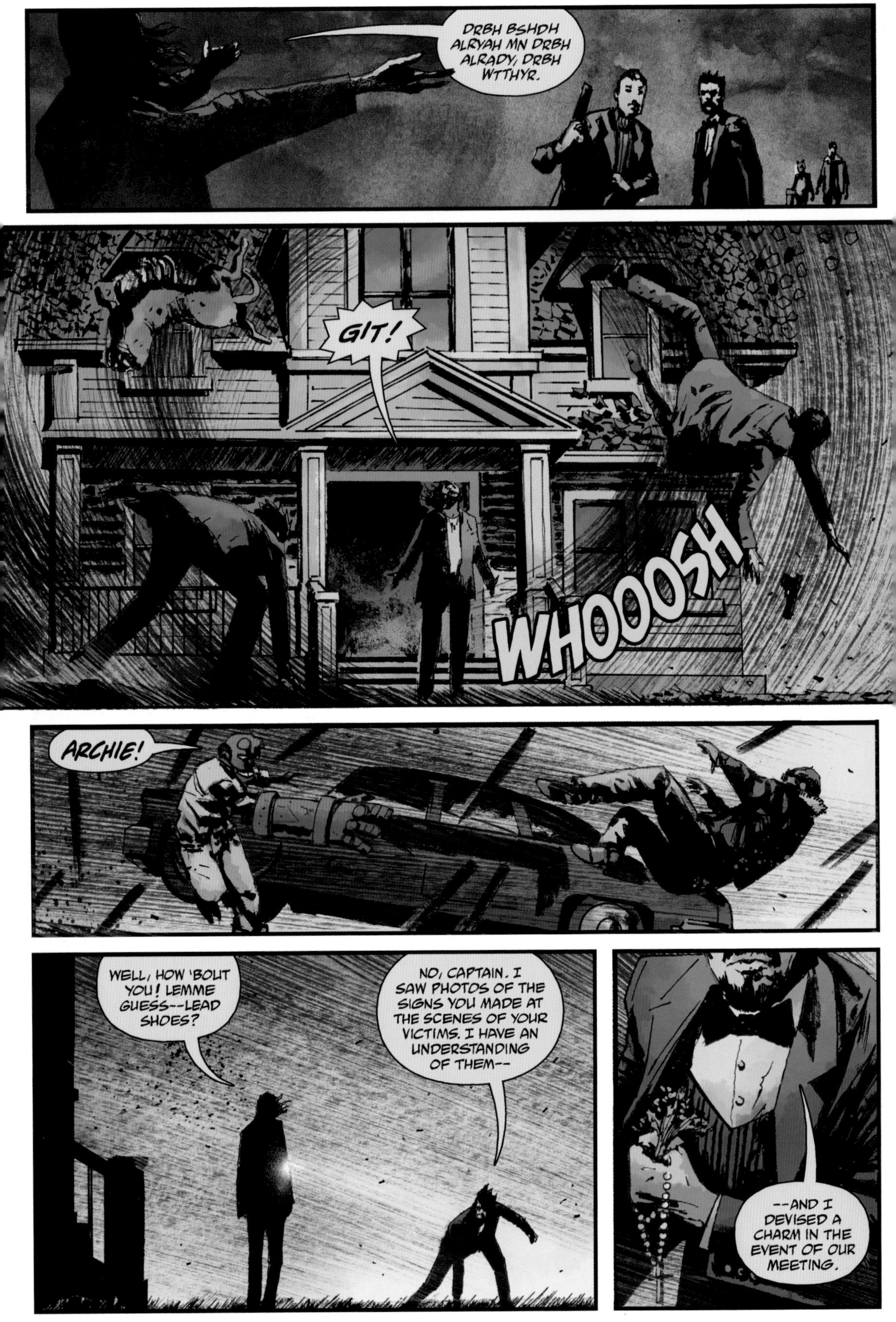
DRBH BSHDH ALRYAH MN DRBH ALRADY, DRBH WTTHYR.
GIT!
WHOOOSH
ARCHIE!
WELL, HOW 'BOUT YOU! LEMME GUESS--LEAD SHOES?
NO, CAPTAIN. I SAW PHOTOS OF THE SIGNS YOU MADE AT THE SCENES OF YOUR VICTIMS. I HAVE AN UNDERSTANDING OF THEM--
--AND I DEVISED A CHARM IN THE EVENT OF OUR MEETING.

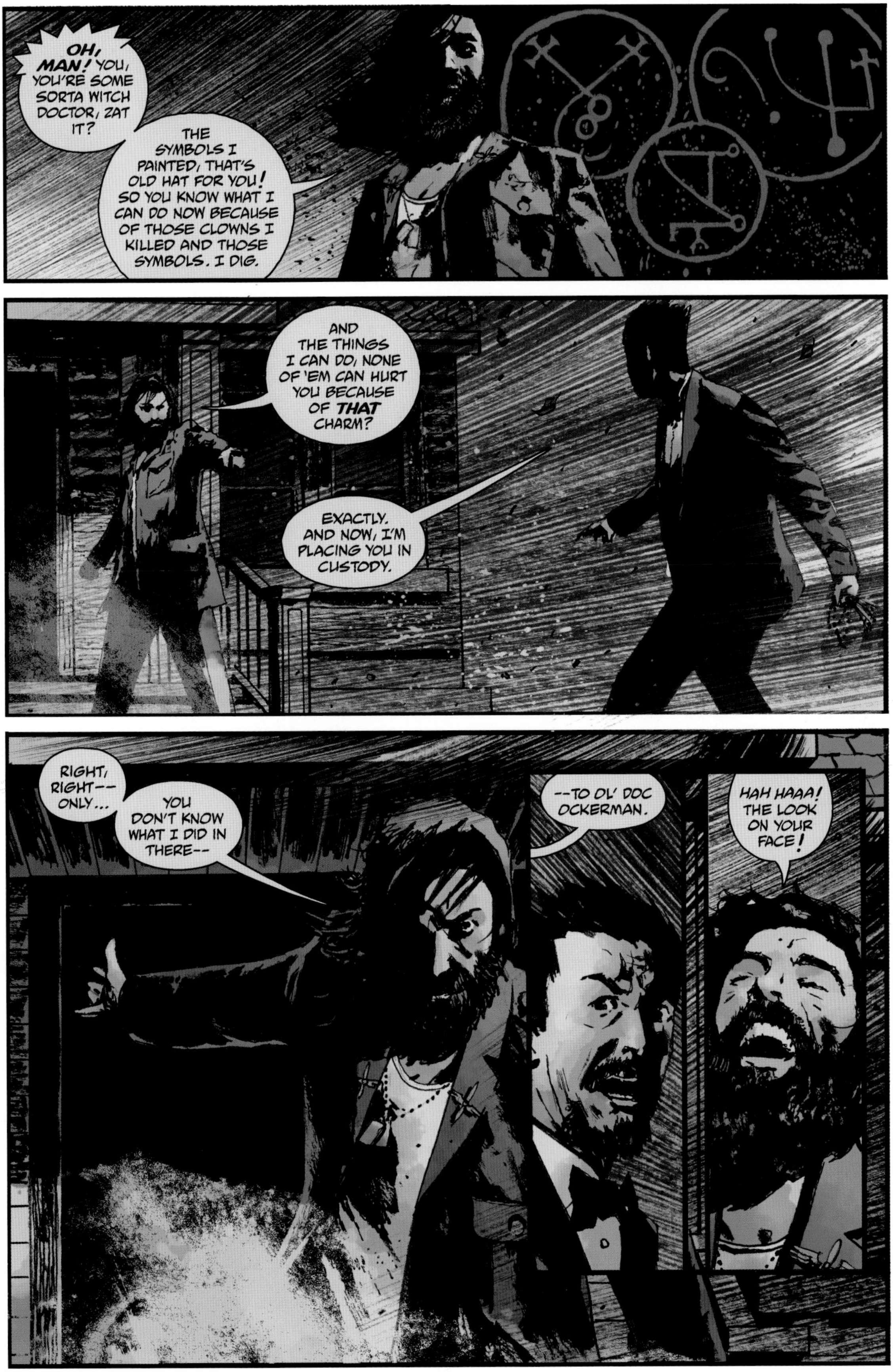
OH, MAN! YOU, YOU'RE SOME SORTA WITCH DOCTOR, ZAT IT?
THE SYMBOLS I PAINTED, THAT'S OLD HAT FOR YOU! SO YOU KNOW WHAT I CAN DO NOW BECAUSE OF THOSE CLOWNS I KILLED AND THOSE SYMBOLS. I DIG.
AND THE THINGS I CAN DO, NONE OF 'EM CAN HURT YOU BECAUSE OF THAT CHARM?
EXACTLY. AND NOW, I'M PLACING YOU IN CUSTODY.
RIGHT, RIGHT-- ONLY...
YOU DON'T KNOW WHAT I DID IN THERE--
--TO OL' DOC OCKERMAN.
HAH HAAA! THE LOOK ON YOUR FACE!

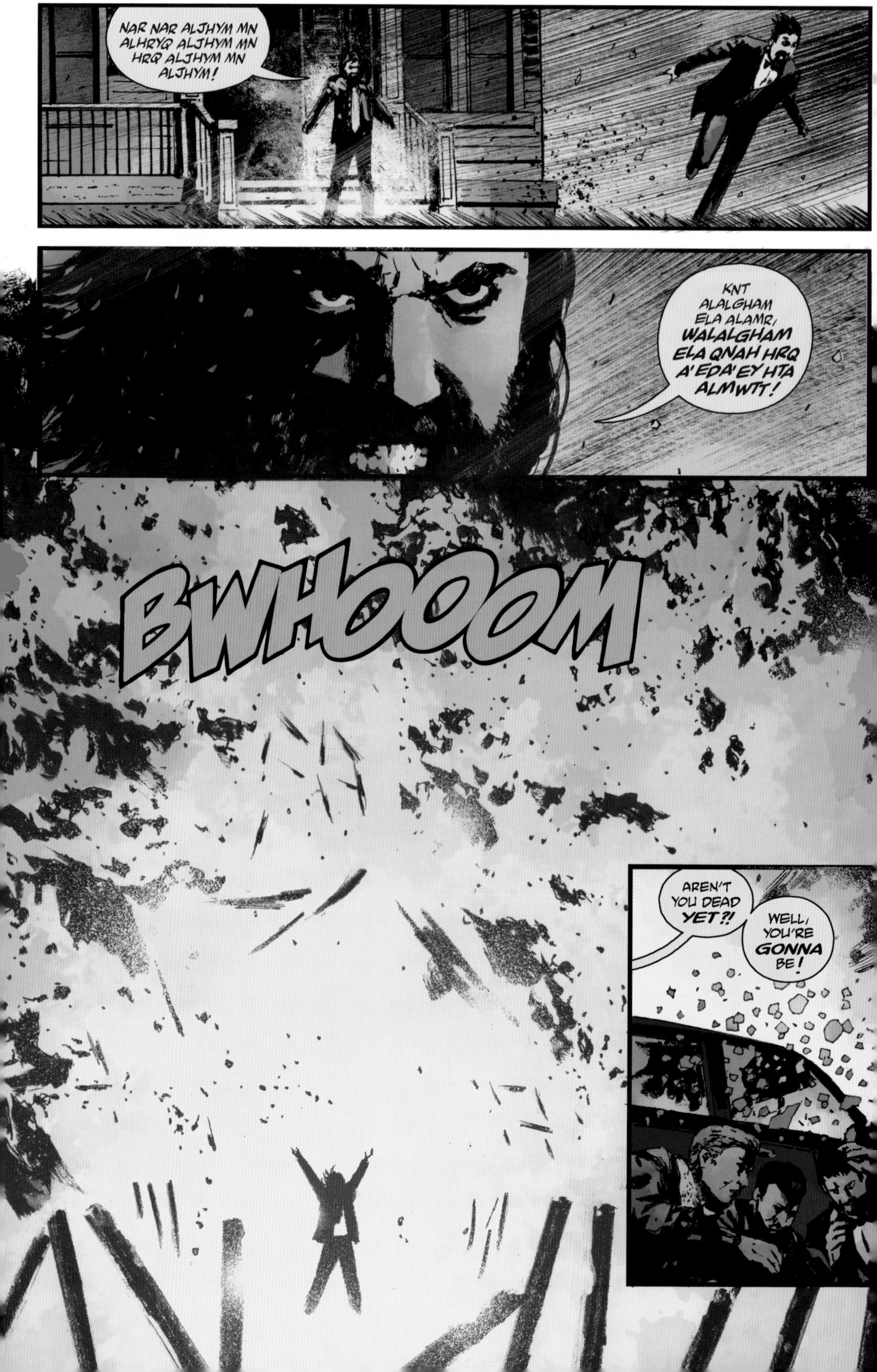
NAR NAR ALJHYM MN ALHRYQ ALJHYM MN HRQ ALJHYM MN ALJHYM!
KNT ALALGHAM ELA ALAMR, WALALGHAM ELA QNAH HRQ A'EDA'EY HTA ALMWTT!
BWHOOOM
AREN'T YOU DEAD YET?!
WELL, YOU'RE GONNA BE!

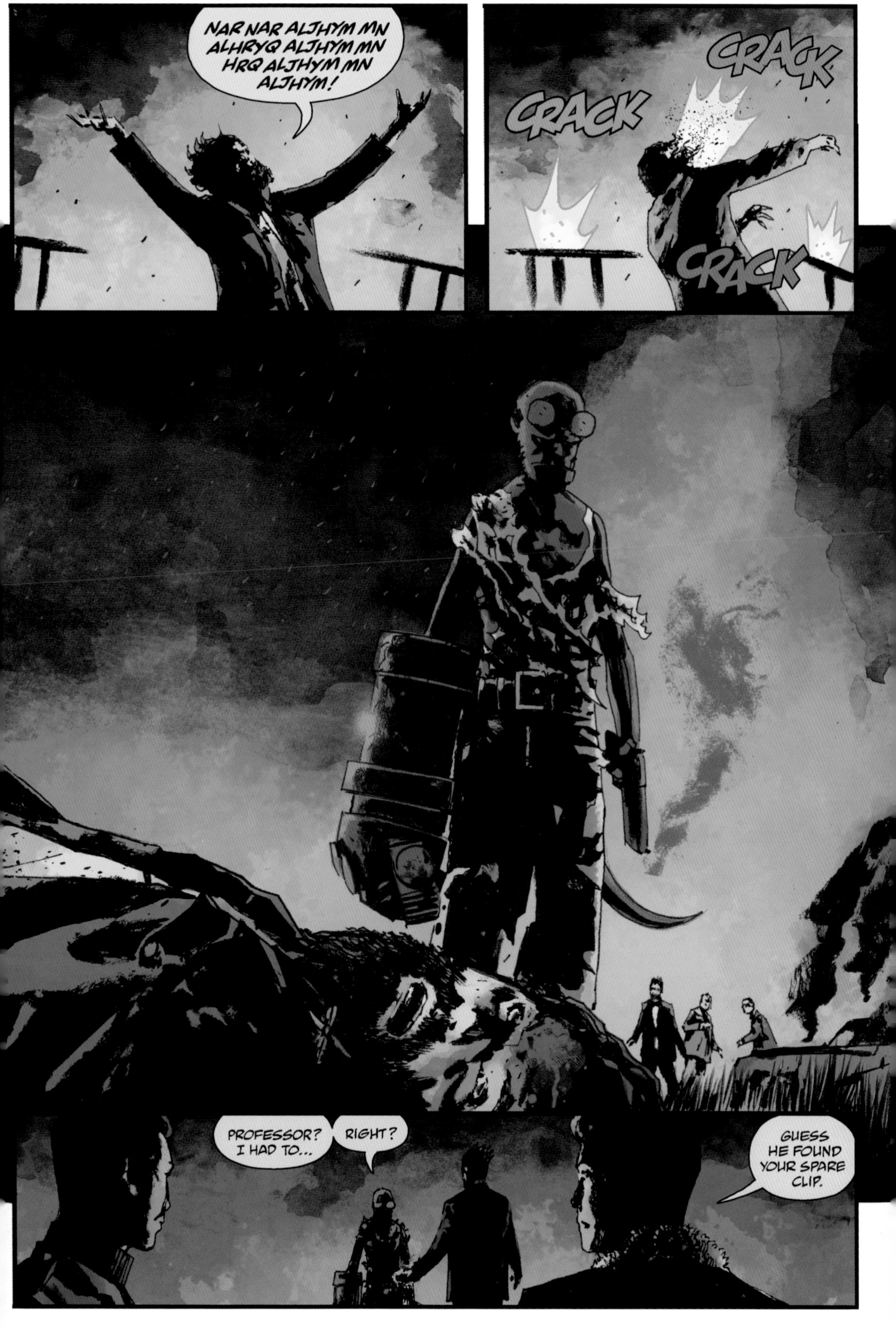
NAR NAR ALJHYM MN ALHRYQ ALJHYM MN HRQ ALJHYM MN ALJHYM!
CRACK
CRACK
CRACK
PROFESSOR? I HAD TO...
RIGHT?
GUESS HE FOUND YOUR SPARE CLIP.

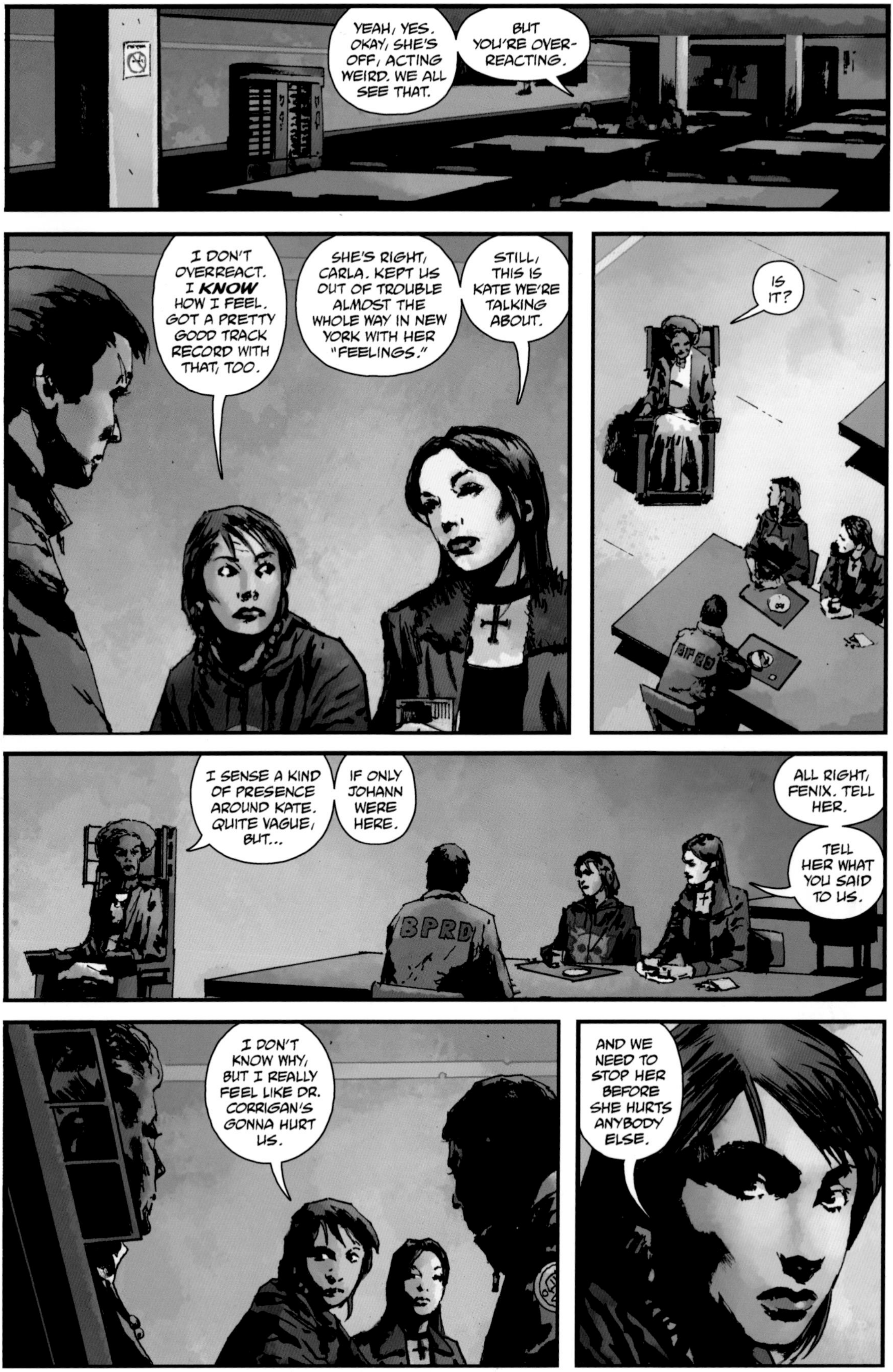
YEAH, YES. OKAY, SHE'S OFF, ACTING WEIRD. WE ALL SEE THAT.
BUT YOU'RE OVER-REACTING.
I DON'T OVERREACT. I **KNOW** HOW I FEEL. GOT A PRETTY GOOD TRACK RECORD WITH THAT, TOO.
SHE'S RIGHT, CARLA. KEPT US OUT OF TROUBLE ALMOST THE WHOLE WAY IN NEW YORK WITH HER "FEELINGS."
STILL, THIS IS KATE WE'RE TALKING ABOUT.
IS IT?
I SENSE A KIND OF PRESENCE AROUND KATE. QUITE VAGUE, BUT...
IF ONLY JOHANN WERE HERE.
ALL RIGHT, FENIX. TELL HER.
TELL HER WHAT YOU SAID TO US.
BPRD
I DON'T KNOW WHY, BUT I REALLY FEEL LIKE DR. CORRIGAN'S GONNA HURT US.
AND WE NEED TO STOP HER BEFORE SHE HURTS ANYBODY ELSE.

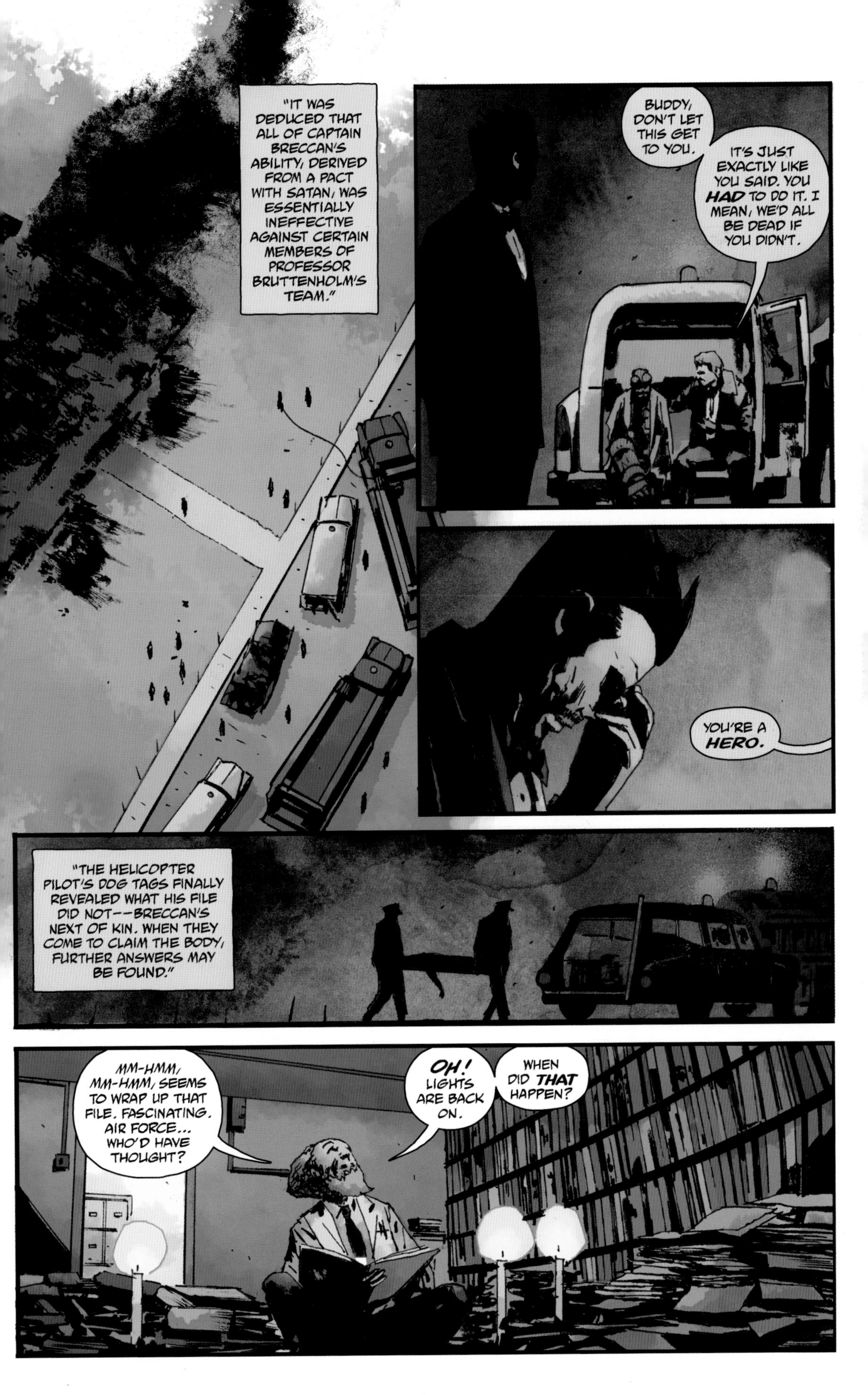
"IT WAS DEDUCED THAT ALL OF CAPTAIN BRECCAN'S ABILITY, DERIVED FROM A PACT WITH SATAN, WAS ESSENTIALLY INEFFECTIVE AGAINST CERTAIN MEMBERS OF PROFESSOR BRUTTENHOLM'S TEAM."
BUDDY, DON'T LET THIS GET TO YOU.
IT'S JUST EXACTLY LIKE YOU SAID. YOU HAD TO DO IT. I MEAN, WE'D ALL BE DEAD IF YOU DIDN'T.
YOU'RE A HERO.
"THE HELICOPTER PILOT'S DOG TAGS FINALLY REVEALED WHAT HIS FILE DID NOT--BRECCAN'S NEXT OF KIN. WHEN THEY COME TO CLAIM THE BODY, FURTHER ANSWERS MAY BE FOUND."
MM-HMM, MM-HMM, SEEMS TO WRAP UP THAT FILE. FASCINATING. AIR FORCE... WHO'D HAVE THOUGHT?
OH! LIGHTS ARE BACK ON.
WHEN DID THAT HAPPEN?

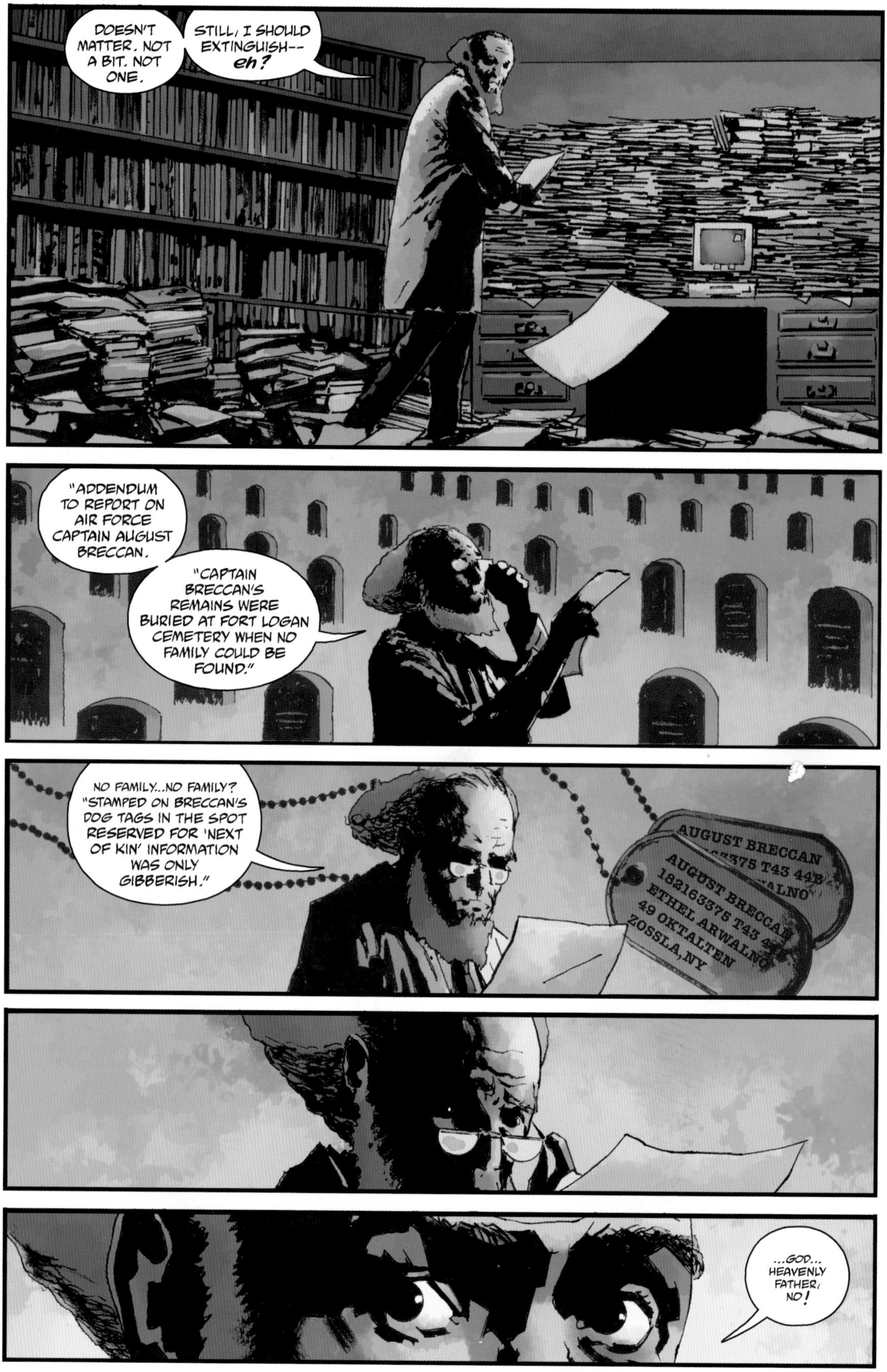
DOESN'T MATTER. NOT A BIT. NOT ONE.
STILL, I SHOULD EXTINGUISH-- eh?
"ADDENDUM TO REPORT ON AIR FORCE CAPTAIN AUGUST BRECCAN.
"CAPTAIN BRECCAN'S REMAINS WERE BURIED AT FORT LOGAN CEMETERY WHEN NO FAMILY COULD BE FOUND."
NO FAMILY...NO FAMILY? "STAMPED ON BRECCAN'S DOG TAGS IN THE SPOT RESERVED FOR 'NEXT OF KIN' INFORMATION WAS ONLY GIBBERISH."
AUGUST BRECCAN
AUGUST BRECCAN
182163375 T43
ETHEL ARWALNO
49 OKTALTEN
ZOSSLA, NY
...GOD... HEAVENLY FATHER, NO!

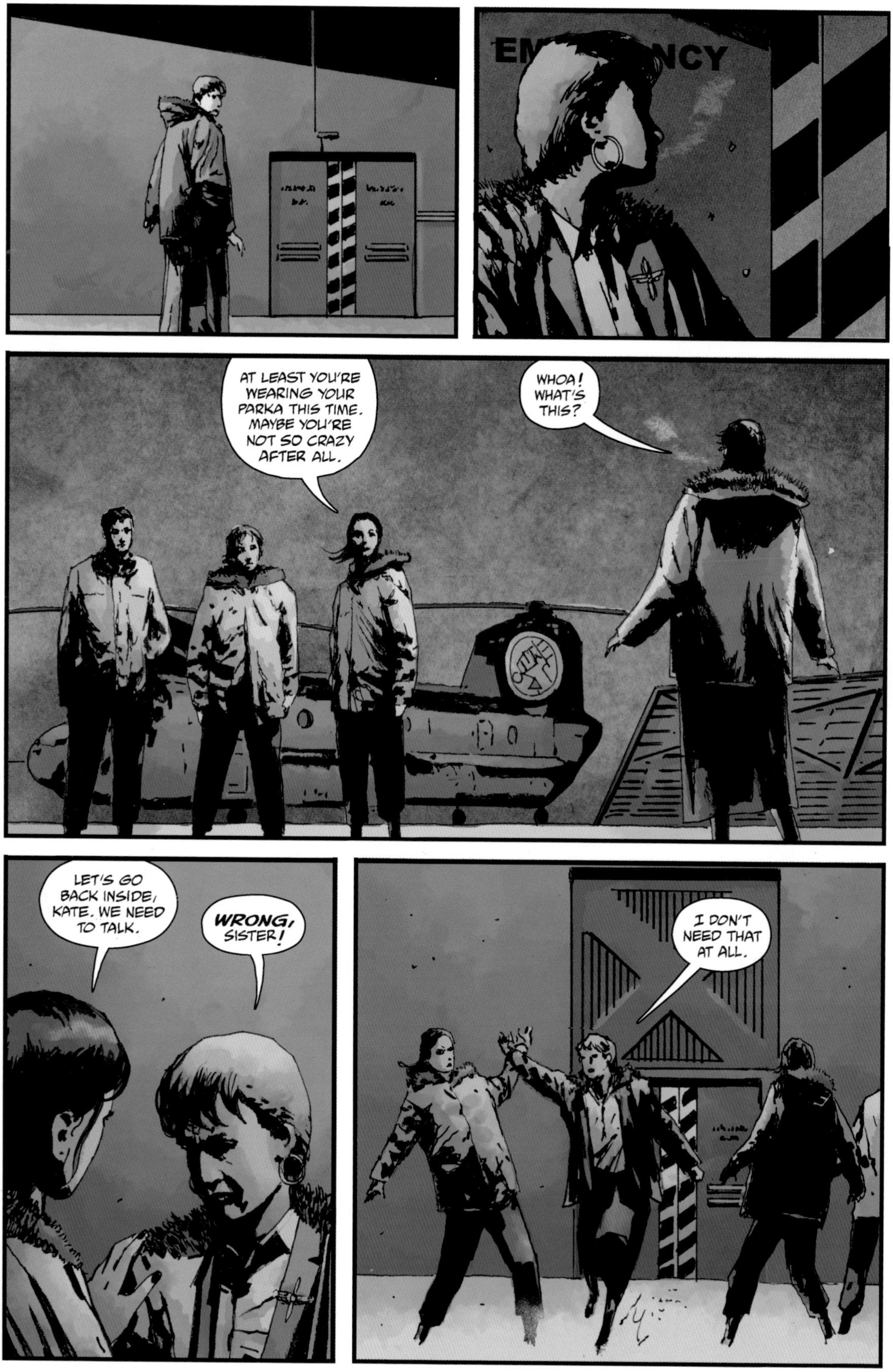
EM NCY
AT LEAST YOU'RE WEARING YOUR PARKA THIS TIME. MAYBE YOU'RE NOT SO CRAZY AFTER ALL.
WHOA! WHAT'S THIS?
LET'S GO BACK INSIDE, KATE. WE NEED TO TALK.
WRONG, SISTER!
I DON'T NEED THAT AT ALL.

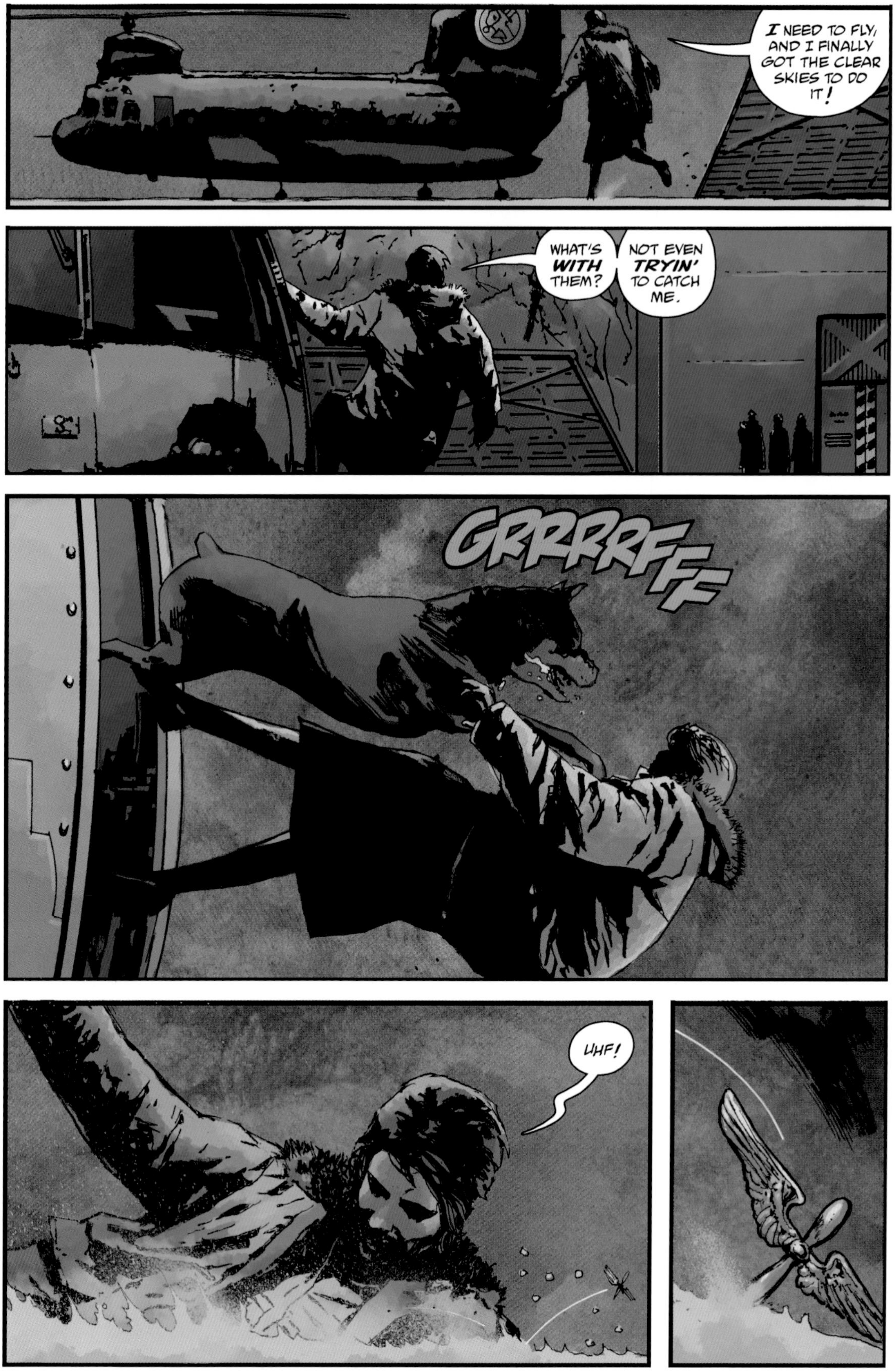
I NEED TO FLY, AND I FINALLY GOT THE CLEAR SKIES TO DO IT!
WHAT'S WITH THEM?
NOT EVEN TRYIN' TO CATCH ME.
GRRRRFFF
UHF!

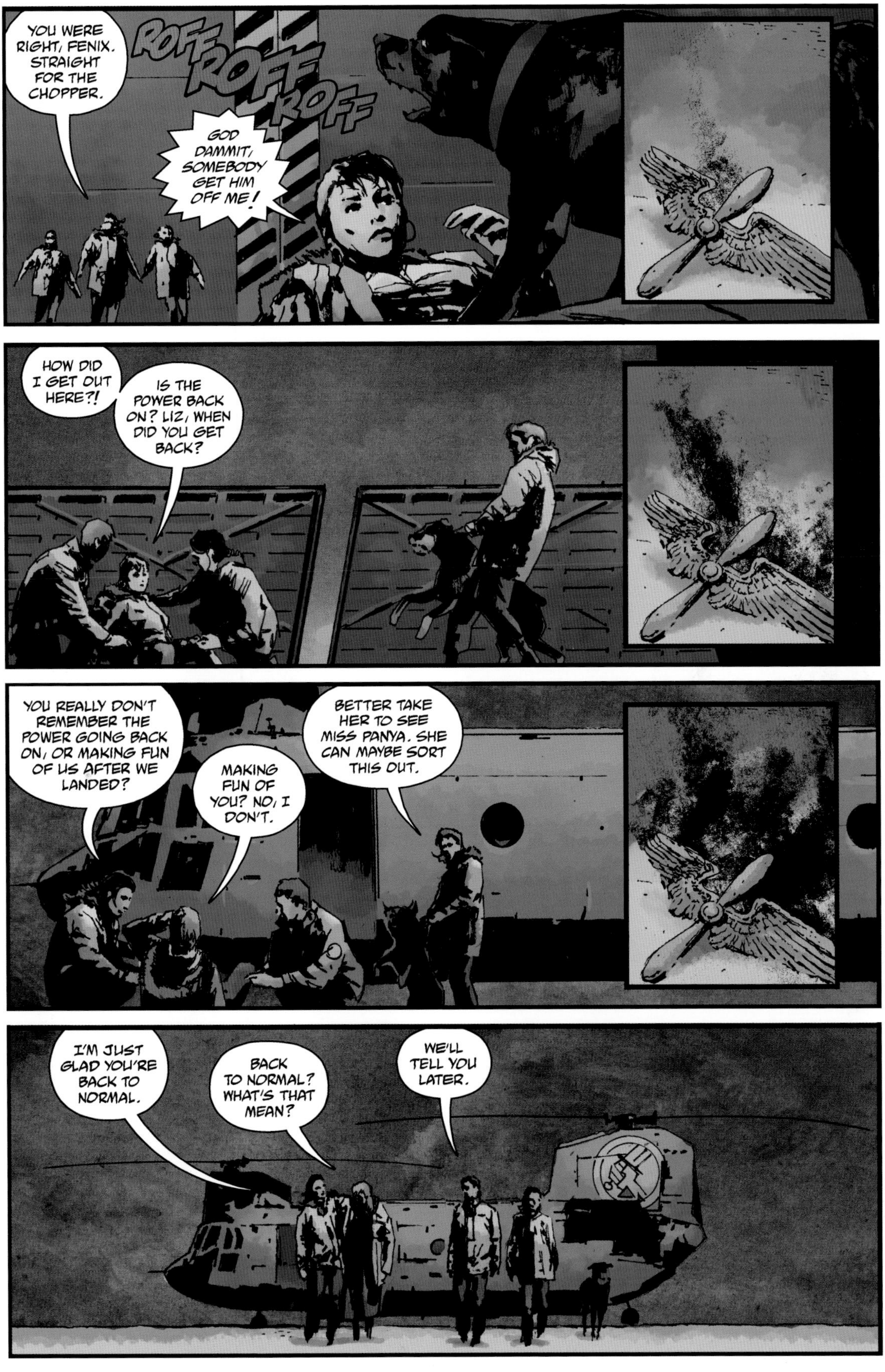
YOU WERE RIGHT, FENIX. STRAIGHT FOR THE CHOPPER.
ROFF ROFF ROFF
GOD DAMMIT, SOMEBODY GET HIM OFF ME!
HOW DID I GET OUT HERE?!
IS THE POWER BACK ON? LIZ, WHEN DID YOU GET BACK?
YOU REALLY DON'T REMEMBER THE POWER GOING BACK ON, OR MAKING FUN OF US AFTER WE LANDED?
MAKING FUN OF YOU? NO, I DON'T.
BETTER TAKE HER TO SEE MISS PANYA. SHE CAN MAYBE SORT THIS OUT.
I'M JUST GLAD YOU'RE BACK TO NORMAL.
BACK TO NORMAL? WHAT'S THAT MEAN?
WE'LL TELL YOU LATER.

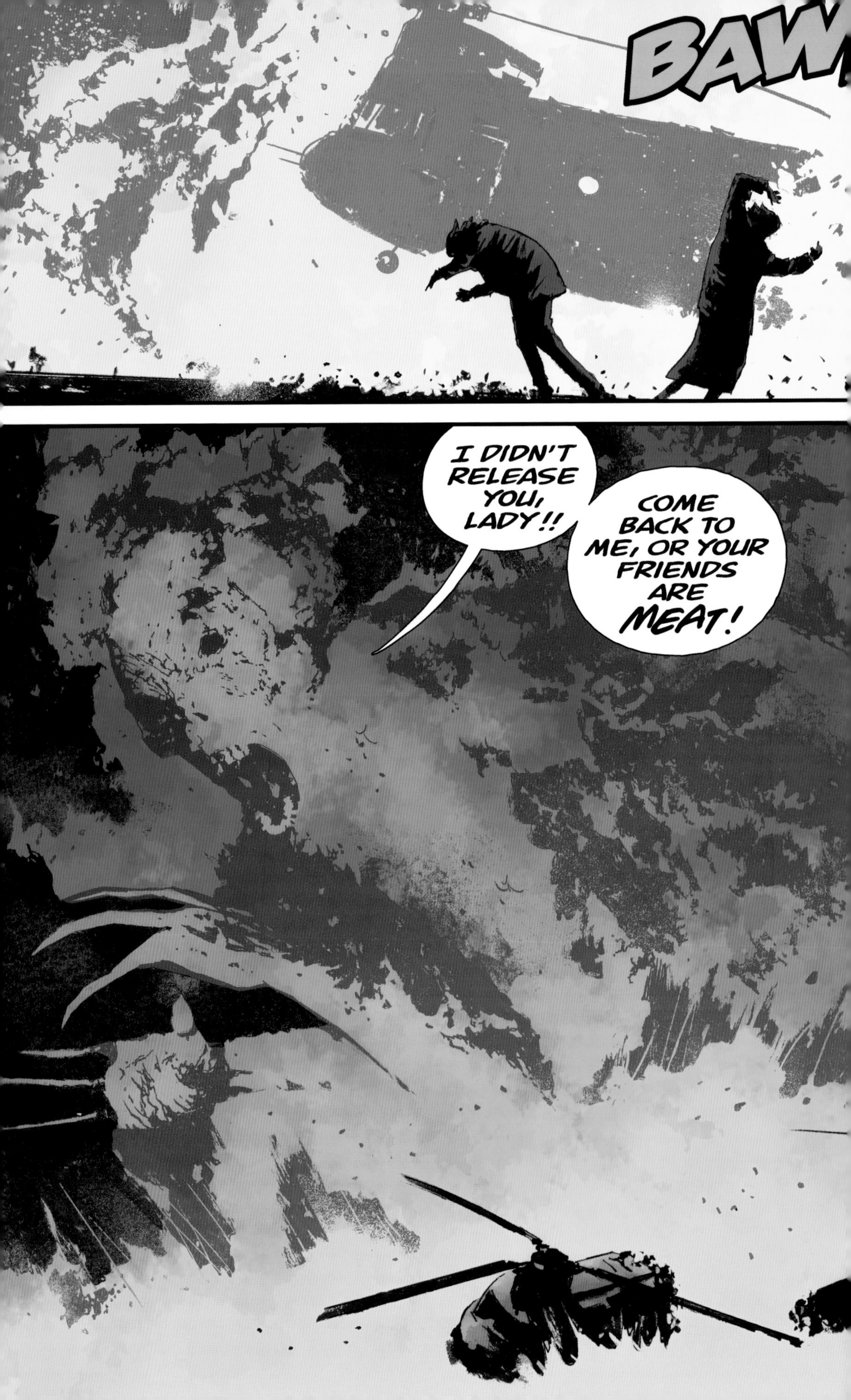
BAW
I DIDN'T RELEASE YOU, LADY!!
COME BACK TO ME, OR YOUR FRIENDS ARE MEAT!

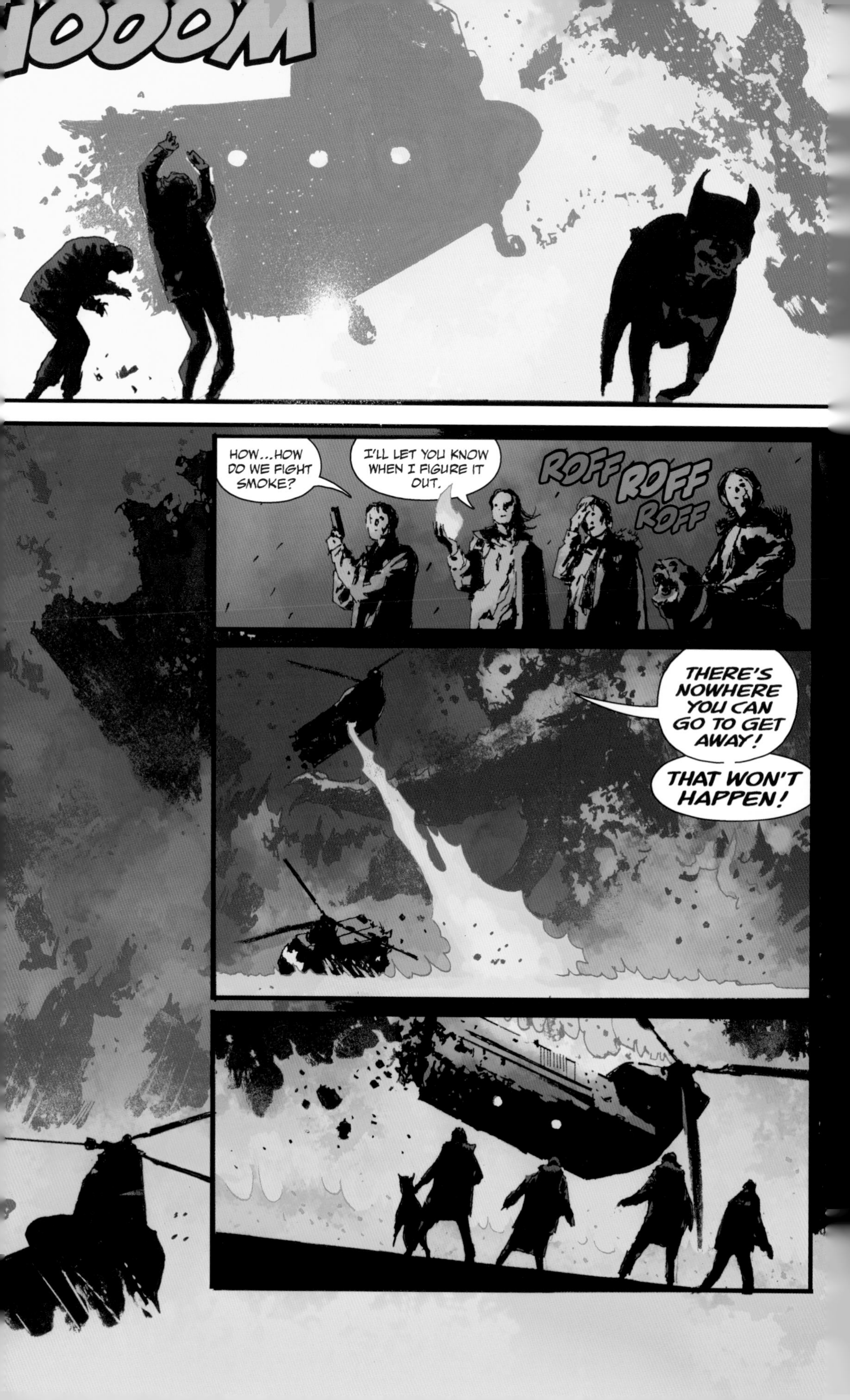
OOOM
HOW...HOW DO WE FIGHT SMOKE?
I'LL LET YOU KNOW WHEN I FIGURE IT OUT.
ROFF ROFF ROFF
THERE'S NOWHERE YOU CAN GO TO GET AWAY!
THAT WON'T HAPPEN!

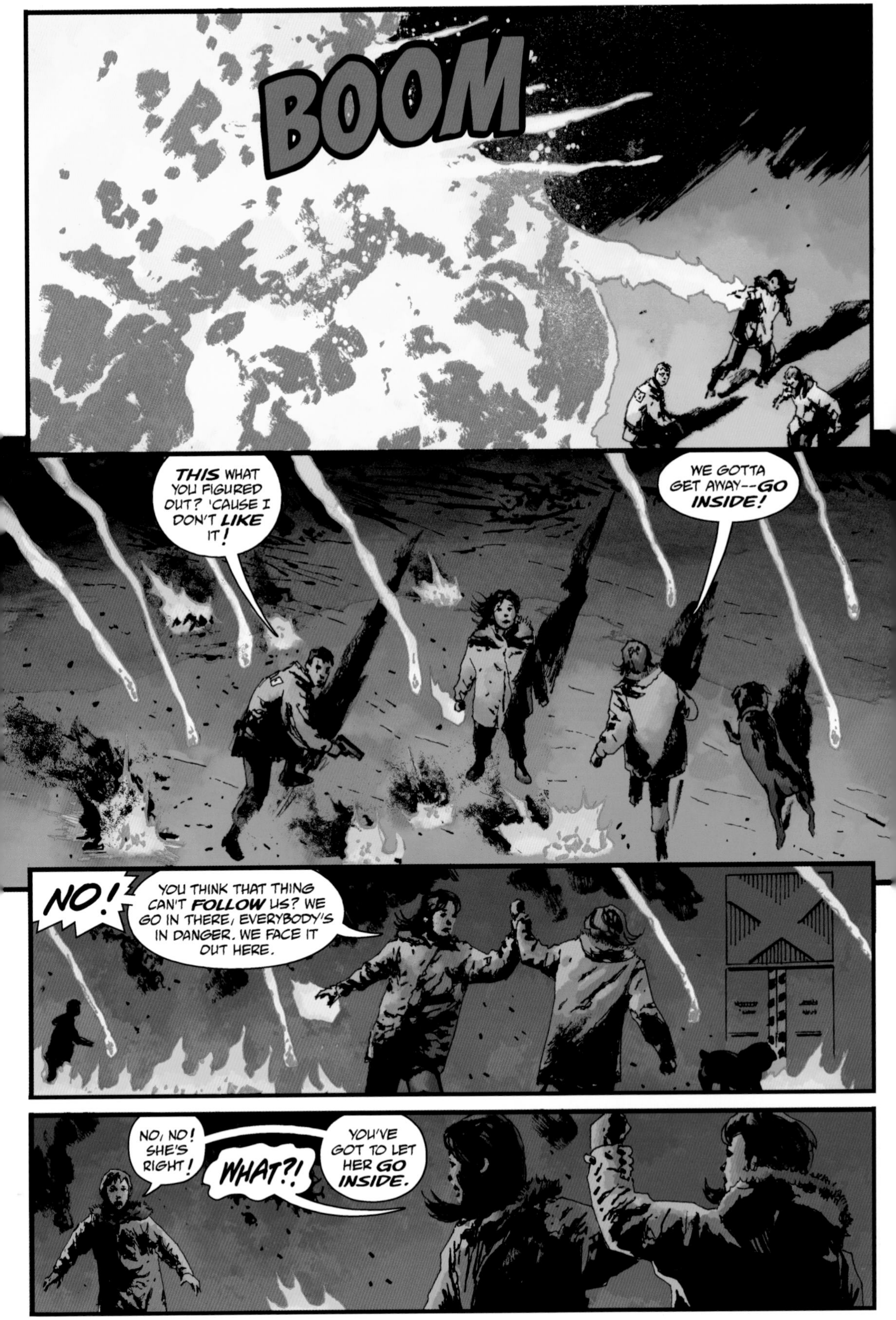
BOOM
THIS WHAT YOU FIGURED OUT? 'CAUSE I DON'T LIKE IT!
WE GOTTA GET AWAY--GO INSIDE!
NO!
YOU THINK THAT THING CAN'T FOLLOW US? WE GO IN THERE, EVERYBODY'S IN DANGER. WE FACE IT OUT HERE.
NO, NO! SHE'S RIGHT!
WHAT?!
YOU'VE GOT TO LET HER GO INSIDE.

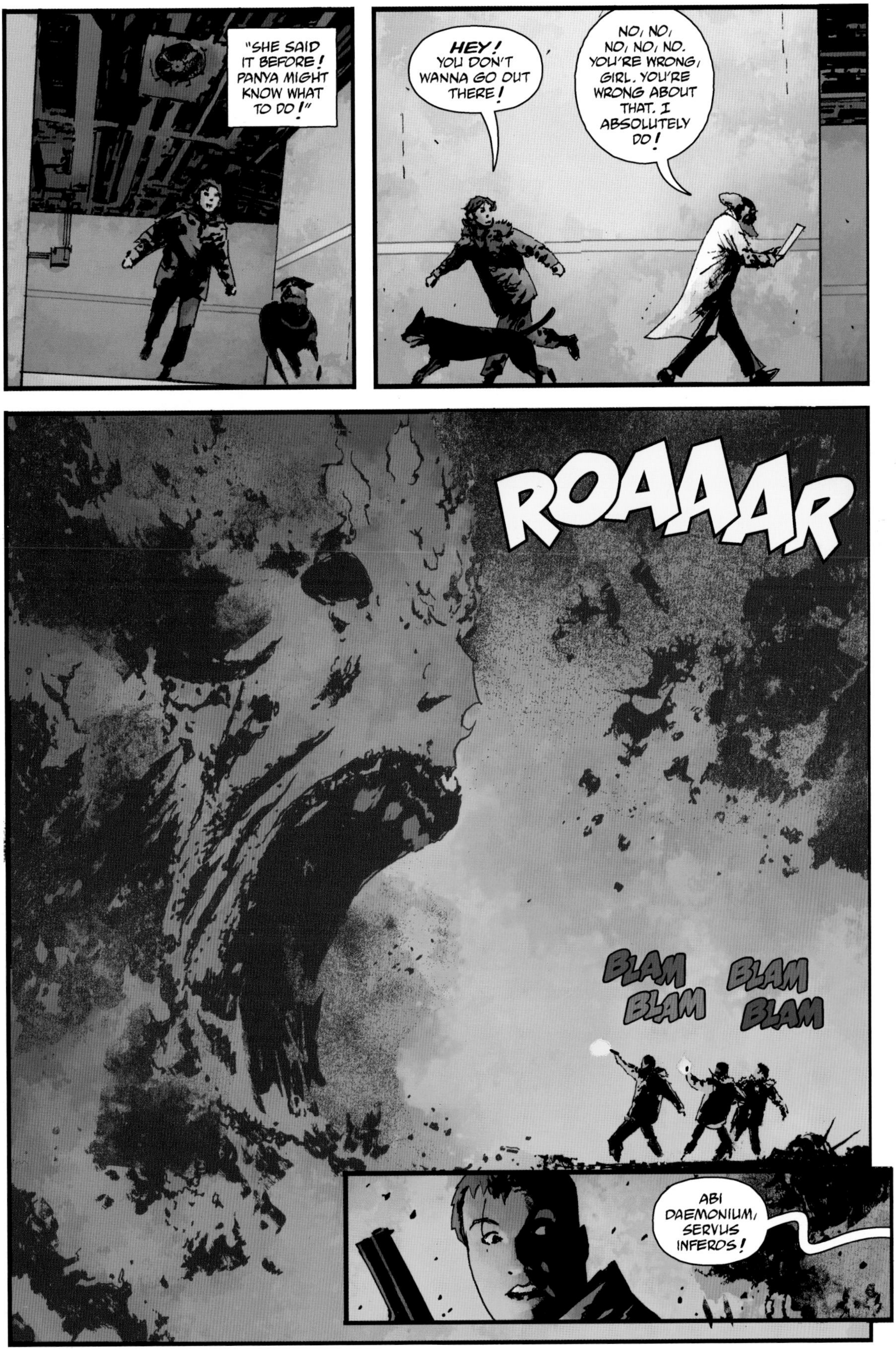
"SHE SAID IT BEFORE! PANYA MIGHT KNOW WHAT TO DO!"
HEY! YOU DON'T WANNA GO OUT THERE!
NO, NO, NO, NO, NO. YOU'RE WRONG, GIRL. YOU'RE WRONG ABOUT THAT. I ABSOLUTELY DO!
ROAAAR
BLAM BLAM BLAM BLAM
ABI DAEMONIUM, SERVUS INFEROS!

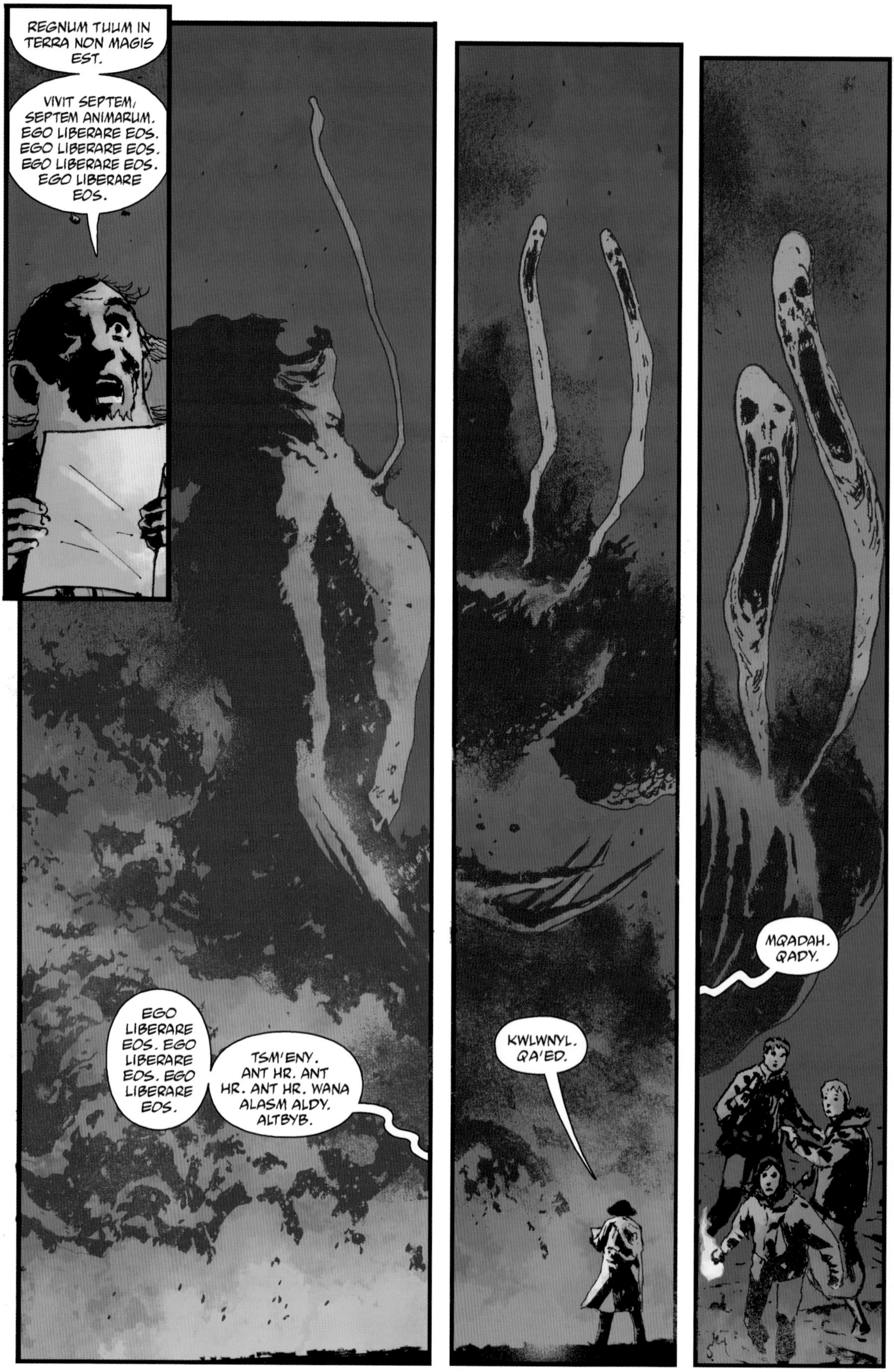
REGNUM TUUM IN TERRA NON MAGIS EST.
VIVIT SEPTEM, SEPTEM ANIMARUM. EGO LIBERARE EOS. EGO LIBERARE EOS. EGO LIBERARE EOS. EGO LIBERARE EOS.
EGO LIBERARE EOS. EGO LIBERARE EOS. EGO LIBERARE EOS.
TSM'ENY. ANT HR. ANT HR. ANT HR. WANA ALASM ALDY. ALTBYB.
KWLWNYL. QA'ED.
MQADAH. QADY.

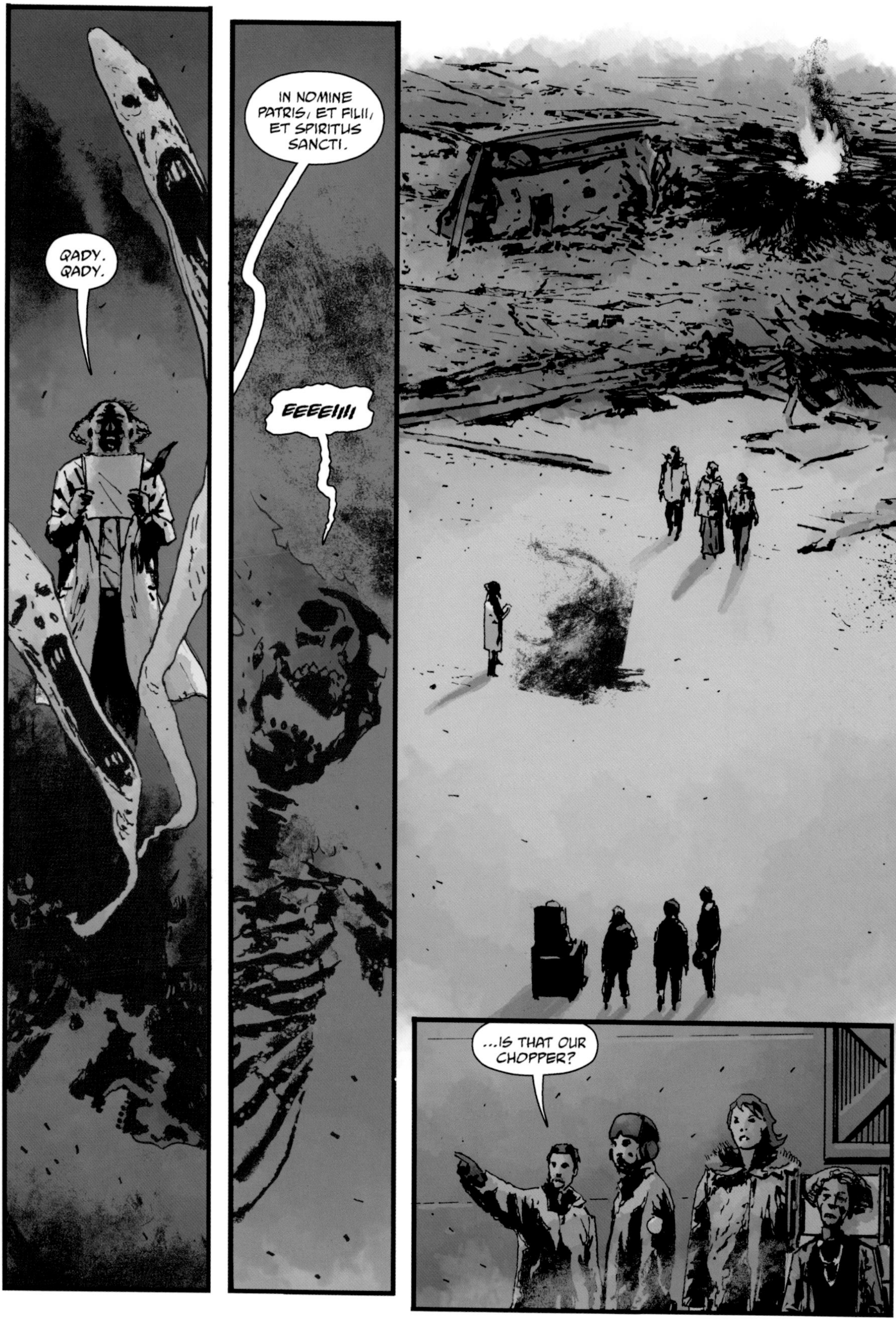
QADY. QADY.
IN NOMINE PATRIS, ET FILII, ET SPIRITUS SANCTI.
EEEEIIII
...IS THAT OUR CHOPPER?

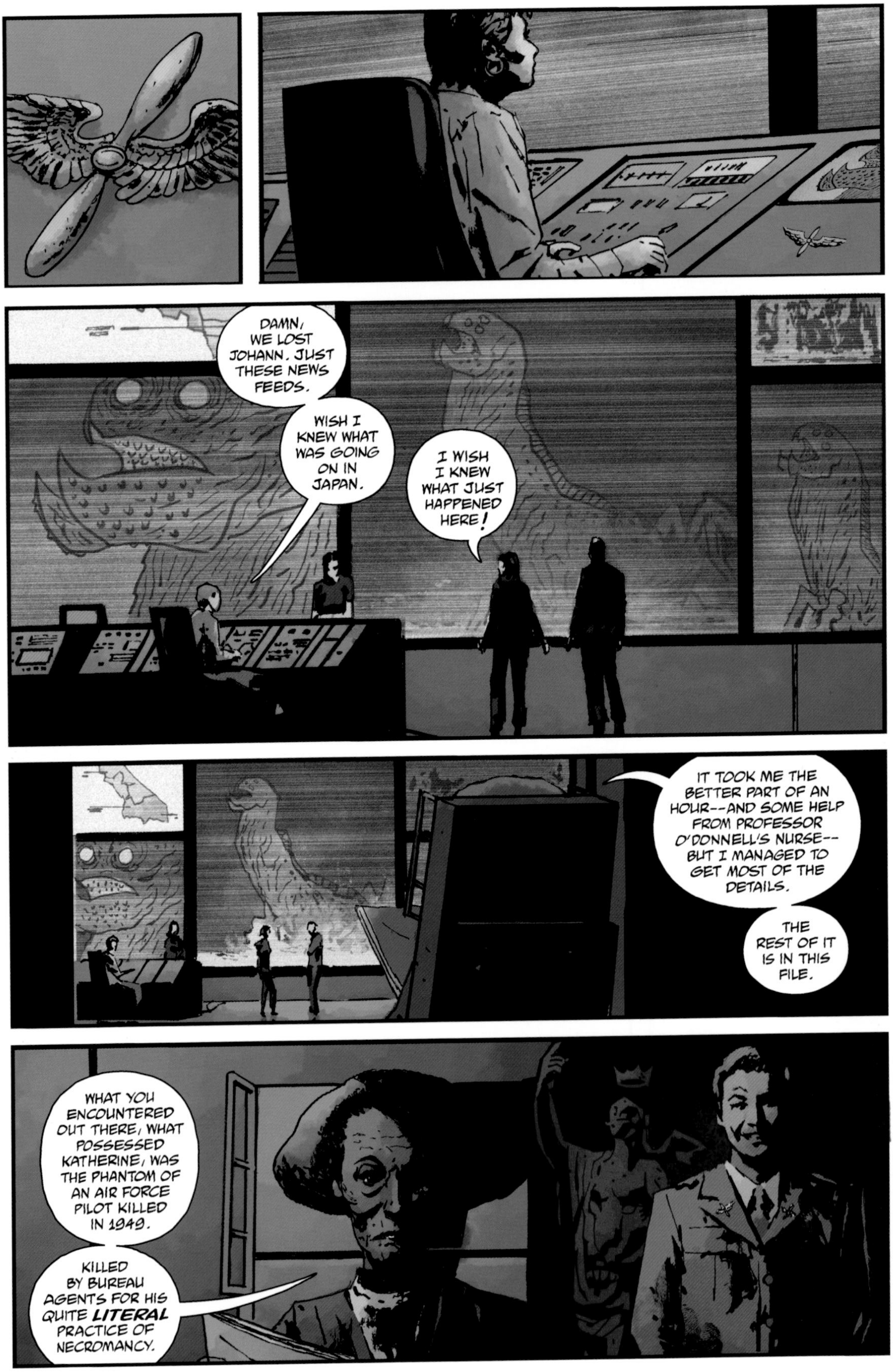
DAMN, WE LOST JOHANN. JUST THESE NEWS FEEDS.
WISH I KNEW WHAT WAS GOING ON IN JAPAN.
I WISH I KNEW WHAT JUST HAPPENED HERE!
IT TOOK ME THE BETTER PART OF AN HOUR--AND SOME HELP FROM PROFESSOR O'DONNELL'S NURSE--BUT I MANAGED TO GET MOST OF THE DETAILS.
THE REST OF IT IS IN THIS FILE.
WHAT YOU ENCOUNTERED OUT THERE, WHAT POSSESSED KATHERINE, WAS THE PHANTOM OF AN AIR FORCE PILOT KILLED IN 1949.
KILLED BY BUREAU AGENTS FOR HIS QUITE ***LITERAL*** PRACTICE OF NECROMANCY.

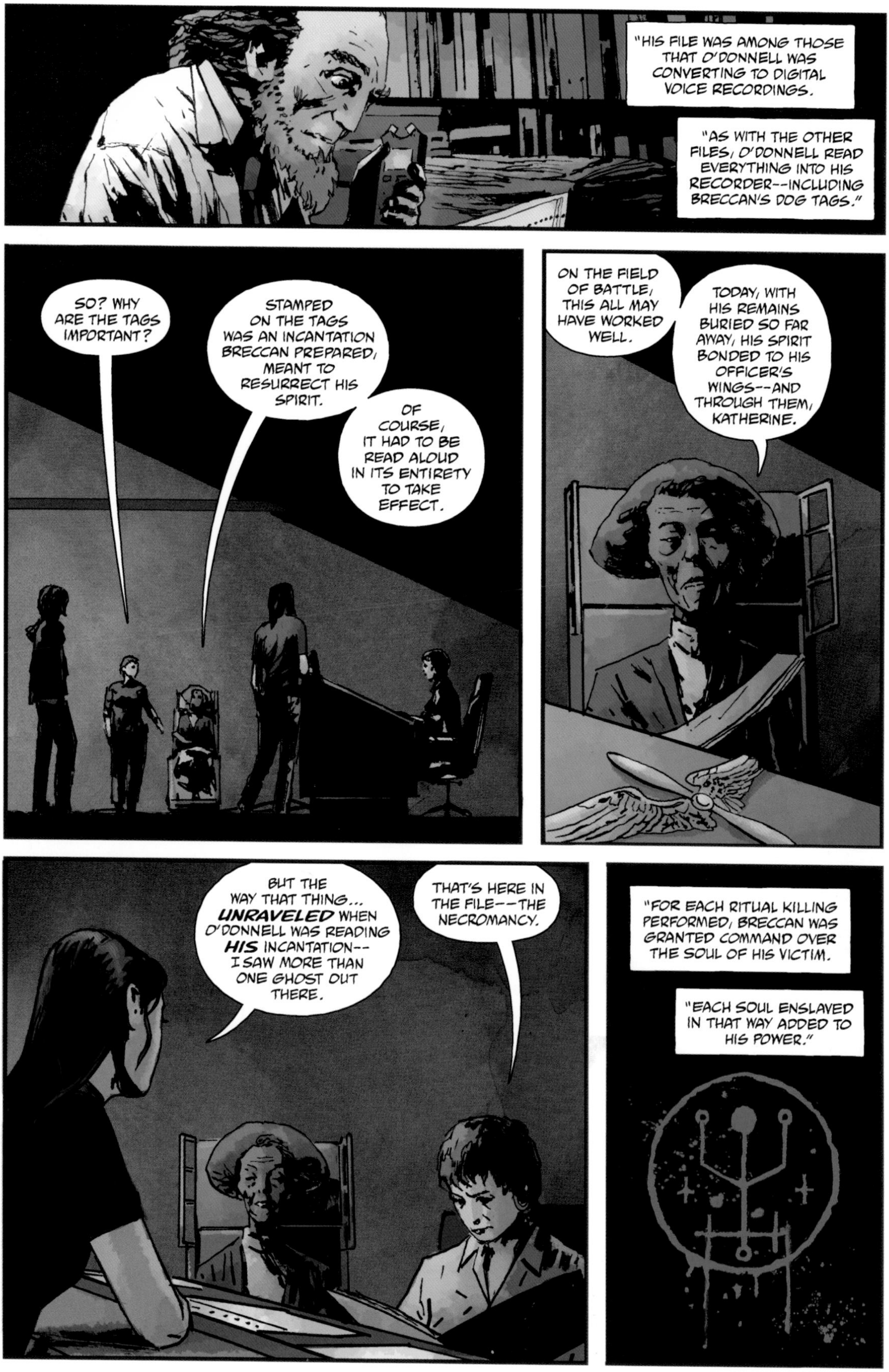
"HIS FILE WAS AMONG THOSE THAT O'DONNELL WAS CONVERTING TO DIGITAL VOICE RECORDINGS.
"AS WITH THE OTHER FILES, O'DONNELL READ EVERYTHING INTO HIS RECORDER--INCLUDING BRECCAN'S DOG TAGS."
SO? WHY ARE THE TAGS IMPORTANT?
STAMPED ON THE TAGS WAS AN INCANTATION BRECCAN PREPARED, MEANT TO RESURRECT HIS SPIRIT.
OF COURSE, IT HAD TO BE READ ALOUD IN ITS ENTIRETY TO TAKE EFFECT.
ON THE FIELD OF BATTLE, THIS ALL MAY HAVE WORKED WELL.
TODAY, WITH HIS REMAINS BURIED SO FAR AWAY, HIS SPIRIT BONDED TO HIS OFFICER'S WINGS--AND THROUGH THEM, KATHERINE.
BUT THE WAY THAT THING... UNRAVELED WHEN O'DONNELL WAS READING HIS INCANTATION--I SAW MORE THAN ONE GHOST OUT THERE.
THAT'S HERE IN THE FILE--THE NECROMANCY.
"FOR EACH RITUAL KILLING PERFORMED, BRECCAN WAS GRANTED COMMAND OVER THE SOUL OF HIS VICTIM.
"EACH SOUL ENSLAVED IN THAT WAY ADDED TO HIS POWER."

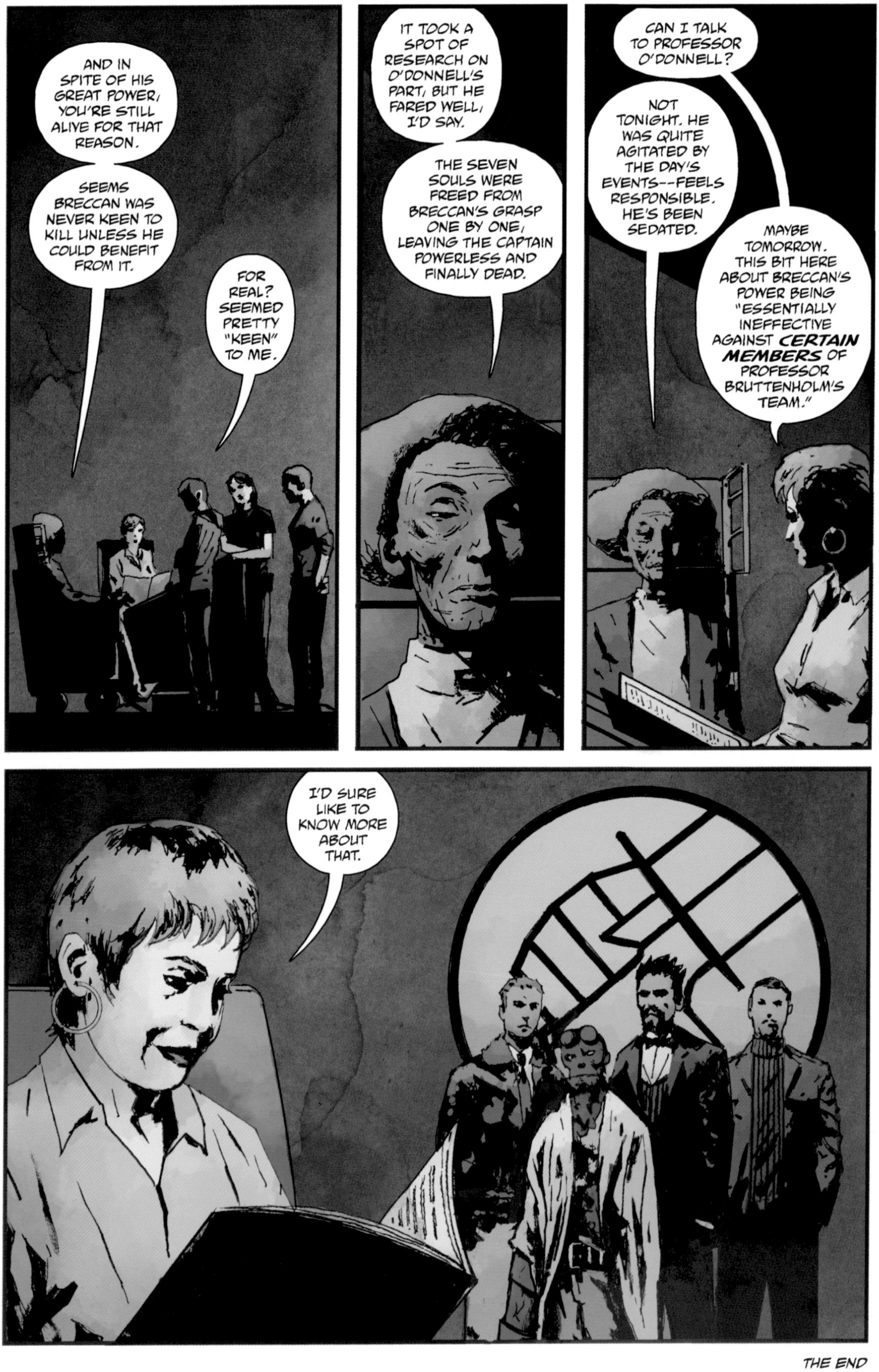
AND IN SPITE OF HIS GREAT POWER, YOU'RE STILL ALIVE FOR THAT REASON.
SEEMS BRECCAN WAS NEVER KEEN TO KILL UNLESS HE COULD BENEFIT FROM IT.
FOR REAL? SEEMED PRETTY "KEEN" TO ME.
IT TOOK A SPOT OF RESEARCH ON O'DONNELL'S PART, BUT HE FARED WELL, I'D SAY.
THE SEVEN SOULS WERE FREED FROM BRECCAN'S GRASP ONE BY ONE, LEAVING THE CAPTAIN POWERLESS AND FINALLY DEAD.
CAN I TALK TO PROFESSOR O'DONNELL?
NOT TONIGHT. HE WAS QUITE AGITATED BY THE DAY'S EVENTS--FEELS RESPONSIBLE. HE'S BEEN SEDATED.
MAYBE TOMORROW. THIS BIT HERE ABOUT BRECCAN'S POWER BEING "ESSENTIALLY INEFFECTIVE AGAINST ***CERTAIN MEMBERS*** OF PROFESSOR BRUTTENHOLM'S TEAM."
I'D SURE LIKE TO KNOW MORE ABOUT THAT.

THE END

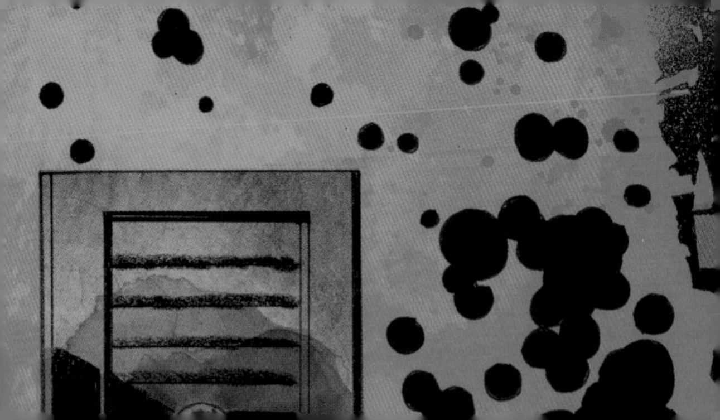

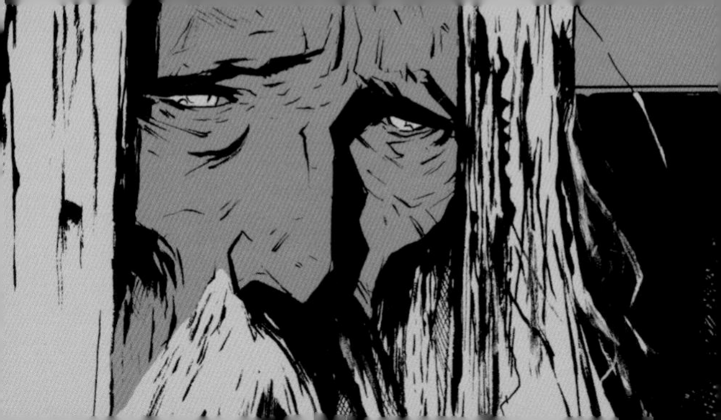

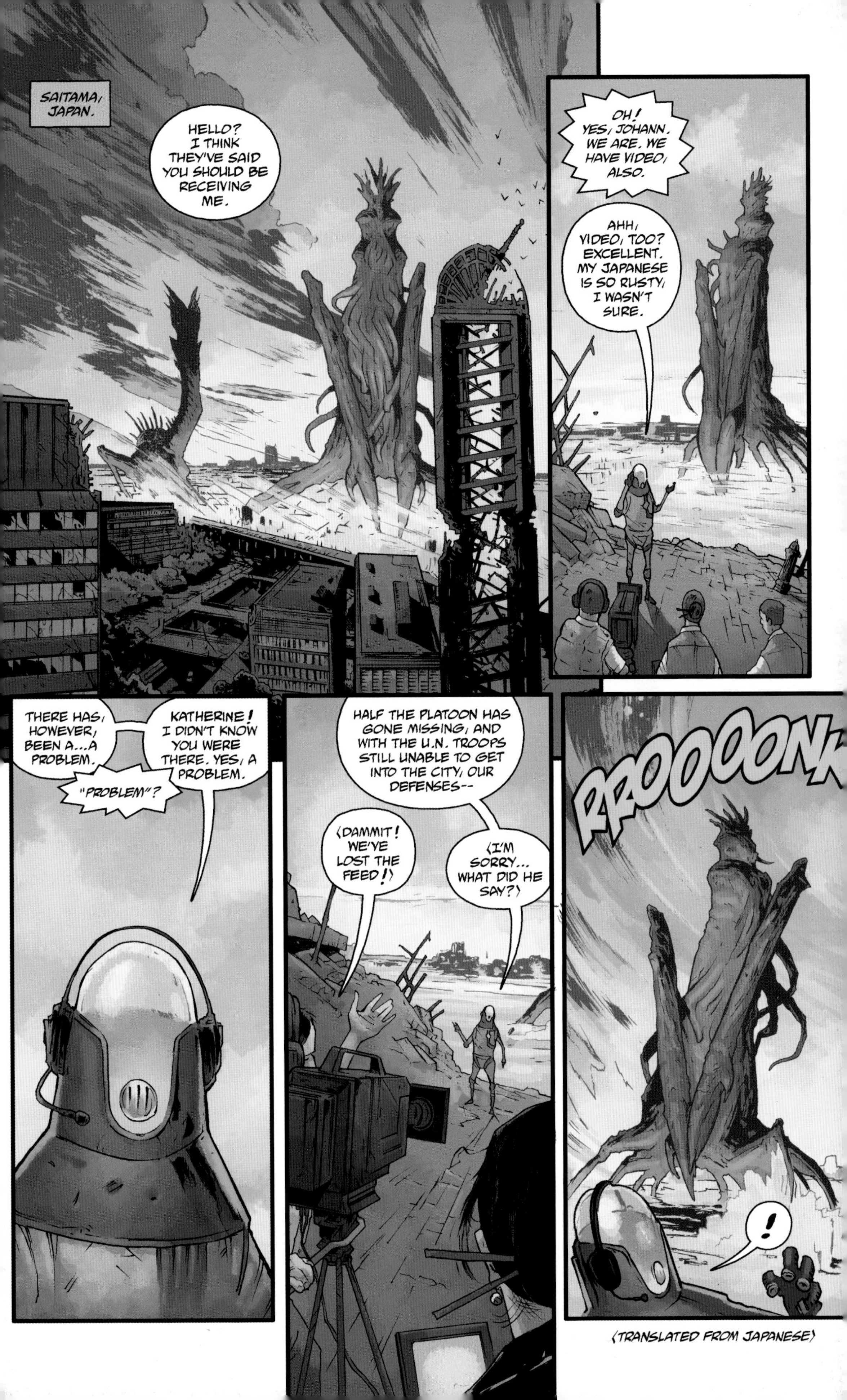
SAITAMA, JAPAN.
HELLO? I THINK THEY'VE SAID YOU SHOULD BE RECEIVING ME.
OH! YES, JOHANN. WE ARE. WE HAVE VIDEO, ALSO.
AHH, VIDEO, TOO? EXCELLENT. MY JAPANESE IS SO RUSTY, I WASN'T SURE.
THERE HAS, HOWEVER, BEEN A...A PROBLEM.
"PROBLEM"?
KATHERINE! I DIDN'T KNOW YOU WERE THERE. YES, A PROBLEM.
HALF THE PLATOON HAS GONE MISSING, AND WITH THE U.N. TROOPS STILL UNABLE TO GET INTO THE CITY, OUR DEFENSES--
‹DAMMIT! WE'VE LOST THE FEED!›
‹I'M SORRY... WHAT DID HE SAY?›
RROOOONK
!
‹TRANSLATED FROM JAPANESE›

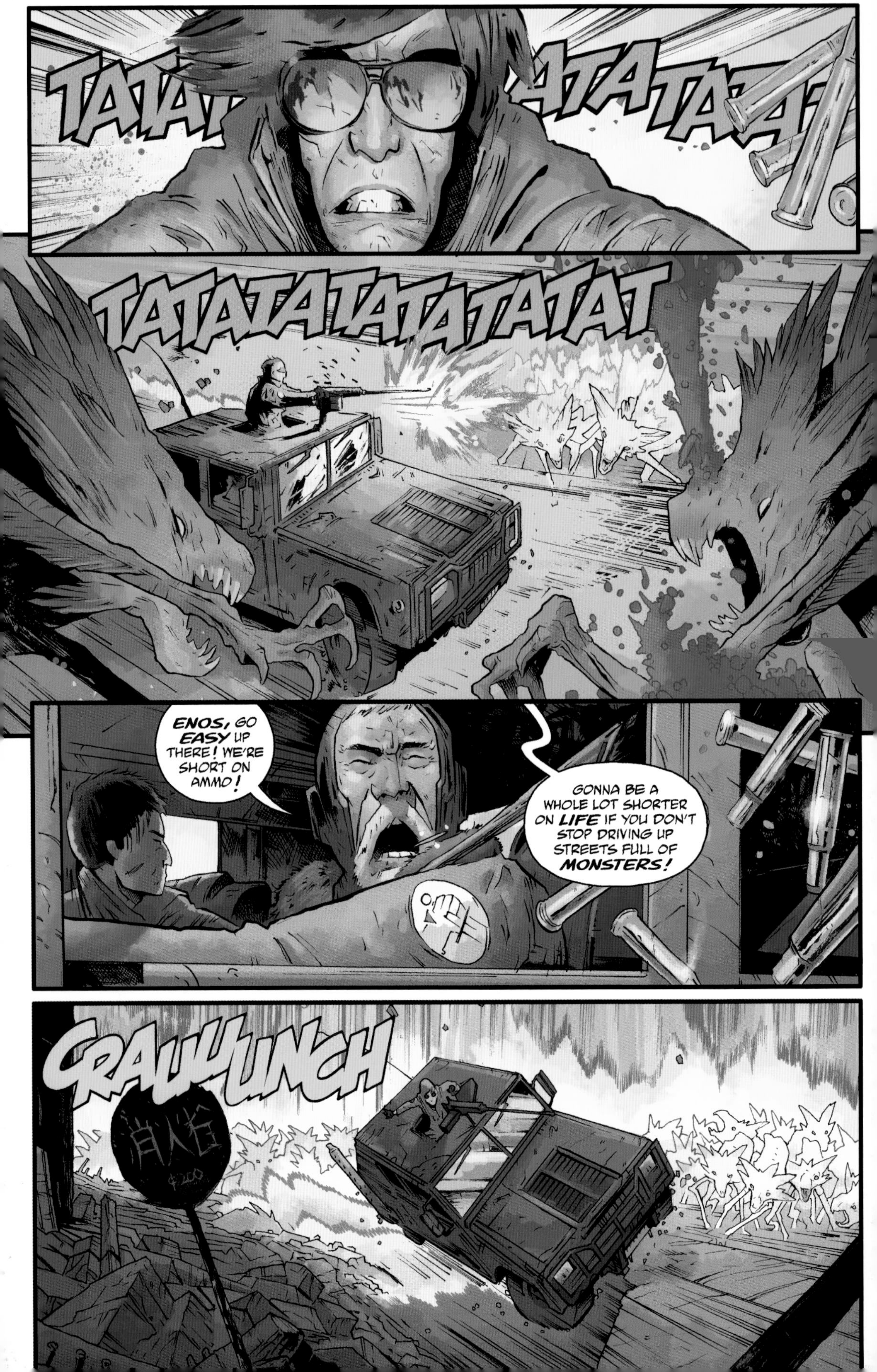
TATATATATATATA
TATATATATATATAT
ENOS, GO EASY UP THERE! WE'RE SHORT ON AMMO!
GONNA BE A WHOLE LOT SHORTER ON LIFE IF YOU DON'T STOP DRIVING UP STREETS FULL OF MONSTERS!
CRAUUUNCH

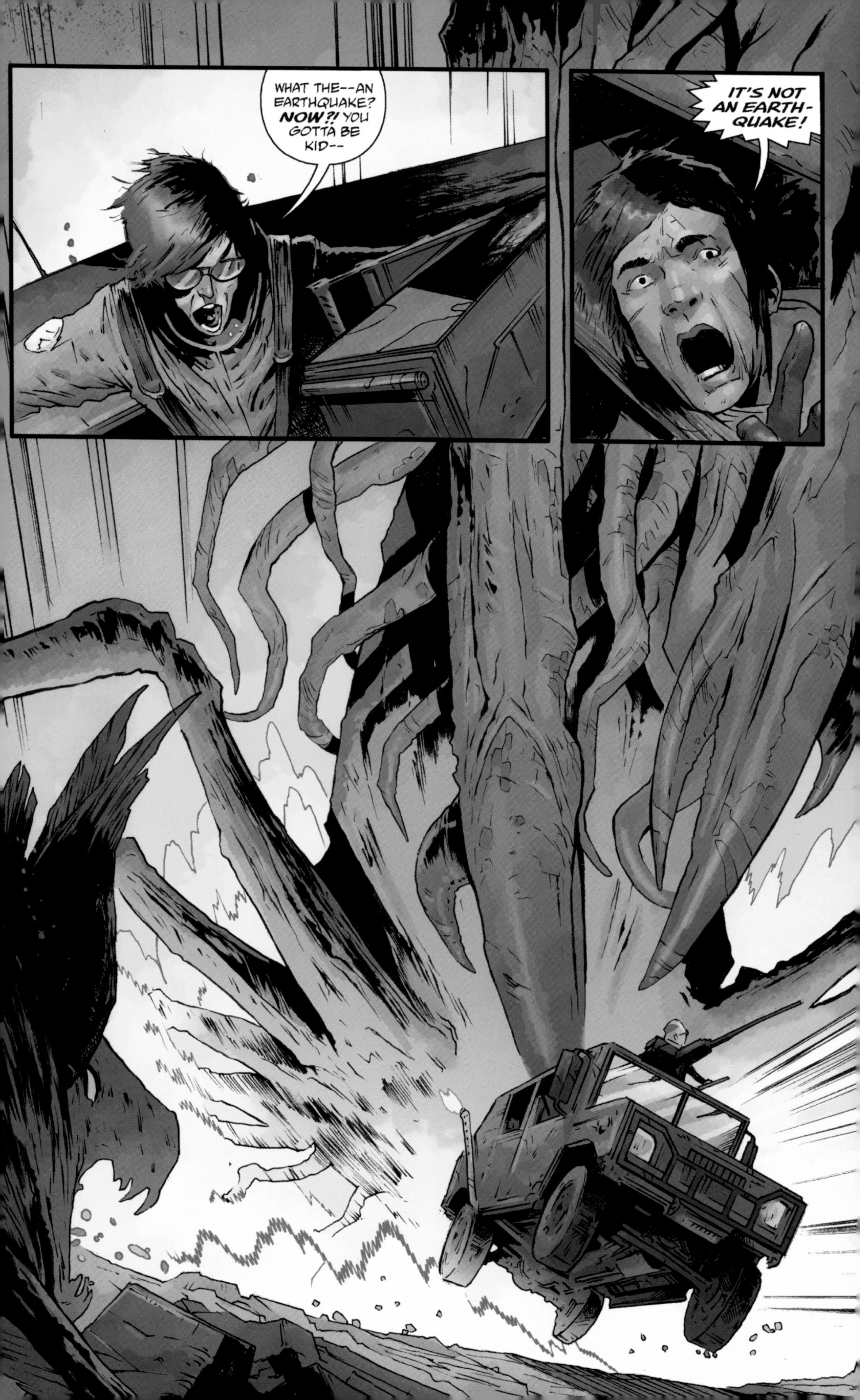
WHAT THE--AN EARTHQUAKE? **NOW?!** YOU GOTTA BE KID--
IT'S NOT AN EARTH-QUAKE!

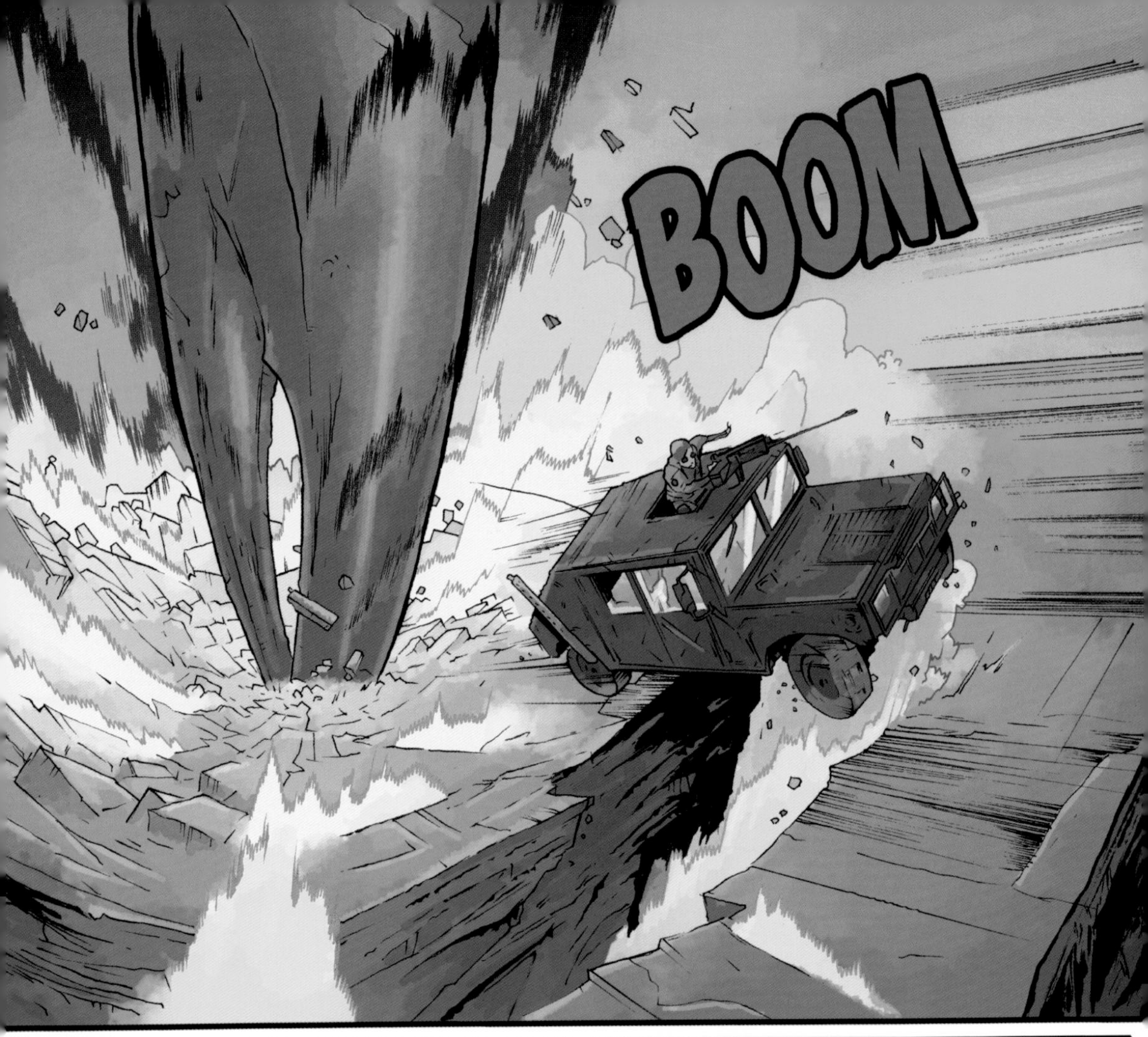
BOOM

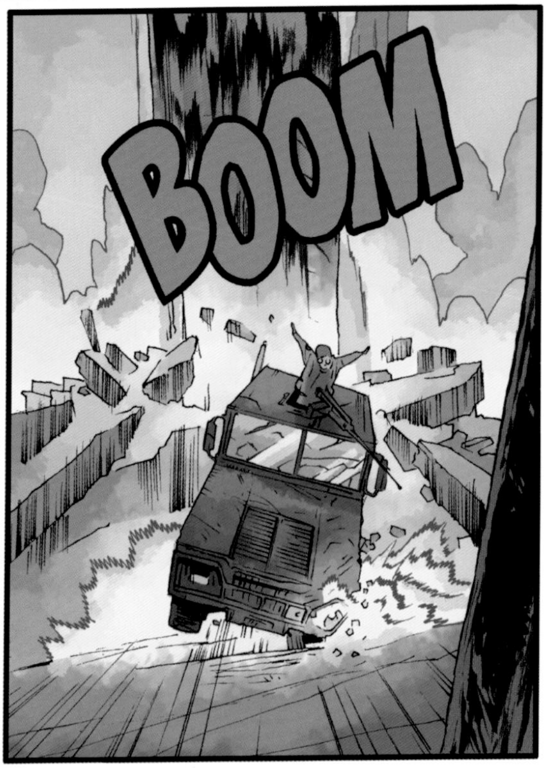
BOOM

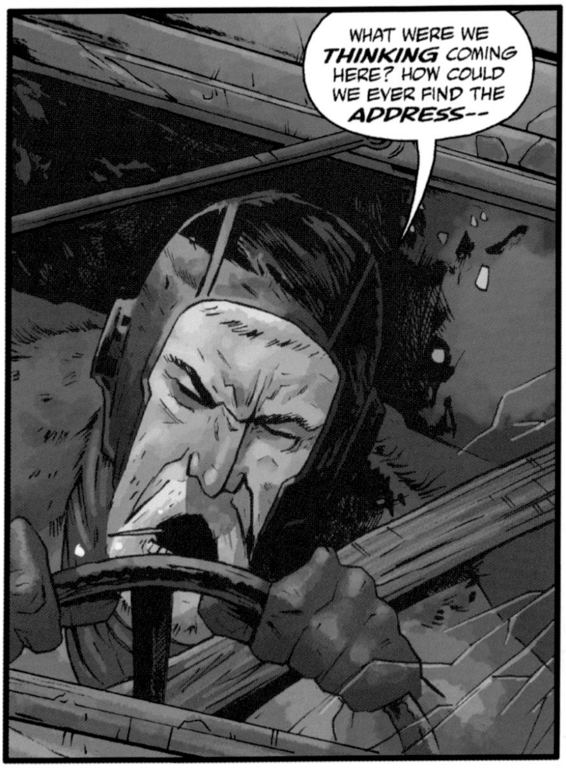
WHAT WERE WE THINKING COMING HERE? HOW COULD WE EVER FIND THE ADDRESS--

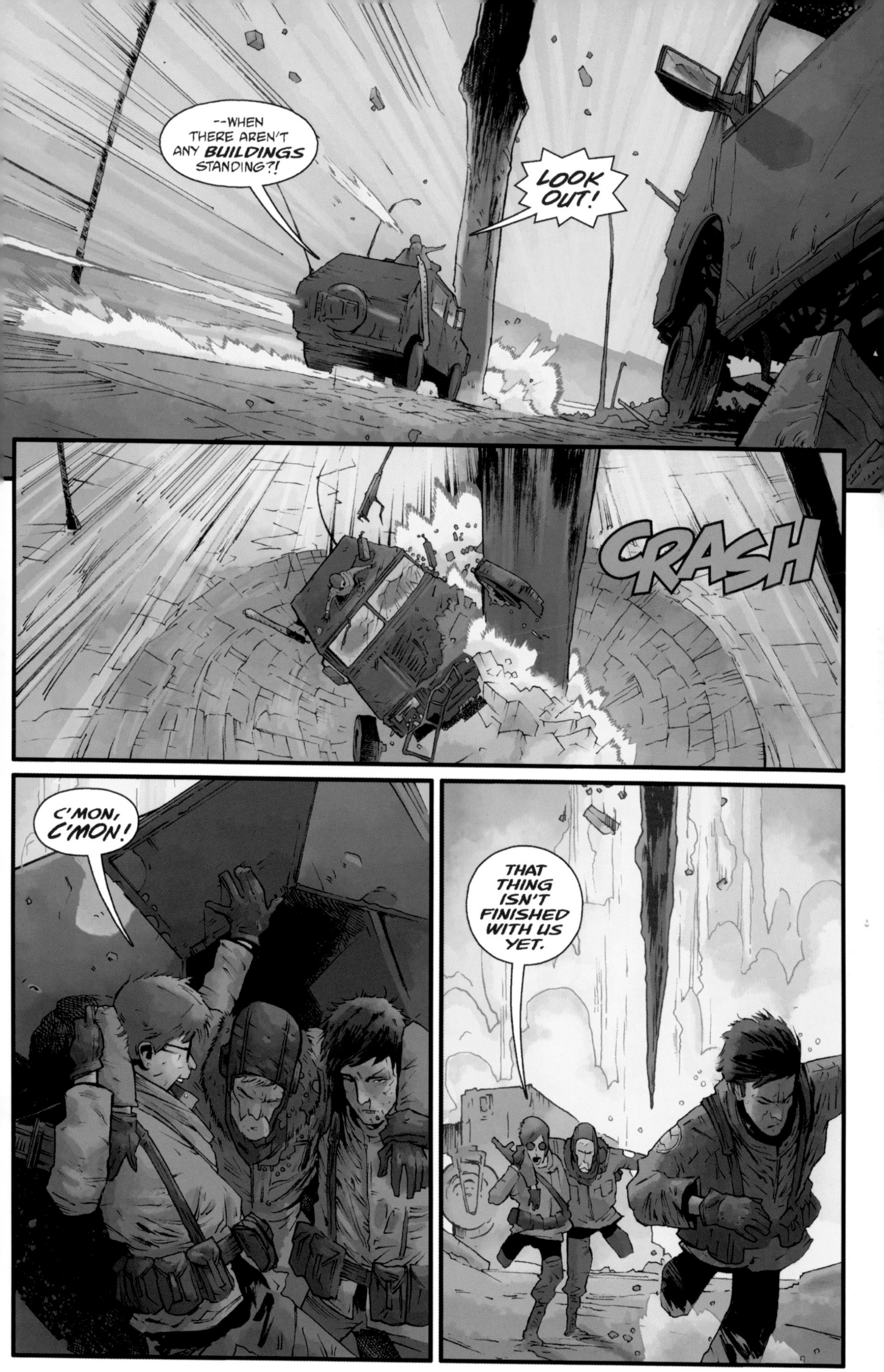
--WHEN THERE AREN'T ANY BUILDINGS STANDING?!
LOOK OUT!
CRASH
C'MON, C'MON!
THAT THING ISN'T FINISHED WITH US YET.

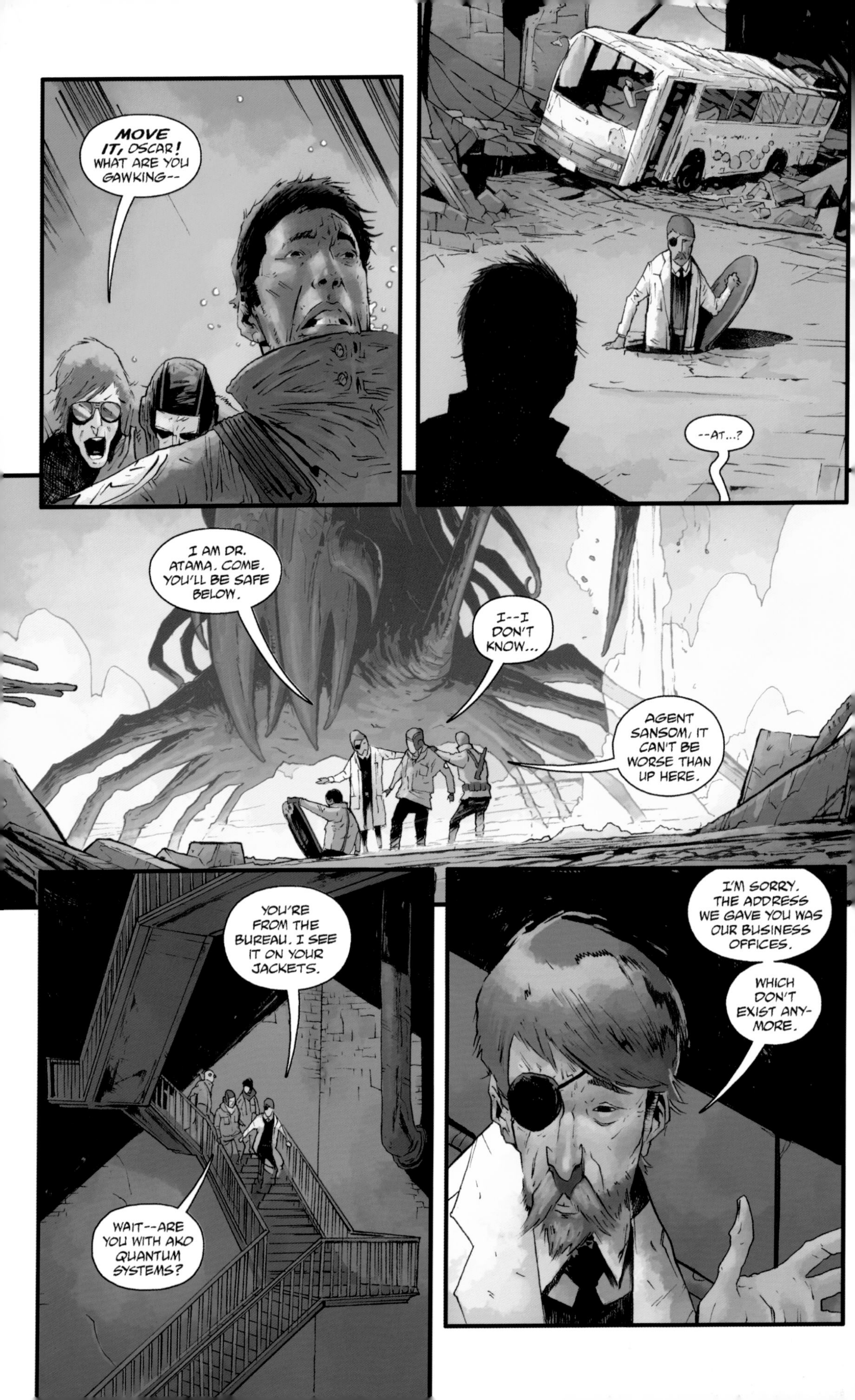
MOVE IT, OSCAR! WHAT ARE YOU GAWKING--
--AT...?
I AM DR. ATAMA. COME. YOU'LL BE SAFE BELOW.
I--I DON'T KNOW...
AGENT SANSOM, IT CAN'T BE WORSE THAN UP HERE.
YOU'RE FROM THE BUREAU. I SEE IT ON YOUR JACKETS.
WAIT--ARE YOU WITH AKO QUANTUM SYSTEMS?
I'M SORRY. THE ADDRESS WE GAVE YOU WAS OUR BUSINESS OFFICES.
WHICH DON'T EXIST ANY-MORE.

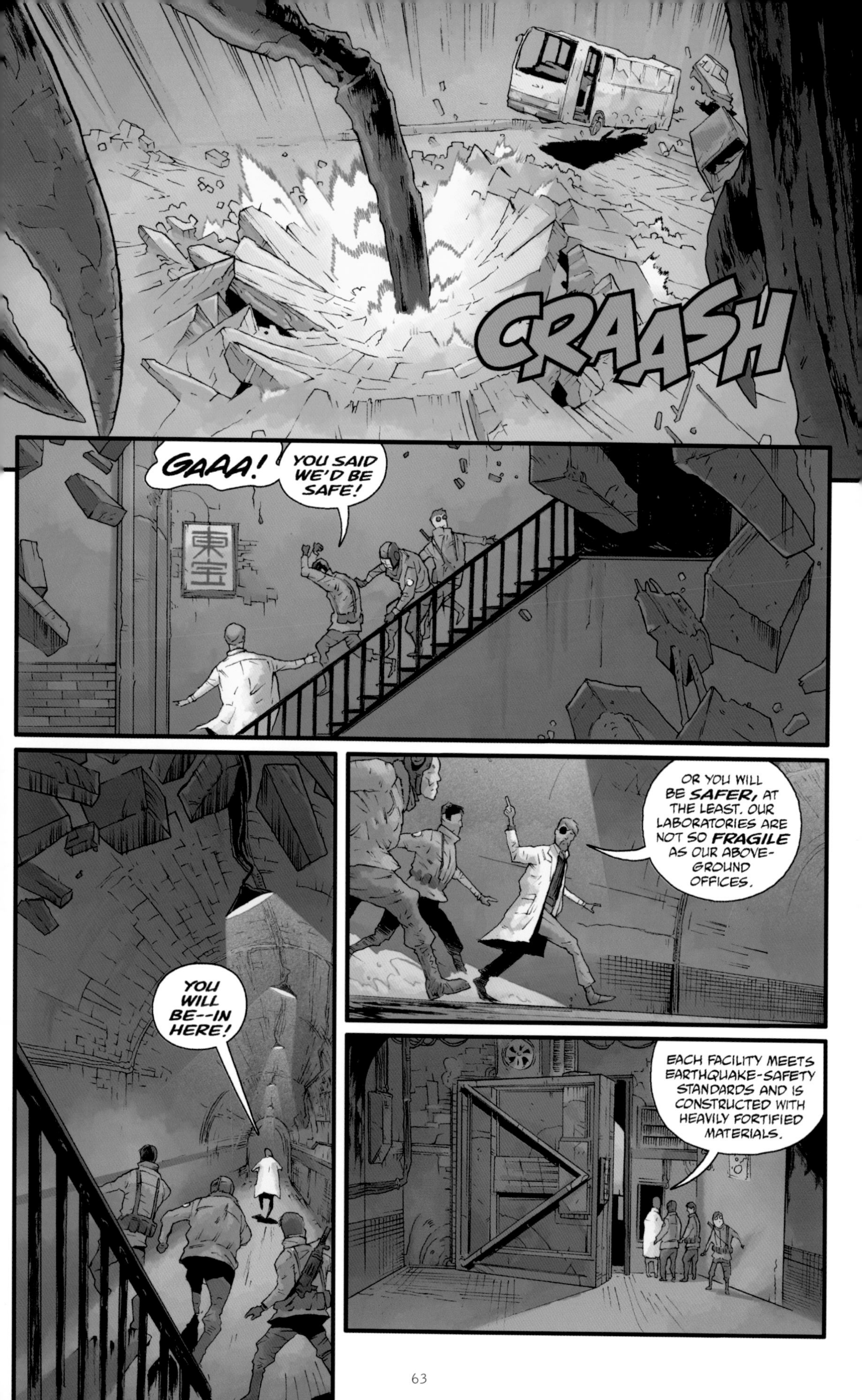
CRAASH
GAAA!
YOU SAID WE'D BE SAFE!
東宝
YOU WILL BE--IN HERE!
OR YOU WILL BE SAFER, AT THE LEAST. OUR LABORATORIES ARE NOT SO FRAGILE AS OUR ABOVE-GROUND OFFICES.
EACH FACILITY MEETS EARTHQUAKE-SAFETY STANDARDS AND IS CONSTRUCTED WITH HEAVILY FORTIFIED MATERIALS.

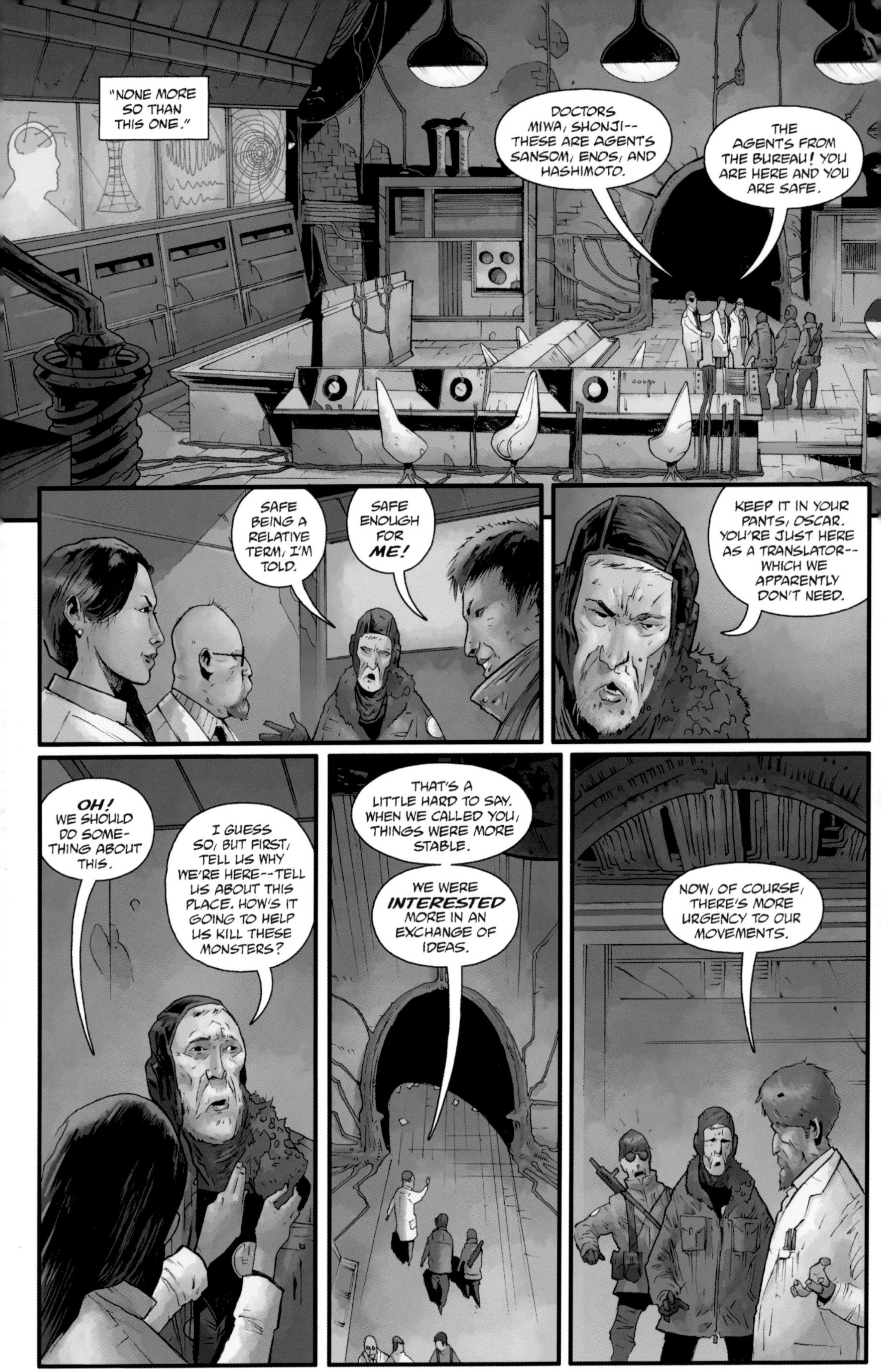
"NONE MORE SO THAN THIS ONE."
DOCTORS MIWA, SHONJI-- THESE ARE AGENTS SANSOM, ENOS, AND HASHIMOTO.
THE AGENTS FROM THE BUREAU! YOU ARE HERE AND YOU ARE SAFE.
SAFE BEING A RELATIVE TERM, I'M TOLD.
SAFE ENOUGH FOR ME!
KEEP IT IN YOUR PANTS, OSCAR. YOU'RE JUST HERE AS A TRANSLATOR-- WHICH WE APPARENTLY DON'T NEED.
OH! WE SHOULD DO SOME-THING ABOUT THIS.
I GUESS SO, BUT FIRST, TELL US WHY WE'RE HERE--TELL US ABOUT THIS PLACE. HOW'S IT GOING TO HELP US KILL THESE MONSTERS?
THAT'S A LITTLE HARD TO SAY. WHEN WE CALLED YOU, THINGS WERE MORE STABLE.
WE WERE INTERESTED MORE IN AN EXCHANGE OF IDEAS.
NOW, OF COURSE, THERE'S MORE URGENCY TO OUR MOVEMENTS.

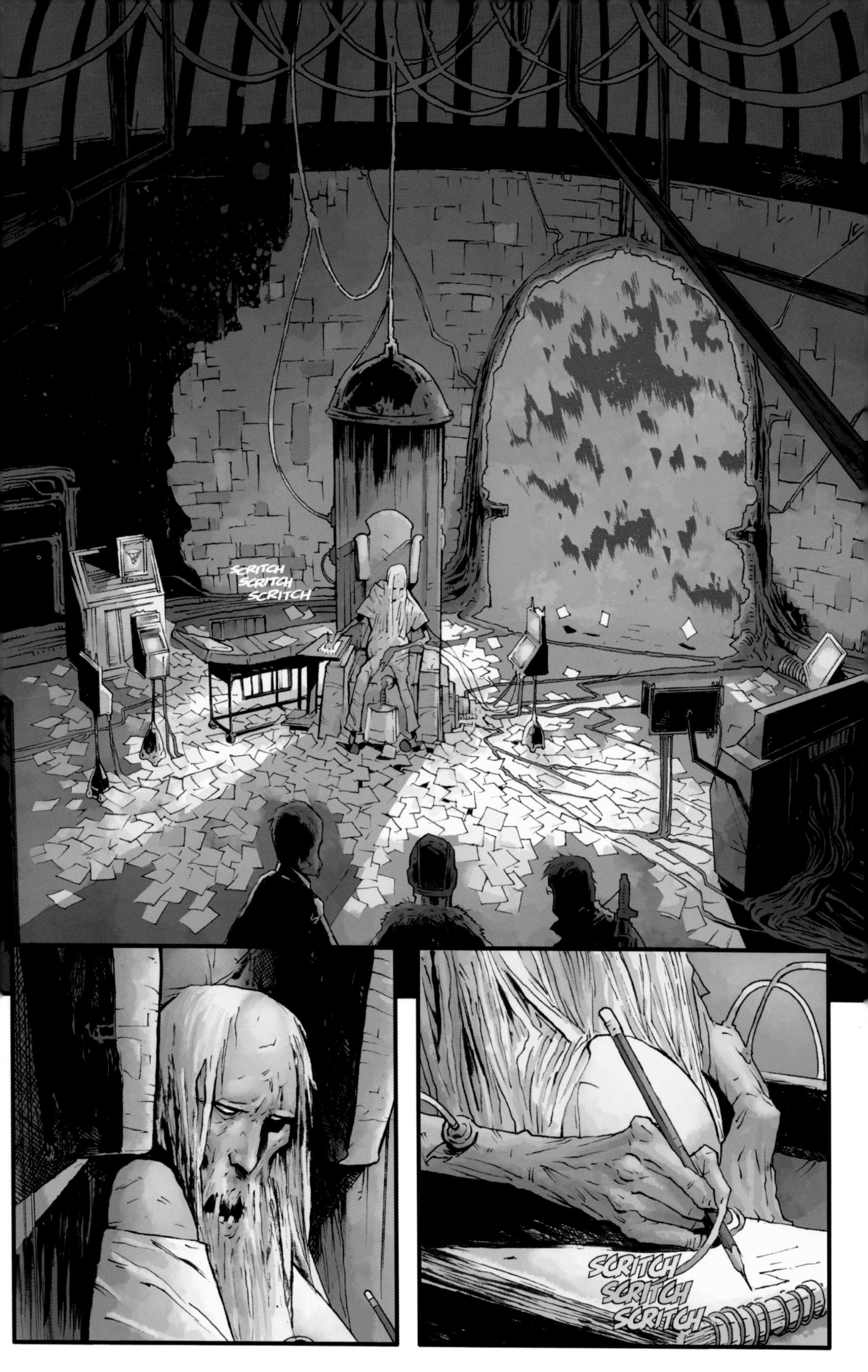
SCRITCH
SCRITCH
SCRITCH
SCRITCH
SCRITCH
SCRITCH

WHAT IN BURNING HELL IS GOING **ON** IN THIS PLACE?!

IT'S A LONG STORY, AGENT SANSOM, BUT I FEEL THAT YOU HAVE THE TIME TO HEAR IT.

"IN 1979, AKO QUANTUM SYSTEMS WAS OPERATING OUTSIDE OF ANY FEDERAL GUIDE-LINES--OR EVEN JURISDICTIONS.

"THE NATIONAL DIET WAS NEVER INFORMED OF OUR PROGRESS. IF WE WERE EVER CAUGHT, THEY WERE TO HAVE PLAUSIBLE DENIABILITY.

"BECAUSE WHAT WE WERE DOING WAS VERY, VERY DANGEROUS.

"YOU'VE HEARD OF PROFESSOR SHUN KUKYO AND HIS CONTROVERSIAL **CONDENSED ENERGY SYSTEM EQUATION** THAT SUGGESTED PARALLEL REALITY ACCESSIBILITY WAS FEASIBLE?

$$\Sigma = i \sum \sqrt{\frac{\hbar w_K}{2 N_M d_V}}$$

"HERE, WE TESTED THAT EQUATION.

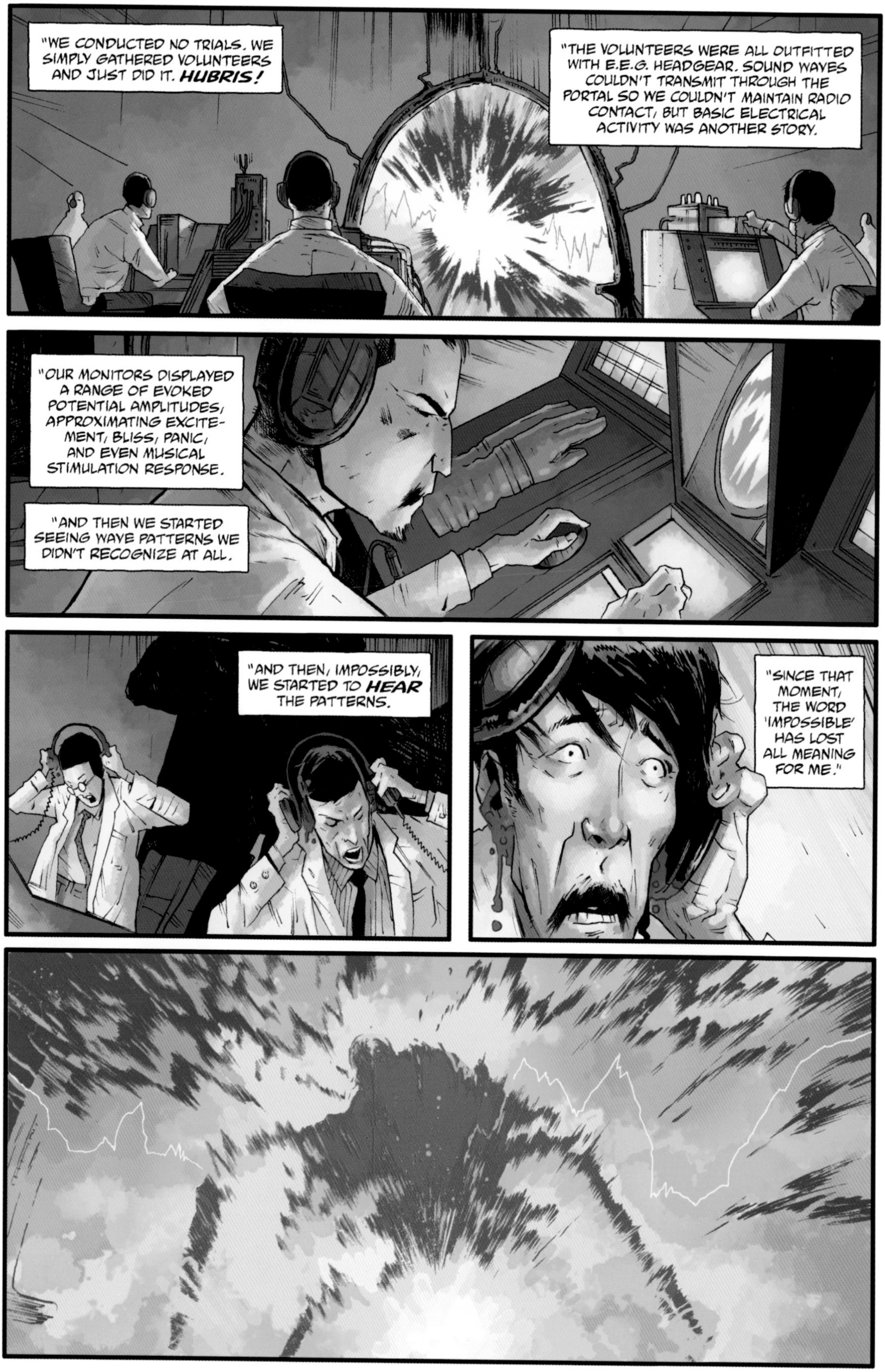
"WE CONDUCTED NO TRIALS. WE SIMPLY GATHERED VOLUNTEERS AND JUST DID IT. HUBRIS!
"THE VOLUNTEERS WERE ALL OUTFITTED WITH E.E.G. HEADGEAR. SOUND WAVES COULDN'T TRANSMIT THROUGH THE PORTAL SO WE COULDN'T MAINTAIN RADIO CONTACT, BUT BASIC ELECTRICAL ACTIVITY WAS ANOTHER STORY.
"OUR MONITORS DISPLAYED A RANGE OF EVOKED POTENTIAL AMPLITUDES, APPROXIMATING EXCITEMENT, BLISS, PANIC, AND EVEN MUSICAL STIMULATION RESPONSE.
"AND THEN WE STARTED SEEING WAVE PATTERNS WE DIDN'T RECOGNIZE AT ALL.
"AND THEN, IMPOSSIBLY, WE STARTED TO HEAR THE PATTERNS.
"SINCE THAT MOMENT, THE WORD 'IMPOSSIBLE' HAS LOST ALL MEANING FOR ME."

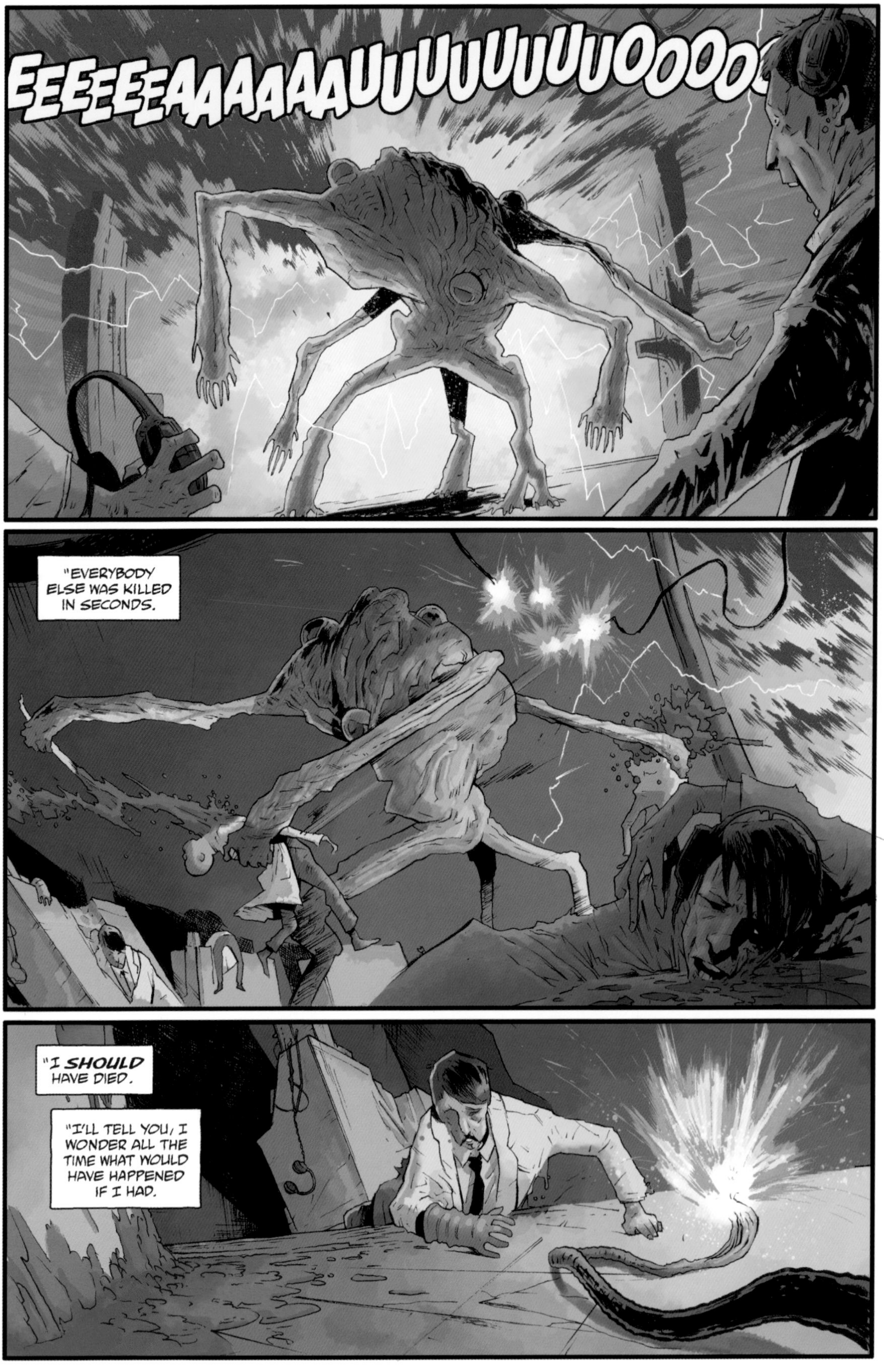
EEEEEEAAAAAAUUUUUUUUUOOOOO
"EVERYBODY ELSE WAS KILLED IN SECONDS.
"I SHOULD HAVE DIED.
"I'LL TELL YOU, I WONDER ALL THE TIME WHAT WOULD HAVE HAPPENED IF I HAD.

"WHAT WOULD THAT CREATURE HAVE DONE HAD I NOT STOPPED IT?"

"WHAT ELSE WOULD HAVE COME THROUGH OUR PORTAL IF IT HAD BEEN LEFT RUNNING?"

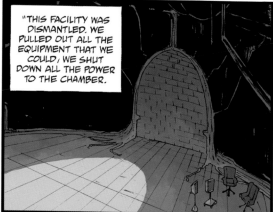

"THIS FACILITY WAS DISMANTLED. WE PULLED OUT ALL THE EQUIPMENT THAT WE COULD; WE SHUT DOWN ALL THE POWER TO THE CHAMBER."

"ITS ENTIRE EXISTENCE WAS ERASED."

"SIX MONTHS LATER, I WAS INFORMED OF AN ANOMALY."

"THE NUCLEAR SAFETY COMMISSION WAS REGISTERING READINGS OF UNUSUAL RADIOACTIVITY UNDER SAITAMA'S SEWERS--"

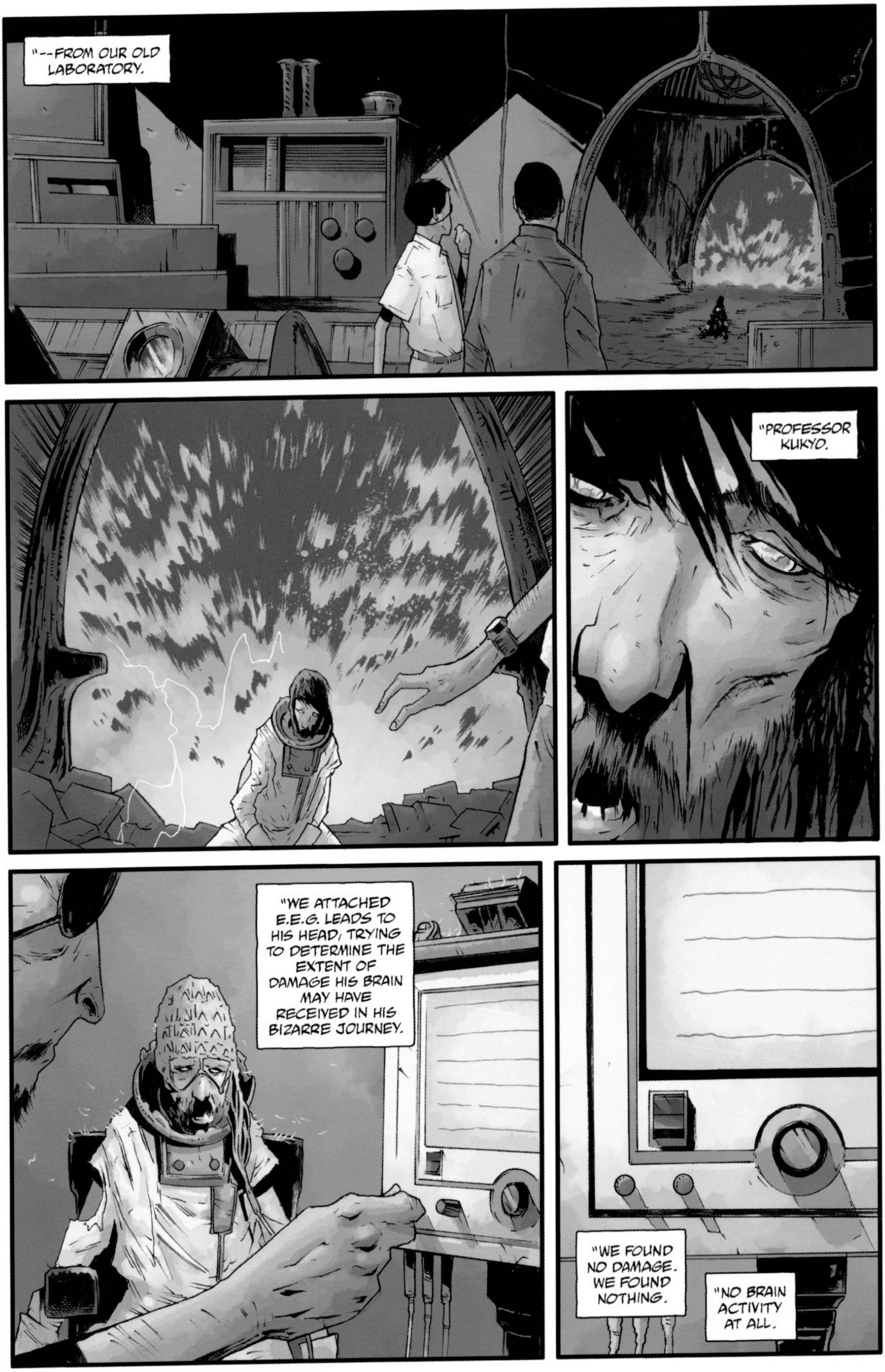
"--FROM OUR OLD LABORATORY.
"PROFESSOR KUKYO.
"WE ATTACHED E.E.G. LEADS TO HIS HEAD, TRYING TO DETERMINE THE EXTENT OF DAMAGE HIS BRAIN MAY HAVE RECEIVED IN HIS BIZARRE JOURNEY.
"WE FOUND NO DAMAGE. WE FOUND NOTHING.
"NO BRAIN ACTIVITY AT ALL.

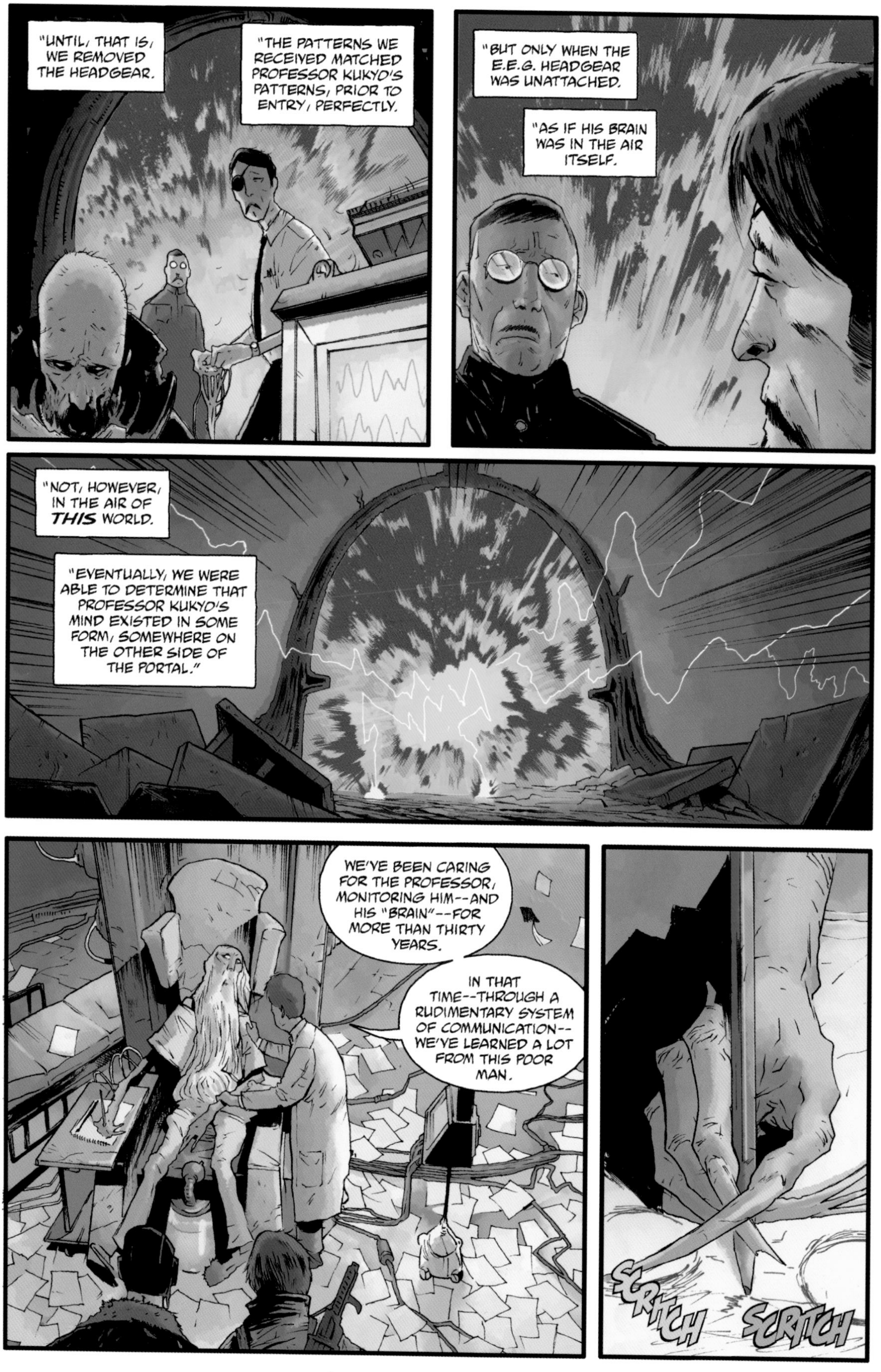
"UNTIL, THAT IS, WE REMOVED THE HEADGEAR.
"THE PATTERNS WE RECEIVED MATCHED PROFESSOR KUKYO'S PATTERNS, PRIOR TO ENTRY, PERFECTLY.
"BUT ONLY WHEN THE E.E.G. HEADGEAR WAS UNATTACHED.
"AS IF HIS BRAIN WAS IN THE AIR ITSELF.
"NOT, HOWEVER, IN THE AIR OF THIS WORLD.
"EVENTUALLY, WE WERE ABLE TO DETERMINE THAT PROFESSOR KUKYO'S MIND EXISTED IN SOME FORM, SOMEWHERE ON THE OTHER SIDE OF THE PORTAL."
WE'VE BEEN CARING FOR THE PROFESSOR, MONITORING HIM--AND HIS "BRAIN"--FOR MORE THAN THIRTY YEARS.
IN THAT TIME--THROUGH A RUDIMENTARY SYSTEM OF COMMUNICATION--WE'VE LEARNED A LOT FROM THIS POOR MAN.
SCRITCH
SCRITCH

HELL OF A STORY--BUT I DON'T SEE WHAT THAT'S GOT TO DO WITH THE BUREAU--UNLESS SOMETHING YOU LEARNED WAS HOW TO **WIPE OUT** THOSE CREATURES OUTSIDE.

AGAIN, WHEN WE CALLED YOU, THINGS WERE DIFFERENT. BUT YOU'RE HERE NOW.

SO I WANT YOU TO LOOK AT SOMETHING.

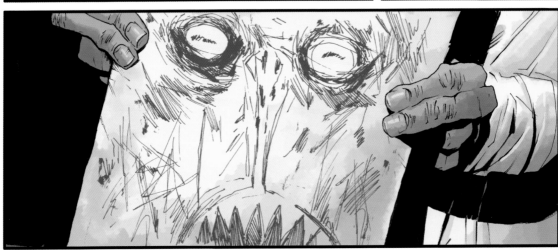

THIS IS WHAT YOU MEANT BY HIS "COMMUNICATING" WITH YOU? HE DRAWS THINGS?

NOT **THINGS.** ONE **THING.**

ONE THING OVER AND OVER. THOUSANDS AND THOUSANDS OF TIMES.

WHAT YOU SEE HERE, THESE ARE NEW. AT FIRST, PROFESSOR KUKYO WOULD ONLY WRITE OUT ENDLESS EQUATIONS.

SOME FAMILIAR, SOME WHOLLY NEW AND INSPIRED, WE THINK, BY HIS EXPOSURE TO THE OTHER SIDE OF OUR PORTAL.

IT WAS A LANGUAGE WE UNDERSTOOD, AND WE HAD A SENSE THAT HE WAS STILL, SOMEHOW, IN HIS RIGHT MIND.

BUT WHEN THE FIRST CREATURES MADE THEIR WAY INTO SAITAMA, THE EQUATIONS STOPPED AND THESE DRAWINGS STARTED.

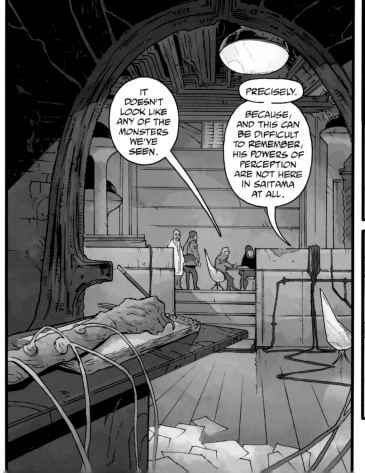

IT DOESN'T LOOK LIKE ANY OF THE MONSTERS WE'VE SEEN.

PRECISELY.

BECAUSE, AND THIS CAN BE DIFFICULT TO REMEMBER, HIS POWERS OF PERCEPTION ARE NOT HERE IN SAITAMA AT ALL.

THEY'RE SOMEWHERE UNREACHABLE, AND UNKNOWABLE TO US.

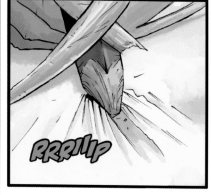

RRRIIP

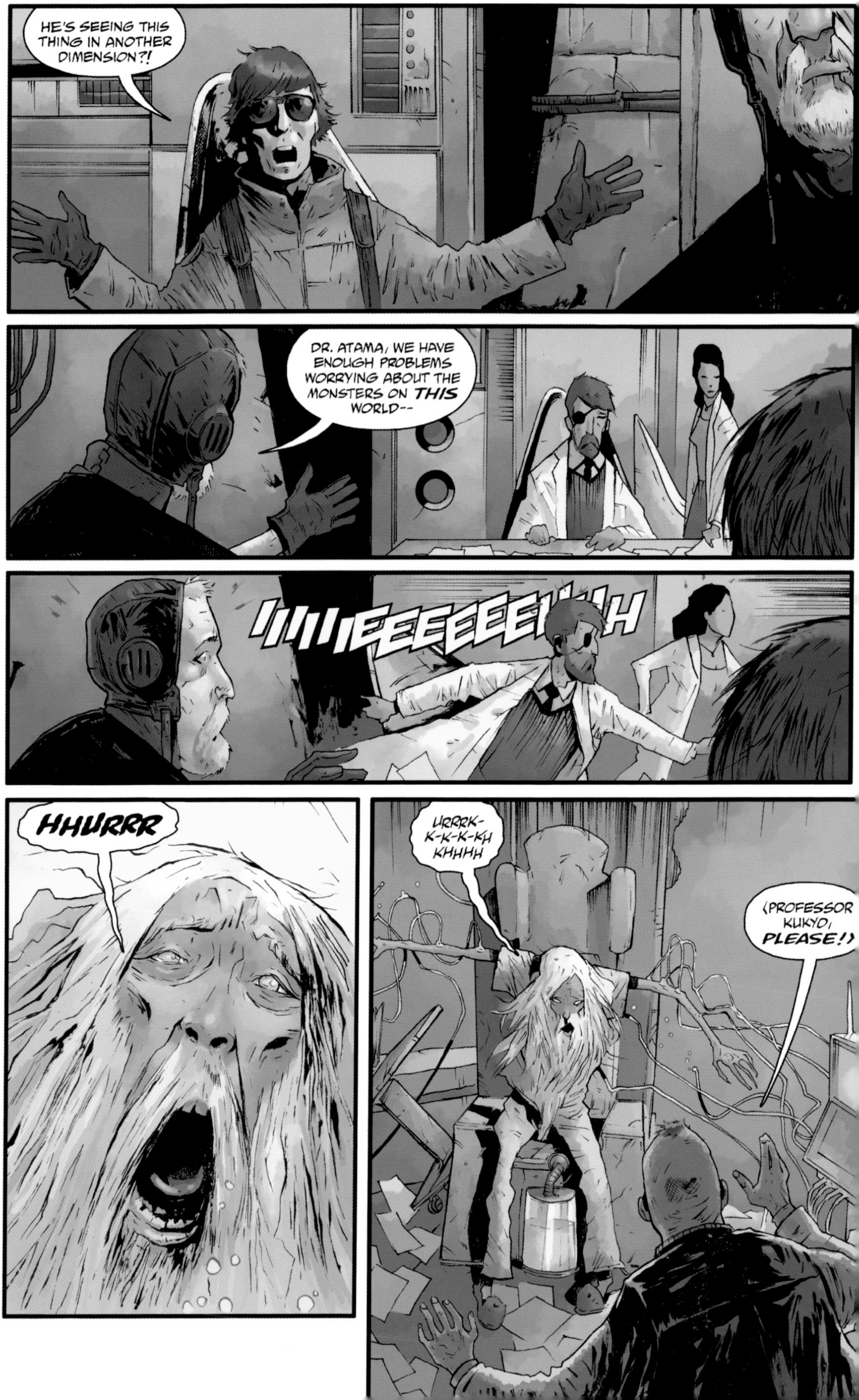
HE'S SEEING THIS THING IN ANOTHER DIMENSION?!
DR. ATAMA, WE HAVE ENOUGH PROBLEMS WORRYING ABOUT THE MONSTERS ON THIS WORLD--
HHURRR
URRRK-K-K-K-KH KHHHH
‹PROFESSOR KUKYO, PLEASE!›

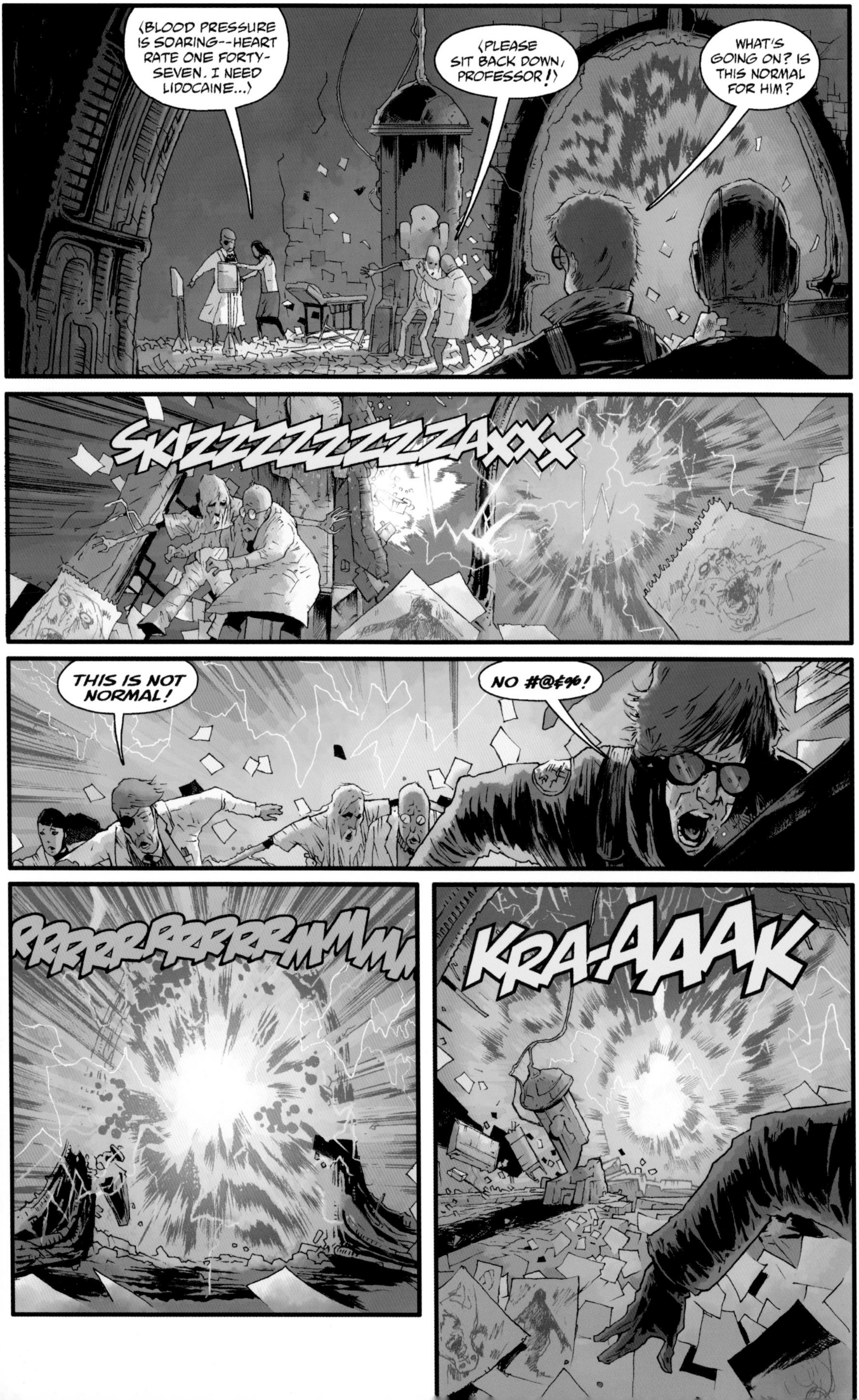
⟨BLOOD PRESSURE IS SOARING--HEART RATE ONE FORTY-SEVEN. I NEED LIDOCAINE...⟩
⟨PLEASE SIT BACK DOWN, PROFESSOR!⟩
WHAT'S GOING ON? IS THIS NORMAL FOR HIM?
SKIZZZZZZZZZAXXX
THIS IS NOT NORMAL!
NO #@¢%!
RRRRRRRRRRRRMMMM
KRA-AAAK

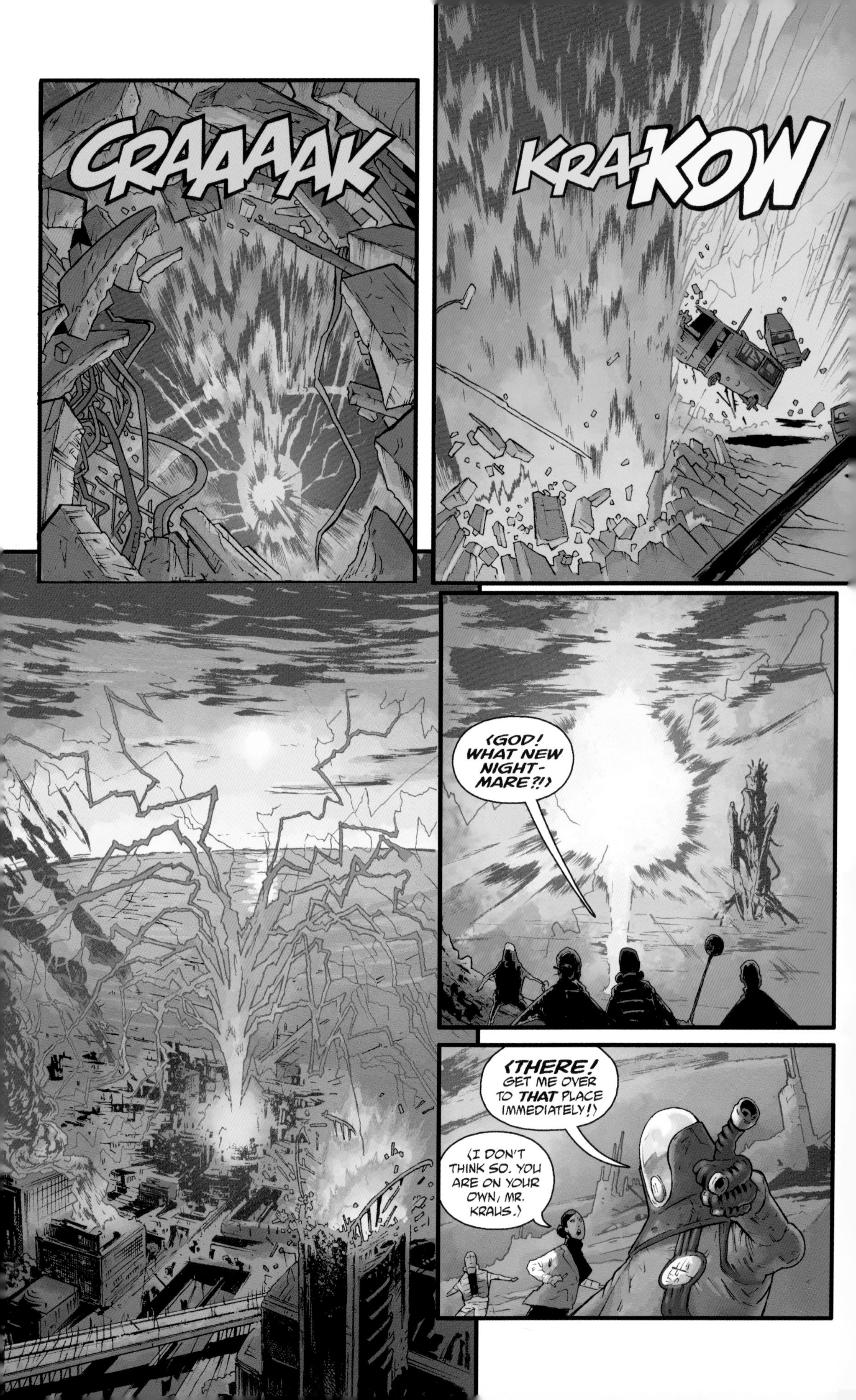
CRAAAAK
KRA-KOW
‹GOD! WHAT NEW NIGHT-MARE?!›
‹THERE! GET ME OVER TO THAT PLACE IMMEDIATELY!›
‹I DON'T THINK SO. YOU ARE ON YOUR OWN, MR. KRAUS.›

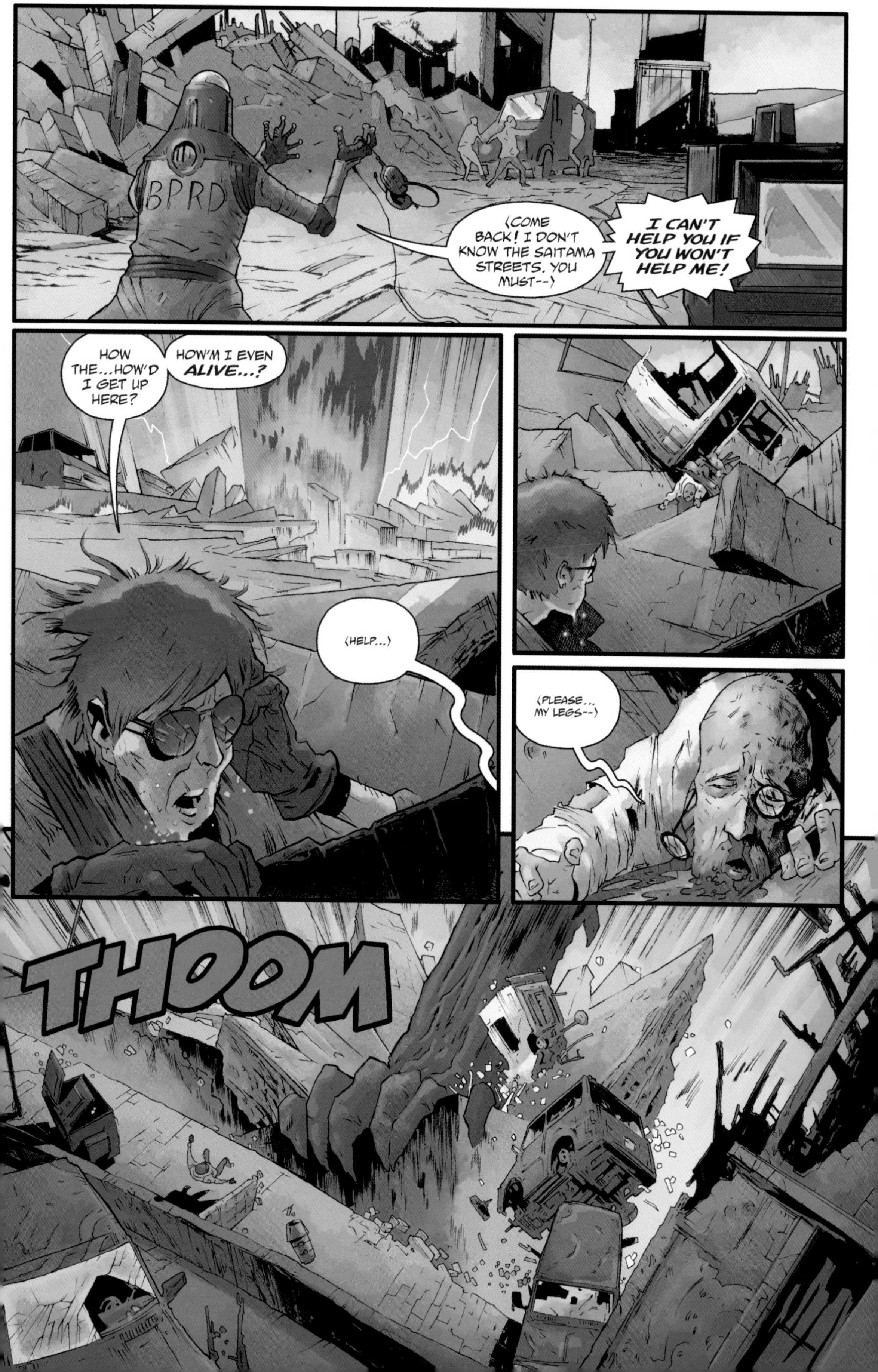

⟨COME BACK! I DON'T KNOW THE SAITAMA STREETS. YOU MUST--⟩
I CAN'T HELP YOU IF YOU WON'T HELP ME!
HOW THE...HOW'D I GET UP HERE?
HOW'M I EVEN ALIVE...?
⟨HELP...⟩
⟨PLEASE... MY LEGS--⟩
THOOM

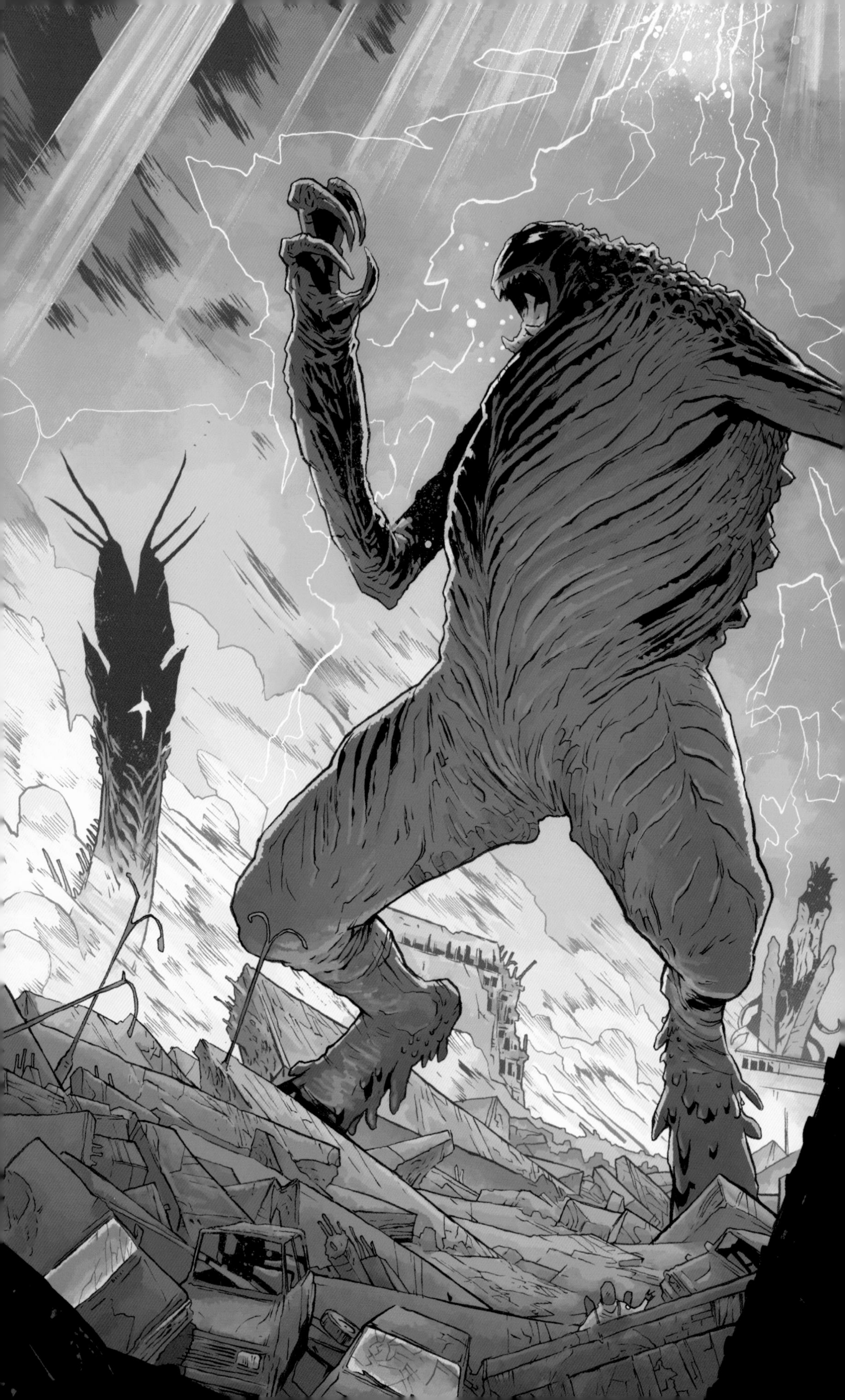

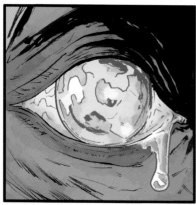

--CAN'T FIND AGENT ENOS! AND WHAT HAPPENED TO THE OTHER *JAPANESE* GUY?

〈SHONJI! SHONJI, WHERE ARE YOU?〉

LOOKS LIKE WE LOST A COUPLE OF MEN. MY AGENT AND YOUR DR. SHONJI.

WE SHOULD CONDUCT A SEARCH.

I DON'T THINK SO.

NO. NO *WAY.* TOO DANGEROUS. WE STAY DOWN HERE MUCH LONGER, WE COULD *ALL* GO MISSING.

I'M SORRY, DR. MIWA.

BUT...BUT DR. ATAMA, HOW CAN WE JUST--

ATAMA...?

HIDEKI ATAMA? IS THAT YOU?

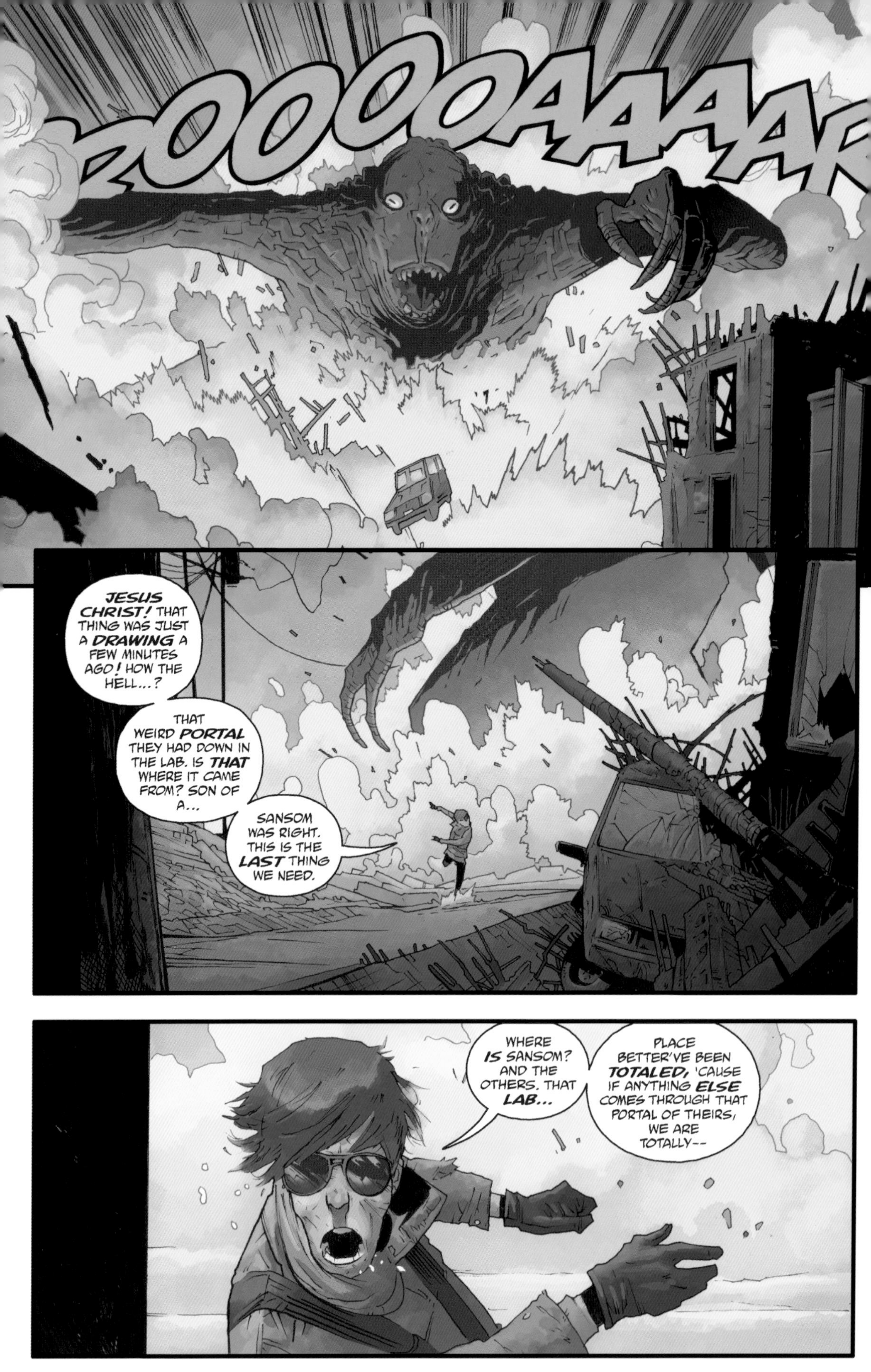
ROOOOAAAAR
JESUS CHRIST! THAT THING WAS JUST A DRAWING A FEW MINUTES AGO! HOW THE HELL...?
THAT WEIRD PORTAL THEY HAD DOWN IN THE LAB. IS THAT WHERE IT CAME FROM? SON OF A...
SANSOM WAS RIGHT. THIS IS THE LAST THING WE NEED.
WHERE IS SANSOM? AND THE OTHERS. THAT LAB...
PLACE BETTER'VE BEEN TOTALED, 'CAUSE IF ANYTHING ELSE COMES THROUGH THAT PORTAL OF THEIRS, WE ARE TOTALLY--

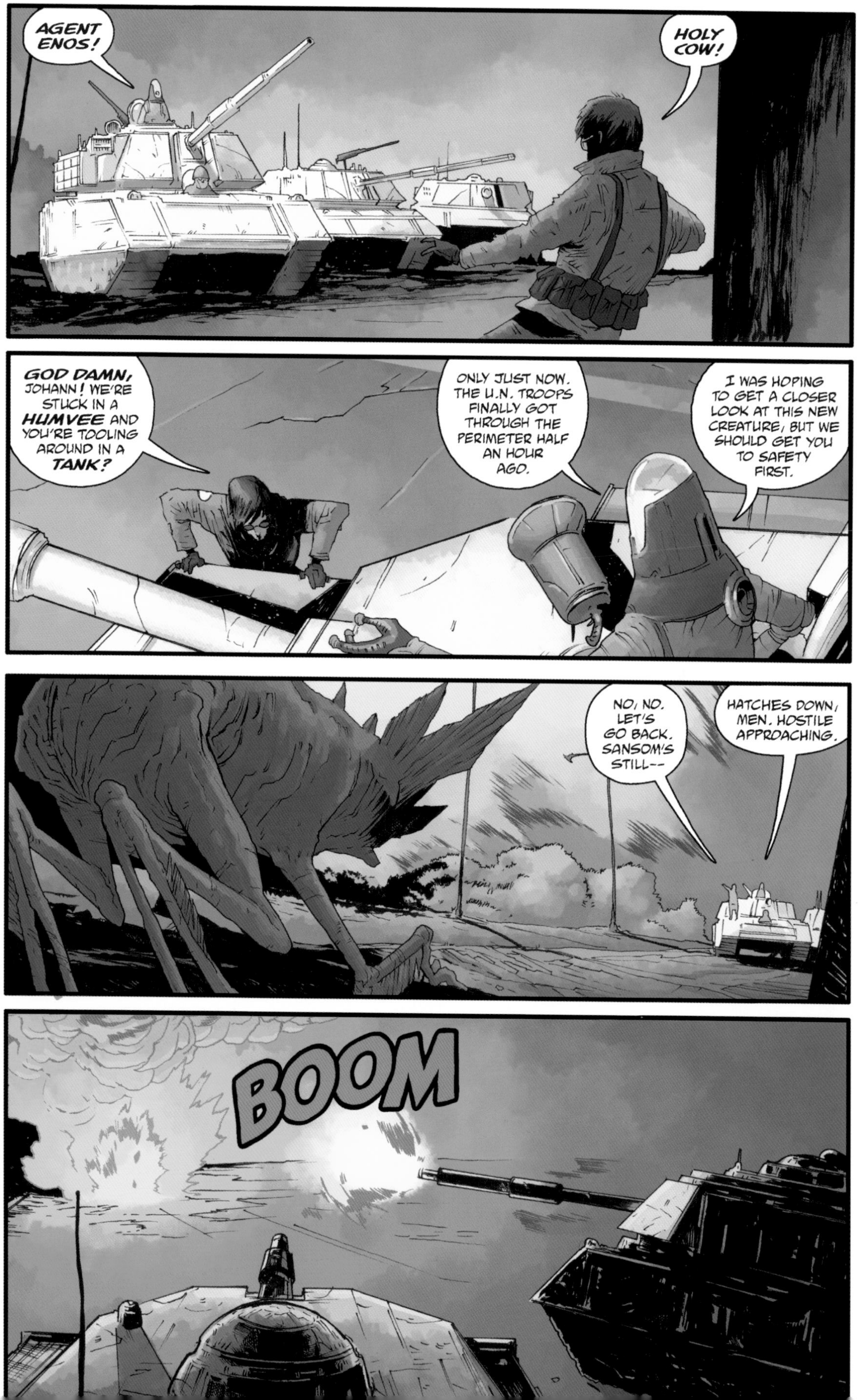
AGENT ENOS!
HOLY COW!
GOD DAMN, JOHANN! WE'RE STUCK IN A HUMVEE AND YOU'RE TOOLING AROUND IN A TANK?
ONLY JUST NOW. THE U.N. TROOPS FINALLY GOT THROUGH THE PERIMETER HALF AN HOUR AGO.
I WAS HOPING TO GET A CLOSER LOOK AT THIS NEW CREATURE, BUT WE SHOULD GET YOU TO SAFETY FIRST.
NO, NO. LET'S GO BACK. SANSOM'S STILL--
HATCHES DOWN, MEN. HOSTILE APPROACHING.
BOOM

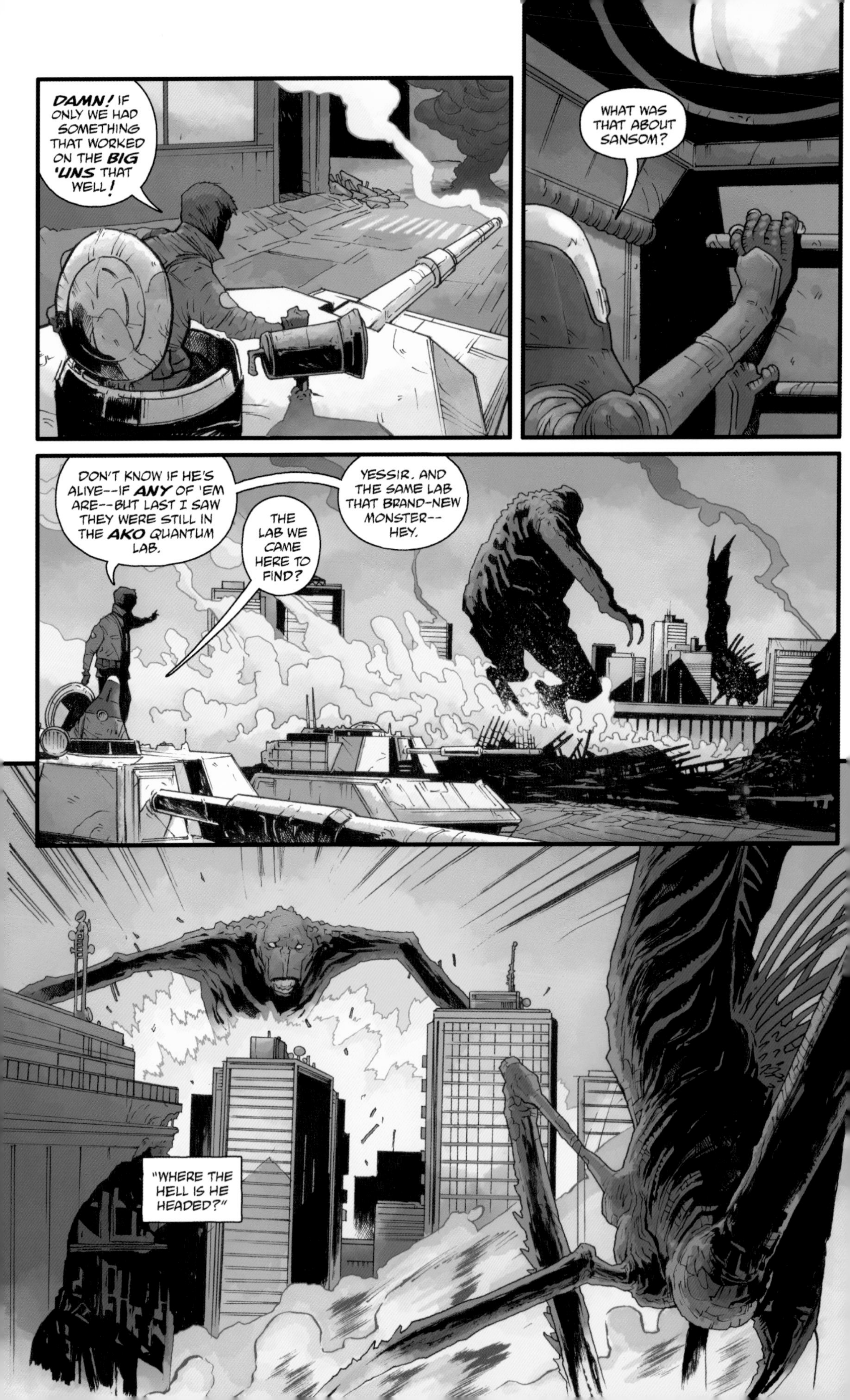
DAMN! IF ONLY WE HAD SOMETHING THAT WORKED ON THE BIG 'UNS THAT WELL!
WHAT WAS THAT ABOUT SANSOM?
DON'T KNOW IF HE'S ALIVE--IF ANY OF 'EM ARE--BUT LAST I SAW THEY WERE STILL IN THE AKO QUANTUM LAB.
THE LAB WE CAME HERE TO FIND?
YESSIR. AND THE SAME LAB THAT BRAND-NEW MONSTER-- HEY.
"WHERE THE HELL IS HE HEADED?"

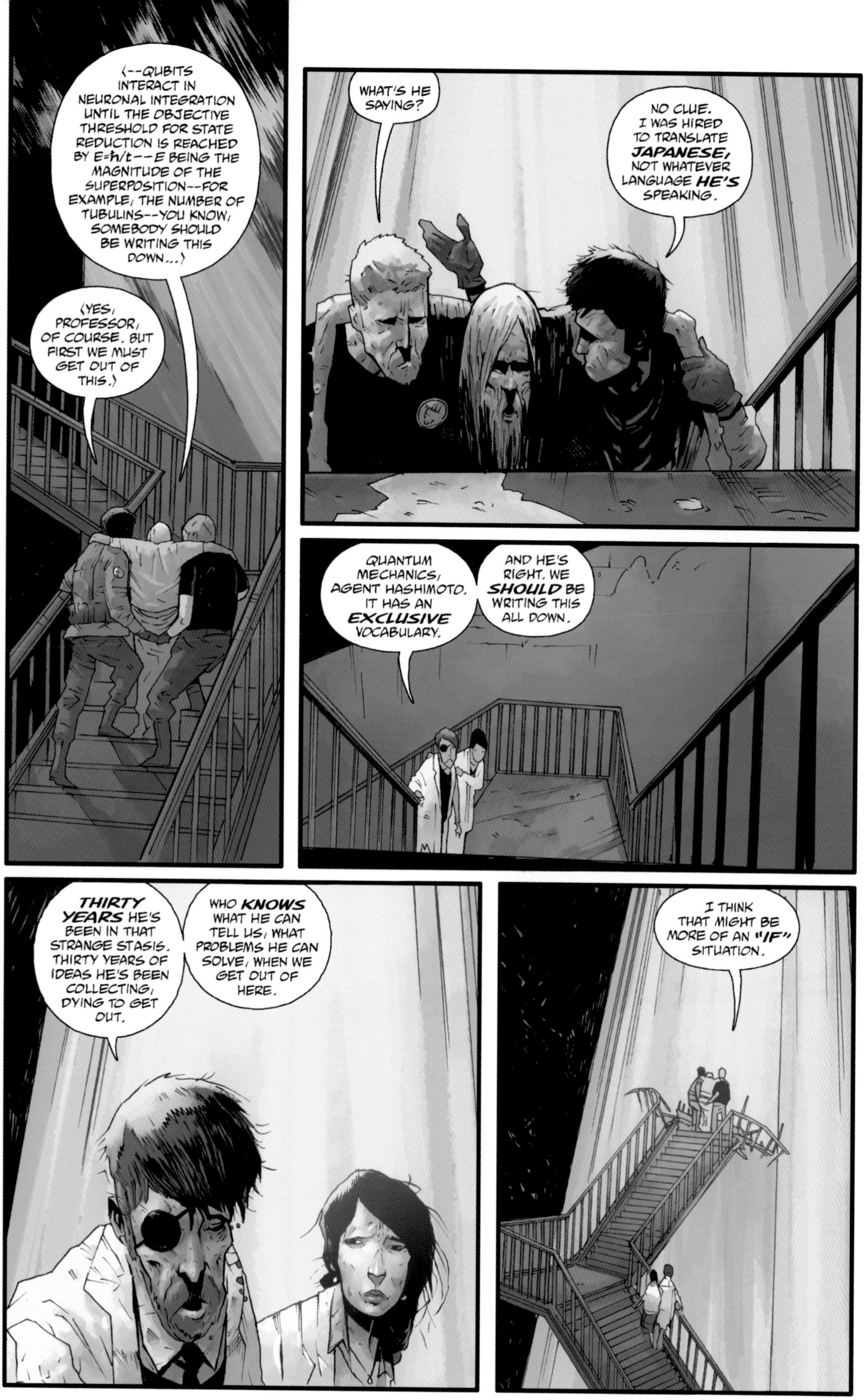
⟨--QUBITS INTERACT IN NEURONAL INTEGRATION UNTIL THE OBJECTIVE THRESHOLD FOR STATE REDUCTION IS REACHED BY E=ħ/t--E BEING THE MAGNITUDE OF THE SUPERPOSITION--FOR EXAMPLE, THE NUMBER OF TUBULINS--YOU KNOW, SOMEBODY SHOULD BE WRITING THIS DOWN...⟩
⟨YES, PROFESSOR, OF COURSE. BUT FIRST WE MUST GET OUT OF THIS.⟩
WHAT'S HE SAYING?
NO CLUE. I WAS HIRED TO TRANSLATE JAPANESE, NOT WHATEVER LANGUAGE HE'S SPEAKING.
QUANTUM MECHANICS, AGENT HASHIMOTO. IT HAS AN EXCLUSIVE VOCABULARY.
AND HE'S RIGHT. WE SHOULD BE WRITING THIS ALL DOWN.
THIRTY YEARS HE'S BEEN IN THAT STRANGE STASIS. THIRTY YEARS OF IDEAS HE'S BEEN COLLECTING, DYING TO GET OUT.
WHO KNOWS WHAT HE CAN TELL US, WHAT PROBLEMS HE CAN SOLVE, WHEN WE GET OUT OF HERE.
I THINK THAT MIGHT BE MORE OF AN "IF" SITUATION.

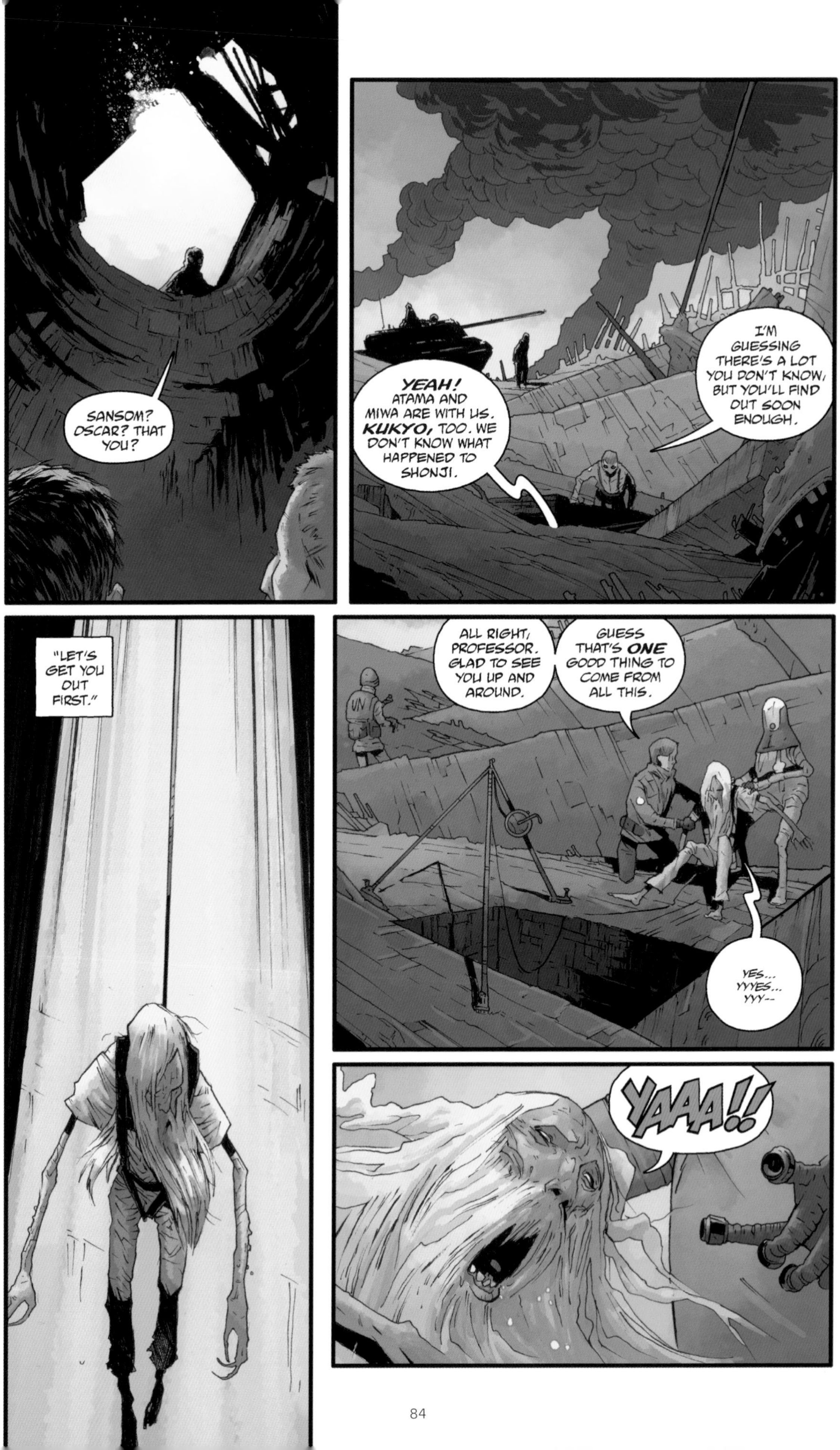
SANSOM? OSCAR? THAT YOU?
YEAH! ATAMA AND MIWA ARE WITH US. KUKYO, TOO. WE DON'T KNOW WHAT HAPPENED TO SHONJI.
I'M GUESSING THERE'S A LOT YOU DON'T KNOW, BUT YOU'LL FIND OUT SOON ENOUGH.
"LET'S GET YOU OUT FIRST."
ALL RIGHT, PROFESSOR. GLAD TO SEE YOU UP AND AROUND.
GUESS THAT'S ONE GOOD THING TO COME FROM ALL THIS.
YES... YYYES... YYY--
YAAA!!

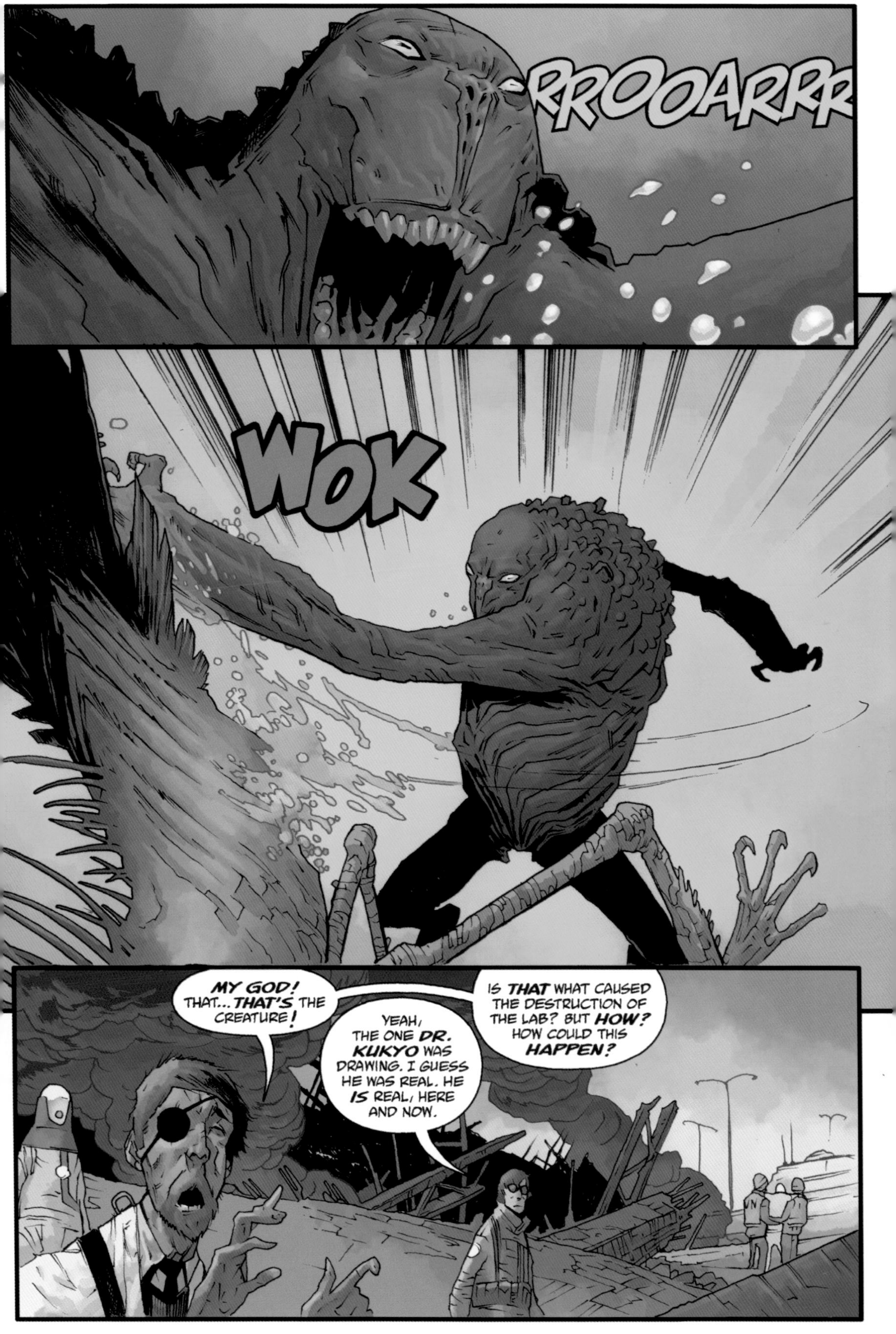
RROOARRR
WOK
MY GOD! THAT... THAT'S THE CREATURE!
YEAH, THE ONE DR. KUKYO WAS DRAWING. I GUESS HE WAS REAL. HE IS REAL, HERE AND NOW.
IS THAT WHAT CAUSED THE DESTRUCTION OF THE LAB? BUT HOW? HOW COULD THIS HAPPEN?

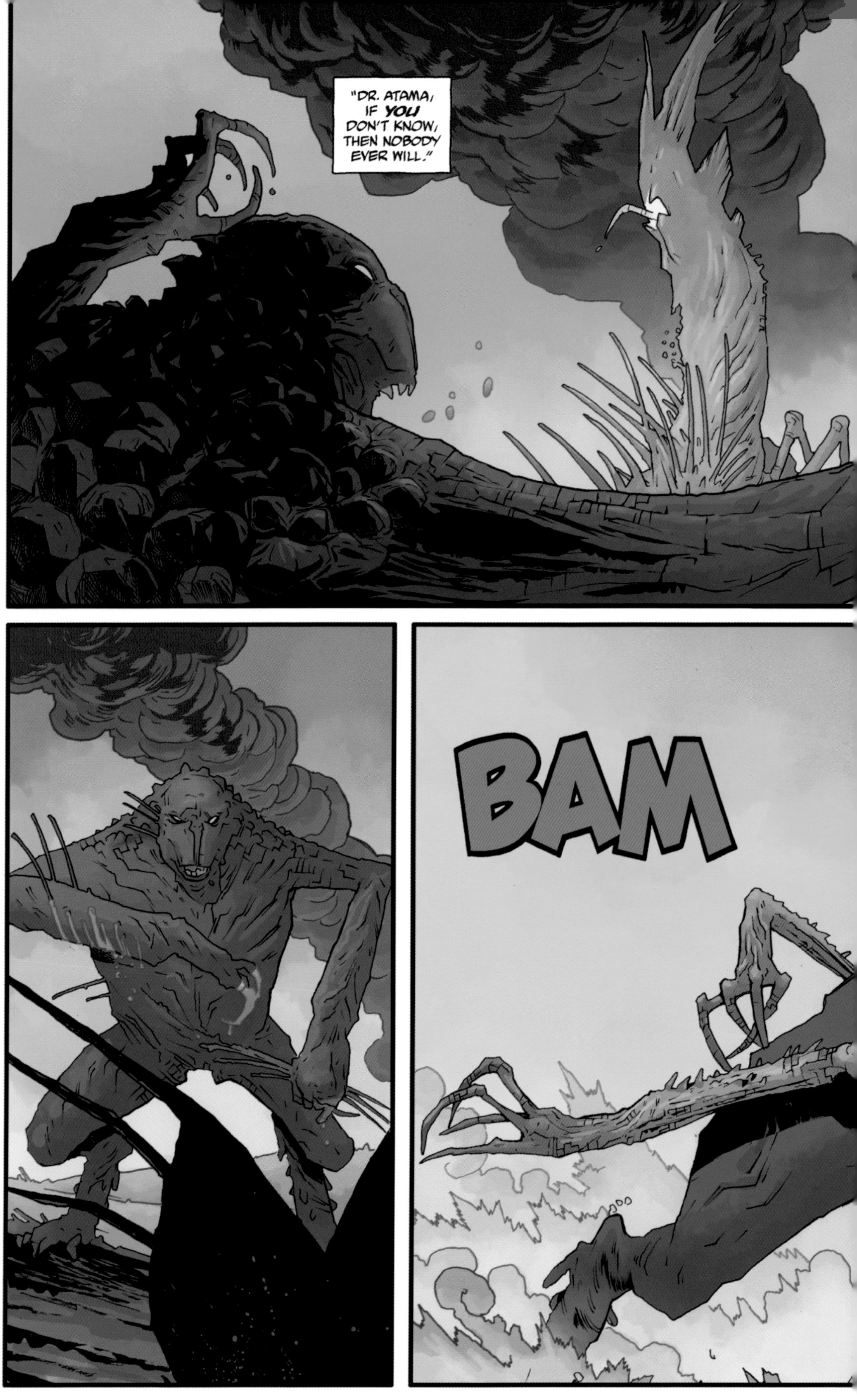
"DR. ATAMA, IF YOU DON'T KNOW, THEN NOBODY EVER WILL."
BAM

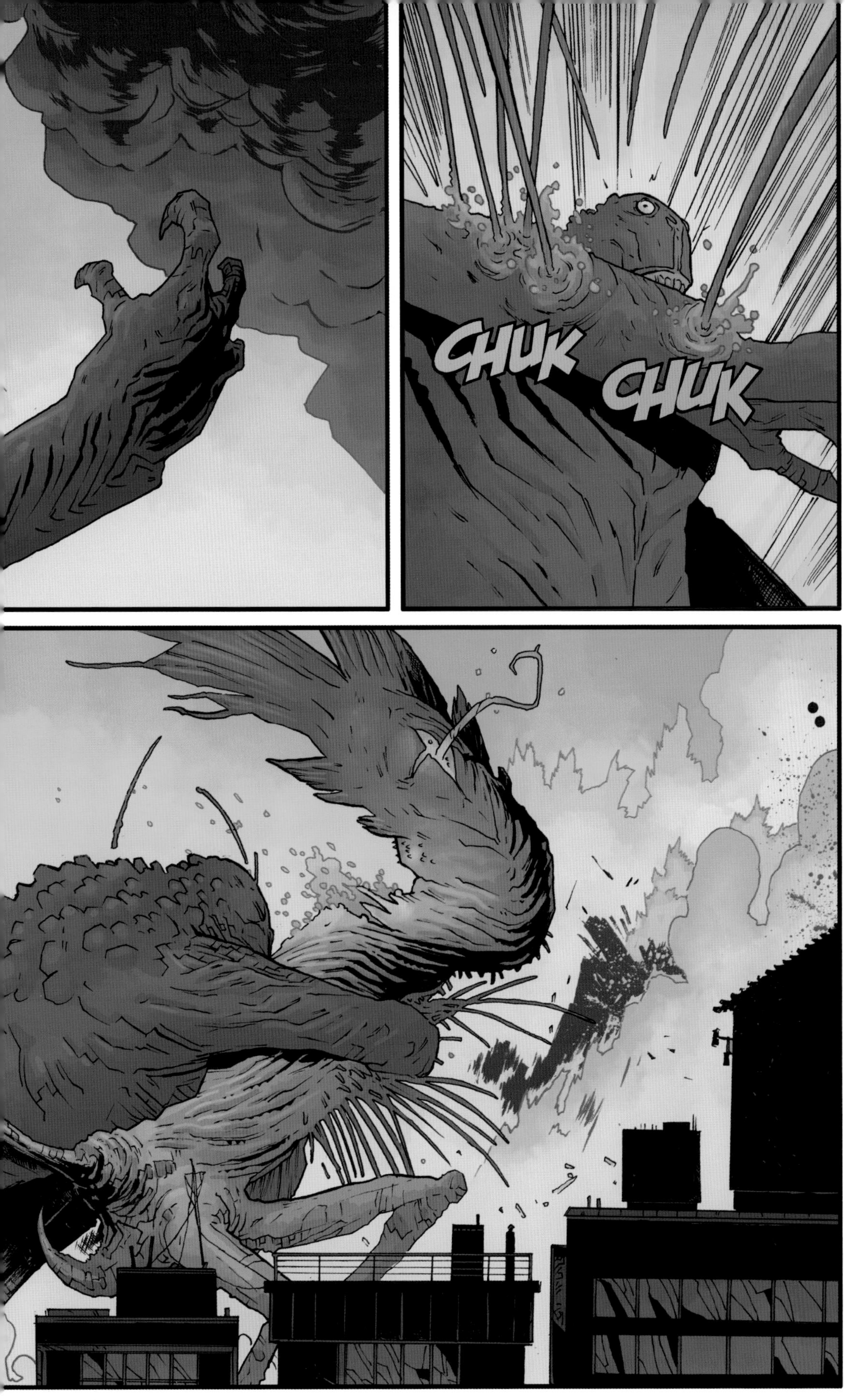
CHUK
CHUK

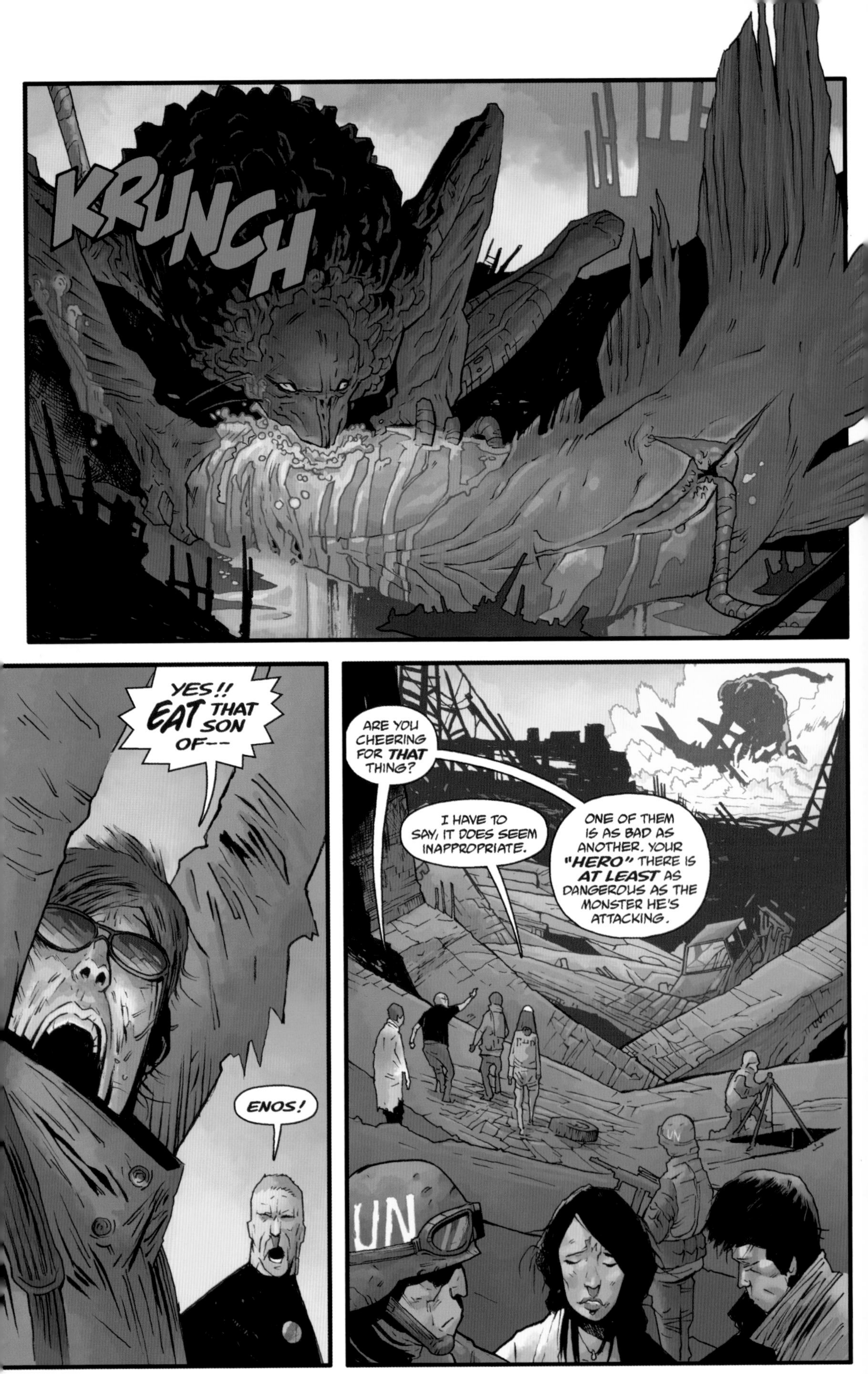
KRUNCH
YES!! EAT THAT SON OF--
ENOS!
ARE YOU CHEERING FOR THAT THING?
I HAVE TO SAY, IT DOES SEEM INAPPROPRIATE.
ONE OF THEM IS AS BAD AS ANOTHER. YOUR "HERO" THERE IS AT LEAST AS DANGEROUS AS THE MONSTER HE'S ATTACKING.
UN

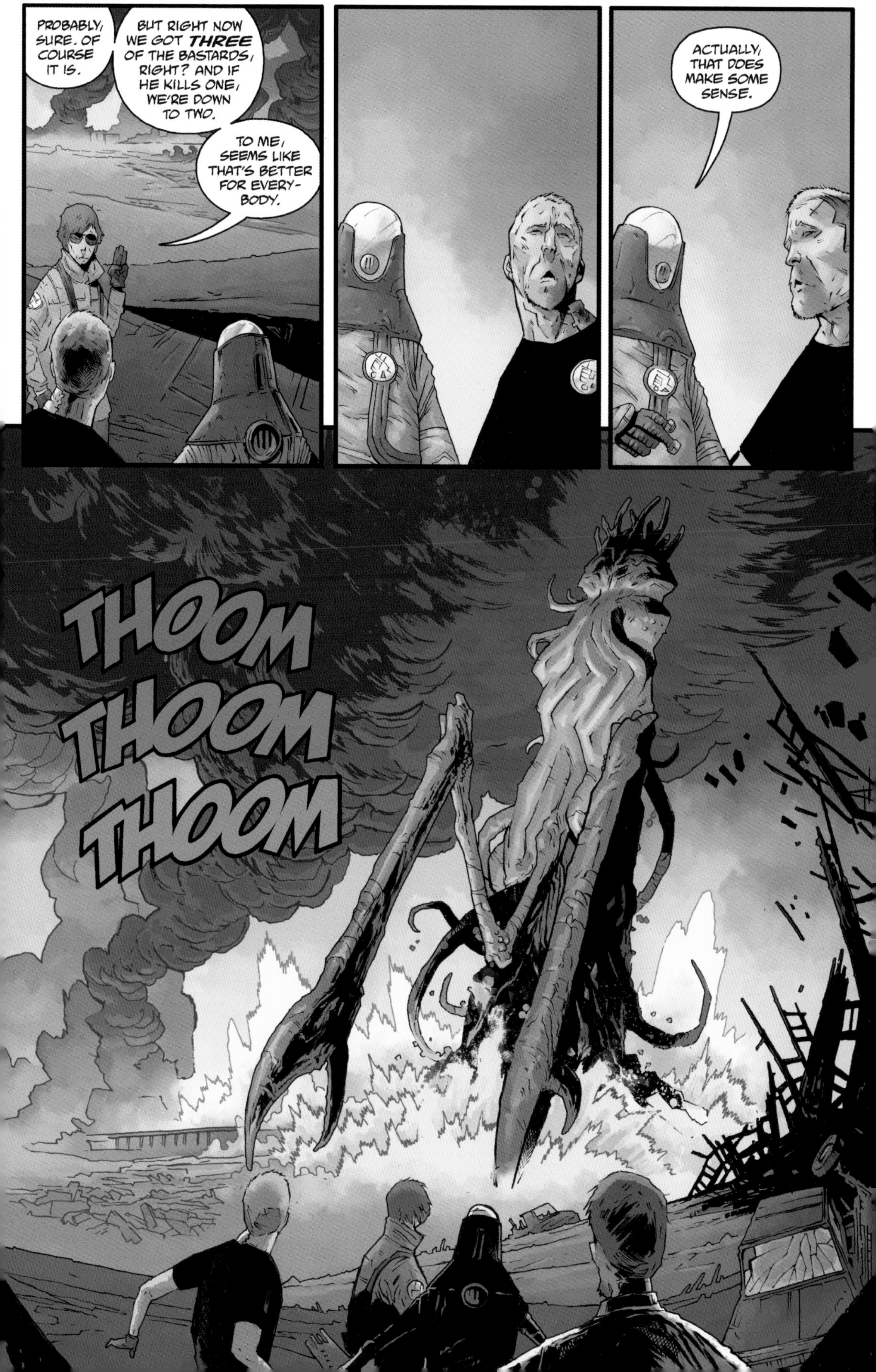
PROBABLY, SURE. OF COURSE IT IS.
BUT RIGHT NOW WE GOT ***THREE*** OF THE BASTARDS, RIGHT? AND IF HE KILLS ONE, WE'RE DOWN TO TWO.
TO ME, SEEMS LIKE THAT'S BETTER FOR EVERY-BODY.
ACTUALLY, THAT DOES MAKE SOME SENSE.
THOOM
THOOM
THOOM

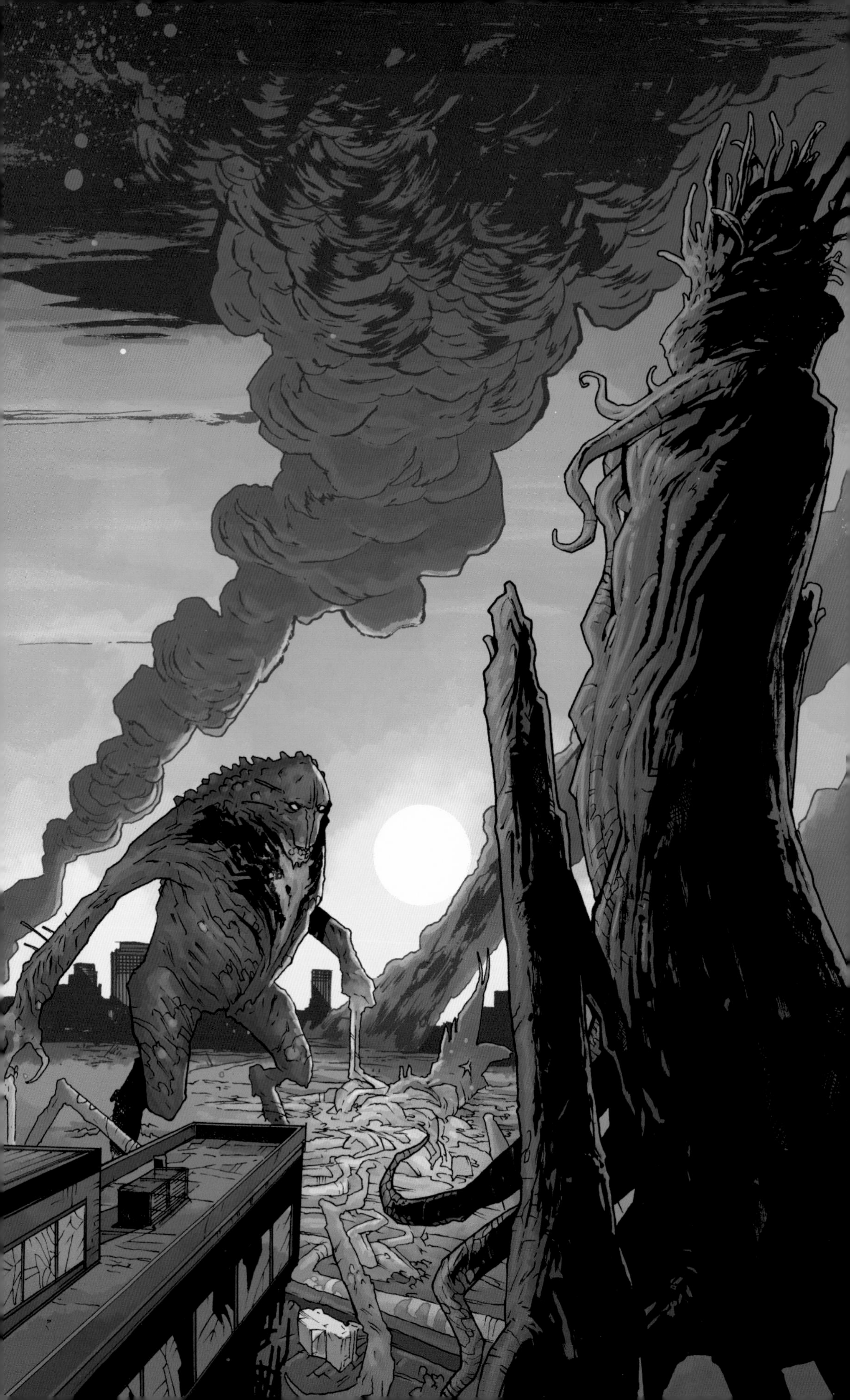

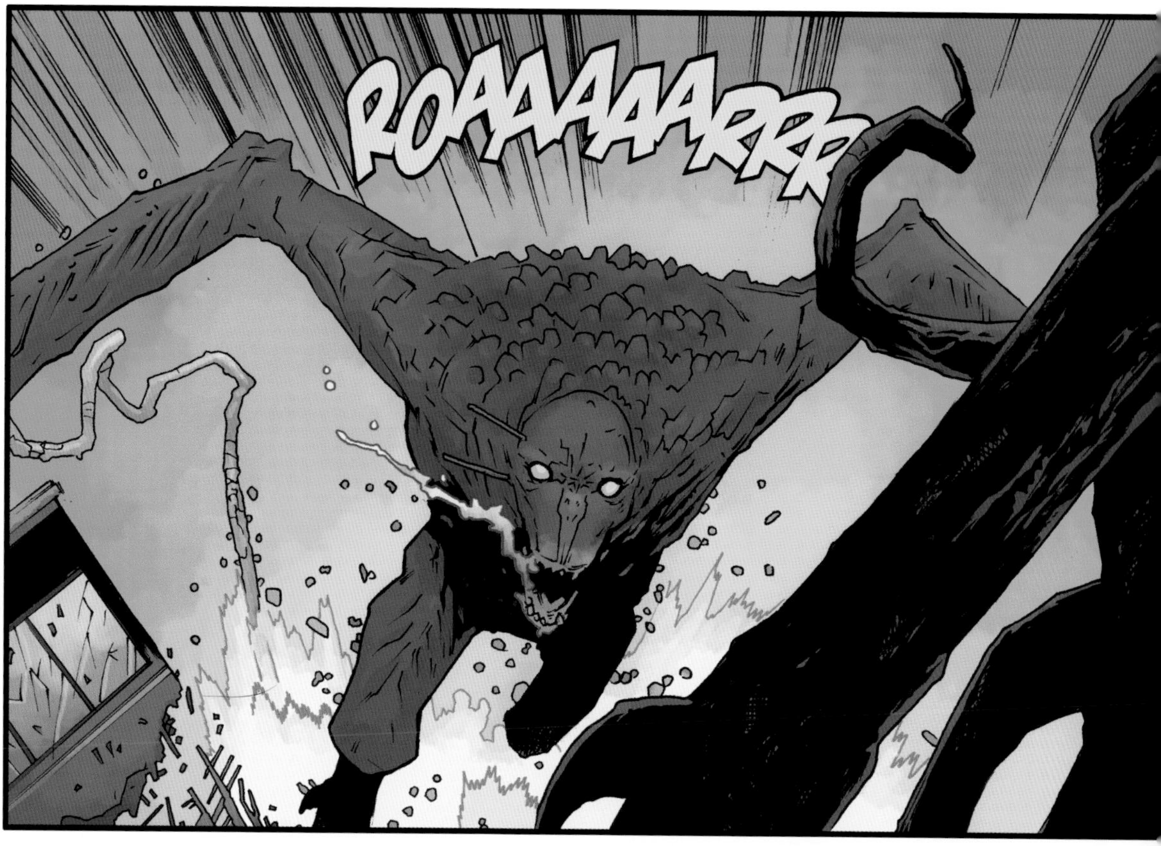
ROAAAAAARRR

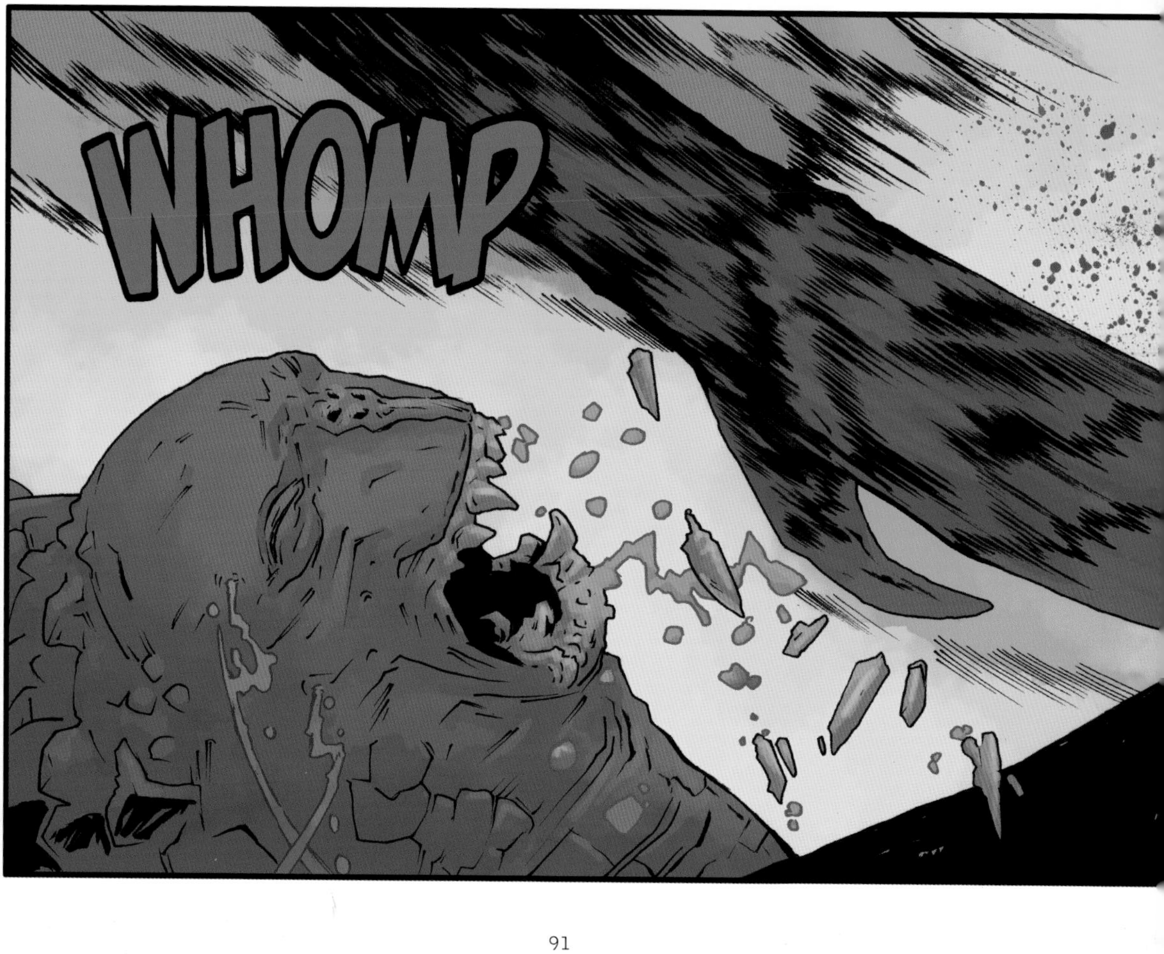
WHOMP

BOOM

...DAMN.

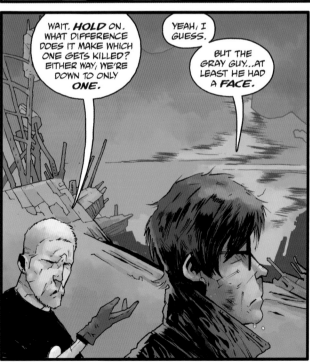

WAIT. **HOLD** ON. WHAT DIFFERENCE DOES IT MAKE WHICH ONE GETS KILLED? EITHER WAY, WE'RE DOWN TO ONLY **ONE.**

YEAH, I GUESS.

BUT THE GRAY GUY...AT LEAST HE HAD A **FACE.**

COME. WE SHOULD NOT JUST BE STANDING AROUND HERE ANYWAY.

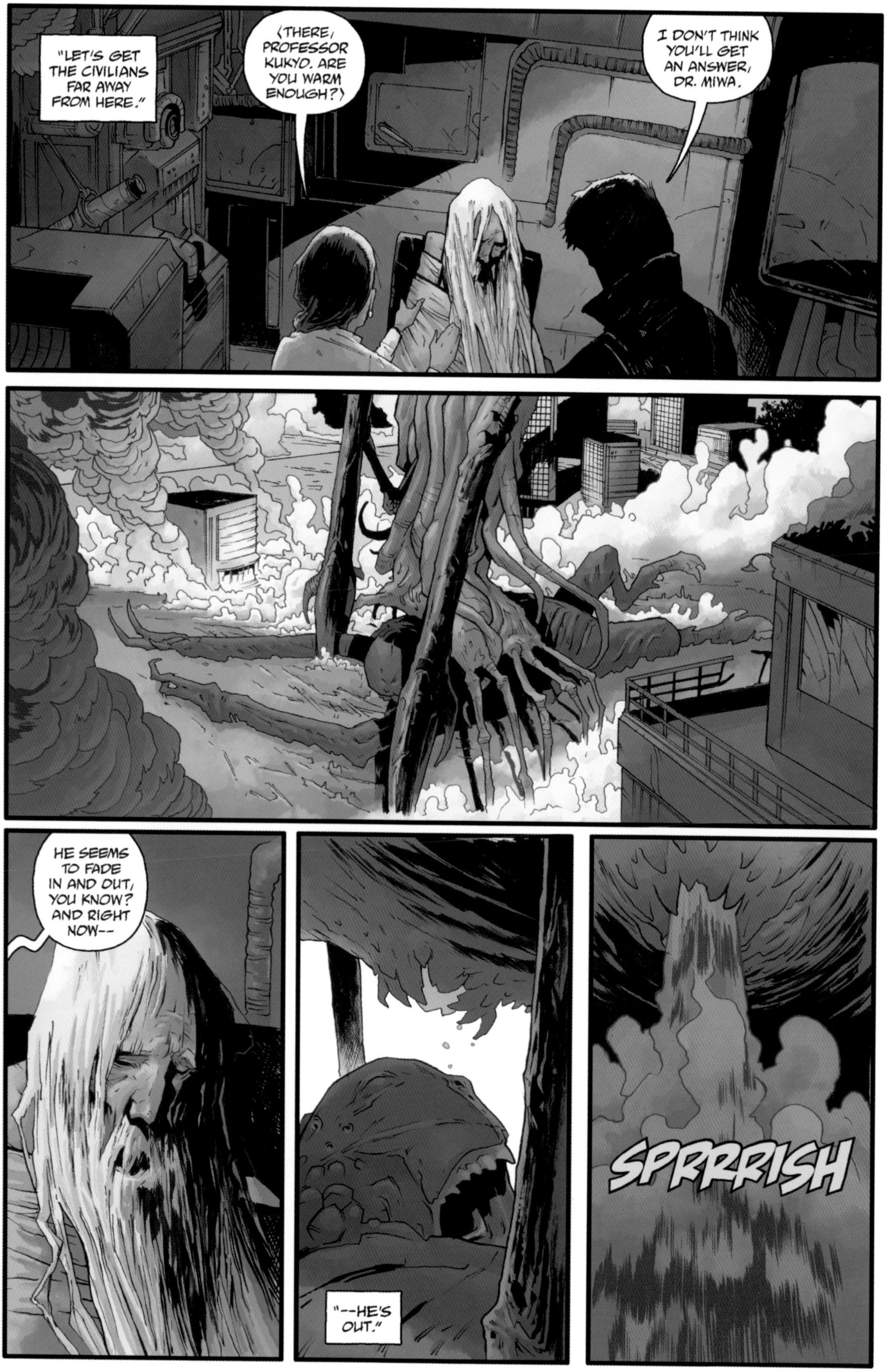
"LET'S GET THE CIVILIANS FAR AWAY FROM HERE."
⟨THERE, PROFESSOR KUKYO. ARE YOU WARM ENOUGH?⟩
I DON'T THINK YOU'LL GET AN ANSWER, DR. MIWA.
HE SEEMS TO FADE IN AND OUT, YOU KNOW? AND RIGHT NOW--
"--HE'S OUT."
SPRRRISH

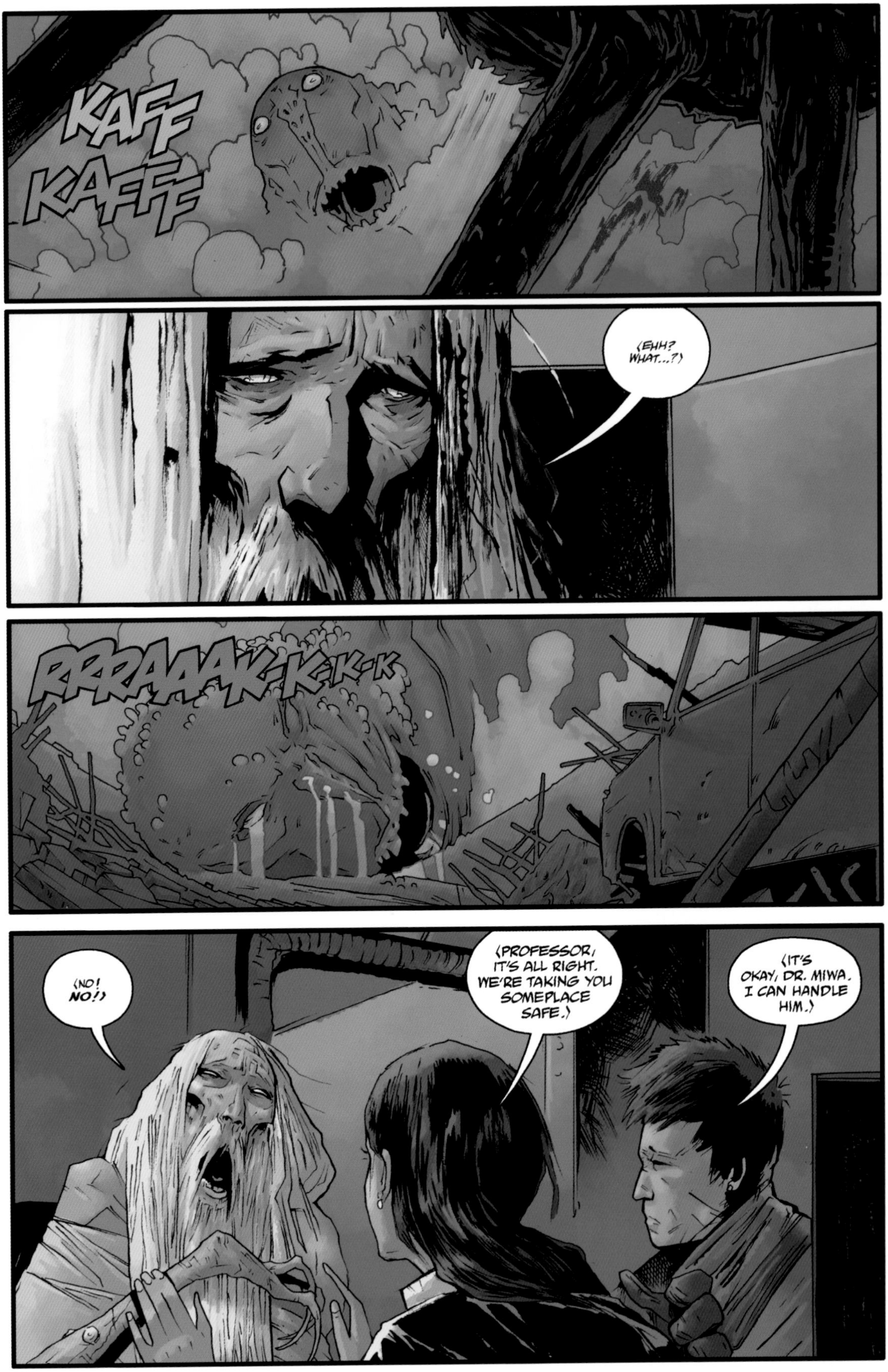
KAFF
KAFFF
‹EHH? WHAT...?›
RRRAAAK-K-K-K
‹NO! NO!›
‹PROFESSOR, IT'S ALL RIGHT. WE'RE TAKING YOU SOMEPLACE SAFE.›
‹IT'S OKAY, DR. MIWA. I CAN HANDLE HIM.›

⟨IT ISN'T... THIS ISN'T RIGHT...⟩

⟨TAKE IT EASY, PROFESSOR, OKAY? YOU'RE NOT CAREFUL, YOU MIGHT GET HURT.⟩

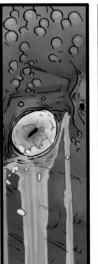

⟨NOT RIGHT!⟩

GAAAH!

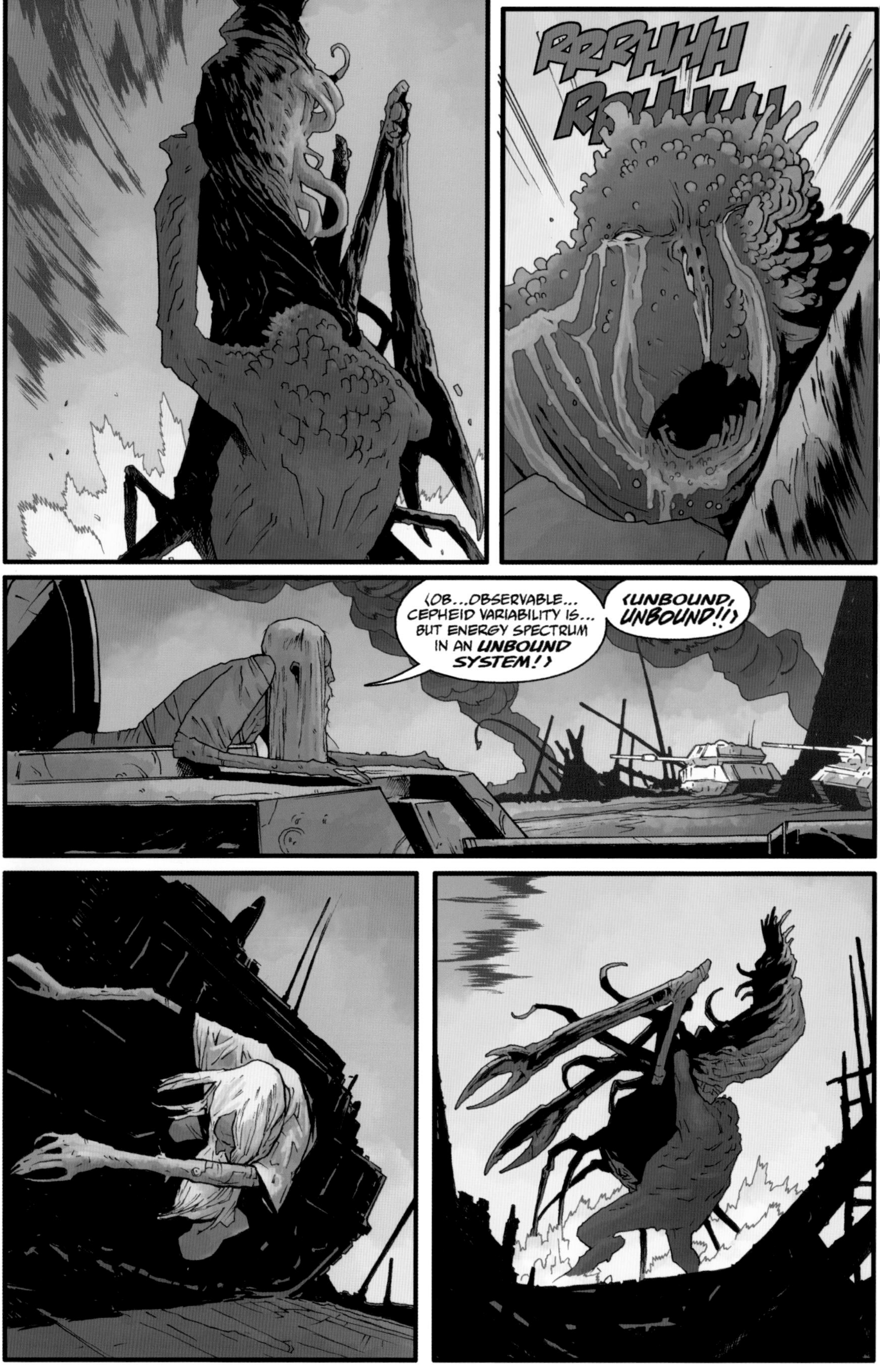
RRRHHH
‹OB...OBSERVABLE... CEPHEID VARIABILITY IS... BUT ENERGY SPECTRUM IN AN UNBOUND SYSTEM!›
‹UNBOUND, UNBOUND!!›

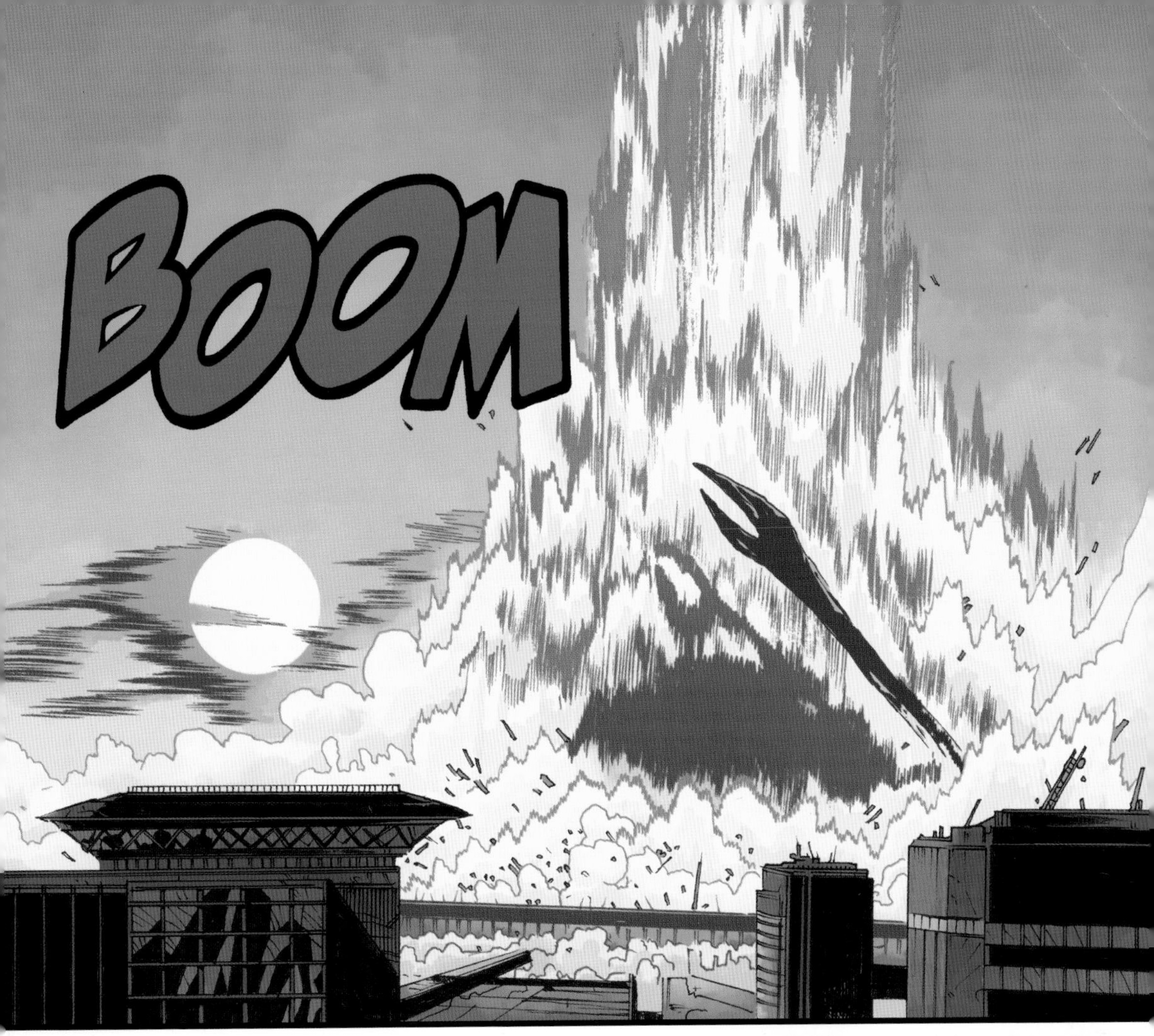
BOOM

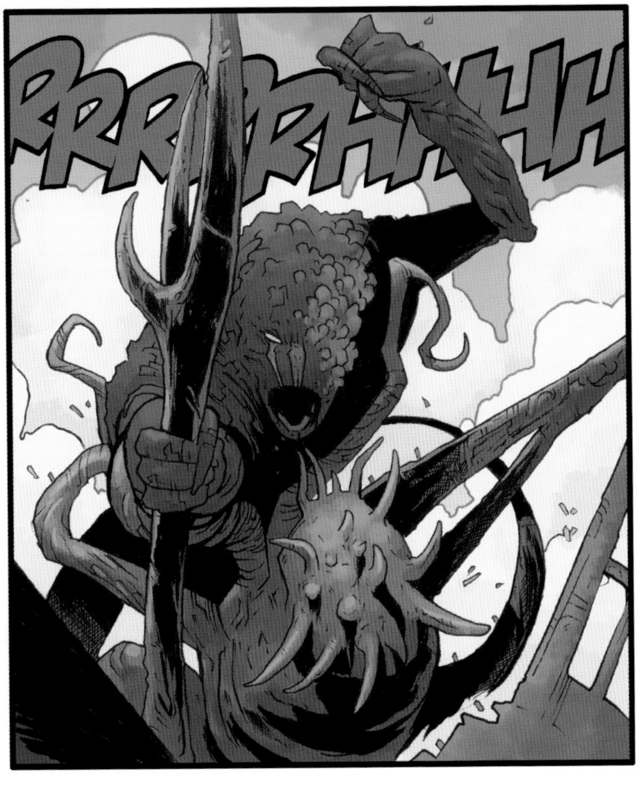

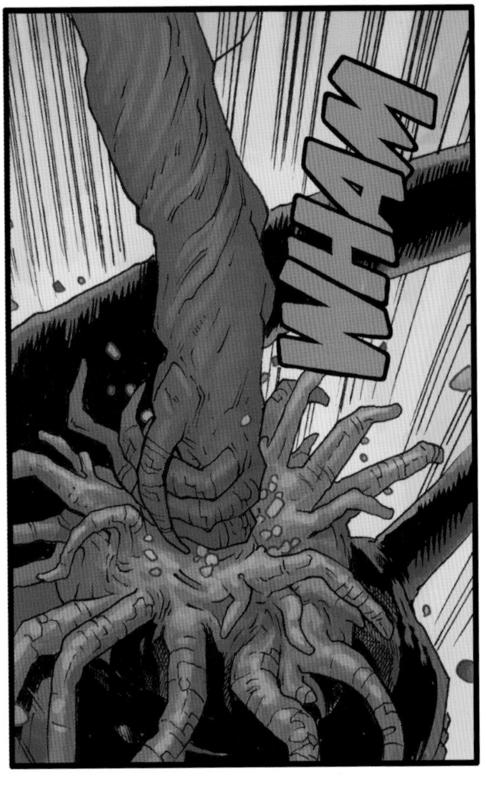
WHAM

KRONCH

UNBOUND...

KRON

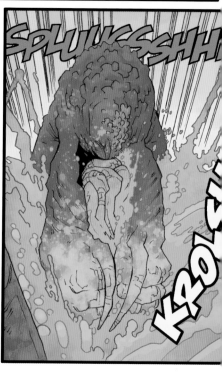

SPLUUKSSHH

KROLSH

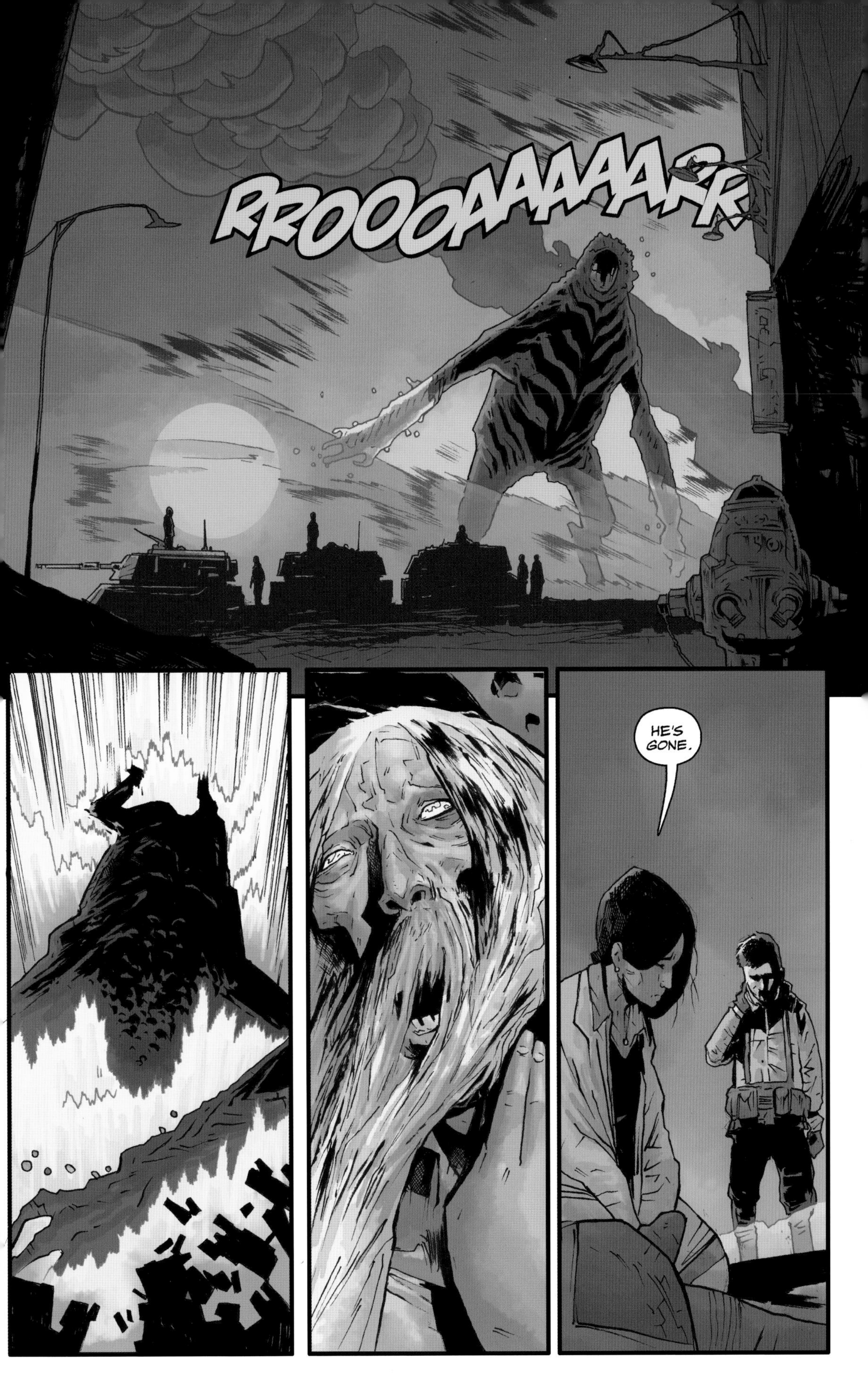
RROOOAAAAARR
HE'S GONE.

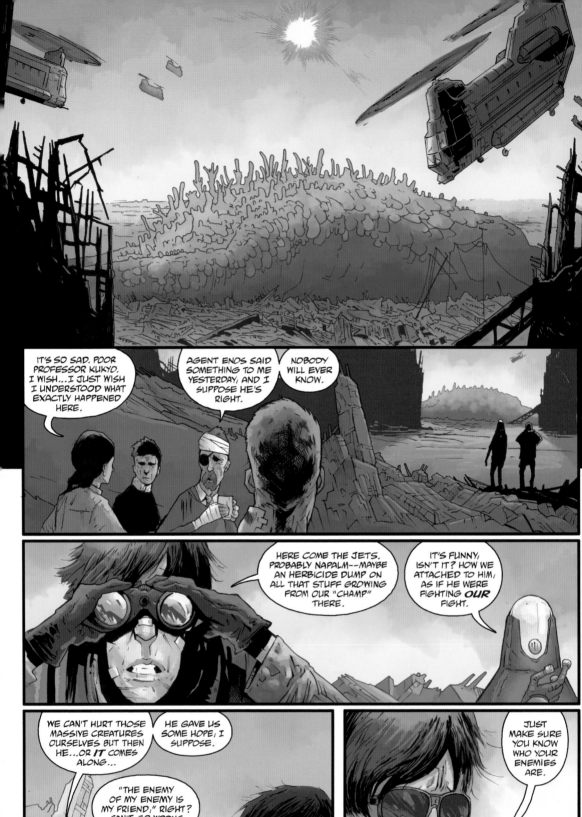

IT'S SO SAD. POOR PROFESSOR KUKYO. I WISH...I JUST WISH I UNDERSTOOD WHAT EXACTLY HAPPENED HERE.

AGENT ENOS SAID SOMETHING TO ME YESTERDAY, AND I SUPPOSE HE'S RIGHT.

NOBODY WILL EVER KNOW.

HERE COME THE JETS. PROBABLY NAPALM--MAYBE AN HERBICIDE DUMP ON ALL THAT STUFF GROWING FROM OUR "CHAMP" THERE.

IT'S FUNNY, ISN'T IT? HOW WE ATTACHED TO HIM, AS IF HE WERE FIGHTING *OUR* FIGHT.

WE CAN'T HURT THOSE MASSIVE CREATURES OURSELVES BUT THEN HE...OR *IT* COMES ALONG...

HE GAVE US SOME HOPE, I SUPPOSE.

"THE ENEMY OF MY ENEMY IS MY FRIEND," RIGHT? CAN'T GO WRONG WITH THAT.

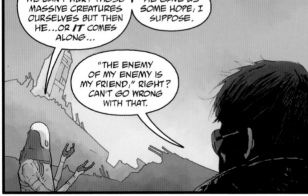

JUST MAKE SURE YOU KNOW WHO YOUR ENEMIES ARE.

THE END

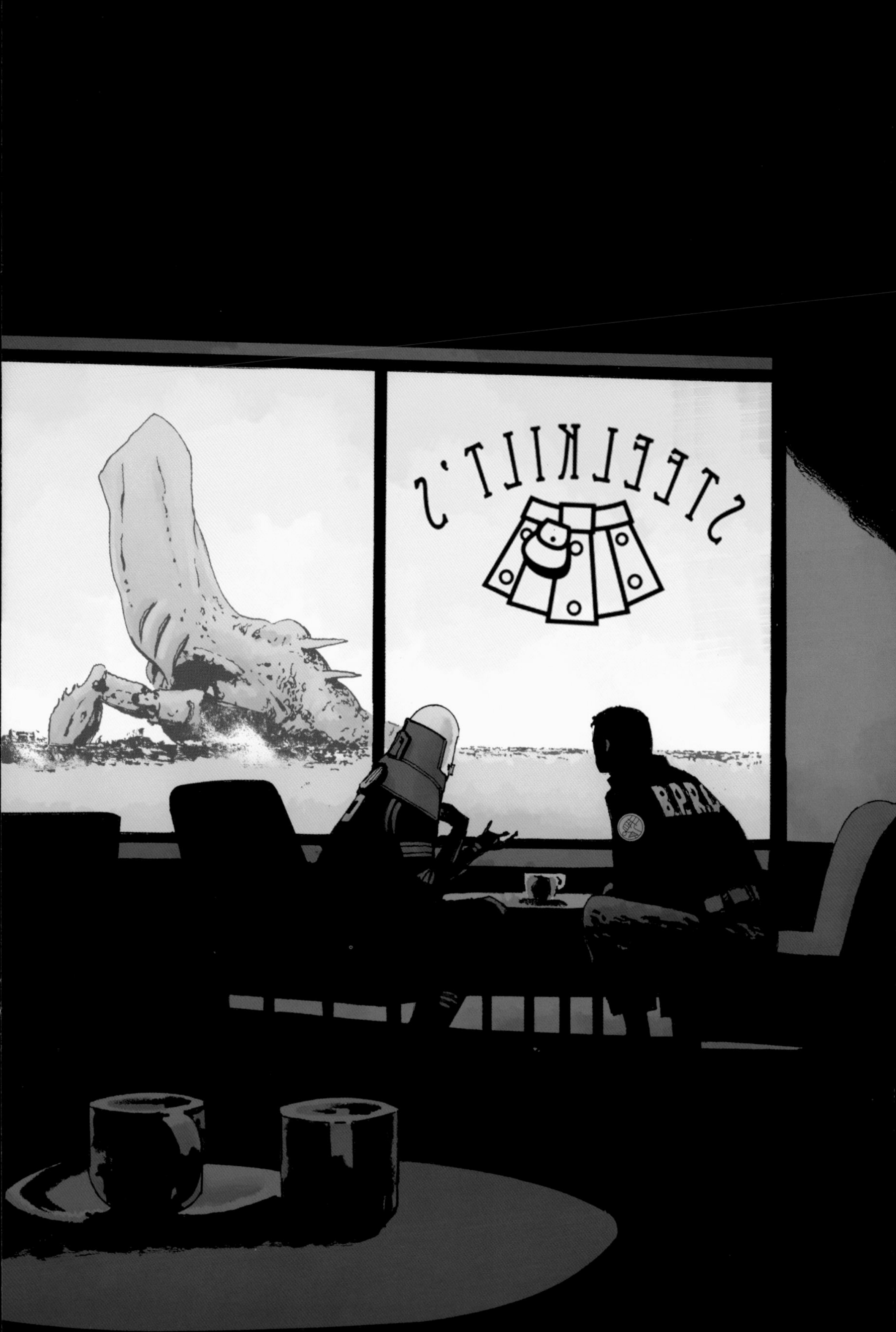
STEELKILT'S

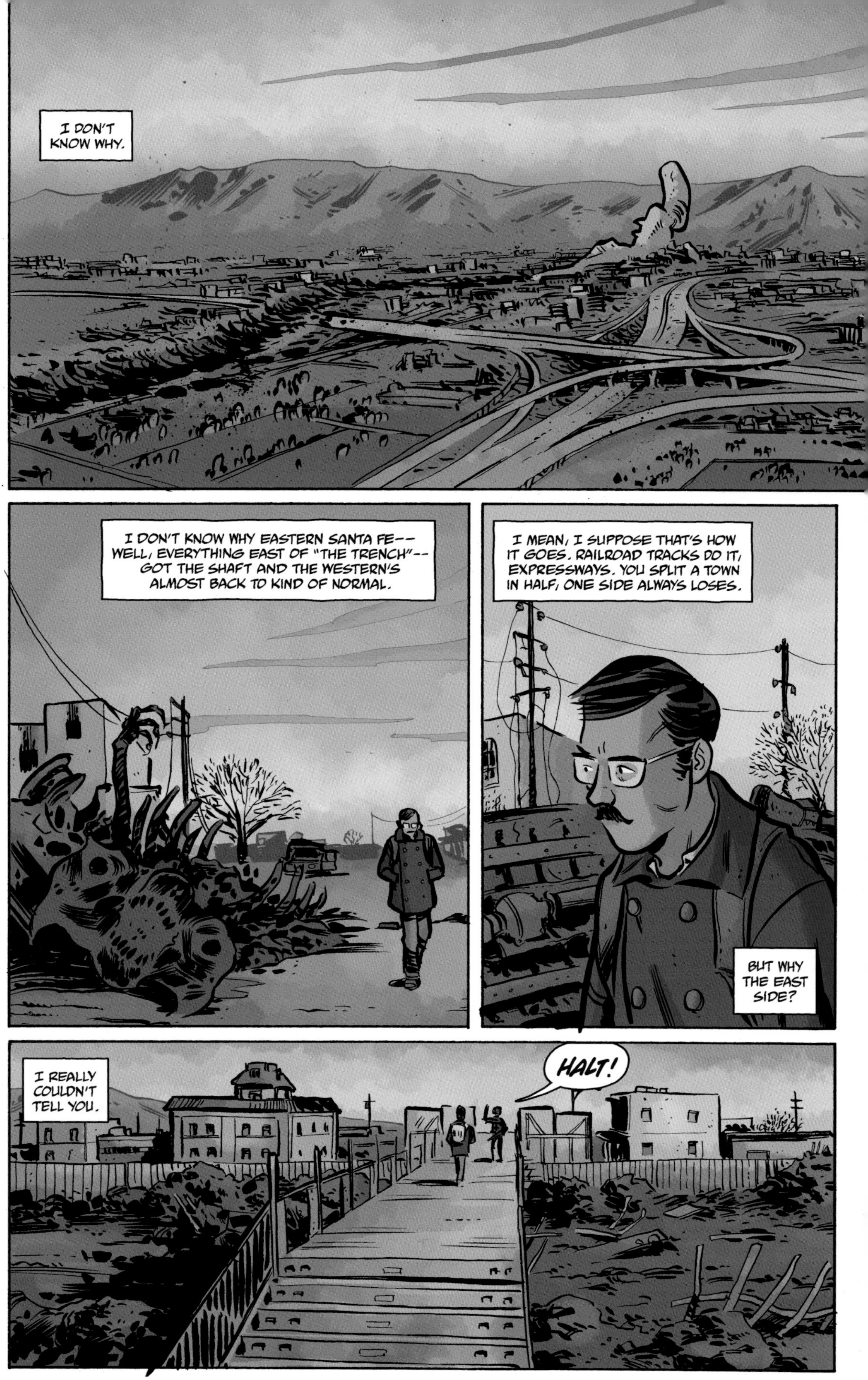
I DON'T KNOW WHY.
I DON'T KNOW WHY EASTERN SANTA FE-- WELL, EVERYTHING EAST OF "THE TRENCH"-- GOT THE SHAFT AND THE WESTERN'S ALMOST BACK TO KIND OF NORMAL.
I MEAN, I SUPPOSE THAT'S HOW IT GOES. RAILROAD TRACKS DO IT, EXPRESSWAYS. YOU SPLIT A TOWN IN HALF, ONE SIDE ALWAYS LOSES.
BUT WHY THE EAST SIDE?
I REALLY COULDN'T TELL YOU.
HALT!

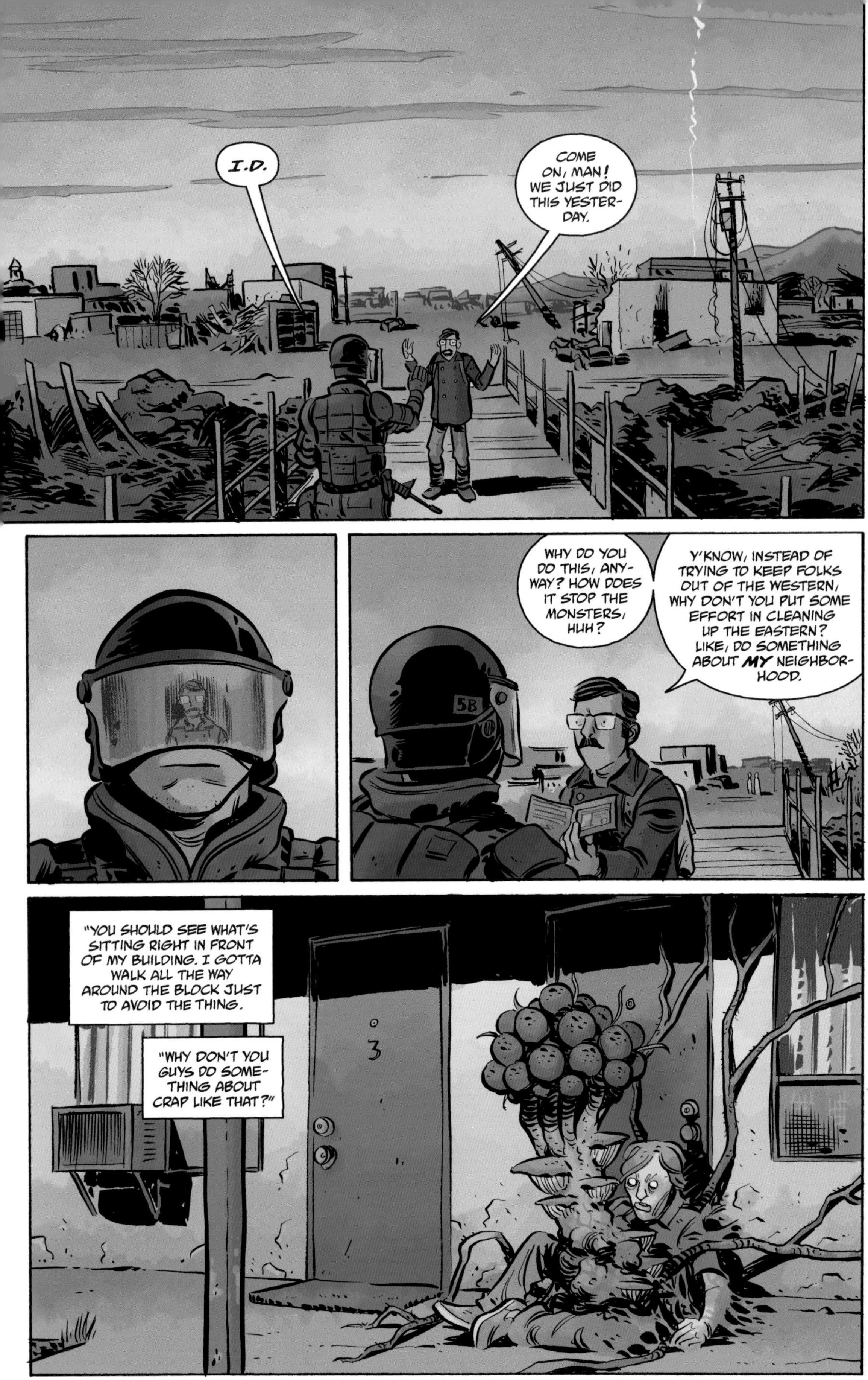
I.D.
COME ON, MAN! WE JUST DID THIS YESTER-DAY.
5B
WHY DO YOU DO THIS, ANY-WAY? HOW DOES IT STOP THE MONSTERS, HUH?
Y'KNOW, INSTEAD OF TRYING TO KEEP FOLKS OUT OF THE WESTERN, WHY DON'T YOU PUT SOME EFFORT IN CLEANING UP THE EASTERN? LIKE, DO SOMETHING ABOUT MY NEIGHBOR-HOOD.
"YOU SHOULD SEE WHAT'S SITTING RIGHT IN FRONT OF MY BUILDING. I GOTTA WALK ALL THE WAY AROUND THE BLOCK JUST TO AVOID THE THING.
"WHY DON'T YOU GUYS DO SOME-THING ABOUT CRAP LIKE THAT?"
3

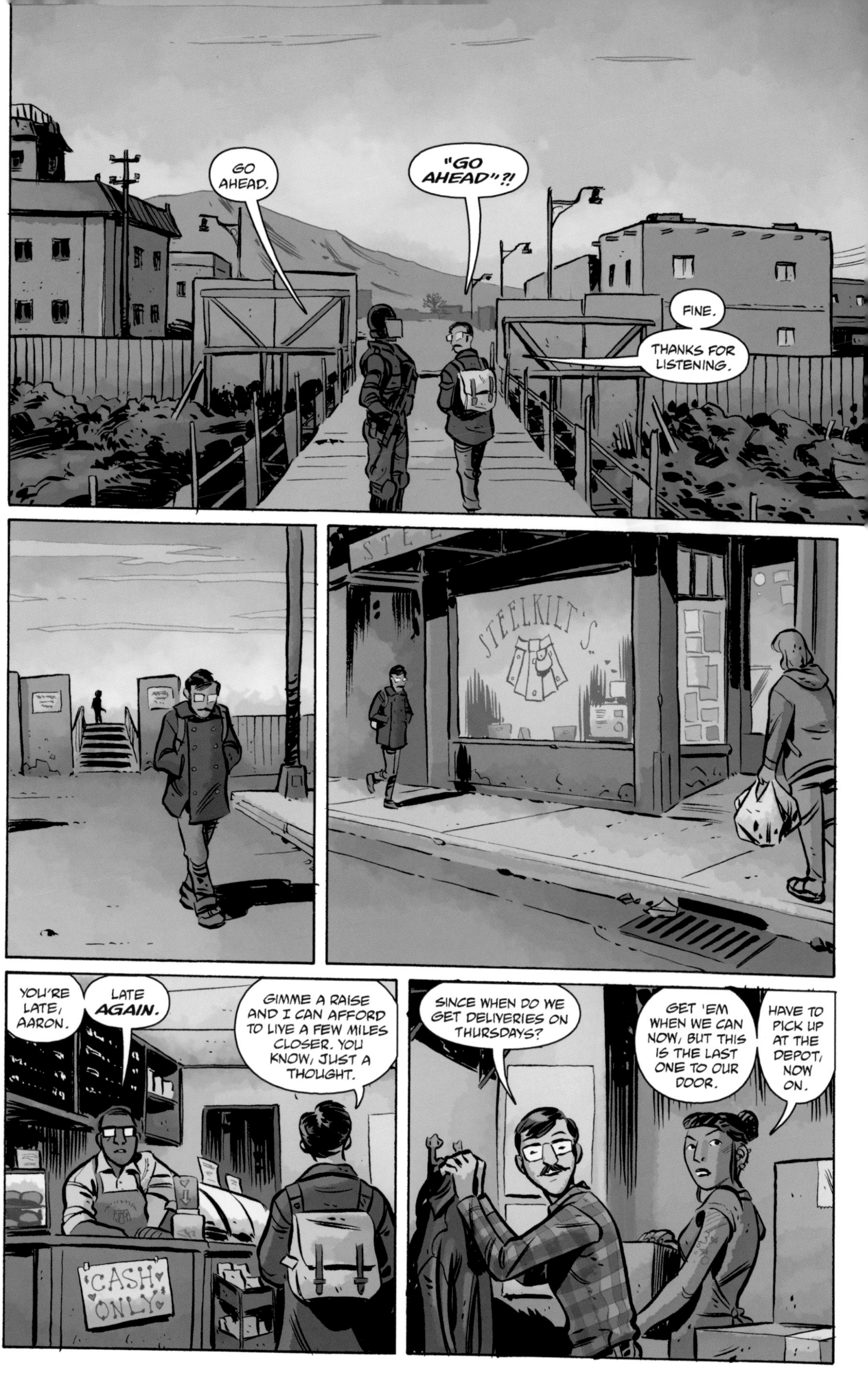
GO AHEAD.
"GO AHEAD"?!
FINE.
THANKS FOR LISTENING.
STEELKILT'S
YOU'RE LATE, AARON.
LATE AGAIN.
GIMME A RAISE AND I CAN AFFORD TO LIVE A FEW MILES CLOSER. YOU KNOW, JUST A THOUGHT.
CASH ONLY
SINCE WHEN DO WE GET DELIVERIES ON THURSDAYS?
GET 'EM WHEN WE CAN NOW, BUT THIS IS THE LAST ONE TO OUR DOOR.
HAVE TO PICK UP AT THE DEPOT, NOW ON.

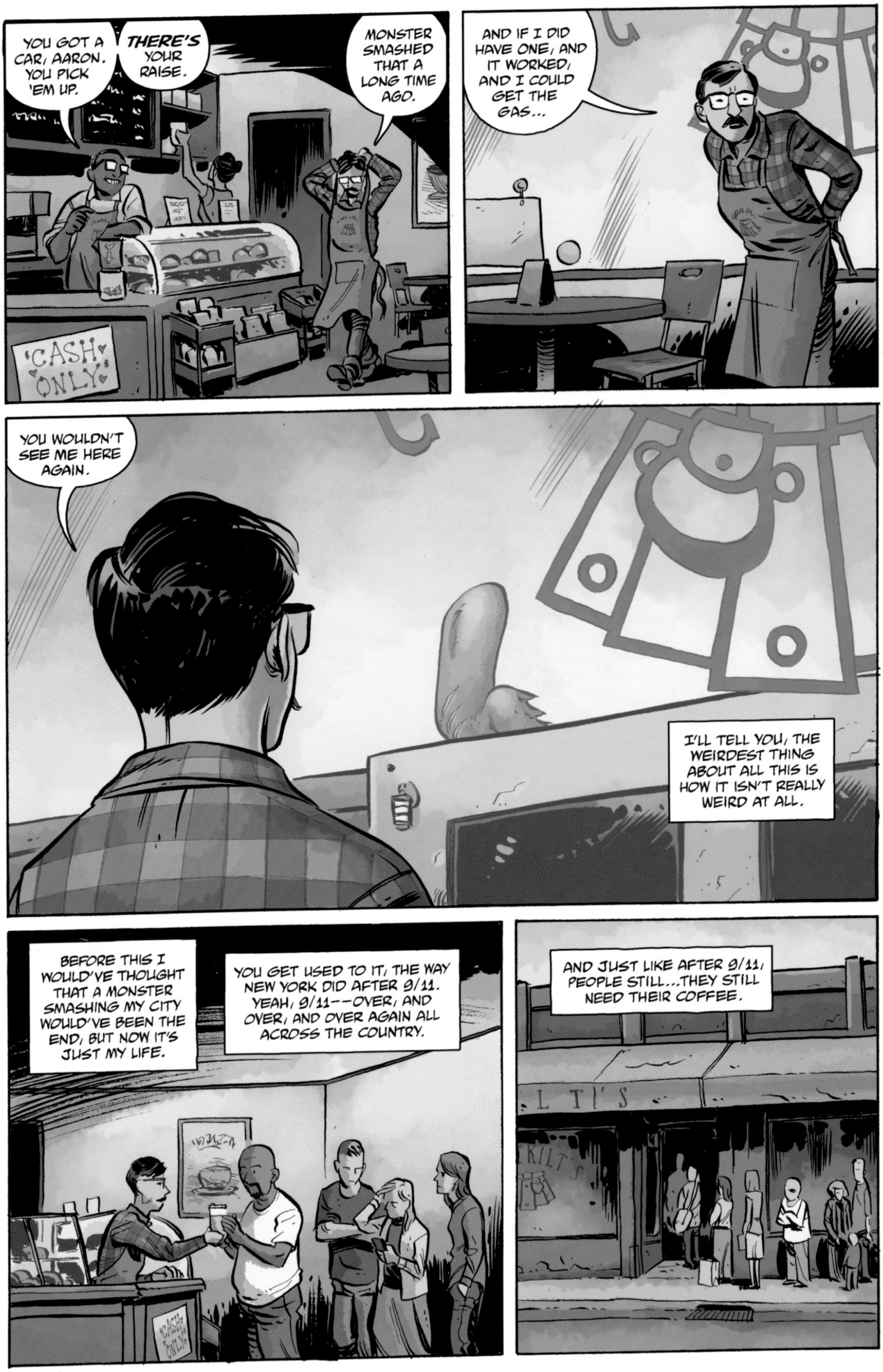
YOU GOT A CAR, AARON. YOU PICK 'EM UP.
THERE'S YOUR RAISE.
MONSTER SMASHED THAT A LONG TIME AGO.
CASH ONLY
AND IF I DID HAVE ONE, AND IT WORKED, AND I COULD GET THE GAS...
YOU WOULDN'T SEE ME HERE AGAIN.
I'LL TELL YOU, THE WEIRDEST THING ABOUT ALL THIS IS HOW IT ISN'T REALLY WEIRD AT ALL.
BEFORE THIS I WOULD'VE THOUGHT THAT A MONSTER SMASHING MY CITY WOULD'VE BEEN THE END, BUT NOW IT'S JUST MY LIFE.
YOU GET USED TO IT, THE WAY NEW YORK DID AFTER 9/11. YEAH, 9/11--OVER, AND OVER, AND OVER AGAIN ALL ACROSS THE COUNTRY.
CASH ONLY
AND JUST LIKE AFTER 9/11, PEOPLE STILL...THEY STILL NEED THEIR COFFEE.

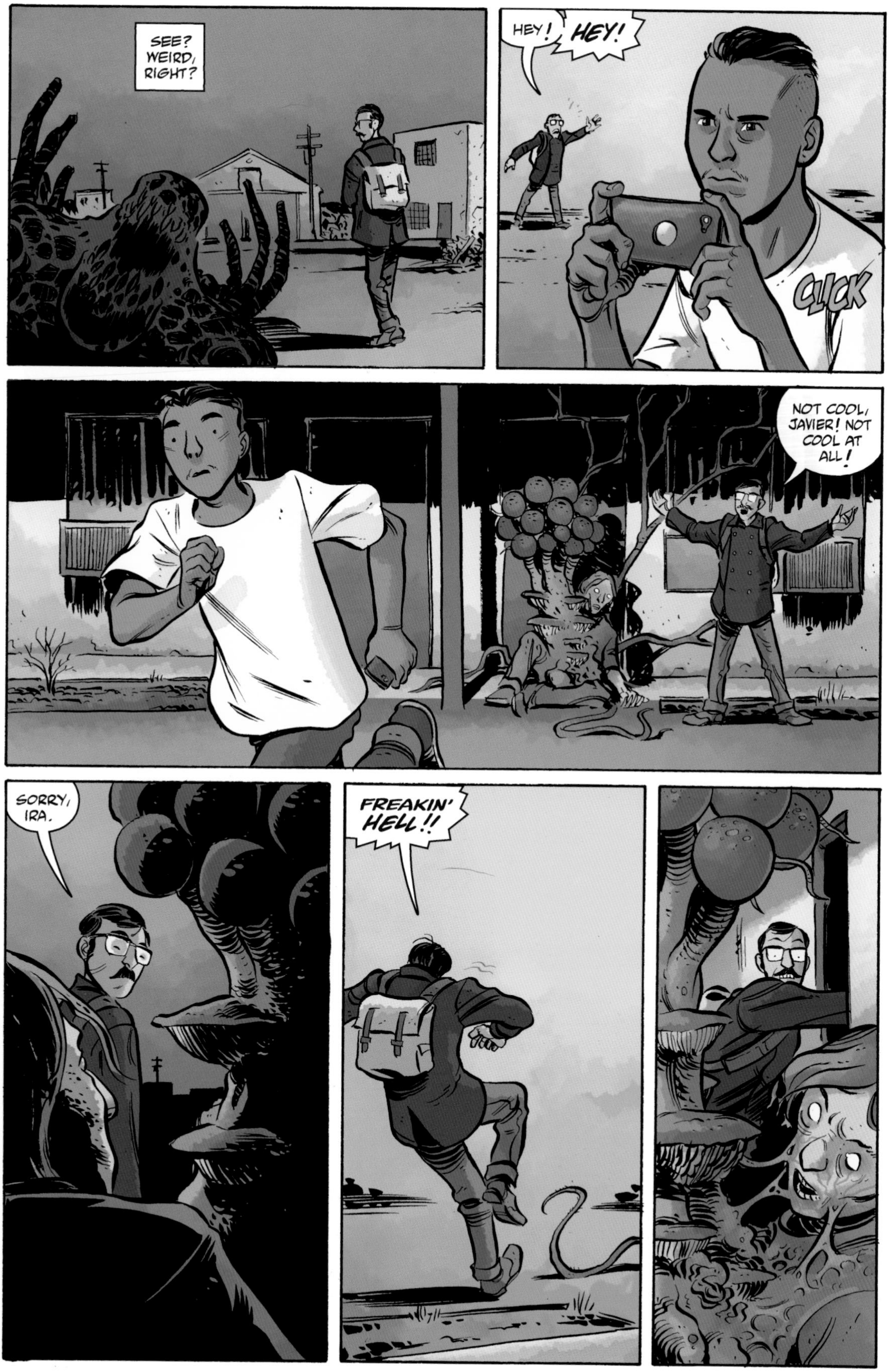
SEE? WEIRD, RIGHT?
HEY!
HEY!
CLICK
NOT COOL, JAVIER! NOT COOL AT ALL!
SORRY, IRA.
FREAKIN' HELL!!

NO, I GUESS YOU DON'T EVER REALLY GET USED TO IT.

OR I DON'T. NOT AT NIGHT.

BECAUSE IT'S NOT BUILDINGS FALLING AND THEN REBUILDING.

THE THINGS THAT KNOCKED DOWN THE BUILDINGS, THAT KILLED MY FRIENDS, THEY'RE STILL HERE.

SLISSSSS SLISSSSS SLISSSSS

I HEAR THEM AT NIGHT, SOMETIMES FAR AWAY, SOMETIMES CLOSER.

HOW CAN ANYBODY SLEEP? YOU CAN'T. NOT FOR DAYS ON END.

BUT THE ANXIETY, IT'S EXHAUSTING, AND EVENTUALLY, YOU FINALLY JUST...

SLISSSSSS SLISSSSSS SLISSSSSS

WHUP WHUP WHUP WHUP

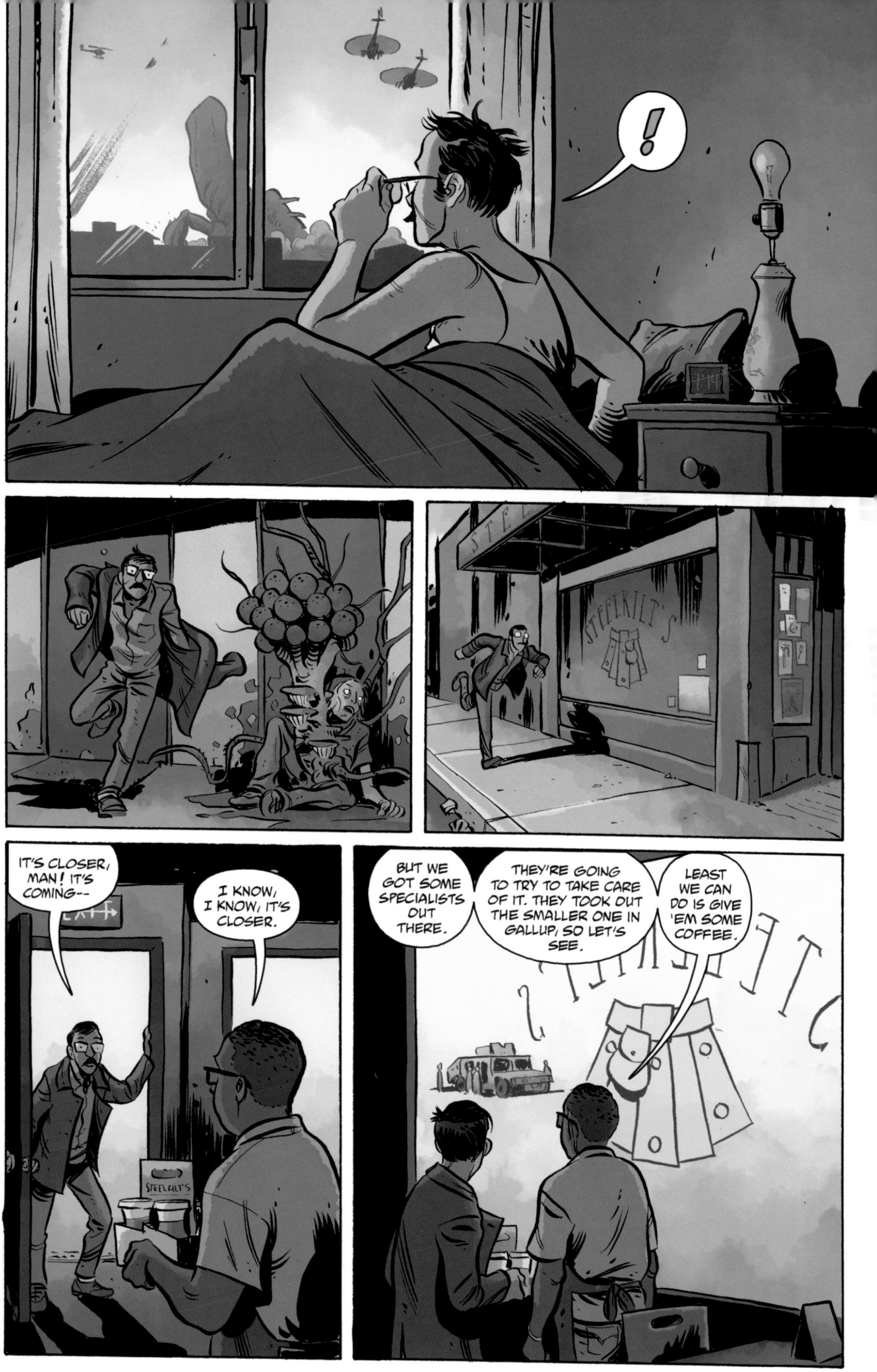
!
STEELKILT'S
IT'S CLOSER, MAN! IT'S COMING--
I KNOW, I KNOW, IT'S CLOSER.
STEELKILT'S
BUT WE GOT SOME SPECIALISTS OUT THERE.
THEY'RE GOING TO TRY TO TAKE CARE OF IT. THEY TOOK OUT THE SMALLER ONE IN GALLUP, SO LET'S SEE.
LEAST WE CAN DO IS GIVE 'EM SOME COFFEE.

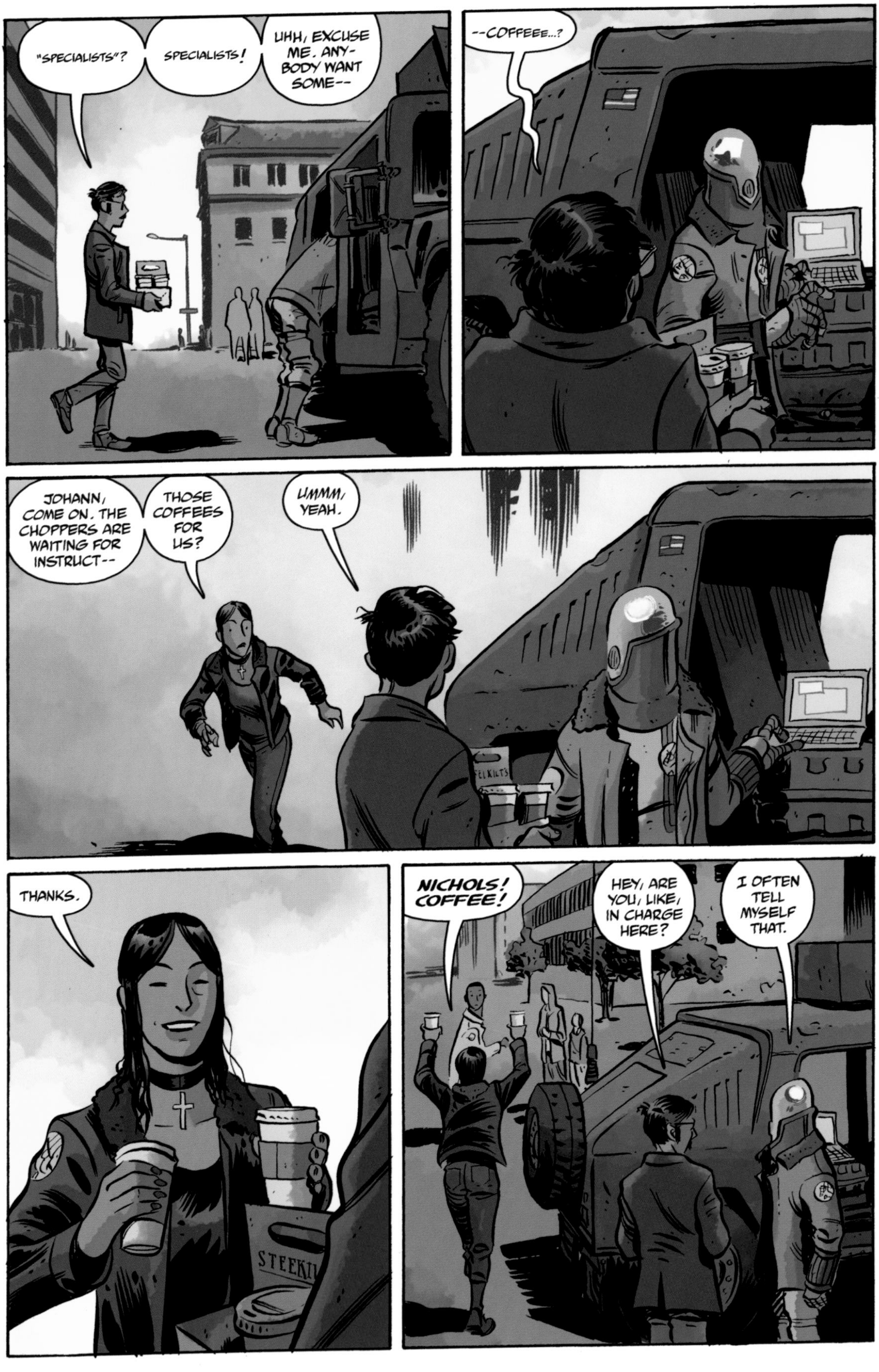
"SPECIALISTS"?
SPECIALISTS!
UHH, EXCUSE ME. ANY-BODY WANT SOME--
--COFFEEE...?
JOHANN, COME ON. THE CHOPPERS ARE WAITING FOR INSTRUCT--
THOSE COFFEES FOR US?
UMMM, YEAH.
THANKS.
STEEKIL
NICHOLS! COFFEE!
HEY, ARE YOU, LIKE, IN CHARGE HERE?
I OFTEN TELL MYSELF THAT.

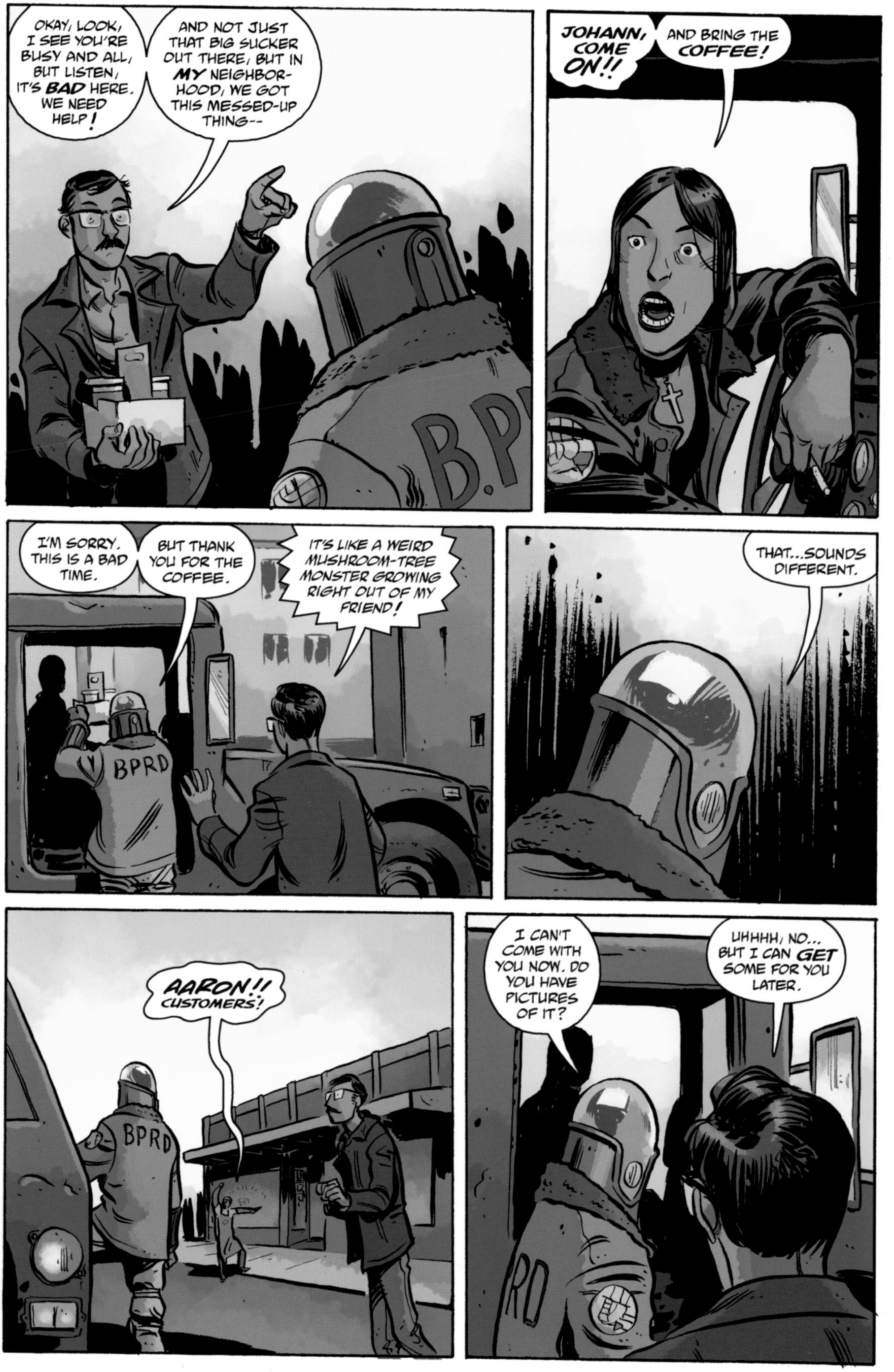
OKAY, LOOK, I SEE YOU'RE BUSY AND ALL, BUT LISTEN, IT'S BAD HERE. WE NEED HELP!
AND NOT JUST THAT BIG SUCKER OUT THERE, BUT IN MY NEIGHBOR-HOOD, WE GOT THIS MESSED-UP THING--
JOHANN, COME ON!!
AND BRING THE COFFEE!
I'M SORRY. THIS IS A BAD TIME.
BUT THANK YOU FOR THE COFFEE.
IT'S LIKE A WEIRD MUSHROOM-TREE MONSTER GROWING RIGHT OUT OF MY FRIEND!
BPRD
THAT...SOUNDS DIFFERENT.
AARON!! CUSTOMERS!
BPRD
I CAN'T COME WITH YOU NOW. DO YOU HAVE PICTURES OF IT?
UHHHH, NO... BUT I CAN GET SOME FOR YOU LATER.

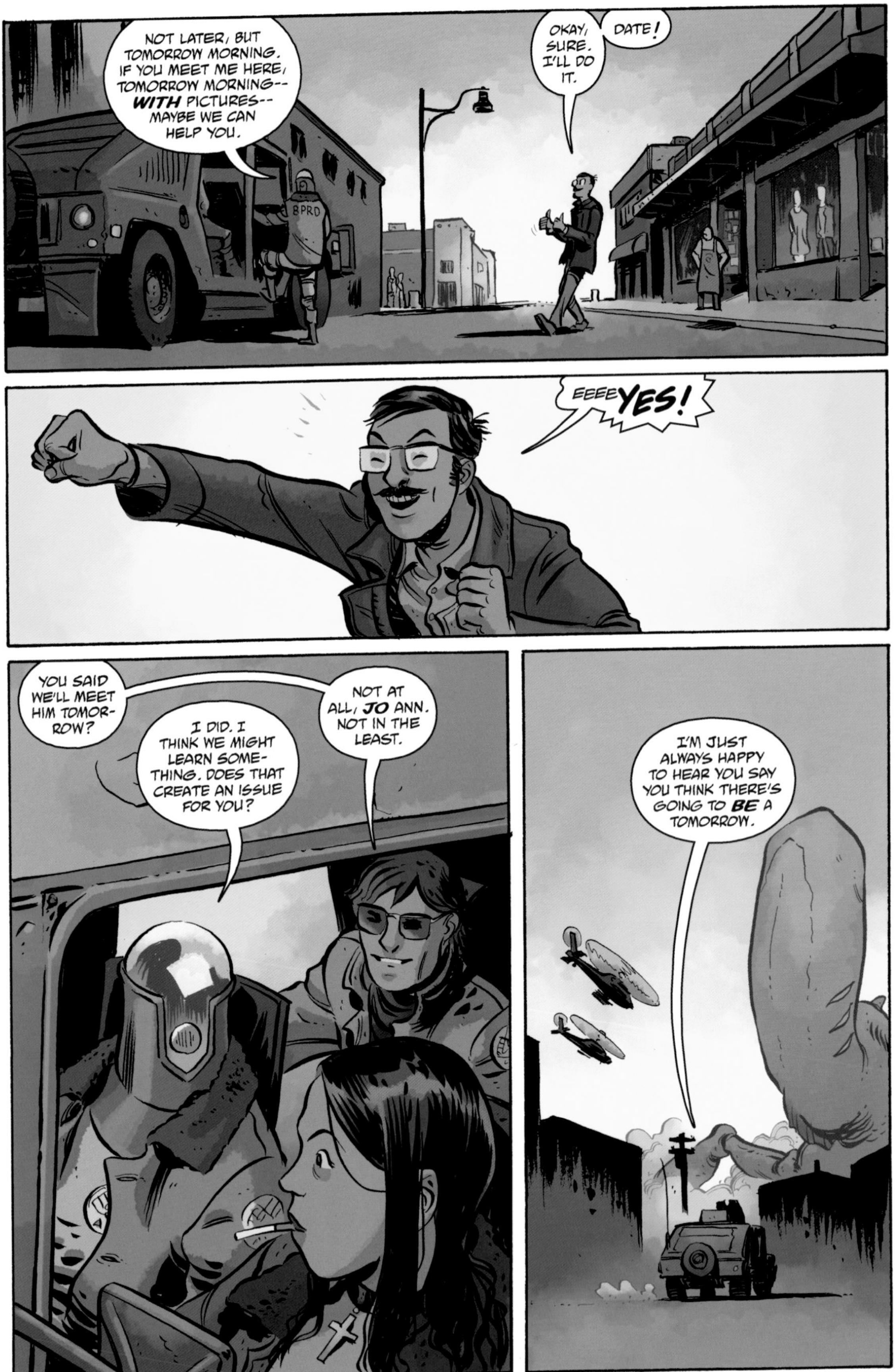
NOT LATER, BUT TOMORROW MORNING. IF YOU MEET ME HERE, TOMORROW MORNING-- WITH PICTURES-- MAYBE WE CAN HELP YOU.
BPRD
OKAY, SURE. I'LL DO IT.
DATE!
EEEEYES!
YOU SAID WE'LL MEET HIM TOMORROW?
I DID. I THINK WE MIGHT LEARN SOMETHING. DOES THAT CREATE AN ISSUE FOR YOU?
NOT AT ALL, JO ANN. NOT IN THE LEAST.
I'M JUST ALWAYS HAPPY TO HEAR YOU SAY YOU THINK THERE'S GOING TO BE A TOMORROW.

NO DECAF?! WHY'D YOU STOP CARRYING IT?

YOU'RE THE ONLY ONE WHO EVER ASKS FOR IT, MISS ORLANDA.

LISTEN, OBVIOUSLY IF THAT THING GETS ANY CLOSER, WE'LL HAVE TO CLOSE.

BUT THEY MIGHT *KILL* IT!

RIGHT, MAYBE, BUT THERE'S A STEELKILT'S IN ALBUQUERQUE LOOKING FOR A MANAGER THAT I MIGHT TAKE, AND IF *YOU* WANT A LIFT OUT OF TOWN--

IT'S HAPPENING!

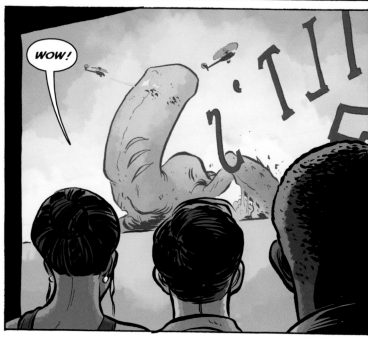

WOW!

I DON'T KNOW. THEY BOMBED IT FOR A WEEK LAST DECEMBER, THEN JUST LEFT IT.

HOW IS THIS GOING TO GO ANY BETTER?

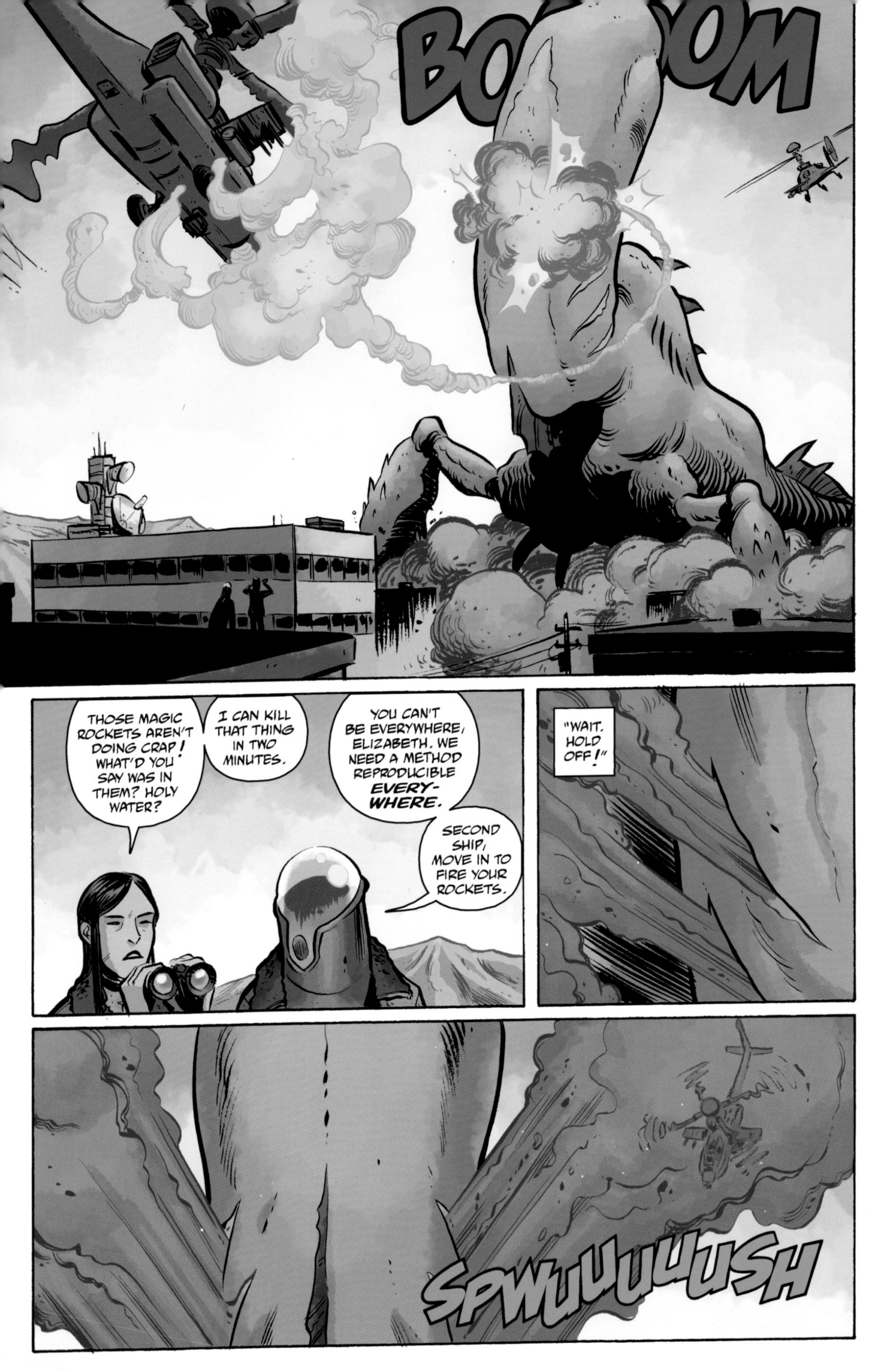
BOOOOM
THOSE MAGIC ROCKETS AREN'T DOING CRAP! WHAT'D YOU SAY WAS IN THEM? HOLY WATER?
I CAN KILL THAT THING IN TWO MINUTES.
YOU CAN'T BE EVERYWHERE, ELIZABETH. WE NEED A METHOD REPRODUCIBLE EVERY- WHERE.
SECOND SHIP, MOVE IN TO FIRE YOUR ROCKETS.
"WAIT. HOLD OFF!"
SPWUUUUUSH

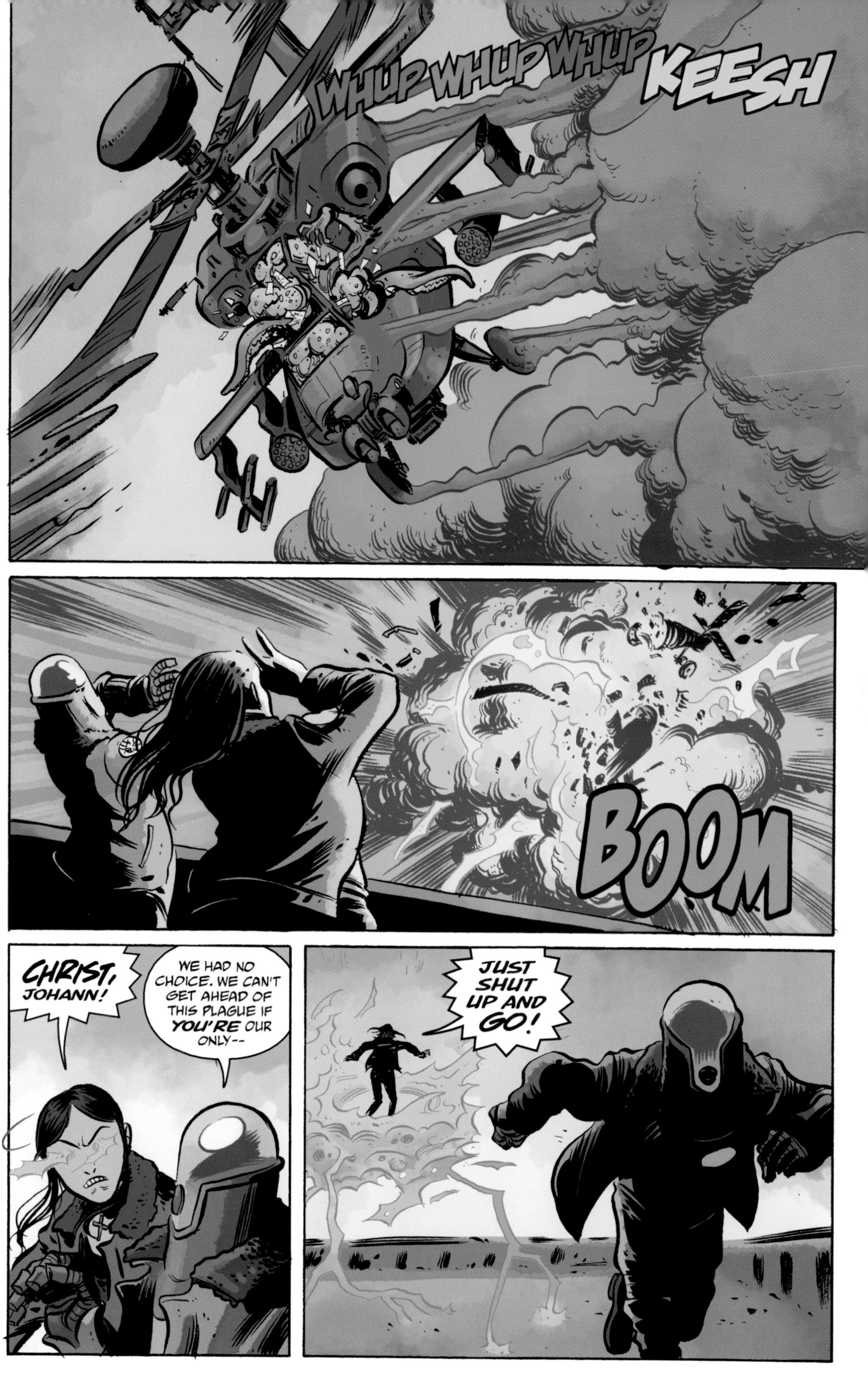
WHUP WHUP WHUP
KEESH
BOOM
CHRIST, JOHANN!
WE HAD NO CHOICE. WE CAN'T GET AHEAD OF THIS PLAGUE IF YOU'RE OUR ONLY--
JUST SHUT UP AND GO!

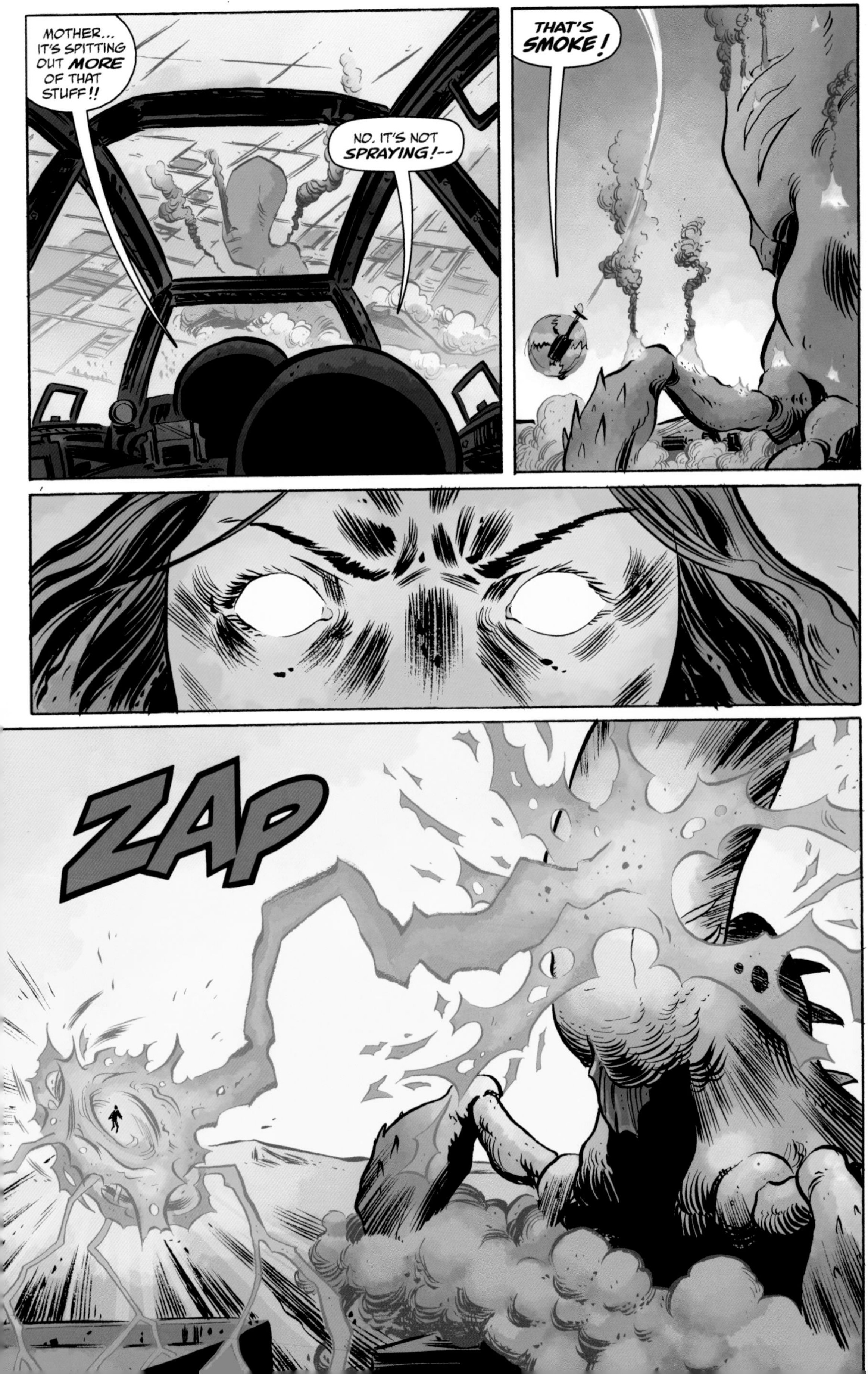
MOTHER... IT'S SPITTING OUT MORE OF THAT STUFF!!
NO. IT'S NOT SPRAYING!--
THAT'S SMOKE!
ZAP

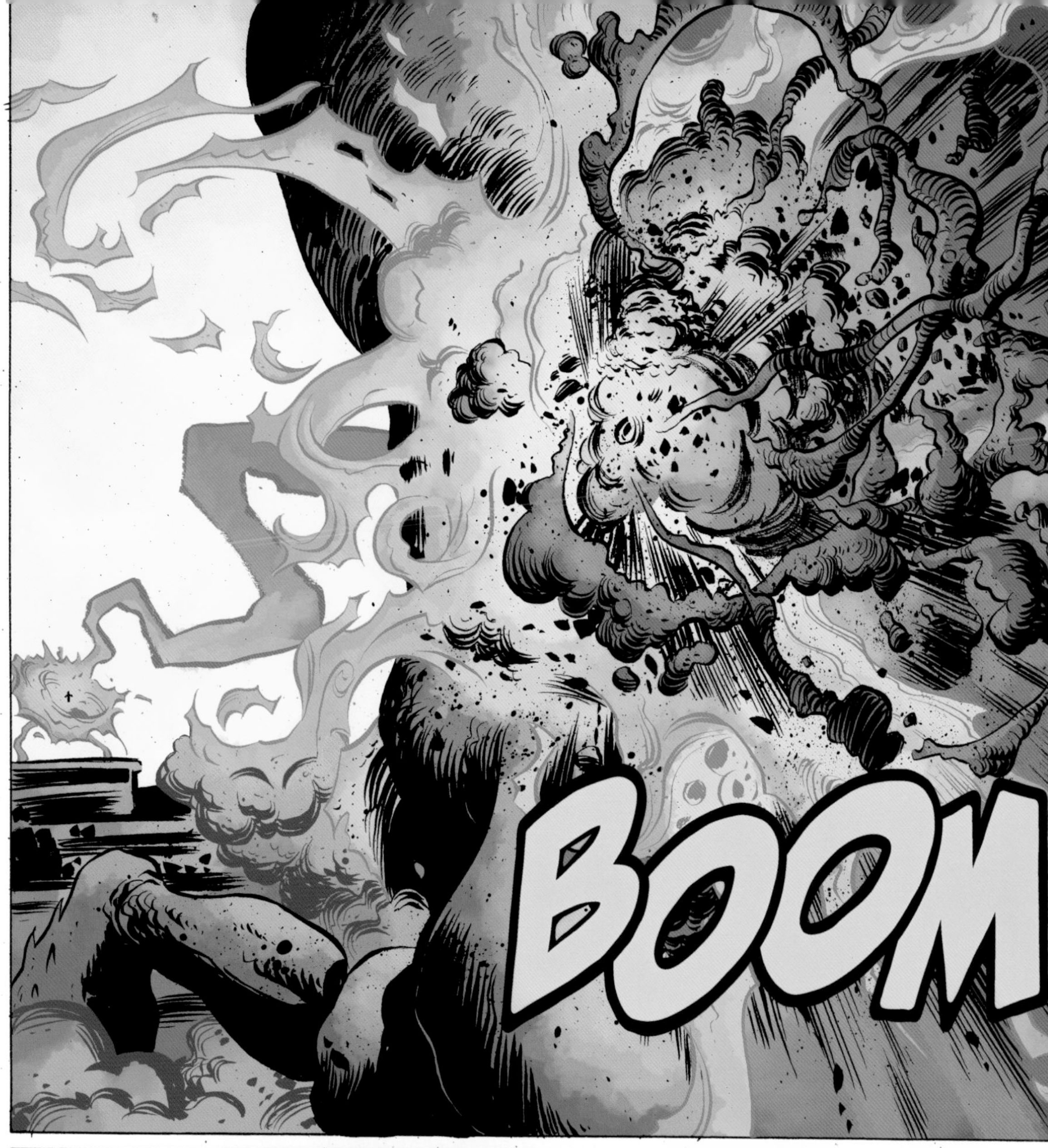
BOOM

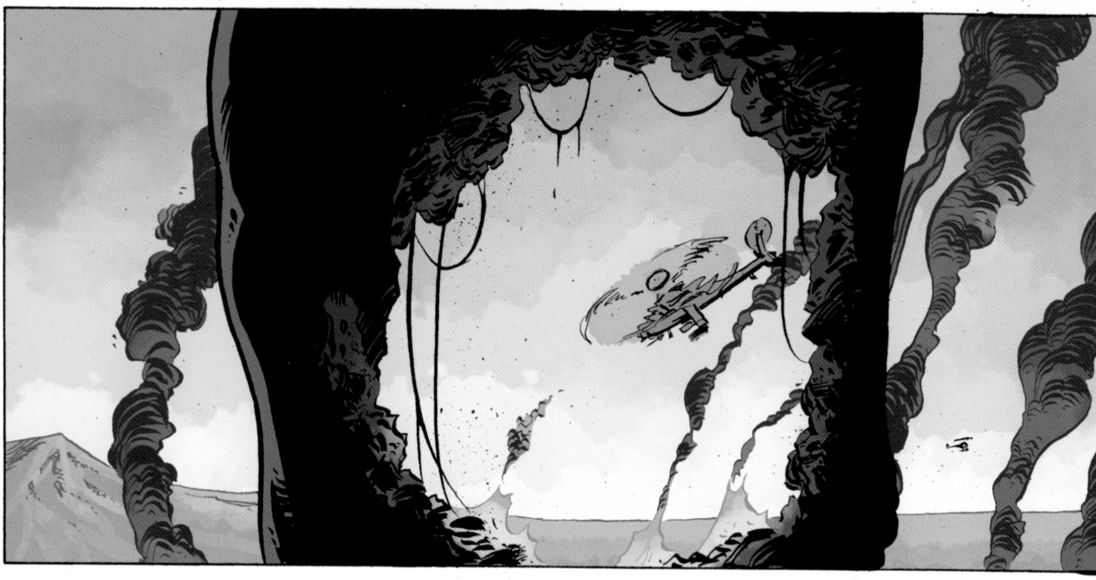

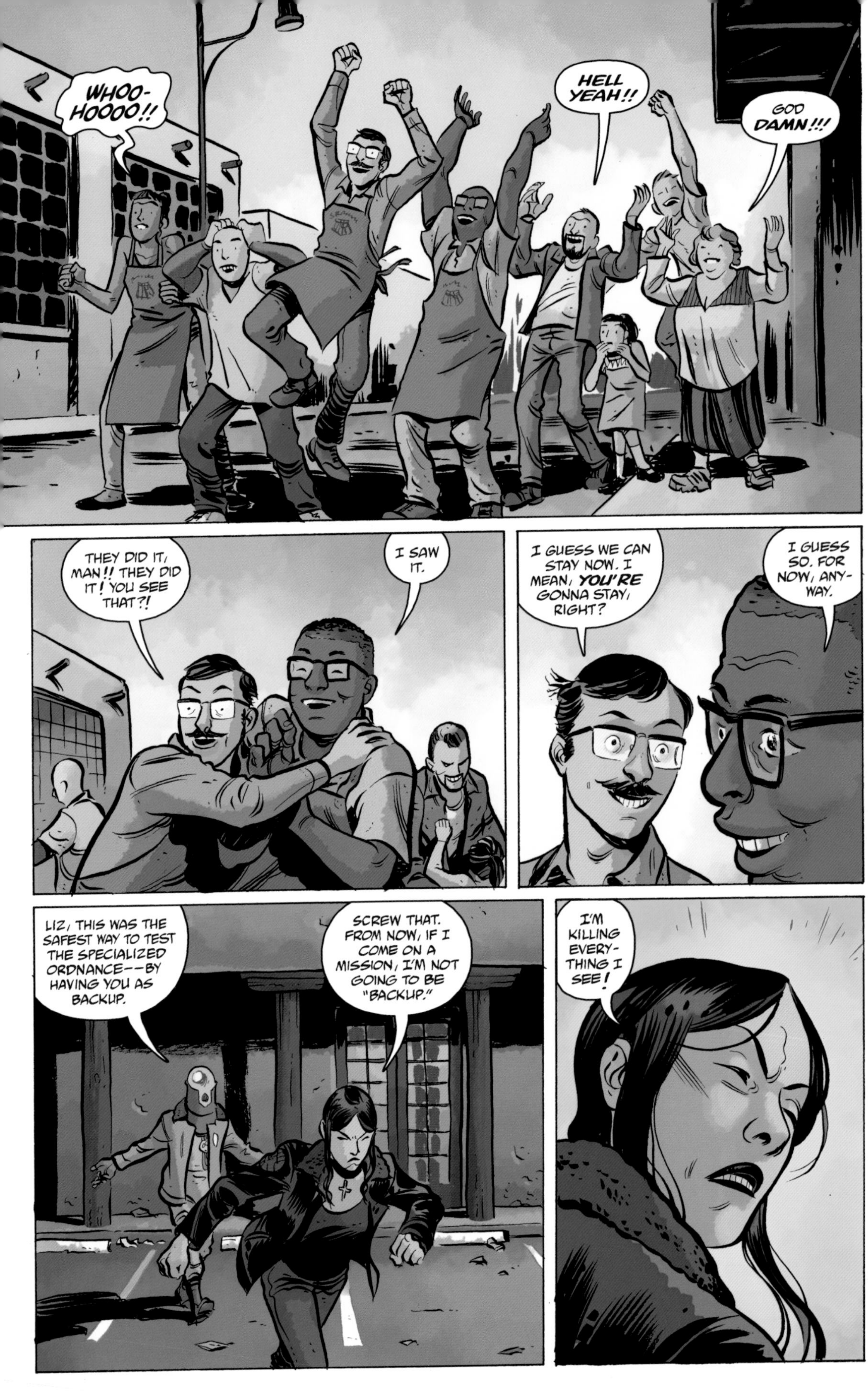
WHOO-HOOOO!!
HELL YEAH!!
GOD DAMN!!!
THEY DID IT, MAN!! THEY DID IT! YOU SEE THAT?!
I SAW IT.
I GUESS WE CAN STAY NOW. I MEAN, YOU'RE GONNA STAY, RIGHT?
I GUESS SO. FOR NOW, ANYWAY.
LIZ, THIS WAS THE SAFEST WAY TO TEST THE SPECIALIZED ORDNANCE--BY HAVING YOU AS BACKUP.
SCREW THAT. FROM NOW, IF I COME ON A MISSION, I'M NOT GOING TO BE "BACKUP."
I'M KILLING EVERYTHING I SEE!

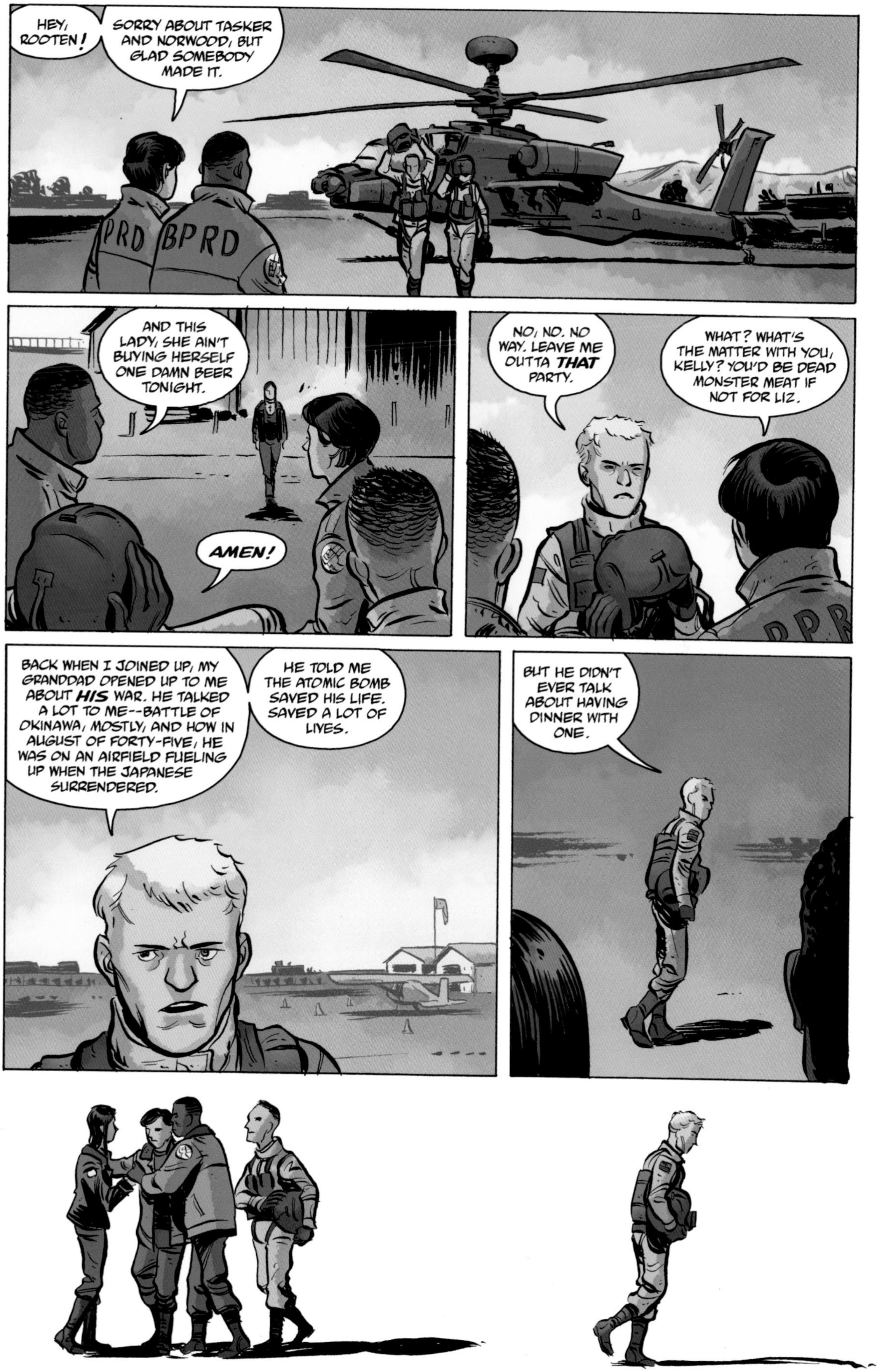
HEY, ROOTEN!
SORRY ABOUT TASKER AND NORWOOD, BUT GLAD SOMEBODY MADE IT.
PRD
BPRD
AND THIS LADY, SHE AIN'T BUYING HERSELF ONE DAMN BEER TONIGHT.
AMEN!
NO, NO. NO WAY. LEAVE ME OUTTA THAT PARTY.
WHAT? WHAT'S THE MATTER WITH YOU, KELLY? YOU'D BE DEAD MONSTER MEAT IF NOT FOR LIZ.
BACK WHEN I JOINED UP, MY GRANDDAD OPENED UP TO ME ABOUT HIS WAR. HE TALKED A LOT TO ME--BATTLE OF OKINAWA, MOSTLY, AND HOW IN AUGUST OF FORTY-FIVE, HE WAS ON AN AIRFIELD FUELING UP WHEN THE JAPANESE SURRENDERED.
HE TOLD ME THE ATOMIC BOMB SAVED HIS LIFE. SAVED A LOT OF LIVES.
BUT HE DIDN'T EVER TALK ABOUT HAVING DINNER WITH ONE.

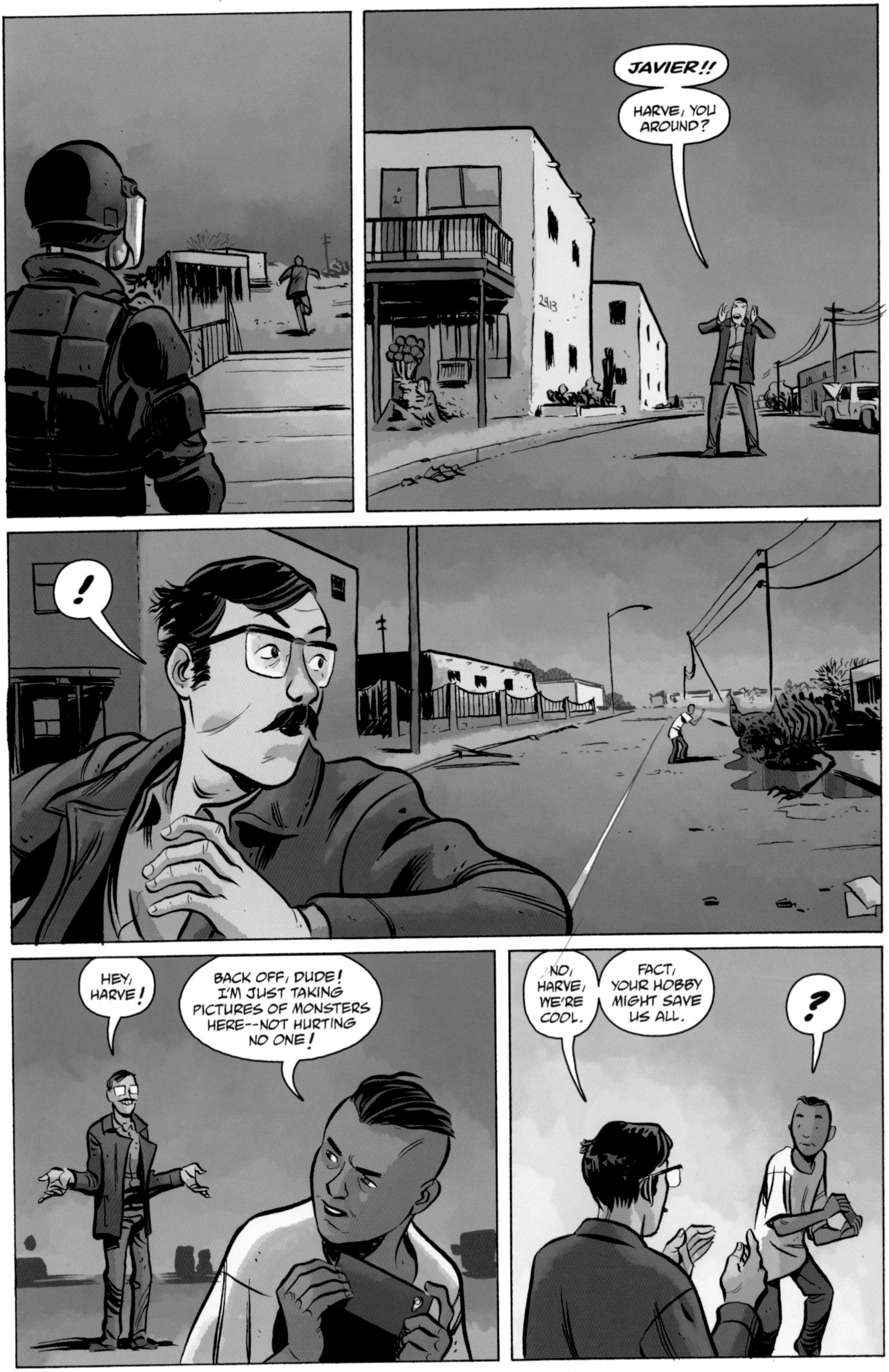
JAVIER!!
HARVE, YOU AROUND?
2413
!
HEY, HARVE!
BACK OFF, DUDE! I'M JUST TAKING PICTURES OF MONSTERS HERE--NOT HURTING NO ONE!
NO, HARVE, WE'RE COOL.
FACT, YOUR HOBBY MIGHT SAVE US ALL.
?

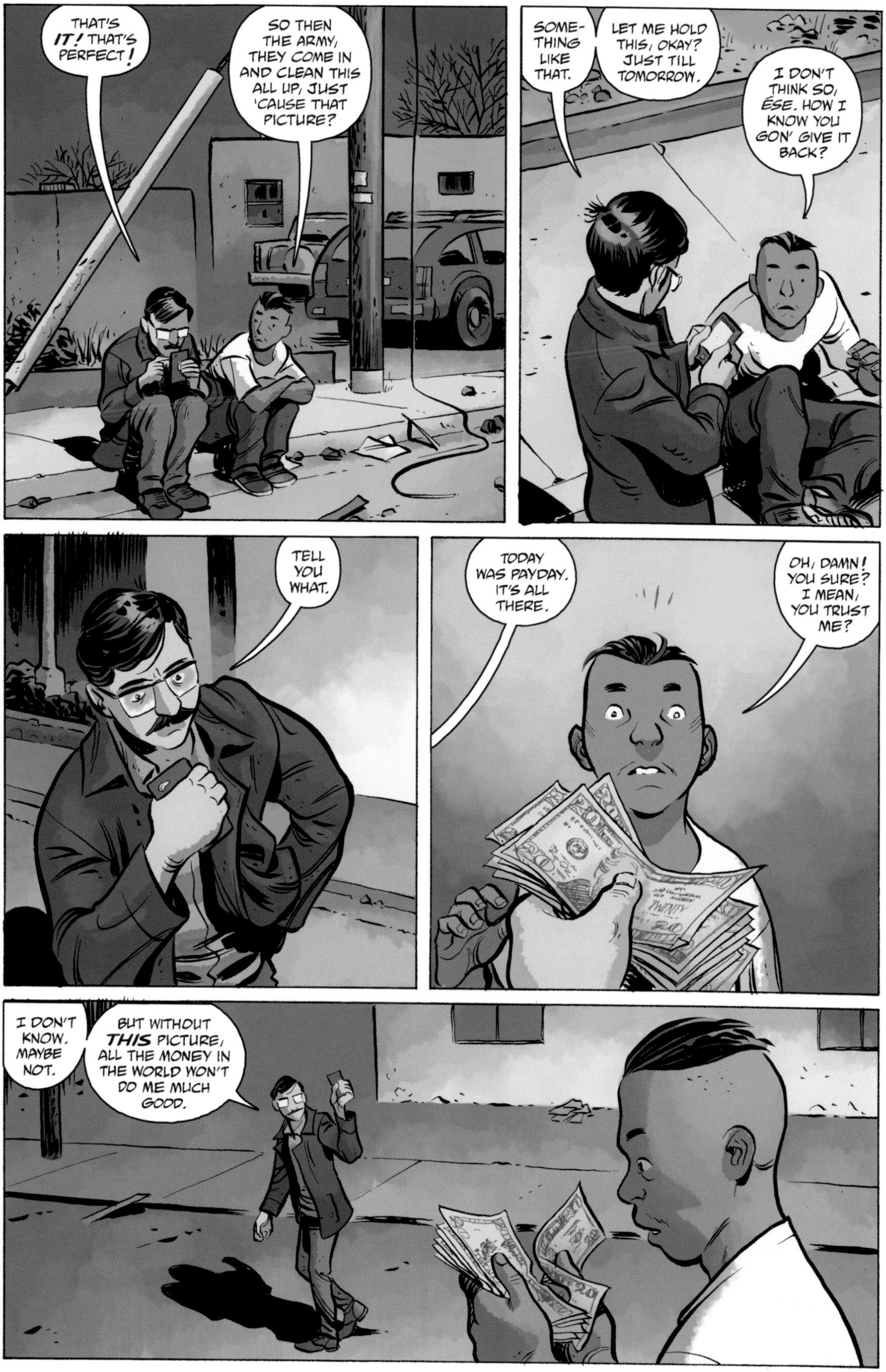
THAT'S IT! THAT'S PERFECT!
SO THEN THE ARMY, THEY COME IN AND CLEAN THIS ALL UP, JUST 'CAUSE THAT PICTURE?
SOME-THING LIKE THAT.
LET ME HOLD THIS, OKAY? JUST TILL TOMORROW.
I DON'T THINK SO, ÉSE. HOW I KNOW YOU GON' GIVE IT BACK?
TELL YOU WHAT.
TODAY WAS PAYDAY. IT'S ALL THERE.
OH, DAMN! YOU SURE? I MEAN, YOU TRUST ME?
I DON'T KNOW. MAYBE NOT.
BUT WITHOUT THIS PICTURE, ALL THE MONEY IN THE WORLD WON'T DO ME MUCH GOOD.

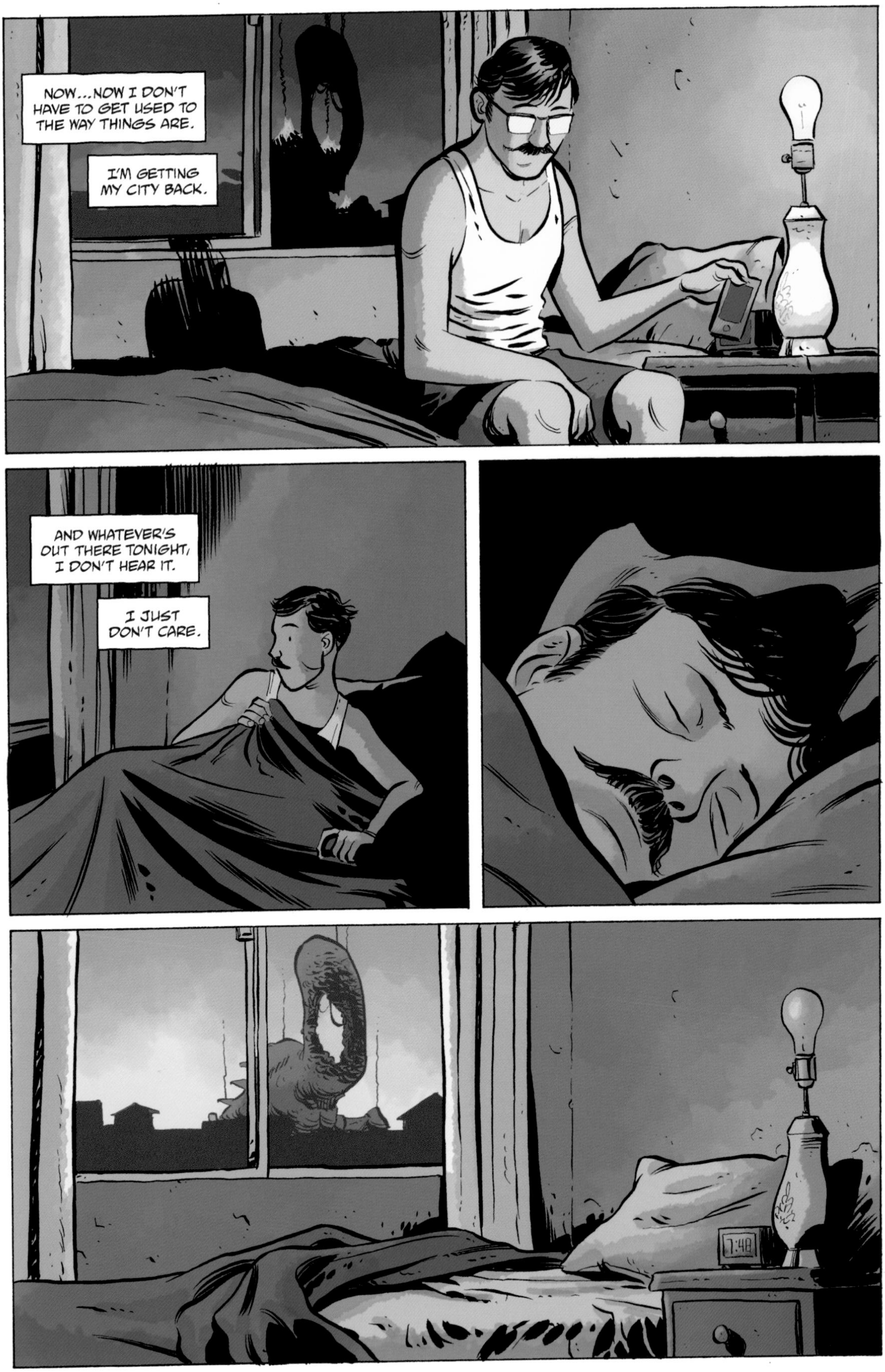
NOW...NOW I DON'T HAVE TO GET USED TO THE WAY THINGS ARE.
I'M GETTING MY CITY BACK.
AND WHATEVER'S OUT THERE TONIGHT, I DON'T HEAR IT.
I JUST DON'T CARE.

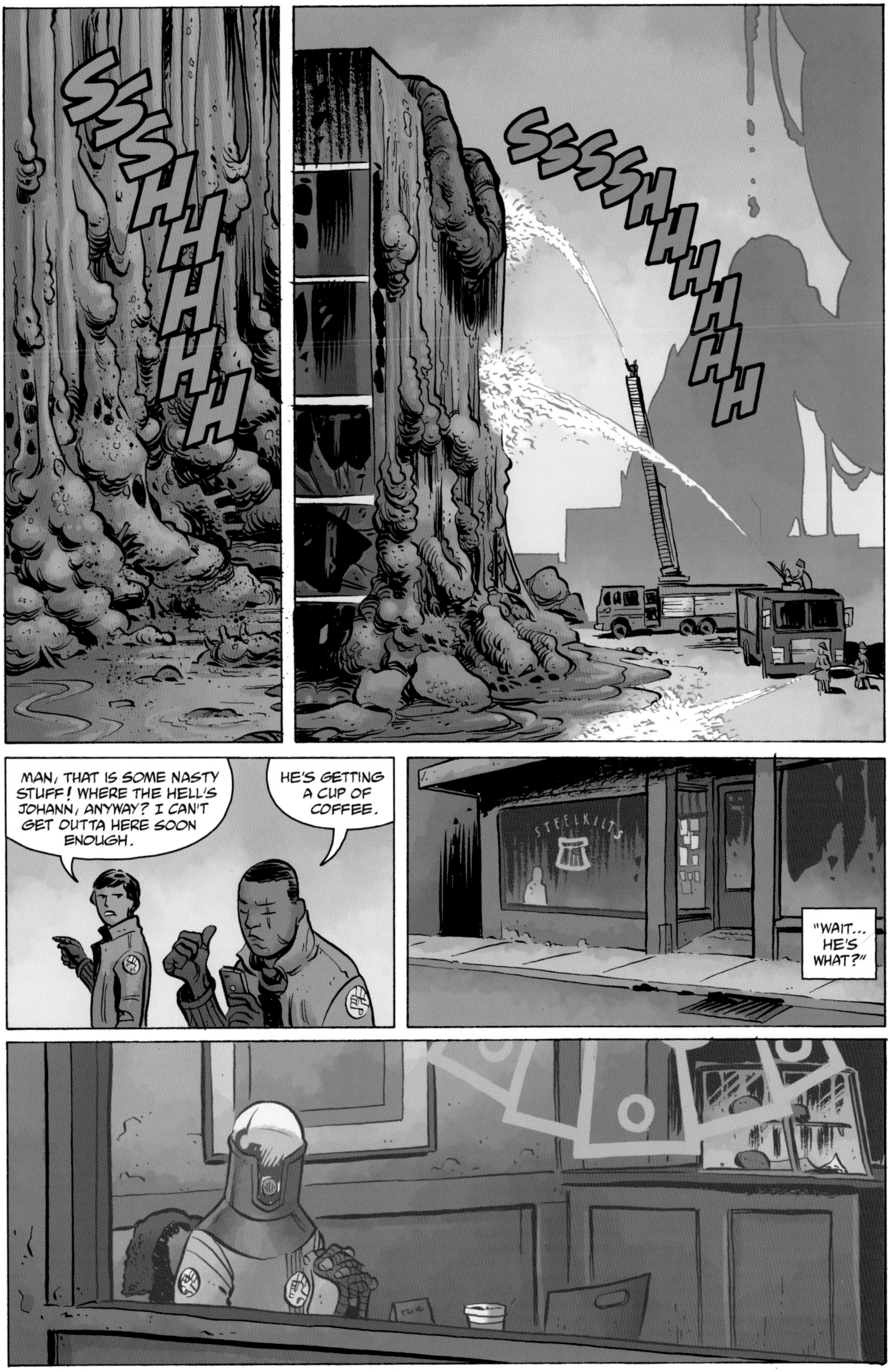
SSSHHHHHH
SSSSSHHHHHHH
MAN, THAT IS SOME NASTY STUFF! WHERE THE HELL'S JOHANN, ANYWAY? I CAN'T GET OUTTA HERE SOON ENOUGH.
HE'S GETTING A CUP OF COFFEE.
STEELKILTS
"WAIT... HE'S WHAT?"

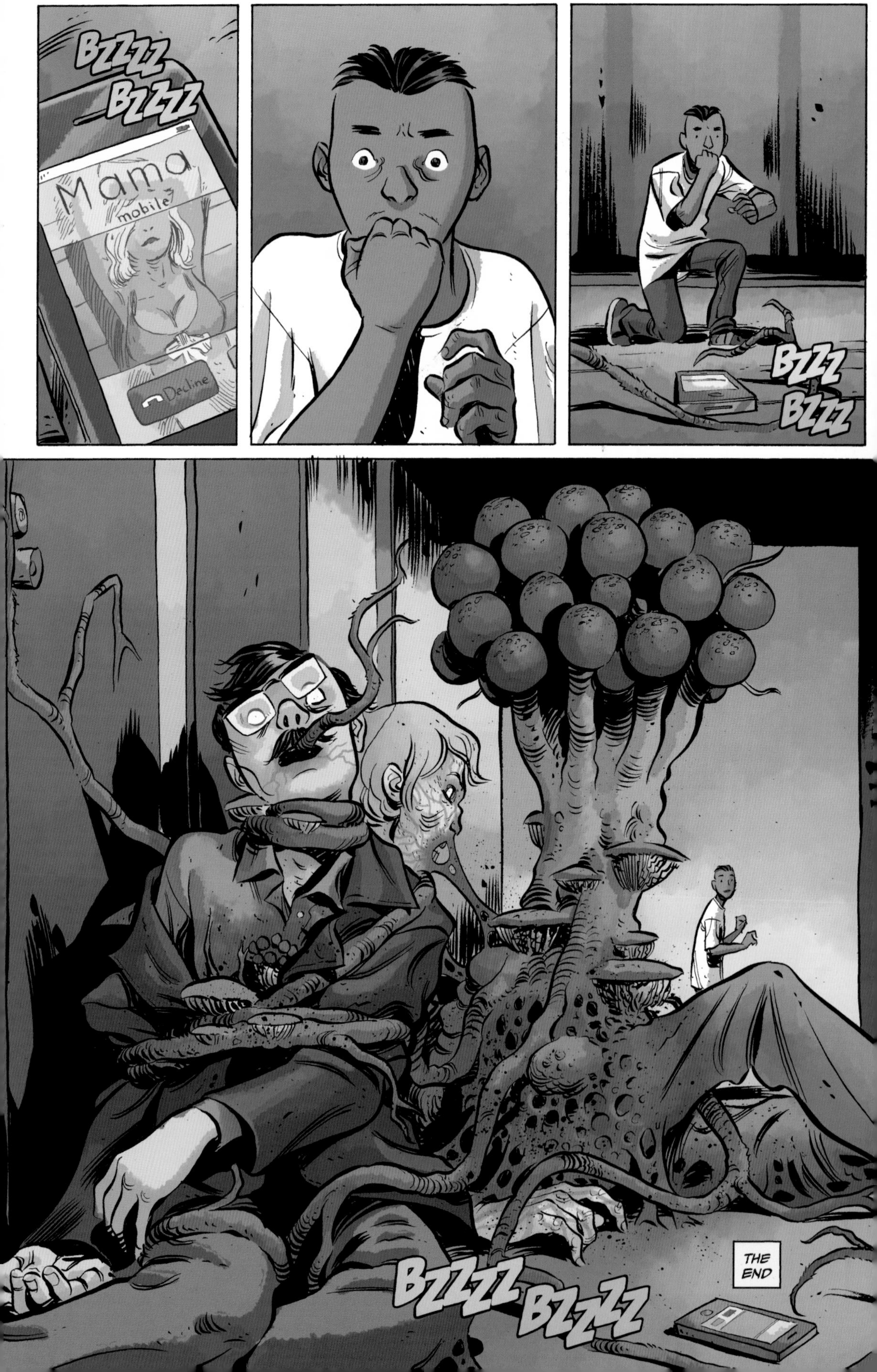
BZZZZ
BZZZZ
Mama
mobile
Decline
BZZZ
BZZZ
BZZZZ
BZZZZ
THE END

FLESH AND STONE CHAPTER ONE

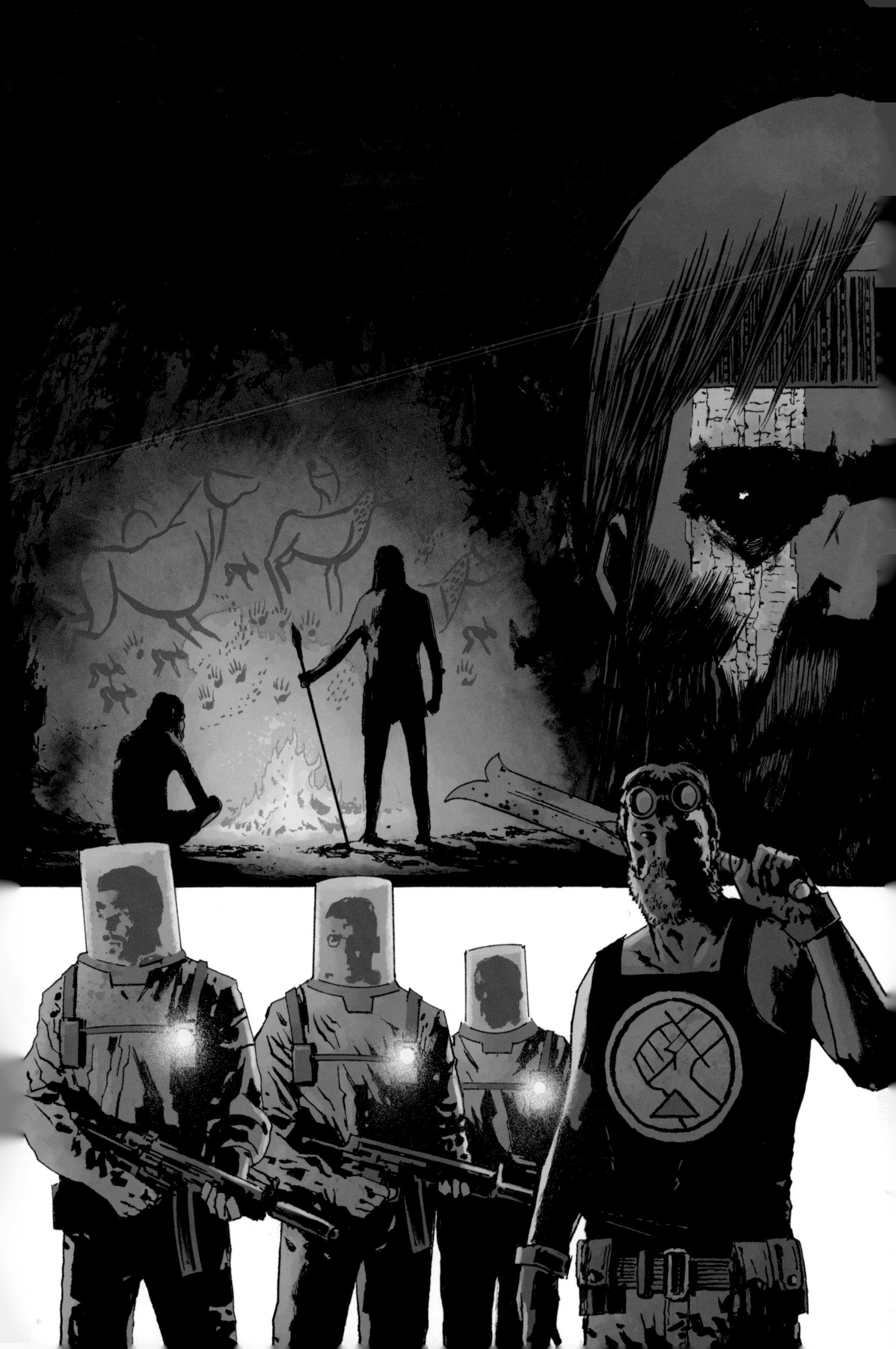

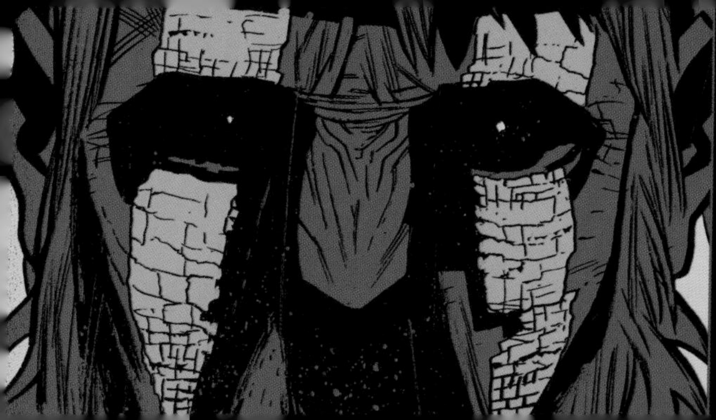

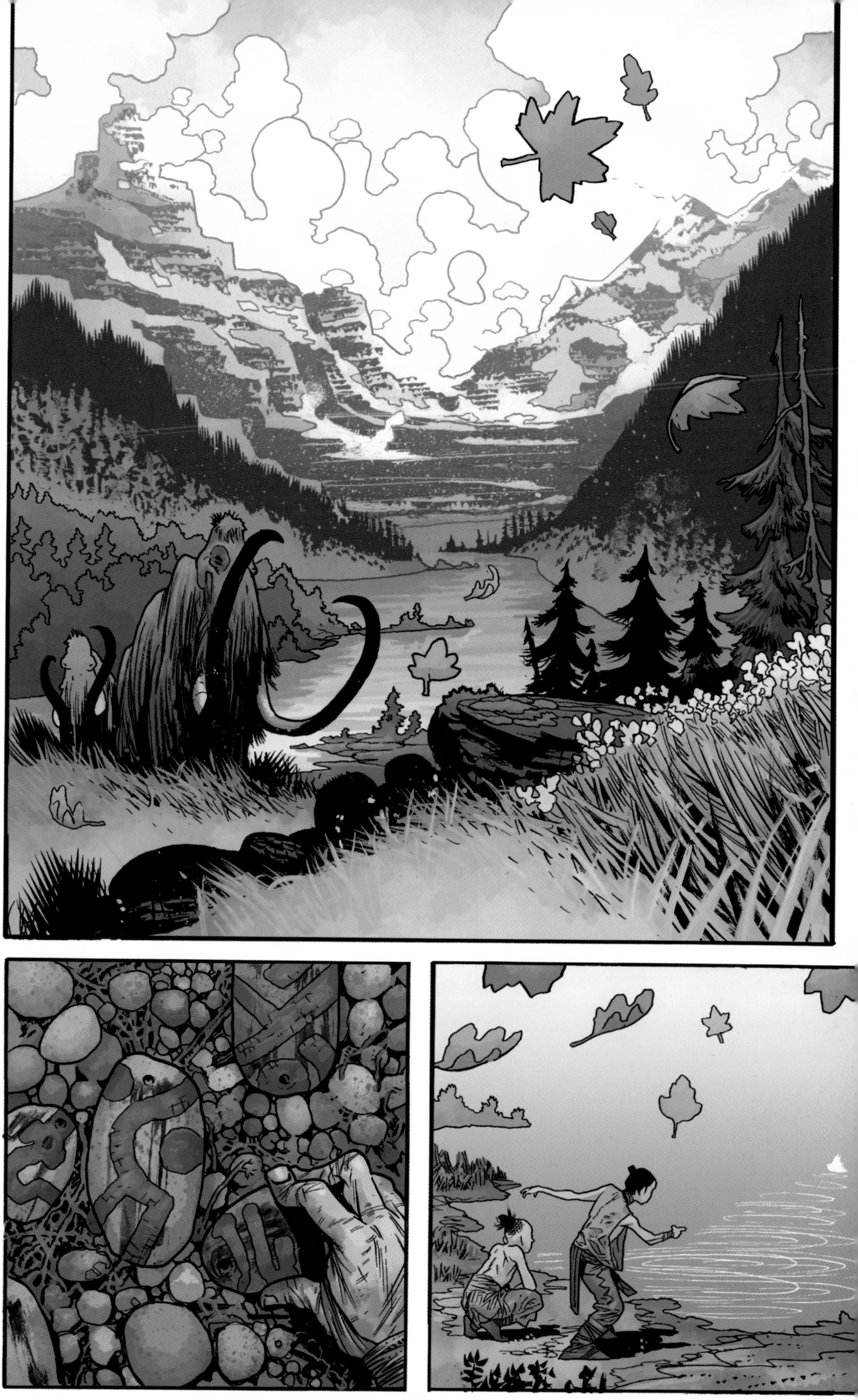

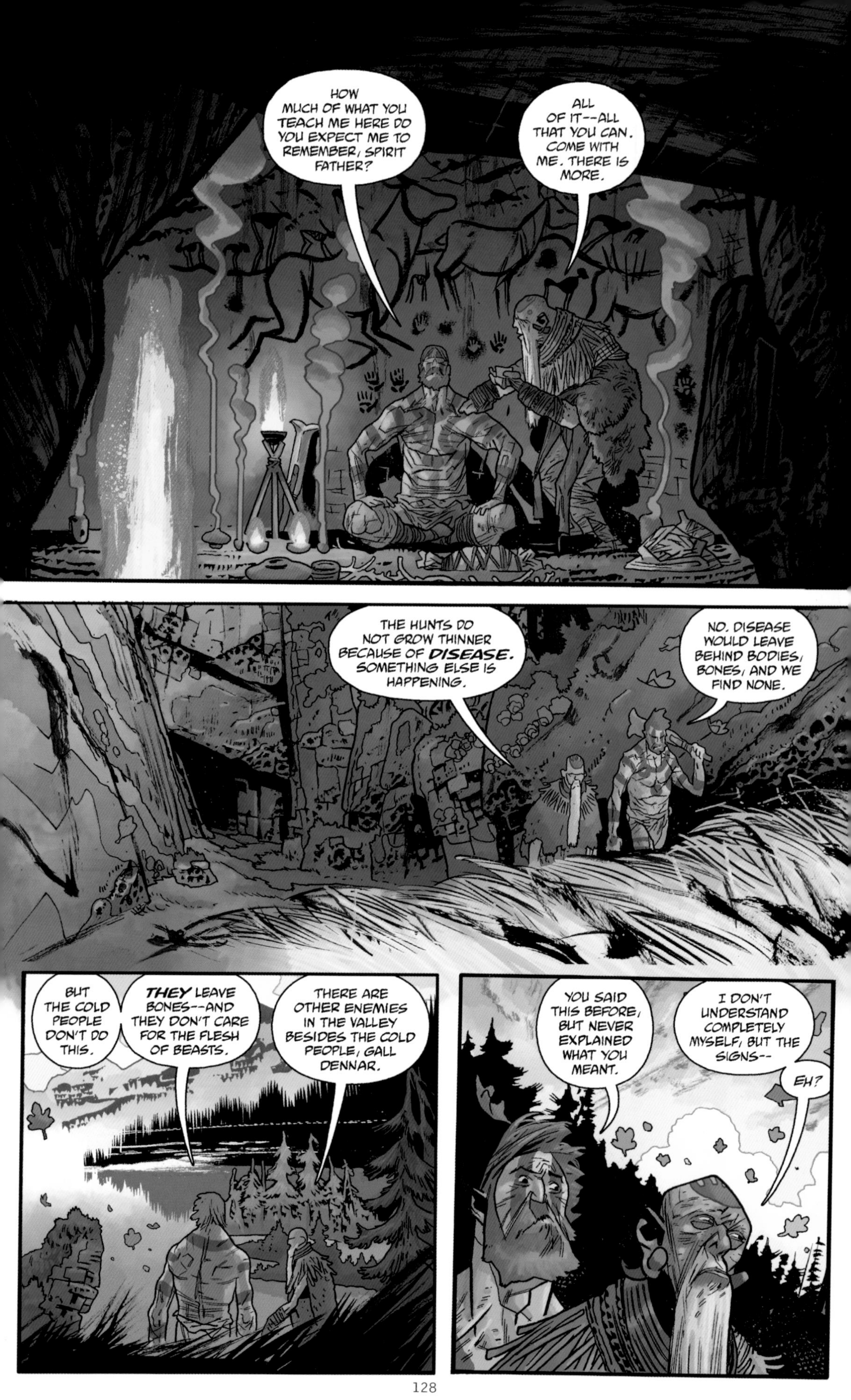
HOW MUCH OF WHAT YOU TEACH ME HERE DO YOU EXPECT ME TO REMEMBER, SPIRIT FATHER?
ALL OF IT--ALL THAT YOU CAN. COME WITH ME. THERE IS MORE.
THE HUNTS DO NOT GROW THINNER BECAUSE OF DISEASE. SOMETHING ELSE IS HAPPENING.
NO. DISEASE WOULD LEAVE BEHIND BODIES, BONES, AND WE FIND NONE.
BUT THE COLD PEOPLE DON'T DO THIS.
THEY LEAVE BONES--AND THEY DON'T CARE FOR THE FLESH OF BEASTS.
THERE ARE OTHER ENEMIES IN THE VALLEY BESIDES THE COLD PEOPLE, GALL DENNAR.
YOU SAID THIS BEFORE, BUT NEVER EXPLAINED WHAT YOU MEANT.
I DON'T UNDERSTAND COMPLETELY MYSELF, BUT THE SIGNS--
EH?

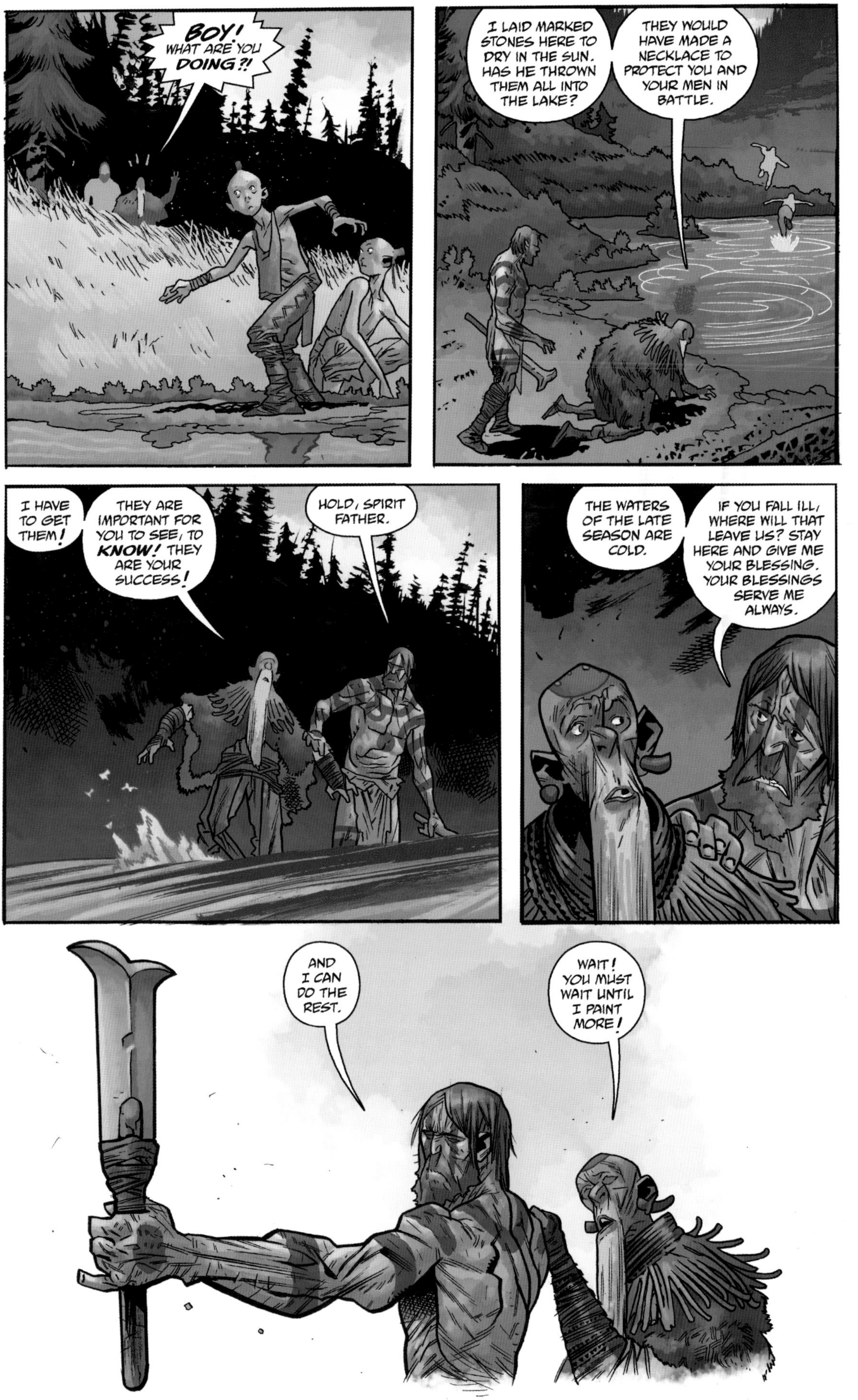
BOY! WHAT ARE YOU DOING?!
I LAID MARKED STONES HERE TO DRY IN THE SUN. HAS HE THROWN THEM ALL INTO THE LAKE?
THEY WOULD HAVE MADE A NECKLACE TO PROTECT YOU AND YOUR MEN IN BATTLE.
I HAVE TO GET THEM!
THEY ARE IMPORTANT FOR YOU TO SEE, TO KNOW! THEY ARE YOUR SUCCESS!
HOLD, SPIRIT FATHER.
THE WATERS OF THE LATE SEASON ARE COLD.
IF YOU FALL ILL, WHERE WILL THAT LEAVE US? STAY HERE AND GIVE ME YOUR BLESSING. YOUR BLESSINGS SERVE ME ALWAYS.
AND I CAN DO THE REST.
WAIT! YOU MUST WAIT UNTIL I PAINT MORE!

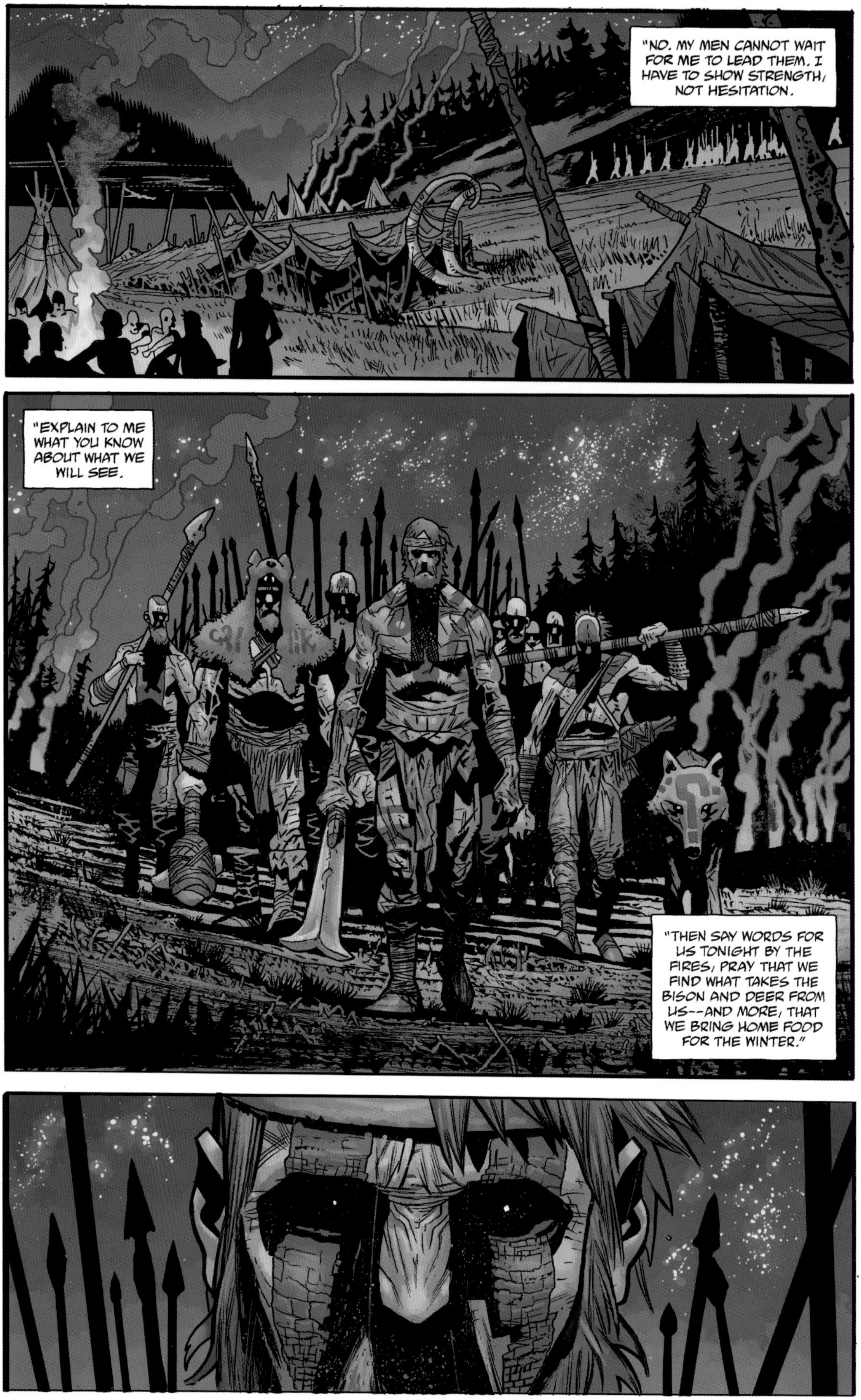
"NO. MY MEN CANNOT WAIT FOR ME TO LEAD THEM. I HAVE TO SHOW STRENGTH, NOT HESITATION.
"EXPLAIN TO ME WHAT YOU KNOW ABOUT WHAT WE WILL SEE.
"THEN SAY WORDS FOR US TONIGHT BY THE FIRES, PRAY THAT WE FIND WHAT TAKES THE BISON AND DEER FROM US--AND MORE, THAT WE BRING HOME FOOD FOR THE WINTER."

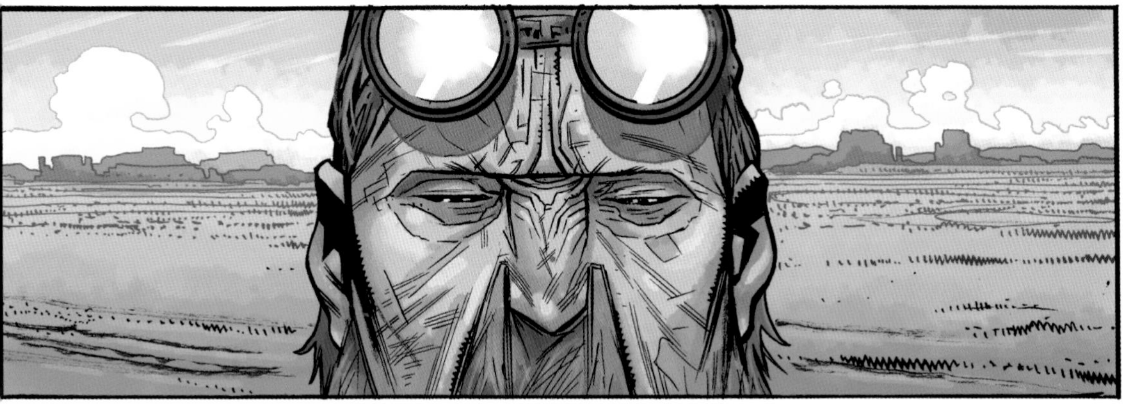

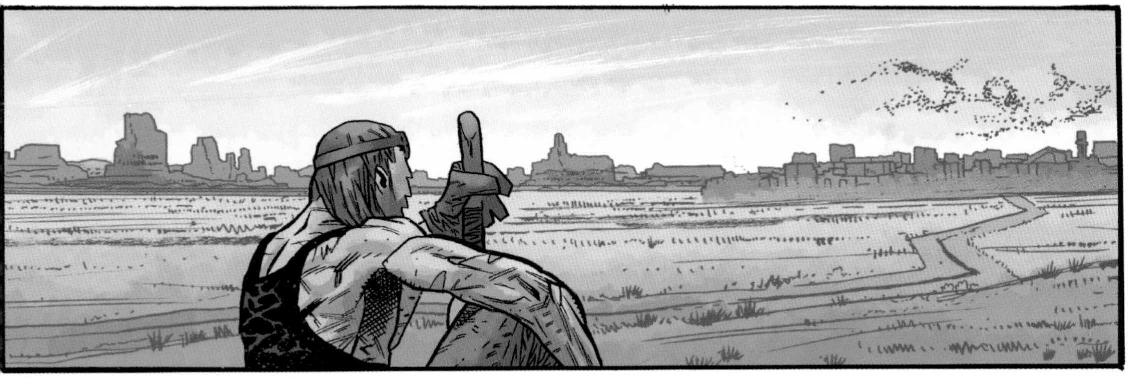

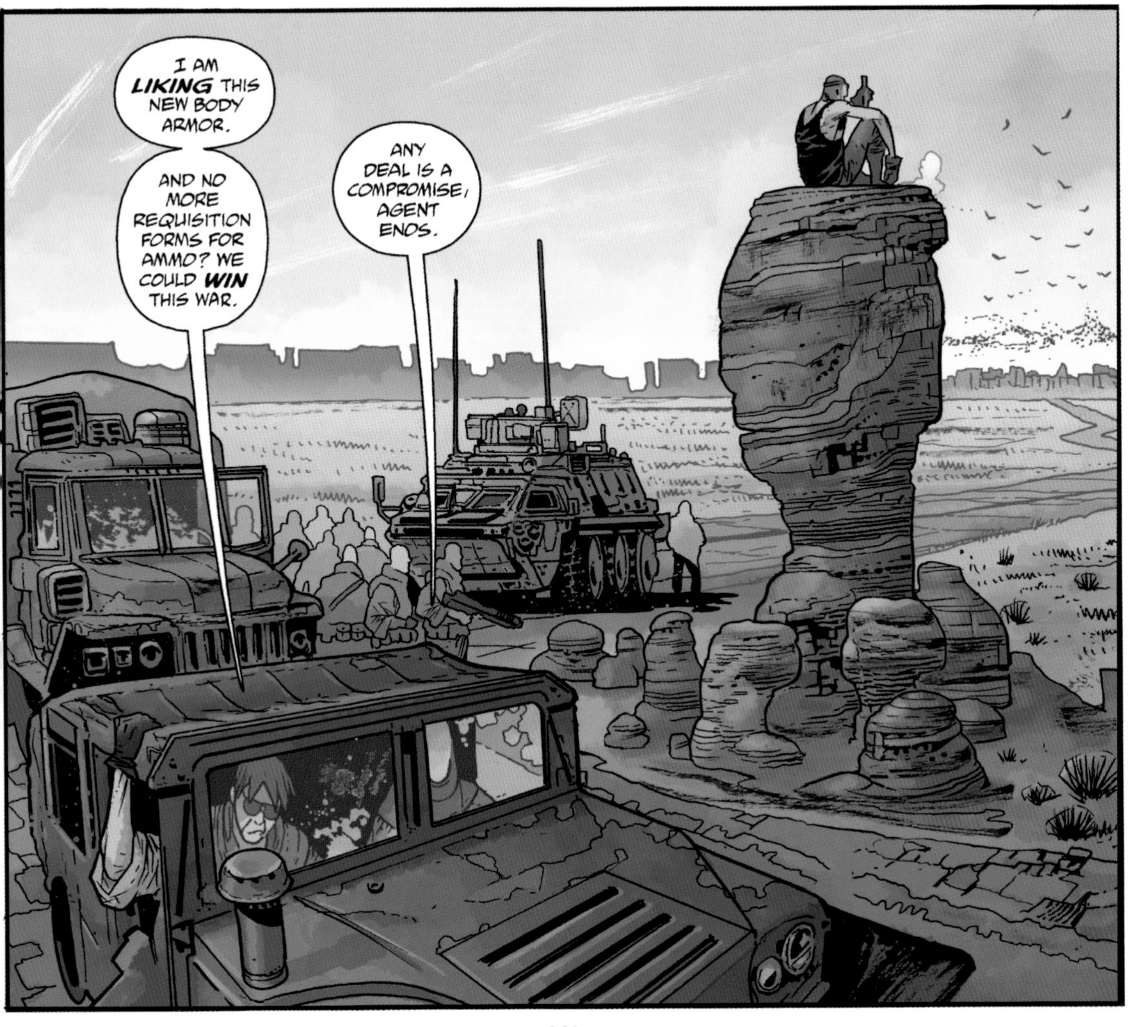
I AM LIKING THIS NEW BODY ARMOR.
AND NO MORE REQUISITION FORMS FOR AMMO? WE COULD WIN THIS WAR.
ANY DEAL IS A COMPROMISE, AGENT ENOS.

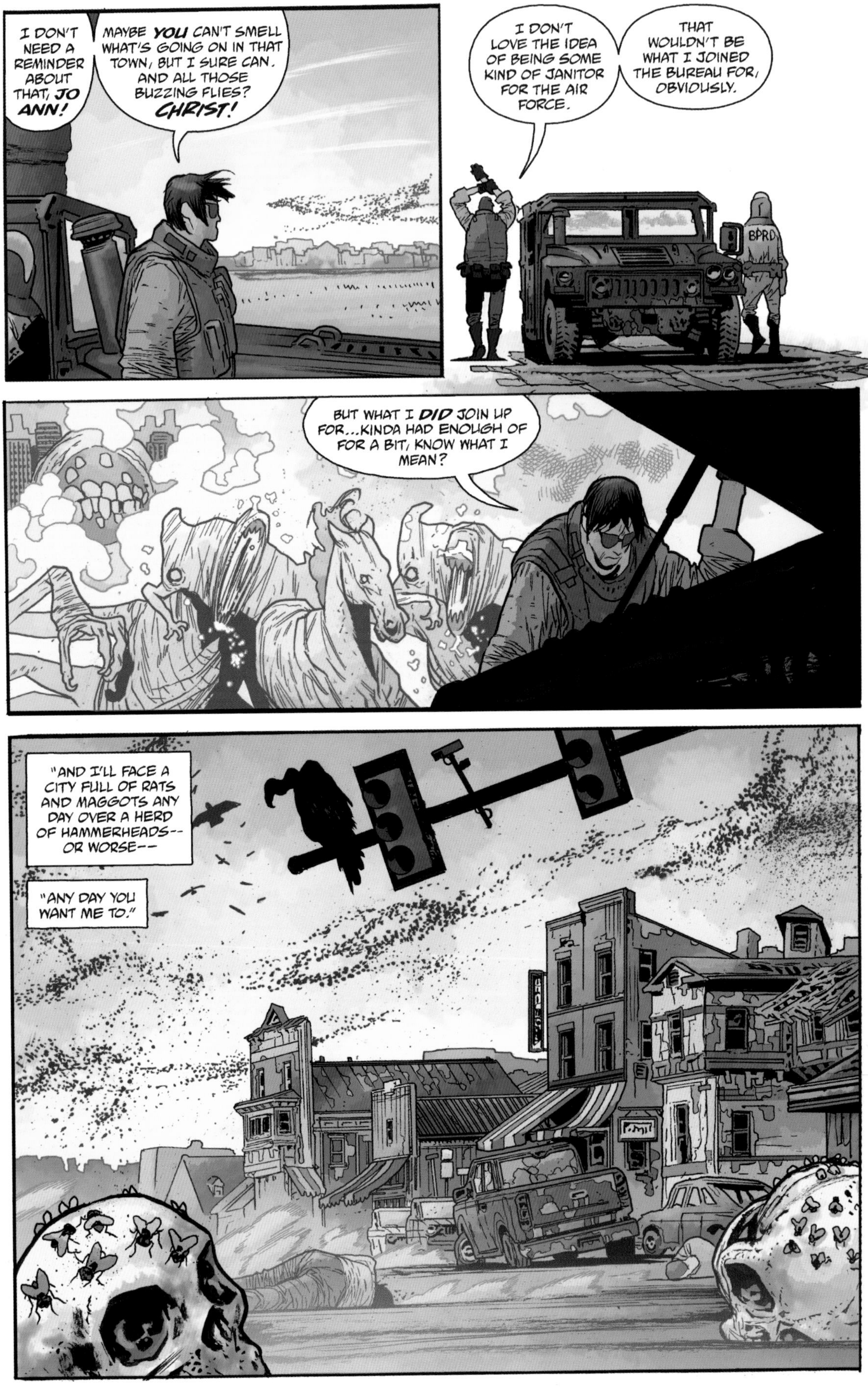
I DON'T NEED A REMINDER ABOUT THAT, JO ANN!
MAYBE YOU CAN'T SMELL WHAT'S GOING ON IN THAT TOWN, BUT I SURE CAN. AND ALL THOSE BUZZING FLIES? CHRIST!
I DON'T LOVE THE IDEA OF BEING SOME KIND OF JANITOR FOR THE AIR FORCE.
THAT WOULDN'T BE WHAT I JOINED THE BUREAU FOR, OBVIOUSLY.
BPRD
BUT WHAT I DID JOIN UP FOR...KINDA HAD ENOUGH OF FOR A BIT, KNOW WHAT I MEAN?
"AND I'LL FACE A CITY FULL OF RATS AND MAGGOTS ANY DAY OVER A HERD OF HAMMERHEADS--OR WORSE--
"ANY DAY YOU WANT ME TO."

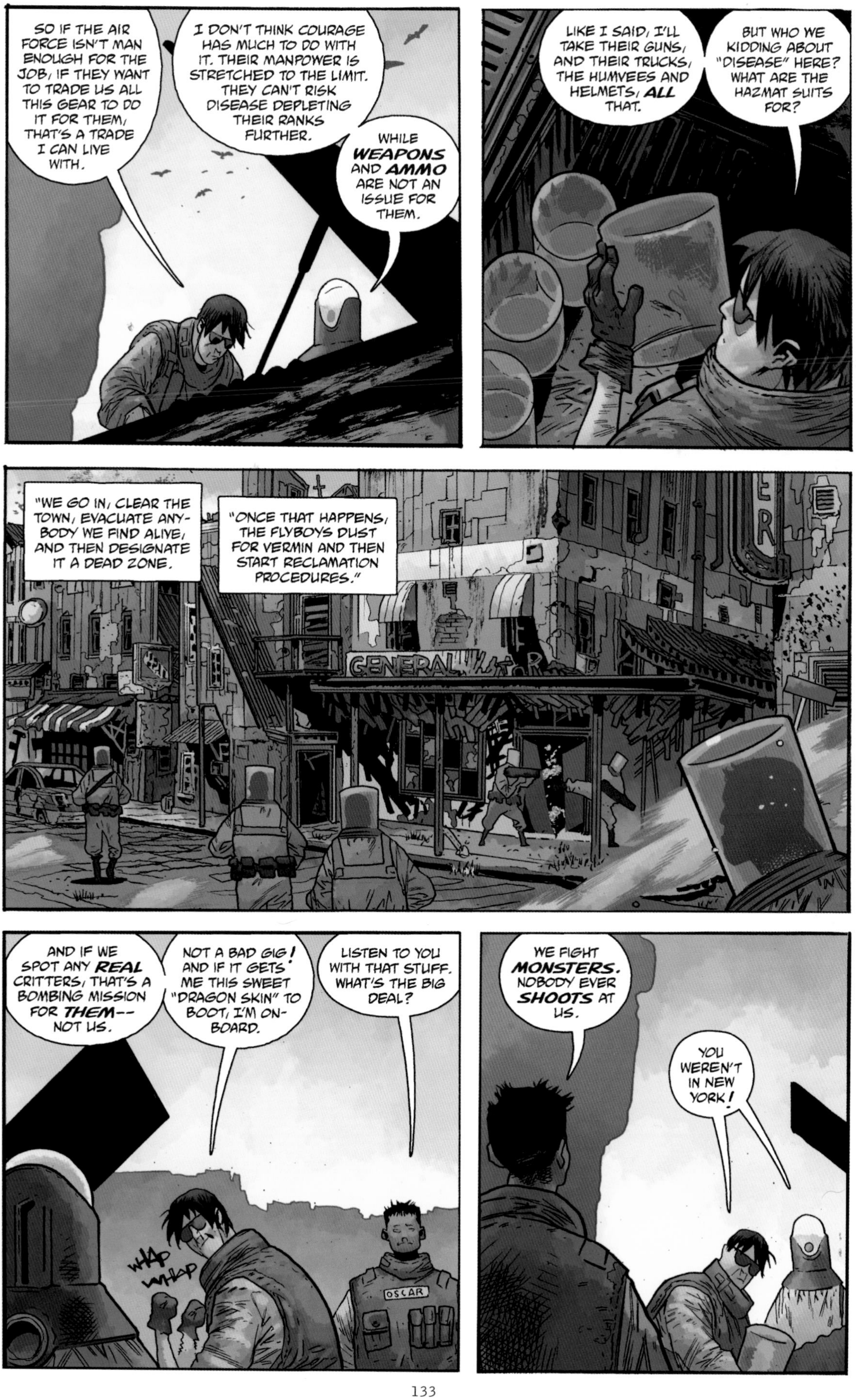
SO IF THE AIR FORCE ISN'T MAN ENOUGH FOR THE JOB, IF THEY WANT TO TRADE US ALL THIS GEAR TO DO IT FOR THEM, THAT'S A TRADE I CAN LIVE WITH.
I DON'T THINK COURAGE HAS MUCH TO DO WITH IT. THEIR MANPOWER IS STRETCHED TO THE LIMIT. THEY CAN'T RISK DISEASE DEPLETING THEIR RANKS FURTHER.
WHILE WEAPONS AND AMMO ARE NOT AN ISSUE FOR THEM.
LIKE I SAID, I'LL TAKE THEIR GUNS, AND THEIR TRUCKS, THE HUMVEES AND HELMETS, ALL THAT.
BUT WHO WE KIDDING ABOUT "DISEASE" HERE? WHAT ARE THE HAZMAT SUITS FOR?
"WE GO IN, CLEAR THE TOWN, EVACUATE ANYBODY WE FIND ALIVE, AND THEN DESIGNATE IT A DEAD ZONE.
"ONCE THAT HAPPENS, THE FLYBOYS DUST FOR VERMIN AND THEN START RECLAMATION PROCEDURES."
GENERAL
AND IF WE SPOT ANY REAL CRITTERS, THAT'S A BOMBING MISSION FOR THEM-- NOT US.
NOT A BAD GIG! AND IF IT GETS ME THIS SWEET "DRAGON SKIN" TO BOOT, I'M ON-BOARD.
LISTEN TO YOU WITH THAT STUFF. WHAT'S THE BIG DEAL?
WHAP WHAP
OSCAR
WE FIGHT MONSTERS. NOBODY EVER SHOOTS AT US.
YOU WEREN'T IN NEW YORK!

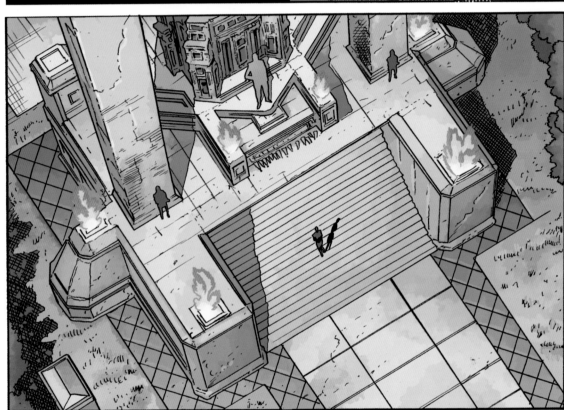

ISAIAH MARSTEN

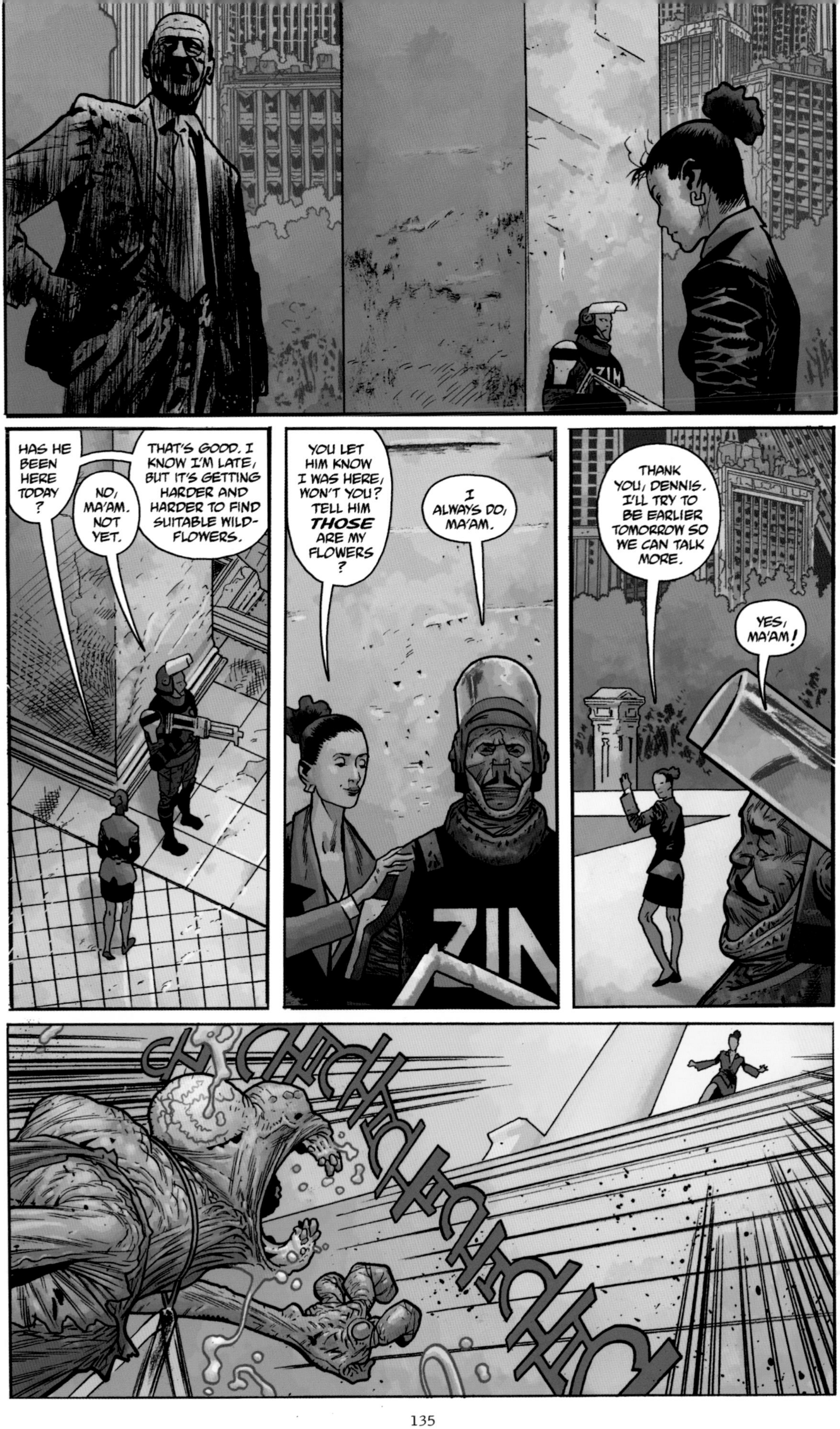

HAS HE BEEN HERE TODAY?
NO, MA'AM. NOT YET.
THAT'S GOOD. I KNOW I'M LATE, BUT IT'S GETTING HARDER AND HARDER TO FIND SUITABLE WILD-FLOWERS.
YOU LET HIM KNOW I WAS HERE, WON'T YOU? TELL HIM THOSE ARE MY FLOWERS?
I ALWAYS DO, MA'AM.
ZIN
THANK YOU, DENNIS. I'LL TRY TO BE EARLIER TOMORROW SO WE CAN TALK MORE.
YES, MA'AM!
CHCHCHCHCHCHCHCHCHCH

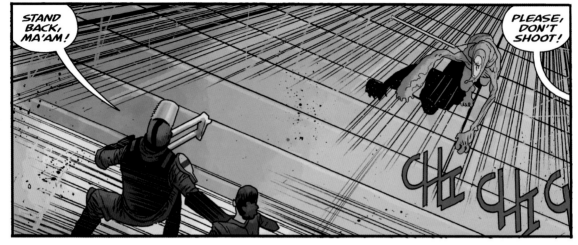

STAND BACK, MA'AM!

PLEASE, DON'T SHOOT!

CHIK CHIK

THIS ONE'S OURS!

DON'T WORRY. WE *GOT* HIM!

CHICHICHIK UHK

SORRY ABOUT THAT! VERY, *VERY* SORRY.

IT'S JUST THAT WE HAVE SO *FEW* OF THE MUTATED MEN IN THE CITY--THE FOGS NEVER REACHED MANHATTAN, AND TO CATCH ONE *ALIVE*...VERY DIFFICULT.

THIS ONE TRICKLED IN FROM THE BRONX, WE THINK.

PRETTY GOOD SHAPE, TOO.

GLUK CHIK CHIK AHH

AND WHY WOULD YOU NEED A *LIVING MUTANT,* HIRSCH?

MA'AM.

I DON'T RECALL YOU OR ANYBODY ELSE FROM *RED* SUBMITTING PAPERWORK ABOUT THIS.

MA'AM.

EVELYN!

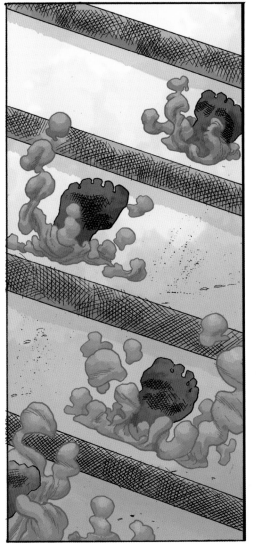

137

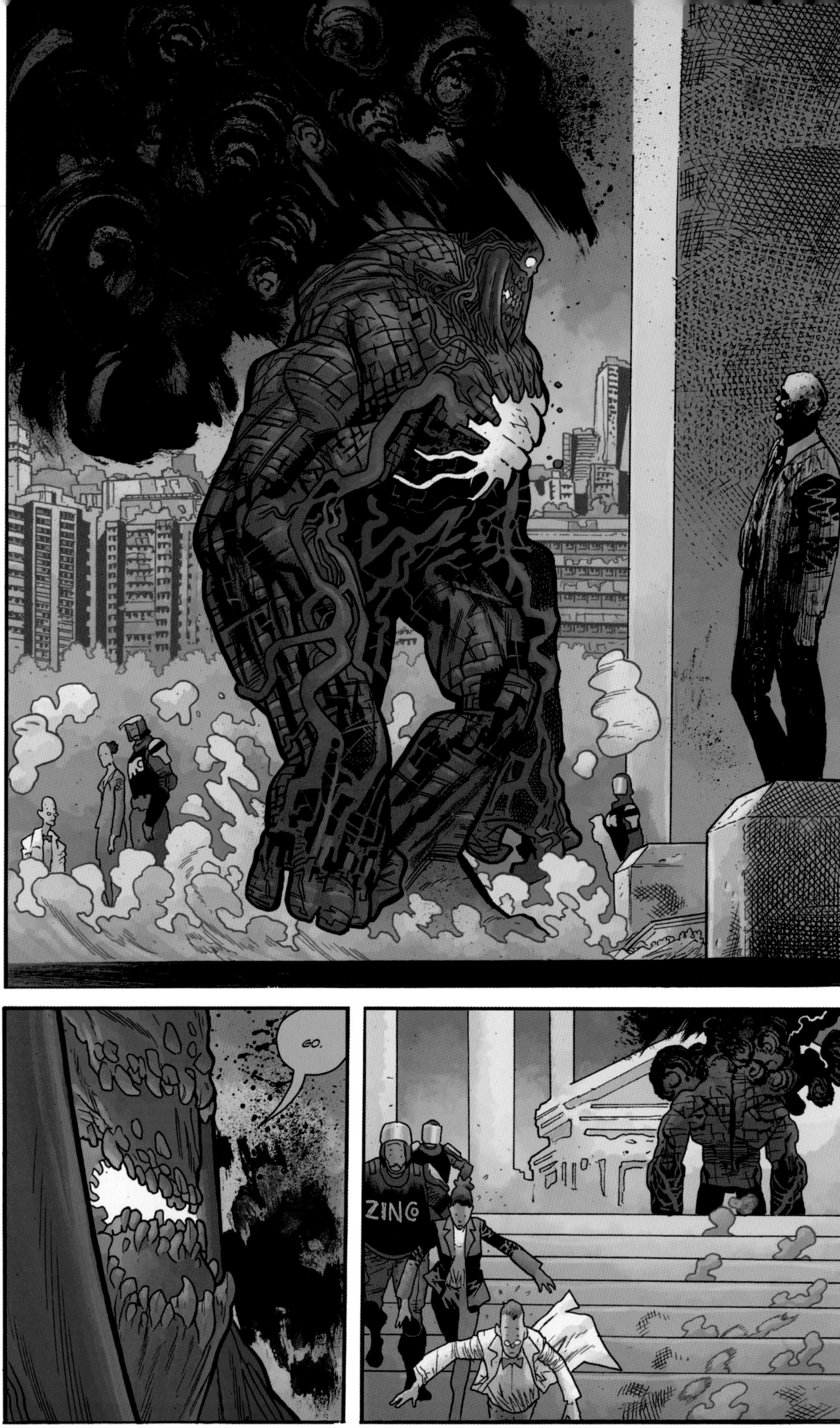
GO.

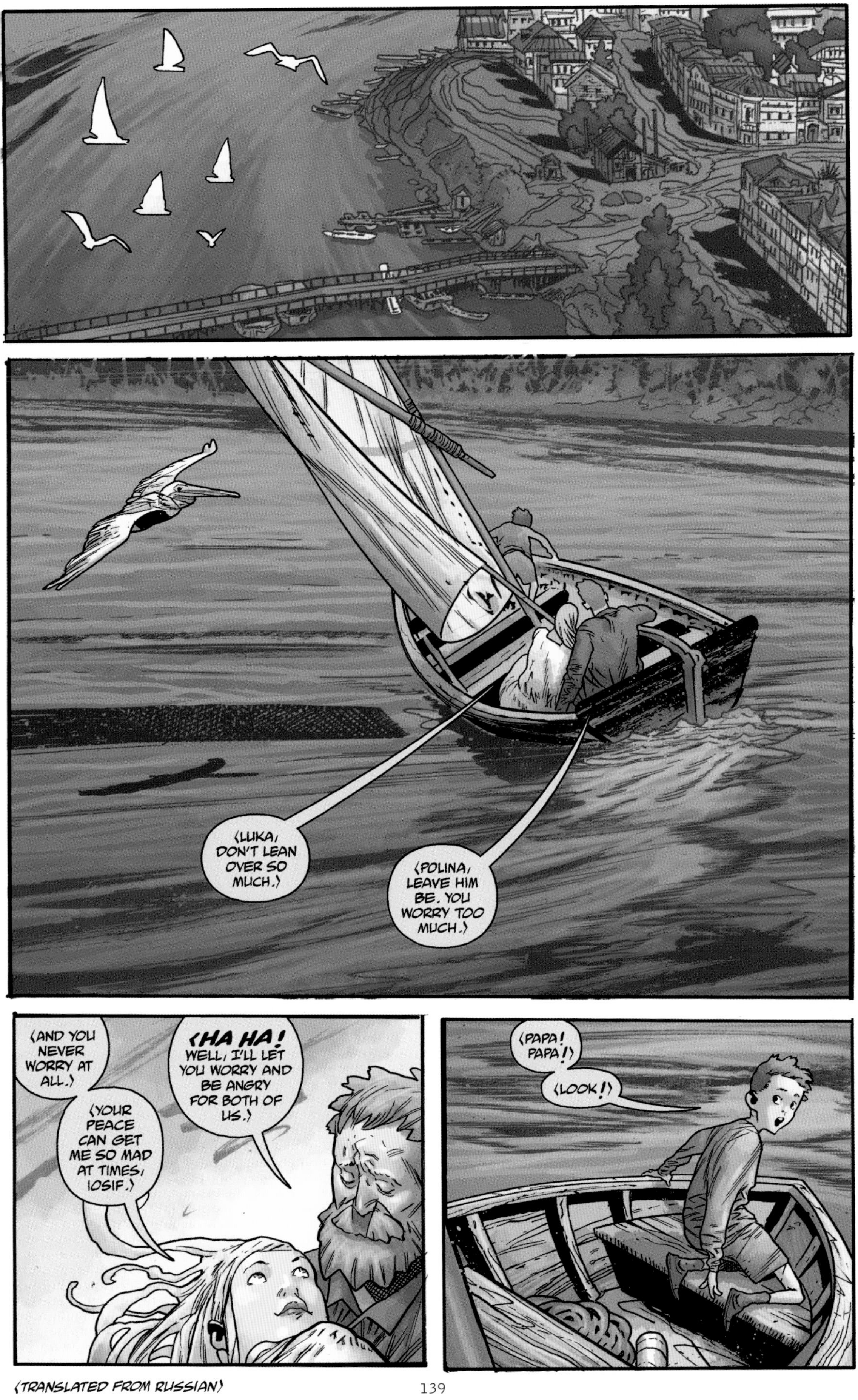
‹LUKA, DON'T LEAN OVER SO MUCH.›
‹POLINA, LEAVE HIM BE. YOU WORRY TOO MUCH.›
‹AND YOU NEVER WORRY AT ALL.›
‹YOUR PEACE CAN GET ME SO MAD AT TIMES, IOSIF.›
‹HA HA! WELL, I'LL LET YOU WORRY AND BE ANGRY FOR BOTH OF US.›
‹PAPA! PAPA!›
‹LOOK!›

‹TRANSLATED FROM RUSSIAN›

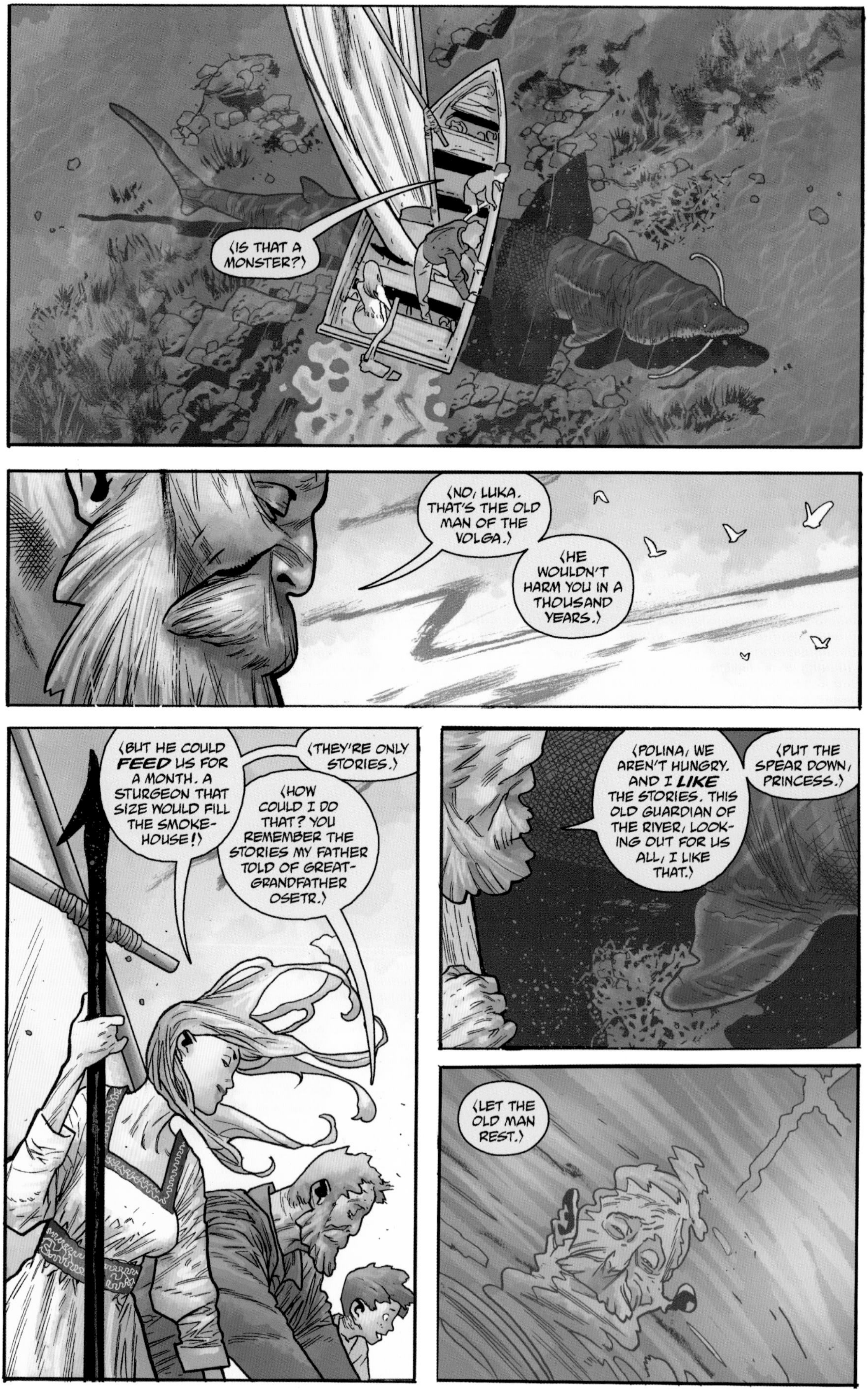
⟨IS THAT A MONSTER?⟩
⟨NO, LUKA. THAT'S THE OLD MAN OF THE VOLGA.⟩
⟨HE WOULDN'T HARM YOU IN A THOUSAND YEARS.⟩
⟨BUT HE COULD FEED US FOR A MONTH. A STURGEON THAT SIZE WOULD FILL THE SMOKE-HOUSE!⟩
⟨THEY'RE ONLY STORIES.⟩
⟨HOW COULD I DO THAT? YOU REMEMBER THE STORIES MY FATHER TOLD OF GREAT-GRANDFATHER OSETR.⟩
⟨POLINA, WE AREN'T HUNGRY. AND I LIKE THE STORIES. THIS OLD GUARDIAN OF THE RIVER, LOOKING OUT FOR US ALL, I LIKE THAT.⟩
⟨PUT THE SPEAR DOWN, PRINCESS.⟩
⟨LET THE OLD MAN REST.⟩

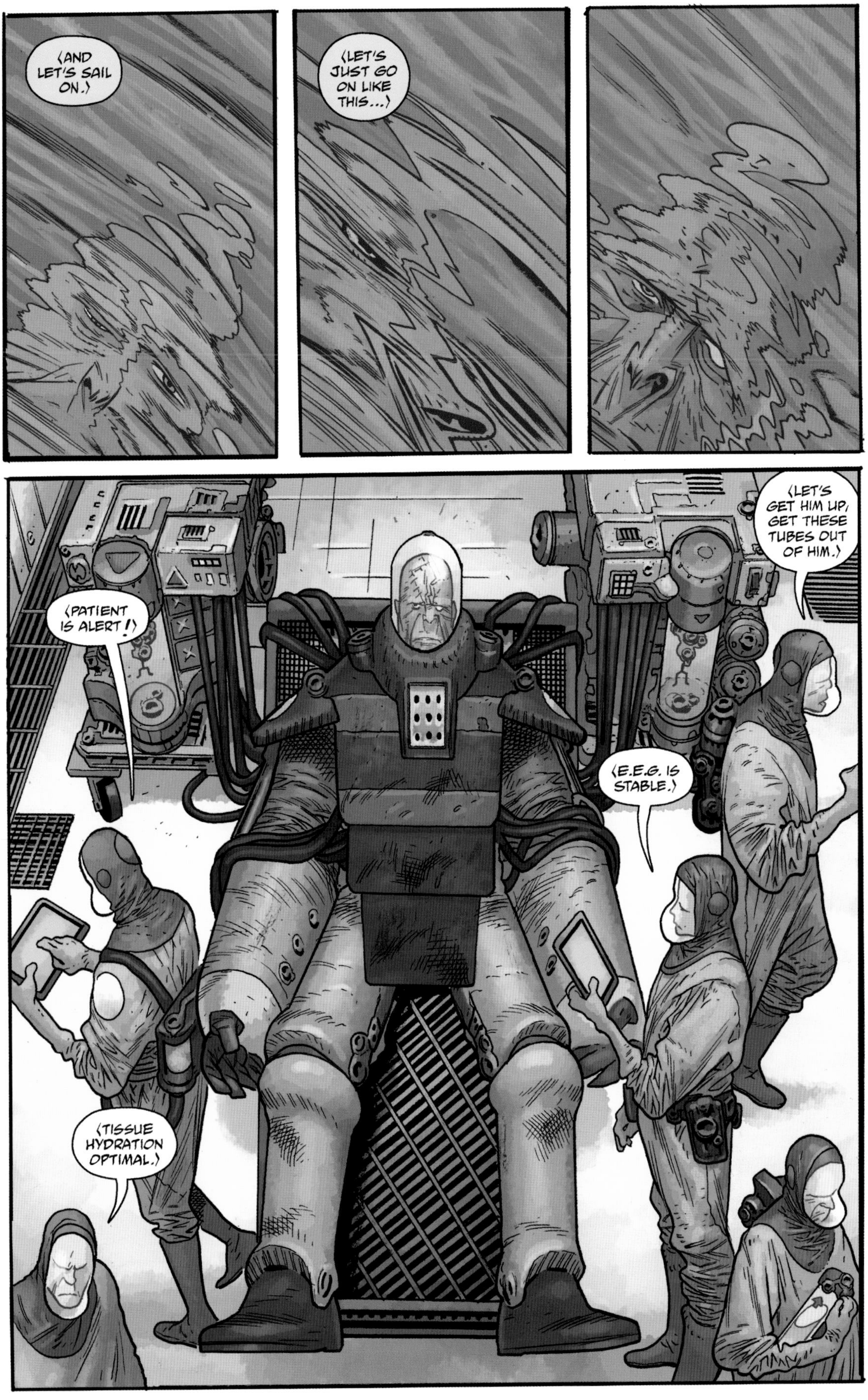

⟨AND LET'S SAIL ON.⟩
⟨LET'S JUST GO ON LIKE THIS...⟩
⟨PATIENT IS ALERT!⟩
⟨LET'S GET HIM UP, GET THESE TUBES OUT OF HIM.⟩
⟨E.E.G. IS STABLE.⟩
⟨TISSUE HYDRATION OPTIMAL.⟩

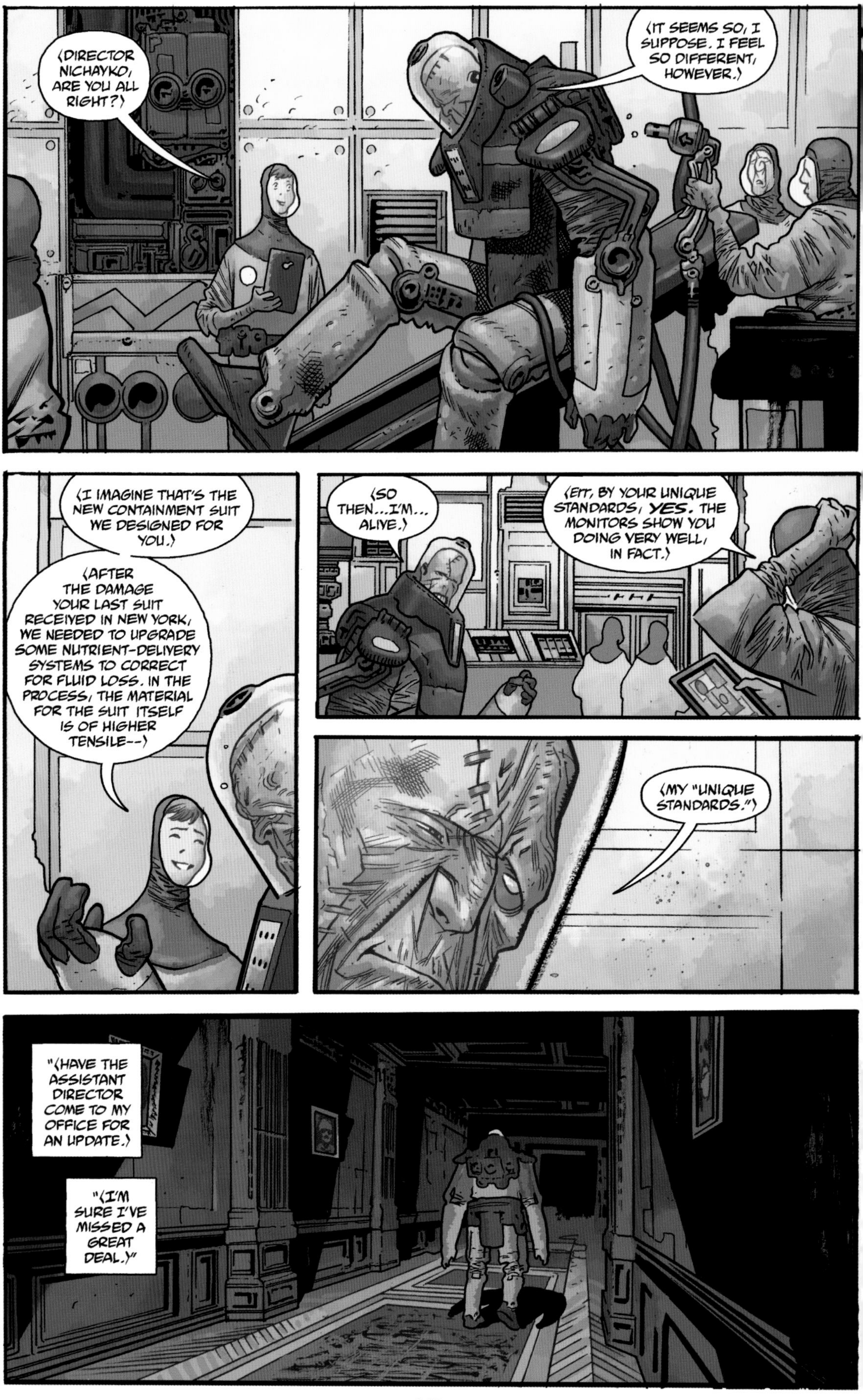

⟨DIRECTOR NICHAYKO, ARE YOU ALL RIGHT?⟩
⟨IT SEEMS SO, I SUPPOSE. I FEEL SO DIFFERENT, HOWEVER.⟩
⟨I IMAGINE THAT'S THE NEW CONTAINMENT SUIT WE DESIGNED FOR YOU.⟩
⟨AFTER THE DAMAGE YOUR LAST SUIT RECEIVED IN NEW YORK, WE NEEDED TO UPGRADE SOME NUTRIENT-DELIVERY SYSTEMS TO CORRECT FOR FLUID LOSS. IN THE PROCESS, THE MATERIAL FOR THE SUIT ITSELF IS OF HIGHER TENSILE--⟩
⟨SO THEN...I'M... ALIVE.⟩
⟨ER, BY YOUR UNIQUE STANDARDS, **YES.** THE MONITORS SHOW YOU DOING VERY WELL, IN FACT.⟩
⟨MY "UNIQUE STANDARDS."⟩
"⟨HAVE THE ASSISTANT DIRECTOR COME TO MY OFFICE FOR AN UPDATE.⟩
"⟨I'M SURE I'VE MISSED A GREAT DEAL.⟩"

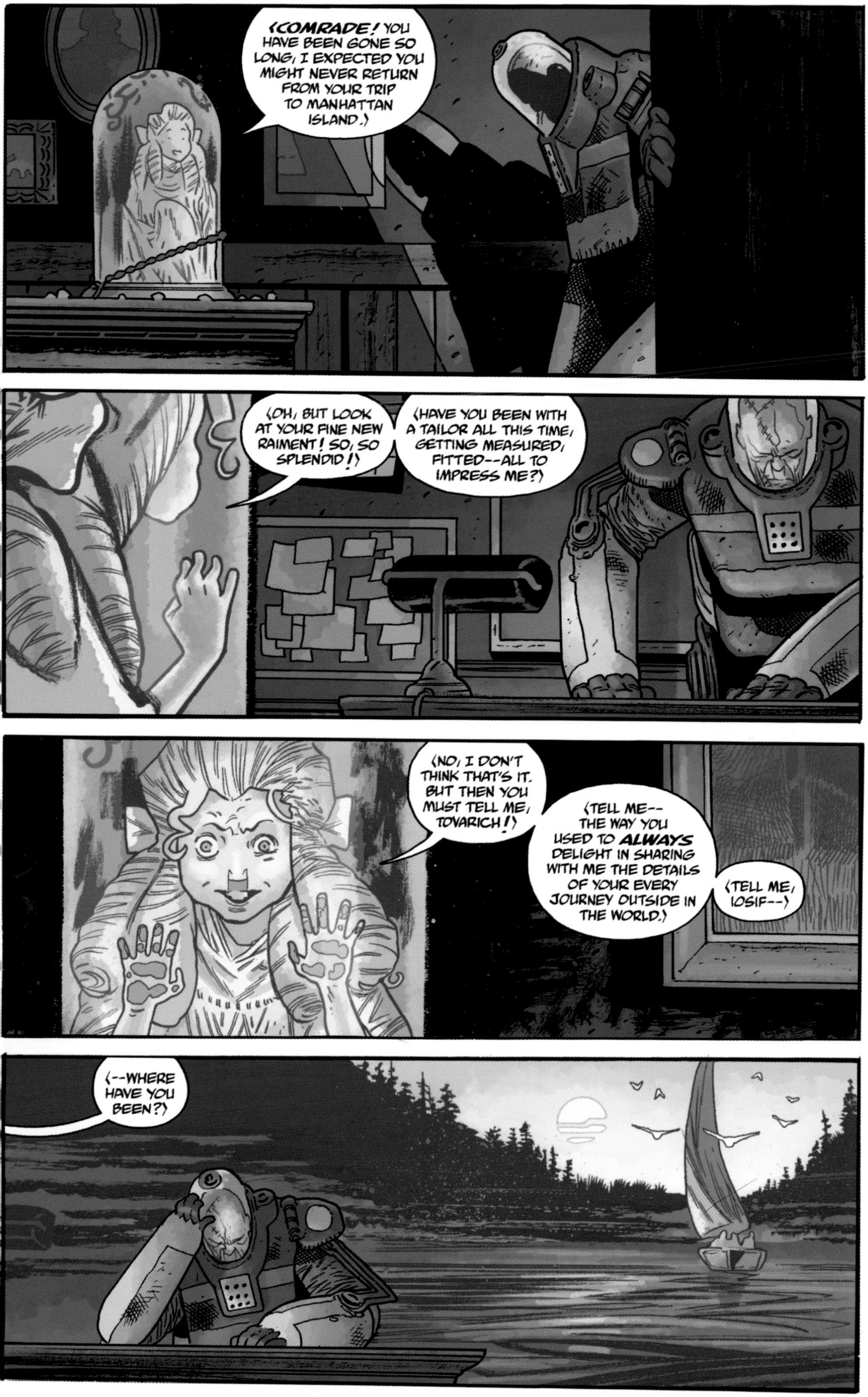
⟨COMRADE! YOU HAVE BEEN GONE SO LONG, I EXPECTED YOU MIGHT NEVER RETURN FROM YOUR TRIP TO MANHATTAN ISLAND.⟩
⟨OH, BUT LOOK AT YOUR FINE NEW RAIMENT! SO, SO SPLENDID!⟩
⟨HAVE YOU BEEN WITH A TAILOR ALL THIS TIME, GETTING MEASURED, FITTED--ALL TO IMPRESS ME?⟩
⟨NO, I DON'T THINK THAT'S IT. BUT THEN YOU MUST TELL ME, TOVARICH!⟩
⟨TELL ME-- THE WAY YOU USED TO ALWAYS DELIGHT IN SHARING WITH ME THE DETAILS OF YOUR EVERY JOURNEY OUTSIDE IN THE WORLD.⟩
⟨TELL ME, IOSIF--⟩
⟨--WHERE HAVE YOU BEEN?⟩

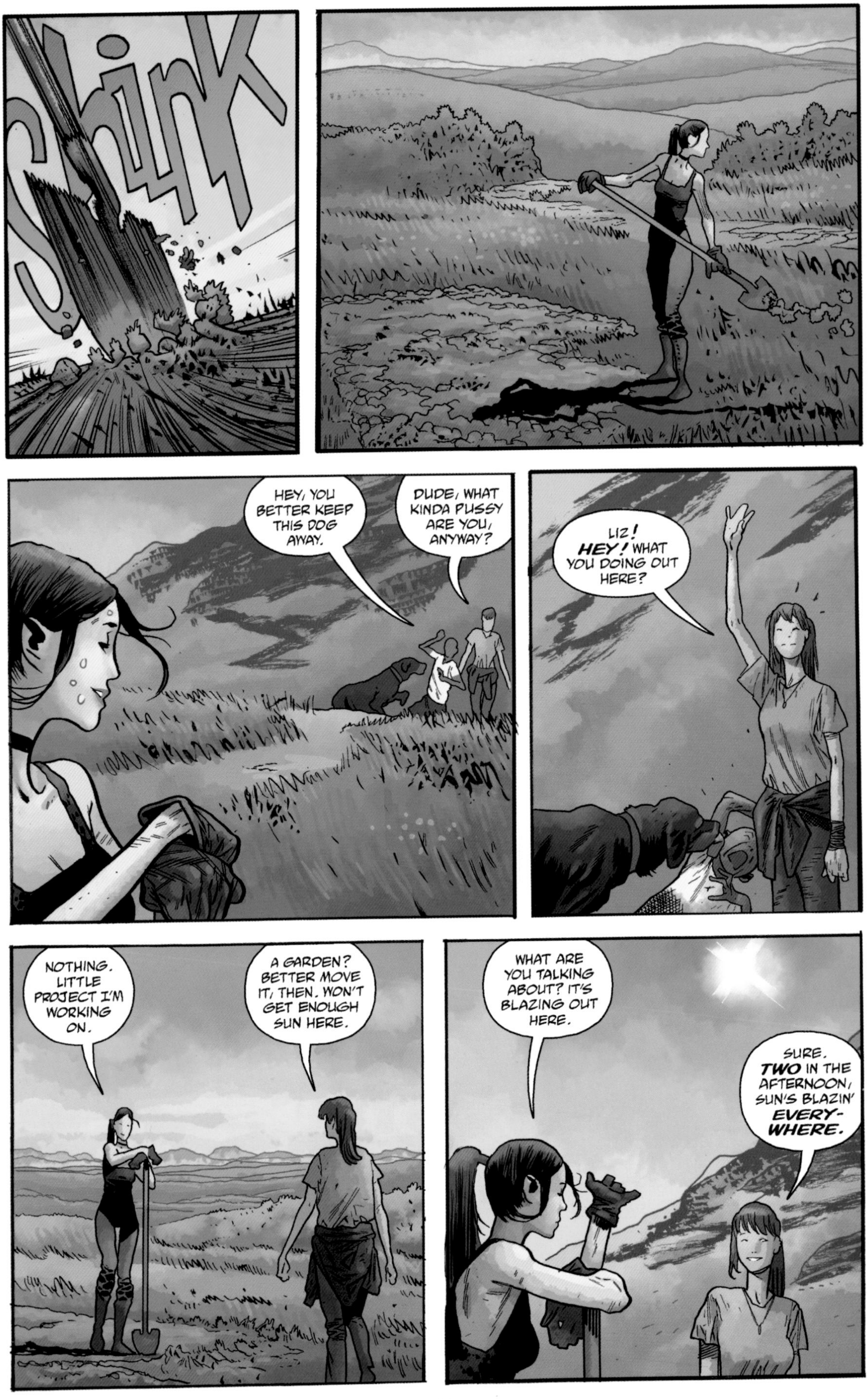
Shink
HEY, YOU BETTER KEEP THIS DOG AWAY.
DUDE, WHAT KINDA PUSSY ARE YOU, ANYWAY?
LIZ! HEY! WHAT YOU DOING OUT HERE?
NOTHING. LITTLE PROJECT I'M WORKING ON.
A GARDEN? BETTER MOVE IT, THEN. WON'T GET ENOUGH SUN HERE.
WHAT ARE YOU TALKING ABOUT? IT'S BLAZING OUT HERE.
SURE. TWO IN THE AFTERNOON, SUN'S BLAZIN' EVERY-WHERE.

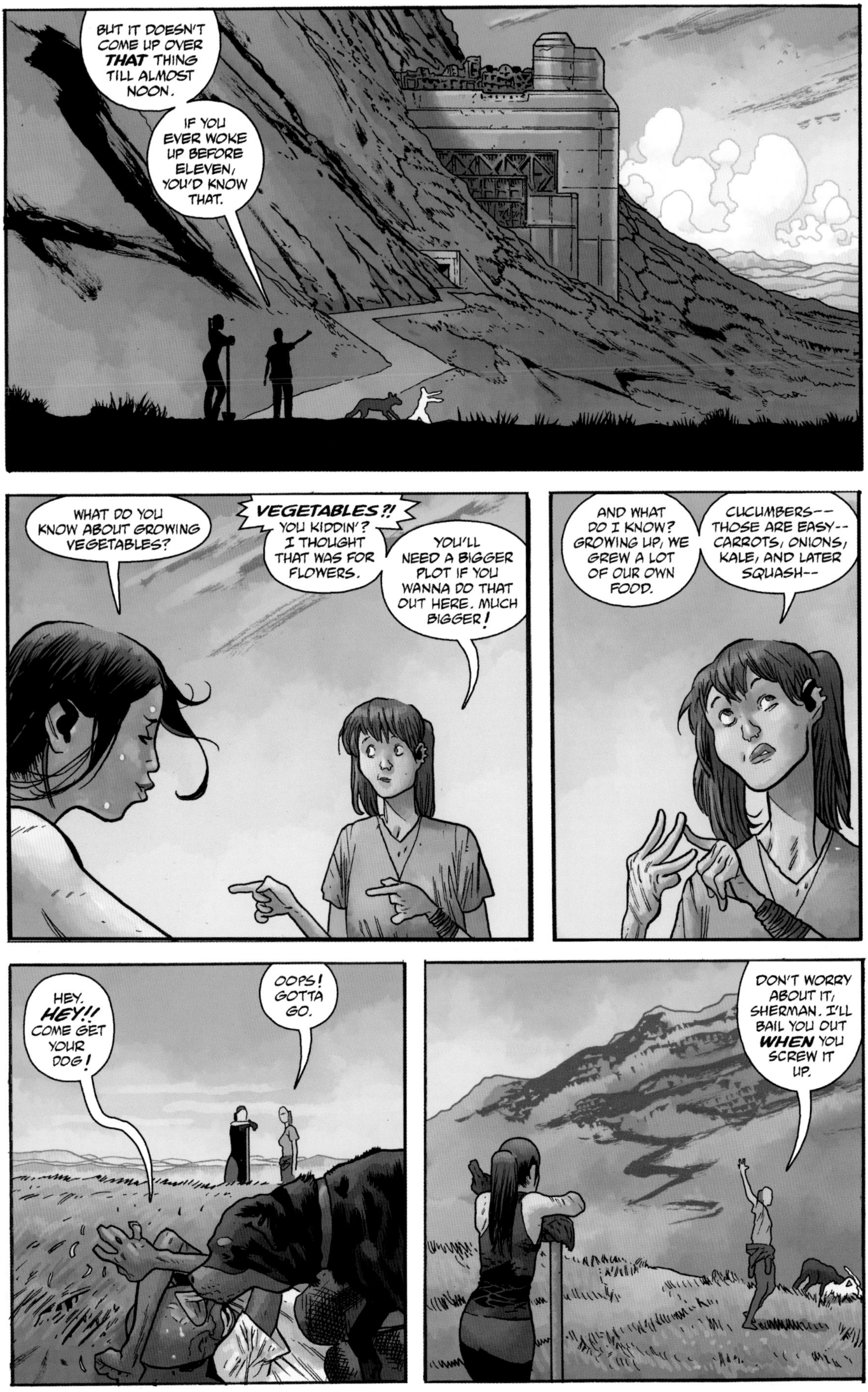
BUT IT DOESN'T COME UP OVER THAT THING TILL ALMOST NOON.
IF YOU EVER WOKE UP BEFORE ELEVEN, YOU'D KNOW THAT.
WHAT DO YOU KNOW ABOUT GROWING VEGETABLES?
VEGETABLES?! YOU KIDDIN'? I THOUGHT THAT WAS FOR FLOWERS.
YOU'LL NEED A BIGGER PLOT IF YOU WANNA DO THAT OUT HERE. MUCH BIGGER!
AND WHAT DO I KNOW? GROWING UP, WE GREW A LOT OF OUR OWN FOOD.
CUCUMBERS-- THOSE ARE EASY-- CARROTS, ONIONS, KALE, AND LATER SQUASH--
HEY. HEY!! COME GET YOUR DOG!
OOPS! GOTTA GO.
DON'T WORRY ABOUT IT, SHERMAN. I'LL BAIL YOU OUT WHEN YOU SCREW IT UP.

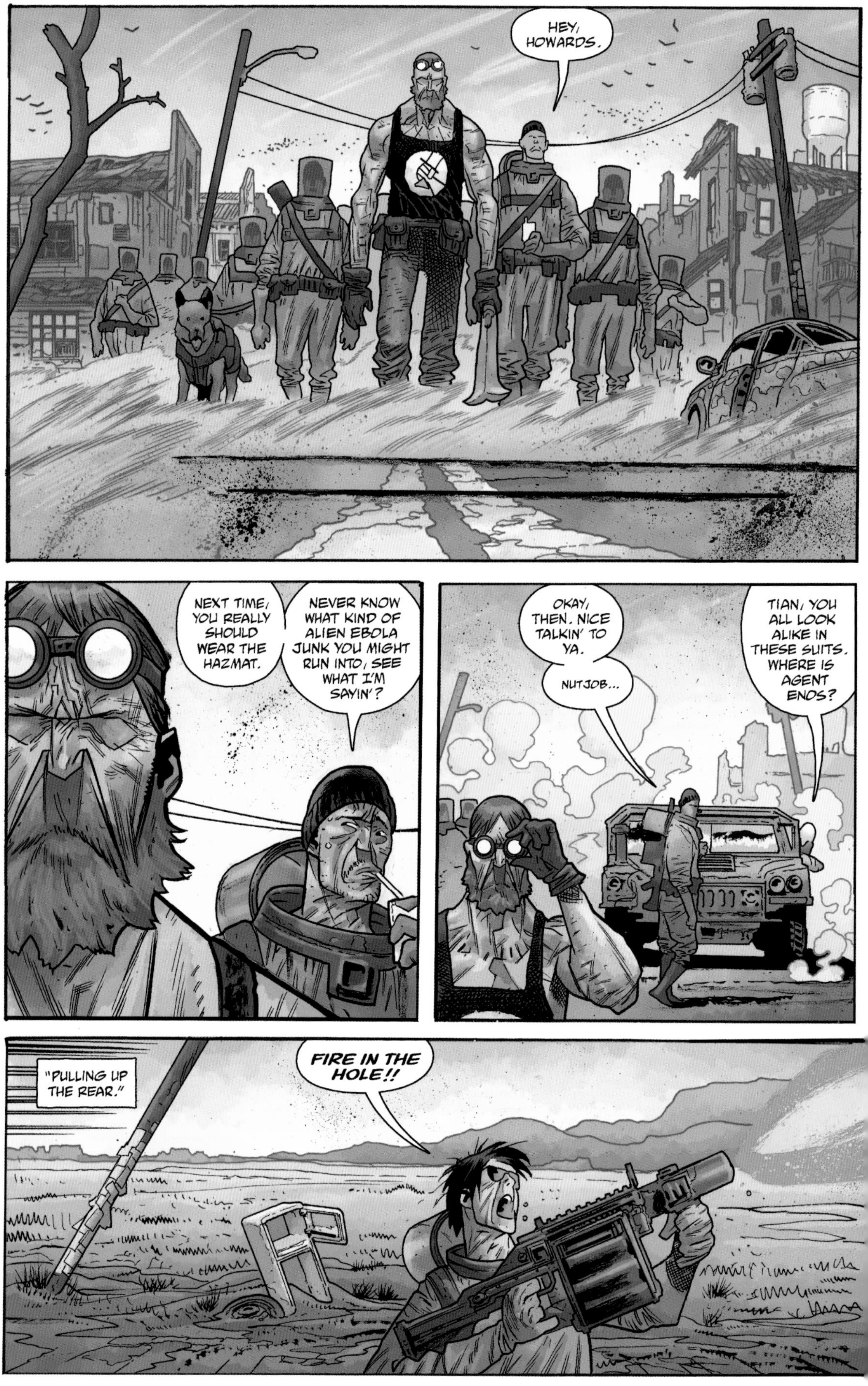
HEY, HOWARDS.
NEXT TIME, YOU REALLY SHOULD WEAR THE HAZMAT.
NEVER KNOW WHAT KIND OF ALIEN EBOLA JUNK YOU MIGHT RUN INTO, SEE WHAT I'M SAYIN'?
OKAY, THEN. NICE TALKIN' TO YA.
NUTJOB...
TIAN, YOU ALL LOOK ALIKE IN THESE SUITS. WHERE IS AGENT ENOS?
"PULLING UP THE REAR."
FIRE IN THE HOLE!!

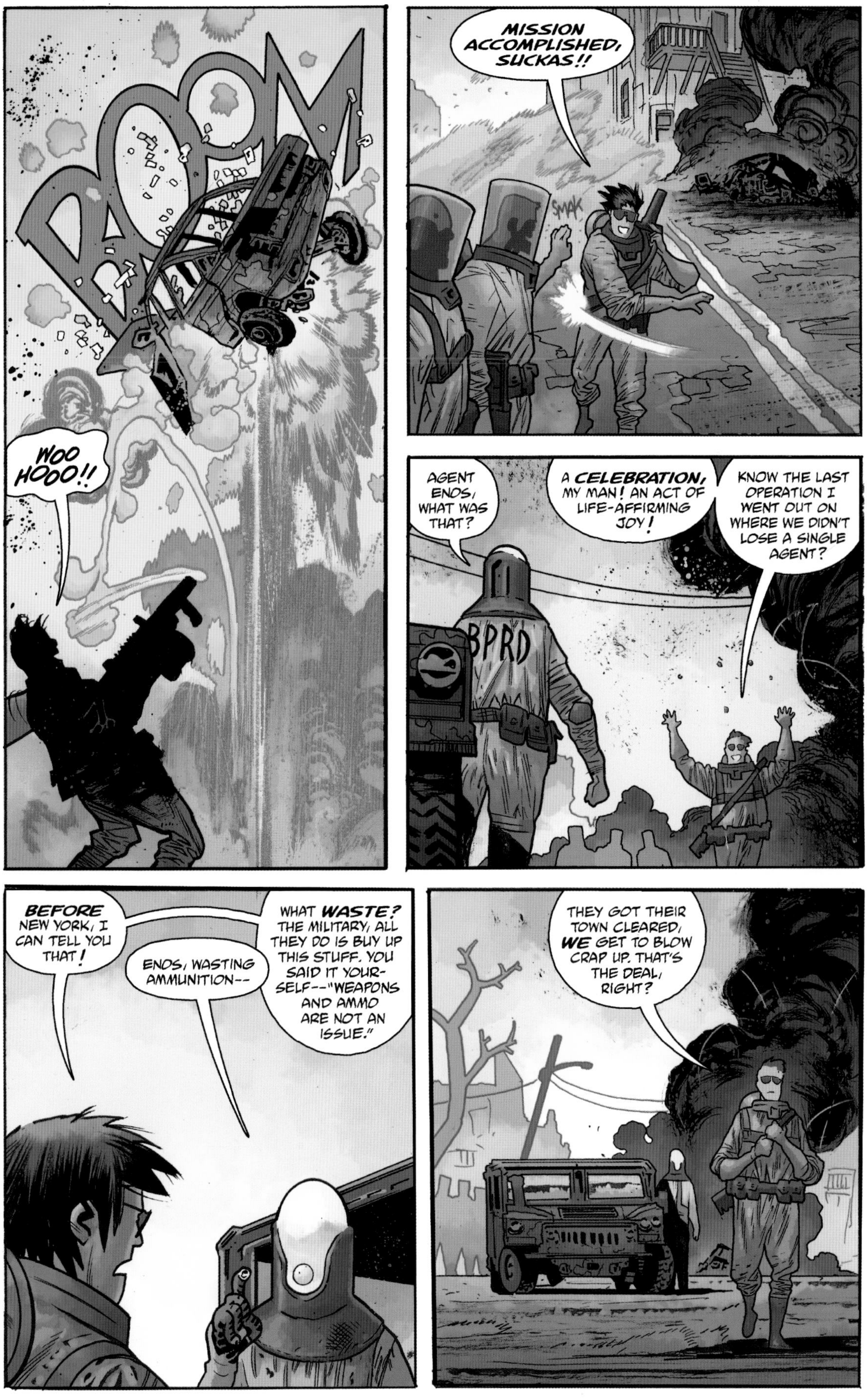
BROOM!
WOO HOOO!!
MISSION ACCOMPLISHED, SUCKAS!!
SMAK
AGENT ENOS, WHAT WAS THAT?
A CELEBRATION, MY MAN! AN ACT OF LIFE-AFFIRMING JOY!
KNOW THE LAST OPERATION I WENT OUT ON WHERE WE DIDN'T LOSE A SINGLE AGENT?
BPRD
BEFORE NEW YORK, I CAN TELL YOU THAT!
ENOS, WASTING AMMUNITION--
WHAT WASTE? THE MILITARY, ALL THEY DO IS BUY UP THIS STUFF. YOU SAID IT YOURSELF--"WEAPONS AND AMMO ARE NOT AN ISSUE."
THEY GOT THEIR TOWN CLEARED, WE GET TO BLOW CRAP UP. THAT'S THE DEAL, RIGHT?

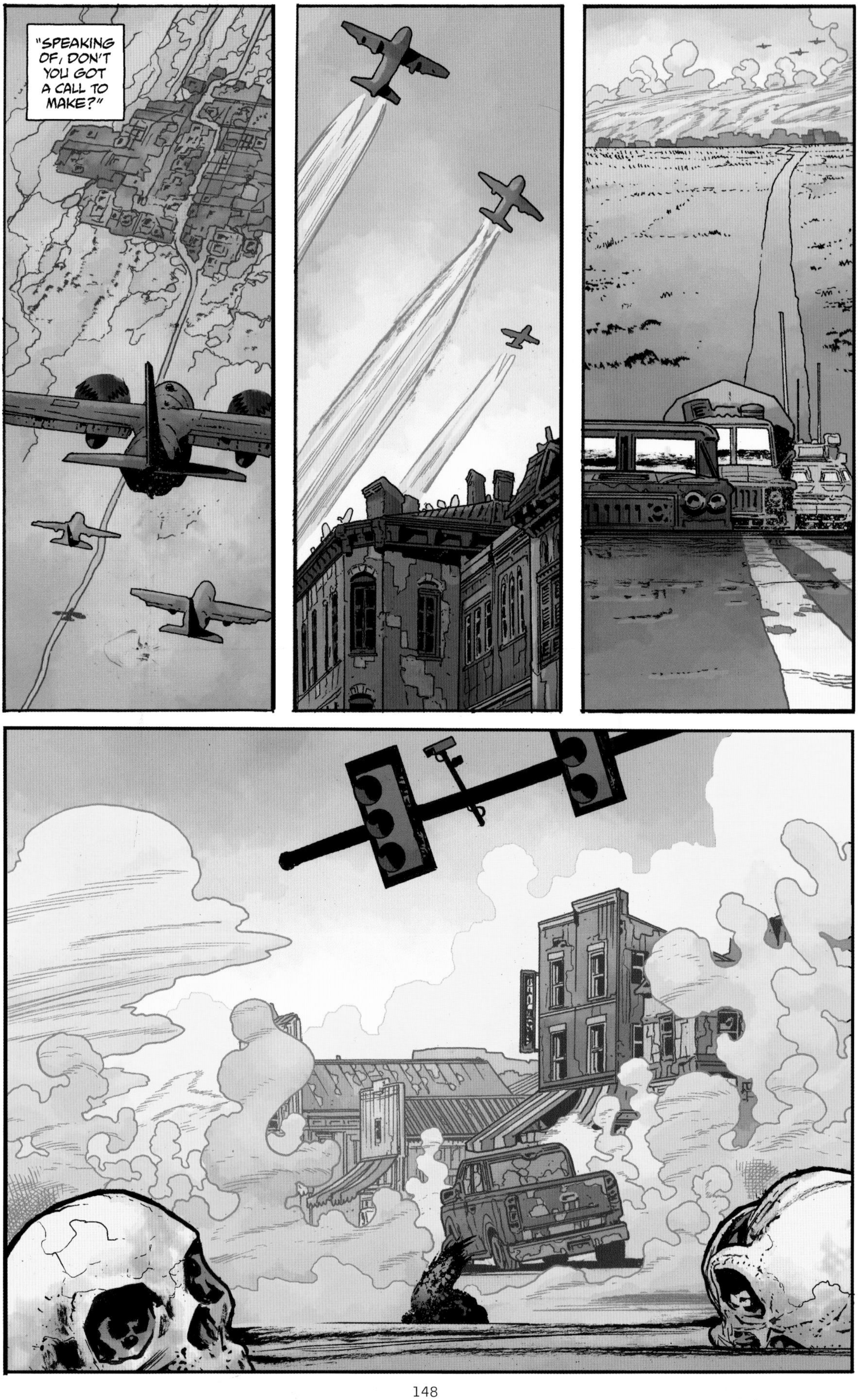
"SPEAKING OF, DON'T YOU GOT A CALL TO MAKE?"

FLESH AND STONE CHAPTER TWO

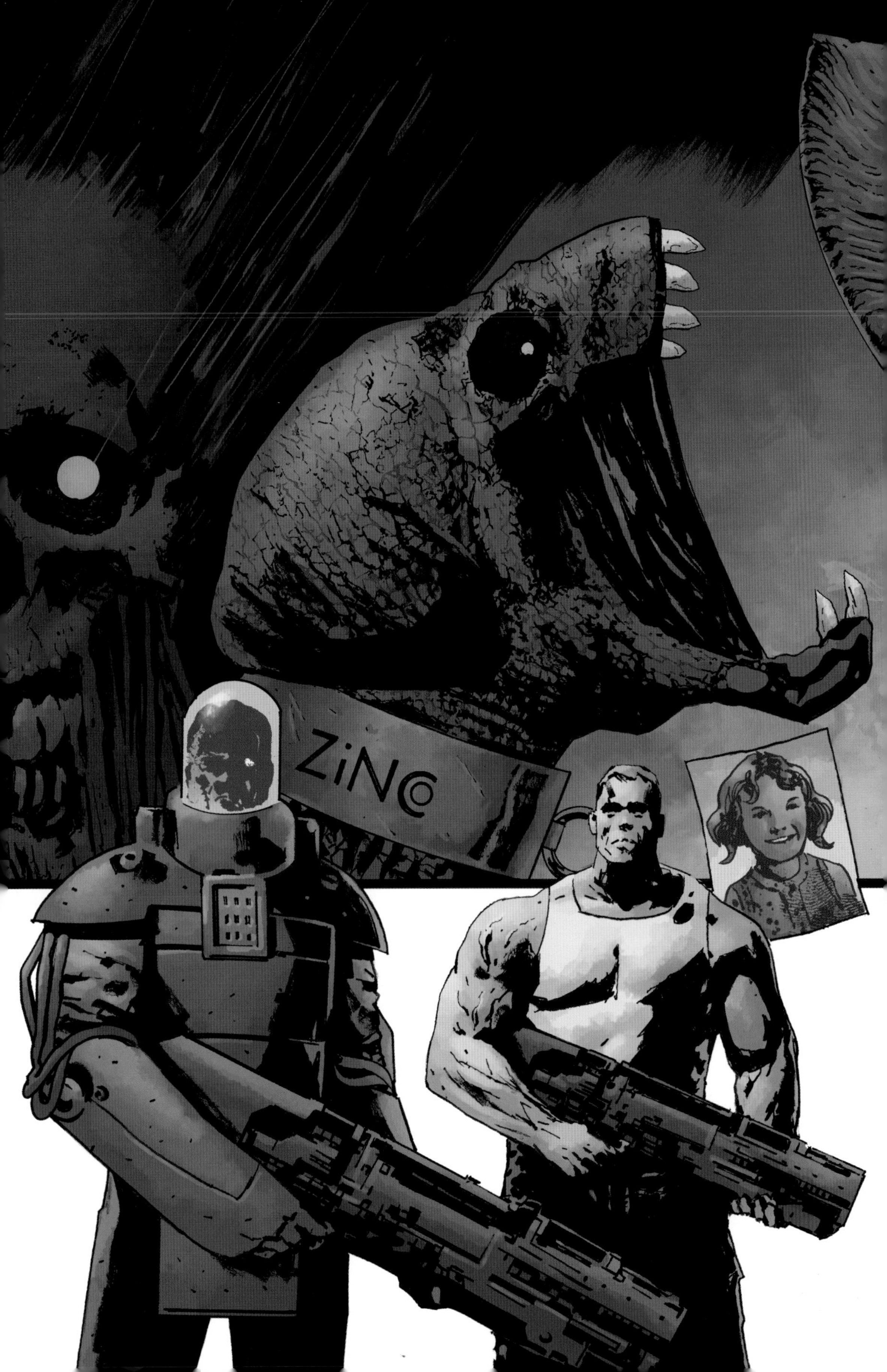
ZiNCO

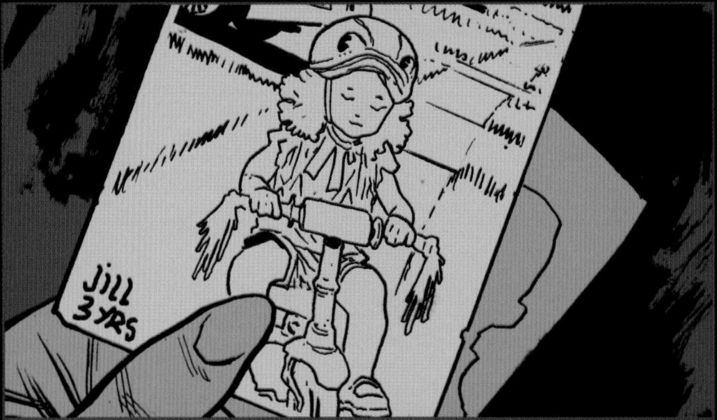
JILL
3 YRS

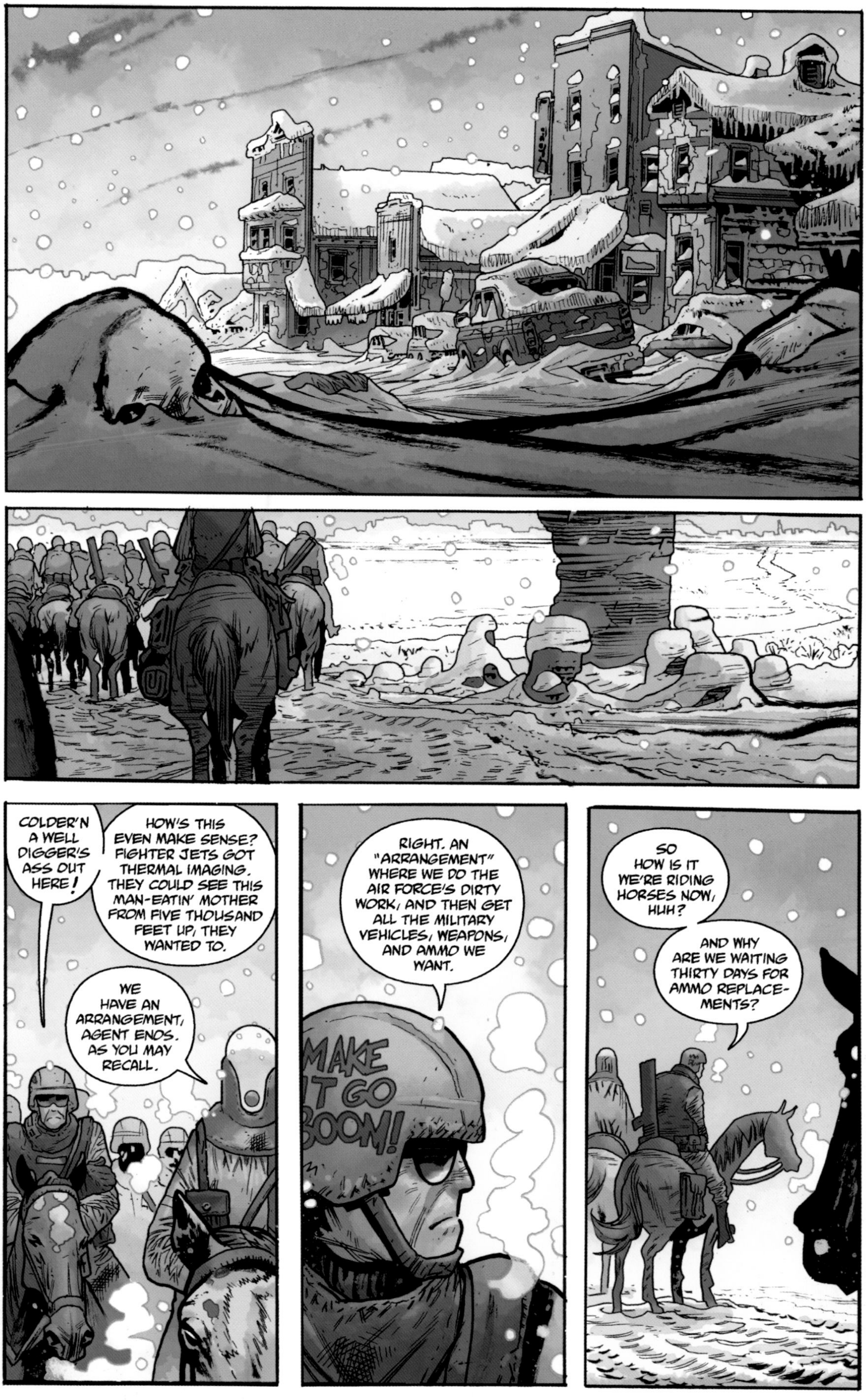

COLDER'N A WELL DIGGER'S ASS OUT HERE!
HOW'S THIS EVEN MAKE SENSE? FIGHTER JETS GOT THERMAL IMAGING. THEY COULD SEE THIS MAN-EATIN' MOTHER FROM FIVE THOUSAND FEET UP, THEY WANTED TO.
WE HAVE AN ARRANGEMENT, AGENT ENOS. AS YOU MAY RECALL.
RIGHT. AN "ARRANGEMENT" WHERE WE DO THE AIR FORCE'S DIRTY WORK, AND THEN GET ALL THE MILITARY VEHICLES, WEAPONS, AND AMMO WE WANT.
MAKE IT GO BOOM!
SO HOW IS IT WE'RE RIDING HORSES NOW, HUH?
AND WHY ARE WE WAITING THIRTY DAYS FOR AMMO REPLACE-MENTS?

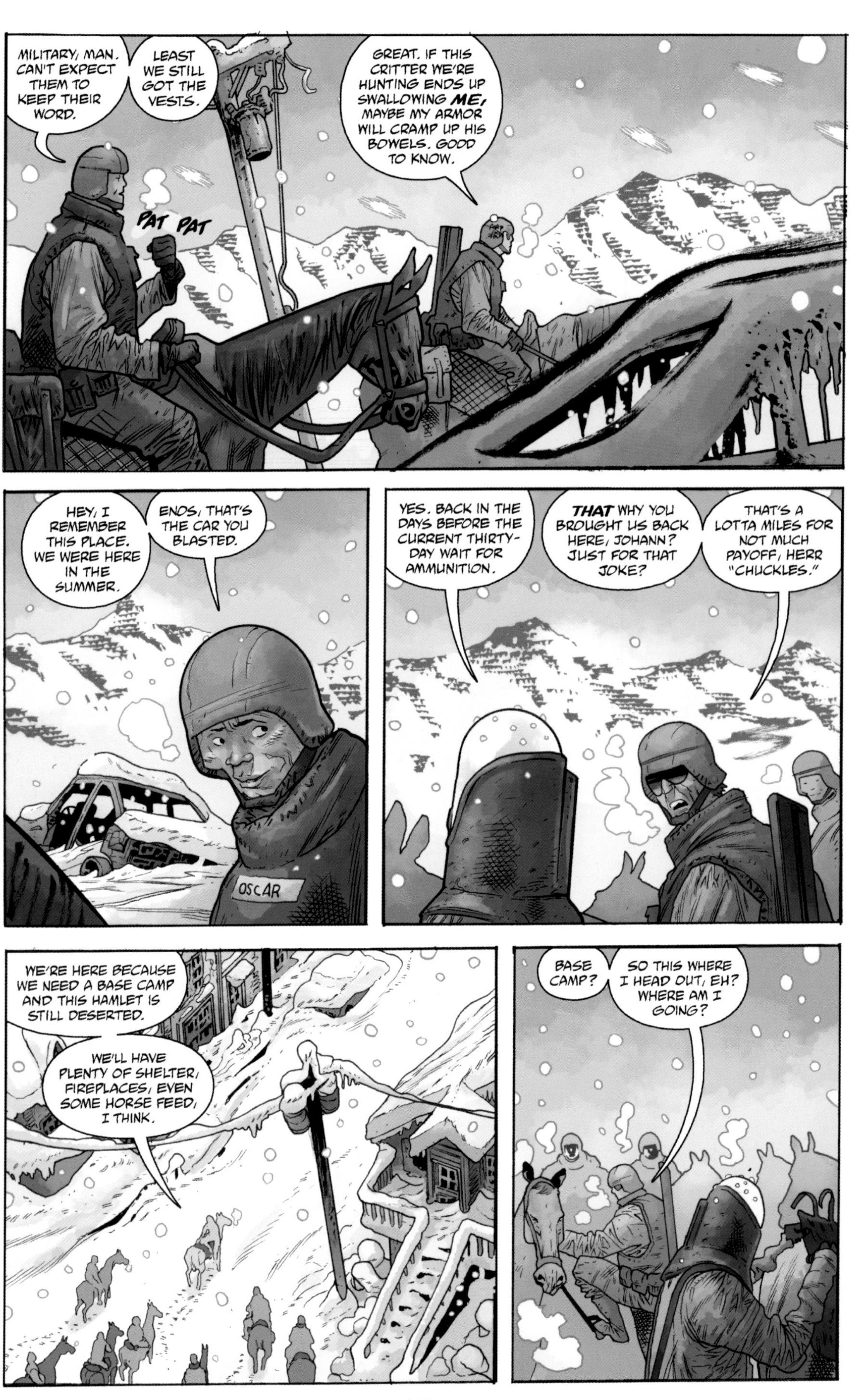
MILITARY, MAN. CAN'T EXPECT THEM TO KEEP THEIR WORD.
LEAST WE STILL GOT THE VESTS.
PAT PAT
GREAT. IF THIS CRITTER WE'RE HUNTING ENDS UP SWALLOWING ME, MAYBE MY ARMOR WILL CRAMP UP HIS BOWELS. GOOD TO KNOW.
HEY, I REMEMBER THIS PLACE. WE WERE HERE IN THE SUMMER.
ENOS, THAT'S THE CAR YOU BLASTED.
OSCAR
YES. BACK IN THE DAYS BEFORE THE CURRENT THIRTY-DAY WAIT FOR AMMUNITION.
THAT WHY YOU BROUGHT US BACK HERE, JOHANN? JUST FOR THAT JOKE?
THAT'S A LOTTA MILES FOR NOT MUCH PAYOFF, HERR "CHUCKLES."
WE'RE HERE BECAUSE WE NEED A BASE CAMP AND THIS HAMLET IS STILL DESERTED.
WE'LL HAVE PLENTY OF SHELTER, FIREPLACES, EVEN SOME HORSE FEED, I THINK.
BASE CAMP?
SO THIS WHERE I HEAD OUT, EH? WHERE AM I GOING?

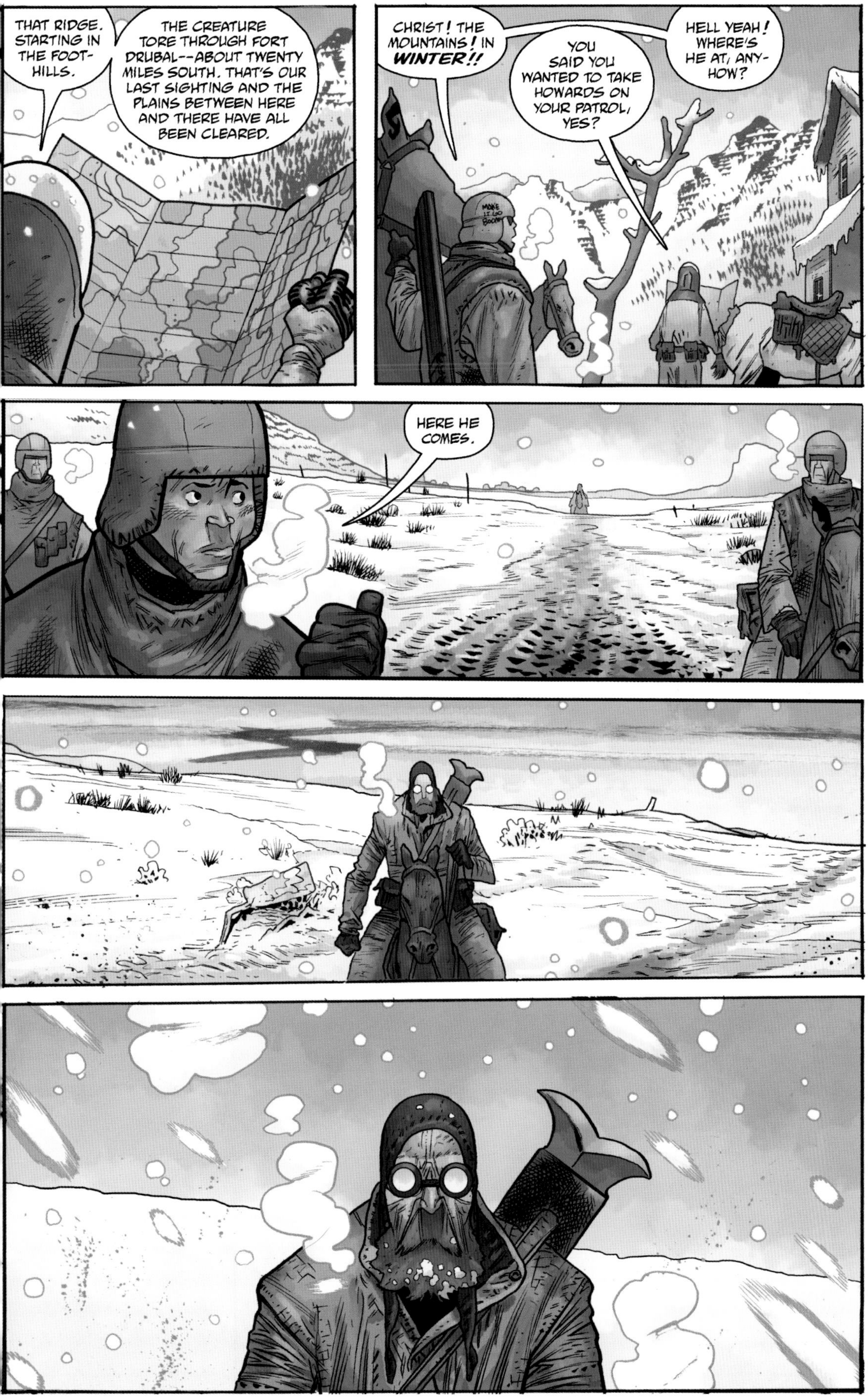
THAT RIDGE. STARTING IN THE FOOT-HILLS.
THE CREATURE TORE THROUGH FORT DRUBAL--ABOUT TWENTY MILES SOUTH. THAT'S OUR LAST SIGHTING AND THE PLAINS BETWEEN HERE AND THERE HAVE ALL BEEN CLEARED.
CHRIST! THE MOUNTAINS! IN WINTER!!
YOU SAID YOU WANTED TO TAKE HOWARDS ON YOUR PATROL, YES?
HELL YEAH! WHERE'S HE AT, ANY-HOW?
MAKE IT GO BOOM
HERE HE COMES.

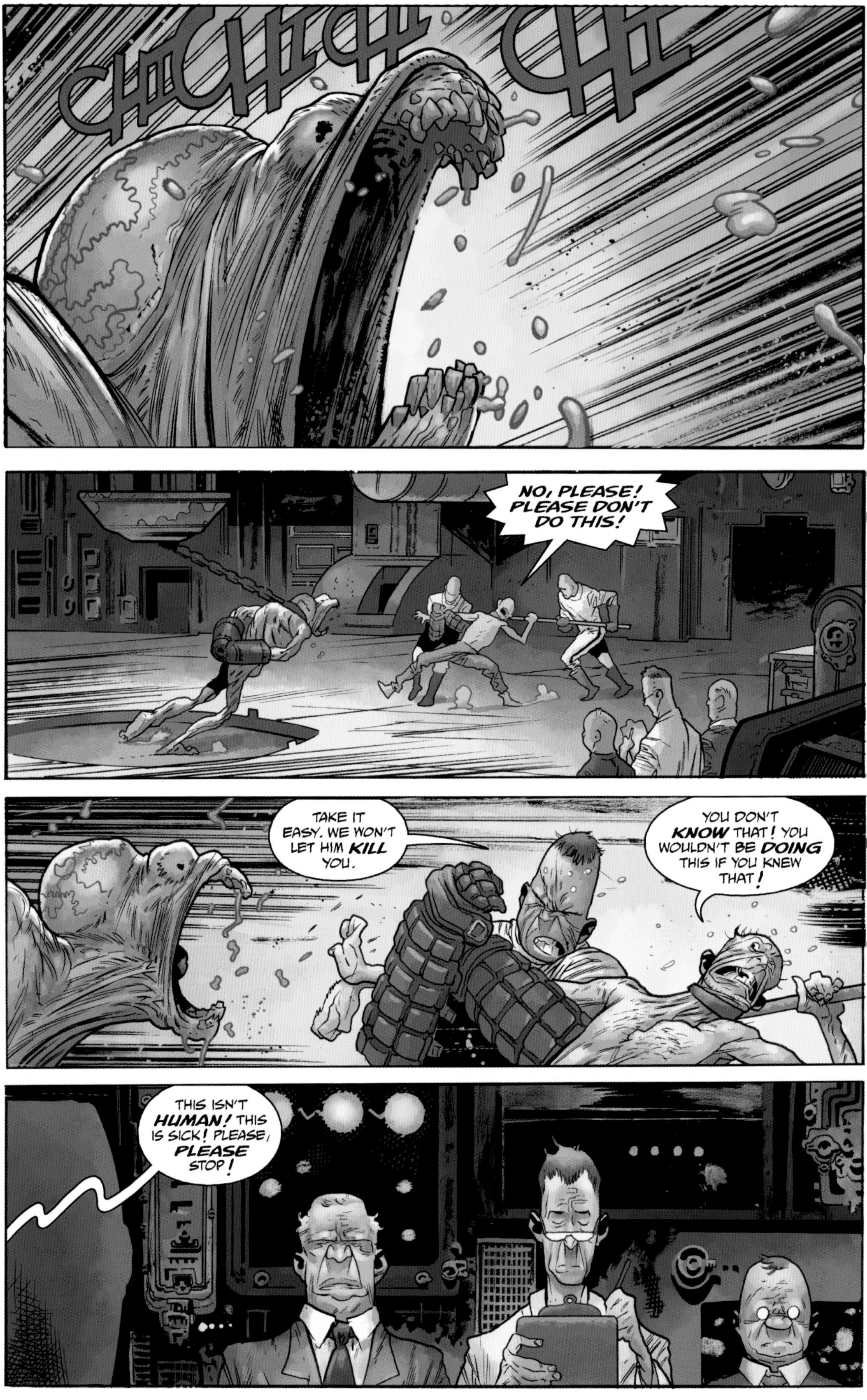
NO, PLEASE! PLEASE DON'T DO THIS!
TAKE IT EASY. WE WON'T LET HIM KILL YOU.
YOU DON'T KNOW THAT! YOU WOULDN'T BE DOING THIS IF YOU KNEW THAT!
THIS ISN'T HUMAN! THIS IS SICK! PLEASE, PLEASE STOP!

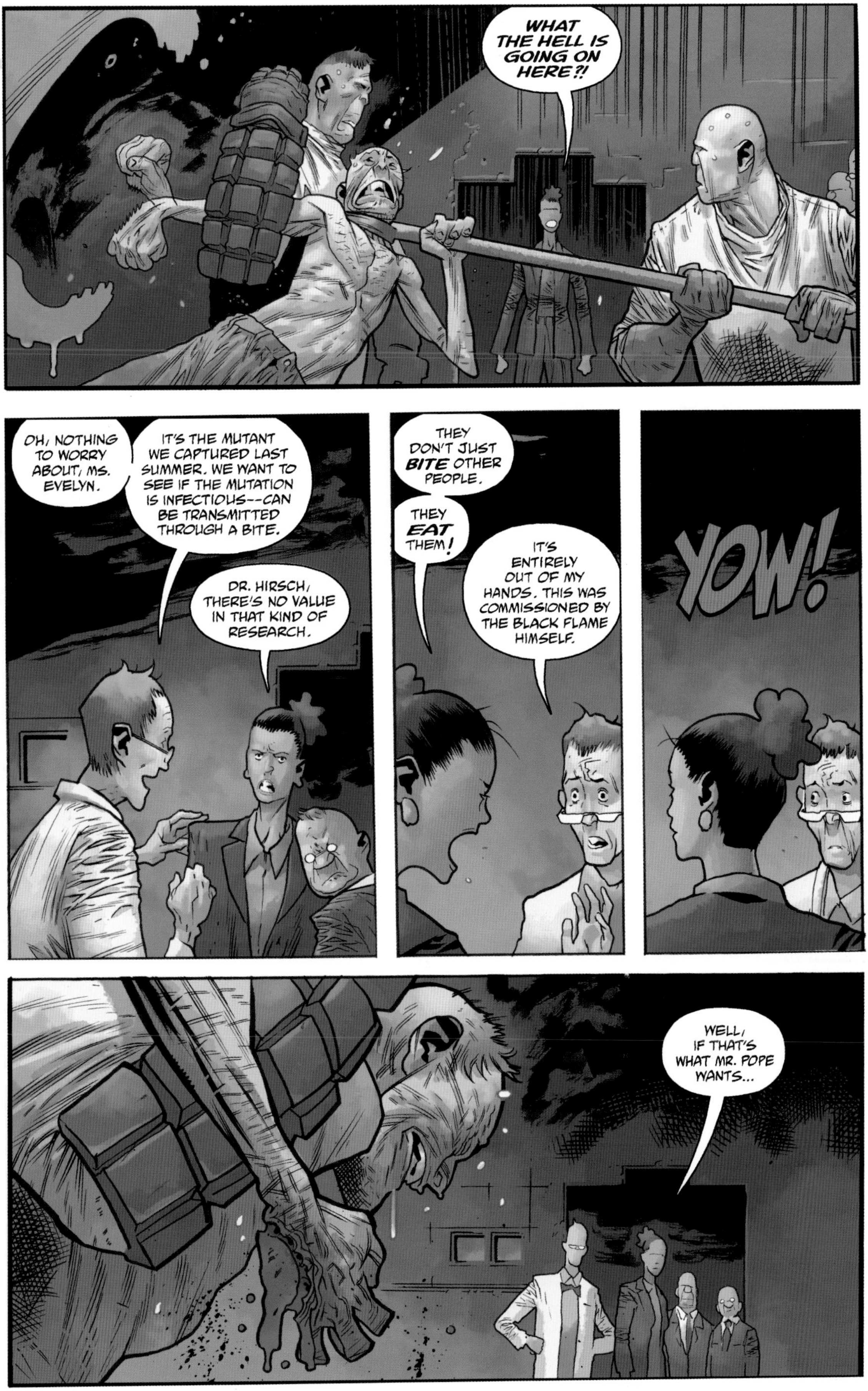
WHAT THE HELL IS GOING ON HERE?!
OH, NOTHING TO WORRY ABOUT, MS. EVELYN.
IT'S THE MUTANT WE CAPTURED LAST SUMMER. WE WANT TO SEE IF THE MUTATION IS INFECTIOUS--CAN BE TRANSMITTED THROUGH A BITE.
DR. HIRSCH, THERE'S NO VALUE IN THAT KIND OF RESEARCH.
THEY DON'T JUST BITE OTHER PEOPLE.
THEY EAT THEM!
IT'S ENTIRELY OUT OF MY HANDS. THIS WAS COMMISSIONED BY THE BLACK FLAME HIMSELF.
YOW!
WELL, IF THAT'S WHAT MR. POPE WANTS...

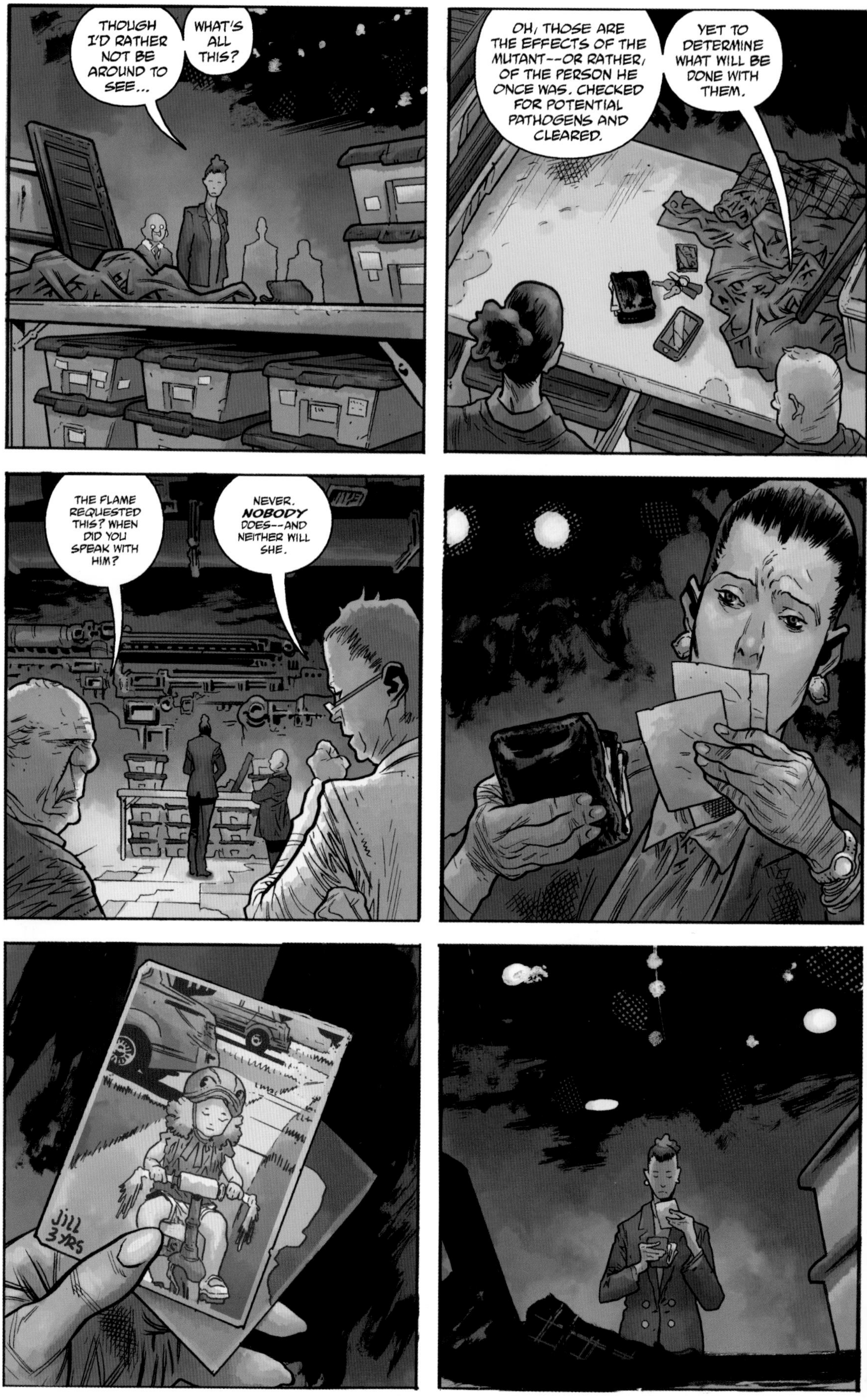
THOUGH I'D RATHER NOT BE AROUND TO SEE...
WHAT'S ALL THIS?
OH, THOSE ARE THE EFFECTS OF THE MUTANT--OR RATHER, OF THE PERSON HE ONCE WAS. CHECKED FOR POTENTIAL PATHOGENS AND CLEARED.
YET TO DETERMINE WHAT WILL BE DONE WITH THEM.
THE FLAME REQUESTED THIS? WHEN DID YOU SPEAK WITH HIM?
NEVER. NOBODY DOES--AND NEITHER WILL SHE.
JILL 3 YRS

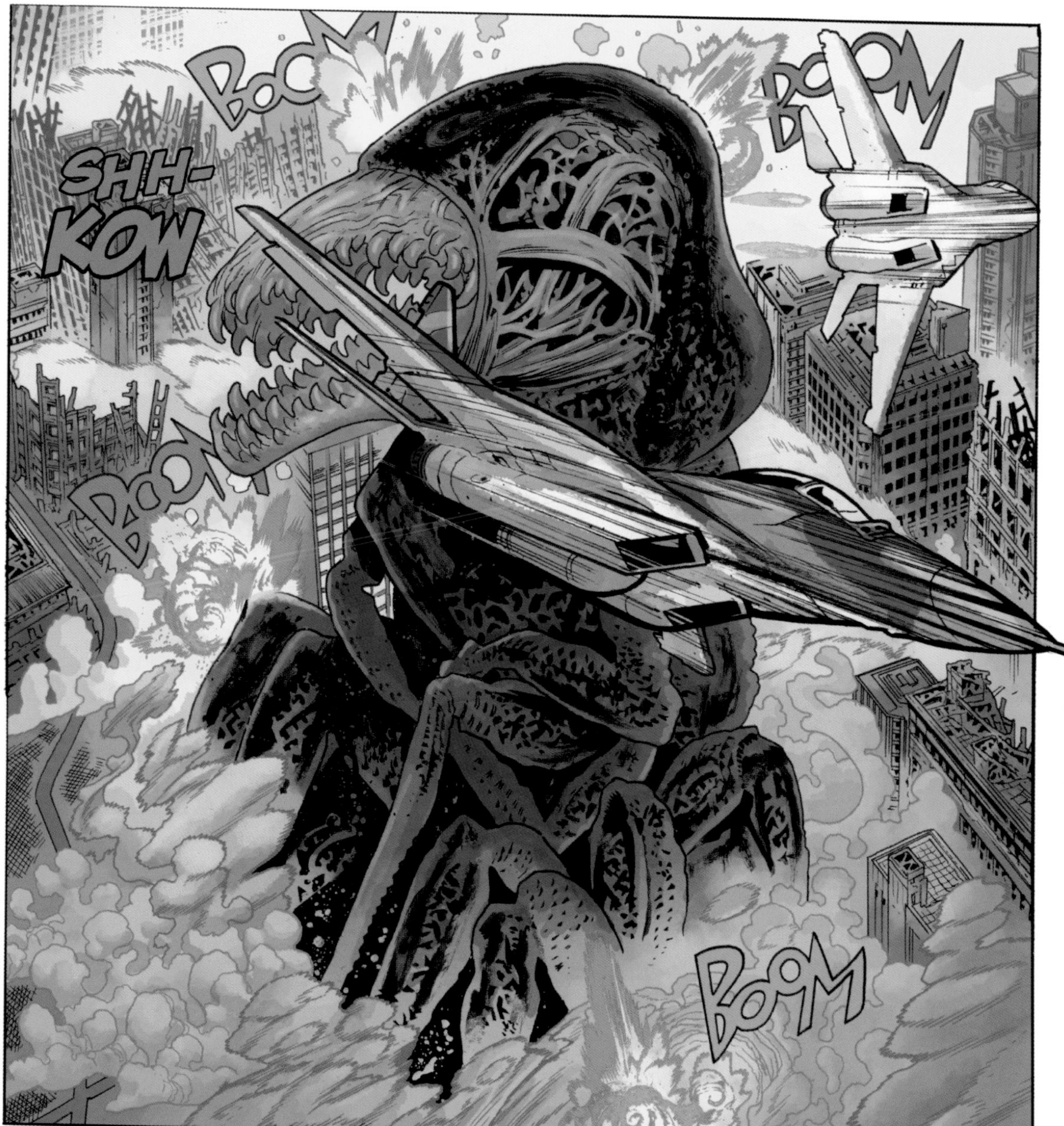
BOOM
SHH-KOW
BOOM
BOOM
BOOM

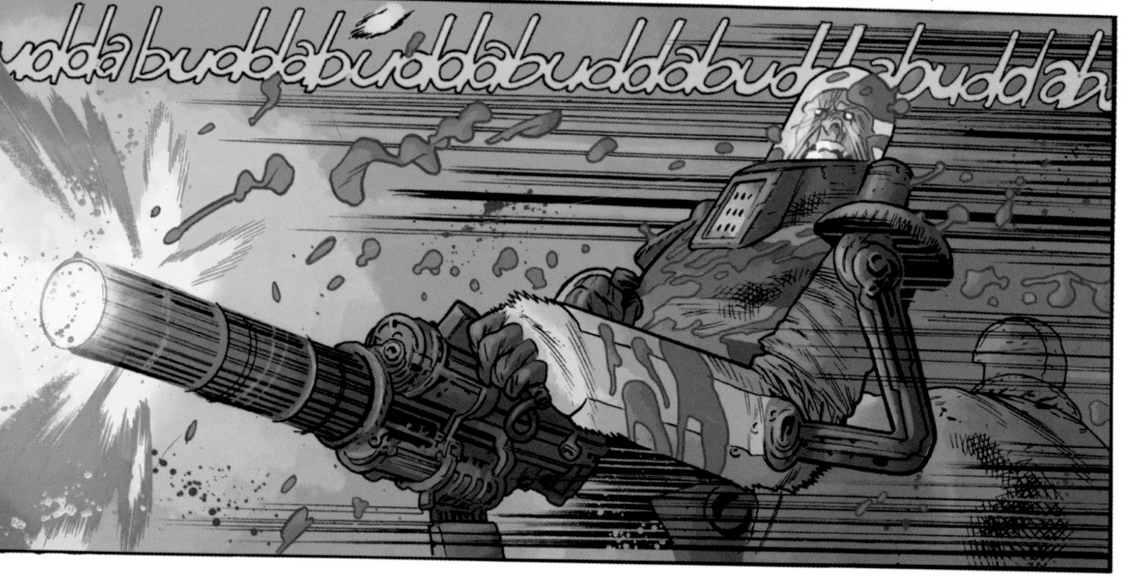
uddabuddabuddabuddabuddabuddah

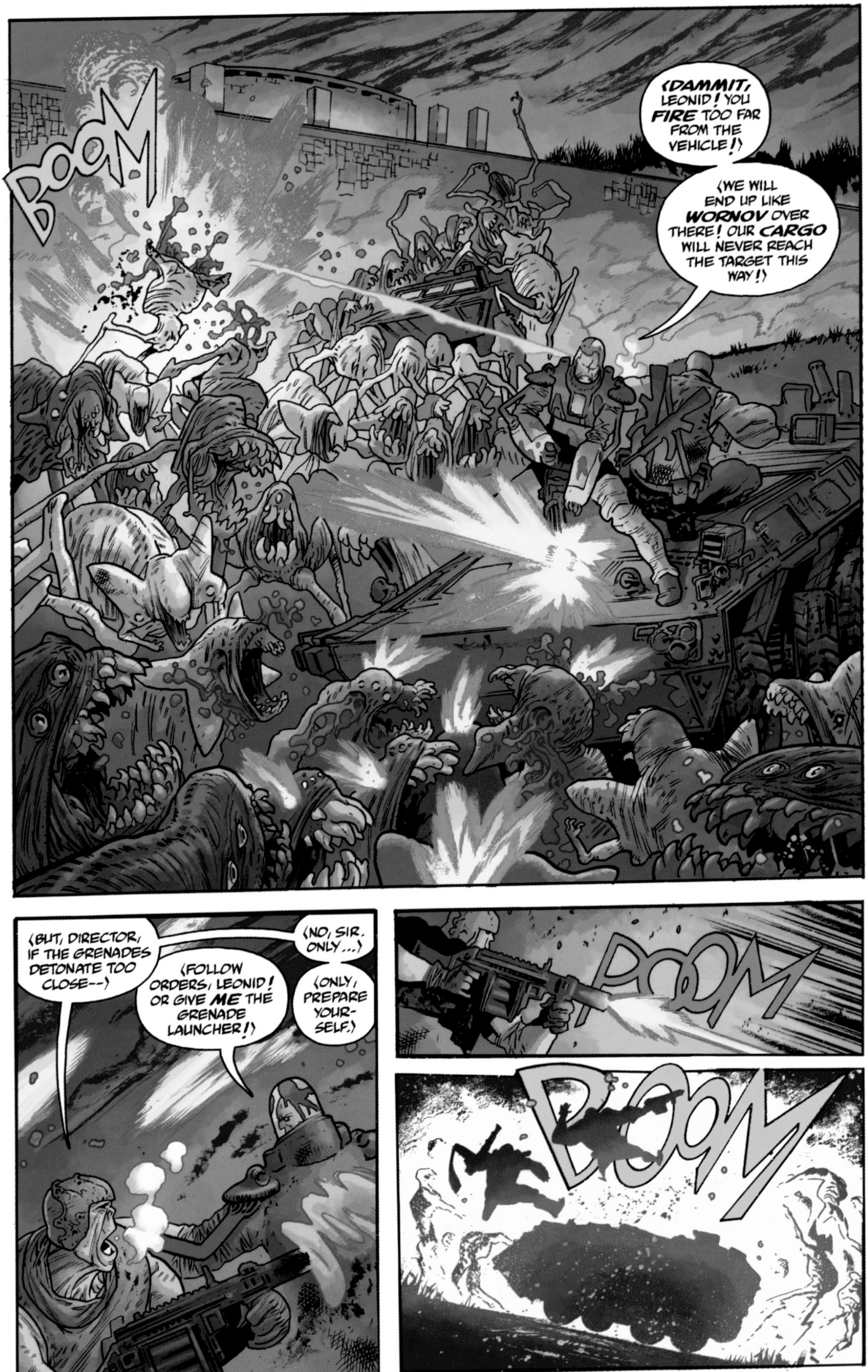
BOOM
(DAMMIT, LEONID! YOU FIRE TOO FAR FROM THE VEHICLE!)
(WE WILL END UP LIKE WORNOV OVER THERE! OUR CARGO WILL NEVER REACH THE TARGET THIS WAY!)
(BUT, DIRECTOR, IF THE GRENADES DETONATE TOO CLOSE--)
(FOLLOW ORDERS, LEONID! OR GIVE ME THE GRENADE LAUNCHER!)
(NO, SIR. ONLY...)
(ONLY, PREPARE YOURSELF.)
POOM
BOOM

(TRANSLATED FROM RUSSIAN)

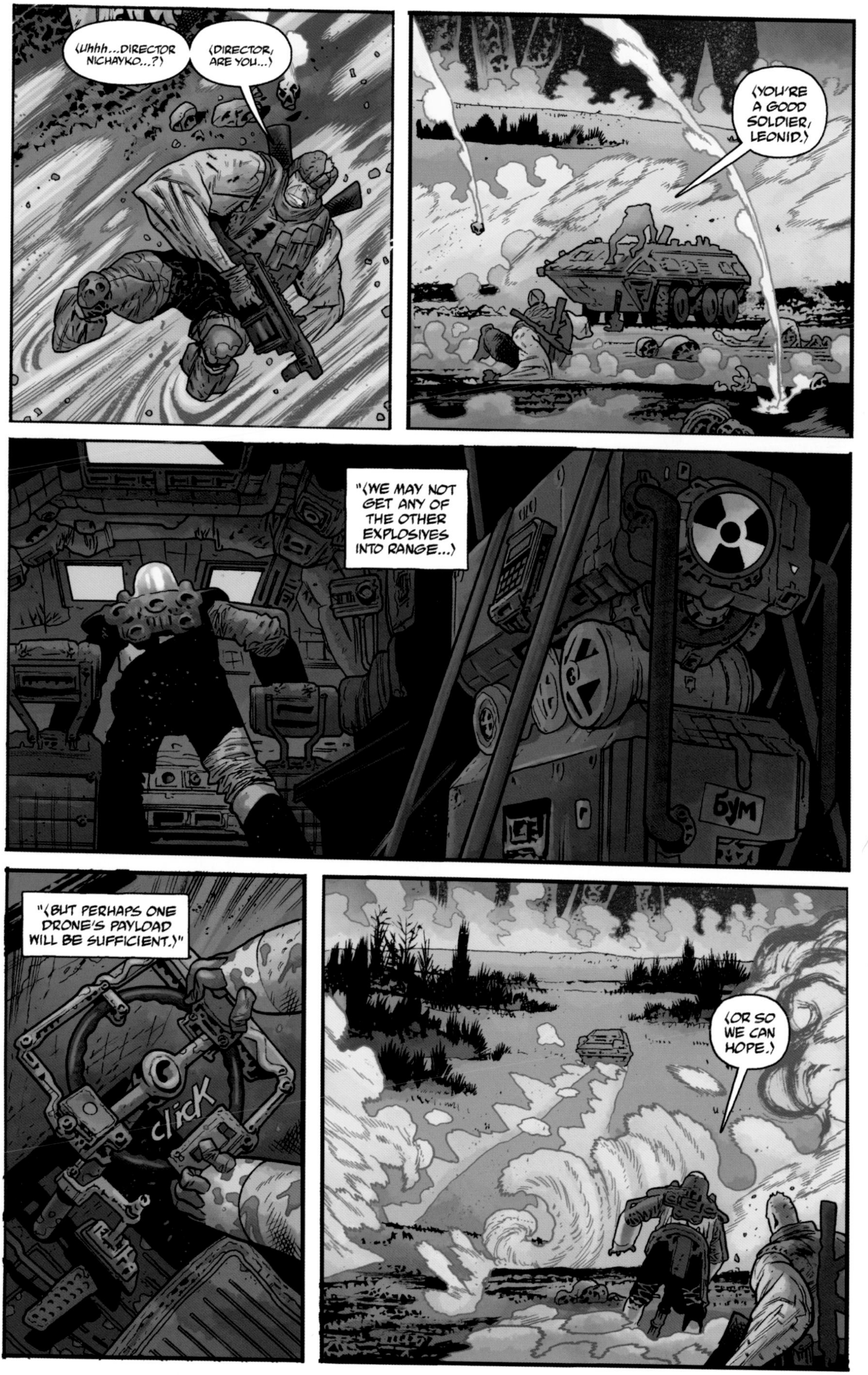
⟨Uhhh...DIRECTOR NICHAYKO...?⟩
⟨DIRECTOR, ARE YOU...⟩
⟨YOU'RE A GOOD SOLDIER, LEONID.⟩
"⟨WE MAY NOT GET ANY OF THE OTHER EXPLOSIVES INTO RANGE...⟩
БУМ
"⟨BUT PERHAPS ONE DRONE'S PAYLOAD WILL BE SUFFICIENT.⟩"
click
⟨OR SO WE CAN HOPE.⟩

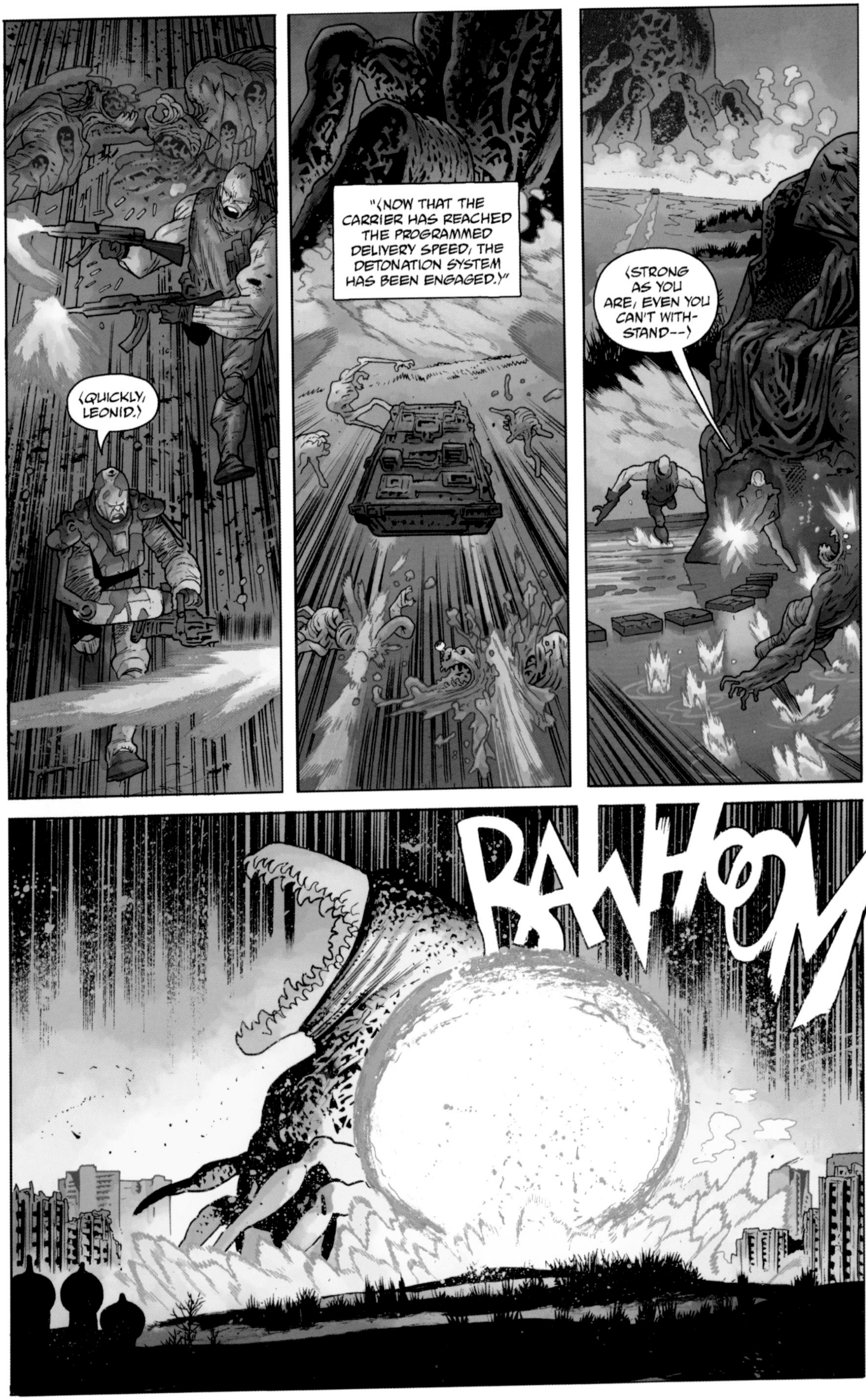
‹QUICKLY, LEONID.›
"‹NOW THAT THE CARRIER HAS REACHED THE PROGRAMMED DELIVERY SPEED, THE DETONATION SYSTEM HAS BEEN ENGAGED.›"
‹STRONG AS YOU ARE, EVEN YOU CAN'T WITH-STAND--›
BAHOOM

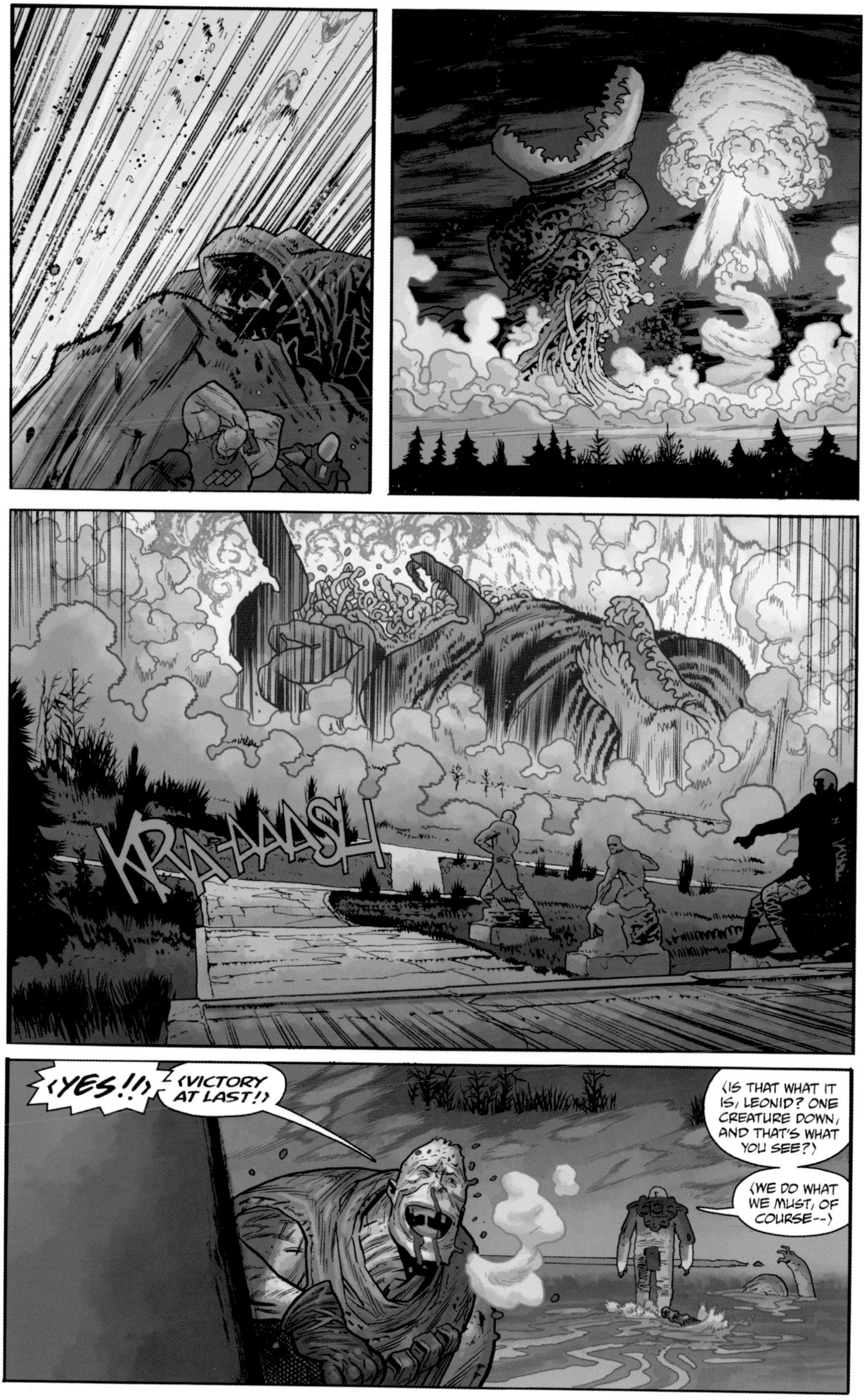
KRAAAASH
‹YES!!›
‹VICTORY AT LAST!›
‹IS THAT WHAT IT IS, LEONID? ONE CREATURE DOWN, AND THAT'S WHAT YOU SEE?›
‹WE DO WHAT WE MUST, OF COURSE--›

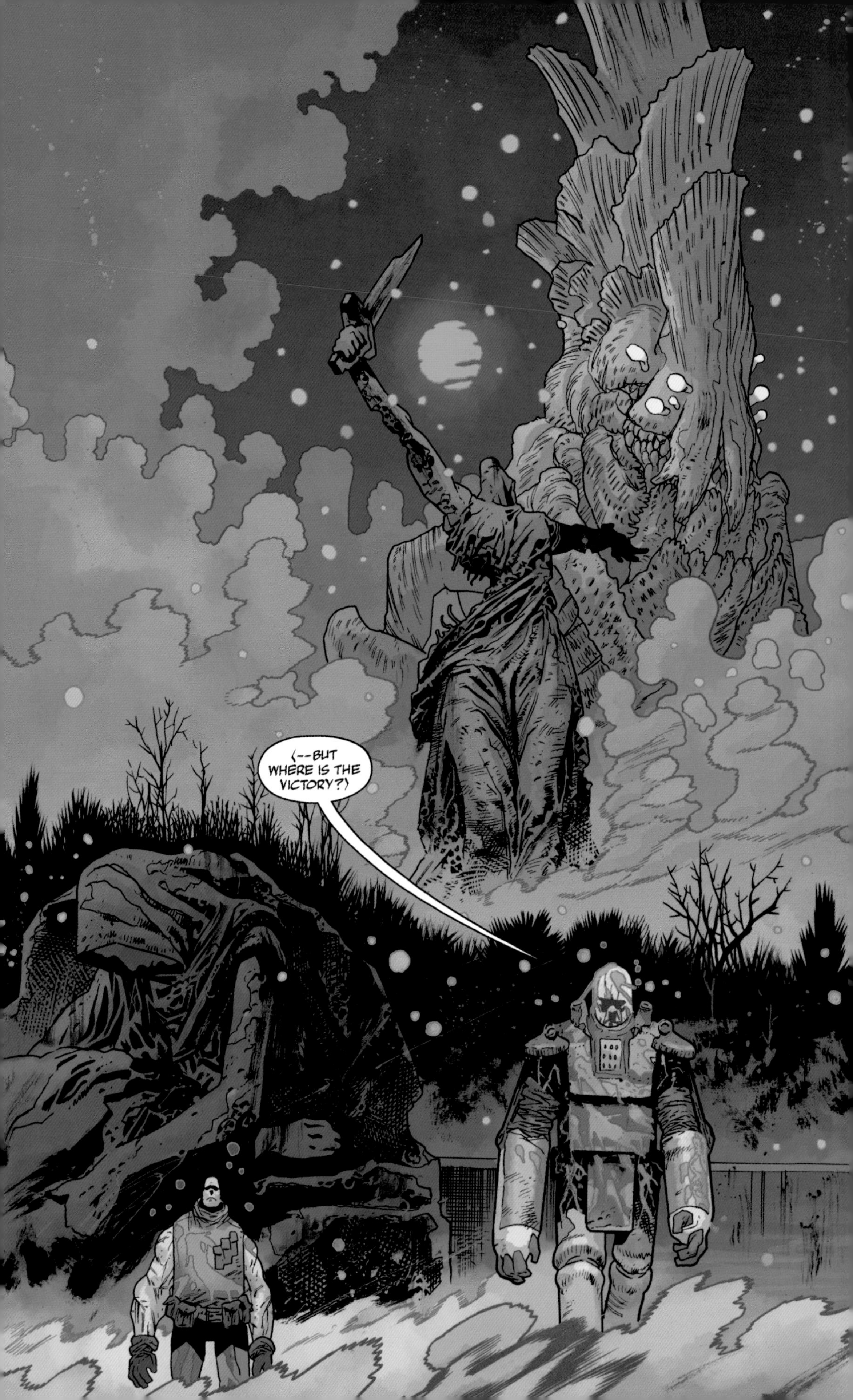
⟨--BUT WHERE IS THE VICTORY?⟩

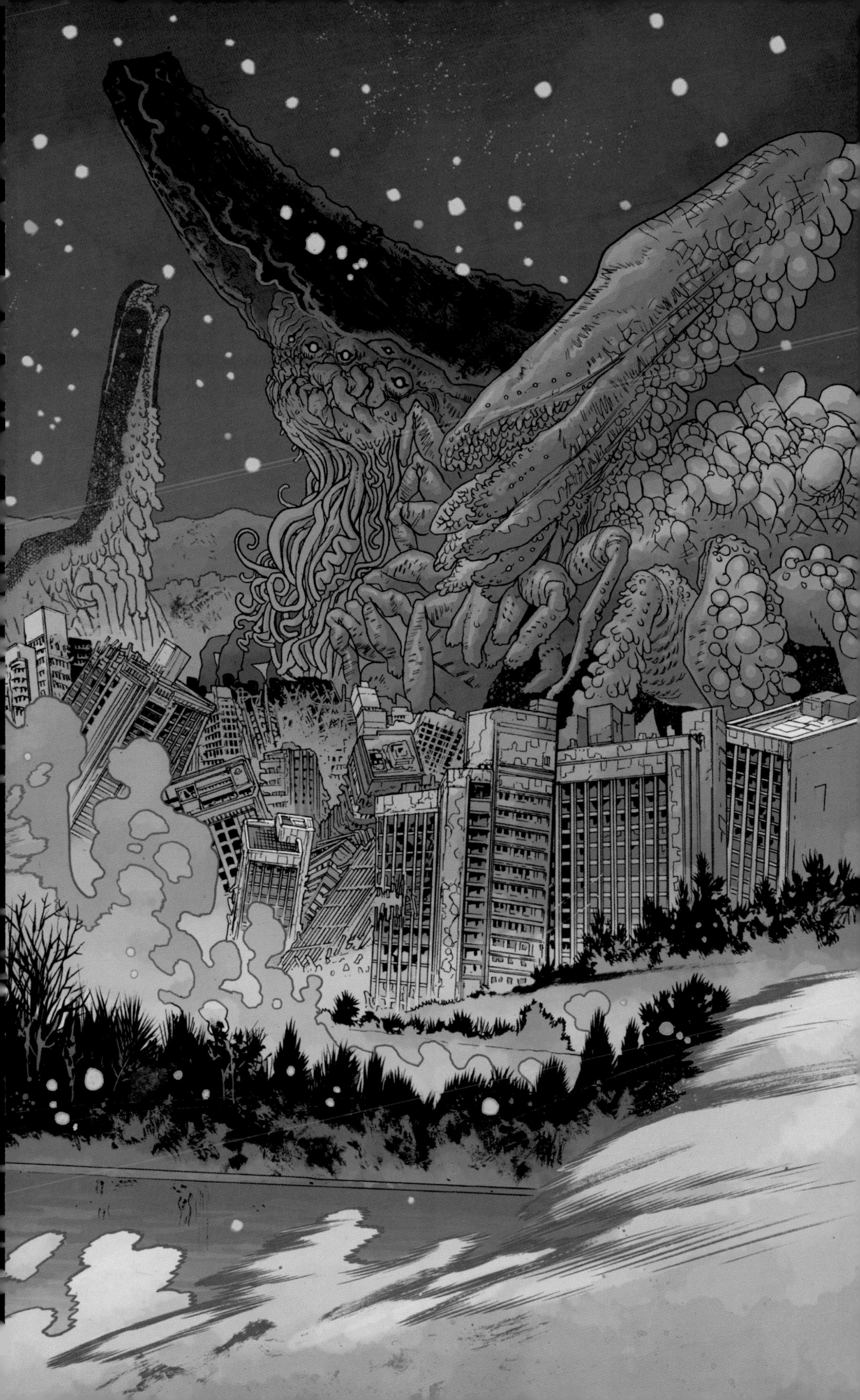

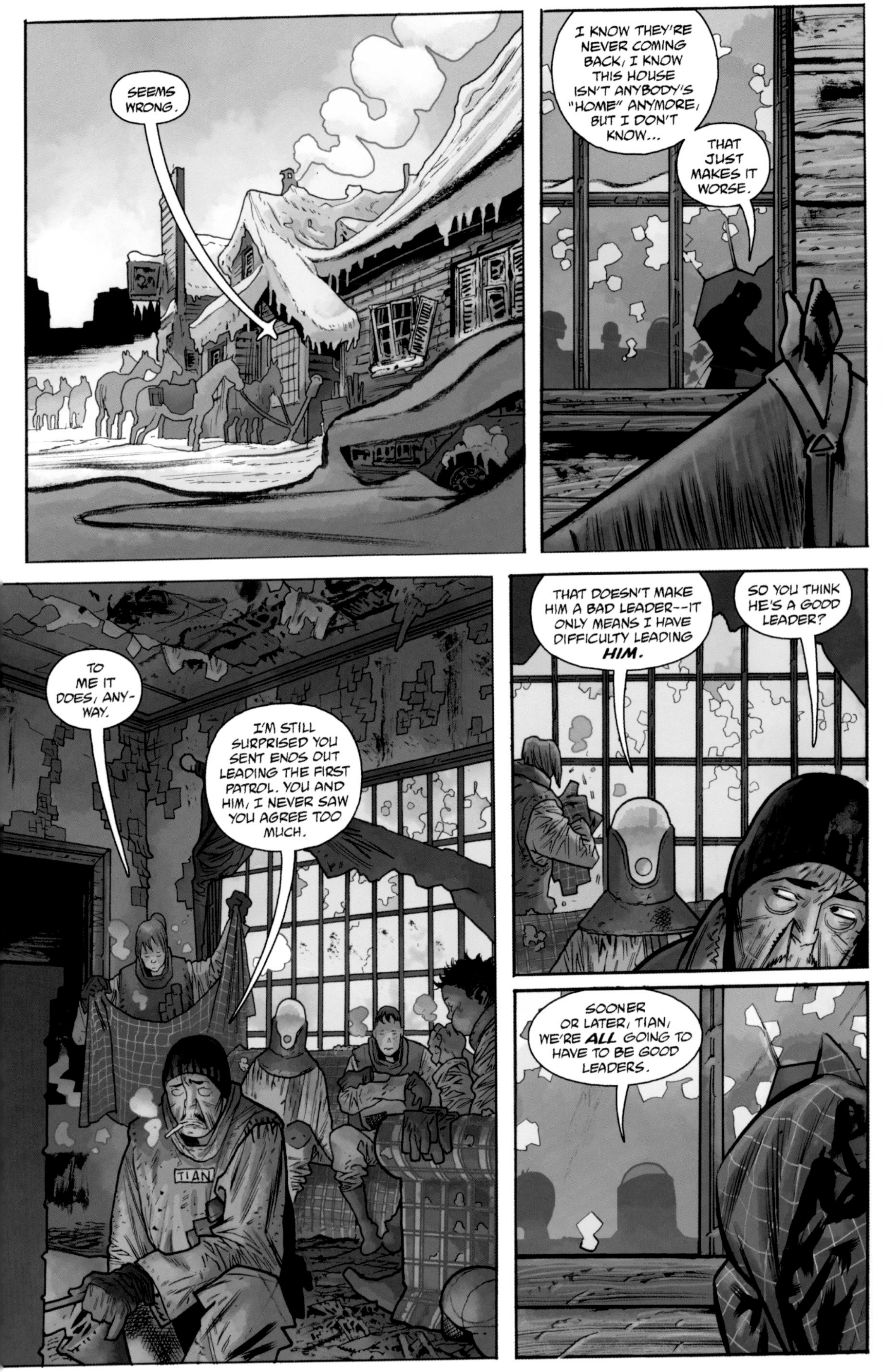
SEEMS WRONG.
I KNOW THEY'RE NEVER COMING BACK, I KNOW THIS HOUSE ISN'T ANYBODY'S "HOME" ANYMORE, BUT I DON'T KNOW...
THAT JUST MAKES IT WORSE.
TO ME IT DOES, ANY-WAY.
I'M STILL SURPRISED YOU SENT ENOS OUT LEADING THE FIRST PATROL. YOU AND HIM, I NEVER SAW YOU AGREE TOO MUCH.
TIAN
THAT DOESN'T MAKE HIM A BAD LEADER--IT ONLY MEANS I HAVE DIFFICULTY LEADING ***HIM***.
SO YOU THINK HE'S A GOOD LEADER?
SOONER OR LATER, TIAN, WE'RE ***ALL*** GOING TO HAVE TO BE GOOD LEADERS.

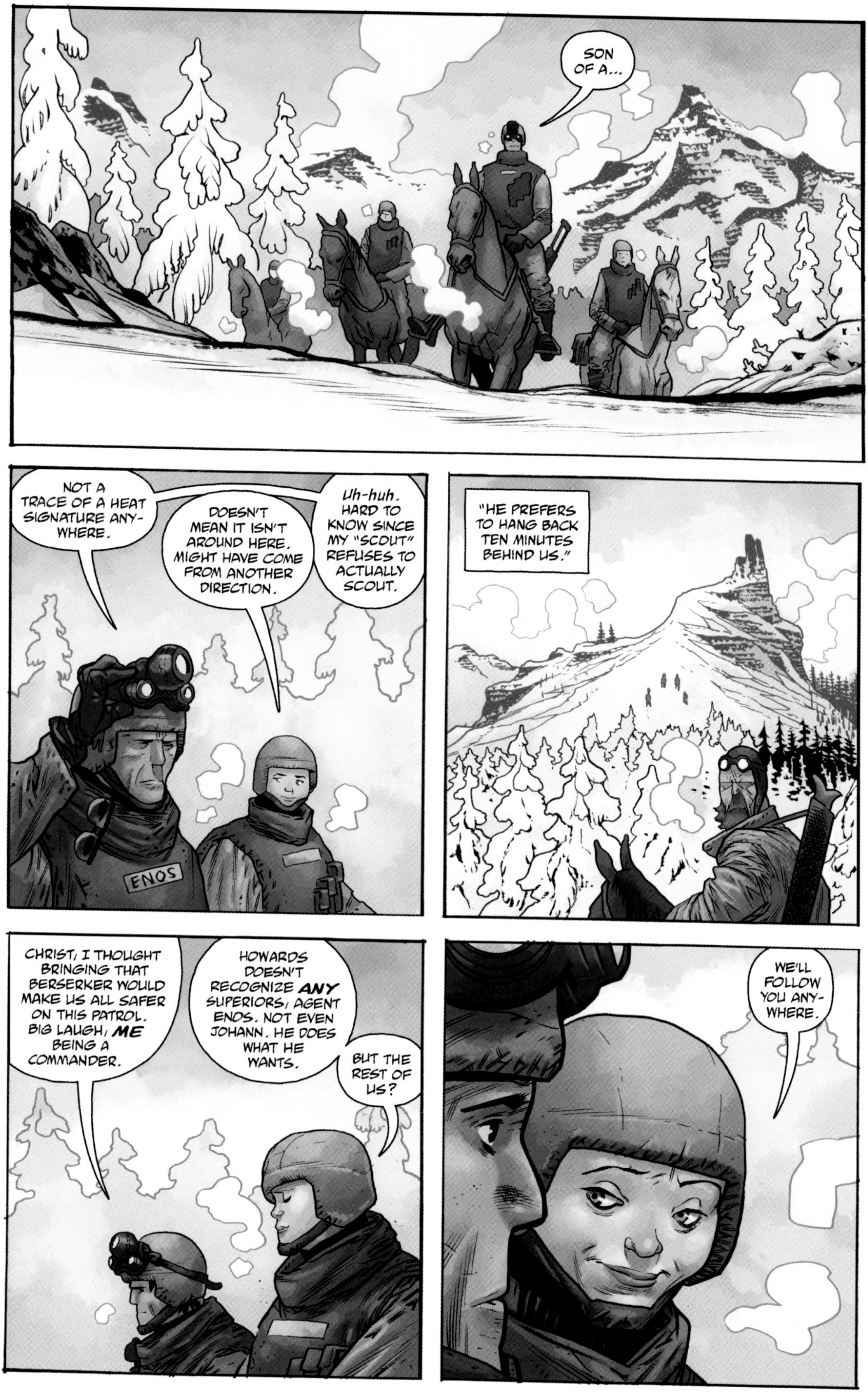
SON OF A...
NOT A TRACE OF A HEAT SIGNATURE ANY-WHERE.
DOESN'T MEAN IT ISN'T AROUND HERE. MIGHT HAVE COME FROM ANOTHER DIRECTION.
Uh-huh. HARD TO KNOW SINCE MY "SCOUT" REFUSES TO ACTUALLY SCOUT.
ENOS
"HE PREFERS TO HANG BACK TEN MINUTES BEHIND US."
CHRIST, I THOUGHT BRINGING THAT BERSERKER WOULD MAKE US ALL SAFER ON THIS PATROL. BIG LAUGH, ME BEING A COMMANDER.
HOWARDS DOESN'T RECOGNIZE ANY SUPERIORS, AGENT ENOS. NOT EVEN JOHANN. HE DOES WHAT HE WANTS.
BUT THE REST OF US?
WE'LL FOLLOW YOU ANY-WHERE.

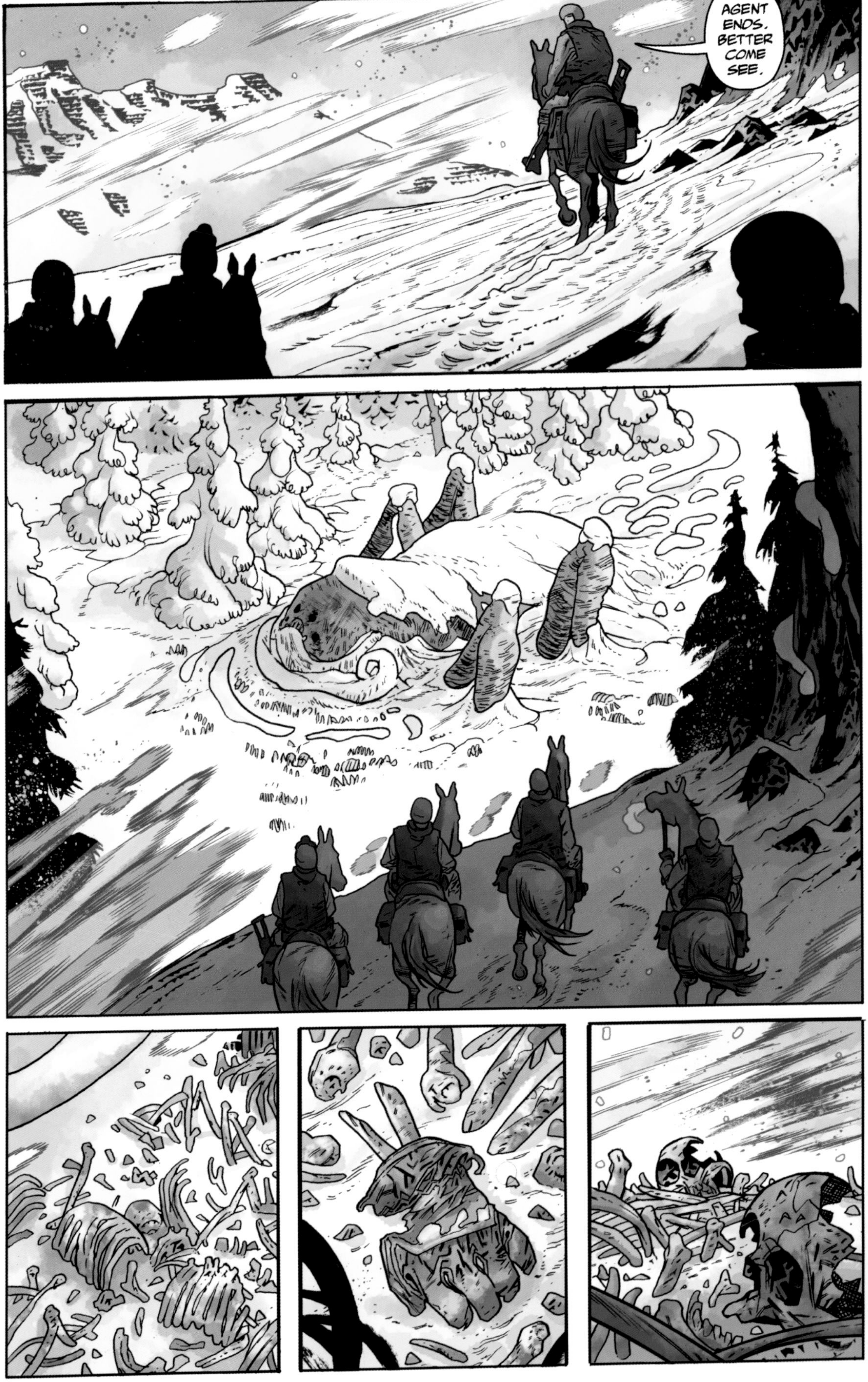
AGENT ENOS, BETTER COME SEE.

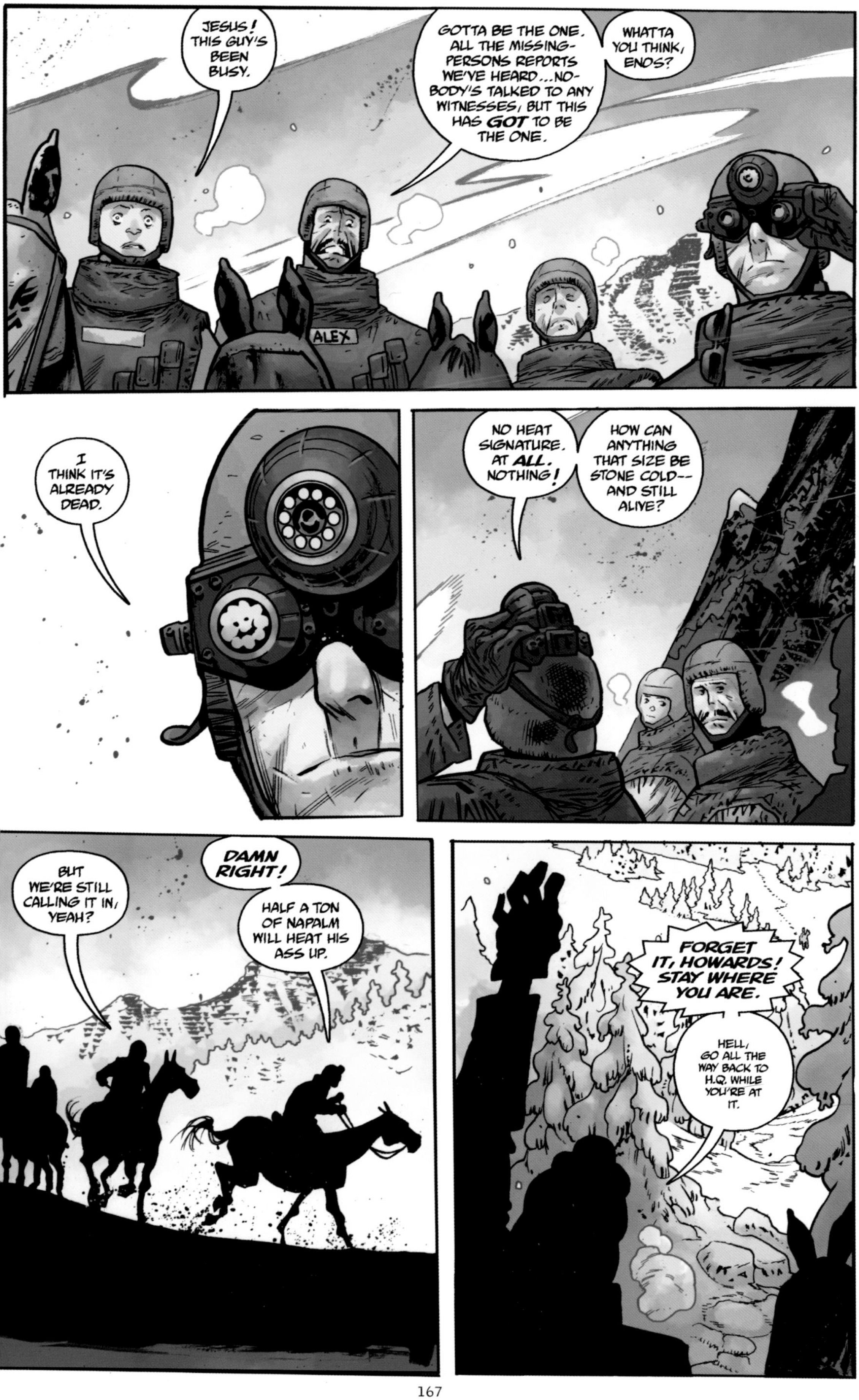
JESUS! THIS GUY'S BEEN BUSY.
GOTTA BE THE ONE. ALL THE MISSING-PERSONS REPORTS WE'VE HEARD...NOBODY'S TALKED TO ANY WITNESSES, BUT THIS HAS GOT TO BE THE ONE.
WHATTA YOU THINK, ENOS?
ALEX
I THINK IT'S ALREADY DEAD.
NO HEAT SIGNATURE. AT ALL. NOTHING!
HOW CAN ANYTHING THAT SIZE BE STONE COLD--AND STILL ALIVE?
BUT WE'RE STILL CALLING IT IN, YEAH?
DAMN RIGHT!
HALF A TON OF NAPALM WILL HEAT HIS ASS UP.
FORGET IT, HOWARDS! STAY WHERE YOU ARE.
HELL, GO ALL THE WAY BACK TO H.Q. WHILE YOU'RE AT IT.

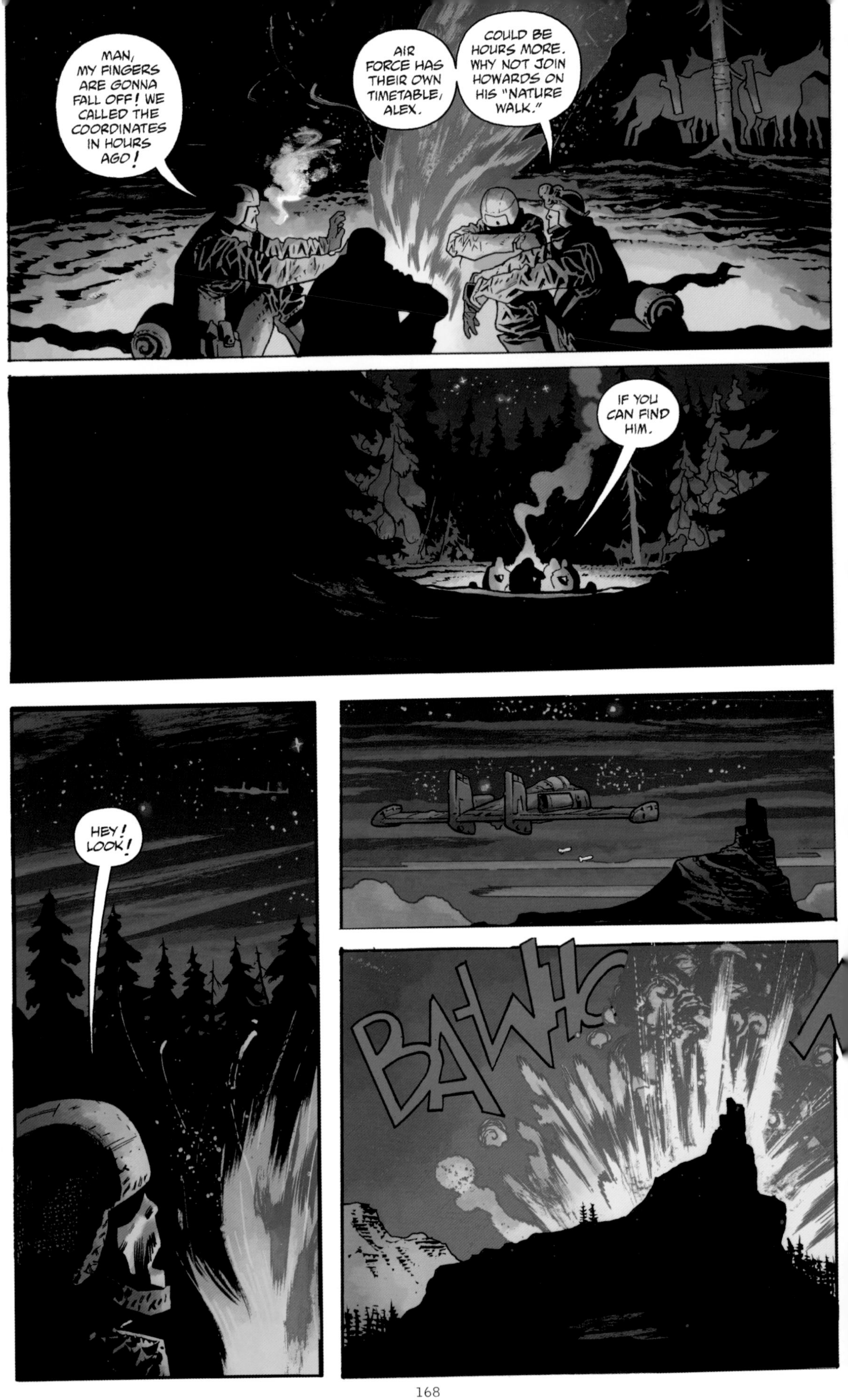
MAN, MY FINGERS ARE GONNA FALL OFF! WE CALLED THE COORDINATES IN HOURS AGO!
AIR FORCE HAS THEIR OWN TIMETABLE, ALEX.
COULD BE HOURS MORE. WHY NOT JOIN HOWARDS ON HIS "NATURE WALK."
IF YOU CAN FIND HIM.
HEY! LOOK!

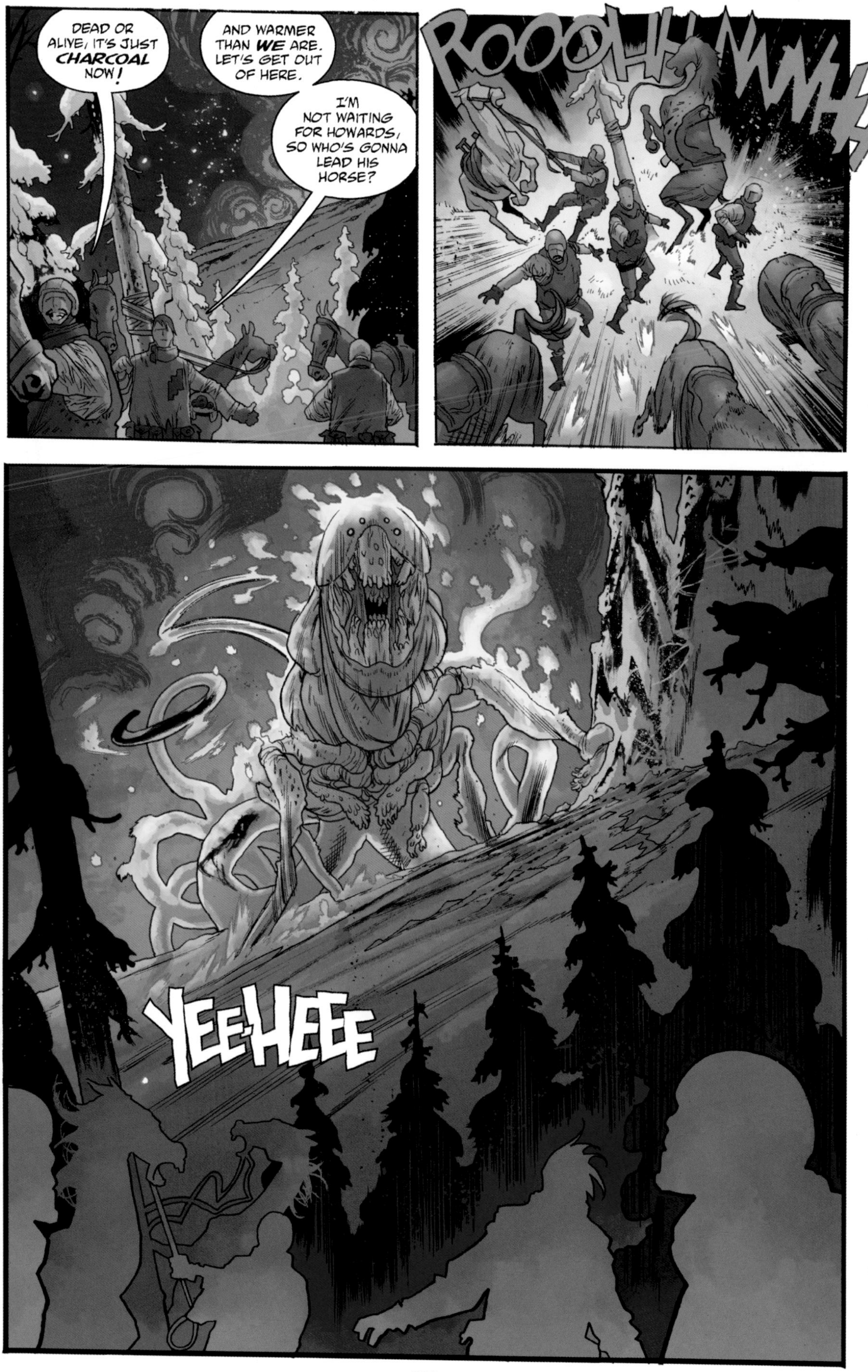
DEAD OR ALIVE, IT'S JUST CHARCOAL NOW!
AND WARMER THAN WE ARE. LET'S GET OUT OF HERE.
I'M NOT WAITING FOR HOWARDS, SO WHO'S GONNA LEAD HIS HORSE?
ROOOHHNWHH
YEE-HEEE

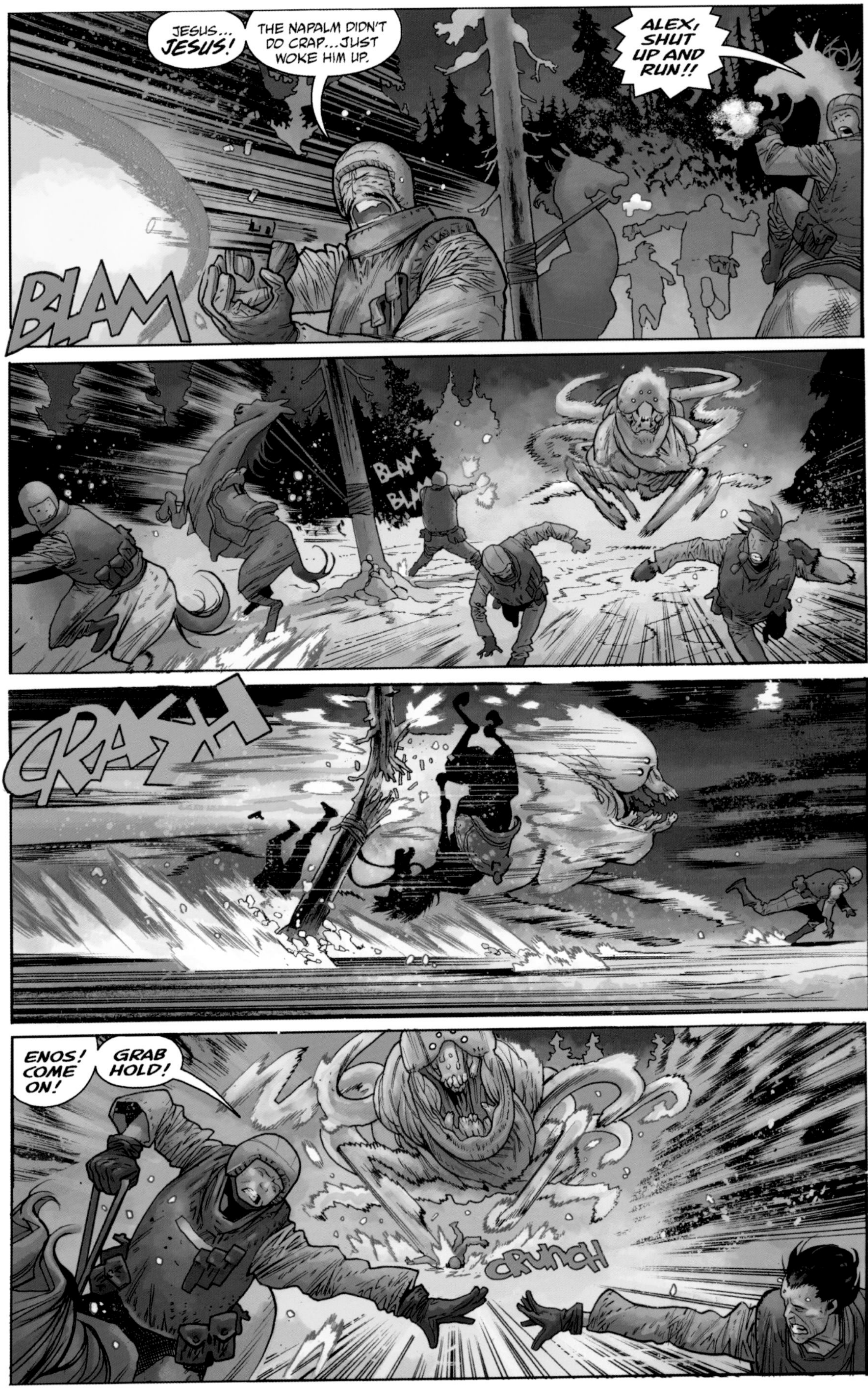
JESUS... JESUS!
THE NAPALM DIDN'T DO CRAP...JUST WOKE HIM UP.
ALEX, SHUT UP AND RUN!!
BLAM
BLAM
BLAM
CRASH
ENOS! COME ON!
GRAB HOLD!
CRUNCH

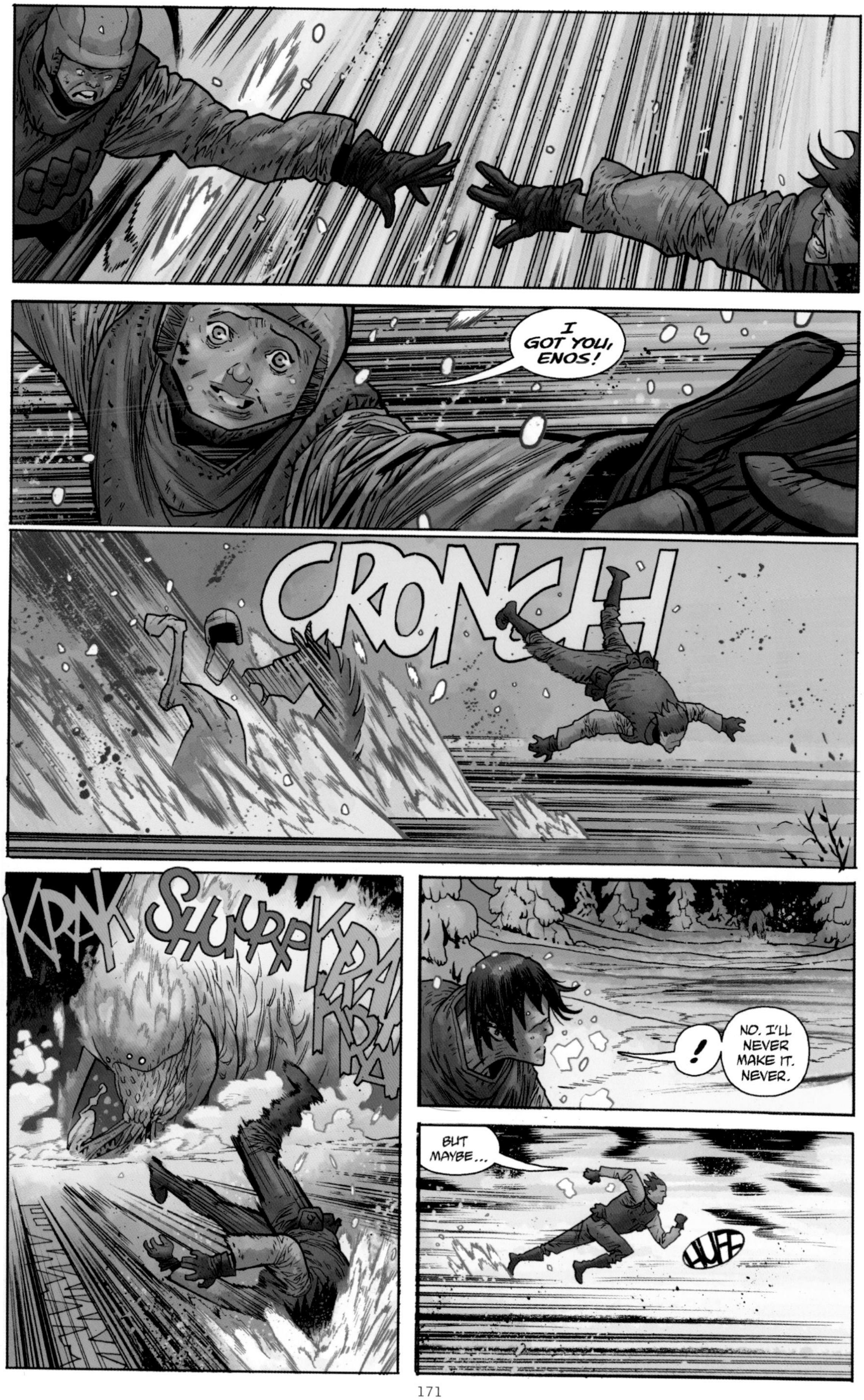
I GOT YOU, ENOS!
CRONCH
KRAK
SHURRP
KRAK
!
NO. I'LL NEVER MAKE IT. NEVER.
BUT MAYBE...
HUFF

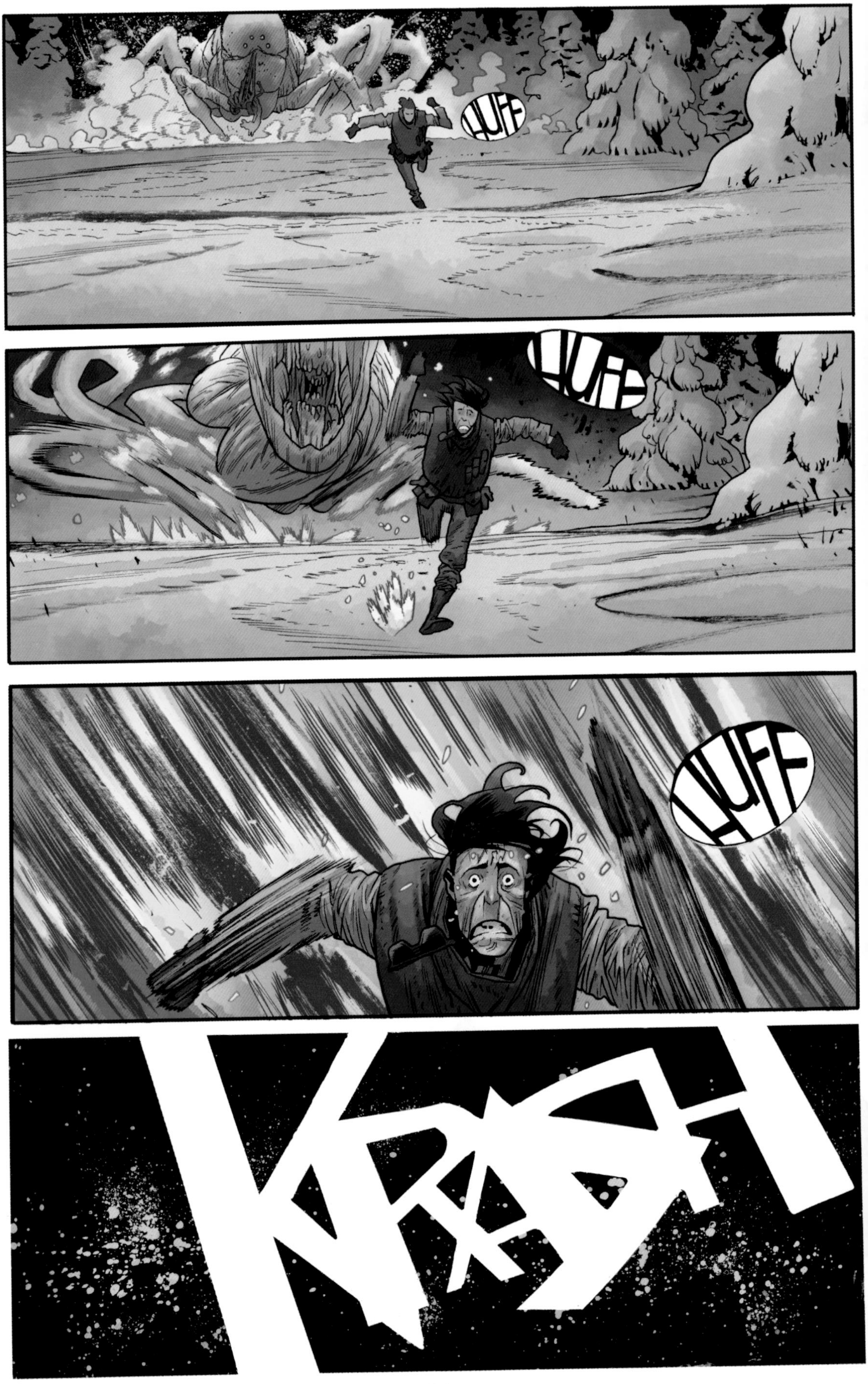
HUFF
HUFF
HUFF
KRASH

FLESH AND STONE CHAPTER THREE

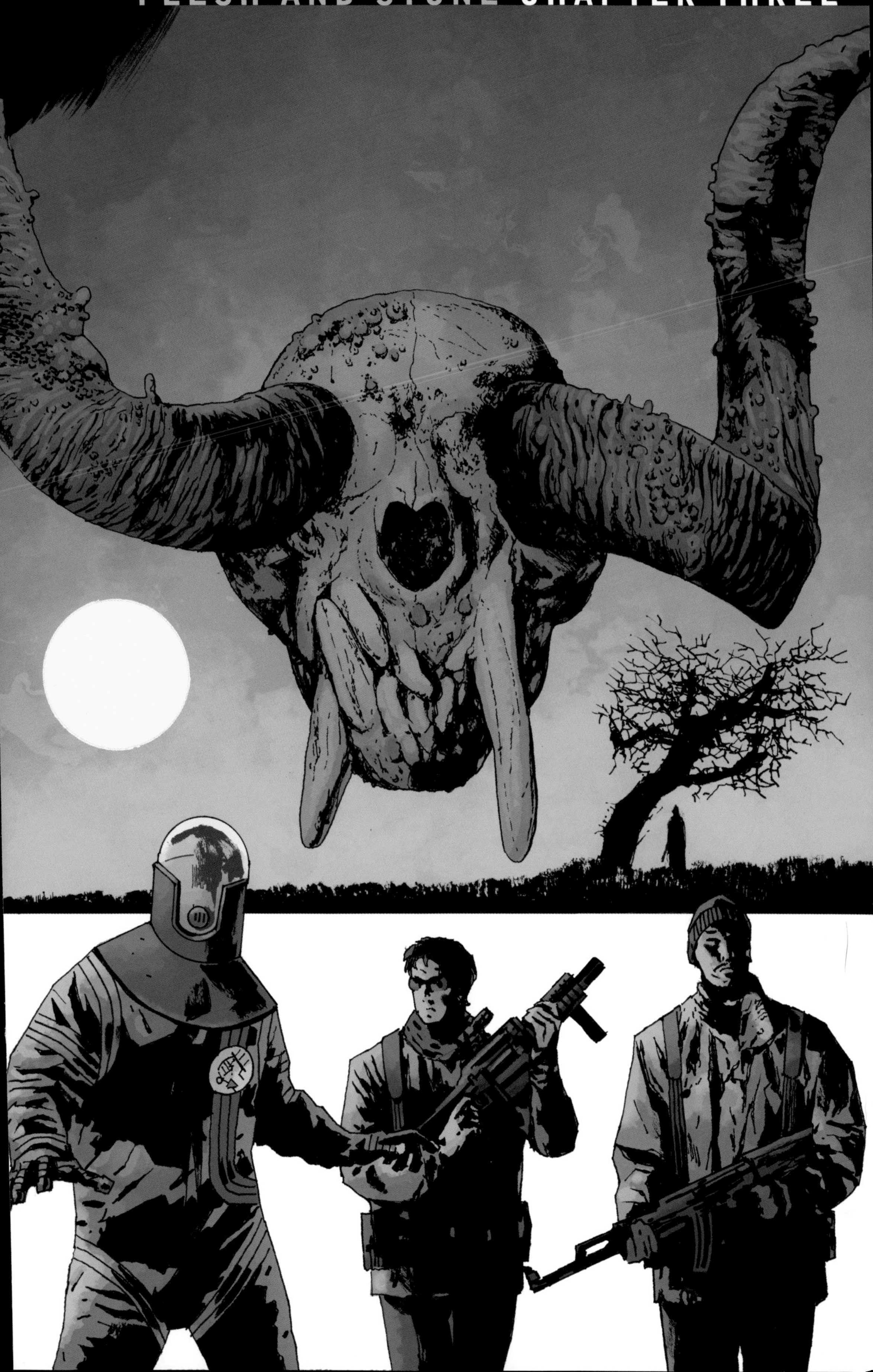

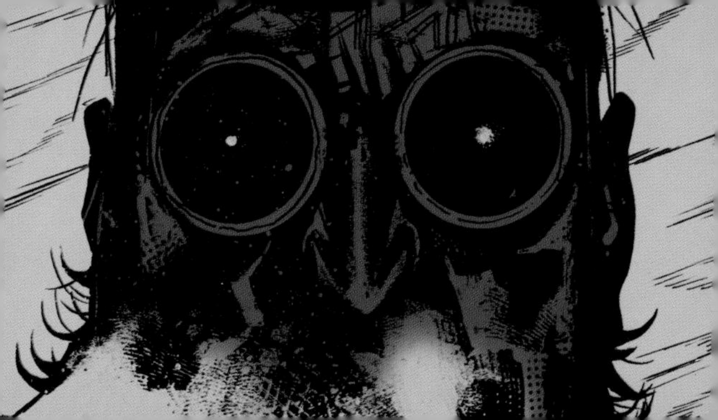

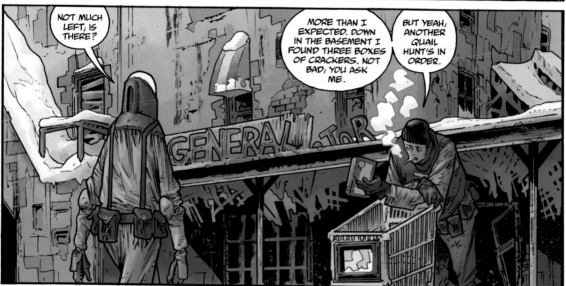

NOT MUCH LEFT, IS THERE?

MORE THAN I EXPECTED. DOWN IN THE BASEMENT I FOUND THREE BOXES OF CRACKERS. NOT BAD, YOU ASK ME.

BUT YEAH, ANOTHER QUAIL HUNT'S IN ORDER.

LISTEN, I'VE BEEN THINKING. WE DON'T **NEED** TO SEND A WHOLE SEARCH PARTY. I'LL DO IT ALONE.

LOOKING AT THE MAP, I SAW THESE VACATION HOMES UP IN THE HILLS--ALL ABANDONED NOW, OF COURSE. THAT'D BE A GOOD PLACE TO START LOOKING.

TIAN, ENOS'S SQUAD WAS TASKED WITH A THREE-DAY MISSION. THIS IS ONLY THE THIRD DAY.

AND I KNOW THE COMPLETE LACK OF RADIO CONTACT SOMEWHAT CHANGES THAT EQUATION. I AM CONCERNED.

BUT THEY ARE NOT YET, TECHNICALLY SPEAKING, MISSING. SO BEFORE I RISK ANY MORE PERSONNEL--

WAIT...

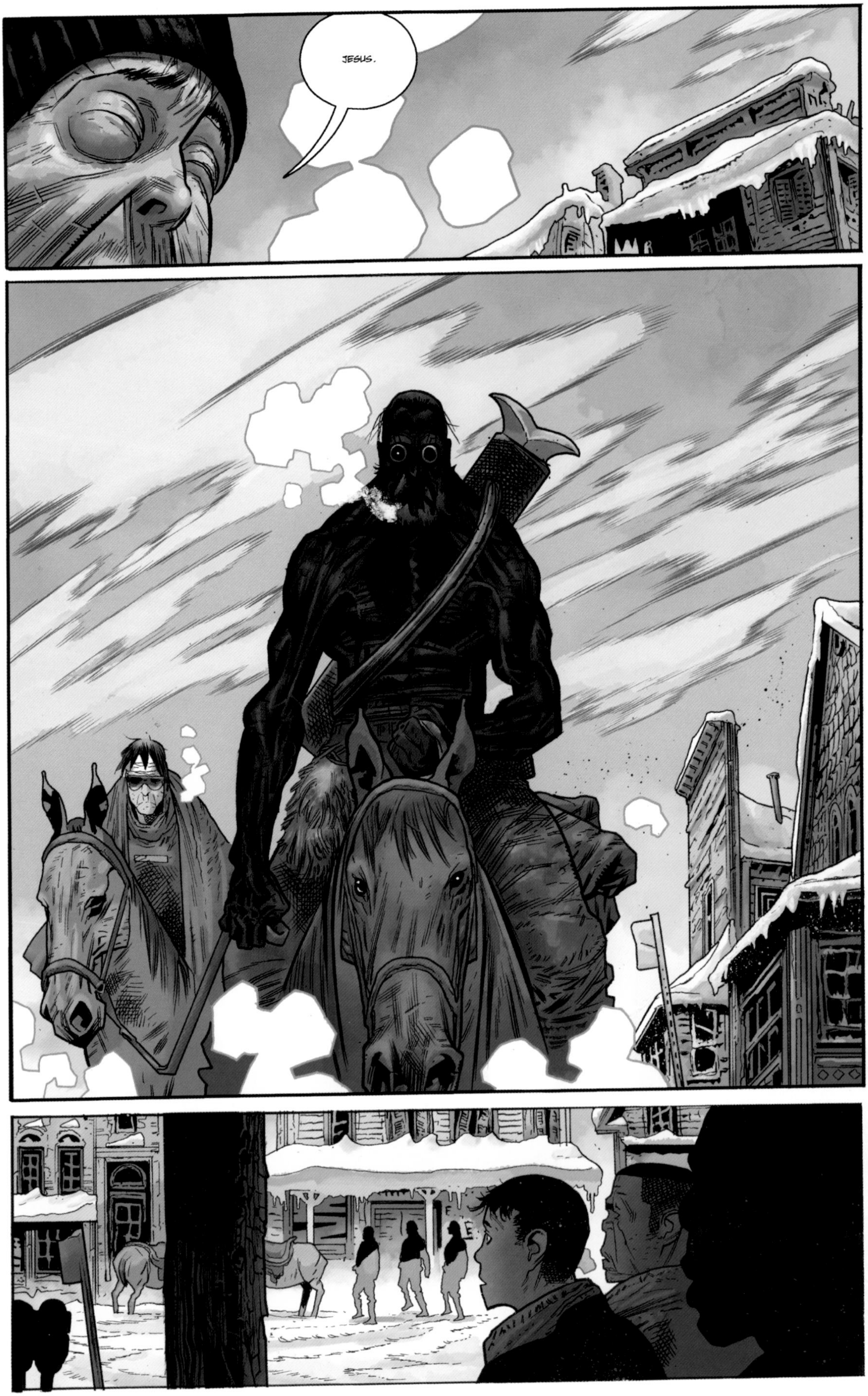
JESUS.

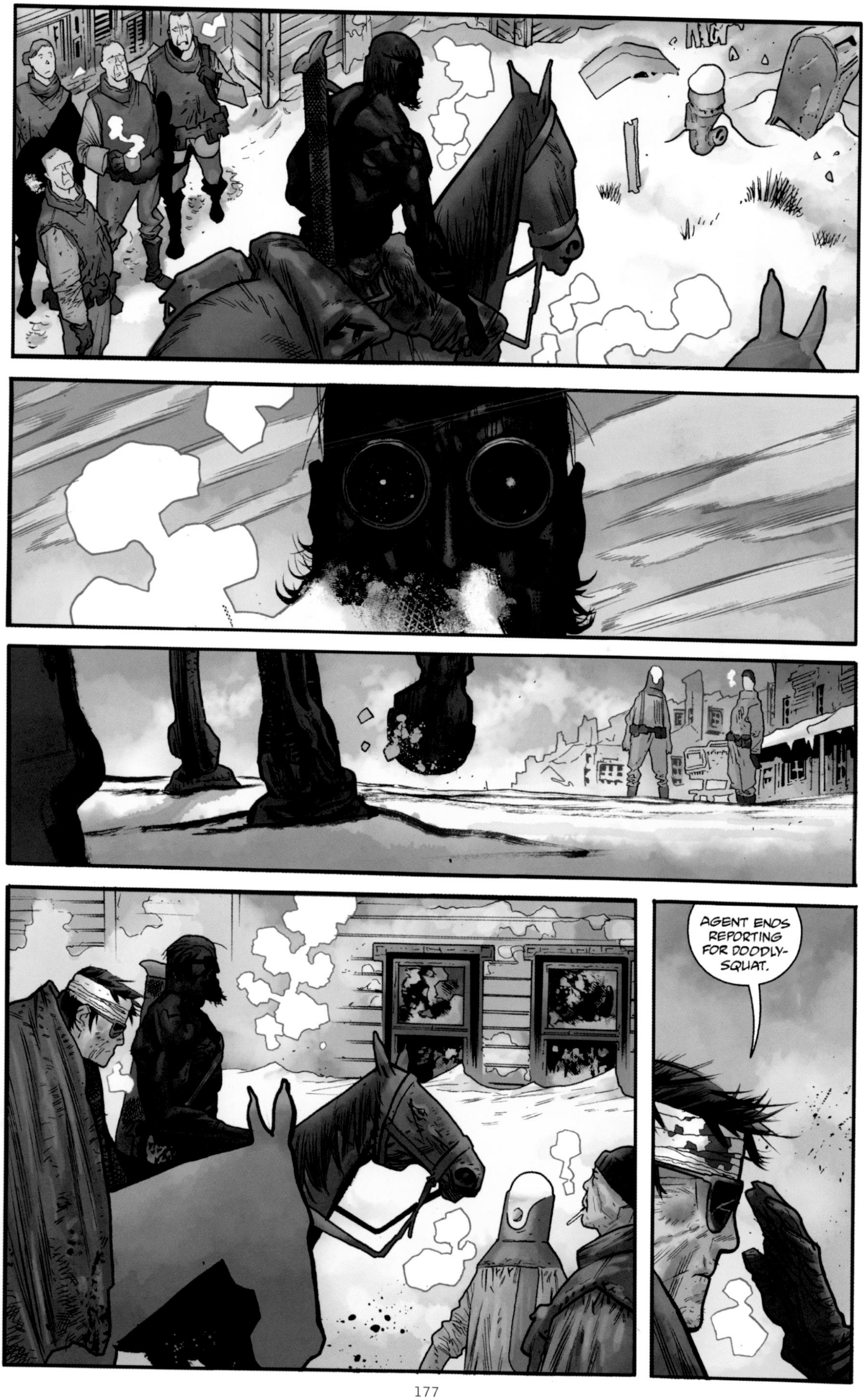
AGENT ENOS REPORTING FOR DOODLY-SQUAT.

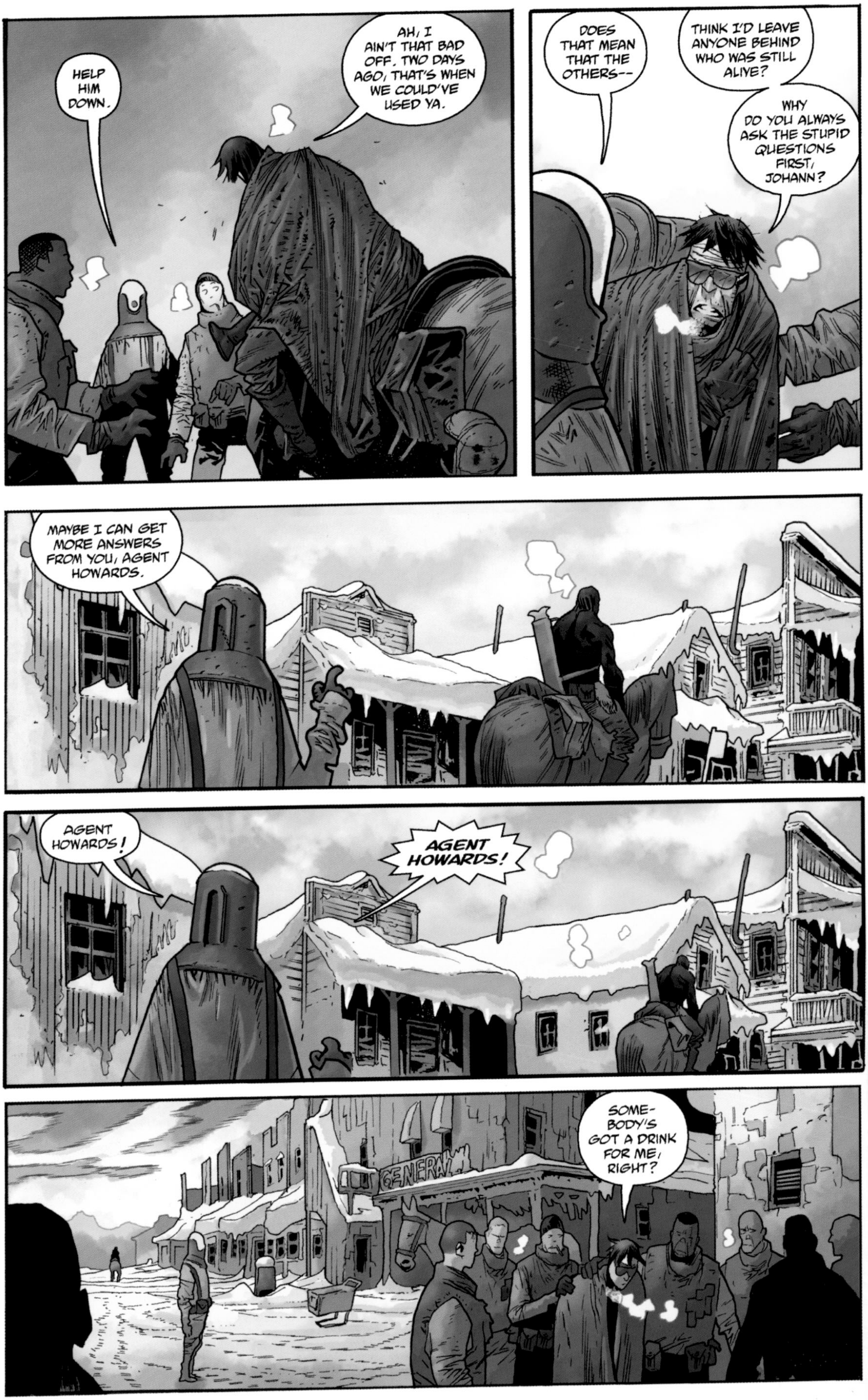

HELP HIM DOWN.
AH, I AIN'T THAT BAD OFF. TWO DAYS AGO, THAT'S WHEN WE COULD'VE USED YA.
DOES THAT MEAN THAT THE OTHERS--
THINK I'D LEAVE ANYONE BEHIND WHO WAS STILL ALIVE?
WHY DO YOU ALWAYS ASK THE STUPID QUESTIONS FIRST, JOHANN?
MAYBE I CAN GET MORE ANSWERS FROM YOU, AGENT HOWARDS.
AGENT HOWARDS!
AGENT HOWARDS!
GENERAL
SOME-BODY'S GOT A DRINK FOR ME, RIGHT?

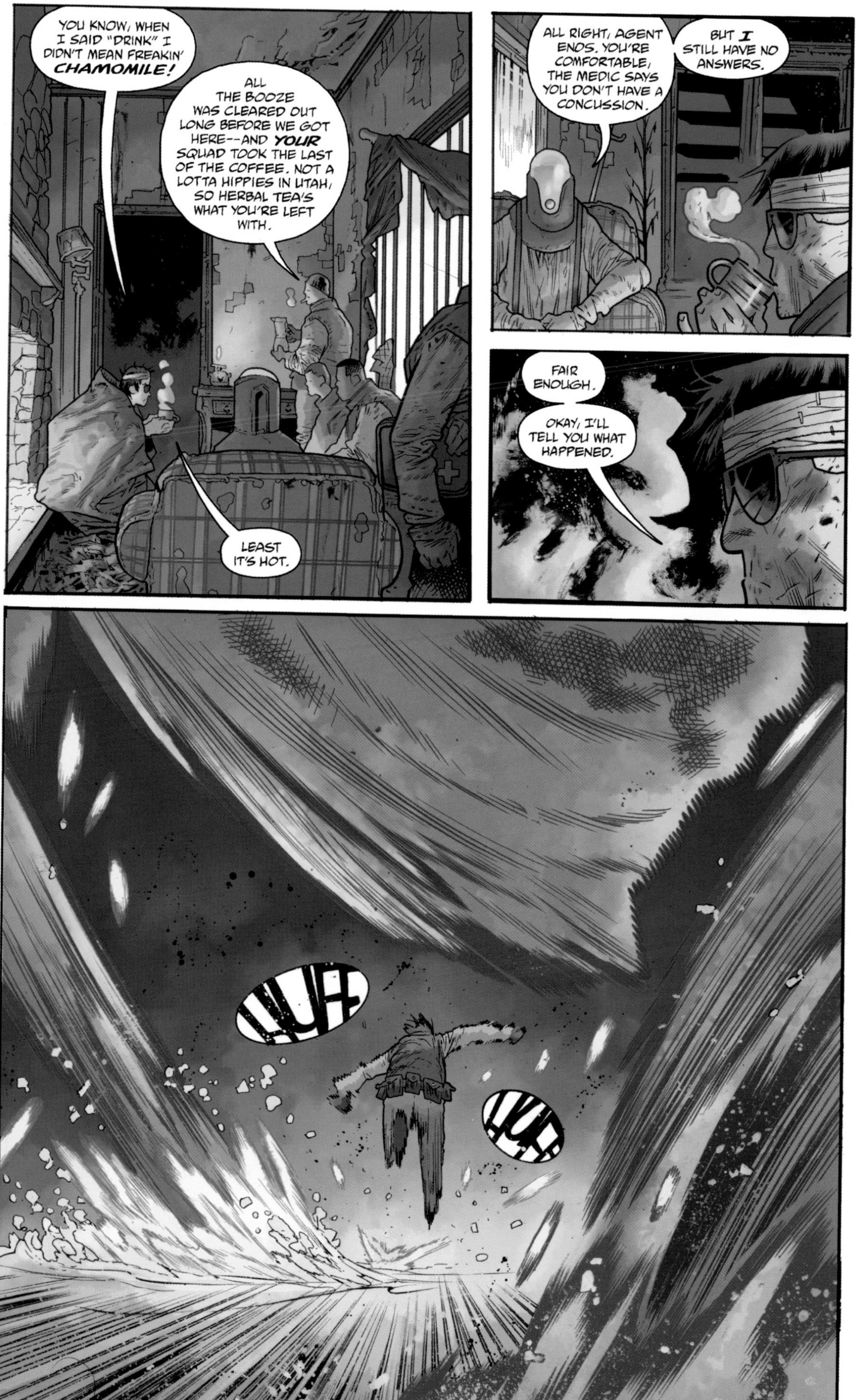
YOU KNOW, WHEN I SAID "DRINK" I DIDN'T MEAN FREAKIN' CHAMOMILE!
ALL THE BOOZE WAS CLEARED OUT LONG BEFORE WE GOT HERE--AND YOUR SQUAD TOOK THE LAST OF THE COFFEE. NOT A LOTTA HIPPIES IN UTAH, SO HERBAL TEA'S WHAT YOU'RE LEFT WITH.
LEAST IT'S HOT.
ALL RIGHT, AGENT ENOS. YOU'RE COMFORTABLE, THE MEDIC SAYS YOU DON'T HAVE A CONCUSSION.
BUT I STILL HAVE NO ANSWERS.
FAIR ENOUGH.
OKAY, I'LL TELL YOU WHAT HAPPENED.
HUF
HUF

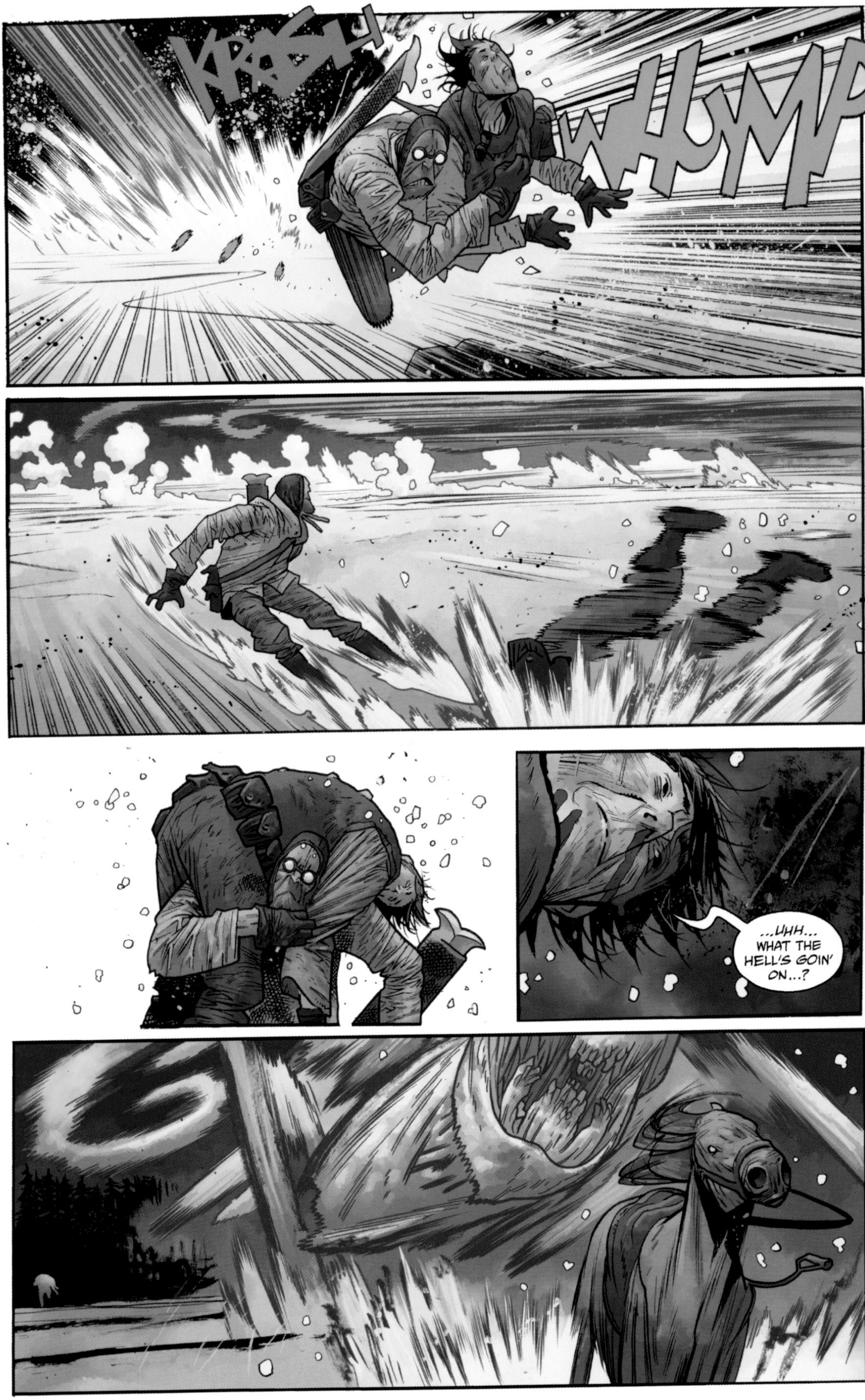
KRASH
WHUMP
...UHH... WHAT THE HELL'S GOIN' ON...?

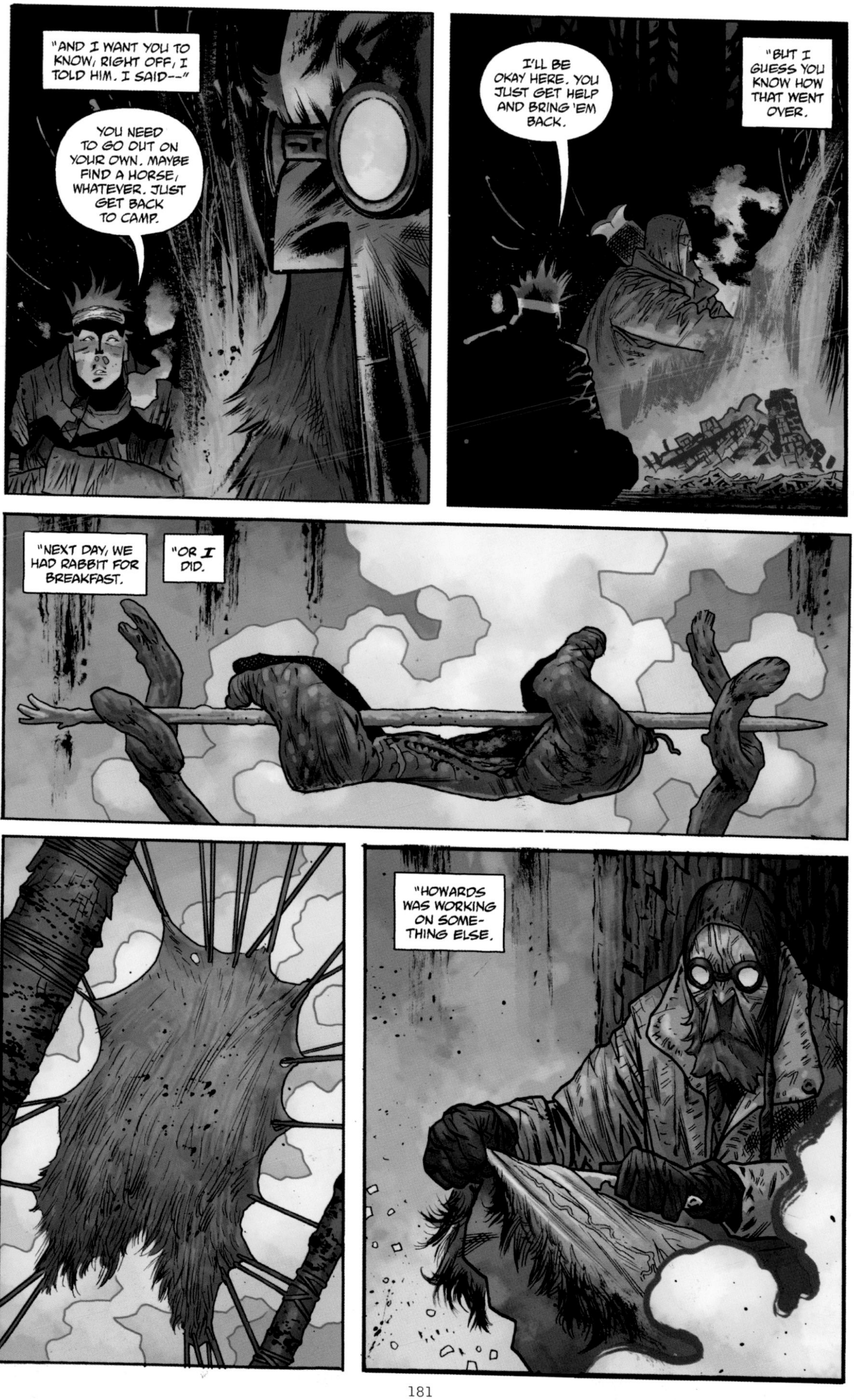
"AND I WANT YOU TO KNOW, RIGHT OFF, I TOLD HIM. I SAID--"
YOU NEED TO GO OUT ON YOUR OWN. MAYBE FIND A HORSE, WHATEVER. JUST GET BACK TO CAMP.
I'LL BE OKAY HERE. YOU JUST GET HELP AND BRING 'EM BACK.
"BUT I GUESS YOU KNOW HOW THAT WENT OVER.
"NEXT DAY, WE HAD RABBIT FOR BREAKFAST.
"OR I DID.
"HOWARDS WAS WORKING ON SOMETHING ELSE.

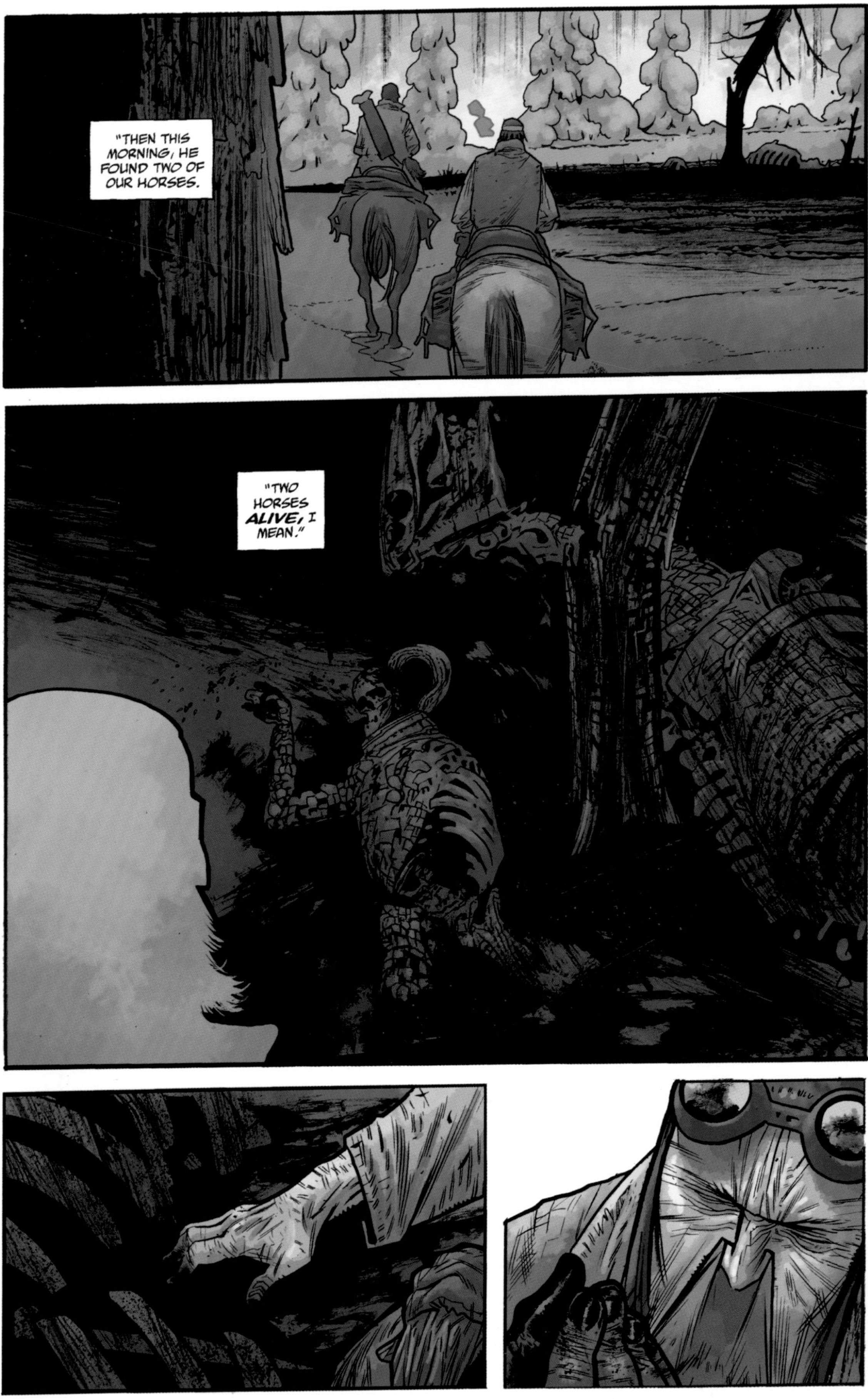
"THEN THIS MORNING, HE FOUND TWO OF OUR HORSES.
"TWO HORSES ALIVE, I MEAN."

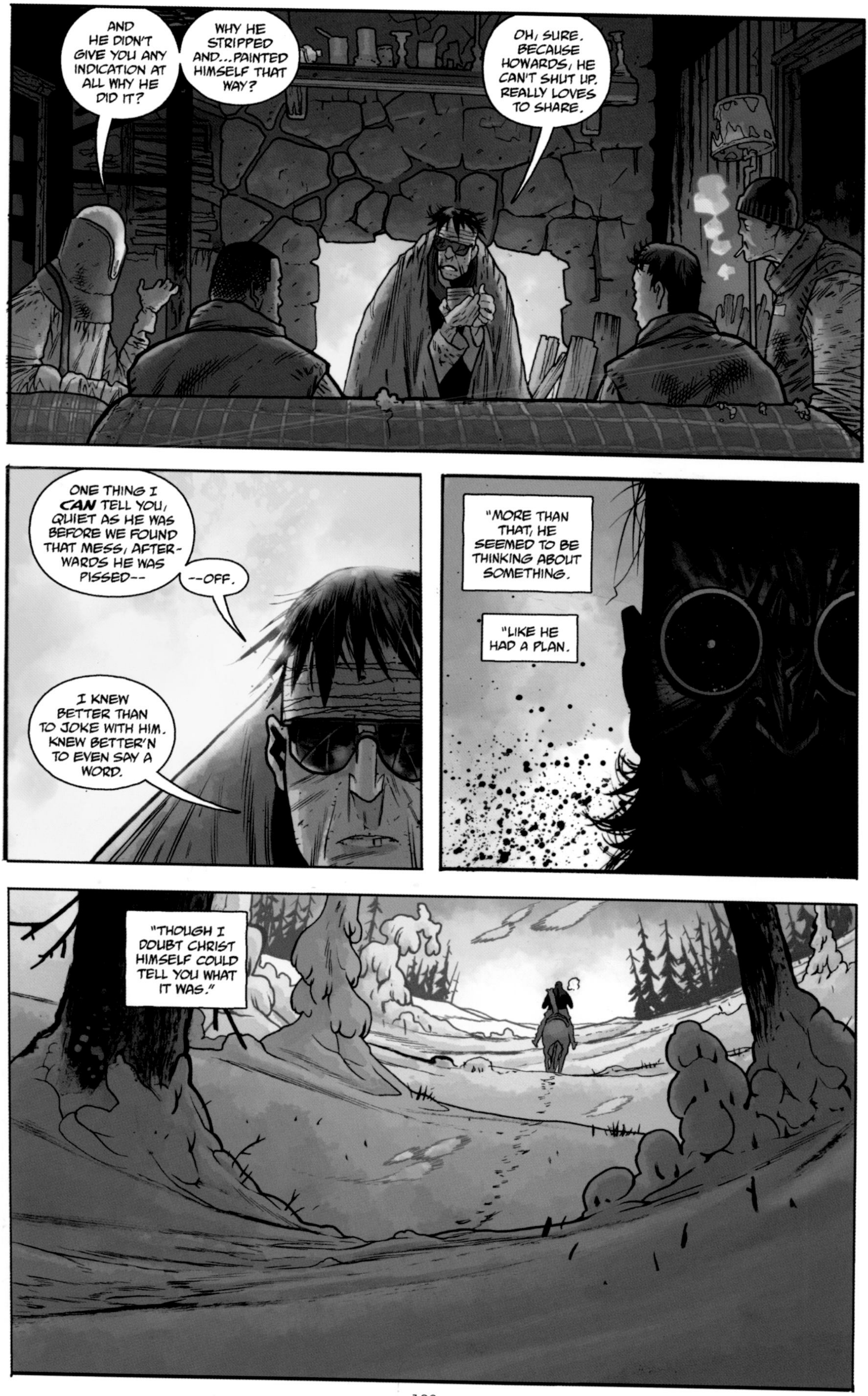
AND HE DIDN'T GIVE YOU ANY INDICATION AT ALL WHY HE DID IT?
WHY HE STRIPPED AND...PAINTED HIMSELF THAT WAY?
OH, SURE. BECAUSE HOWARDS, HE CAN'T SHUT UP. REALLY LOVES TO SHARE.
ONE THING I CAN TELL YOU, QUIET AS HE WAS BEFORE WE FOUND THAT MESS, AFTER-WARDS HE WAS PISSED--
--OFF.
I KNEW BETTER THAN TO JOKE WITH HIM. KNEW BETTER'N TO EVEN SAY A WORD.
"MORE THAN THAT, HE SEEMED TO BE THINKING ABOUT SOMETHING.
"LIKE HE HAD A PLAN.
"THOUGH I DOUBT CHRIST HIMSELF COULD TELL YOU WHAT IT WAS."

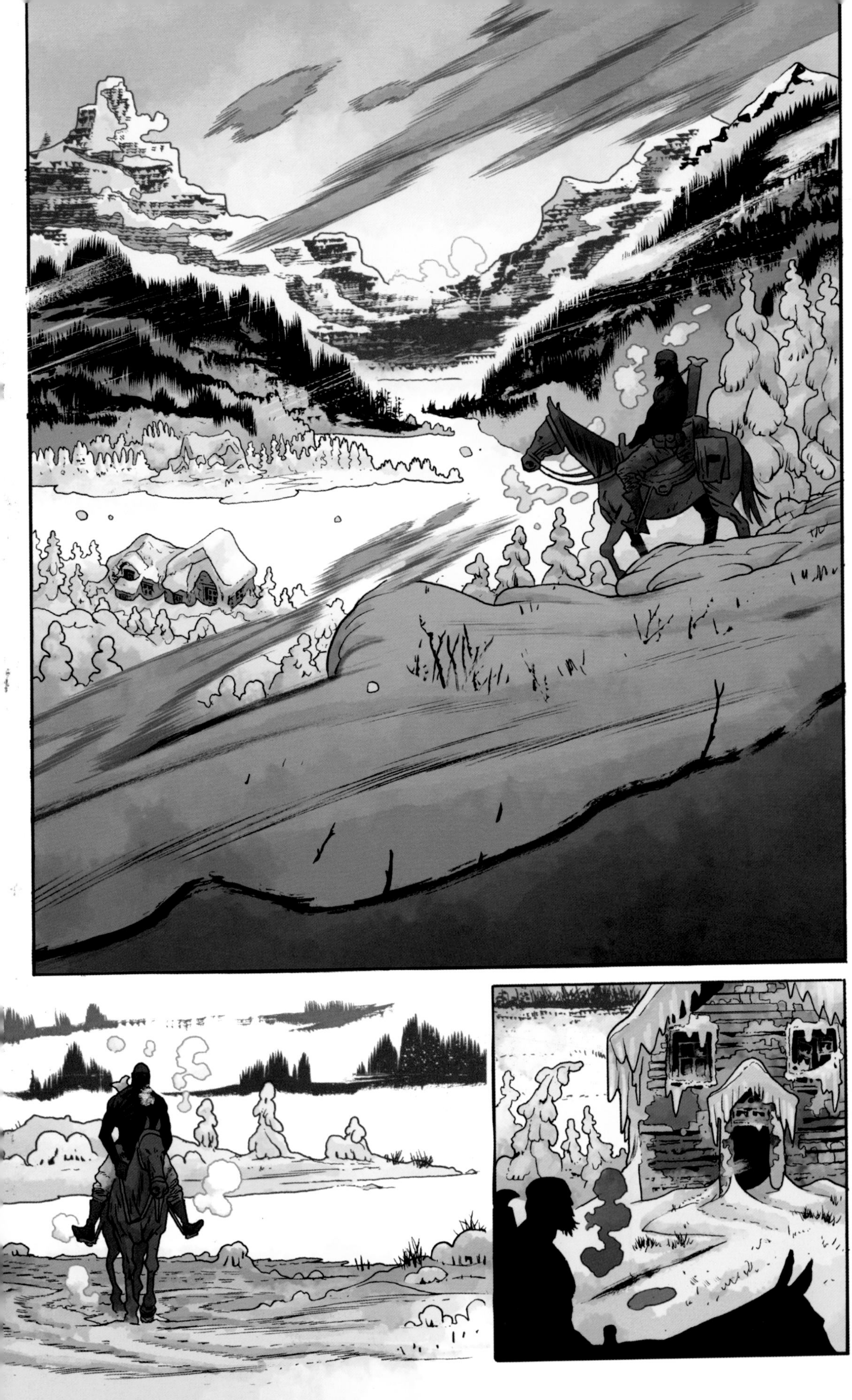

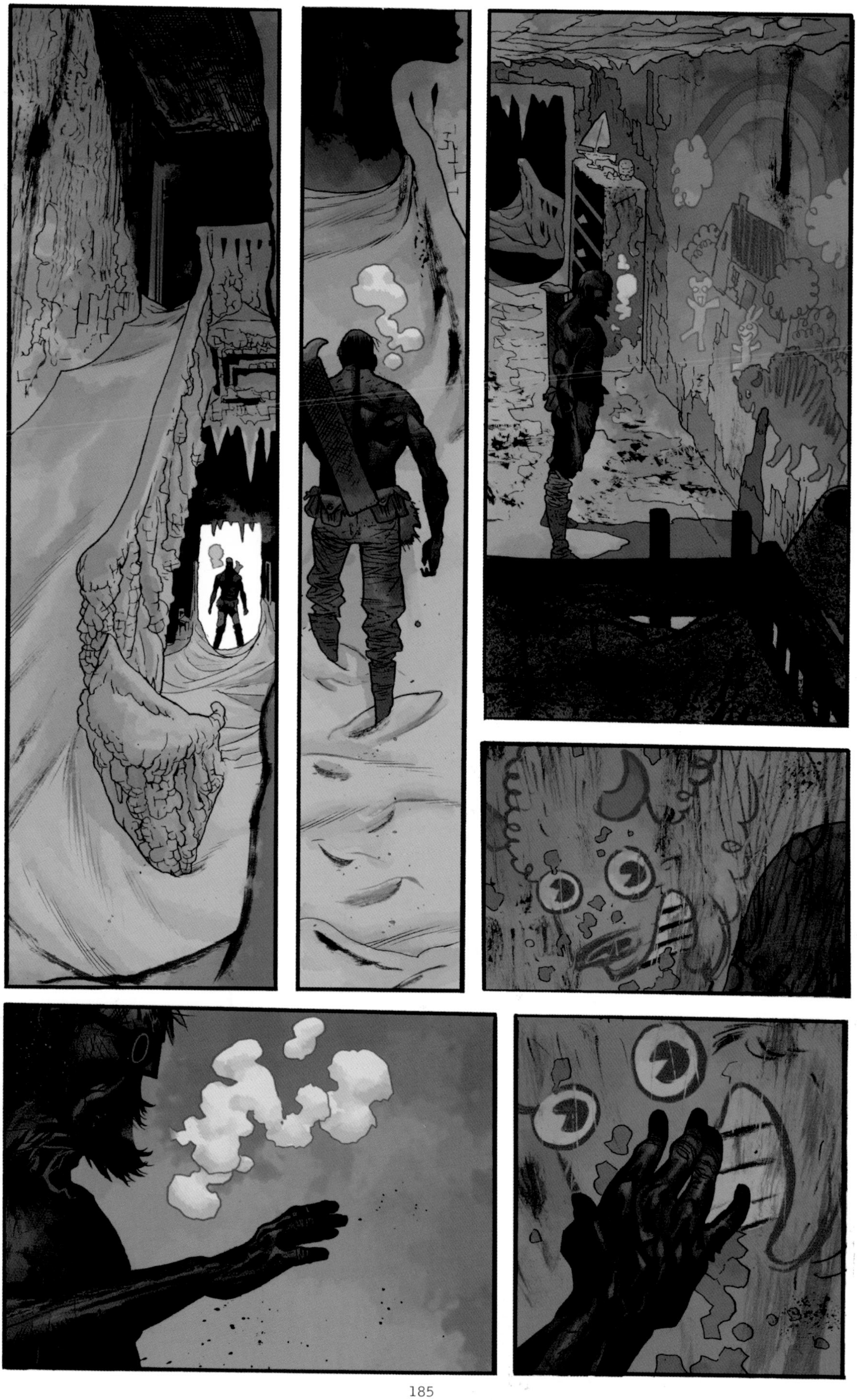

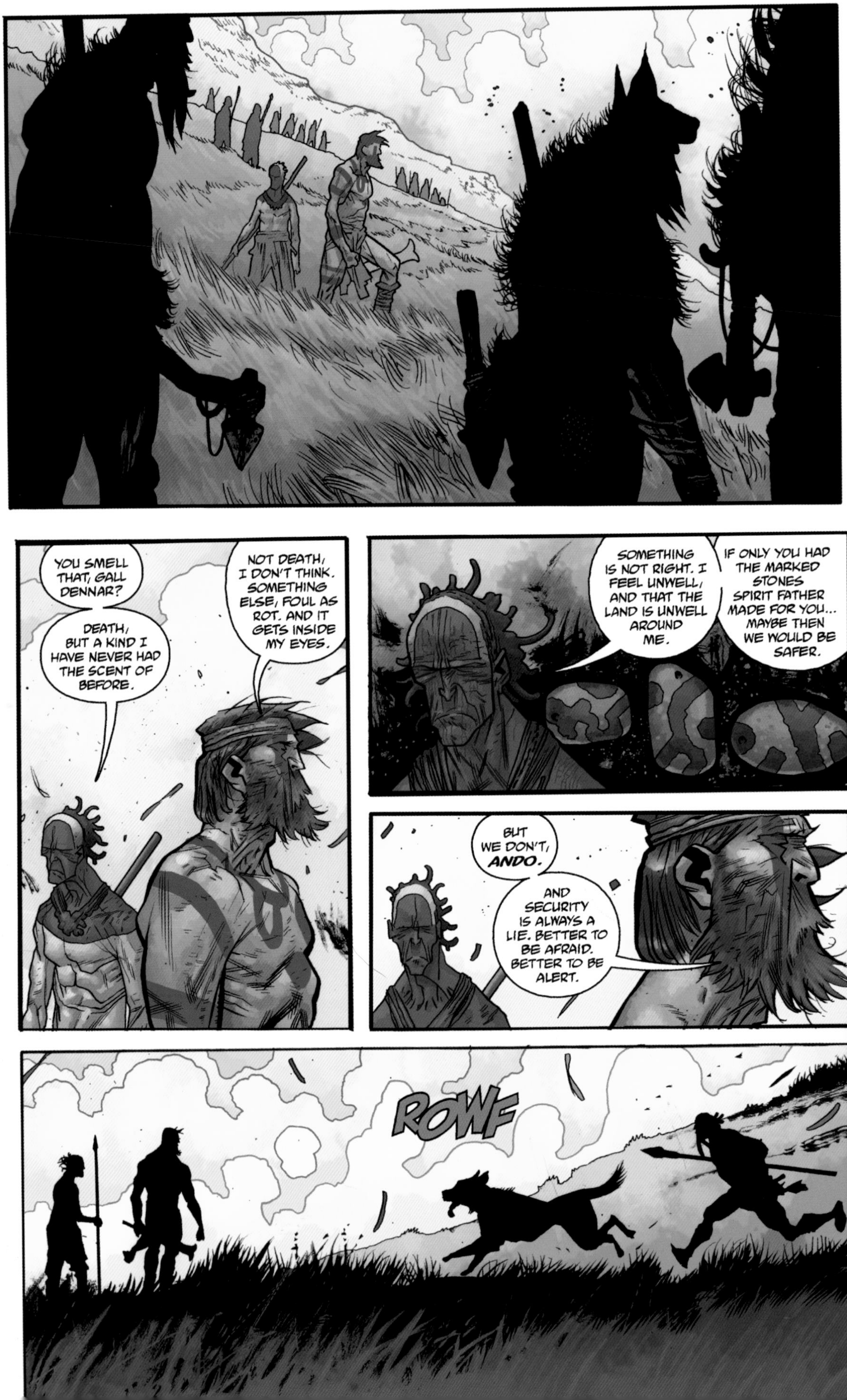
YOU SMELL THAT, GALL DENNAR?
DEATH, BUT A KIND I HAVE NEVER HAD THE SCENT OF BEFORE.
NOT DEATH, I DON'T THINK. SOMETHING ELSE, FOUL AS ROT. AND IT GETS INSIDE MY EYES.
SOMETHING IS NOT RIGHT. I FEEL UNWELL, AND THAT THE LAND IS UNWELL AROUND ME.
IF ONLY YOU HAD THE MARKED STONES SPIRIT FATHER MADE FOR YOU... MAYBE THEN WE WOULD BE SAFER.
BUT WE DON'T, ***ANDO***.
AND SECURITY IS ALWAYS A LIE. BETTER TO BE AFRAID. BETTER TO BE ALERT.
ROWF

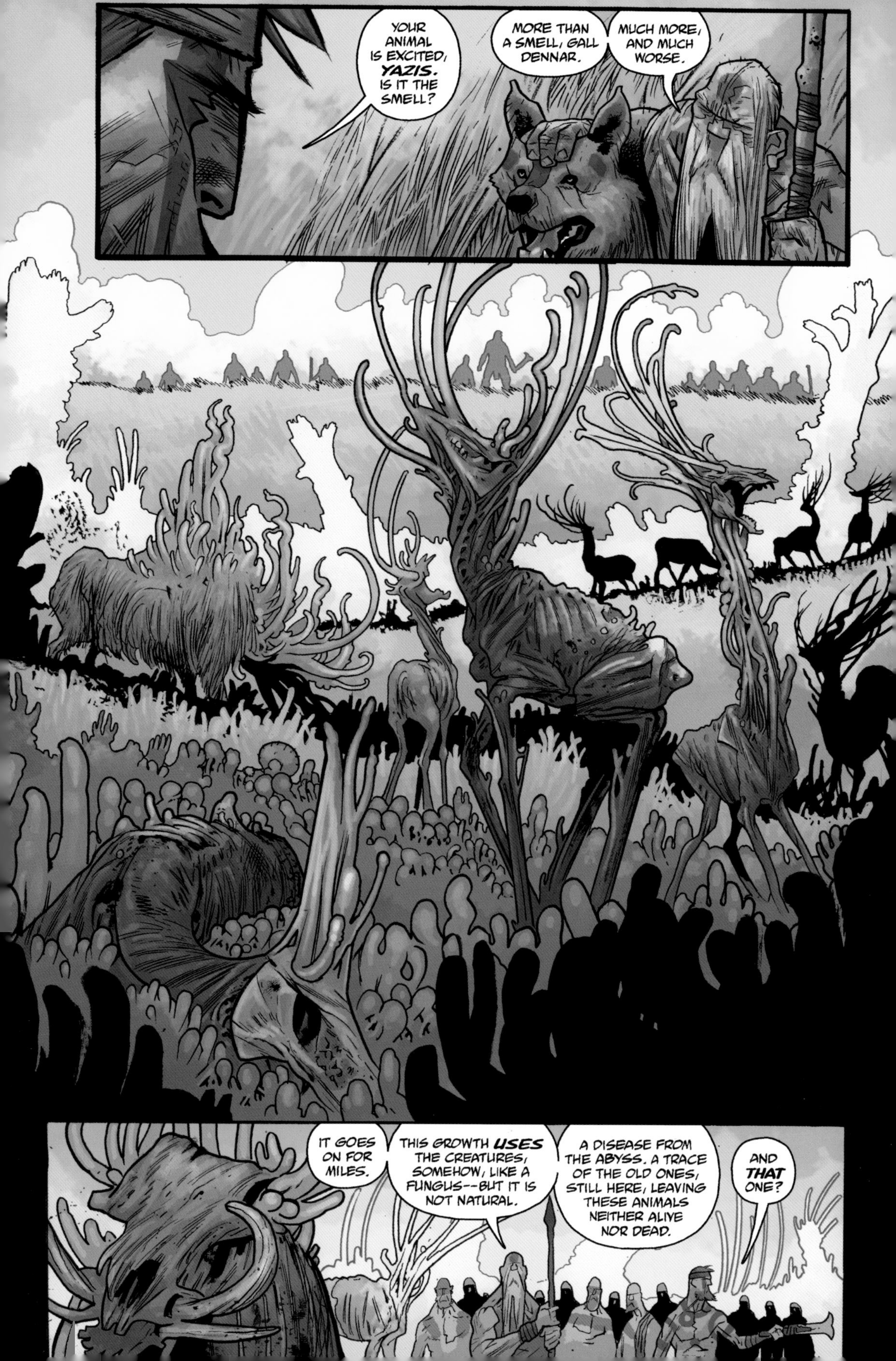
YOUR ANIMAL IS EXCITED, YAZIS. IS IT THE SMELL?
MORE THAN A SMELL, GALL DENNAR.
MUCH MORE, AND MUCH WORSE.
IT GOES ON FOR MILES.
THIS GROWTH USES THE CREATURES, SOMEHOW, LIKE A FUNGUS--BUT IT IS NOT NATURAL.
A DISEASE FROM THE ABYSS. A TRACE OF THE OLD ONES, STILL HERE, LEAVING THESE ANIMALS NEITHER ALIVE NOR DEAD.
AND THAT ONE?

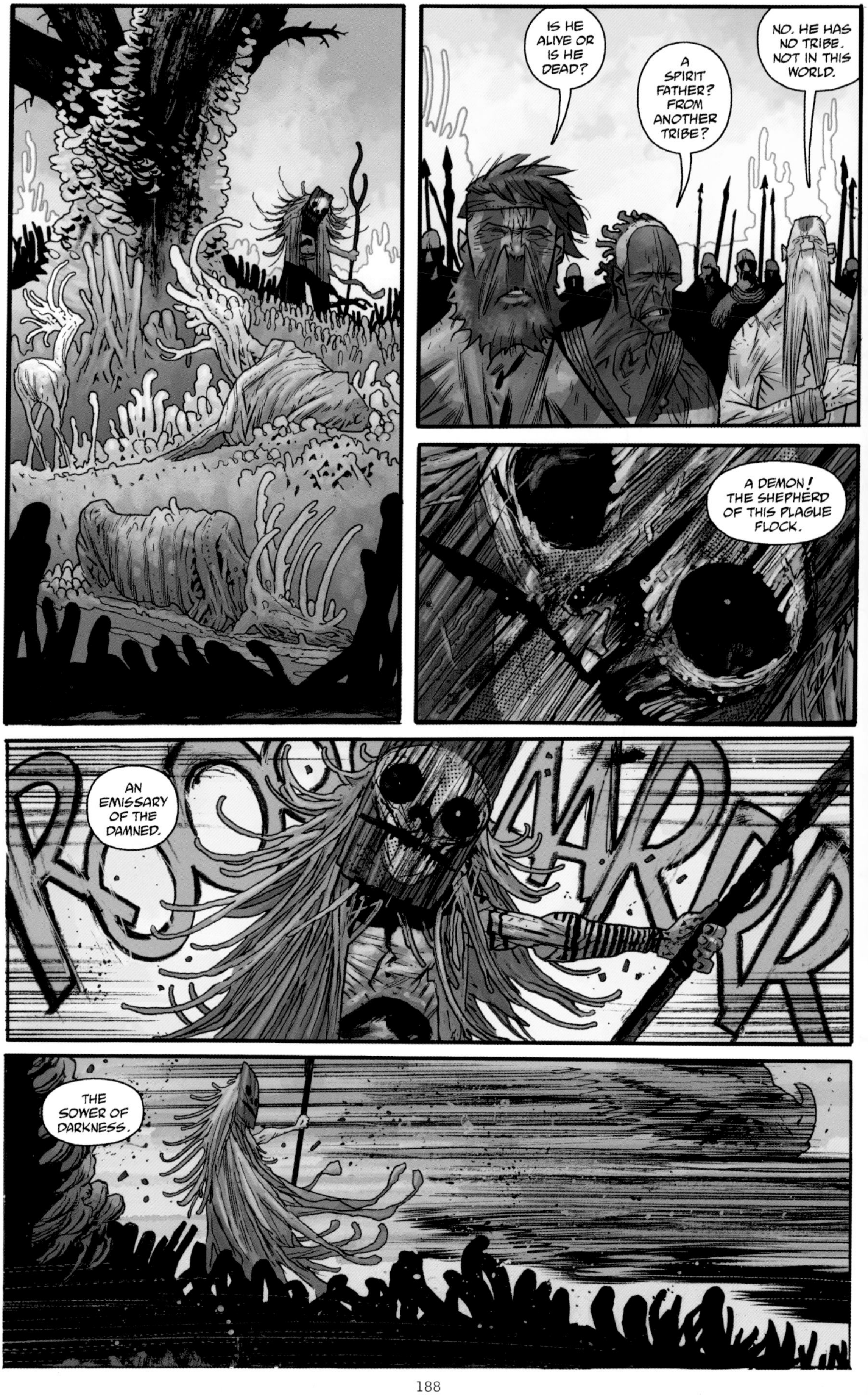
IS HE ALIVE OR IS HE DEAD?
A SPIRIT FATHER? FROM ANOTHER TRIBE?
NO. HE HAS NO TRIBE. NOT IN THIS WORLD.
A DEMON! THE SHEPHERD OF THIS PLAGUE FLOCK.
AN EMISSARY OF THE DAMNED.
THE SOWER OF DARKNESS.

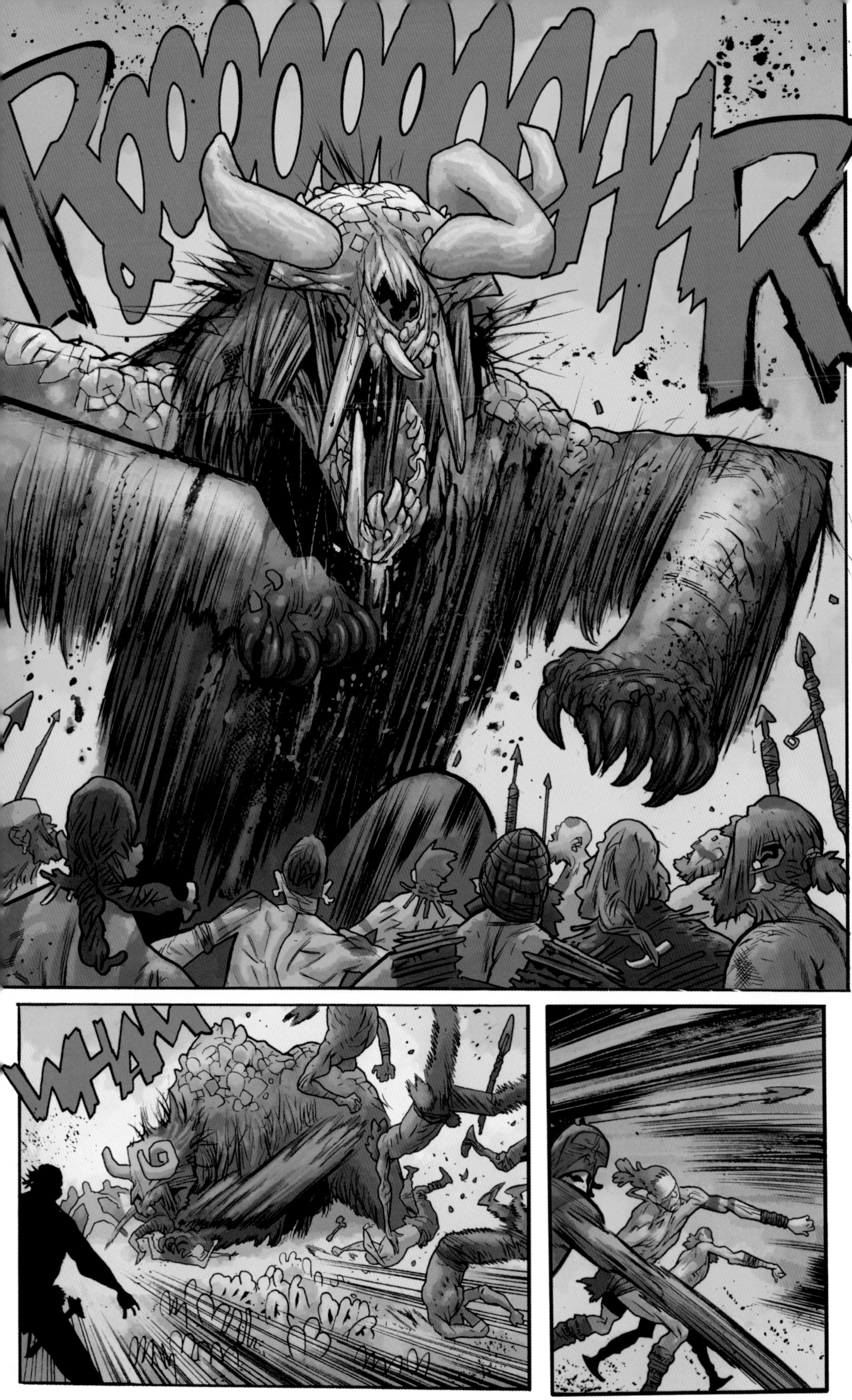
ROOOOOOOOAAR
WHAM

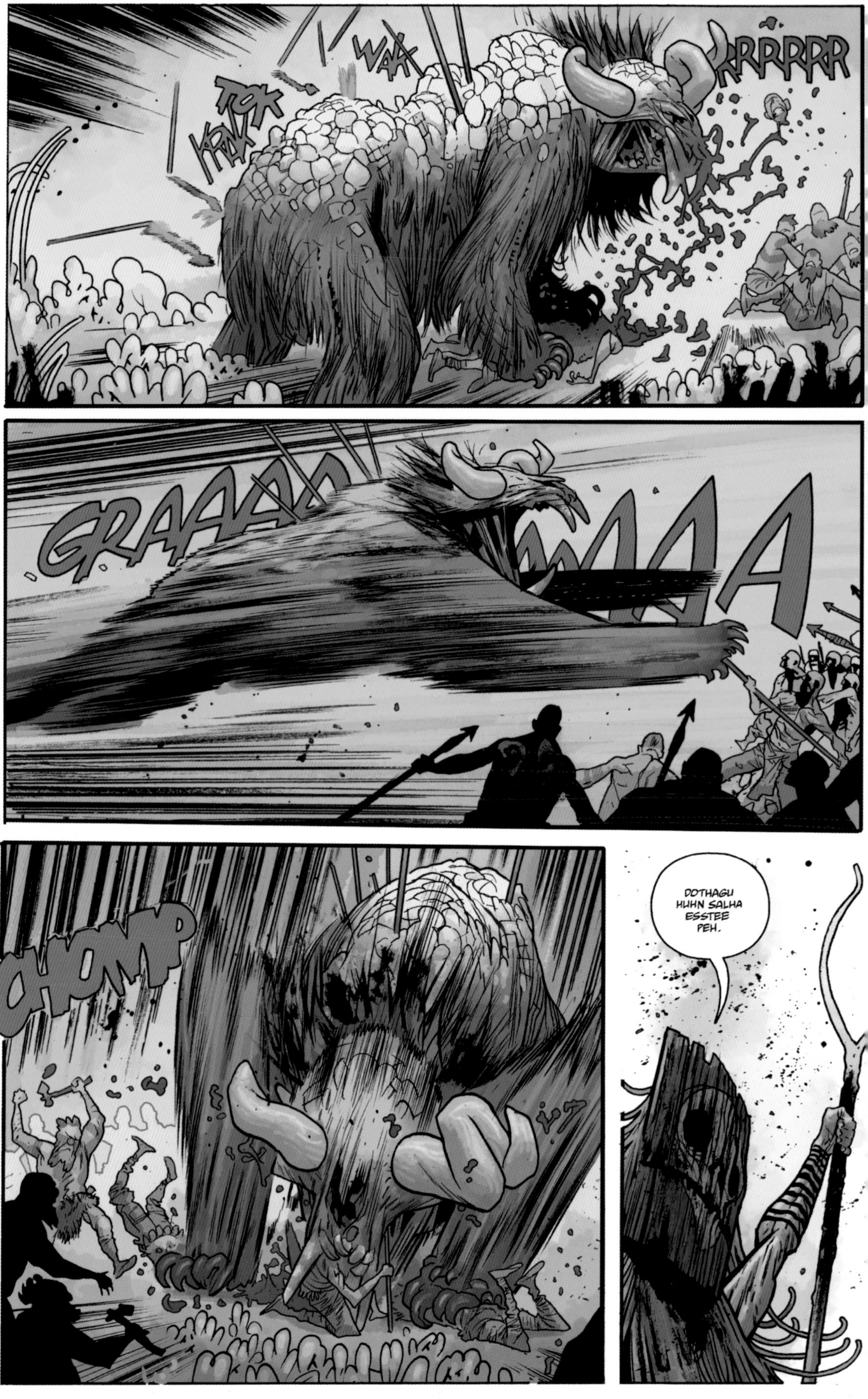
TOK
KRAK
WAK
RRRRRR
GRAAAAAAAAAA
CHOMP
DOTHAGU HUHN SALHA ESSTEE PEH.

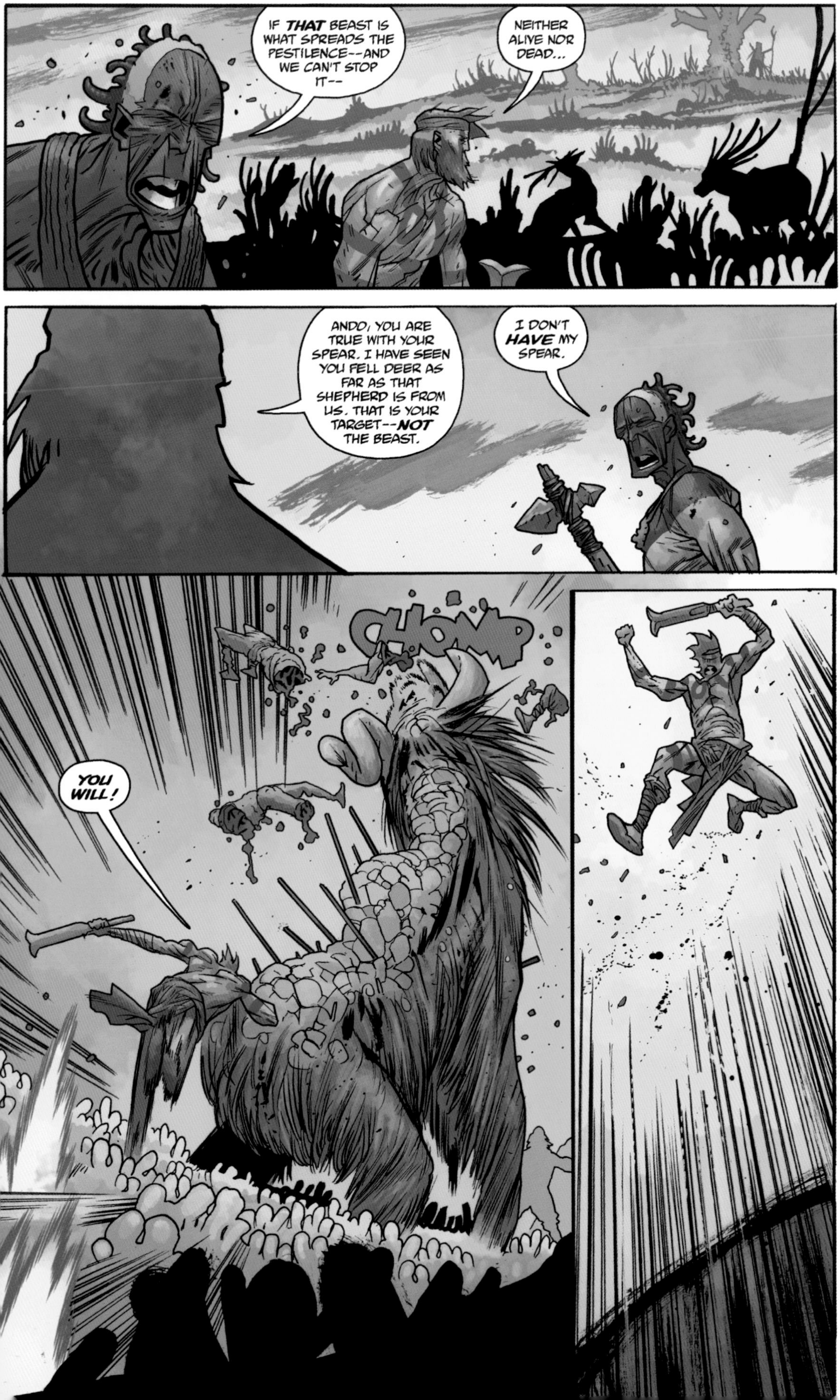
IF THAT BEAST IS WHAT SPREADS THE PESTILENCE--AND WE CAN'T STOP IT--
NEITHER ALIVE NOR DEAD...
ANDO, YOU ARE TRUE WITH YOUR SPEAR. I HAVE SEEN YOU FELL DEER AS FAR AS THAT SHEPHERD IS FROM US. THAT IS YOUR TARGET--NOT THE BEAST.
I DON'T HAVE MY SPEAR.
CHOMP
YOU WILL!

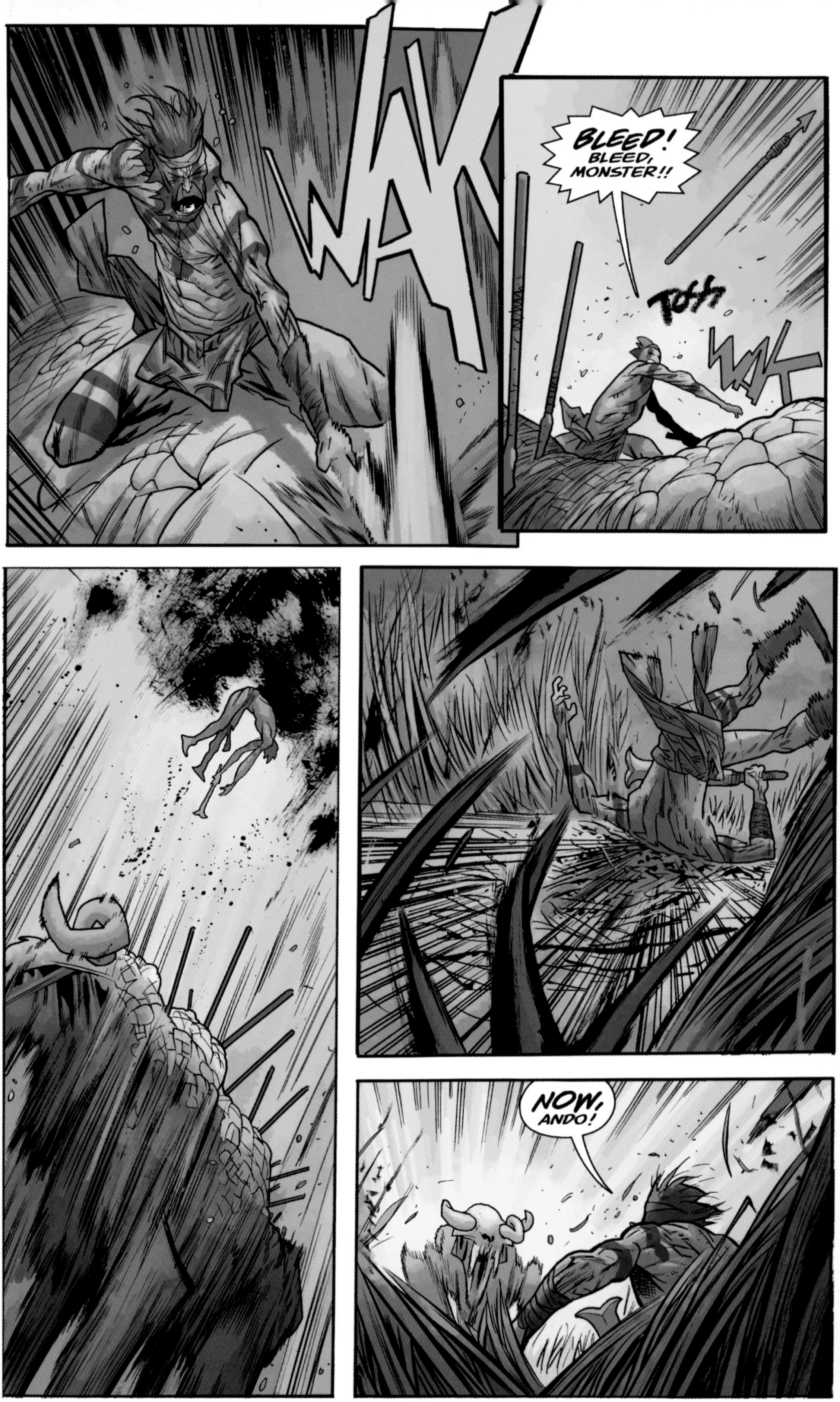
WAK
BLEED! BLEED, MONSTER!!
TOSS
WAK
NOW, ANDO!

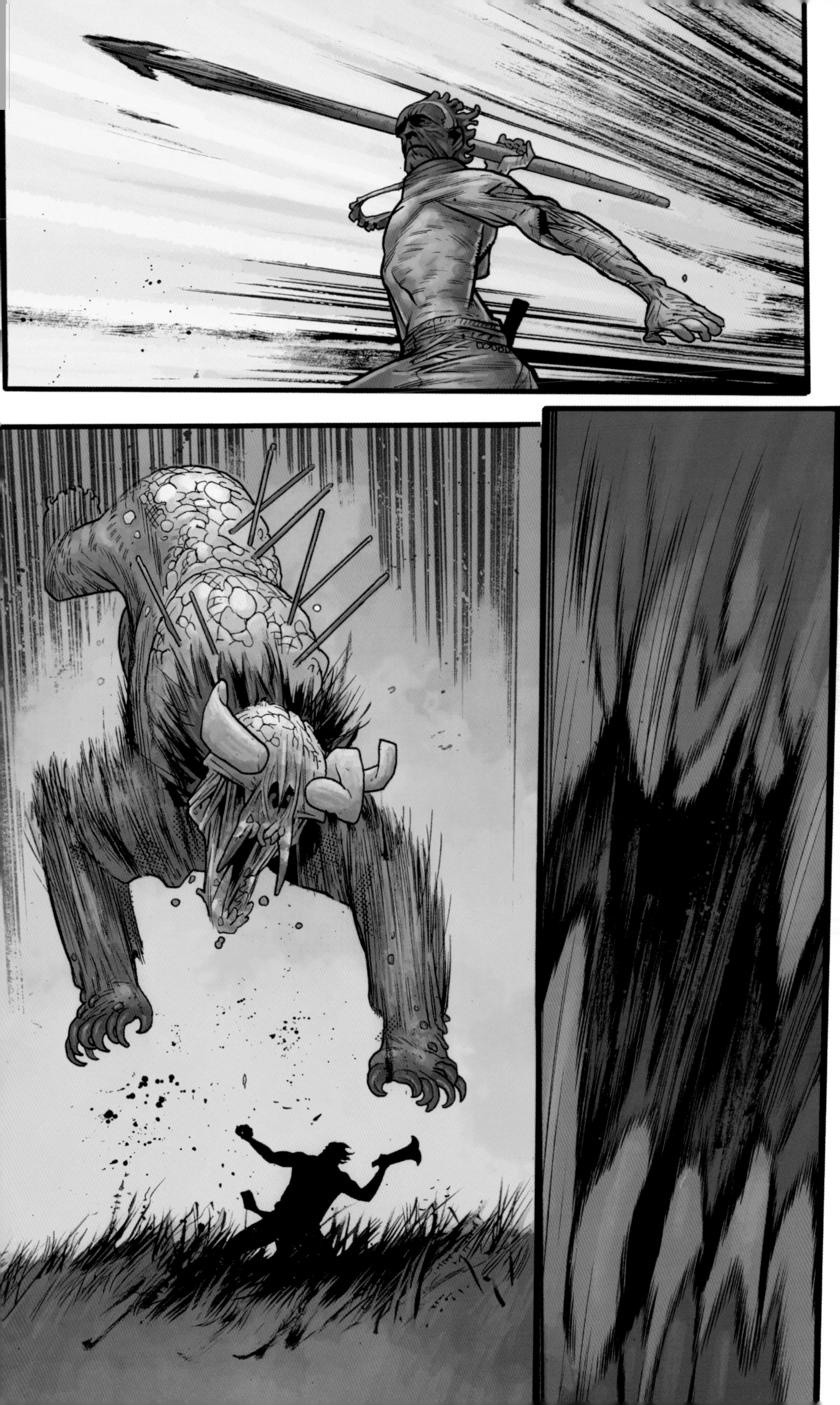

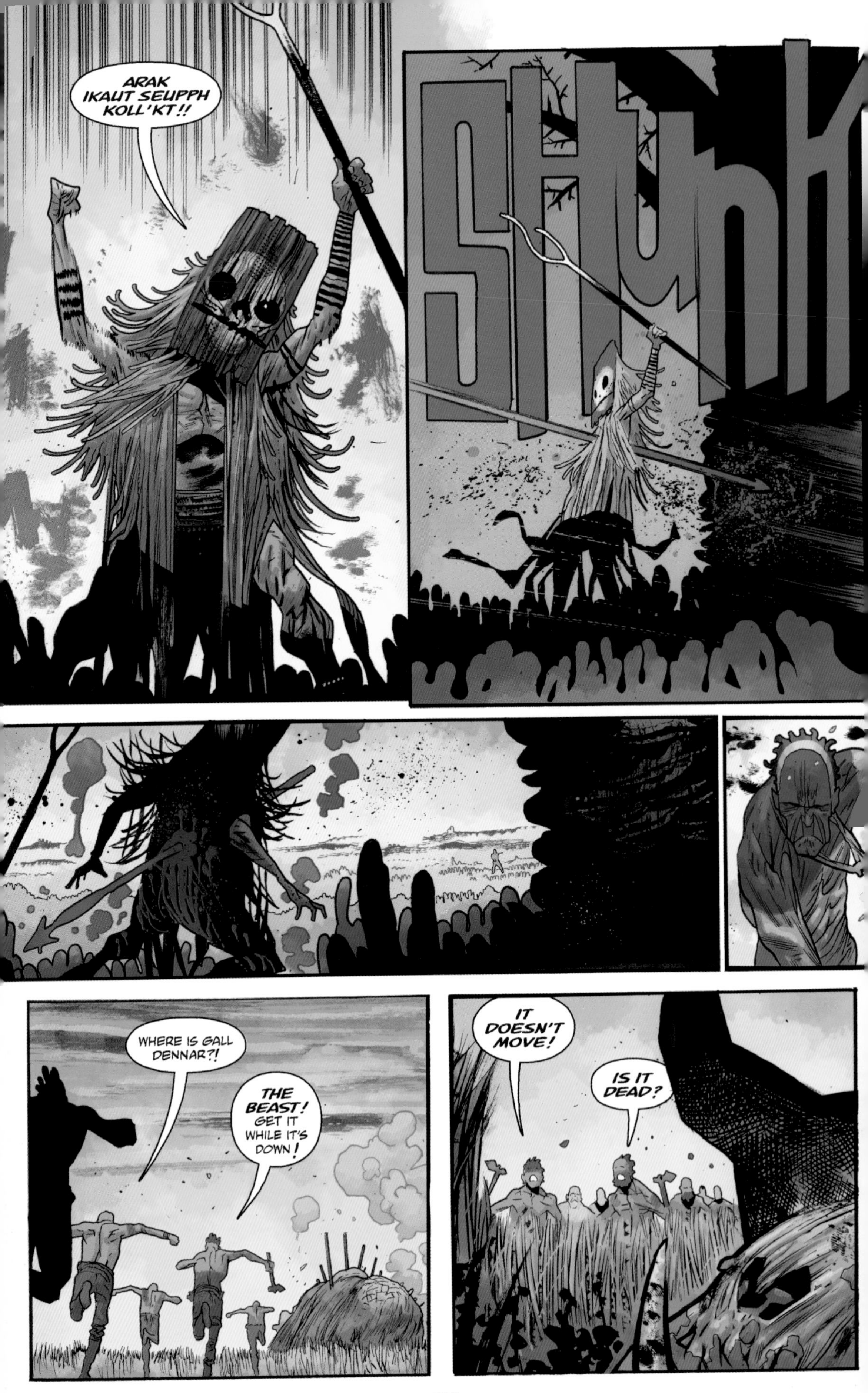
ARAK IKAUT SEUPPH KOLL'KT!!
SHUNK
WHERE IS GALL DENNAR?!
THE BEAST! GET IT WHILE IT'S DOWN!
IT DOESN'T MOVE!
IS IT DEAD?

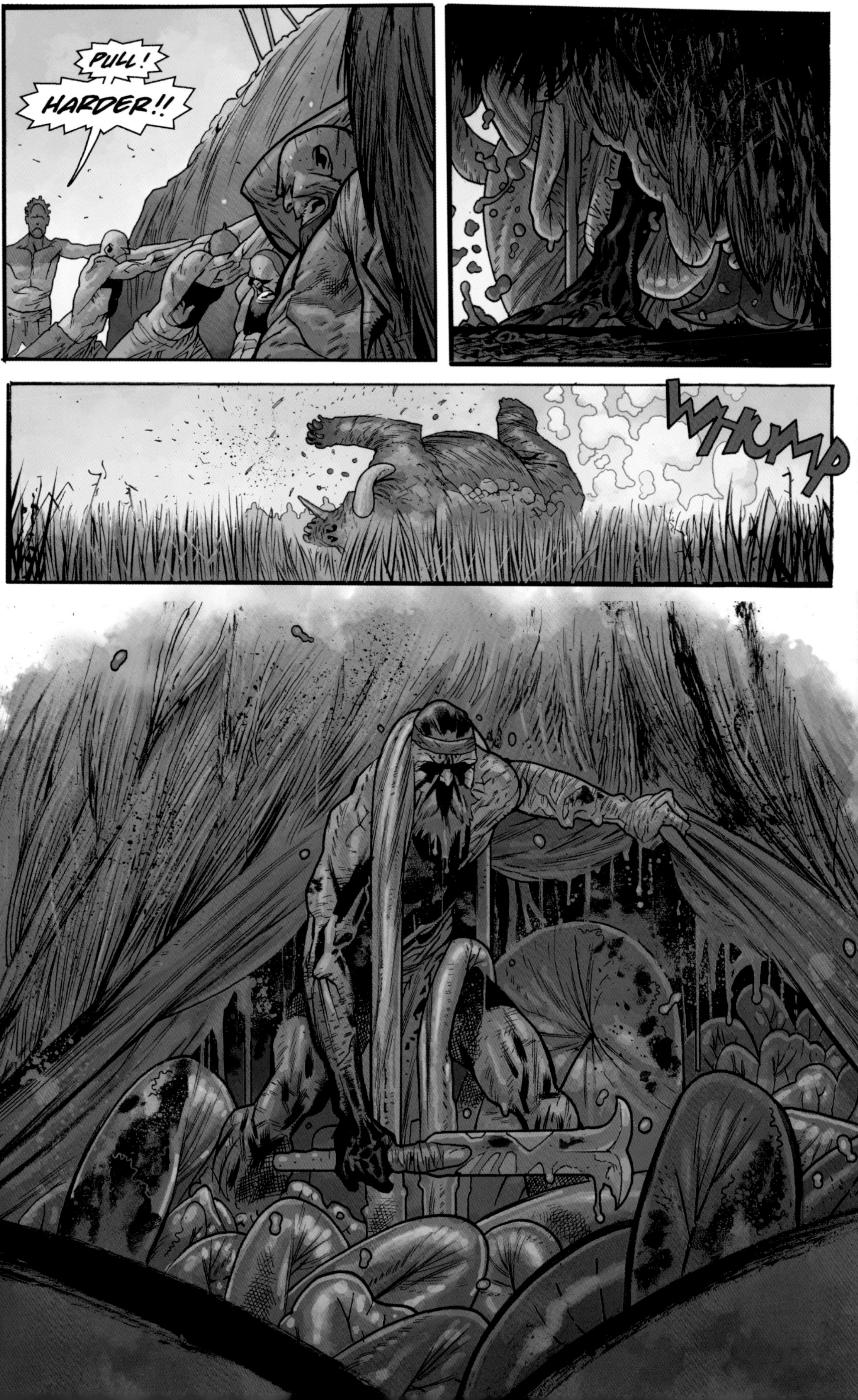
PULL!
HARDER!!
WHUMP

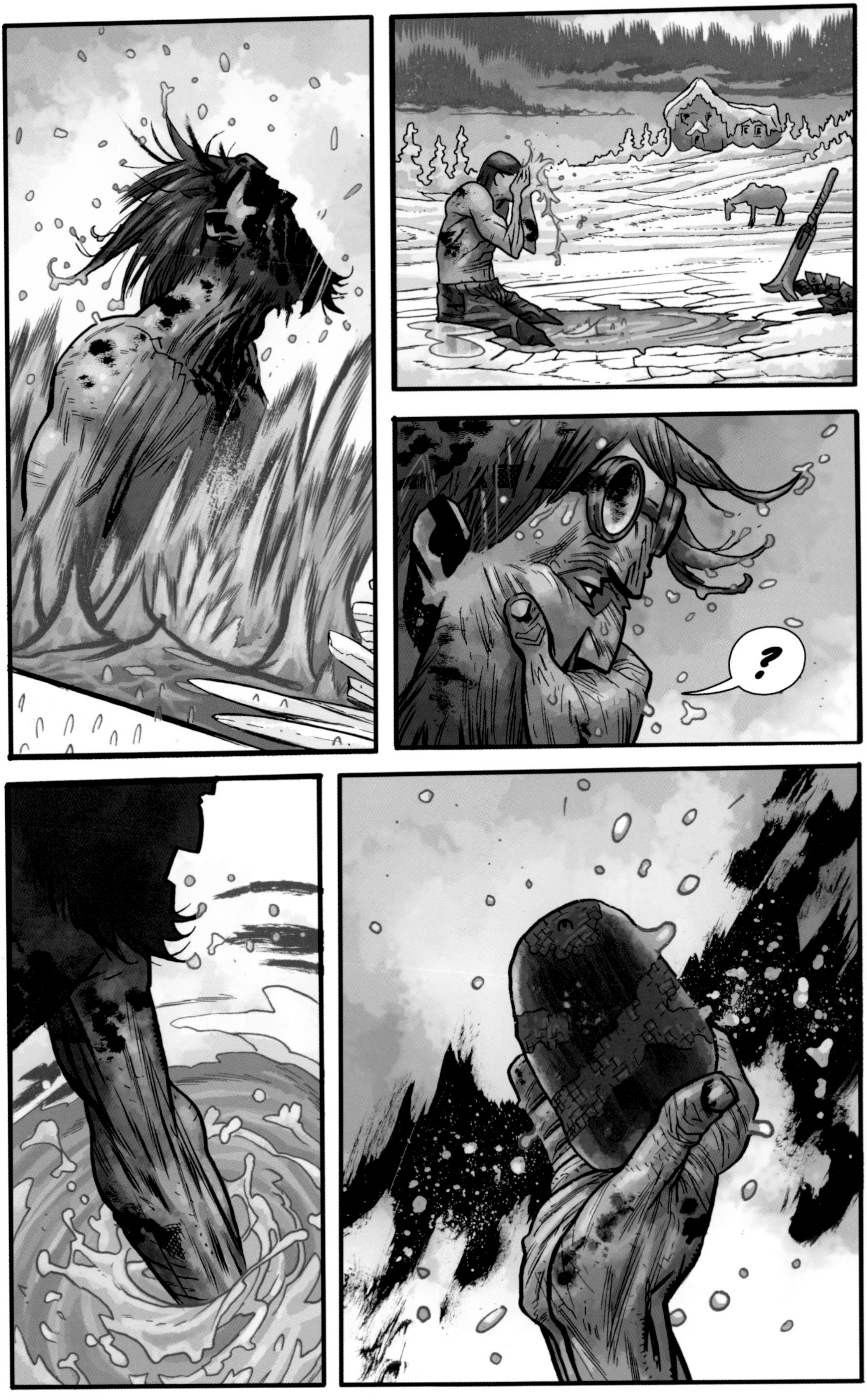
?

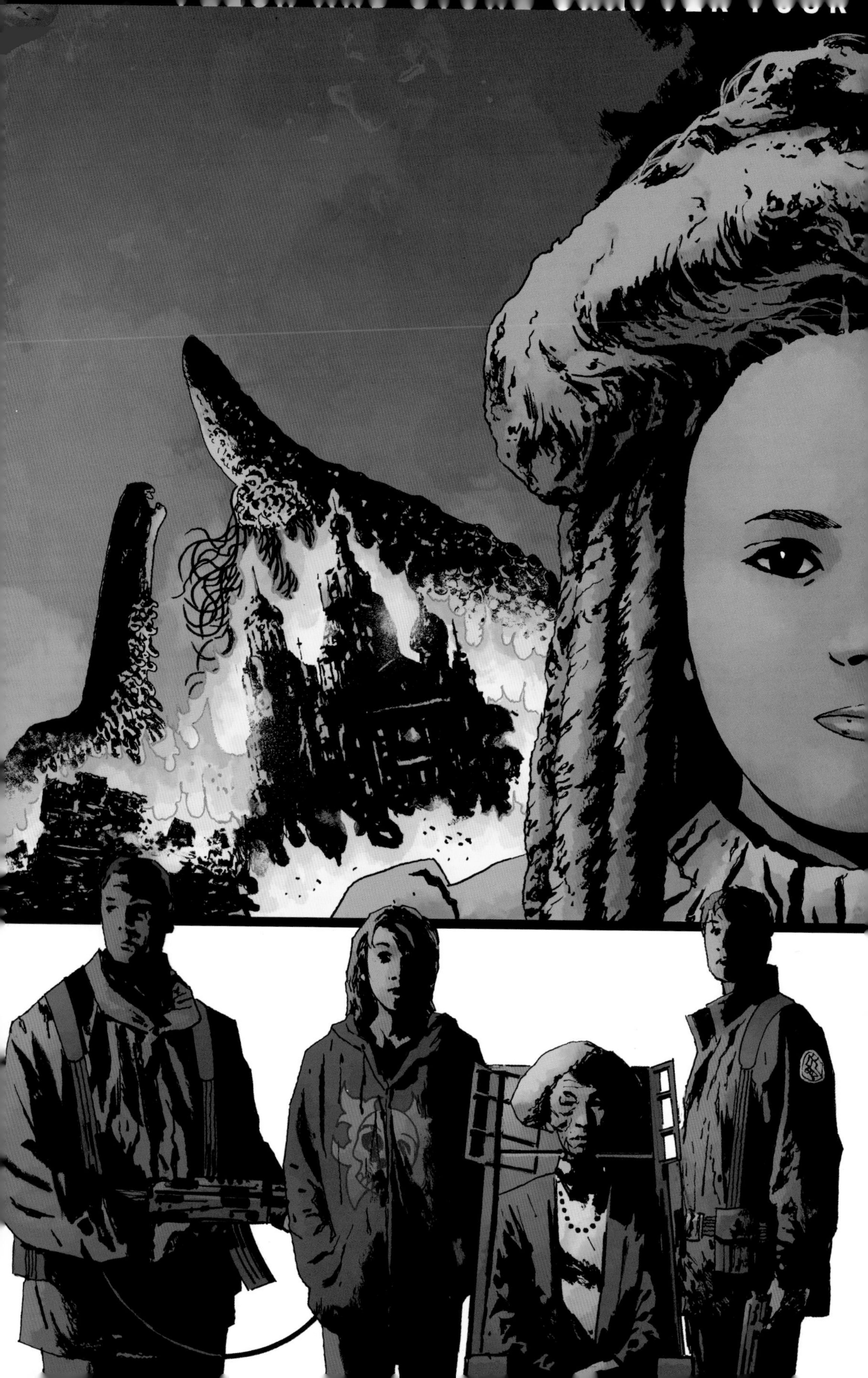

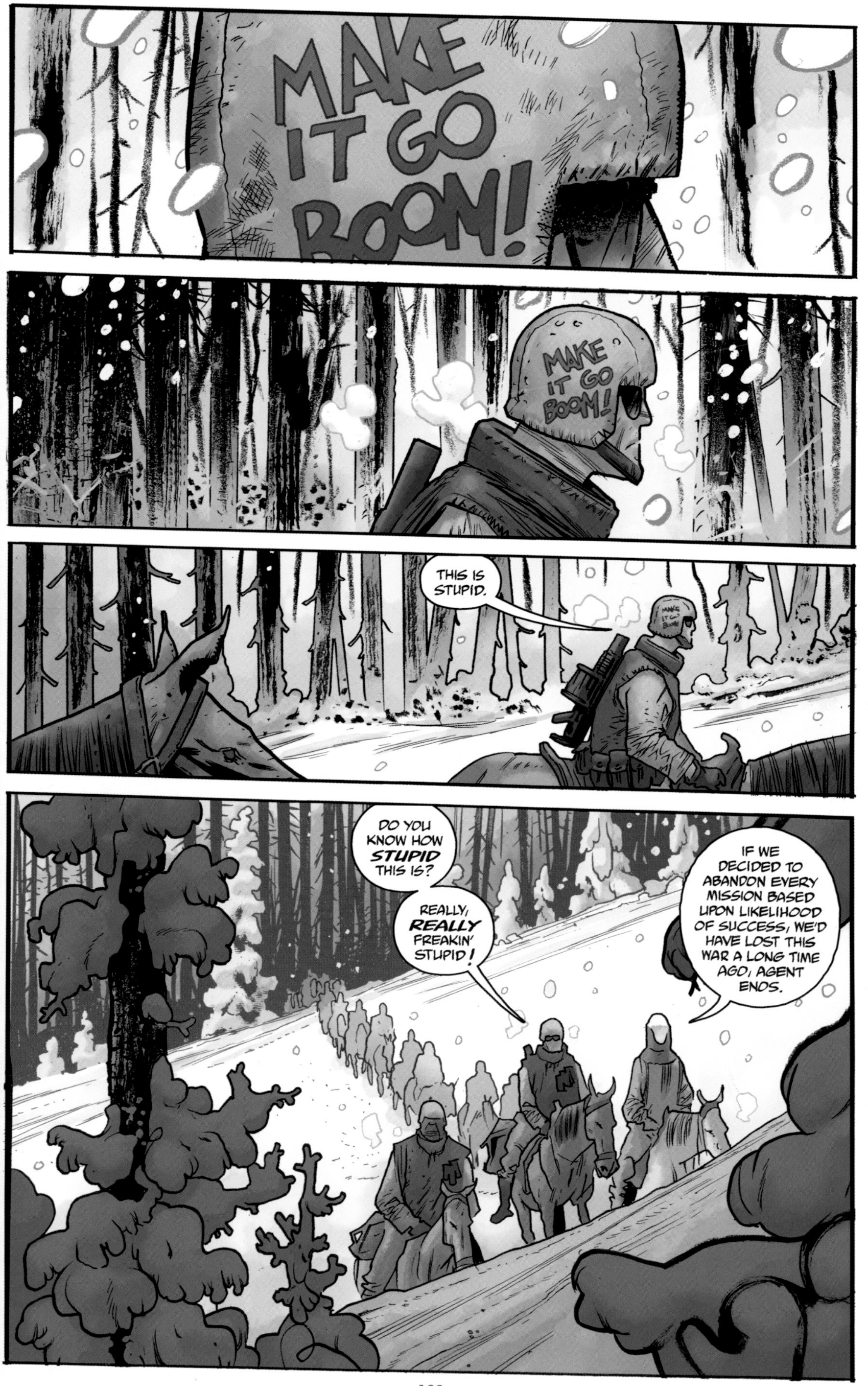
MAKE IT GO BOOM!
MAKE IT GO BOOM!
THIS IS STUPID.
DO YOU KNOW HOW STUPID THIS IS?
REALLY, REALLY FREAKIN' STUPID!
IF WE DECIDED TO ABANDON EVERY MISSION BASED UPON LIKELIHOOD OF SUCCESS, WE'D HAVE LOST THIS WAR A LONG TIME AGO, AGENT ENOS.

BUT I TOLD YOU! NAPALM DIDN'T DO A *THING* TO THE BIG BASTARD. *HELPED* IT, IN FACT!

WHICH IS WHY I PUT IN THE EMERGENCY REQUEST FOR HIGH EXPLOSIVES.

INCENDIARY WEAPONS MAY NOT HAVE BEEN SUFFICIENT TO DESTROY IT, BUT BLASTING IT TO PIECES MIGHT, YES?

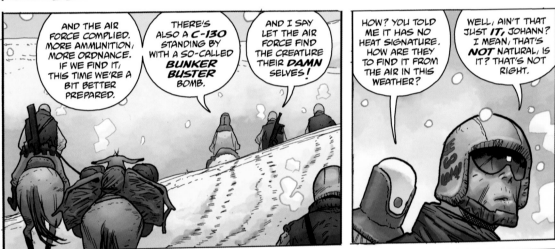

AND THE AIR FORCE COMPLIED. MORE AMMUNITION, MORE ORDNANCE. IF WE FIND IT, THIS TIME WE'RE A BIT BETTER PREPARED.

THERE'S ALSO A *C-130* STANDING BY WITH A SO-CALLED *BUNKER BUSTER* BOMB.

AND I SAY LET THE AIR FORCE FIND THE CREATURE THEIR *DAMN* SELVES!

HOW? YOU TOLD ME IT HAS NO HEAT SIGNATURE. HOW ARE THEY TO FIND IT FROM THE AIR IN THIS WEATHER?

WELL, AIN'T THAT JUST *IT*, JOHANN? I MEAN, THAT'S *NOT* NATURAL, IS IT? THAT'S NOT RIGHT.

YOU OF ALL PEOPLE SHOULD UNDER-STAND THAT THE THINGS WE'RE FACING, THEY AREN'T JUST BIOLOGICAL OR PHYSICAL.

THEY DON'T COME FROM *OUR* WORLD, DO THEY? AND THEY BRING... I DON'T KNOW, MAGIC?

WHAT-EVER IT IS, THEY BRING IT *WITH* 'EM.

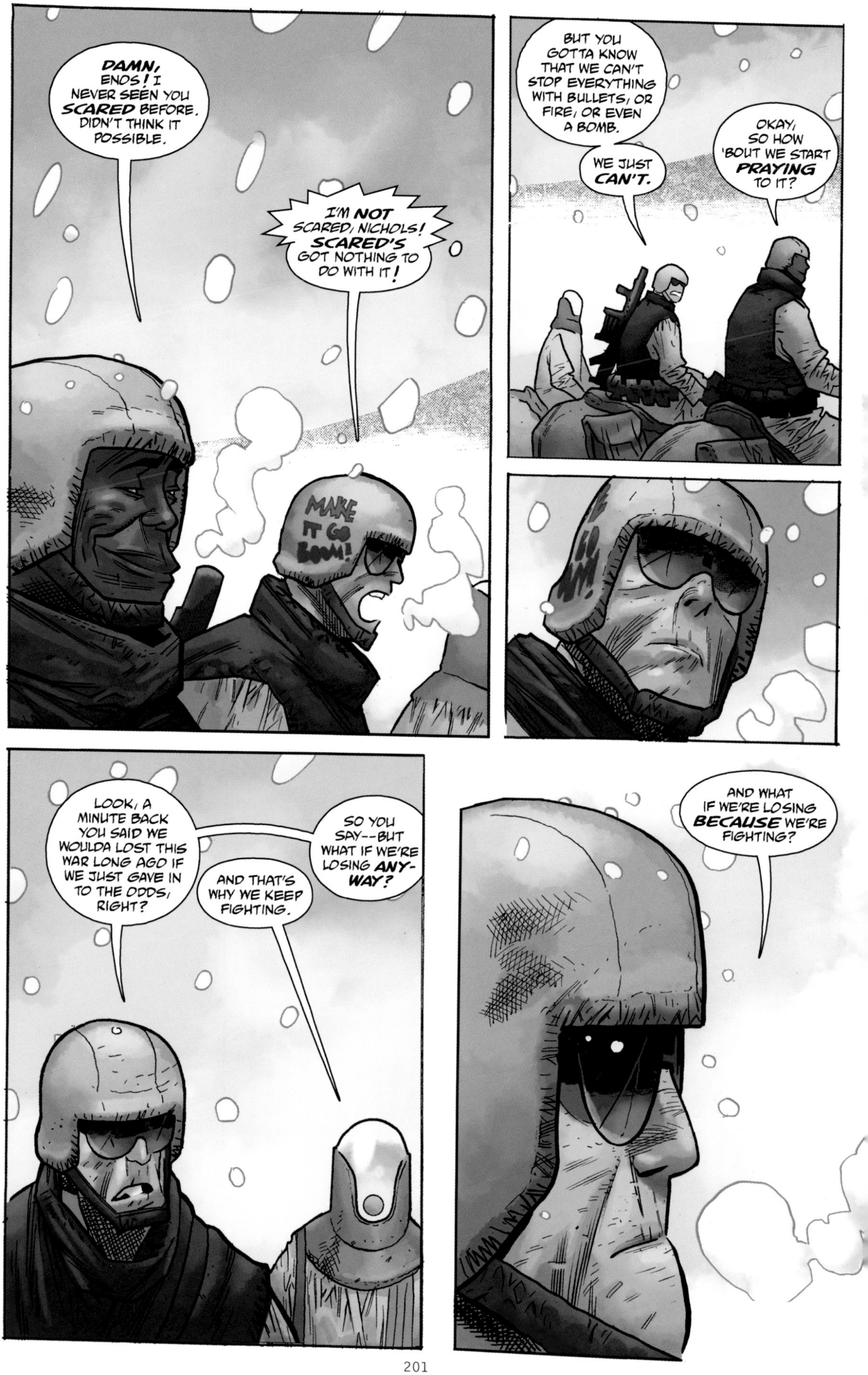

DAMN, ENOS! I NEVER SEEN YOU SCARED BEFORE. DIDN'T THINK IT POSSIBLE.
I'M NOT SCARED, NICHOLS! SCARED'S GOT NOTHING TO DO WITH IT!
MAKE IT GO BOOM!
BUT YOU GOTTA KNOW THAT WE CAN'T STOP EVERYTHING WITH BULLETS, OR FIRE, OR EVEN A BOMB.
WE JUST CAN'T.
OKAY, SO HOW 'BOUT WE START PRAYING TO IT?
LOOK, A MINUTE BACK YOU SAID WE WOULDA LOST THIS WAR LONG AGO IF WE JUST GAVE IN TO THE ODDS, RIGHT?
AND THAT'S WHY WE KEEP FIGHTING.
SO YOU SAY--BUT WHAT IF WE'RE LOSING ANY-WAY?
AND WHAT IF WE'RE LOSING BECAUSE WE'RE FIGHTING?

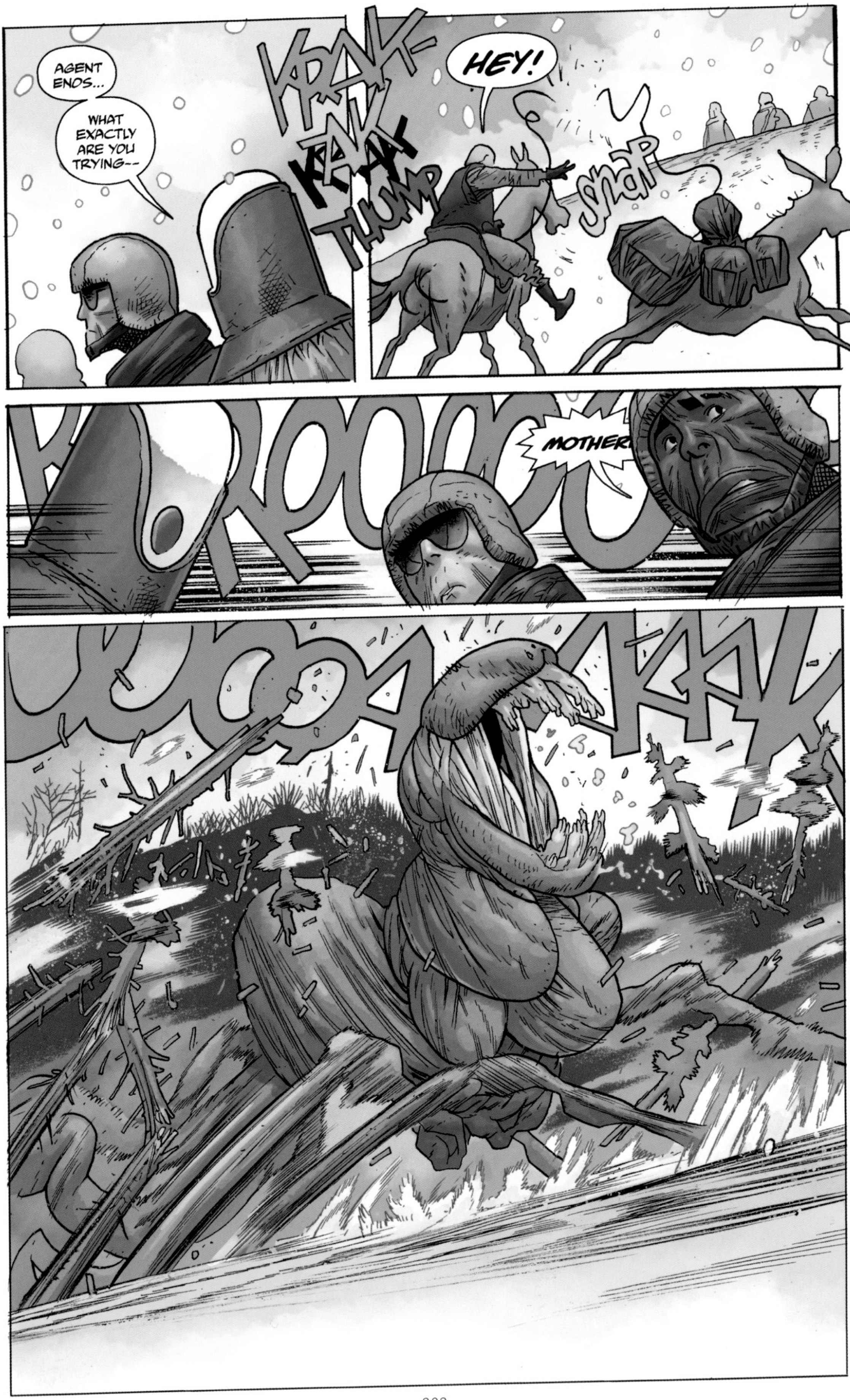
AGENT ENOS...
WHAT EXACTLY ARE YOU TRYING--
KRAK-KRAK KRAK
HEY!
THUMP
SNAP
MOTHER

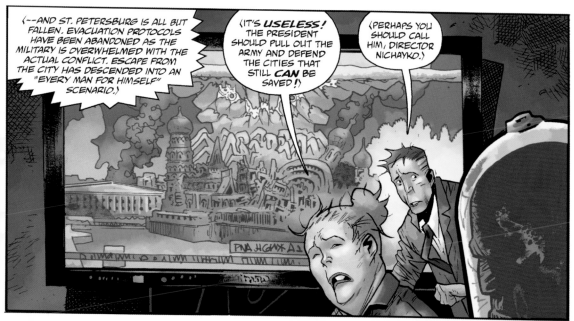

⟨--AND ST. PETERSBURG IS ALL BUT FALLEN. EVACUATION PROTOCOLS HAVE BEEN ABANDONED AS THE MILITARY IS OVERWHELMED WITH THE ACTUAL CONFLICT. ESCAPE FROM THE CITY HAS DESCENDED INTO AN "EVERY MAN FOR HIMSELF" SCENARIO.⟩

⟨IT'S *USELESS!* THE PRESIDENT SHOULD PULL OUT THE ARMY AND DEFEND THE CITIES THAT STILL *CAN* BE SAVED!⟩

⟨PERHAPS YOU SHOULD CALL HIM, DIRECTOR NICHAYKO.⟩

⟨YES, DIRECTOR! YOU *WILL* CALL HIM, WON'T YOU?⟩

CLICK

203

⟨TRANSLATED FROM RUSSIAN⟩

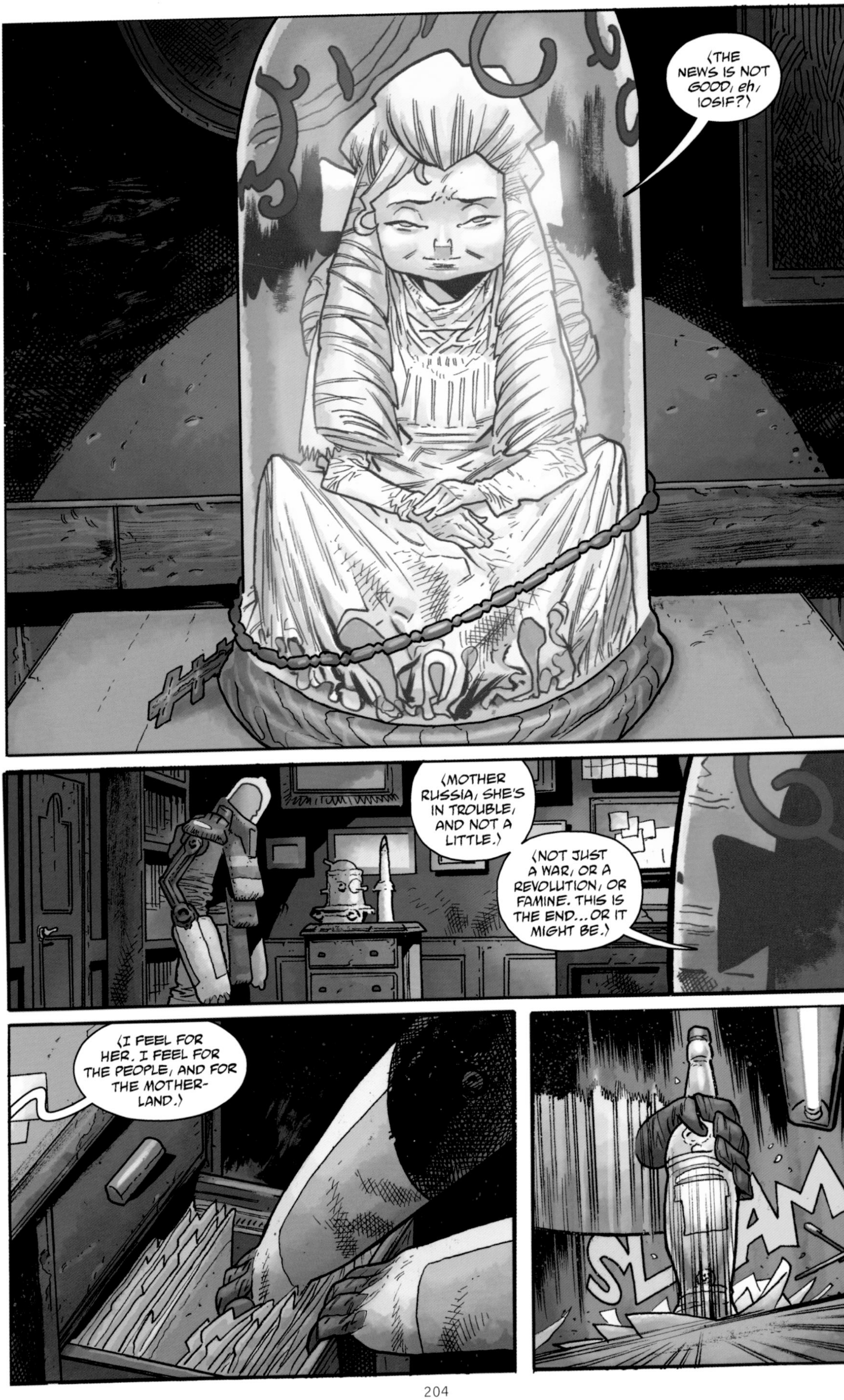
‹THE NEWS IS NOT GOOD, eh, IOSIF?›
‹MOTHER RUSSIA, SHE'S IN TROUBLE, AND NOT A LITTLE.›
‹NOT JUST A WAR, OR A REVOLUTION, OR FAMINE. THIS IS THE END...OR IT MIGHT BE.›
‹I FEEL FOR HER. I FEEL FOR THE PEOPLE, AND FOR THE MOTHER-LAND.›
SLAM

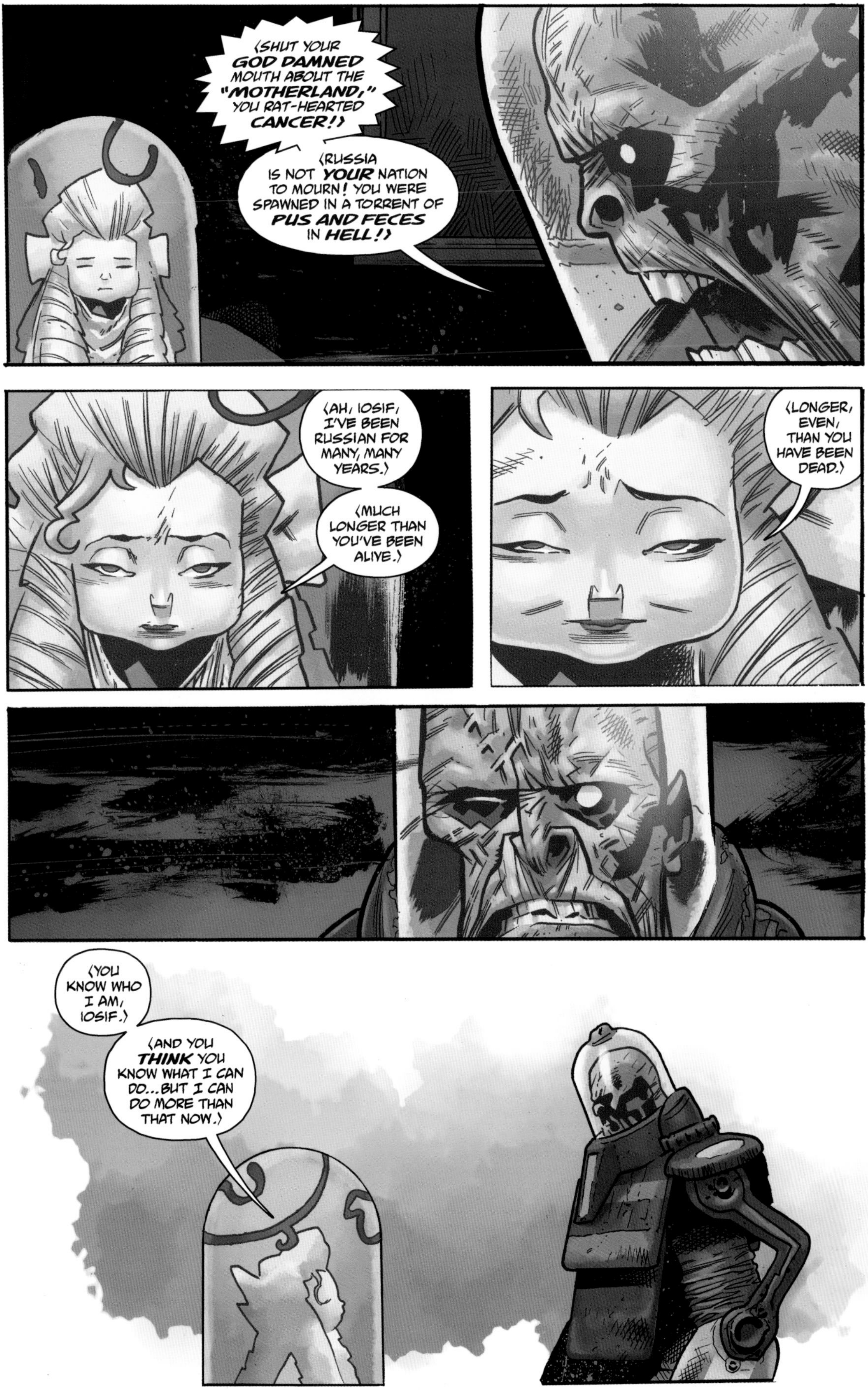
⟨SHUT YOUR GOD DAMNED MOUTH ABOUT THE "MOTHERLAND," YOU RAT-HEARTED CANCER!⟩
⟨RUSSIA IS NOT YOUR NATION TO MOURN! YOU WERE SPAWNED IN A TORRENT OF PUS AND FECES IN HELL!⟩
⟨AH, IOSIF, I'VE BEEN RUSSIAN FOR MANY, MANY YEARS.⟩
⟨MUCH LONGER THAN YOU'VE BEEN ALIVE.⟩
⟨LONGER, EVEN, THAN YOU HAVE BEEN DEAD.⟩
⟨YOU KNOW WHO I AM, IOSIF.⟩
⟨AND YOU THINK YOU KNOW WHAT I CAN DO...BUT I CAN DO MORE THAN THAT NOW.⟩

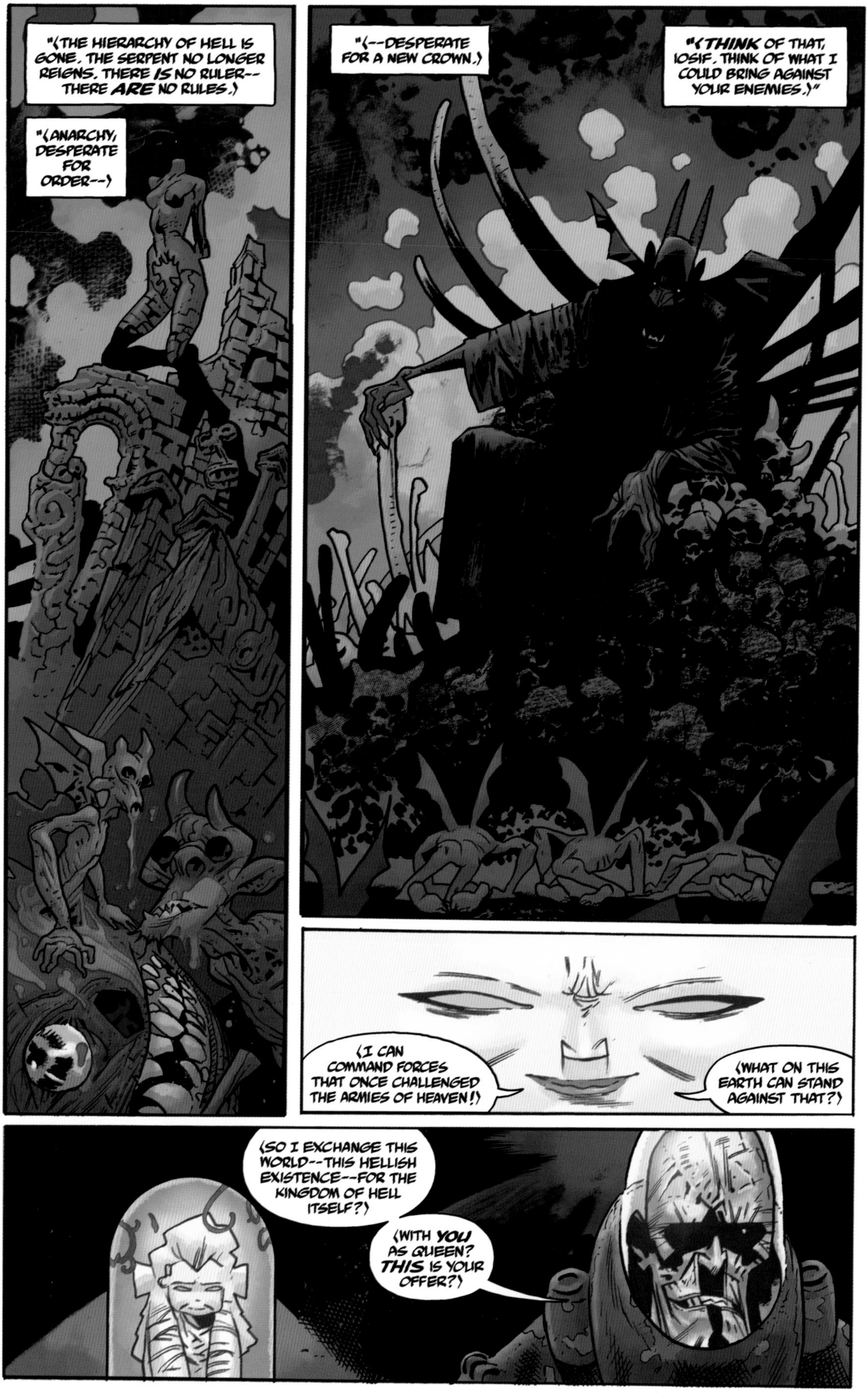
"‹THE HIERARCHY OF HELL IS GONE. THE SERPENT NO LONGER REIGNS. THERE IS NO RULER-- THERE ARE NO RULES.›
"‹ANARCHY, DESPERATE FOR ORDER--›
"‹--DESPERATE FOR A NEW CROWN.›
"‹THINK OF THAT, IOSIF. THINK OF WHAT I COULD BRING AGAINST YOUR ENEMIES.›"
‹I CAN COMMAND FORCES THAT ONCE CHALLENGED THE ARMIES OF HEAVEN!›
‹WHAT ON THIS EARTH CAN STAND AGAINST THAT?›
‹SO I EXCHANGE THIS WORLD--THIS HELLISH EXISTENCE--FOR THE KINGDOM OF HELL ITSELF?›
‹WITH YOU AS QUEEN? THIS IS YOUR OFFER?›

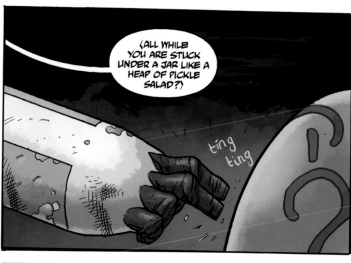

⟨YOU THINK I WOULD HURT THE HUMANS, IS THAT IT? I *LIKE* THEM! THEY'RE FUNNY.⟩

⟨*ALIVE* THEY ARE FUNNY. DEAD, SO DREARY, SO SERIOUS. I WANT NO MORE OF HELL, OF LOST SOULS MOURNING THEMSELVES.⟩

⟨ALL WHILE YOU ARE STUCK UNDER A JAR LIKE A HEAP OF PICKLE SALAD?⟩

ting ting

⟨THIS IS *FOOLISH!* YOU TALK OF YOUR "POWER"?⟩

⟨CRIPPLED BY A FAINT RADIO BROADCAST OF AN AUDIO LOOP--A RECORDING OF A CHANT SPOKEN BY A WOMAN IN HER GRAVE NOW FORTY YEARS *!*⟩

⟨OH, YES! HOW *MIGHTY* YOU ARE!⟩

⟨WHATEVER THIS NEW HELL IS, *YOU'LL* BE NO *ROYALTY* IN IT.⟩

⟨YOU WILL VANISH IN THE INFERNO! YOU WILL MELT AWAY IN AN INSTANT, LITTLE SNOWBALL *!*⟩

⟨I RELEASE YOU...THERE IS ONLY *ONE* THING I CAN TRUST YOU TO DO.⟩

⟨ONLY *ONE* CHILD OF GOD FOR WHOM ALL THIS SUFFERING WILL END.⟩

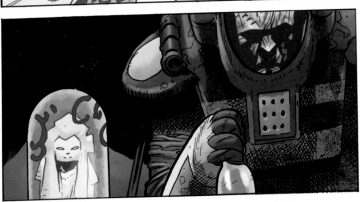

⟨LORD **JESUS!** IF I COULD JUST HAVE A **DRINK!**⟩

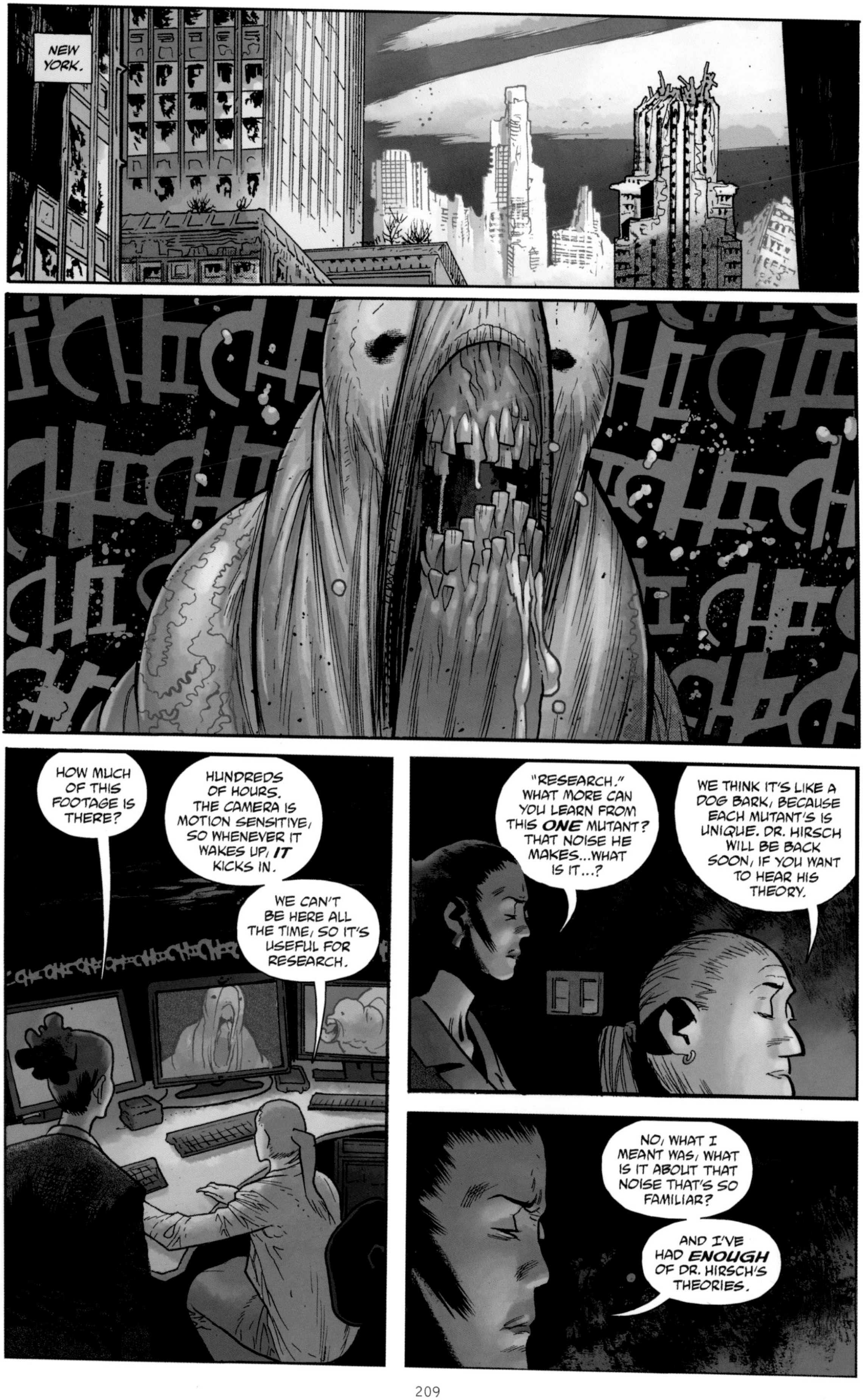
NEW YORK.
HOW MUCH OF THIS FOOTAGE IS THERE?
HUNDREDS OF HOURS. THE CAMERA IS MOTION SENSITIVE, SO WHENEVER IT WAKES UP, IT KICKS IN.
WE CAN'T BE HERE ALL THE TIME, SO IT'S USEFUL FOR RESEARCH.
"RESEARCH." WHAT MORE CAN YOU LEARN FROM THIS ONE MUTANT? THAT NOISE HE MAKES...WHAT IS IT...?
WE THINK IT'S LIKE A DOG BARK, BECAUSE EACH MUTANT'S IS UNIQUE. DR. HIRSCH WILL BE BACK SOON, IF YOU WANT TO HEAR HIS THEORY.
NO, WHAT I MEANT WAS, WHAT IS IT ABOUT THAT NOISE THAT'S SO FAMILIAR?
AND I'VE HAD ENOUGH OF DR. HIRSCH'S THEORIES.

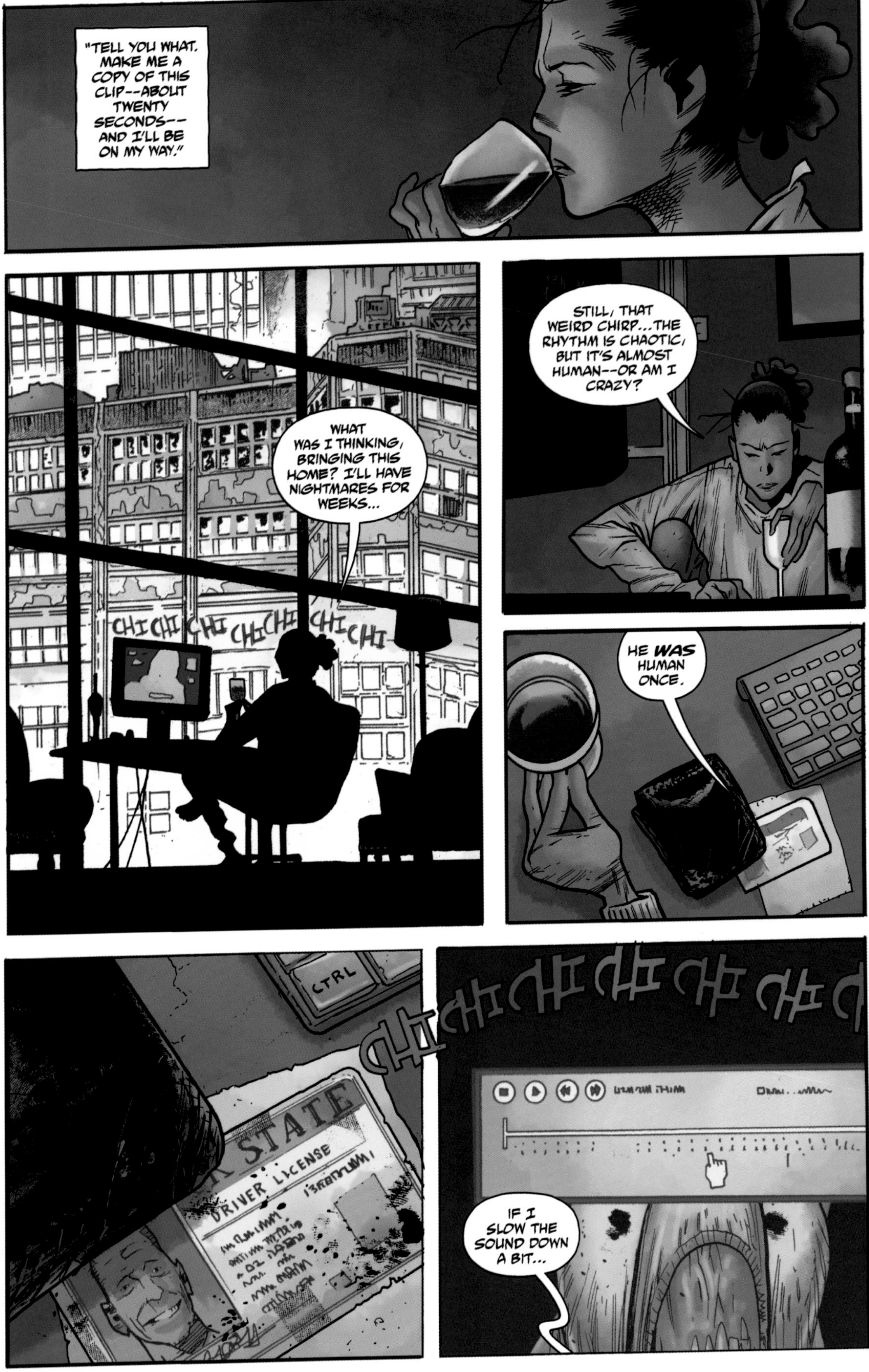
"TELL YOU WHAT. MAKE ME A COPY OF THIS CLIP--ABOUT TWENTY SECONDS-- AND I'LL BE ON MY WAY."
WHAT WAS I THINKING, BRINGING THIS HOME? I'LL HAVE NIGHTMARES FOR WEEKS...
CHI CHI CHI CHI CHI CHI CHI
STILL, THAT WEIRD CHIRP...THE RHYTHM IS CHAOTIC, BUT IT'S ALMOST HUMAN--OR AM I CRAZY?
HE WAS HUMAN ONCE.
CTRL
STATE
DRIVER LICENSE
CHI CHI CHI CHI CHI CHI CHI CHI
IF I SLOW THE SOUND DOWN A BIT...

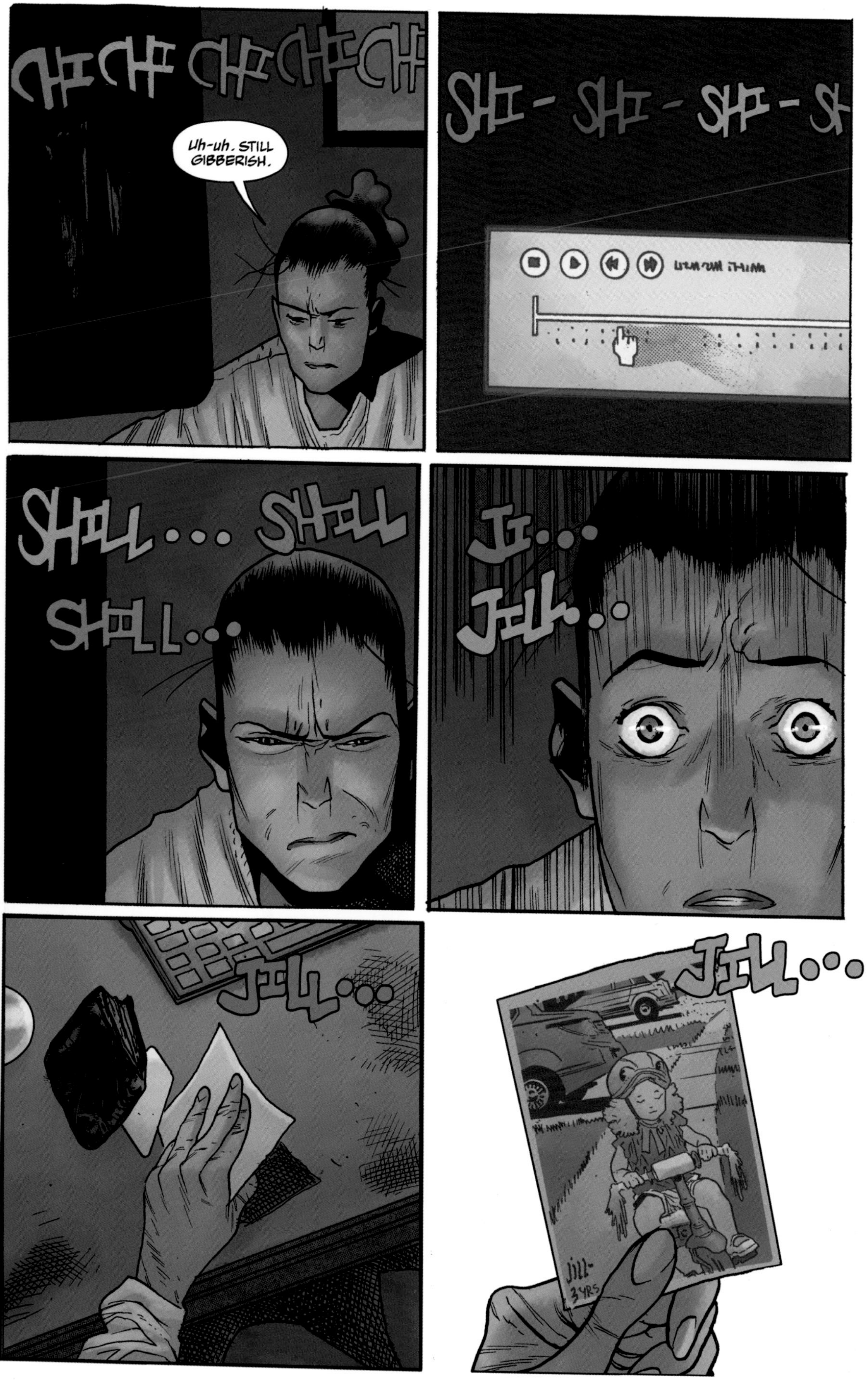
CHICHI CHICHICHI
Uh-uh. STILL GIBBERISH.
SHI - SHI - SHI - SH
SHILL... SHILL
SHILL...
JI...
JILL...
JILL...
JILL...
Jill-
3 YRS

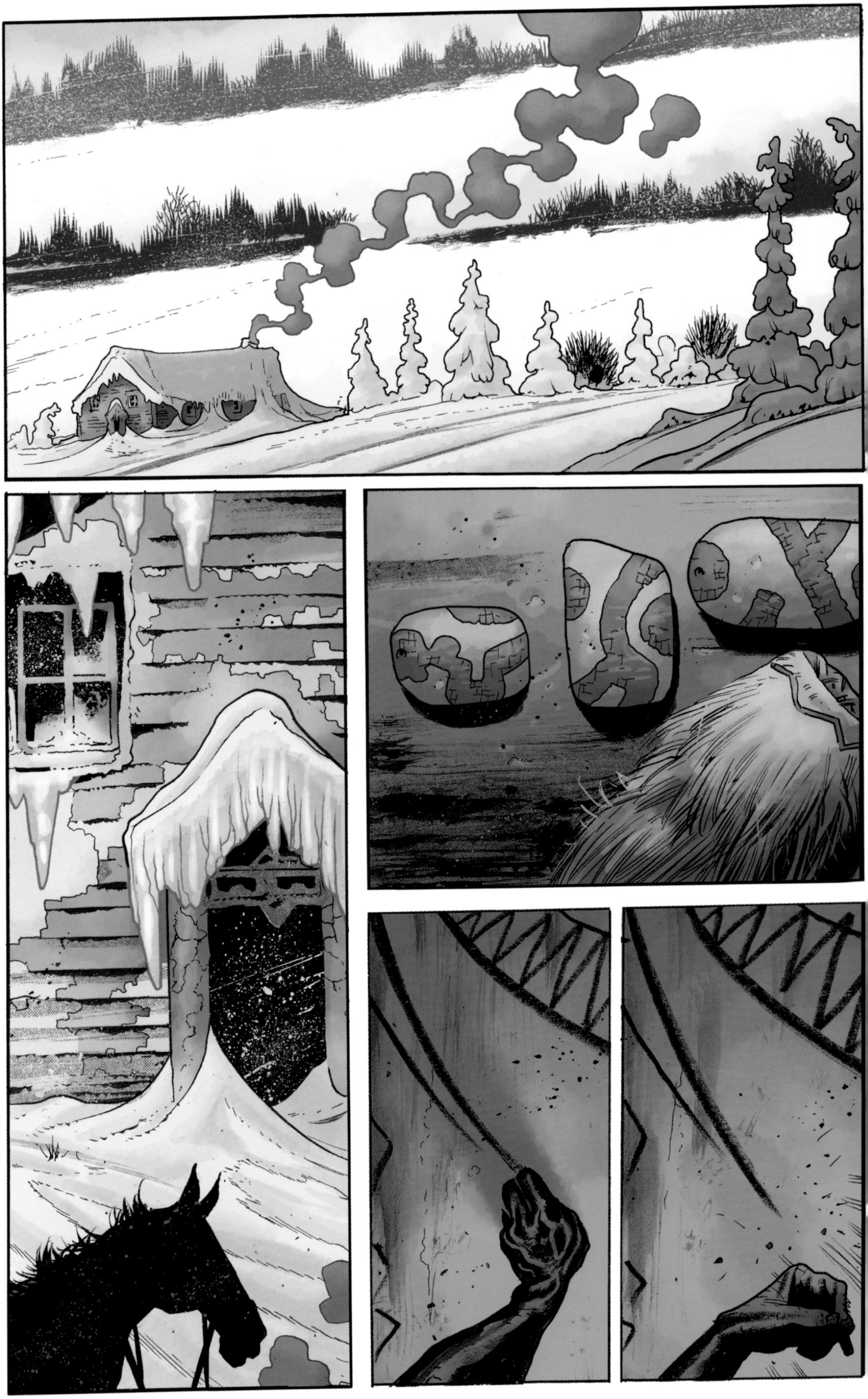

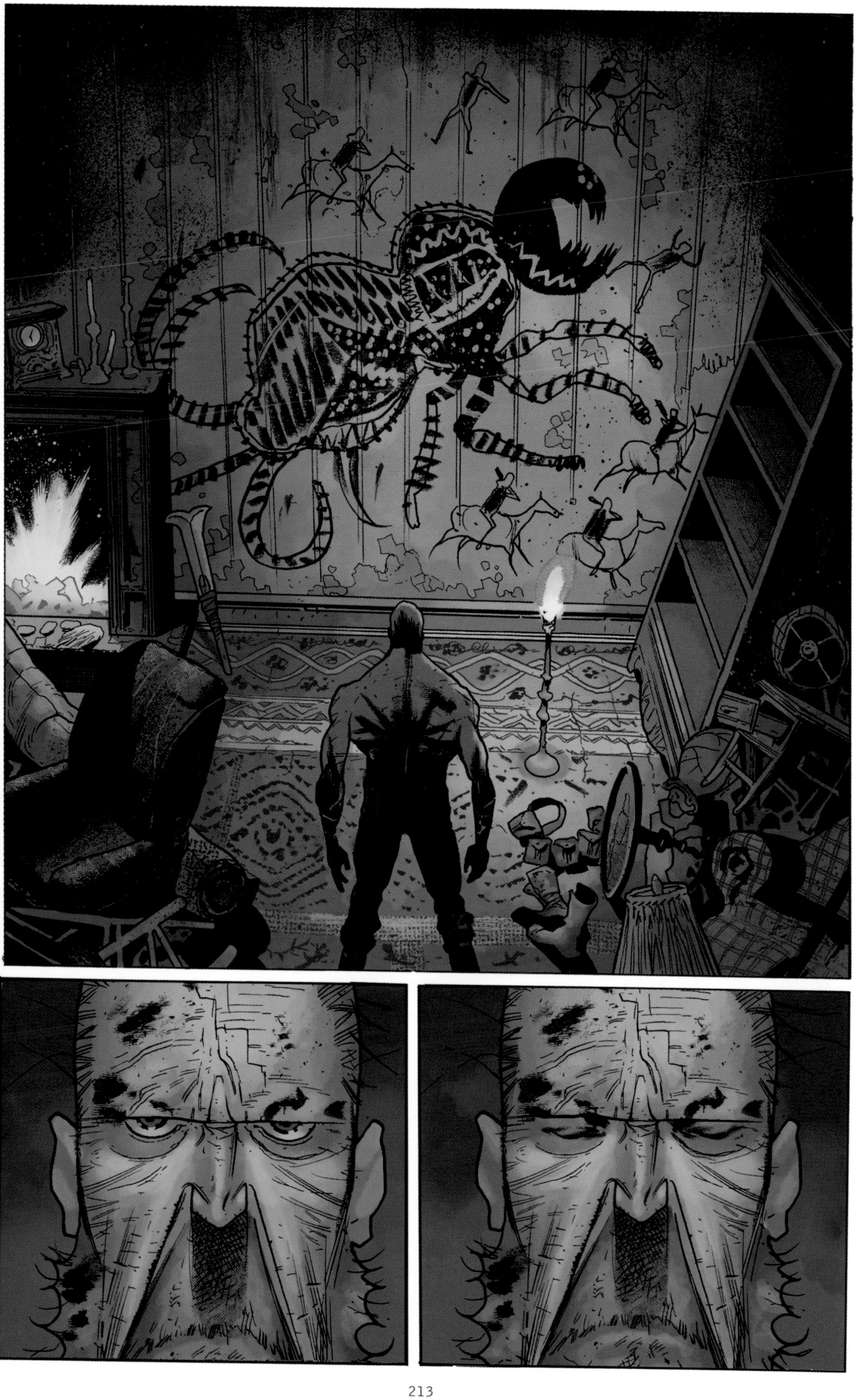

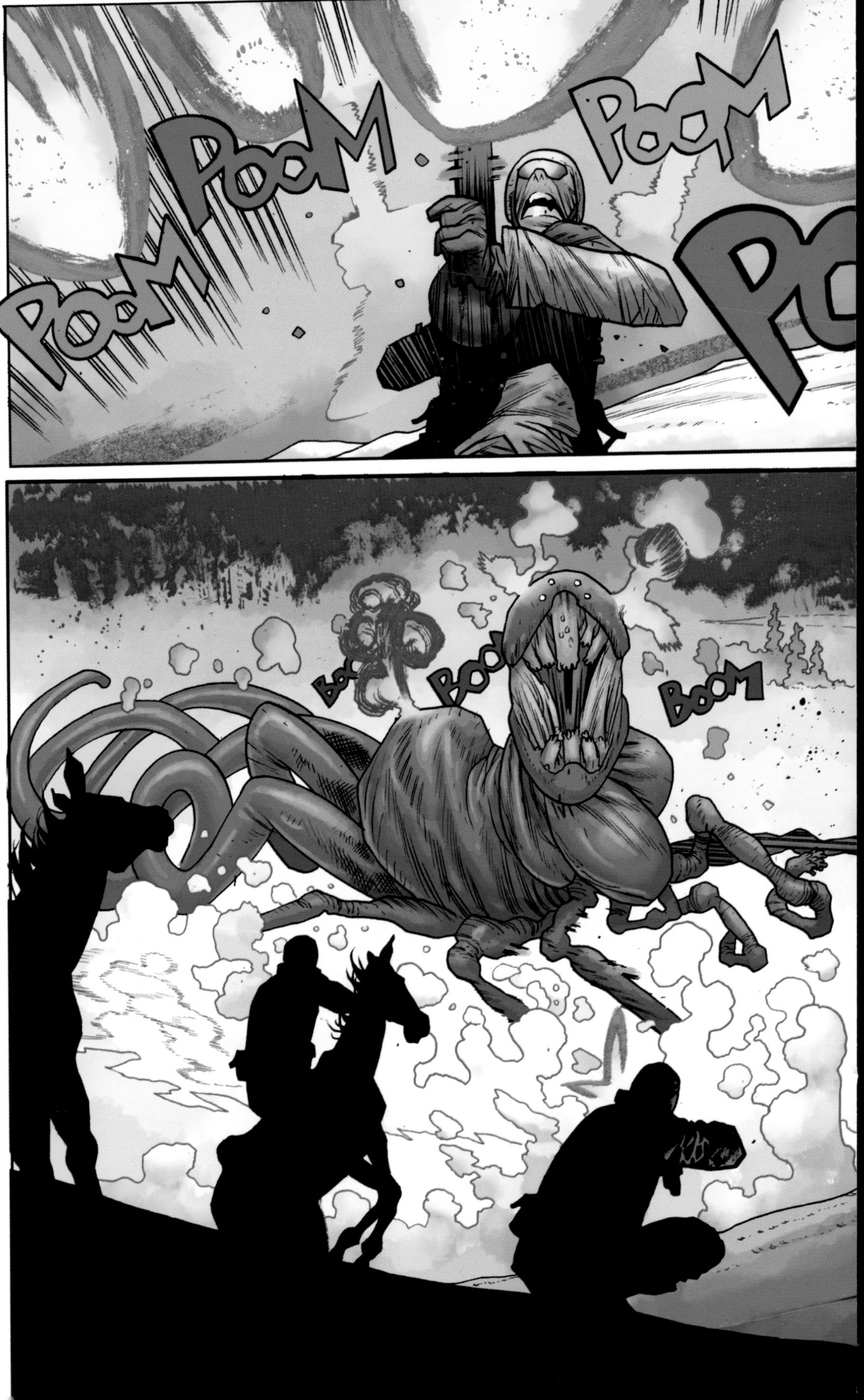
POOM
POOM
POOM
PO
BO
BOO
BOOM

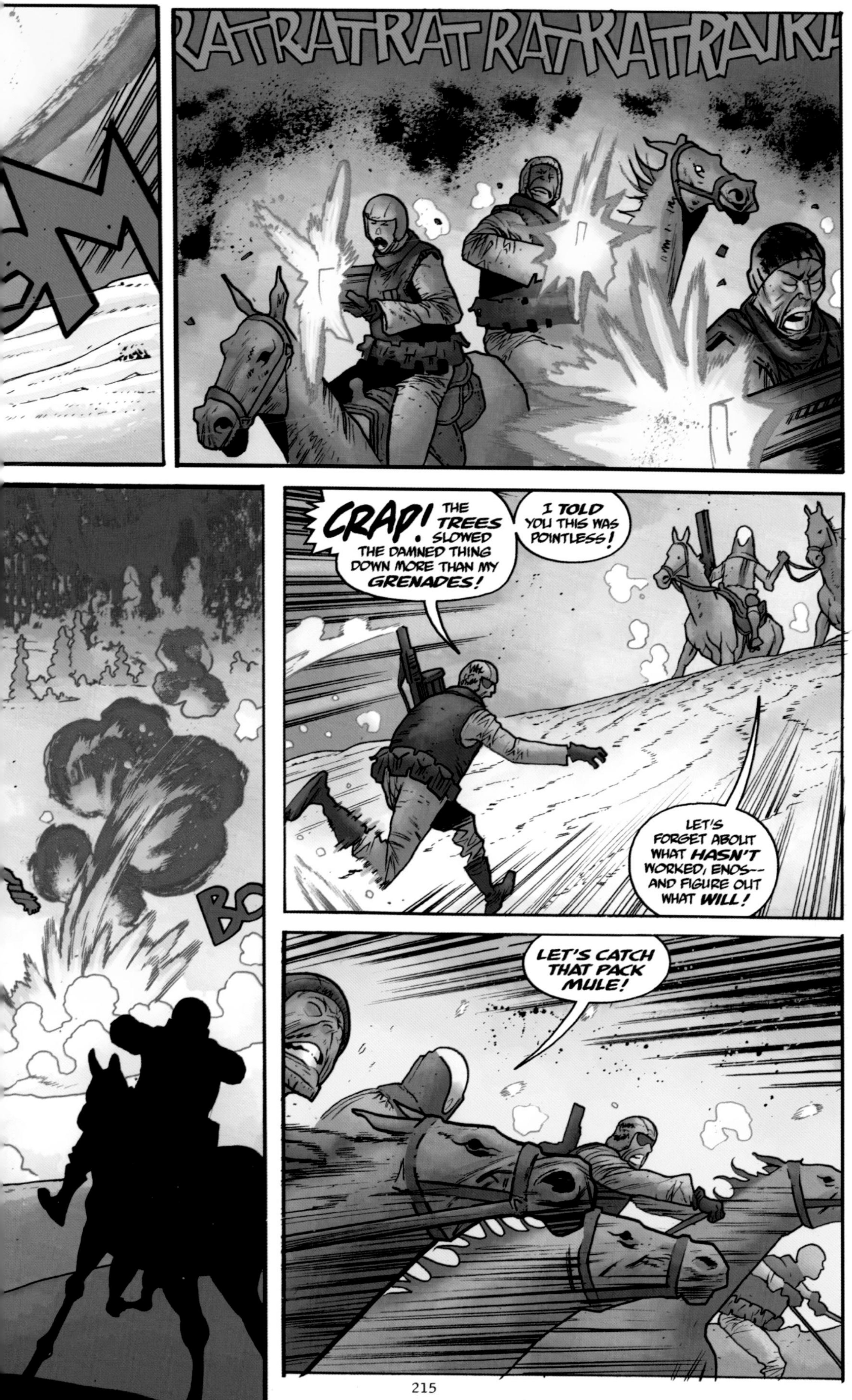
RATRATRATRATRATRATRA
CRAP! THE TREES SLOWED THE DAMNED THING DOWN MORE THAN MY GRENADES!
I TOLD YOU THIS WAS POINTLESS!
LET'S FORGET ABOUT WHAT HASN'T WORKED, ENOS-- AND FIGURE OUT WHAT WILL!
LET'S CATCH THAT PACK MULE!

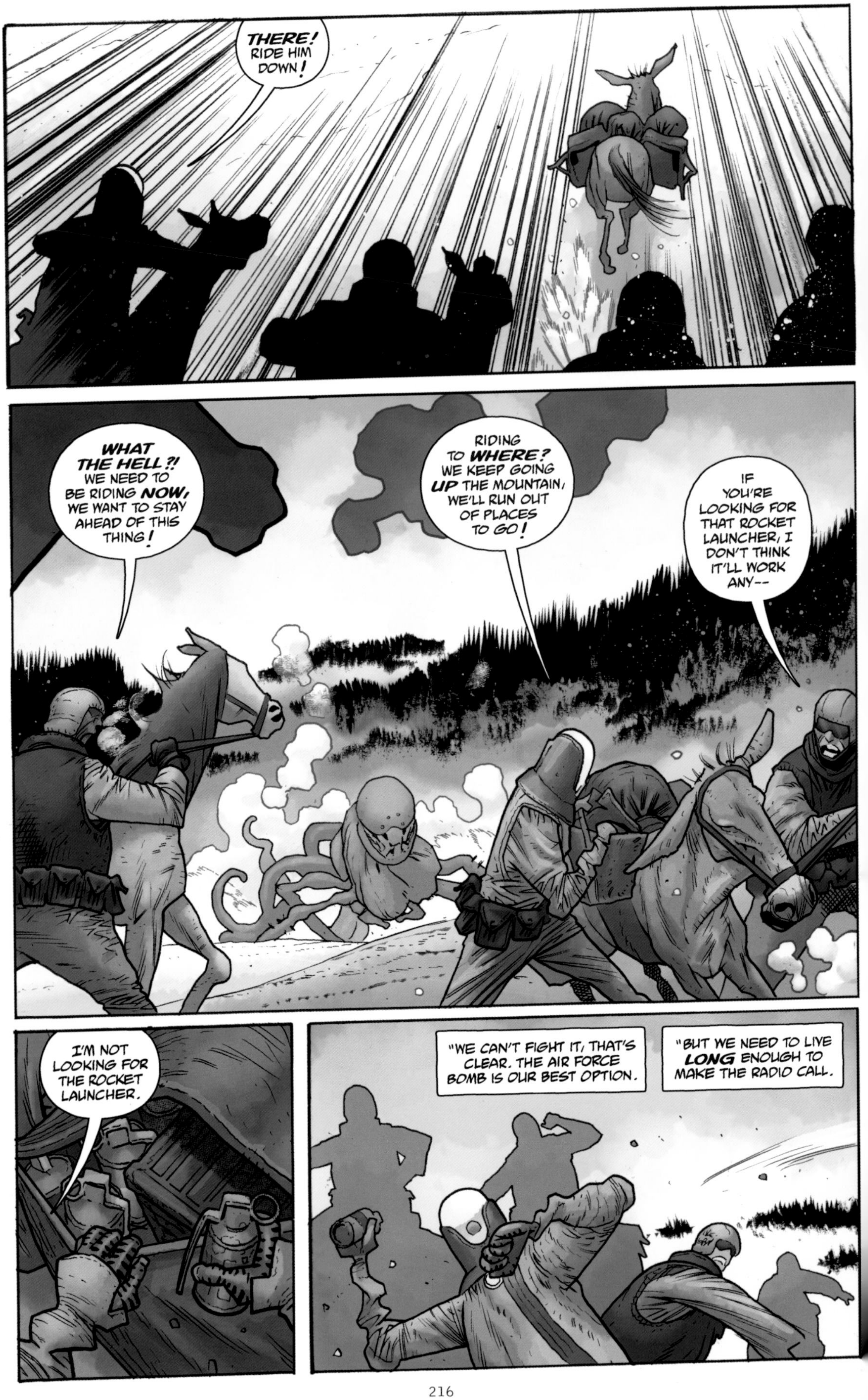
THERE! RIDE HIM DOWN!
WHAT THE HELL?! WE NEED TO BE RIDING NOW, WE WANT TO STAY AHEAD OF THIS THING!
RIDING TO WHERE? WE KEEP GOING UP THE MOUNTAIN, WE'LL RUN OUT OF PLACES TO GO!
IF YOU'RE LOOKING FOR THAT ROCKET LAUNCHER, I DON'T THINK IT'LL WORK ANY--
I'M NOT LOOKING FOR THE ROCKET LAUNCHER.
"WE CAN'T FIGHT IT, THAT'S CLEAR. THE AIR FORCE BOMB IS OUR BEST OPTION.
"BUT WE NEED TO LIVE LONG ENOUGH TO MAKE THE RADIO CALL.

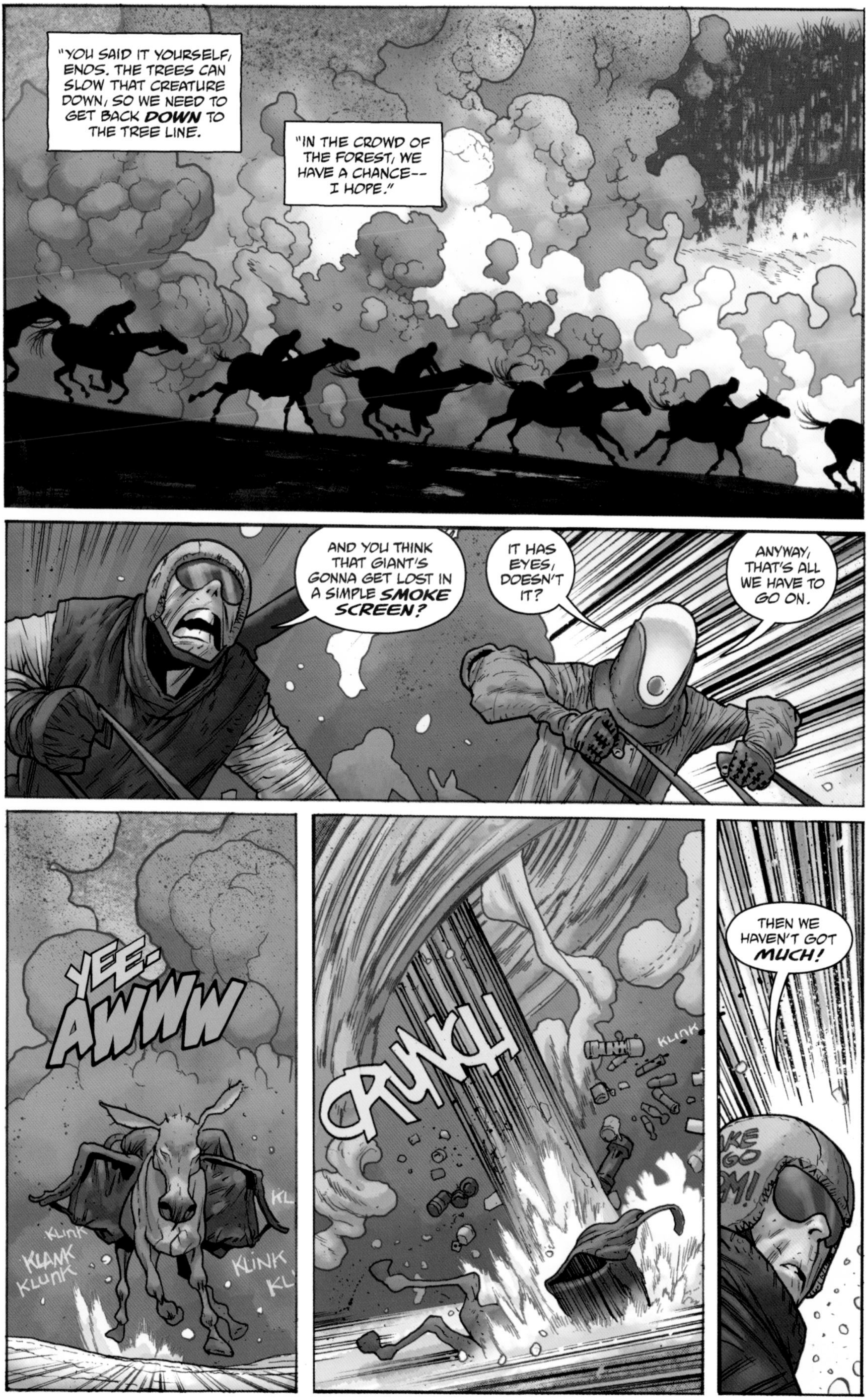
"YOU SAID IT YOURSELF, ENOS. THE TREES CAN SLOW THAT CREATURE DOWN, SO WE NEED TO GET BACK DOWN TO THE TREE LINE.
"IN THE CROWD OF THE FOREST, WE HAVE A CHANCE-- I HOPE."
AND YOU THINK THAT GIANT'S GONNA GET LOST IN A SIMPLE SMOKE SCREEN?
IT HAS EYES, DOESN'T IT?
ANYWAY, THAT'S ALL WE HAVE TO GO ON.
YEE-AWWW
KLINK
KLANK
KLUNK
KLINK
CRUNCH
KLINK
THEN WE HAVEN'T GOT MUCH!

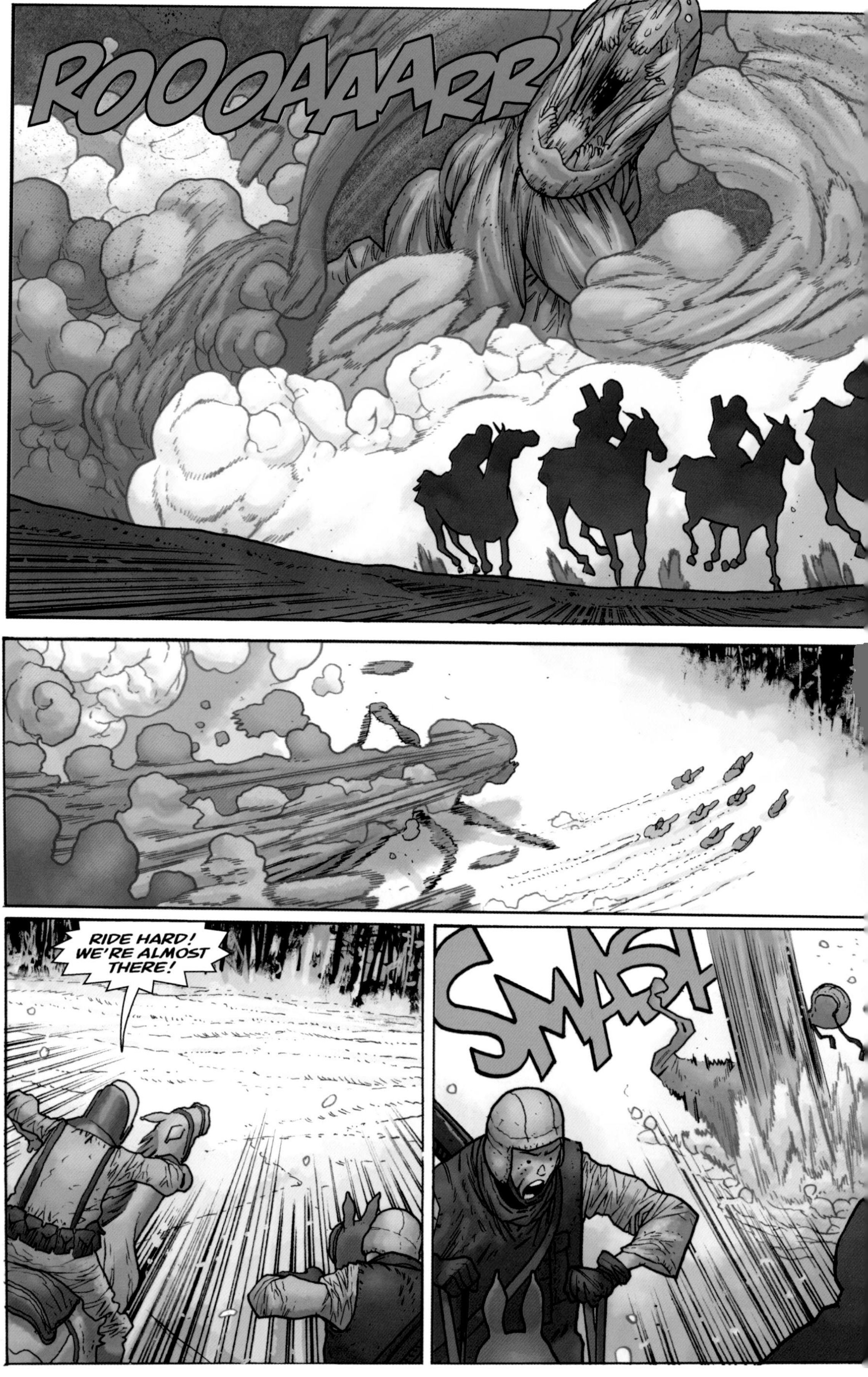
ROOOAAARR
RIDE HARD! WE'RE ALMOST THERE!
SMASH

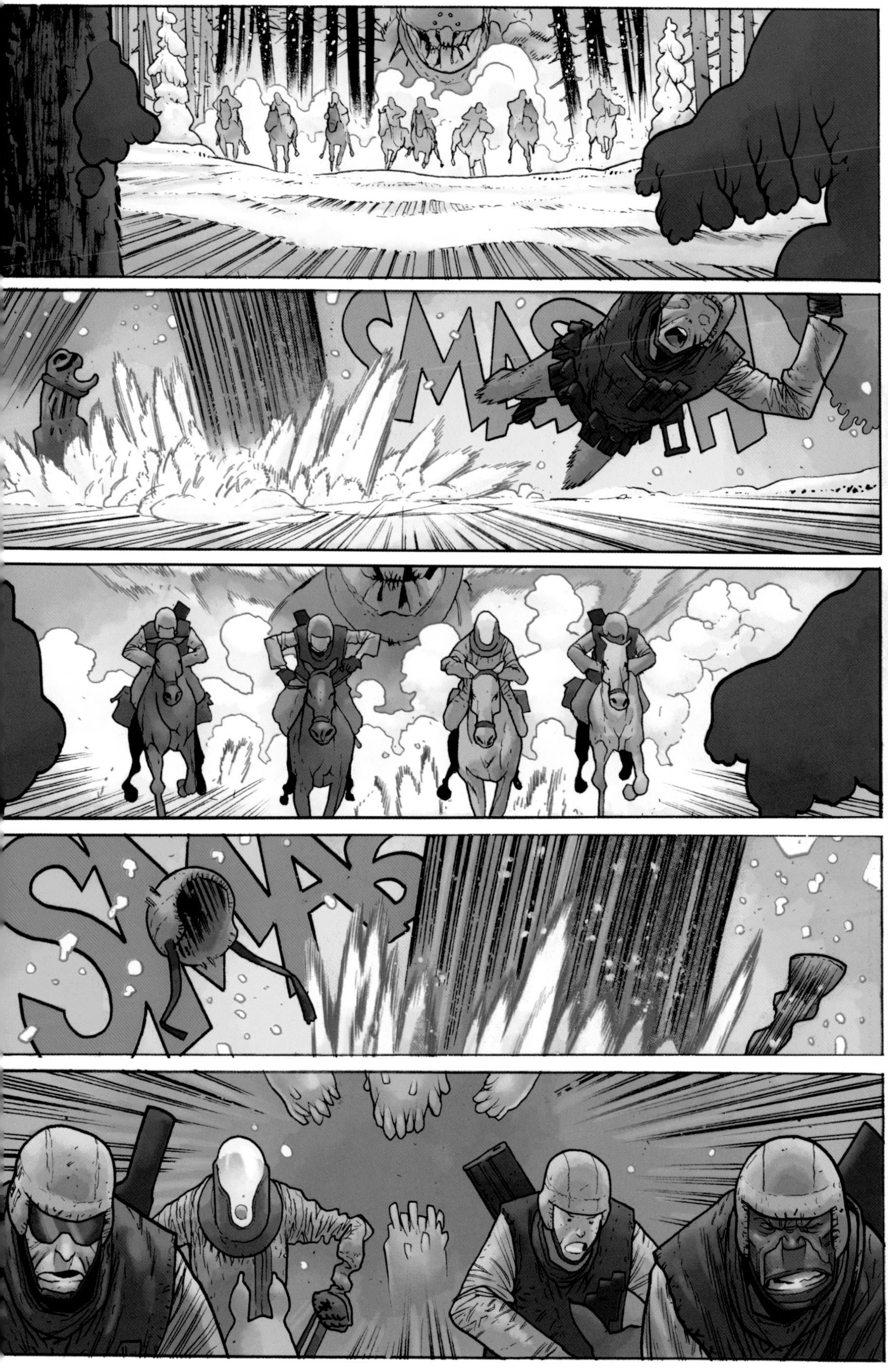

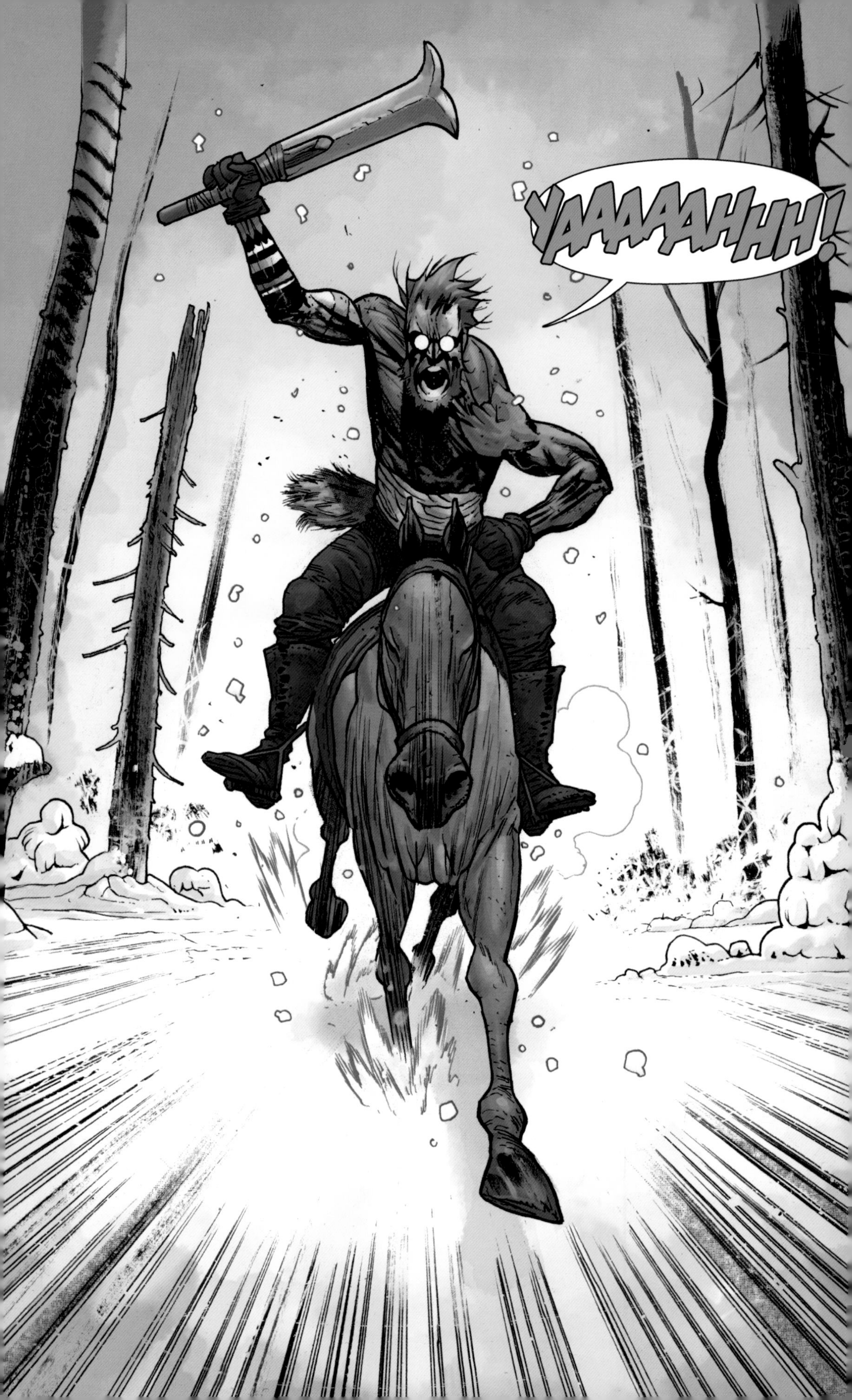
YAAAAAHHH!

FLESH AND STONE CHAPTER FIVE

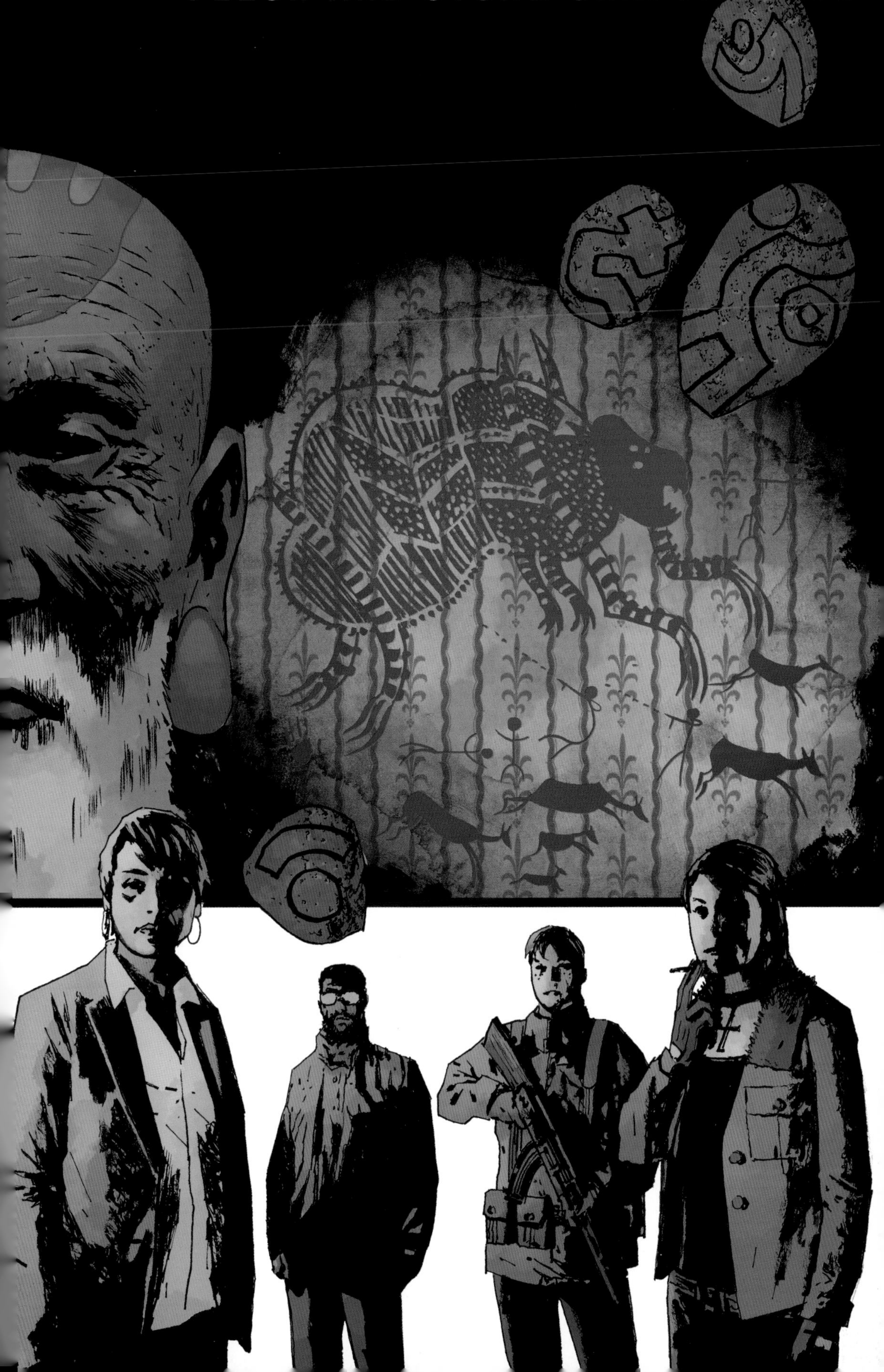

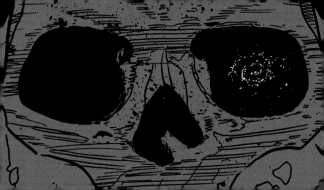

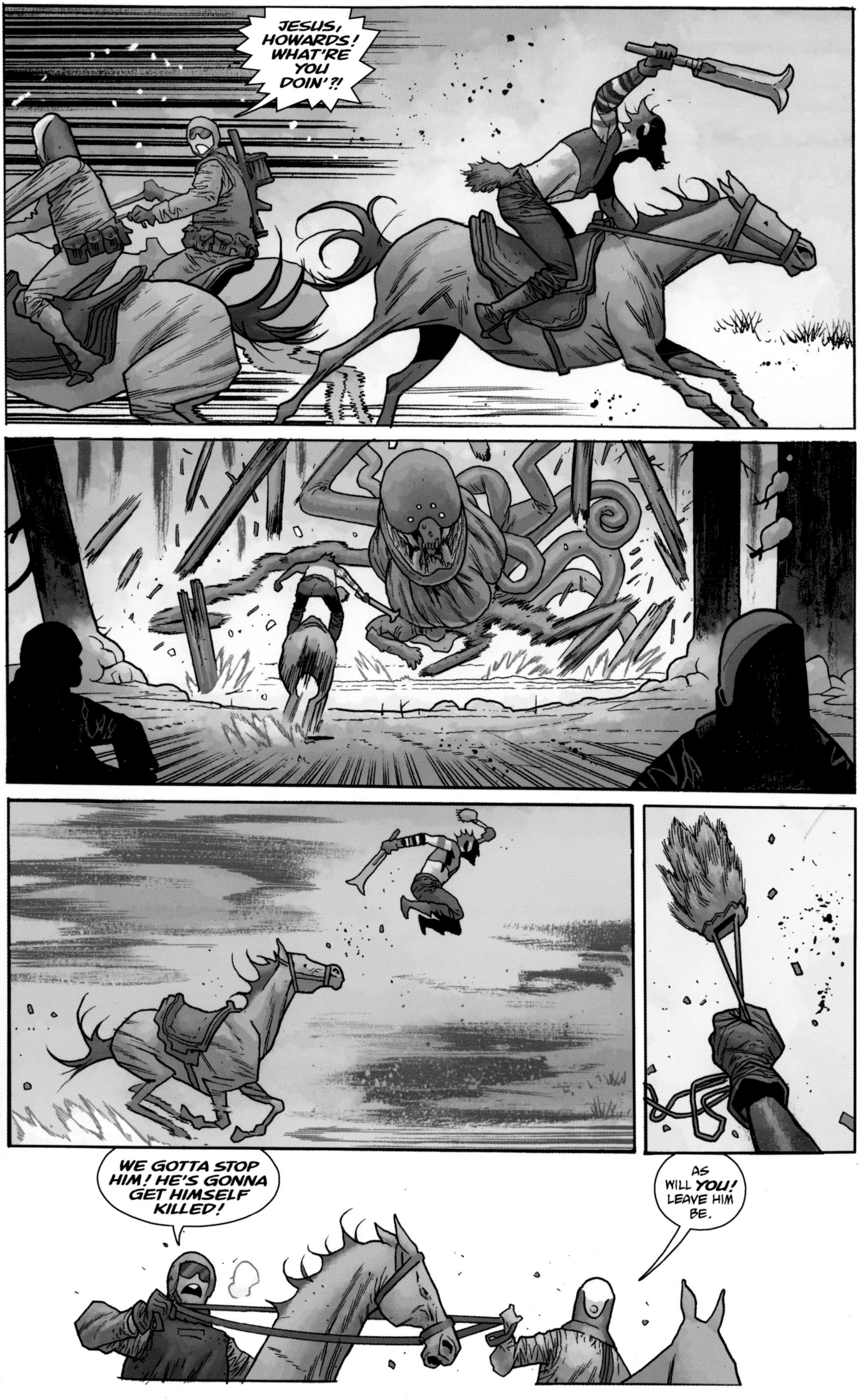

JESUS, HOWARDS! WHAT'RE YOU DOIN'?!
WE GOTTA STOP HIM! HE'S GONNA GET HIMSELF KILLED!
AS WILL YOU! LEAVE HIM BE.

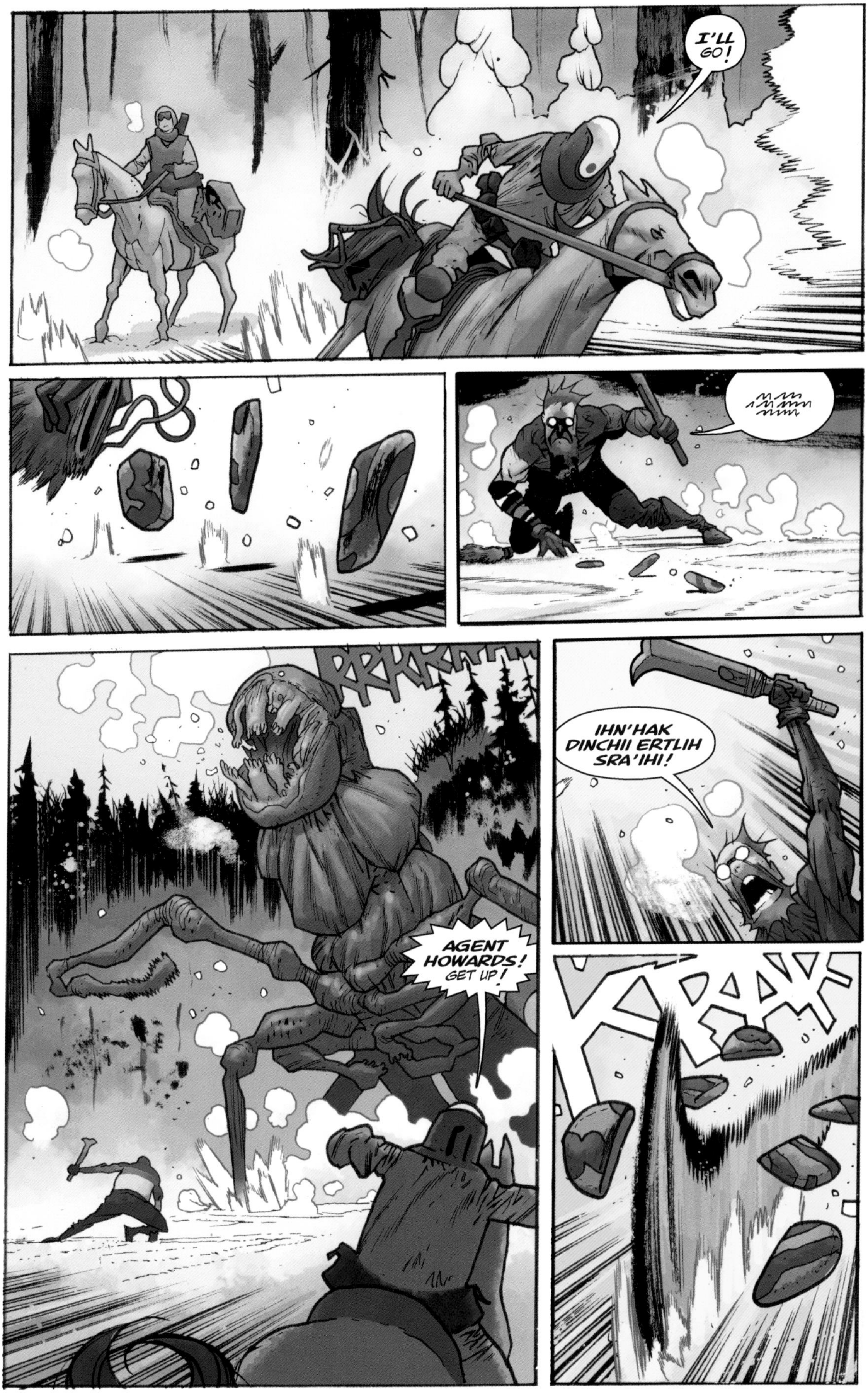
I'LL GO!
IHN'HAK DINCHII ERTLIH SRA'IHI!
AGENT HOWARDS! GET UP!

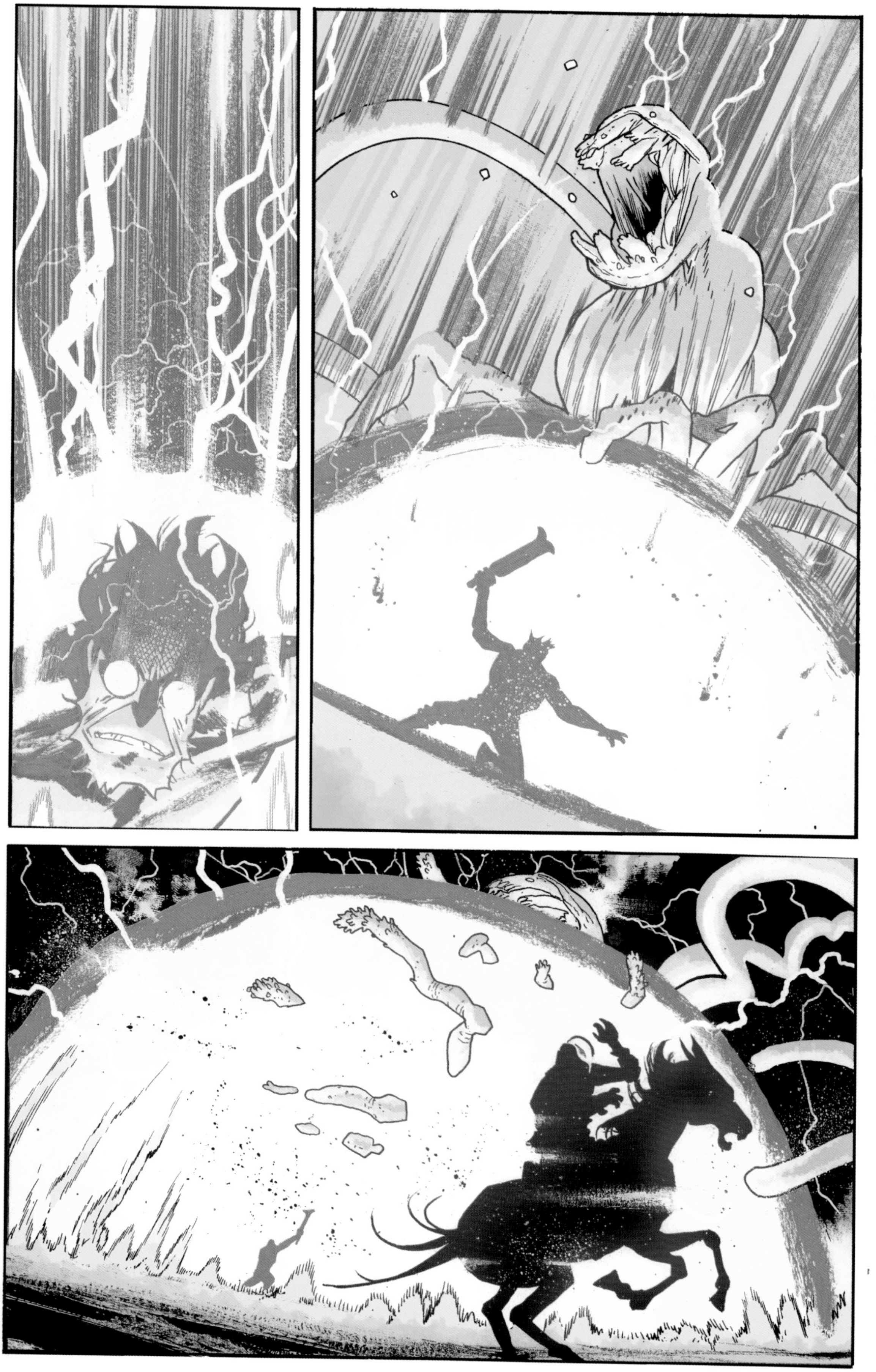

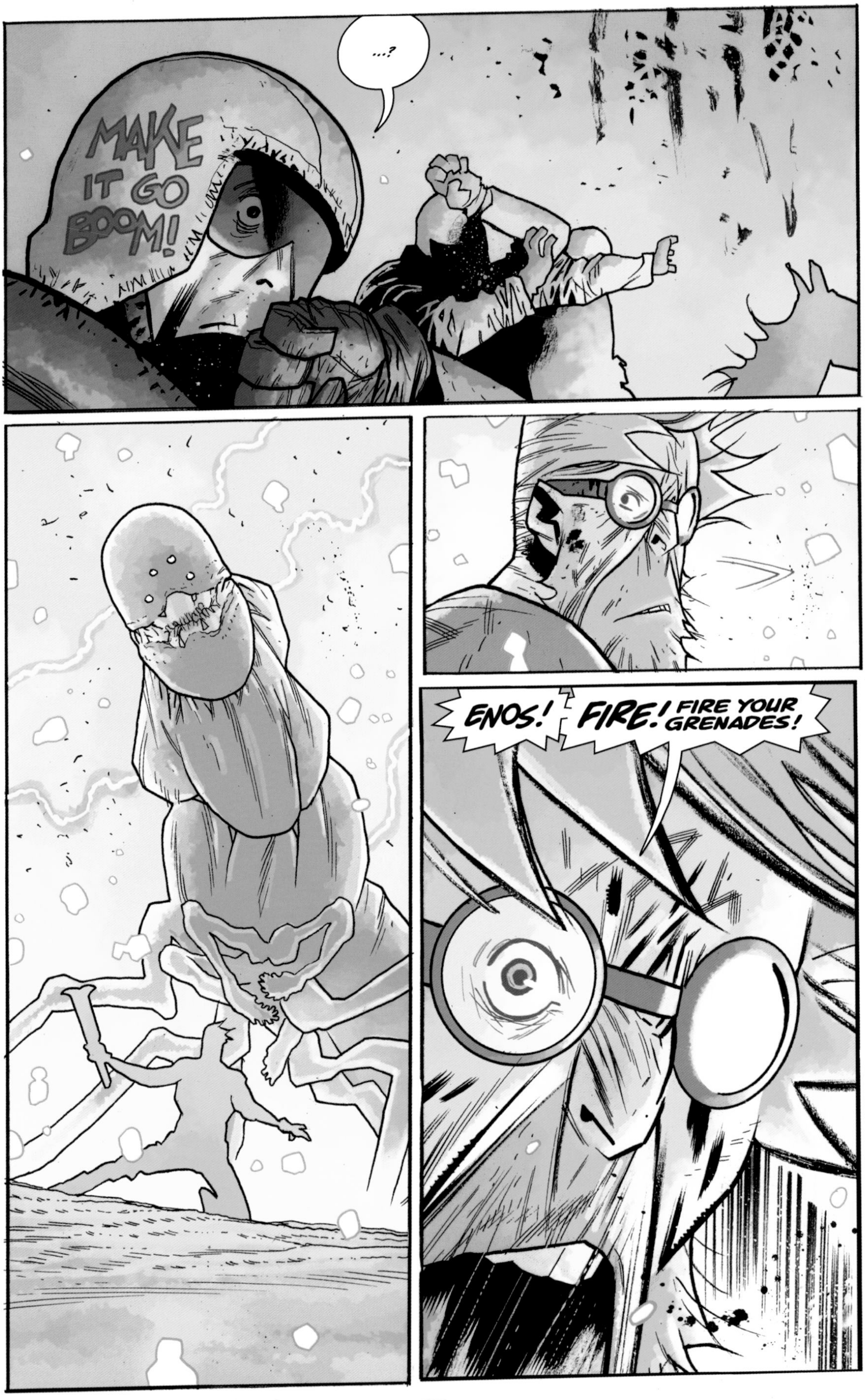

MAKE IT GO BOOM!
...?
ENOS!
FIRE! FIRE YOUR GRENADES!

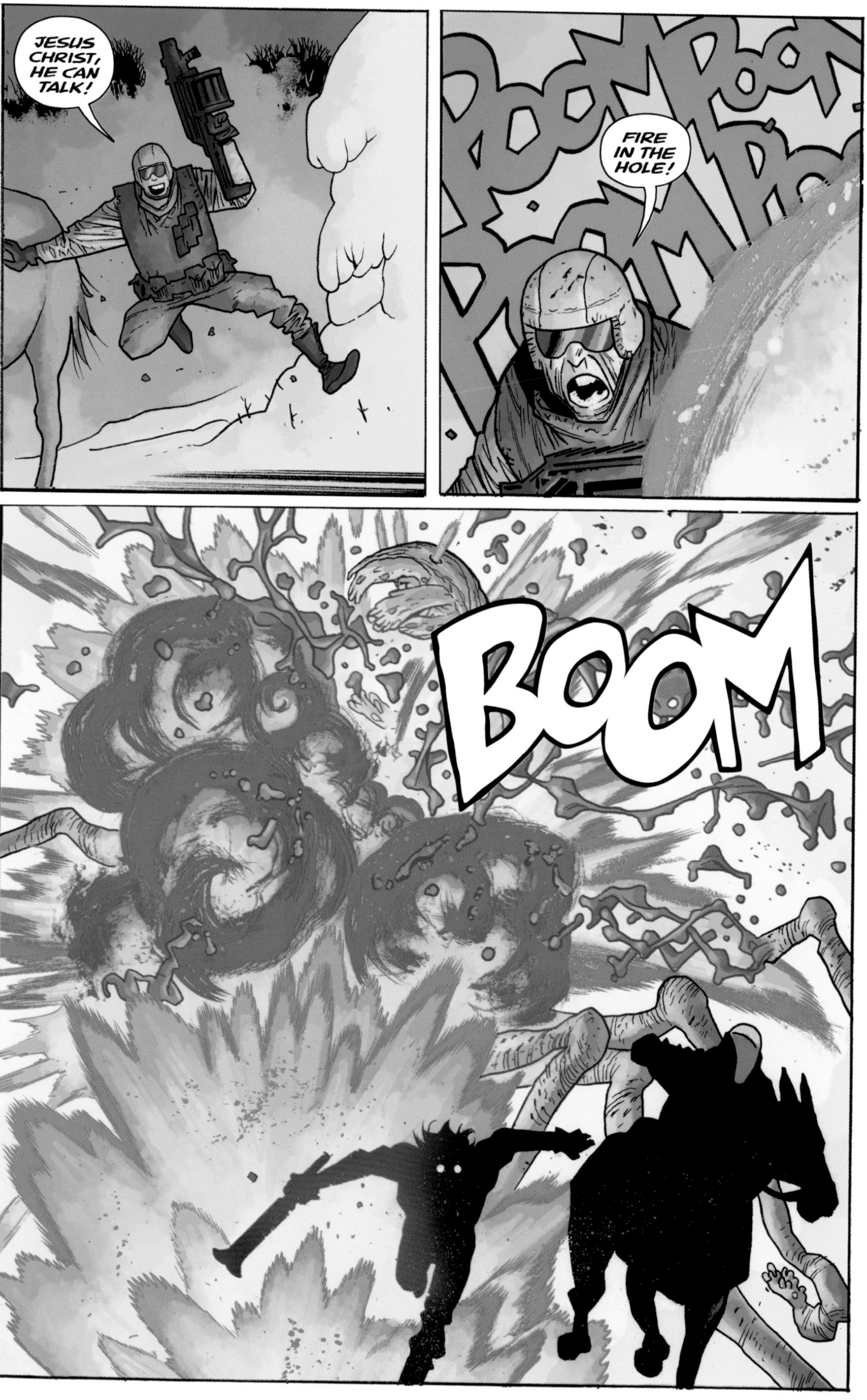
JESUS CHRIST, HE CAN TALK!
FIRE IN THE HOLE!
BOOM

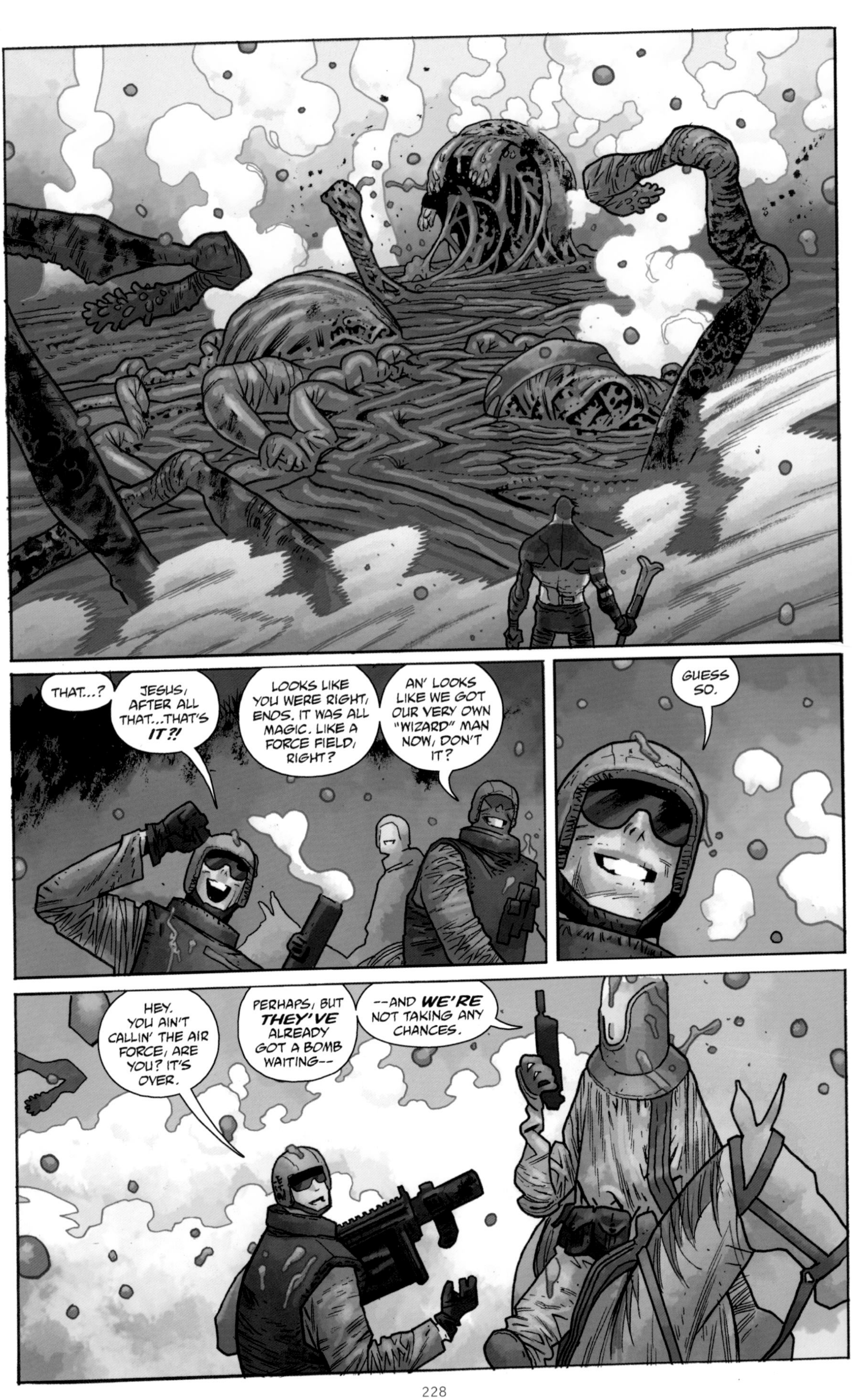
THAT...?
JESUS, AFTER ALL THAT...THAT'S IT?!
LOOKS LIKE YOU WERE RIGHT, ENOS. IT WAS ALL MAGIC. LIKE A FORCE FIELD, RIGHT?
AN' LOOKS LIKE WE GOT OUR VERY OWN "WIZARD" MAN NOW, DON'T IT?
GUESS SO.
HEY. YOU AIN'T CALLIN' THE AIR FORCE, ARE YOU? IT'S OVER.
PERHAPS, BUT THEY'VE ALREADY GOT A BOMB WAITING--
--AND WE'RE NOT TAKING ANY CHANCES.

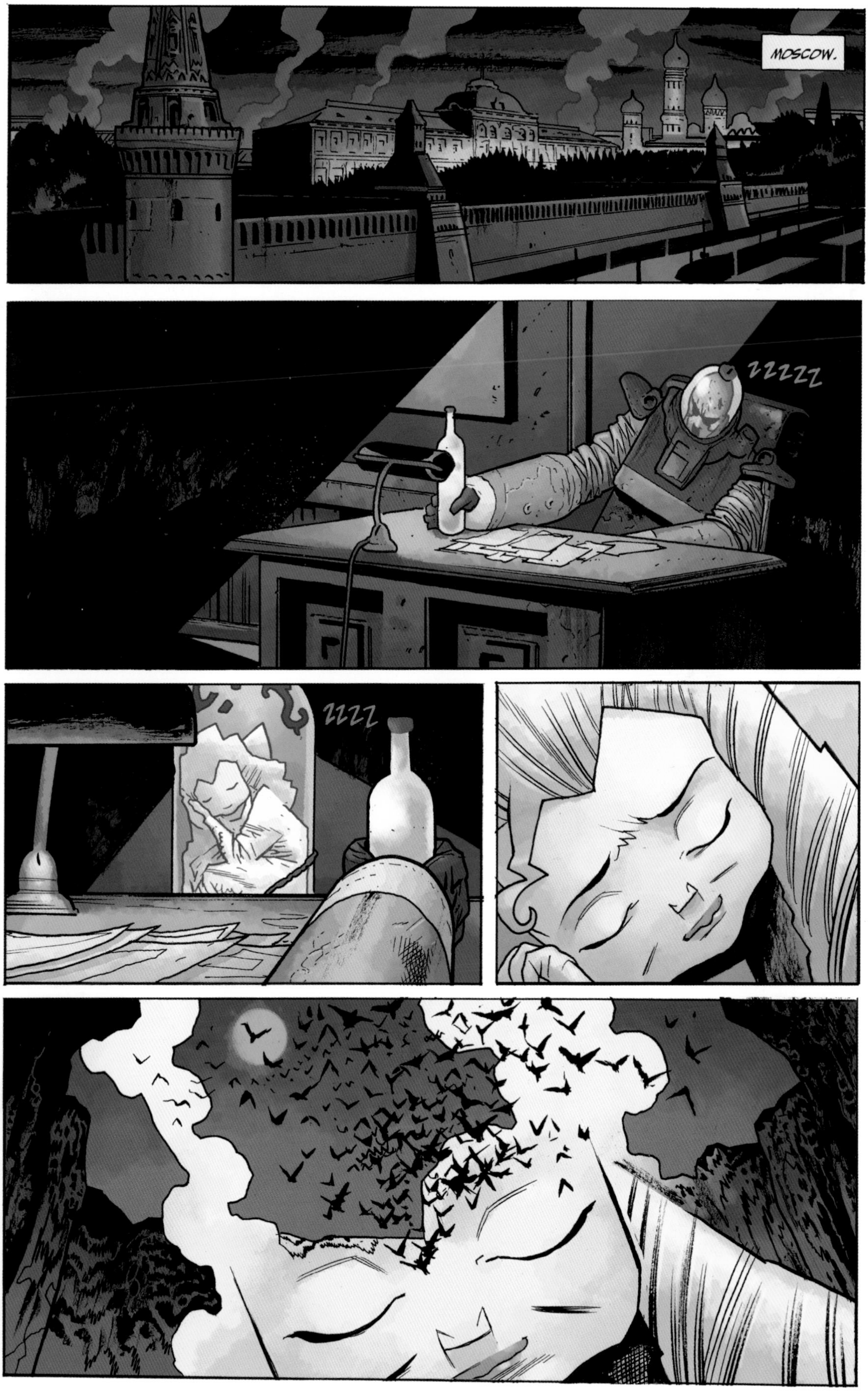
MOSCOW.
ZZZZZ
ZZZZ

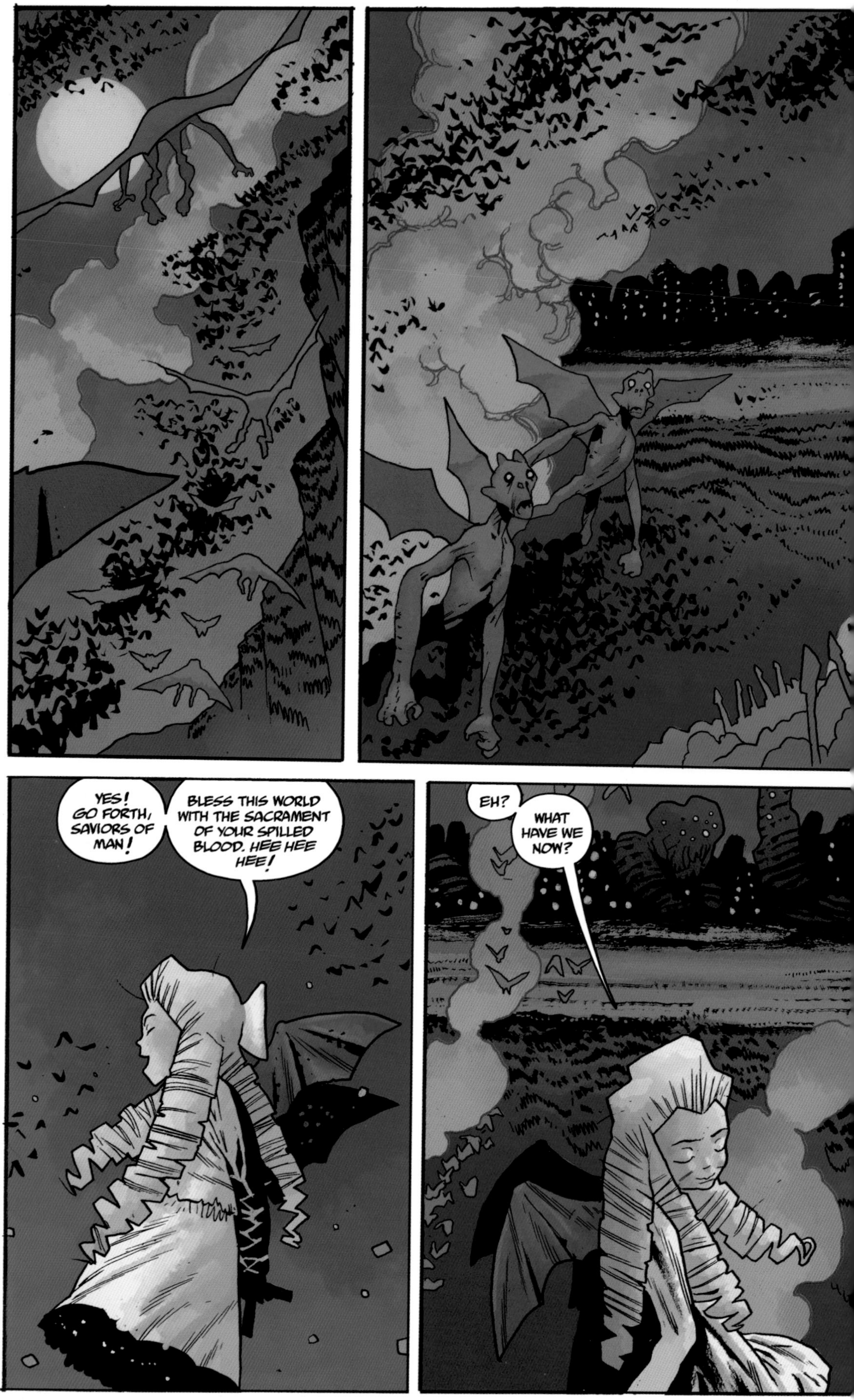
YES! GO FORTH, SAVIORS OF MAN!
BLESS THIS WORLD WITH THE SACRAMENT OF YOUR SPILLED BLOOD. HEE HEE HEE!
EH?
WHAT HAVE WE NOW?

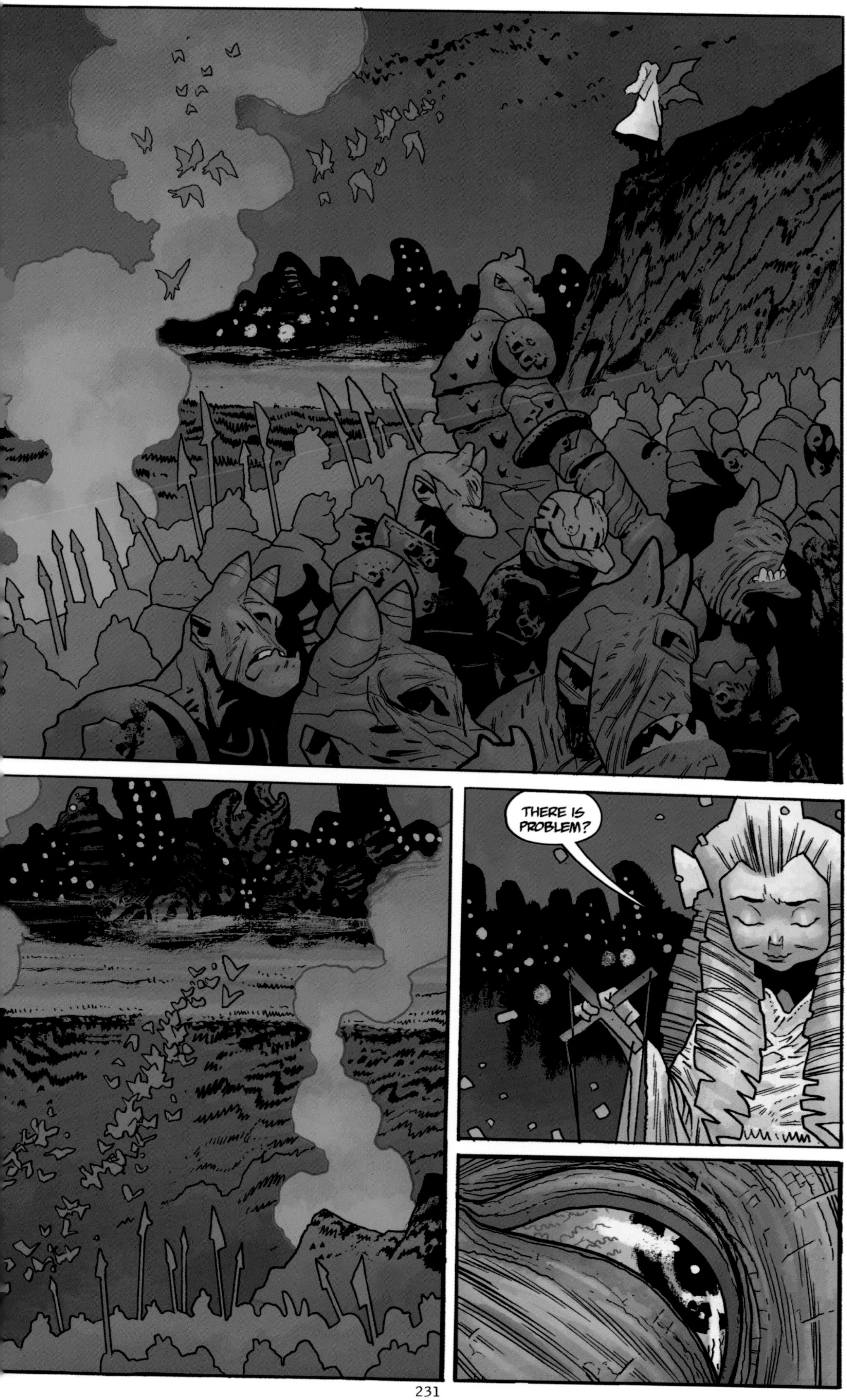
THERE IS PROBLEM?

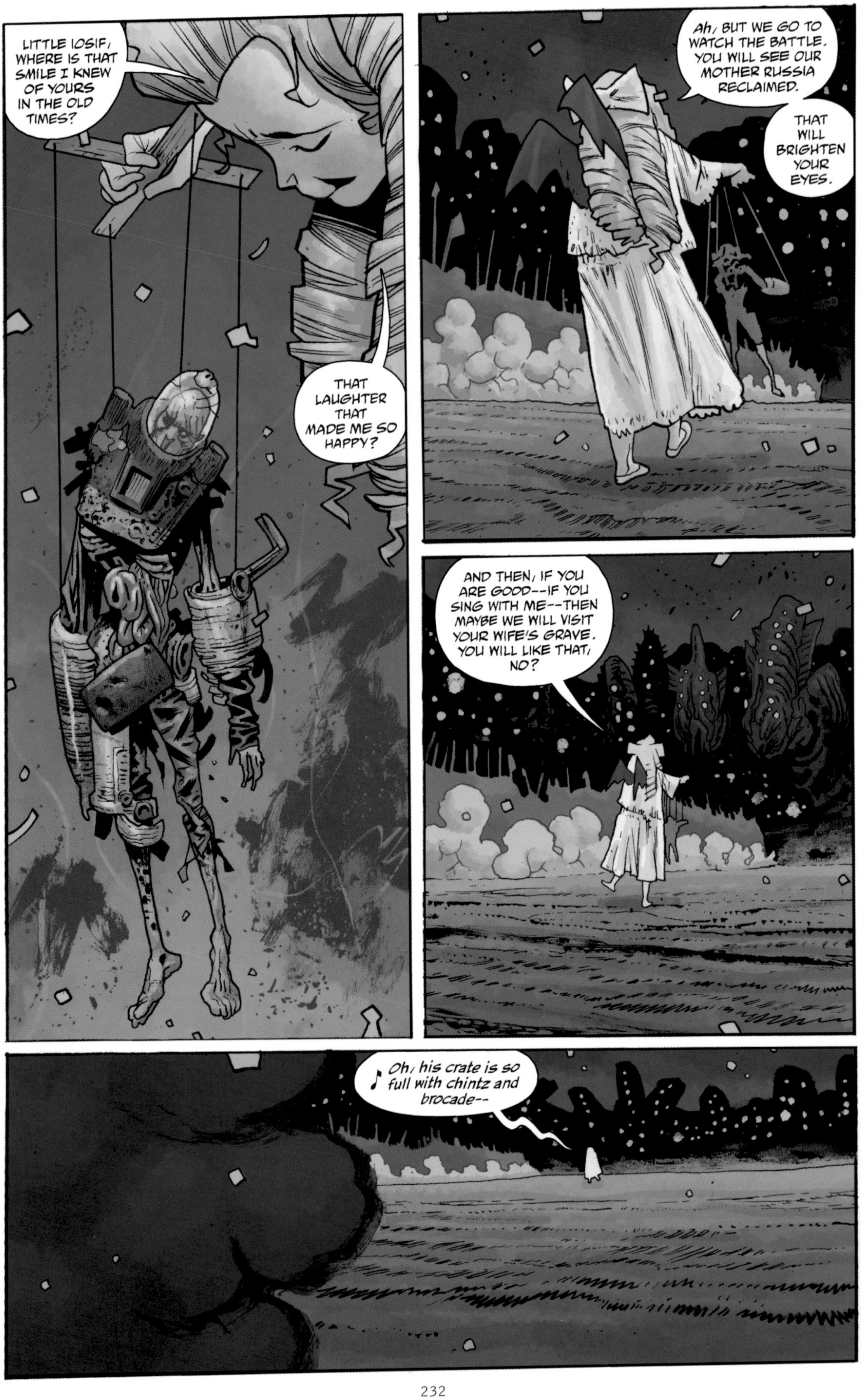
LITTLE IOSIF, WHERE IS THAT SMILE I KNEW OF YOURS IN THE OLD TIMES?
THAT LAUGHTER THAT MADE ME SO HAPPY?
Ah, BUT WE GO TO WATCH THE BATTLE. YOU WILL SEE OUR MOTHER RUSSIA RECLAIMED.
THAT WILL BRIGHTEN YOUR EYES.
AND THEN, IF YOU ARE GOOD--IF YOU SING WITH ME--THEN MAYBE WE WILL VISIT YOUR WIFE'S GRAVE. YOU WILL LIKE THAT, NO?
♪ Oh, his crate is so full with chintz and brocade--

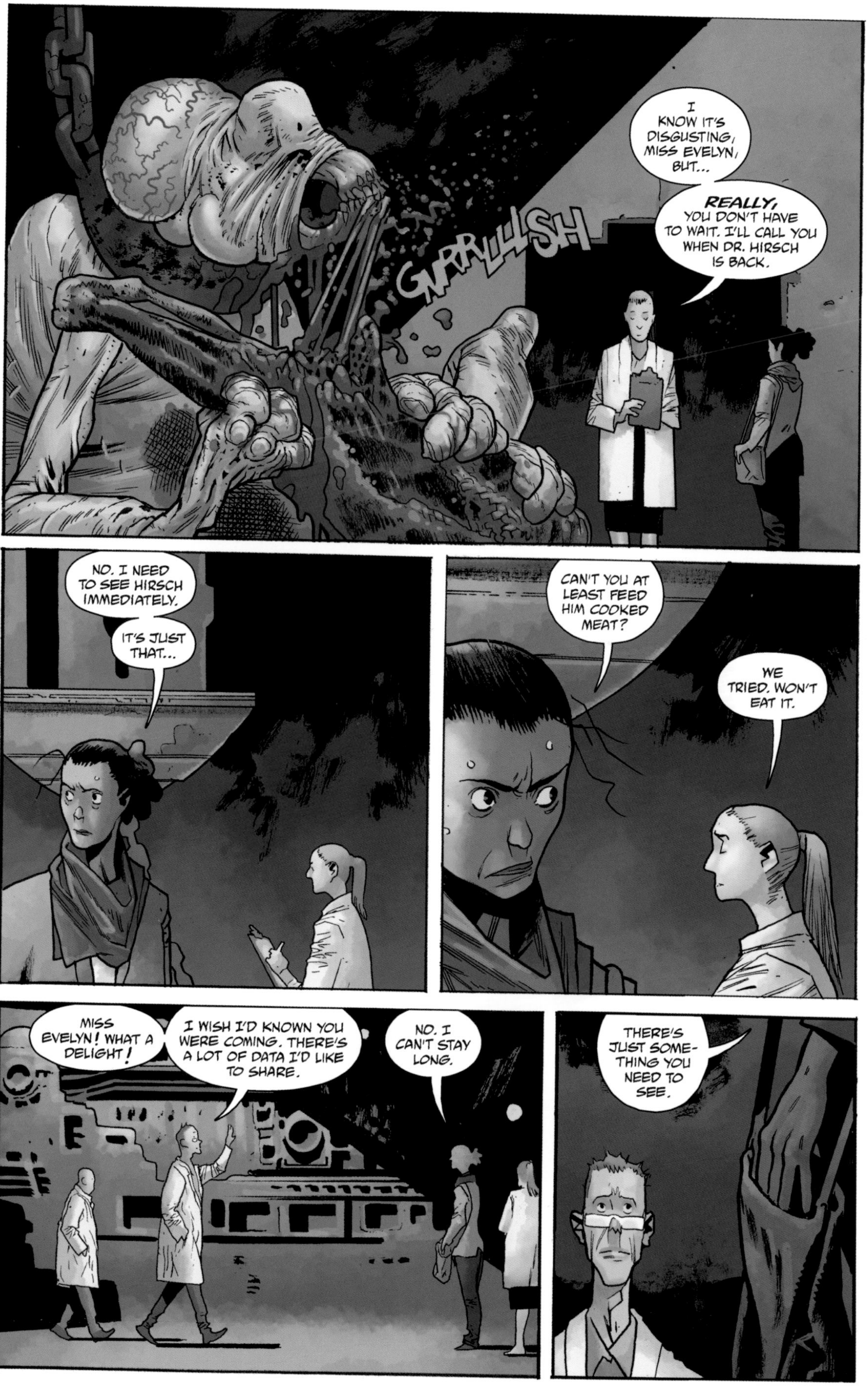
I KNOW IT'S DISGUSTING, MISS EVELYN, BUT...
REALLY, YOU DON'T HAVE TO WAIT. I'LL CALL YOU WHEN DR. HIRSCH IS BACK.
GNRRLLLSH
NO. I NEED TO SEE HIRSCH IMMEDIATELY.
IT'S JUST THAT...
CAN'T YOU AT LEAST FEED HIM COOKED MEAT?
WE TRIED. WON'T EAT IT.
MISS EVELYN! WHAT A DELIGHT!
I WISH I'D KNOWN YOU WERE COMING. THERE'S A LOT OF DATA I'D LIKE TO SHARE.
NO. I CAN'T STAY LONG.
THERE'S JUST SOMETHING YOU NEED TO SEE.

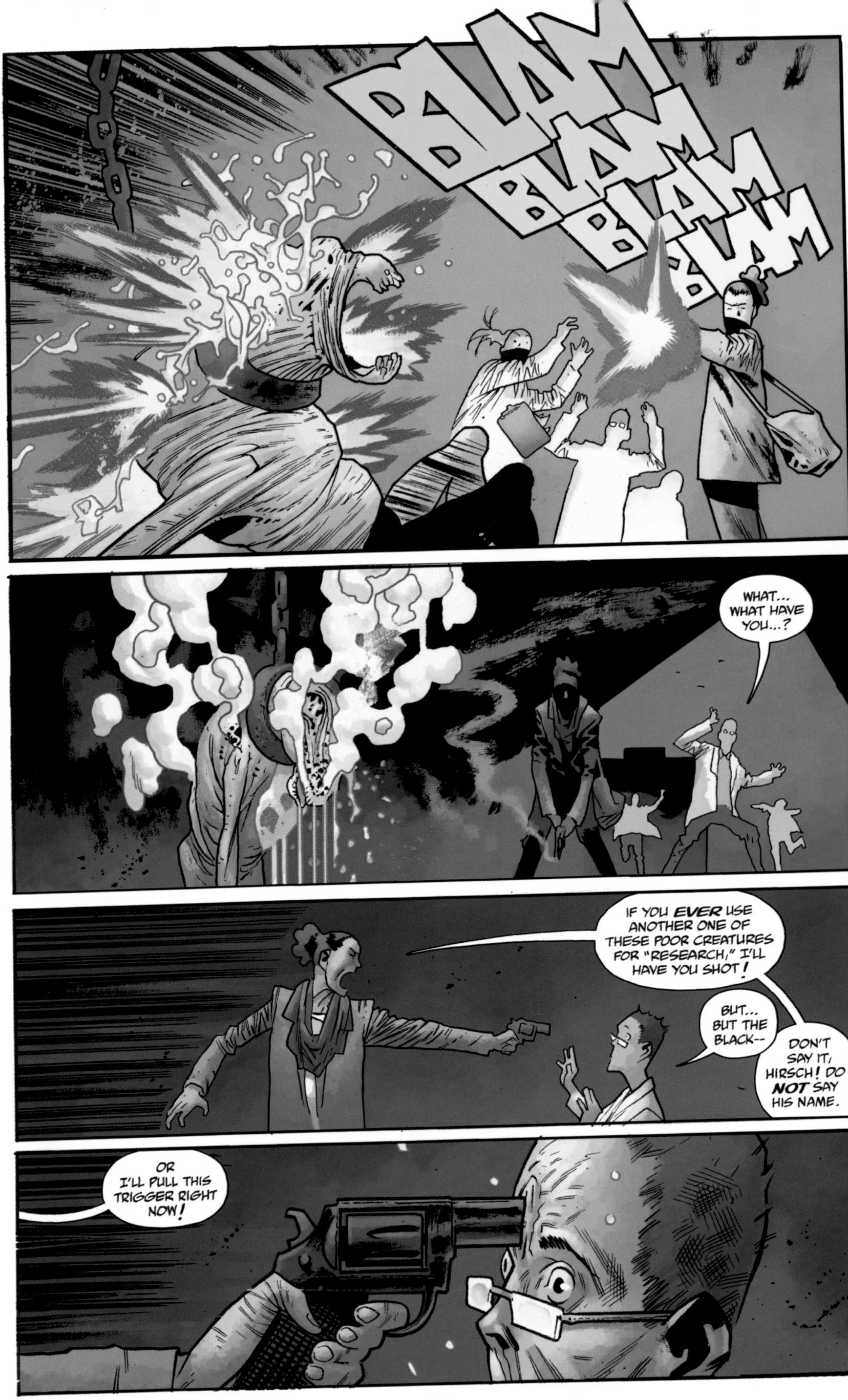
BLAM BLAM BLAM BLAM BLAM
WHAT... WHAT HAVE YOU...?
IF YOU EVER USE ANOTHER ONE OF THESE POOR CREATURES FOR "RESEARCH," I'LL HAVE YOU SHOT!
BUT... BUT THE BLACK--
DON'T SAY IT, HIRSCH! DO NOT SAY HIS NAME.
OR I'LL PULL THIS TRIGGER RIGHT NOW!

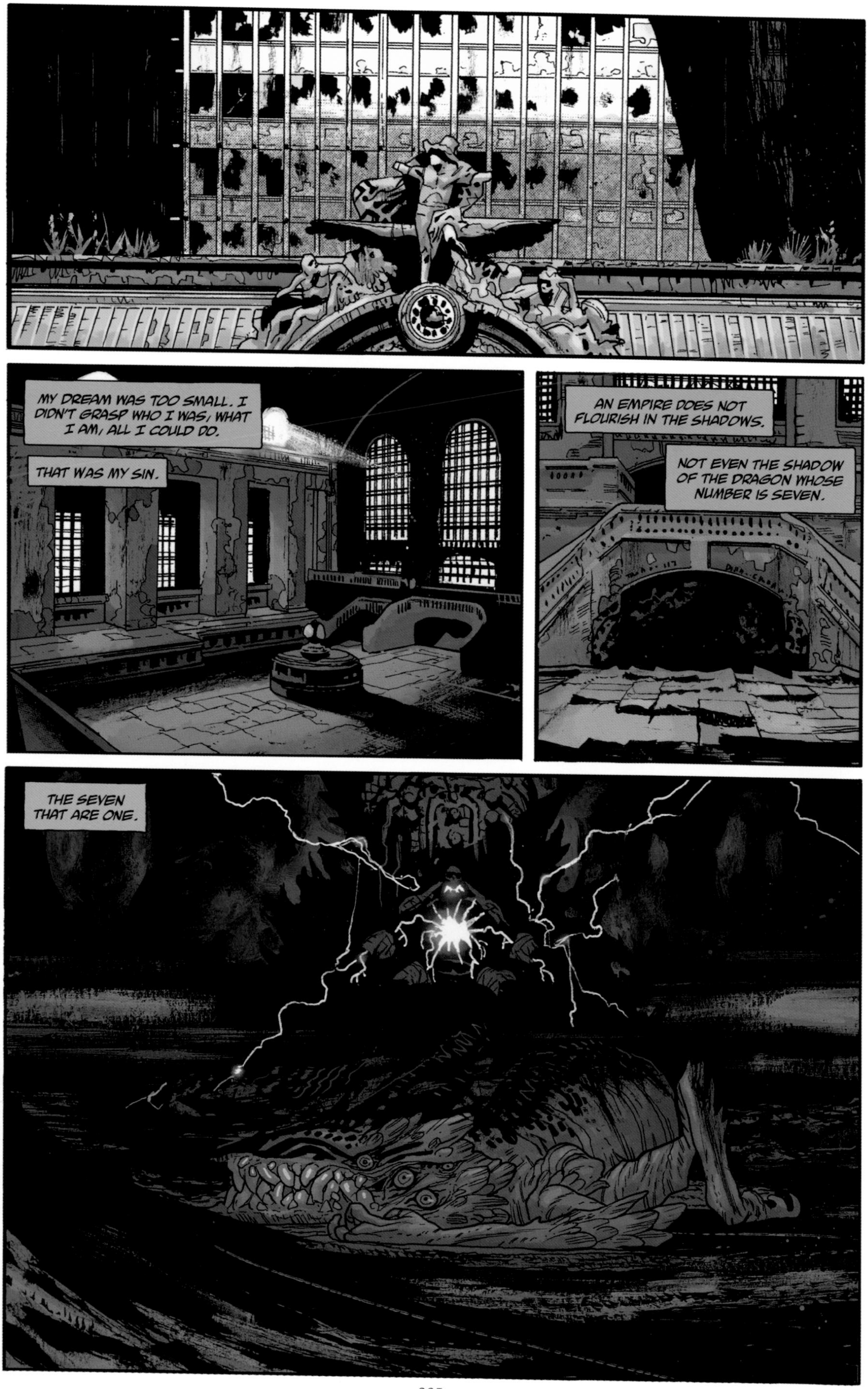
MY DREAM WAS TOO SMALL. I DIDN'T GRASP WHO I WAS, WHAT I AM, ALL I COULD DO.
THAT WAS MY SIN.
AN EMPIRE DOES NOT FLOURISH IN THE SHADOWS.
NOT EVEN THE SHADOW OF THE DRAGON WHOSE NUMBER IS SEVEN.
THE SEVEN THAT ARE ONE.

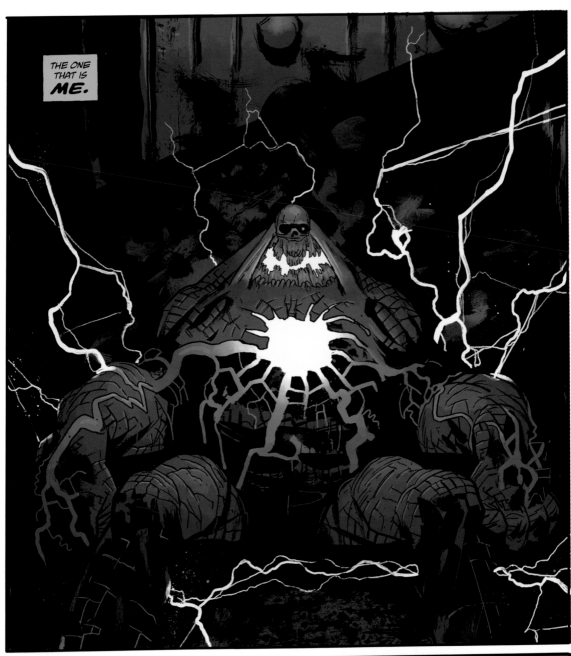

THE ONE
THAT IS
ME.

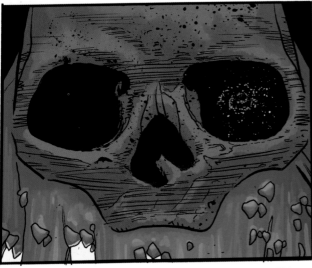

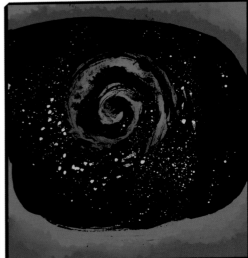

THE SEVEN...

THE SEVEN THAT ARE MINE!

MINE!

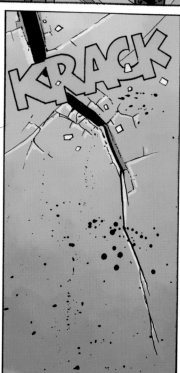

KRACK

KRA-AAK

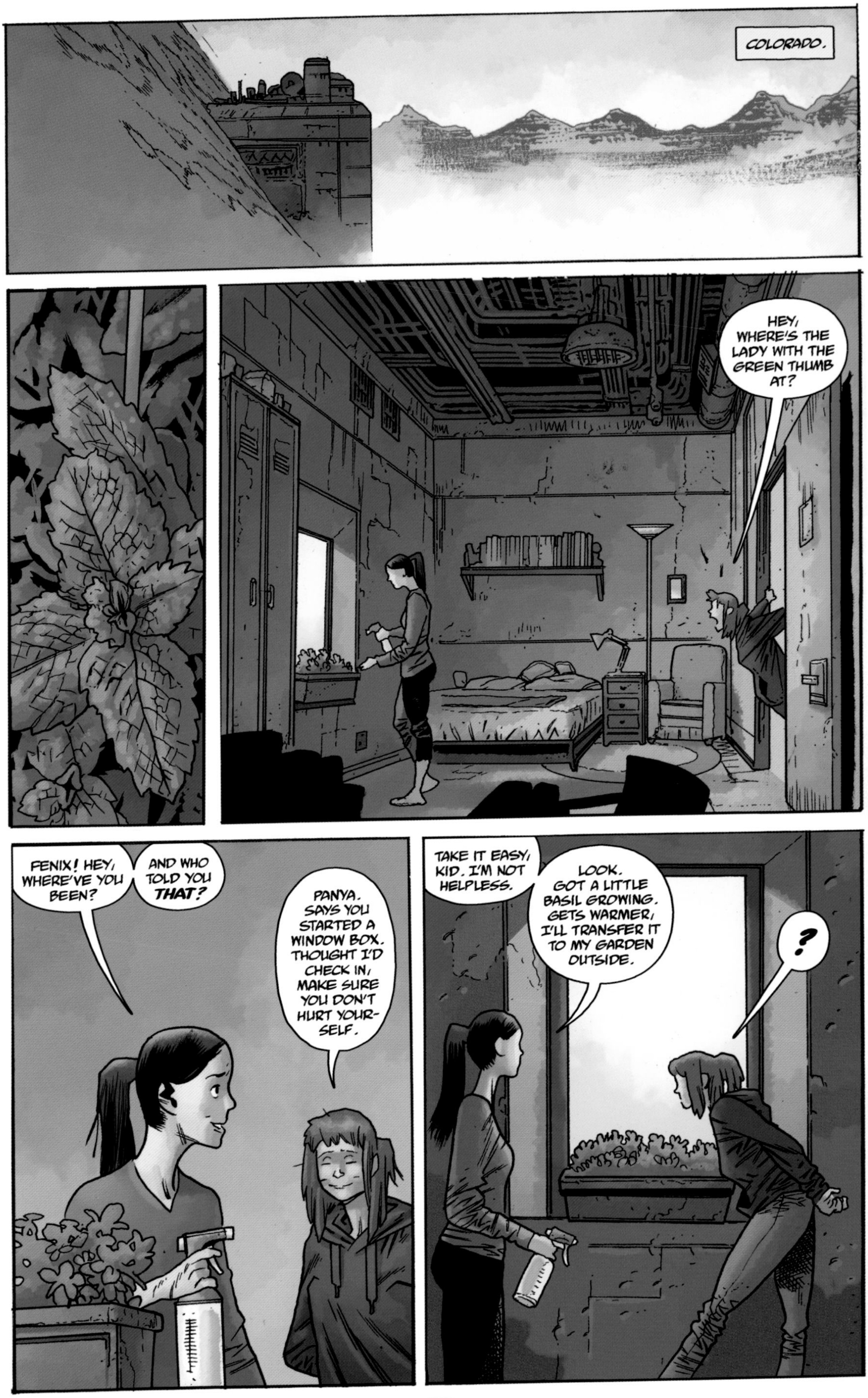
COLORADO.
HEY, WHERE'S THE LADY WITH THE GREEN THUMB AT?
FENIX! HEY, WHERE'VE YOU BEEN?
AND WHO TOLD YOU *THAT?*
PANYA. SAYS YOU STARTED A WINDOW BOX. THOUGHT I'D CHECK IN, MAKE SURE YOU DON'T HURT YOURSELF.
TAKE IT EASY, KID. I'M NOT HELPLESS.
LOOK. GOT A LITTLE BASIL GROWING. GETS WARMER, I'LL TRANSFER IT TO MY GARDEN OUTSIDE.
?

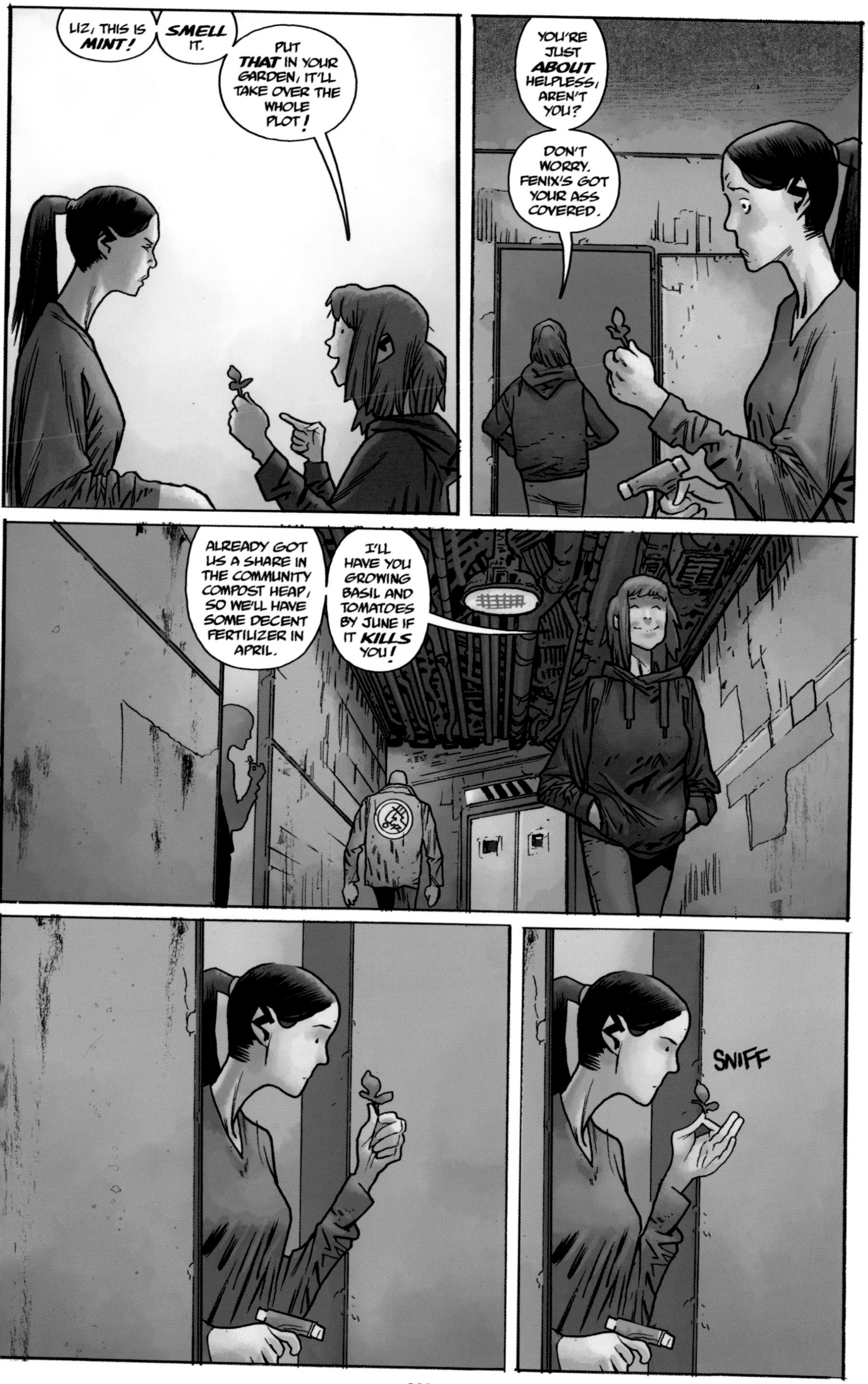
LIZ, THIS IS MINT!
SMELL IT.
PUT THAT IN YOUR GARDEN, IT'LL TAKE OVER THE WHOLE PLOT!
YOU'RE JUST ABOUT HELPLESS, AREN'T YOU?
DON'T WORRY. FENIX'S GOT YOUR ASS COVERED.
ALREADY GOT US A SHARE IN THE COMMUNITY COMPOST HEAP, SO WE'LL HAVE SOME DECENT FERTILIZER IN APRIL.
I'LL HAVE YOU GROWING BASIL AND TOMATOES BY JUNE IF IT KILLS YOU!
SNIFF

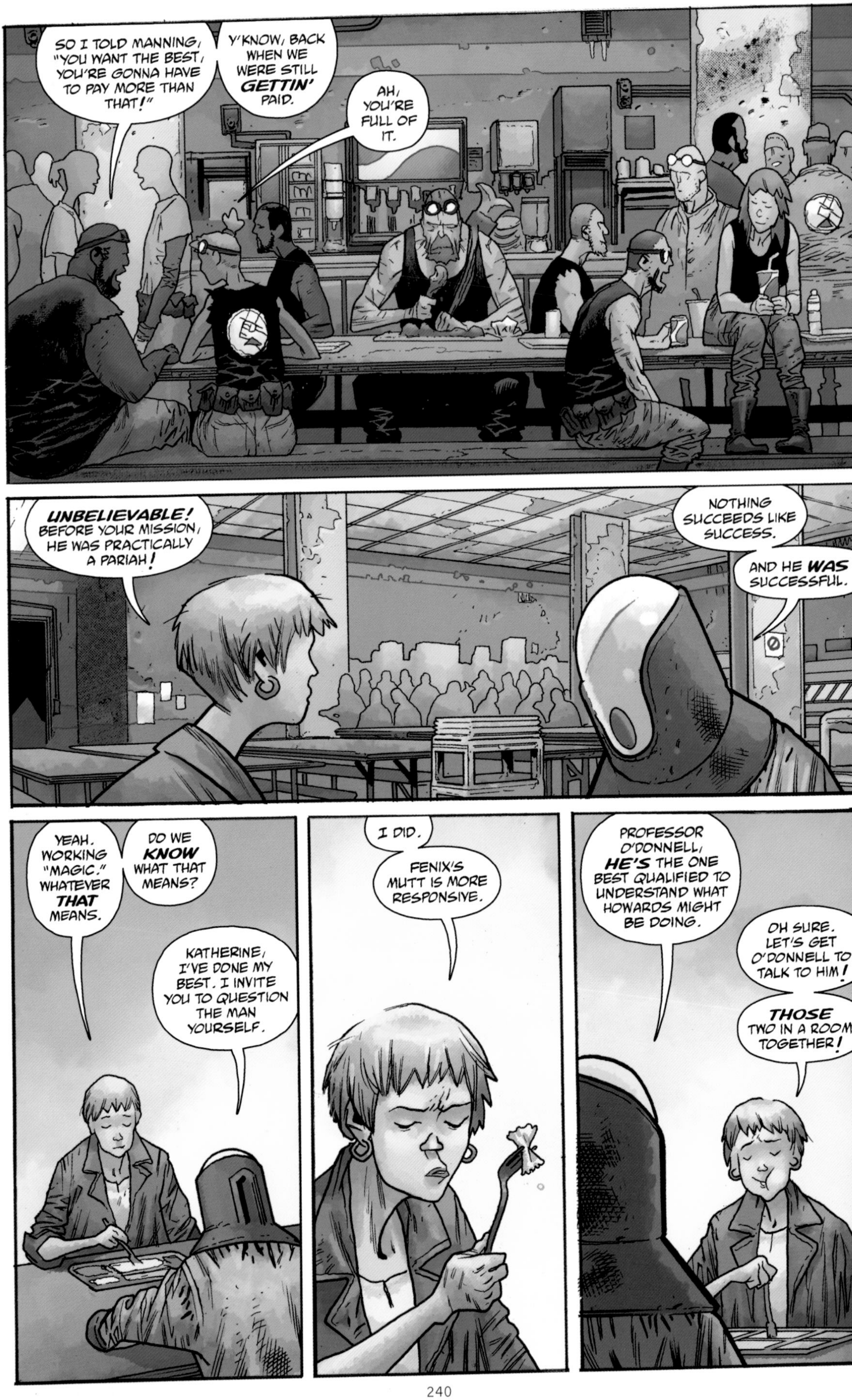
SO I TOLD MANNING, "YOU WANT THE BEST, YOU'RE GONNA HAVE TO PAY MORE THAN THAT!"
Y'KNOW, BACK WHEN WE WERE STILL GETTIN' PAID.
AH, YOU'RE FULL OF IT.
UNBELIEVABLE! BEFORE YOUR MISSION, HE WAS PRACTICALLY A PARIAH!
NOTHING SUCCEEDS LIKE SUCCESS.
AND HE WAS SUCCESSFUL.
YEAH. WORKING "MAGIC." WHATEVER THAT MEANS.
DO WE KNOW WHAT THAT MEANS?
KATHERINE, I'VE DONE MY BEST. I INVITE YOU TO QUESTION THE MAN YOURSELF.
I DID.
FENIX'S MUTT IS MORE RESPONSIVE.
PROFESSOR O'DONNELL, HE'S THE ONE BEST QUALIFIED TO UNDERSTAND WHAT HOWARDS MIGHT BE DOING.
OH SURE. LET'S GET O'DONNELL TO TALK TO HIM!
THOSE TWO IN A ROOM TOGETHER!

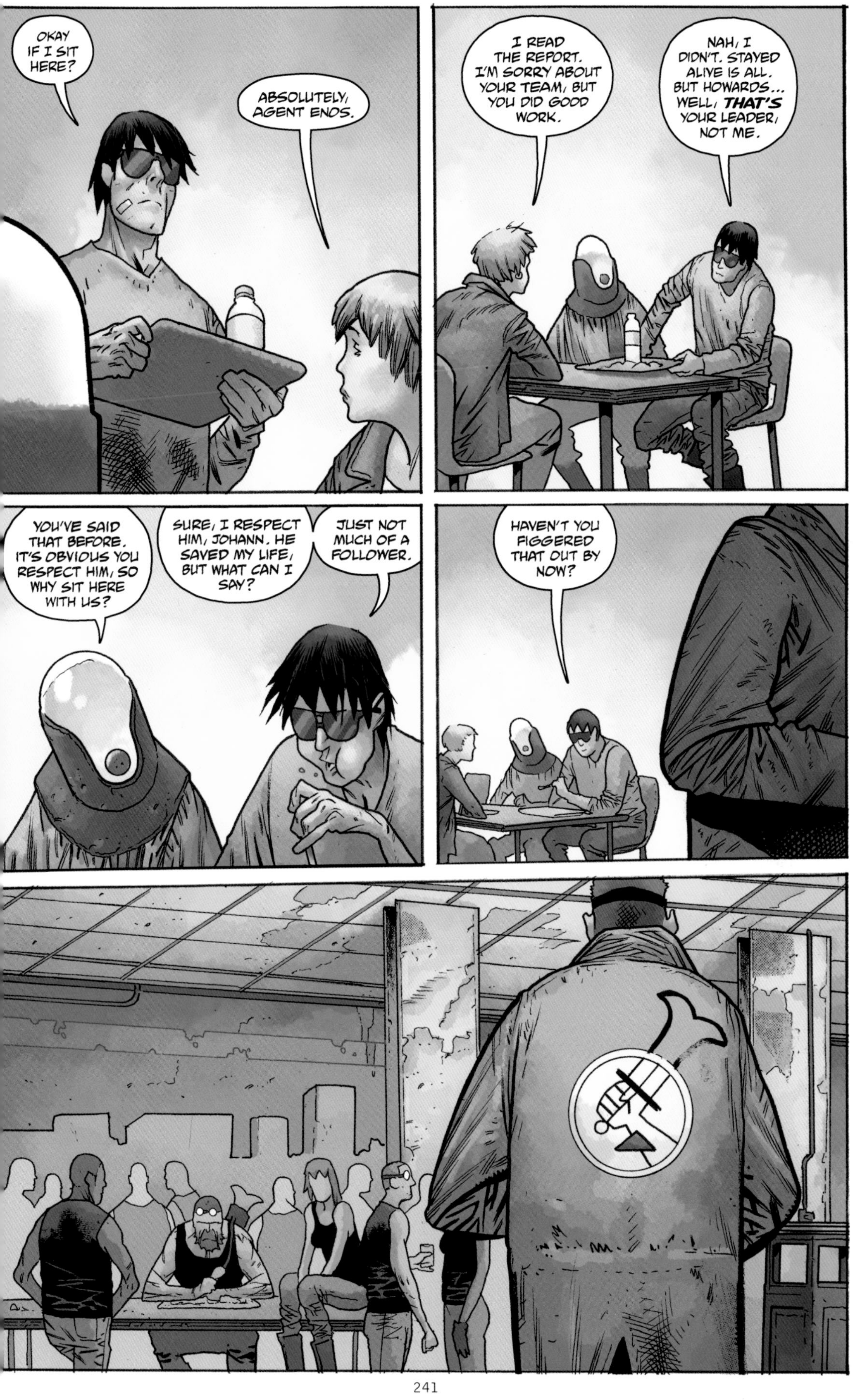
OKAY IF I SIT HERE?
ABSOLUTELY, AGENT ENOS.
I READ THE REPORT. I'M SORRY ABOUT YOUR TEAM, BUT YOU DID GOOD WORK.
NAH, I DIDN'T. STAYED ALIVE IS ALL. BUT HOWARDS... WELL, **THAT'S** YOUR LEADER, NOT ME.
YOU'VE SAID THAT BEFORE. IT'S OBVIOUS YOU RESPECT HIM, SO WHY SIT HERE WITH US?
SURE, I RESPECT HIM, JOHANN. HE SAVED MY LIFE, BUT WHAT CAN I SAY?
JUST NOT MUCH OF A FOLLOWER.
HAVEN'T YOU FIGGERED THAT OUT BY NOW?

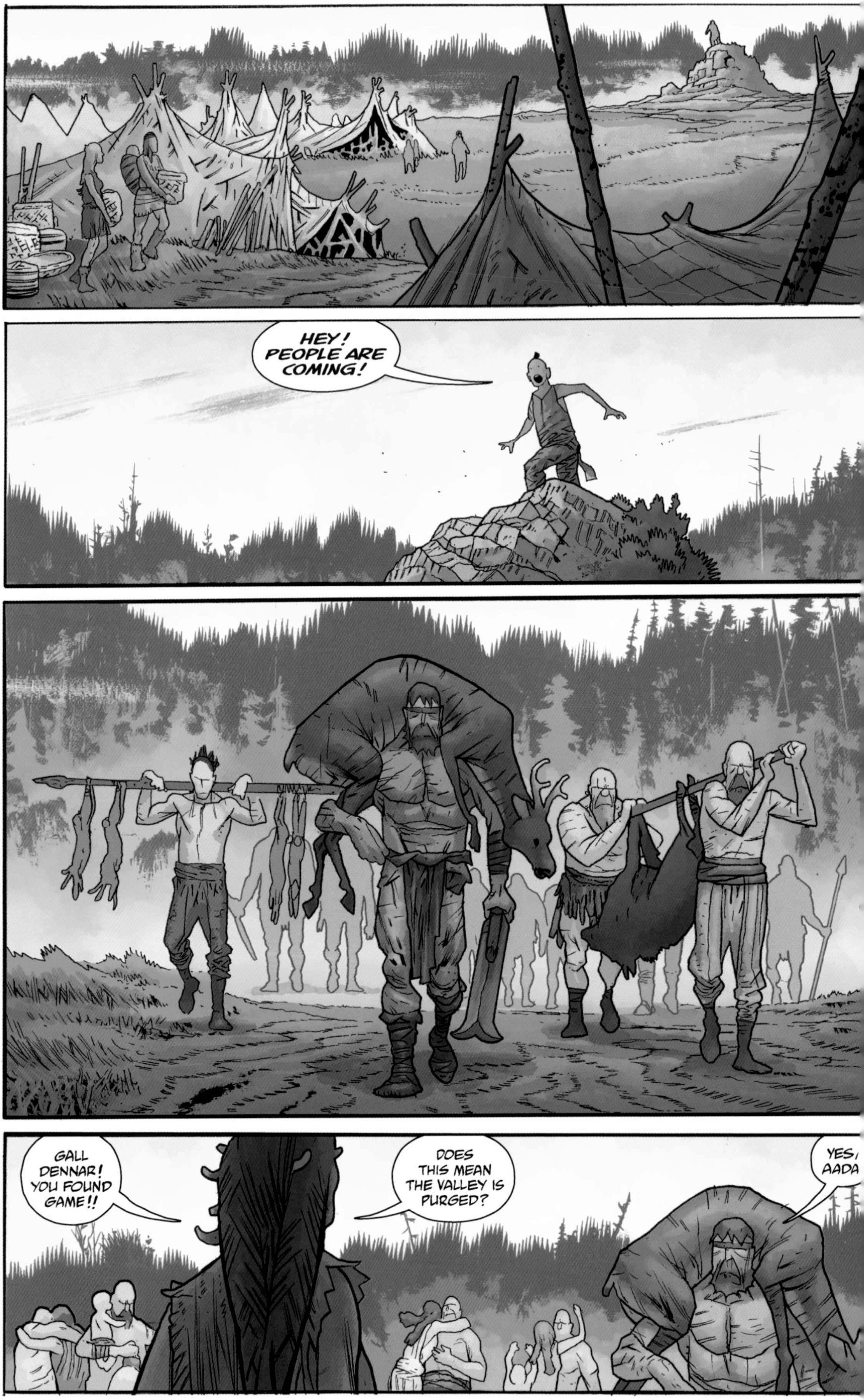
HEY! PEOPLE ARE COMING!
GALL DENNAR! YOU FOUND GAME!!
DOES THIS MEAN THE VALLEY IS PURGED?
YES, AADA

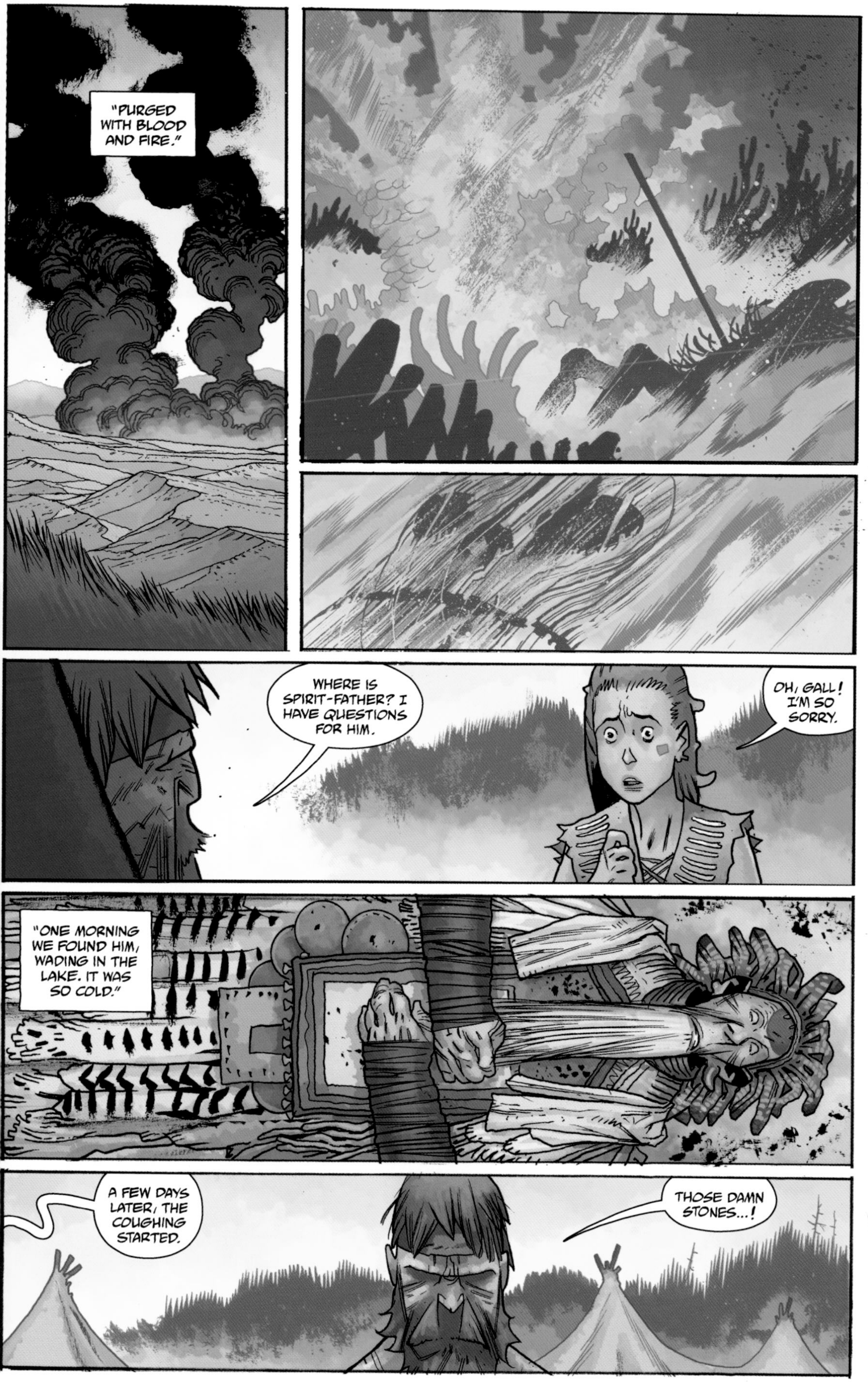
"PURGED WITH BLOOD AND FIRE."
WHERE IS SPIRIT-FATHER? I HAVE QUESTIONS FOR HIM.
OH, GALL! I'M SO SORRY.
"ONE MORNING WE FOUND HIM, WADING IN THE LAKE. IT WAS SO COLD."
A FEW DAYS LATER, THE COUGHING STARTED.
THOSE DAMN STONES...!

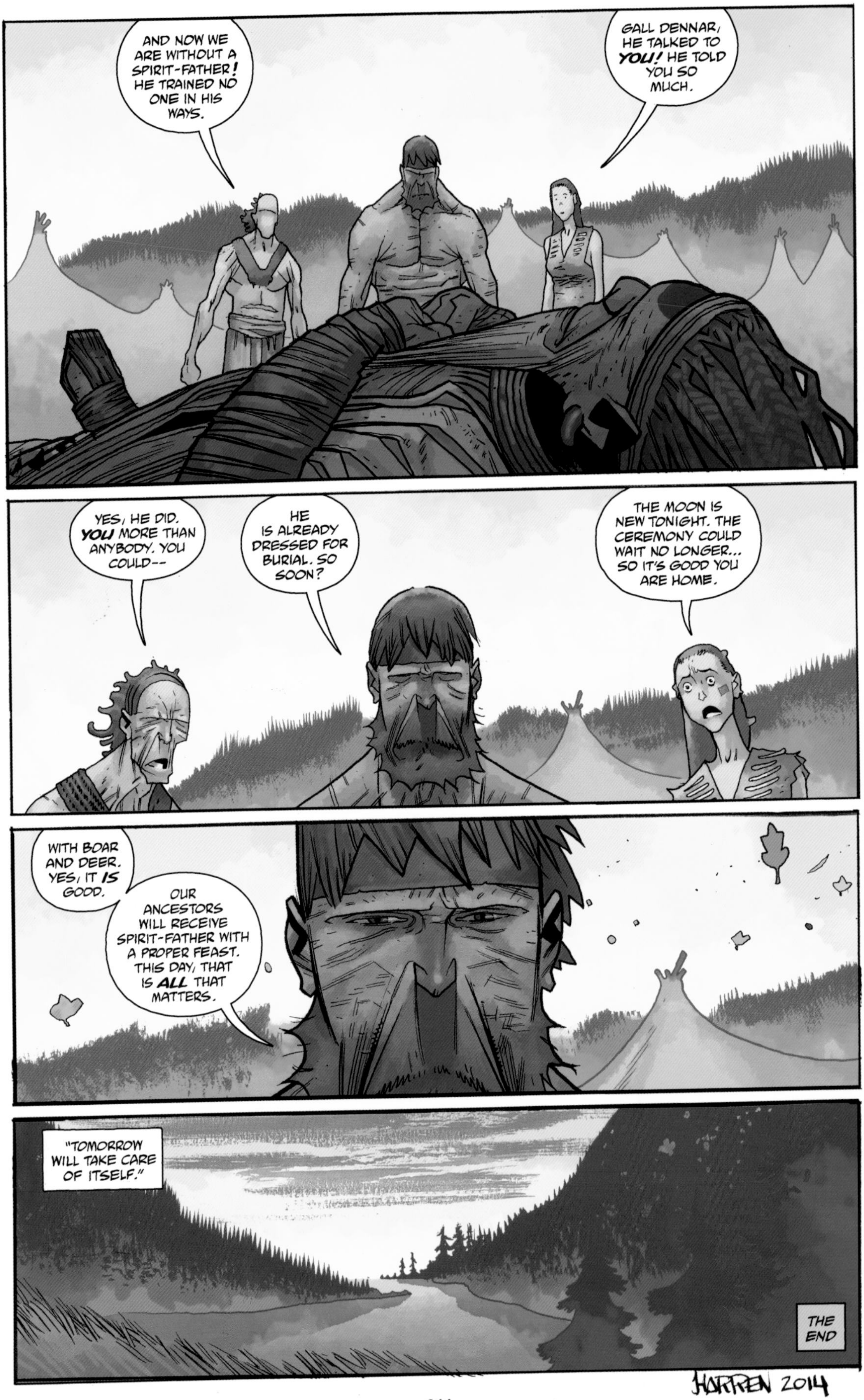
AND NOW WE ARE WITHOUT A SPIRIT-FATHER! HE TRAINED NO ONE IN HIS WAYS.
GALL DENNAR, HE TALKED TO YOU! HE TOLD YOU SO MUCH.
YES, HE DID. YOU MORE THAN ANYBODY. YOU COULD--
HE IS ALREADY DRESSED FOR BURIAL. SO SOON?
THE MOON IS NEW TONIGHT. THE CEREMONY COULD WAIT NO LONGER... SO IT'S GOOD YOU ARE HOME.
WITH BOAR AND DEER. YES, IT IS GOOD.
OUR ANCESTORS WILL RECEIVE SPIRIT-FATHER WITH A PROPER FEAST. THIS DAY, THAT IS ALL THAT MATTERS.
"TOMORROW WILL TAKE CARE OF ITSELF."
THE END
HARREN 2014

EXORCISM

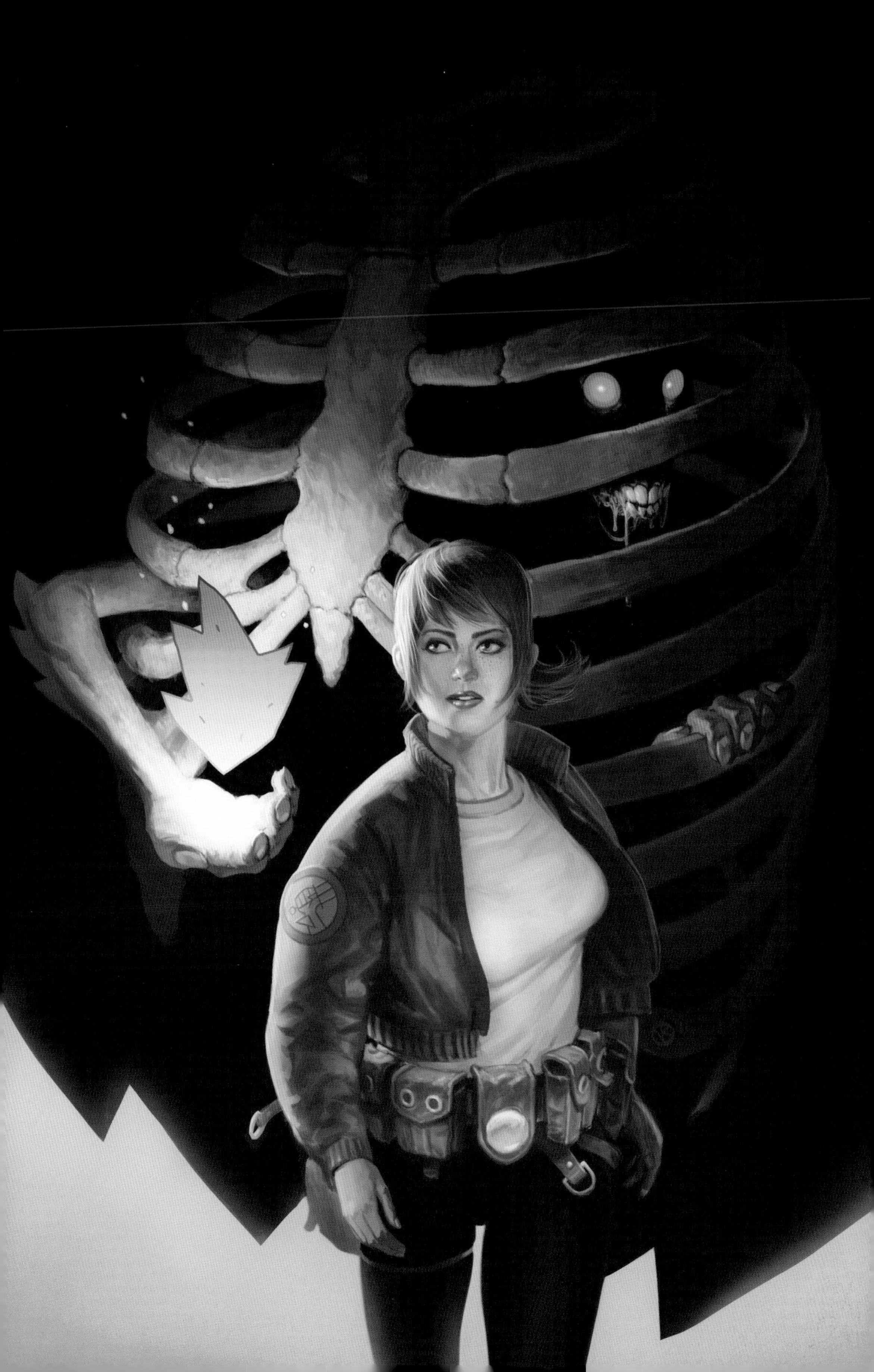

EAST AFRICA, 1890.

JAMES, THIS IS **MADNESS!**

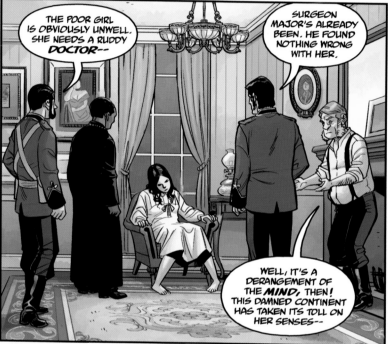

THE POOR GIRL IS OBVIOUSLY UNWELL. SHE NEEDS A RUDDY **DOCTOR--**

SURGEON MAJOR'S ALREADY BEEN. HE FOUND NOTHING WRONG WITH HER.

WELL, IT'S A DERANGEMENT OF THE **MIND,** THEN! THIS DAMNED CONTINENT HAS TAKEN ITS TOLL ON HER SENSES--

YOU WERE RIGHT TO SEND FOR ME. WITHIN THIS WOMAN RESIDES GREAT EVIL.

WE MUST ACT SWIFTLY.

URRRR

WHAT **ROT!** KEATING, THIS IS ABSOLUTE NONSENSE.

I WOULDN'T HAVE THIS FROM AN **ENGLISH** BIBLE BEATER, LET ALONE ONE OF THESE... **FUZZIES** PLAYING DRESS-UP!

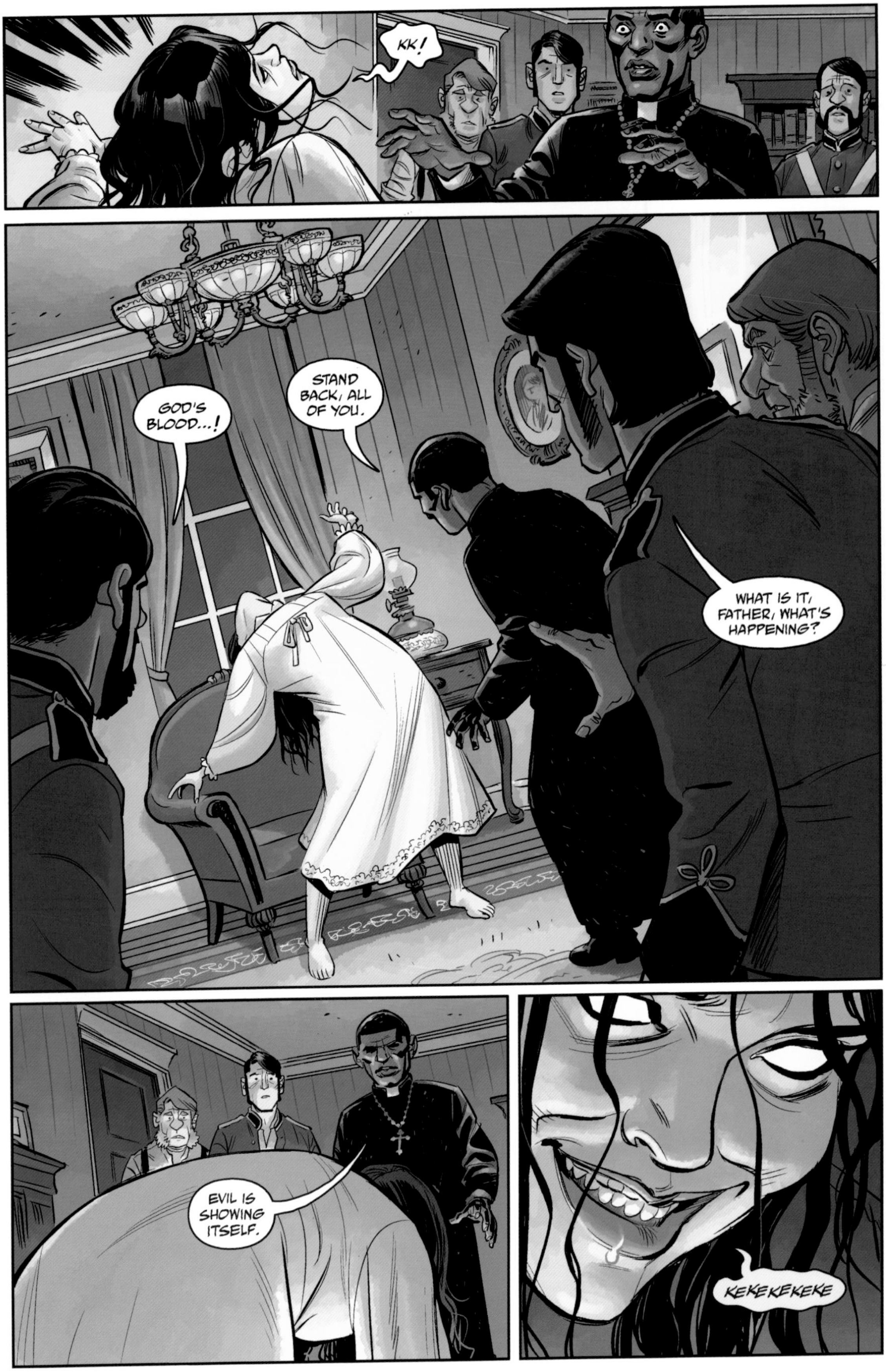
KK!
GOD'S BLOOD...!
STAND BACK, ALL OF YOU.
WHAT IS IT, FATHER, WHAT'S HAPPENING?
EVIL IS SHOWING ITSELF.
KEKEKEKEKE

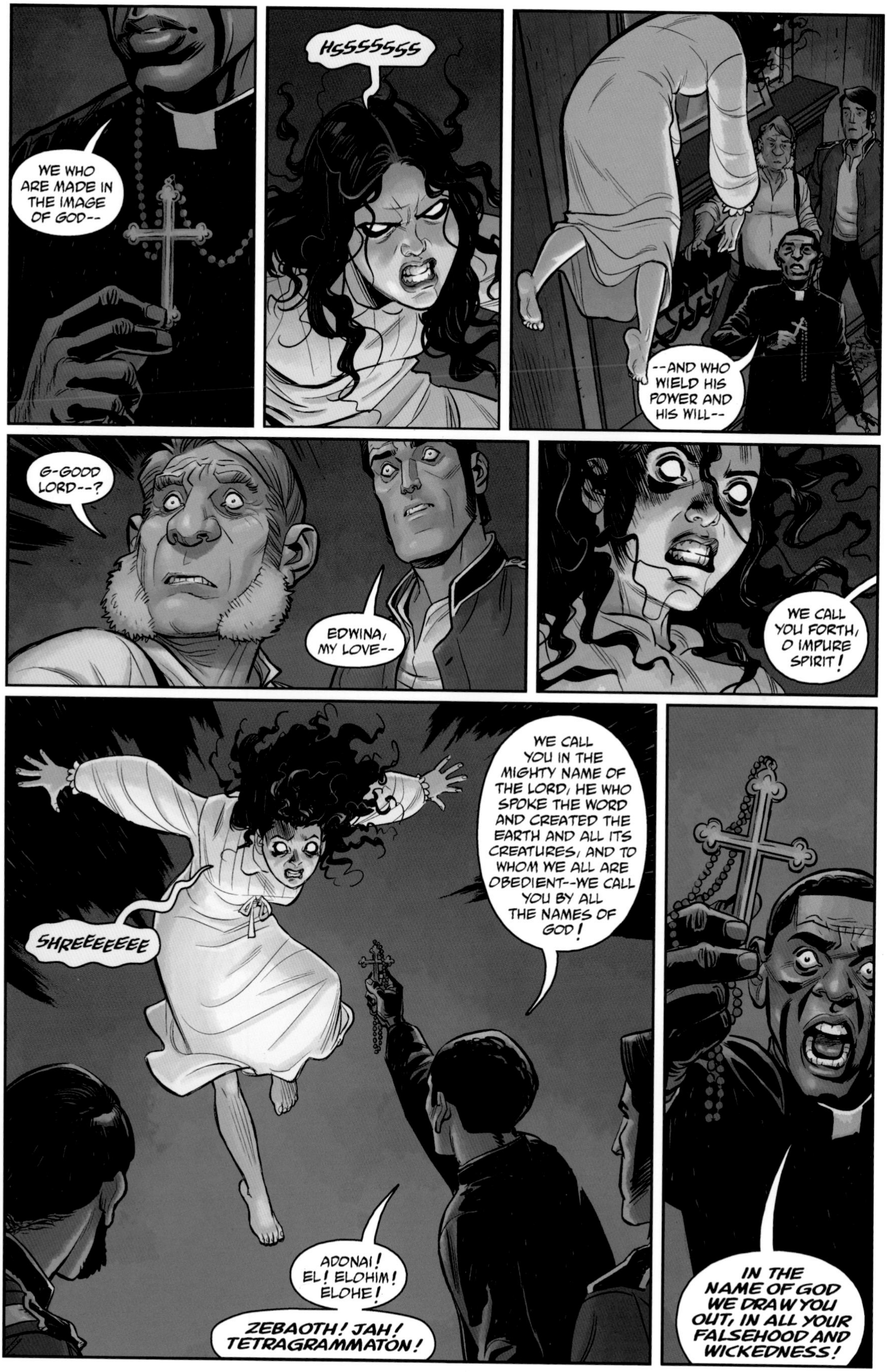
WE WHO ARE MADE IN THE IMAGE OF GOD--
HSSSSSSS
--AND WHO WIELD HIS POWER AND HIS WILL--
G-GOOD LORD--?
EDWINA, MY LOVE--
WE CALL YOU FORTH, O IMPURE SPIRIT!
WE CALL YOU IN THE MIGHTY NAME OF THE LORD, HE WHO SPOKE THE WORD AND CREATED THE EARTH AND ALL ITS CREATURES, AND TO WHOM WE ALL ARE OBEDIENT--WE CALL YOU BY ALL THE NAMES OF GOD!
SHREEEEEEE
ADONAI! EL! ELOHIM! ELOHE!
ZEBAOTH! JAH! TETRAGRAMMATON!
IN THE NAME OF GOD WE DRAW YOU OUT, IN ALL YOUR FALSEHOOD AND WICKEDNESS!

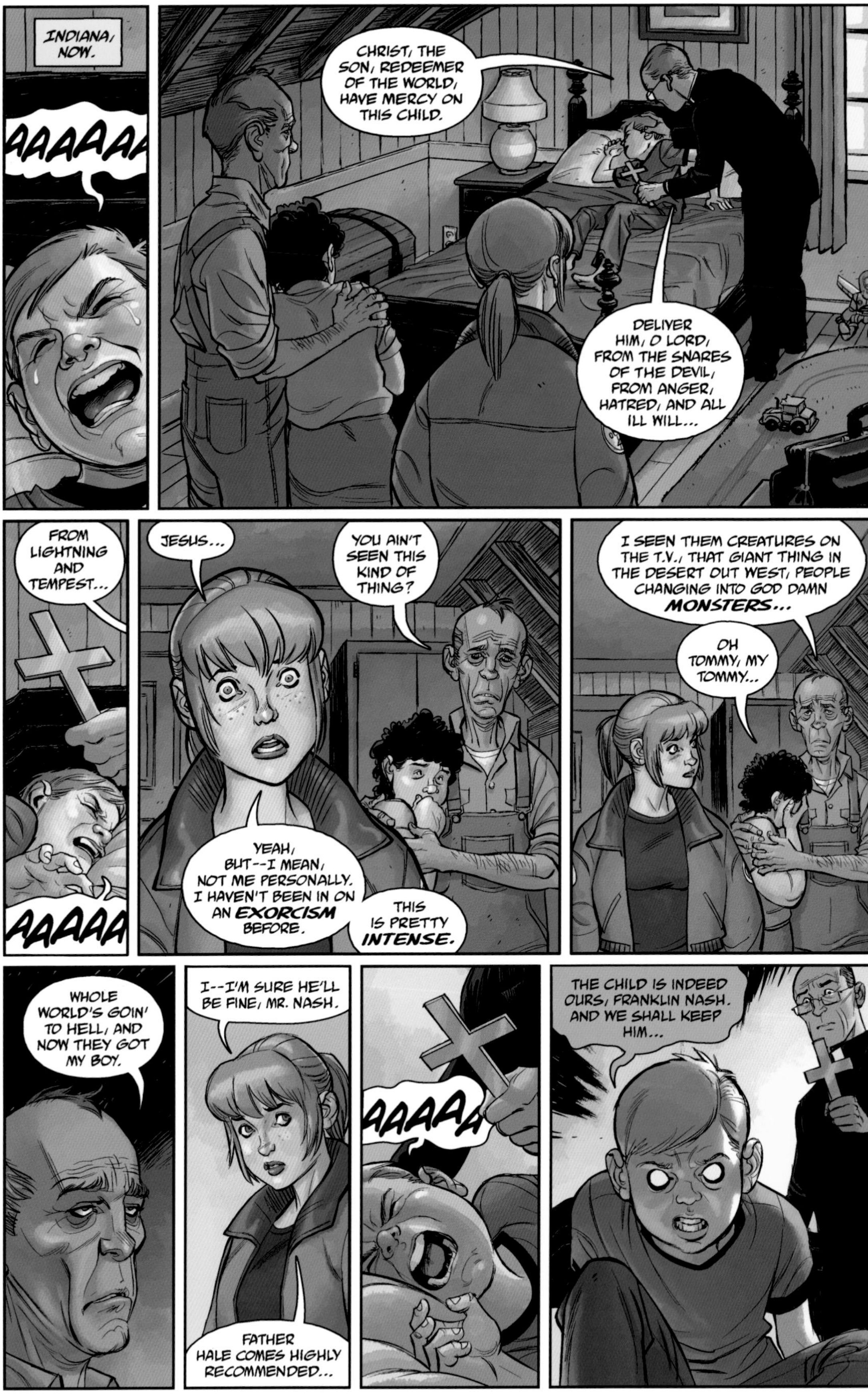
INDIANA, NOW.
AAAAAA
CHRIST, THE SON, REDEEMER OF THE WORLD, HAVE MERCY ON THIS CHILD.
DELIVER HIM, O LORD, FROM THE SNARES OF THE DEVIL, FROM ANGER, HATRED, AND ALL ILL WILL...
FROM LIGHTNING AND TEMPEST...
AAAAA
JESUS...
YOU AIN'T SEEN THIS KIND OF THING?
YEAH, BUT--I MEAN, NOT ME PERSONALLY. I HAVEN'T BEEN IN ON AN EXORCISM BEFORE.
THIS IS PRETTY INTENSE.
I SEEN THEM CREATURES ON THE T.V., THAT GIANT THING IN THE DESERT OUT WEST, PEOPLE CHANGING INTO GOD DAMN MONSTERS...
OH TOMMY, MY TOMMY...
WHOLE WORLD'S GOIN' TO HELL, AND NOW THEY GOT MY BOY.
I--I'M SURE HE'LL BE FINE, MR. NASH.
FATHER HALE COMES HIGHLY RECOMMENDED...
AAAAA
THE CHILD IS INDEED OURS, FRANKLIN NASH. AND WE SHALL KEEP HIM...

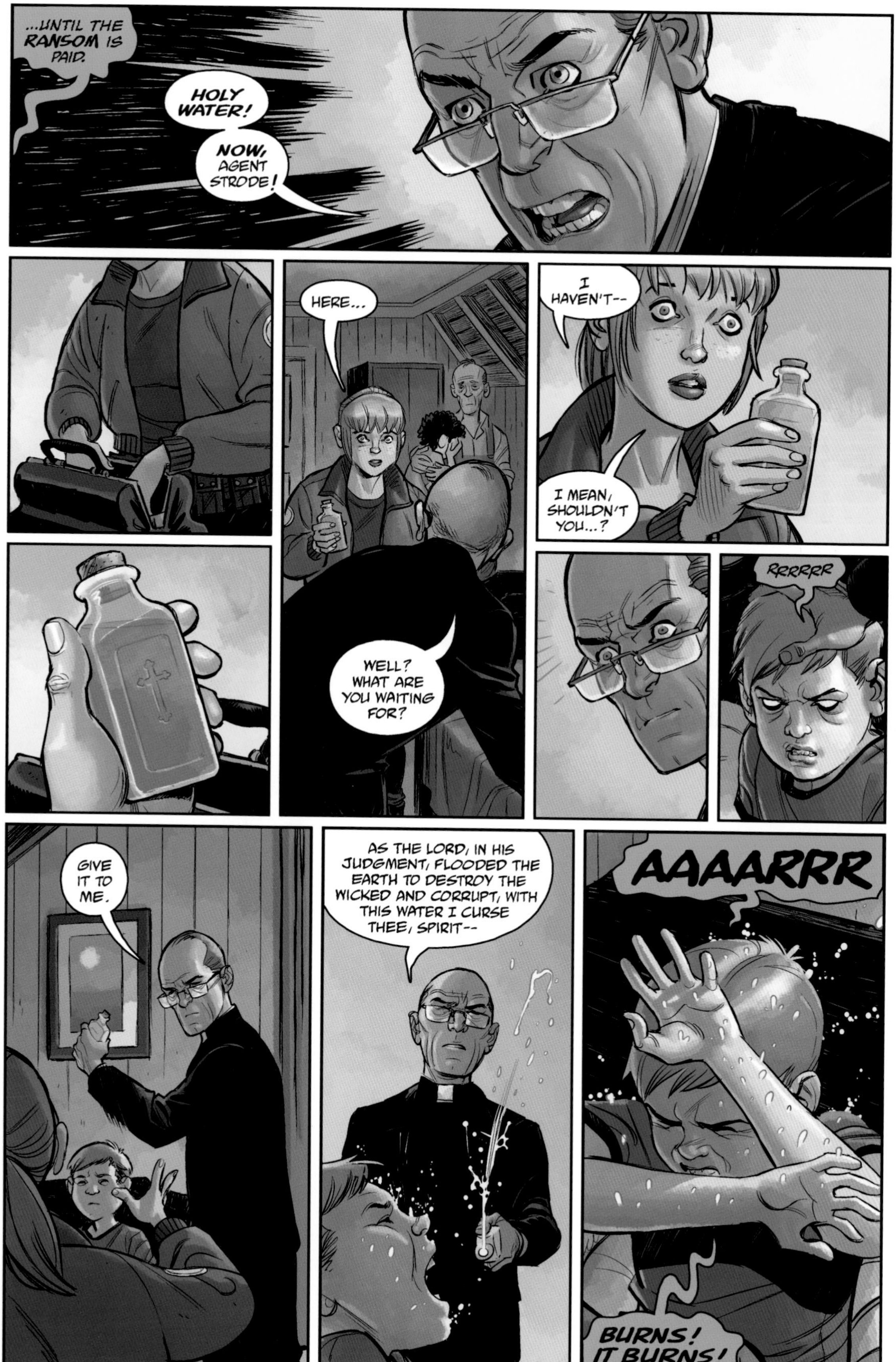

...UNTIL THE RANSOM IS PAID.
HOLY WATER!
NOW, AGENT STRODE!
HERE...
I HAVEN'T--
I MEAN, SHOULDN'T YOU...?
WELL? WHAT ARE YOU WAITING FOR?
RRRRRR
GIVE IT TO ME.
AS THE LORD, IN HIS JUDGMENT, FLOODED THE EARTH TO DESTROY THE WICKED AND CORRUPT, WITH THIS WATER I CURSE THEE, SPIRIT--
AAAARRR
BURNS! IT BURNS!

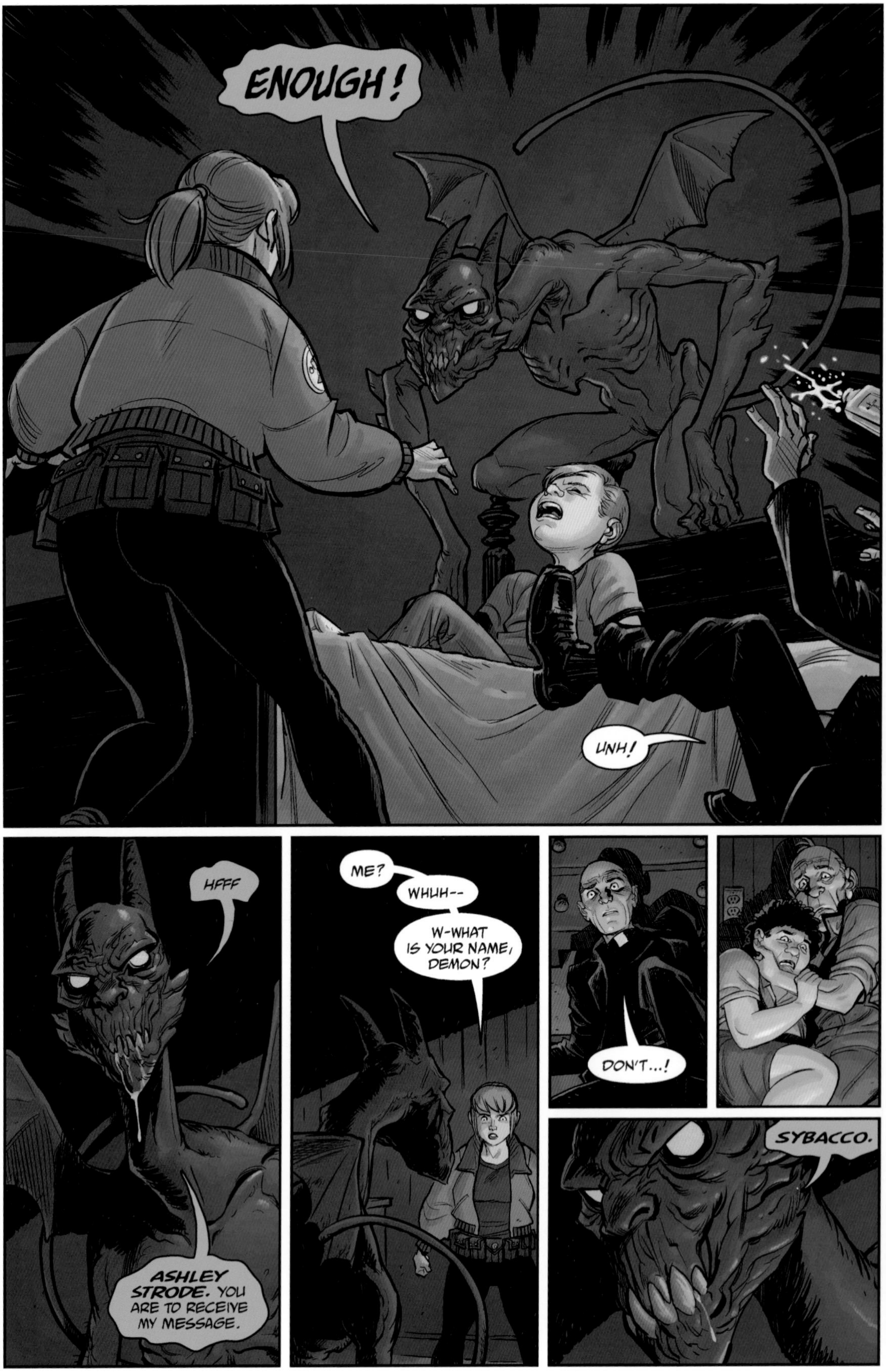
ENOUGH!
UNH!
HFFF
ASHLEY STRODE. YOU ARE TO RECEIVE MY MESSAGE.
ME?
WHUH--
W-WHAT IS YOUR NAME, DEMON?
DON'T...!
SYBACCO.

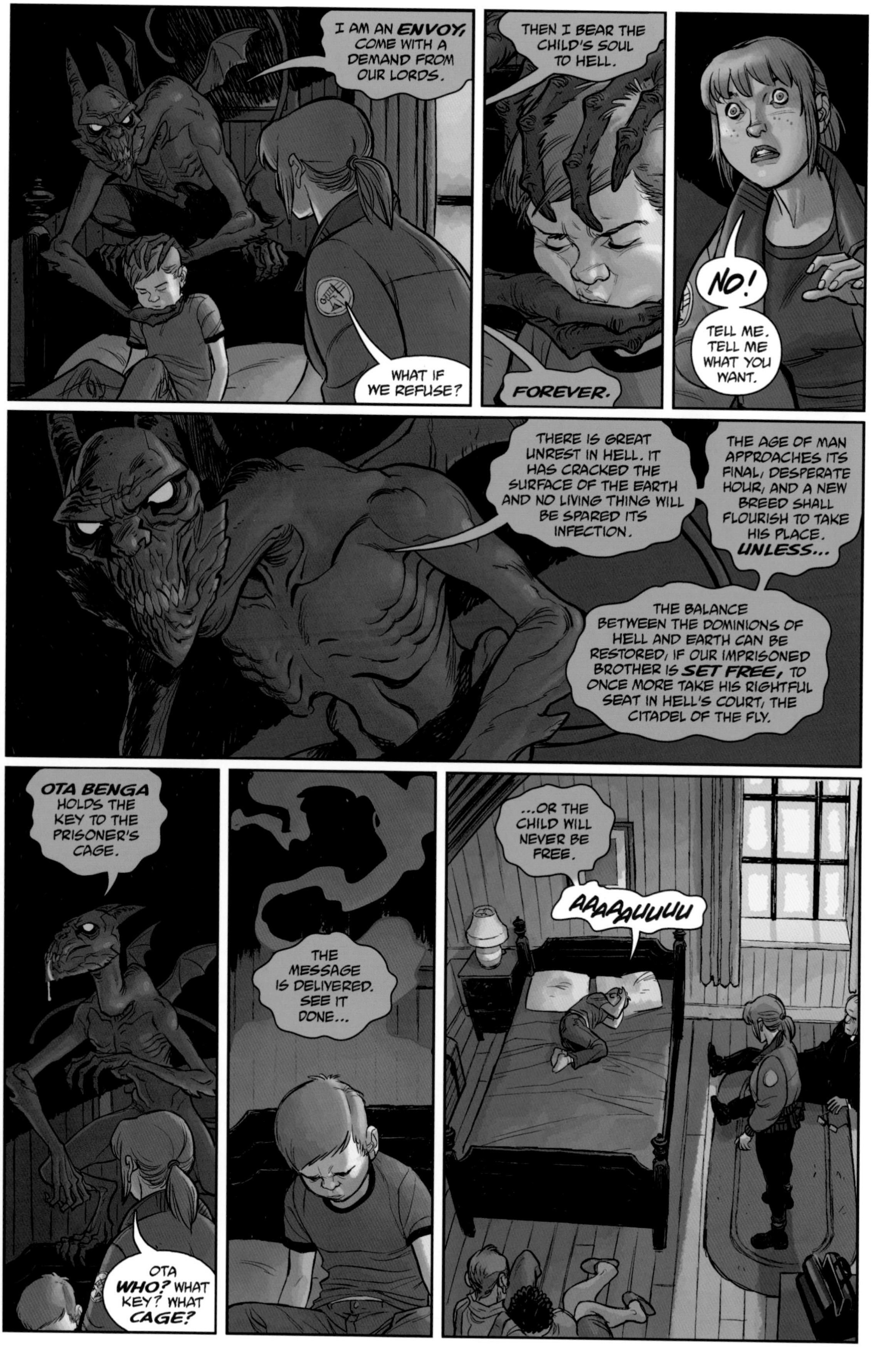
I AM AN ENVOY, COME WITH A DEMAND FROM OUR LORDS.
WHAT IF WE REFUSE?
THEN I BEAR THE CHILD'S SOUL TO HELL.
FOREVER.
NO!
TELL ME. TELL ME WHAT YOU WANT.
THERE IS GREAT UNREST IN HELL. IT HAS CRACKED THE SURFACE OF THE EARTH AND NO LIVING THING WILL BE SPARED ITS INFECTION.
THE AGE OF MAN APPROACHES ITS FINAL, DESPERATE HOUR, AND A NEW BREED SHALL FLOURISH TO TAKE HIS PLACE. UNLESS...
THE BALANCE BETWEEN THE DOMINIONS OF HELL AND EARTH CAN BE RESTORED, IF OUR IMPRISONED BROTHER IS SET FREE, TO ONCE MORE TAKE HIS RIGHTFUL SEAT IN HELL'S COURT, THE CITADEL OF THE FLY.
OTA BENGA HOLDS THE KEY TO THE PRISONER'S CAGE.
OTA WHO? WHAT KEY? WHAT CAGE?
THE MESSAGE IS DELIVERED. SEE IT DONE...
...OR THE CHILD WILL NEVER BE FREE.
AAAAAUUUU

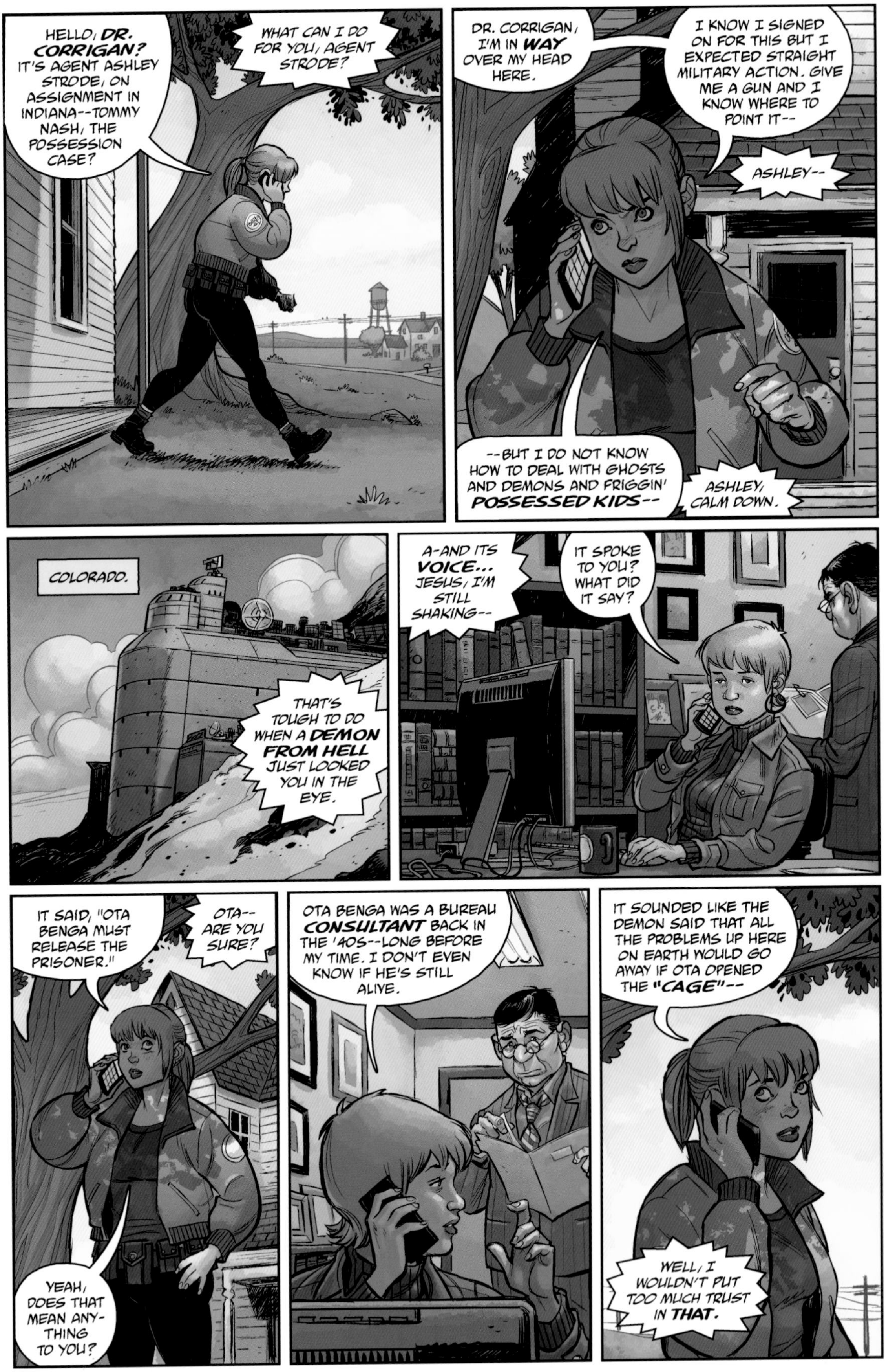
HELLO, DR. CORRIGAN? IT'S AGENT ASHLEY STRODE, ON ASSIGNMENT IN INDIANA--TOMMY NASH, THE POSSESSION CASE?
WHAT CAN I DO FOR YOU, AGENT STRODE?
DR. CORRIGAN, I'M IN WAY OVER MY HEAD HERE.
I KNOW I SIGNED ON FOR THIS BUT I EXPECTED STRAIGHT MILITARY ACTION. GIVE ME A GUN AND I KNOW WHERE TO POINT IT--
ASHLEY--
--BUT I DO NOT KNOW HOW TO DEAL WITH GHOSTS AND DEMONS AND FRIGGIN' POSSESSED KIDS--
ASHLEY, CALM DOWN.
COLORADO.
THAT'S TOUGH TO DO WHEN A DEMON FROM HELL JUST LOOKED YOU IN THE EYE.
A-AND ITS VOICE... JESUS, I'M STILL SHAKING--
IT SPOKE TO YOU? WHAT DID IT SAY?
IT SAID, "OTA BENGA MUST RELEASE THE PRISONER."
OTA-- ARE YOU SURE?
YEAH, DOES THAT MEAN ANYTHING TO YOU?
OTA BENGA WAS A BUREAU CONSULTANT BACK IN THE '40S--LONG BEFORE MY TIME. I DON'T EVEN KNOW IF HE'S STILL ALIVE.
IT SOUNDED LIKE THE DEMON SAID THAT ALL THE PROBLEMS UP HERE ON EARTH WOULD GO AWAY IF OTA OPENED THE "CAGE"--
WELL, I WOULDN'T PUT TOO MUCH TRUST IN THAT.

I'M CURIOUS ABOUT OTA'S CONNECTION TO THIS, THOUGH. I'LL EMAIL ALL THE INFO I CAN DIG UP ON HIS WHEREABOUTS. YOU CAN HEAD OUT IN THE MORNING.

UH, DR. CORRIGAN, ISN'T THERE ANYONE ELSE WHO CAN DO THIS?

I JUST-- I DON'T KNOW IF I FEEL UP TO IT...

THAT'S NOT WHAT *LIZ SHERMAN* SAID ABOUT YOU.

...WAIT, WHAT?

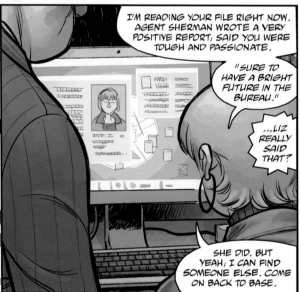

I'M READING YOUR FILE RIGHT NOW. AGENT SHERMAN WROTE A VERY POSITIVE REPORT, SAID YOU WERE TOUGH AND PASSIONATE.

"SURE TO HAVE A BRIGHT FUTURE IN THE BUREAU!"

...LIZ REALLY SAID THAT?

SHE DID. BUT YEAH, I CAN FIND SOMEONE ELSE. COME ON BACK TO BASE.

OKAY, I'LL DO IT. I'LL FIND OTA BENGA.

TERRIFIC. I'LL BE IN TOUCH.

Blp

SHE SOUNDS A LITTLE *GREEN*, BUT IF AGENT SHERMAN APPROVES--

FRANKLY, I DOUBT LIZ EVEN REMEMBERS ASHLEY'S *NAME*.

THE ONLY THING IN THIS FILE ABOUT LIZ SHERMAN IS HOW AGENT STRODE *IDOLIZES* HER.

BUT SHE'S A GOOD KID. SHE CAN HANDLE THIS.

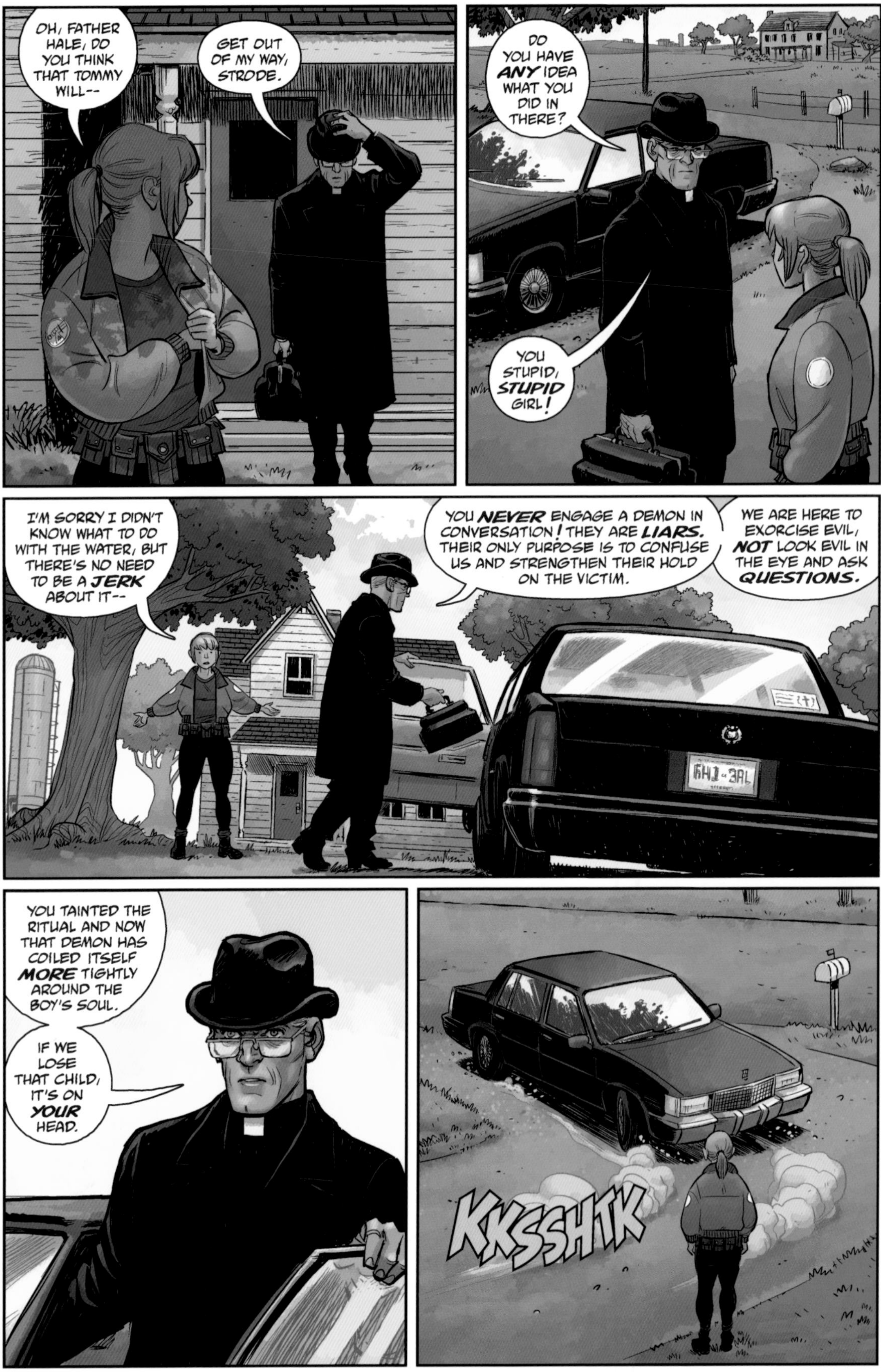
OH, FATHER HALE, DO YOU THINK THAT TOMMY WILL--
GET OUT OF MY WAY, STRODE.
DO YOU HAVE ANY IDEA WHAT YOU DID IN THERE?
YOU STUPID, STUPID GIRL!
I'M SORRY I DIDN'T KNOW WHAT TO DO WITH THE WATER, BUT THERE'S NO NEED TO BE A JERK ABOUT IT--
YOU NEVER ENGAGE A DEMON IN CONVERSATION! THEY ARE LIARS. THEIR ONLY PURPOSE IS TO CONFUSE US AND STRENGTHEN THEIR HOLD ON THE VICTIM.
WE ARE HERE TO EXORCISE EVIL, NOT LOOK EVIL IN THE EYE AND ASK QUESTIONS.
YOU TAINTED THE RITUAL AND NOW THAT DEMON HAS COILED ITSELF MORE TIGHTLY AROUND THE BOY'S SOUL.
IF WE LOSE THAT CHILD, IT'S ON YOUR HEAD.
KKSSHTK

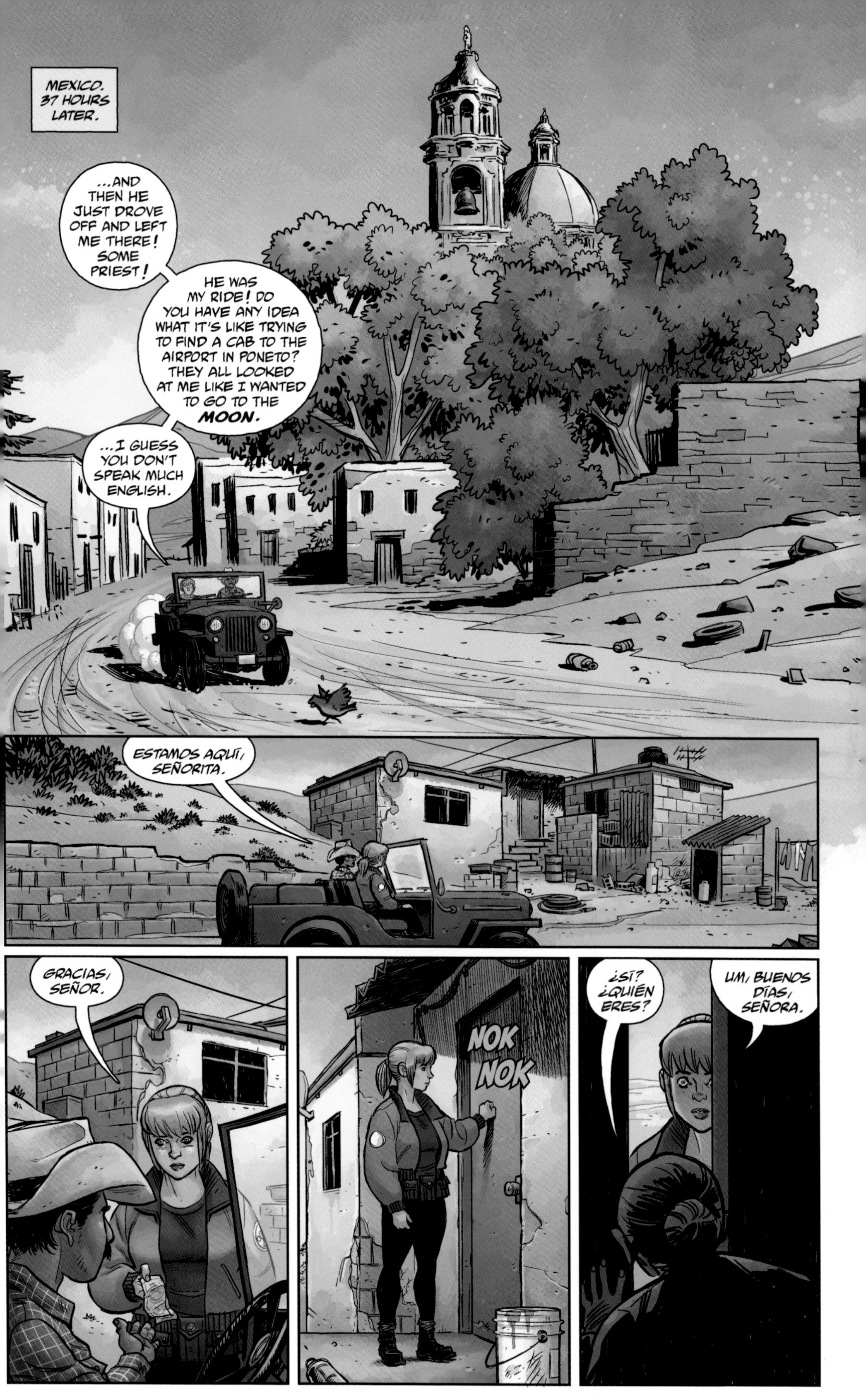

MEXICO. 37 HOURS LATER.
...AND THEN HE JUST DROVE OFF AND LEFT ME THERE! SOME PRIEST!
HE WAS MY RIDE! DO YOU HAVE ANY IDEA WHAT IT'S LIKE TRYING TO FIND A CAB TO THE AIRPORT IN PONETO? THEY ALL LOOKED AT ME LIKE I WANTED TO GO TO THE MOON.
...I GUESS YOU DON'T SPEAK MUCH ENGLISH.
ESTAMOS AQUÍ, SEÑORITA.
GRACIAS, SEÑOR.
NOK NOK
¿SÍ? ¿QUIÉN ERES?
UM, BUENOS DÍAS, SEÑORA.

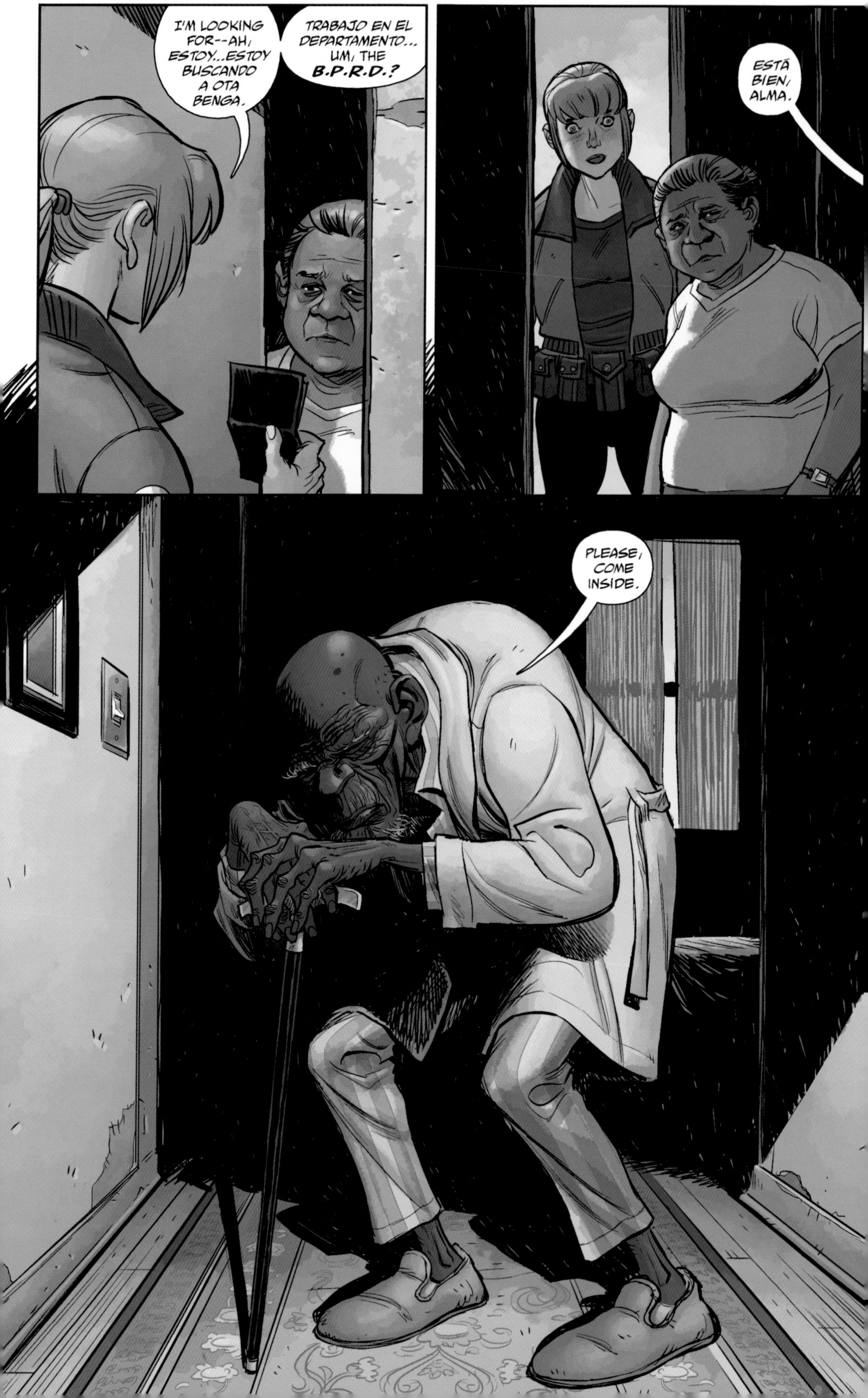
I'M LOOKING FOR--AH, ESTOY...ESTOY BUSCANDO A OTA BENGA.
TRABAJO EN EL DEPARTAMENTO... UM, THE B.P.R.D.?
ESTÁ BIEN, ALMA.
PLEASE, COME INSIDE.

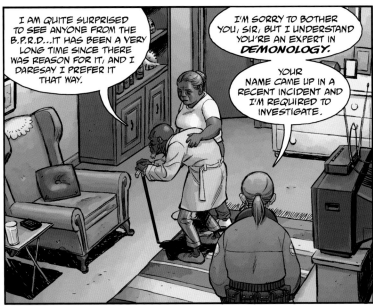

I AM QUITE SURPRISED TO SEE ANYONE FROM THE B.P.R.D...IT HAS BEEN A VERY LONG TIME SINCE THERE WAS REASON FOR IT, AND I DARESAY I PREFER IT THAT WAY.

I'M SORRY TO BOTHER YOU, SIR, BUT I UNDERSTAND YOU'RE AN EXPERT IN *DEMONOLOGY.*

YOUR NAME CAME UP IN A RECENT INCIDENT AND I'M REQUIRED TO INVESTIGATE.

TELL ME--NNGGH-- WHAT KIND OF INCIDENT WOULD BE WORTH DISTURBING AN OLD MAN'S RETIREMENT?

WELL, SIR, IT'S DIFFICULT TO EXPLAIN, BUT I HAD A RUN-IN WITH A DEMON CALLING ITSELF *SYBACCO--*

SYBACCO? HMM. THE NAME IS NOT ONE I KNOW.

HEY, THAT'S PROFESSOR BRUTTENHOLM--

AND IS THAT--

HOW OLD IS THIS PICTURE? HOW OLD ARE *YOU?*

ONE HUNDRED AND FIFTY-FOUR.

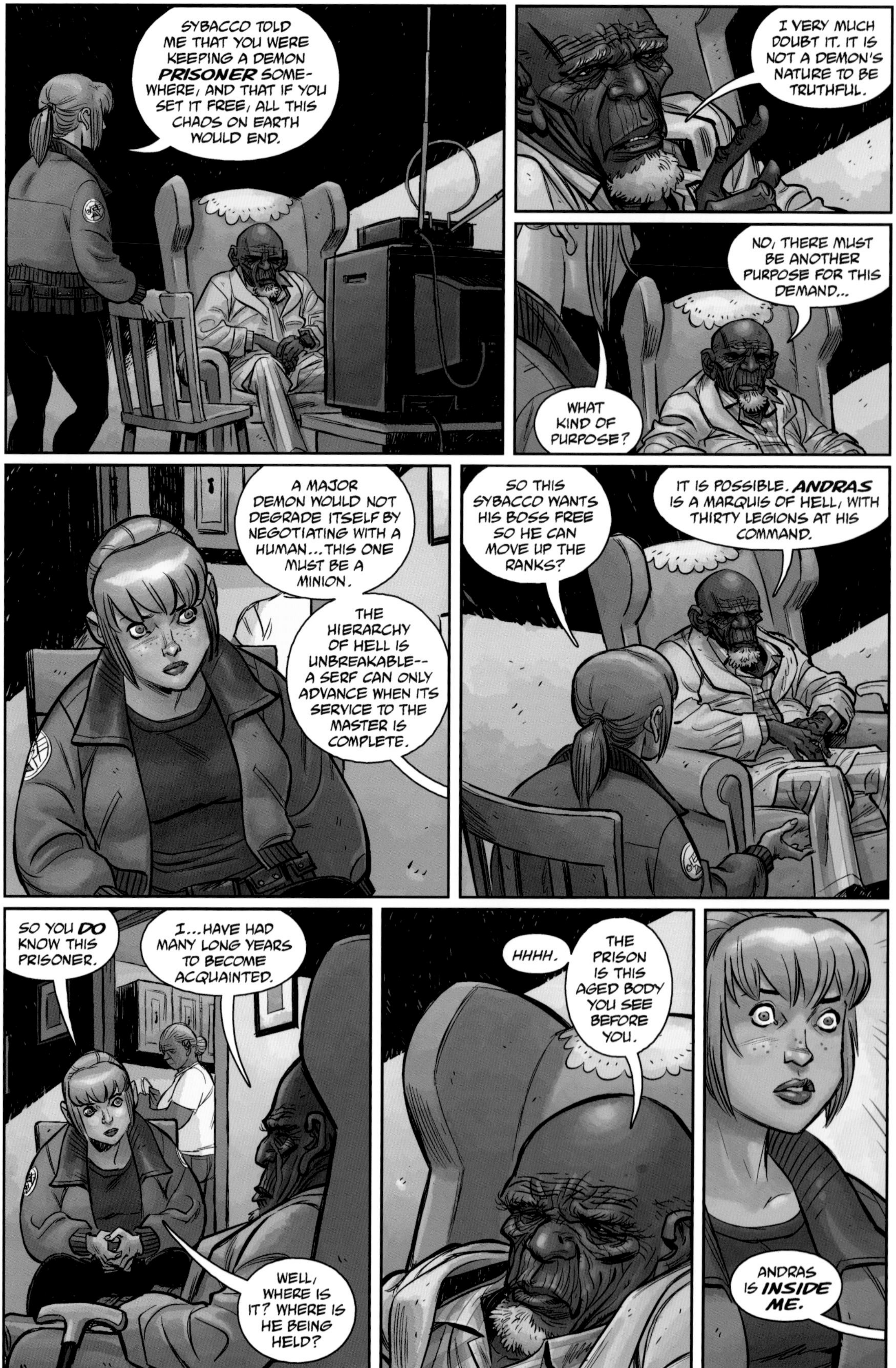
SYBACCO TOLD ME THAT YOU WERE KEEPING A DEMON PRISONER SOMEWHERE, AND THAT IF YOU SET IT FREE, ALL THIS CHAOS ON EARTH WOULD END.
I VERY MUCH DOUBT IT. IT IS NOT A DEMON'S NATURE TO BE TRUTHFUL.
NO, THERE MUST BE ANOTHER PURPOSE FOR THIS DEMAND...
WHAT KIND OF PURPOSE?
A MAJOR DEMON WOULD NOT DEGRADE ITSELF BY NEGOTIATING WITH A HUMAN... THIS ONE MUST BE A MINION.
THE HIERARCHY OF HELL IS UNBREAKABLE-- A SERF CAN ONLY ADVANCE WHEN ITS SERVICE TO THE MASTER IS COMPLETE.
SO THIS SYBACCO WANTS HIS BOSS FREE SO HE CAN MOVE UP THE RANKS?
IT IS POSSIBLE. ANDRAS IS A MARQUIS OF HELL, WITH THIRTY LEGIONS AT HIS COMMAND.
SO YOU DO KNOW THIS PRISONER.
I... HAVE HAD MANY LONG YEARS TO BECOME ACQUAINTED.
WELL, WHERE IS IT? WHERE IS HE BEING HELD?
HHHH.
THE PRISON IS THIS AGED BODY YOU SEE BEFORE YOU.
ANDRAS IS INSIDE ME.

HLSSSLTHSSS

OUT, SPIRIT!

WE DRAW YOU OUT OF THIS WOMAN, THIS SERVANT OF ALMIGHTY GOD, WITHIN WHOM YOU HAVE NO RIGHTFUL RESIDENCE!

SHRREEEE

SKSSSH

KRAK

UNH!

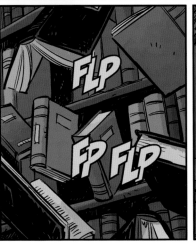

FLP

FP FLP

YOU MUST LEAVE, NOW!

ALL OF YOU, LEAVE BEFORE IT'S TOO LATE!

DOYLE, COME ON!

GOD FORGIVE ME...

SLAM

NOW, DEVIL.

I CALL UPON THE POWER OF THE LORD TO WREST YOU FROM THIS WOMAN.

YOU SHALL NOT HAVE HER, BUT NEITHER SHALL I PERMIT YOU TO RETURN TO HELL.

I DRAW YOU FORTH TO CONTAIN YOUR EVIL AND PROTECT THE INNOCENT FROM ITS CORRUPTION.

I CAST MYSELF A PRISON, FORGED FROM BLOOD AND BONE, SEALED BY GOD'S WILL.

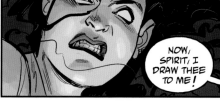

NOW, SPIRIT, I DRAW THEE TO ME!

IN HEAVEN'S NAME I BIND THEE TO ME!

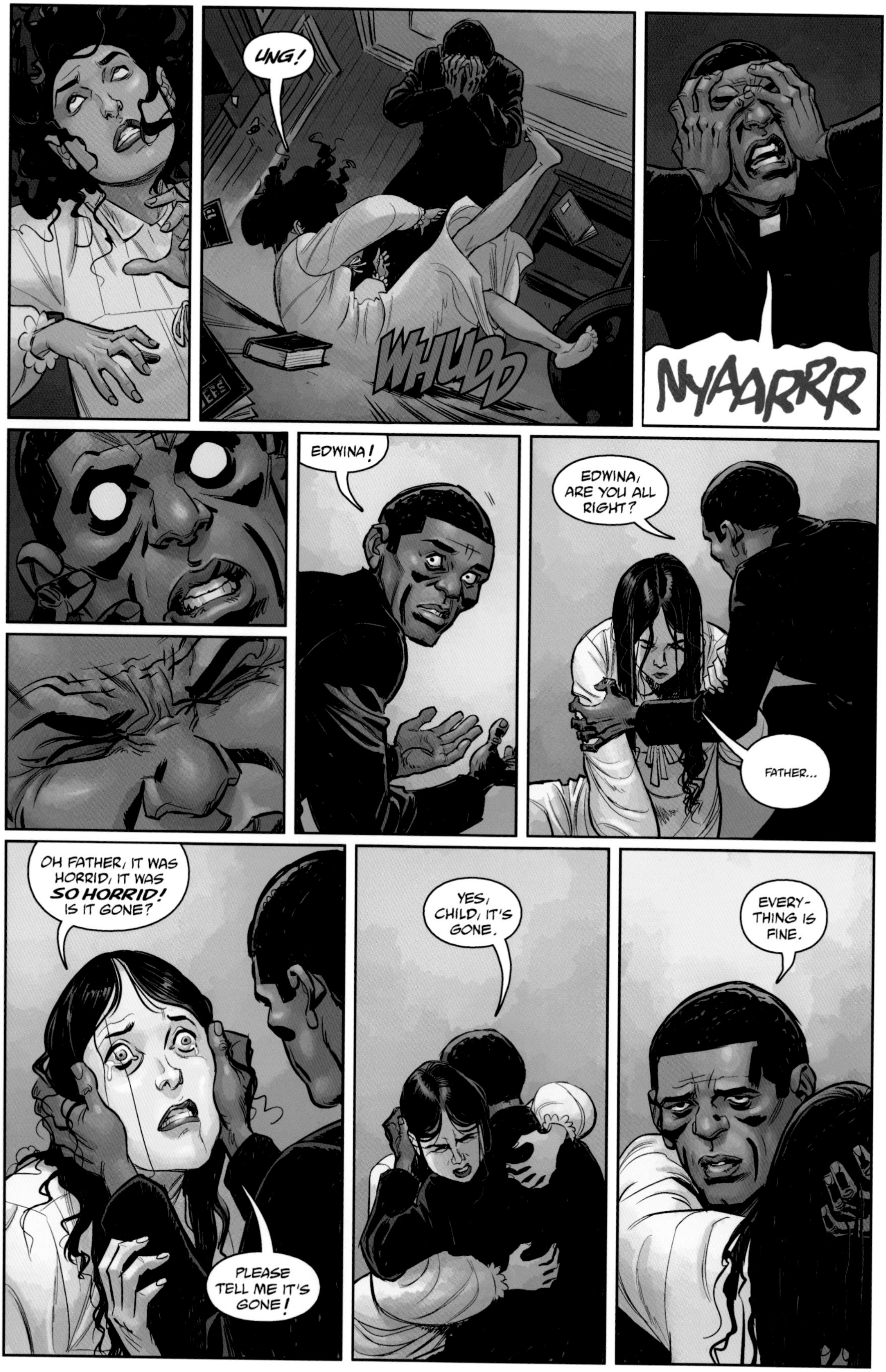
UNG!
WHUDD
NYAARRR
EDWINA!
EDWINA, ARE YOU ALL RIGHT?
FATHER...
OH FATHER, IT WAS HORRID, IT WAS SO HORRID! IS IT GONE?
PLEASE TELL ME IT'S GONE!
YES, CHILD, IT'S GONE.
EVERYTHING IS FINE.

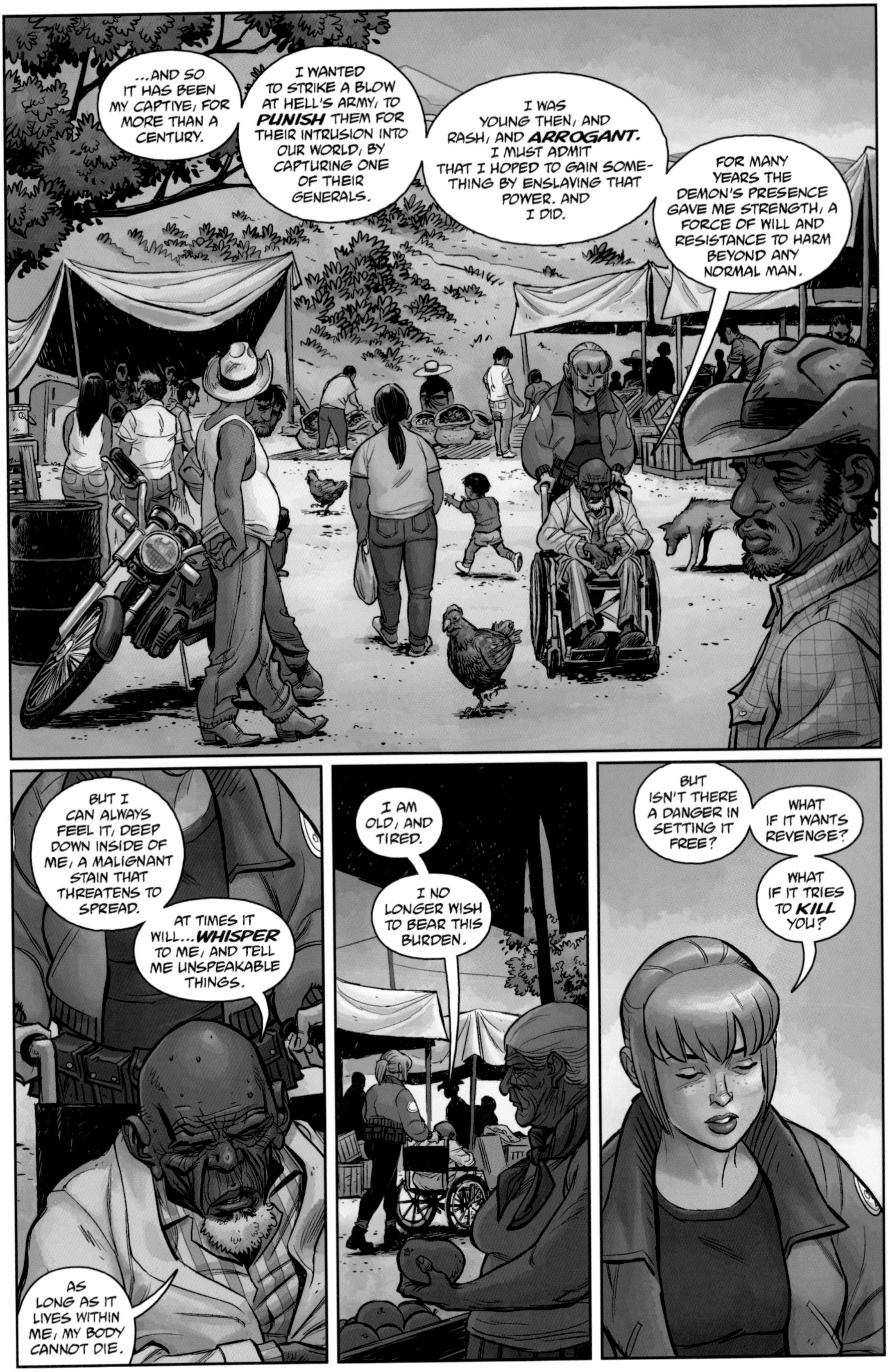
...AND SO IT HAS BEEN MY CAPTIVE, FOR MORE THAN A CENTURY.
I WANTED TO STRIKE A BLOW AT HELL'S ARMY, TO **PUNISH** THEM FOR THEIR INTRUSION INTO OUR WORLD, BY CAPTURING ONE OF THEIR GENERALS.
I WAS YOUNG THEN, AND RASH, AND **ARROGANT.** I MUST ADMIT THAT I HOPED TO GAIN SOMETHING BY ENSLAVING THAT POWER. AND I DID.
FOR MANY YEARS THE DEMON'S PRESENCE GAVE ME STRENGTH, A FORCE OF WILL AND RESISTANCE TO HARM BEYOND ANY NORMAL MAN.
BUT I CAN ALWAYS FEEL IT, DEEP DOWN INSIDE OF ME, A MALIGNANT STAIN THAT THREATENS TO SPREAD.
AT TIMES IT WILL...**WHISPER** TO ME, AND TELL ME UNSPEAKABLE THINGS.
AS LONG AS IT LIVES WITHIN ME, MY BODY CANNOT DIE.
I AM OLD, AND TIRED.
I NO LONGER WISH TO BEAR THIS BURDEN.
BUT ISN'T THERE A DANGER IN SETTING IT FREE?
WHAT IF IT WANTS REVENGE?
WHAT IF IT TRIES TO **KILL** YOU?

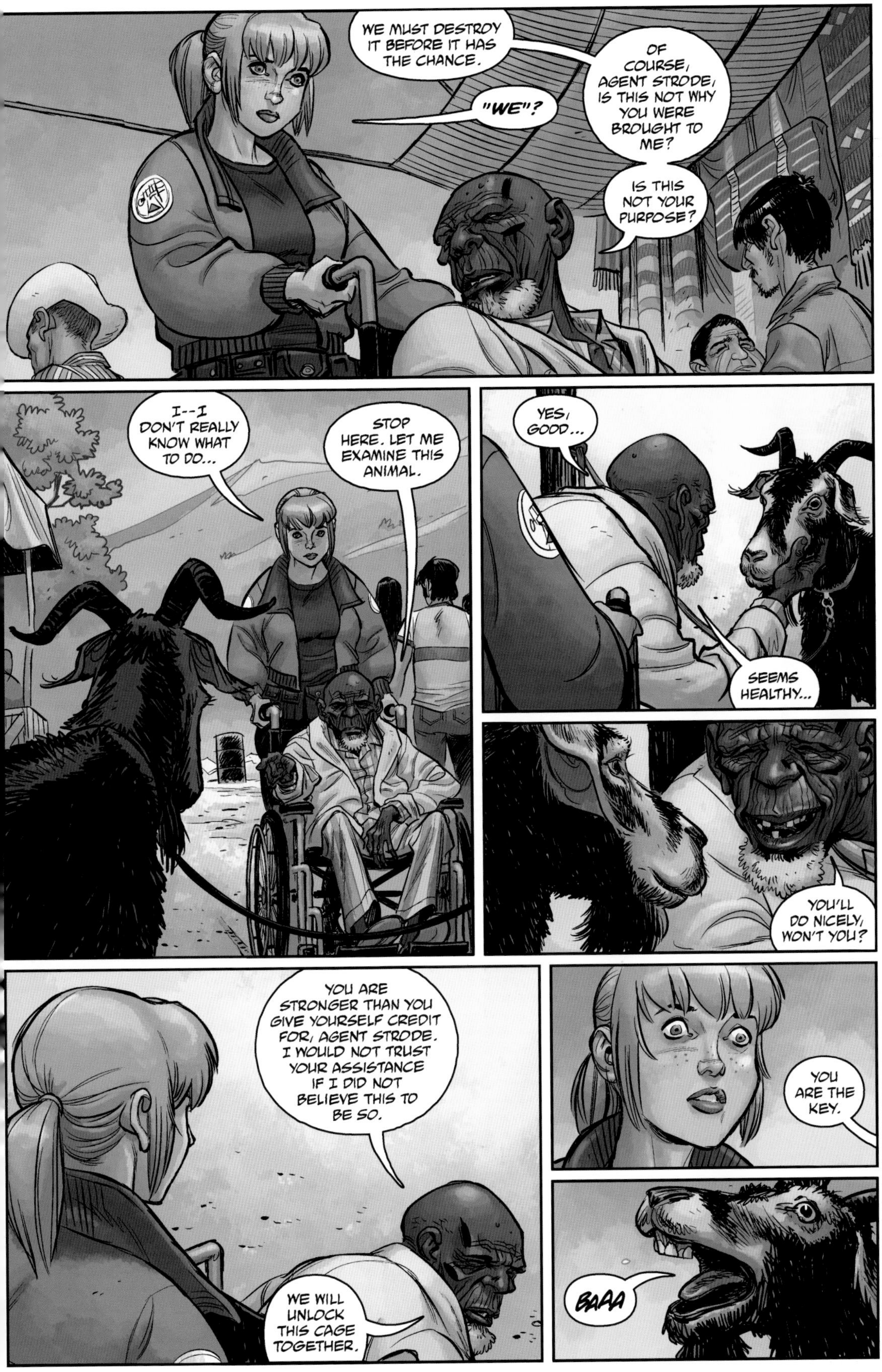
WE MUST DESTROY IT BEFORE IT HAS THE CHANCE.
"WE"?
OF COURSE, AGENT STRODE, IS THIS NOT WHY YOU WERE BROUGHT TO ME?
IS THIS NOT YOUR PURPOSE?
I--I DON'T REALLY KNOW WHAT TO DO...
STOP HERE. LET ME EXAMINE THIS ANIMAL.
YES, GOOD...
SEEMS HEALTHY...
YOU'LL DO NICELY, WON'T YOU?
YOU ARE STRONGER THAN YOU GIVE YOURSELF CREDIT FOR, AGENT STRODE. I WOULD NOT TRUST YOUR ASSISTANCE IF I DID NOT BELIEVE THIS TO BE SO.
WE WILL UNLOCK THIS CAGE TOGETHER.
YOU ARE THE KEY.
BAAA

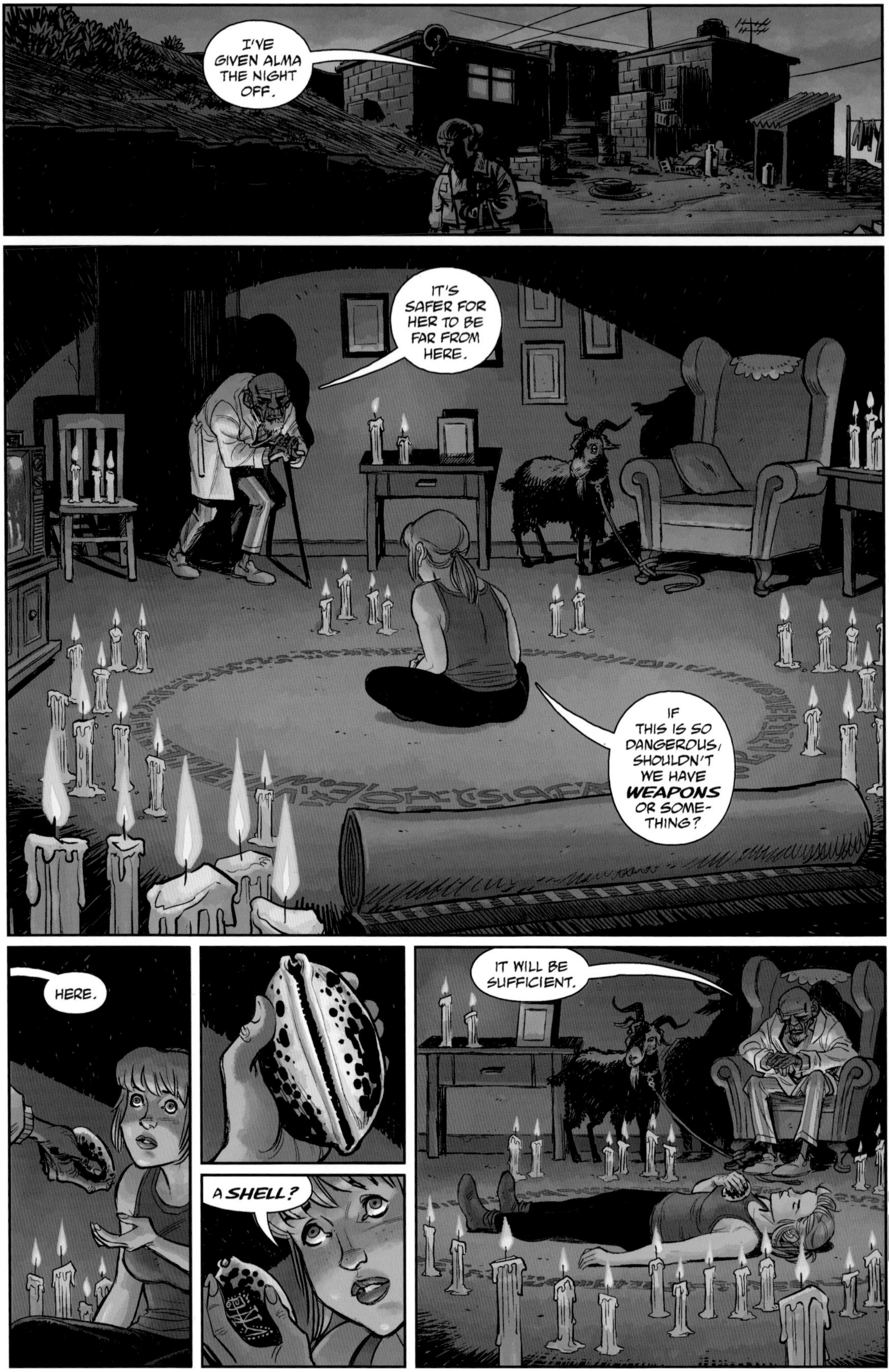
I'VE GIVEN ALMA THE NIGHT OFF.
IT'S SAFER FOR HER TO BE FAR FROM HERE.
IF THIS IS SO DANGEROUS, SHOULDN'T WE HAVE WEAPONS OR SOME-THING?
HERE.
A SHELL?
IT WILL BE SUFFICIENT.

HELLO?

HELLO? OTA, IS THAT YOU?

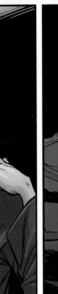

YES, IT IS ME.

OH, YOU...

YOU LOOK YOUNGER.

WHAT IS THIS PLACE? WHERE DID MY CLOTHES GO?

WE ARE IN THE SPIRITUAL PLANE. IT IS ONLY A PSYCHIC PROJECTION.

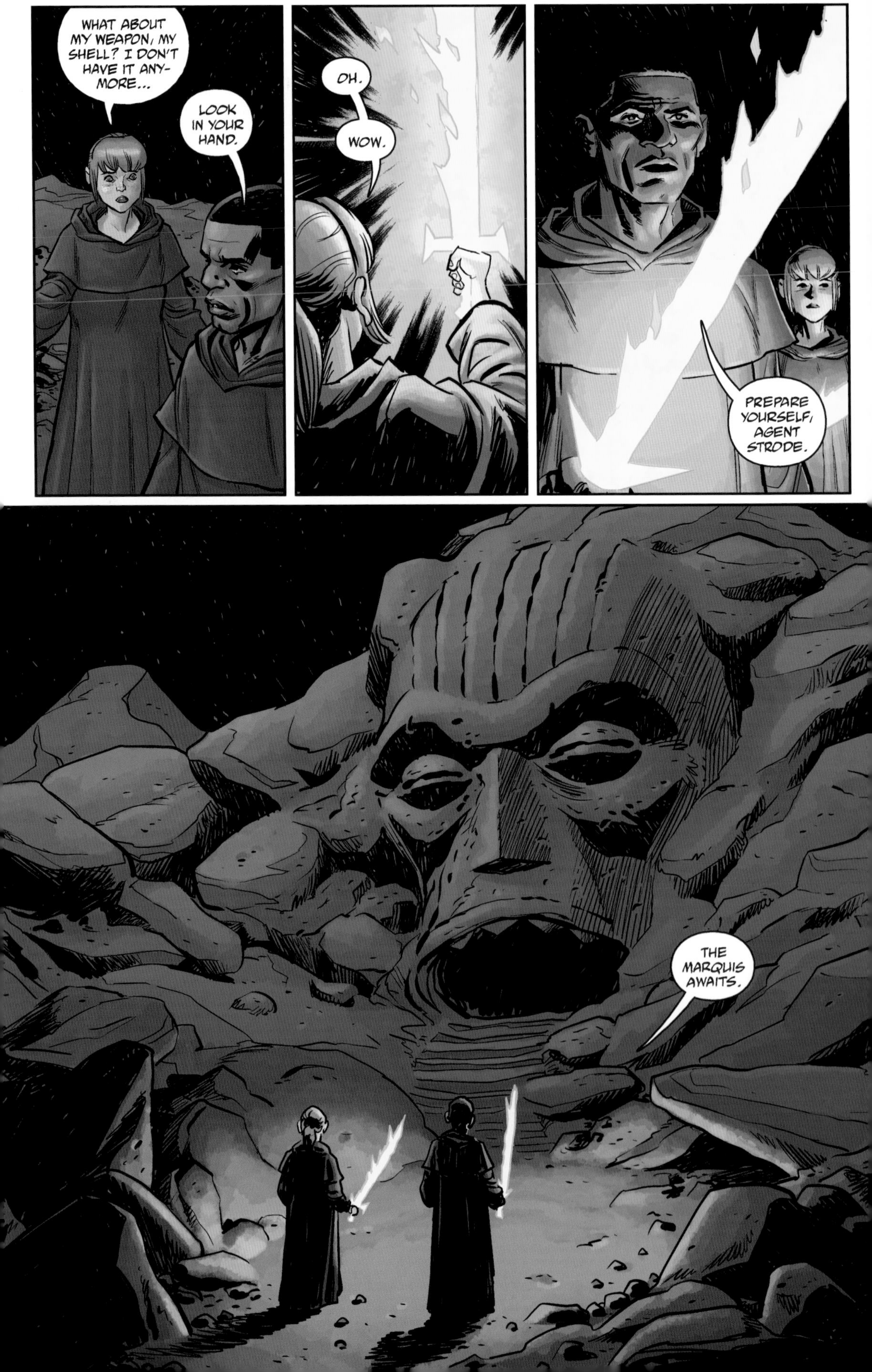
WHAT ABOUT MY WEAPON, MY SHELL? I DON'T HAVE IT ANY-MORE...
LOOK IN YOUR HAND.
OH.
WOW.
PREPARE YOURSELF, AGENT STRODE.
THE MARQUIS AWAITS.

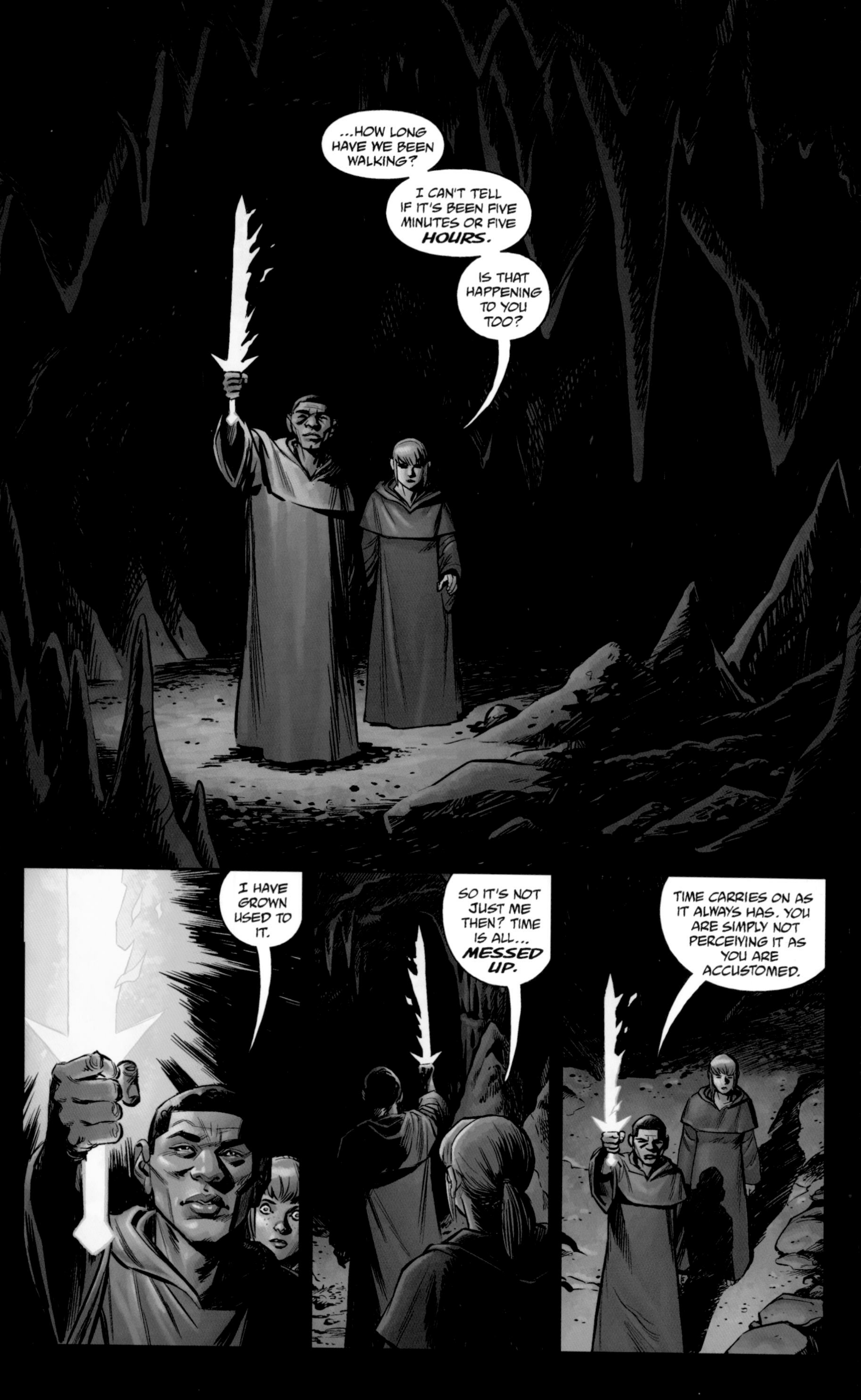

...HOW LONG HAVE WE BEEN WALKING?
I CAN'T TELL IF IT'S BEEN FIVE MINUTES OR FIVE **HOURS.**
IS THAT HAPPENING TO YOU TOO?
I HAVE GROWN USED TO IT.
SO IT'S NOT JUST ME THEN? TIME IS ALL... **MESSED UP.**
TIME CARRIES ON AS IT ALWAYS HAS. YOU ARE SIMPLY NOT PERCEIVING IT AS YOU ARE ACCUSTOMED.

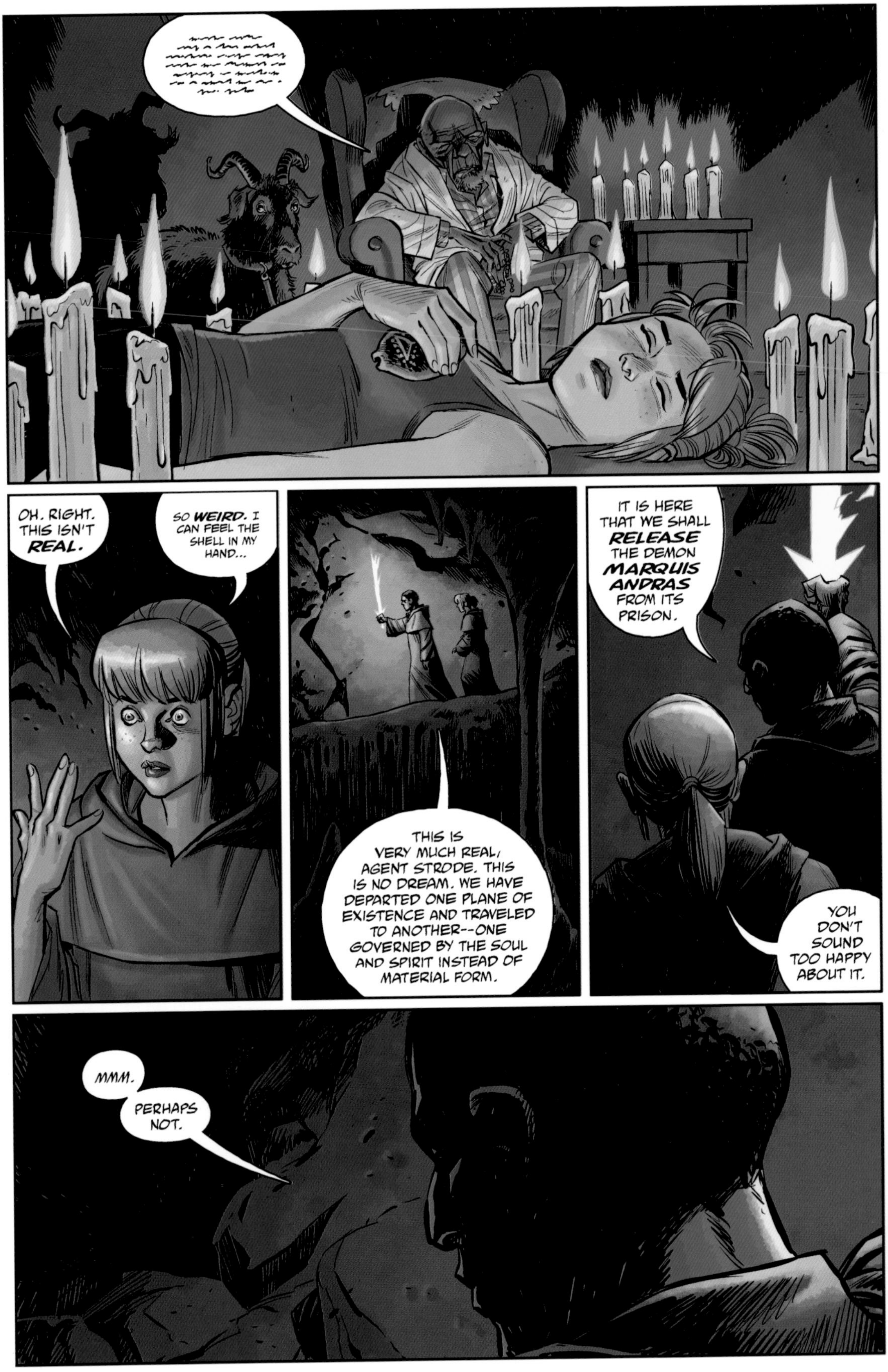
OH. RIGHT. THIS ISN'T **REAL.**
SO **WEIRD.** I CAN FEEL THE SHELL IN MY HAND...
THIS IS VERY MUCH REAL, AGENT STRODE. THIS IS NO DREAM. WE HAVE DEPARTED ONE PLANE OF EXISTENCE AND TRAVELED TO ANOTHER--ONE GOVERNED BY THE SOUL AND SPIRIT INSTEAD OF MATERIAL FORM.
IT IS HERE THAT WE SHALL **RELEASE** THE DEMON **MARQUIS ANDRAS** FROM ITS PRISON.
YOU DON'T SOUND TOO HAPPY ABOUT IT.
MMM.
PERHAPS NOT.

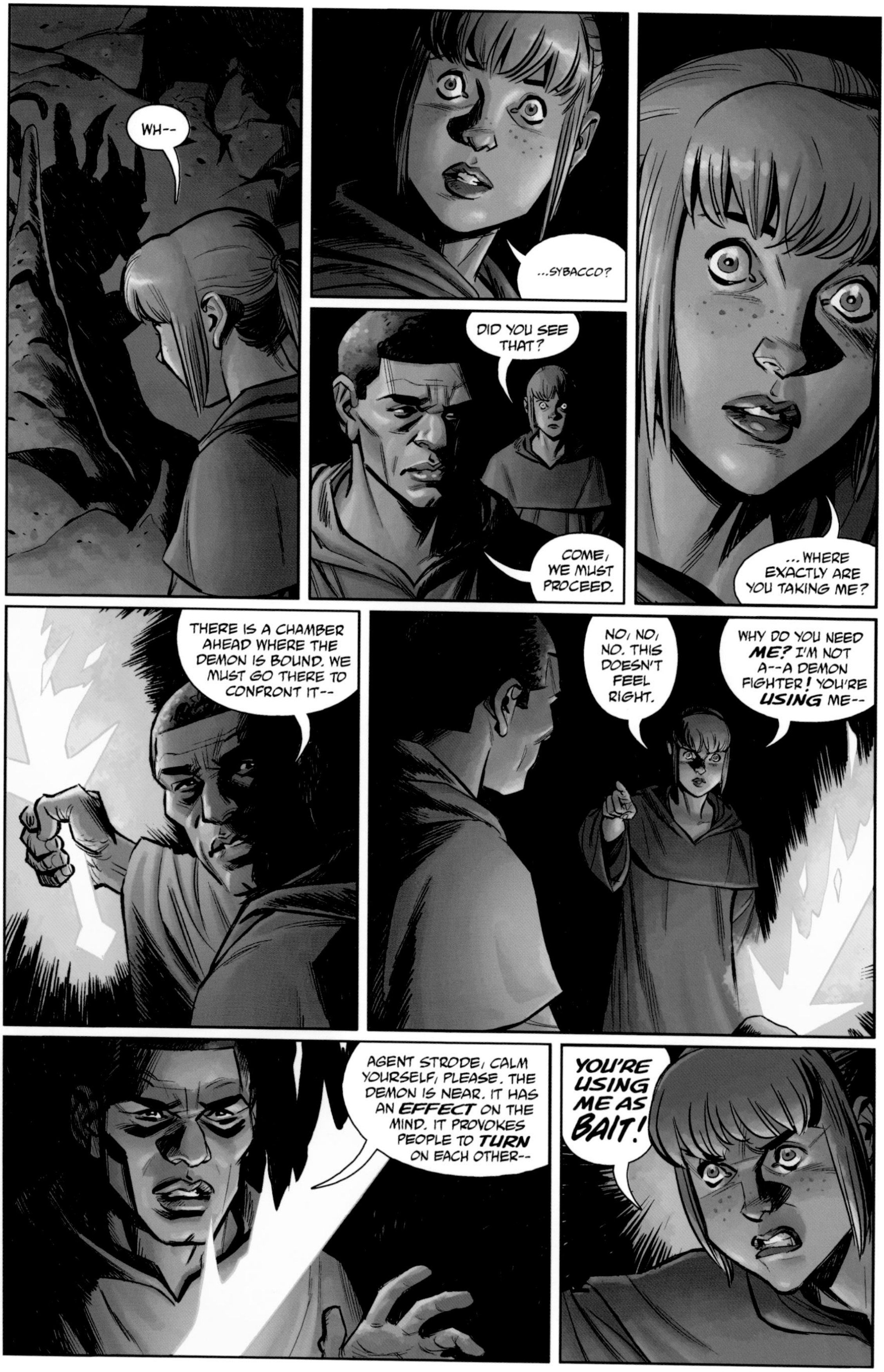
WH--
...SYBACCO?
...WHERE EXACTLY ARE YOU TAKING ME?
DID YOU SEE THAT?
COME, WE MUST PROCEED.
THERE IS A CHAMBER AHEAD WHERE THE DEMON IS BOUND. WE MUST GO THERE TO CONFRONT IT--
NO, NO, NO. THIS DOESN'T FEEL RIGHT.
WHY DO YOU NEED ME? I'M NOT A--A DEMON FIGHTER! YOU'RE USING ME--
AGENT STRODE, CALM YOURSELF, PLEASE. THE DEMON IS NEAR. IT HAS AN EFFECT ON THE MIND. IT PROVOKES PEOPLE TO TURN ON EACH OTHER--
YOU'RE USING ME AS BAIT!

AGENT STRODE, *PLEASE*--

STAY BACK! OR DID YOU FORGET I HAD ONE OF THESE TOO?

AGENT STRODE. *ASHLEY.*

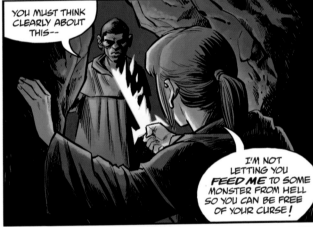

YOU MUST THINK CLEARLY ABOUT THIS--

I'M NOT LETTING YOU *FEED ME* TO SOME MONSTER FROM HELL SO YOU CAN BE FREE OF YOUR CURSE!

YOU THINK I'M SOME DUMB *GRUNT,* JUST LIKE *EVERY-ONE*--

BUT I FIGURED YOU OUT! NOT SO DUMB *NOW,* HUH?!

GOTTA BE A WAY OUT OF HERE--

GOTTA BE...

NNG-- *NGGGH!*

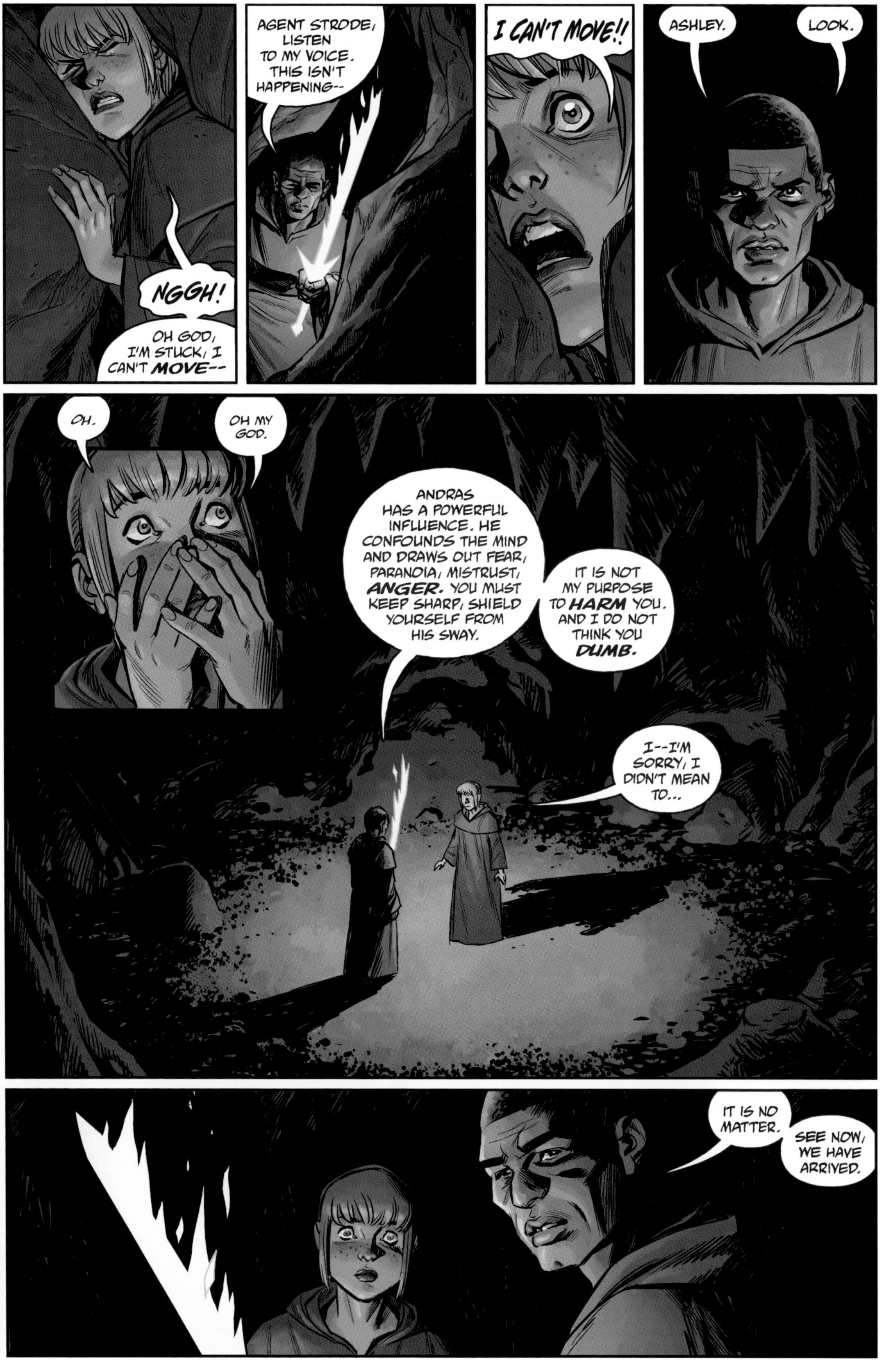
NGGH!
OH GOD, I'M STUCK, I CAN'T MOVE--
AGENT STRODE, LISTEN TO MY VOICE. THIS ISN'T HAPPENING--
I CAN'T MOVE!!
ASHLEY.
LOOK.
OH.
OH MY GOD.
ANDRAS HAS A POWERFUL INFLUENCE. HE CONFOUNDS THE MIND AND DRAWS OUT FEAR, PARANOIA, MISTRUST, ANGER. YOU MUST KEEP SHARP, SHIELD YOURSELF FROM HIS SWAY.
IT IS NOT MY PURPOSE TO HARM YOU. AND I DO NOT THINK YOU DUMB.
I--I'M SORRY, I DIDN'T MEAN TO...
IT IS NO MATTER.
SEE NOW, WE HAVE ARRIVED.

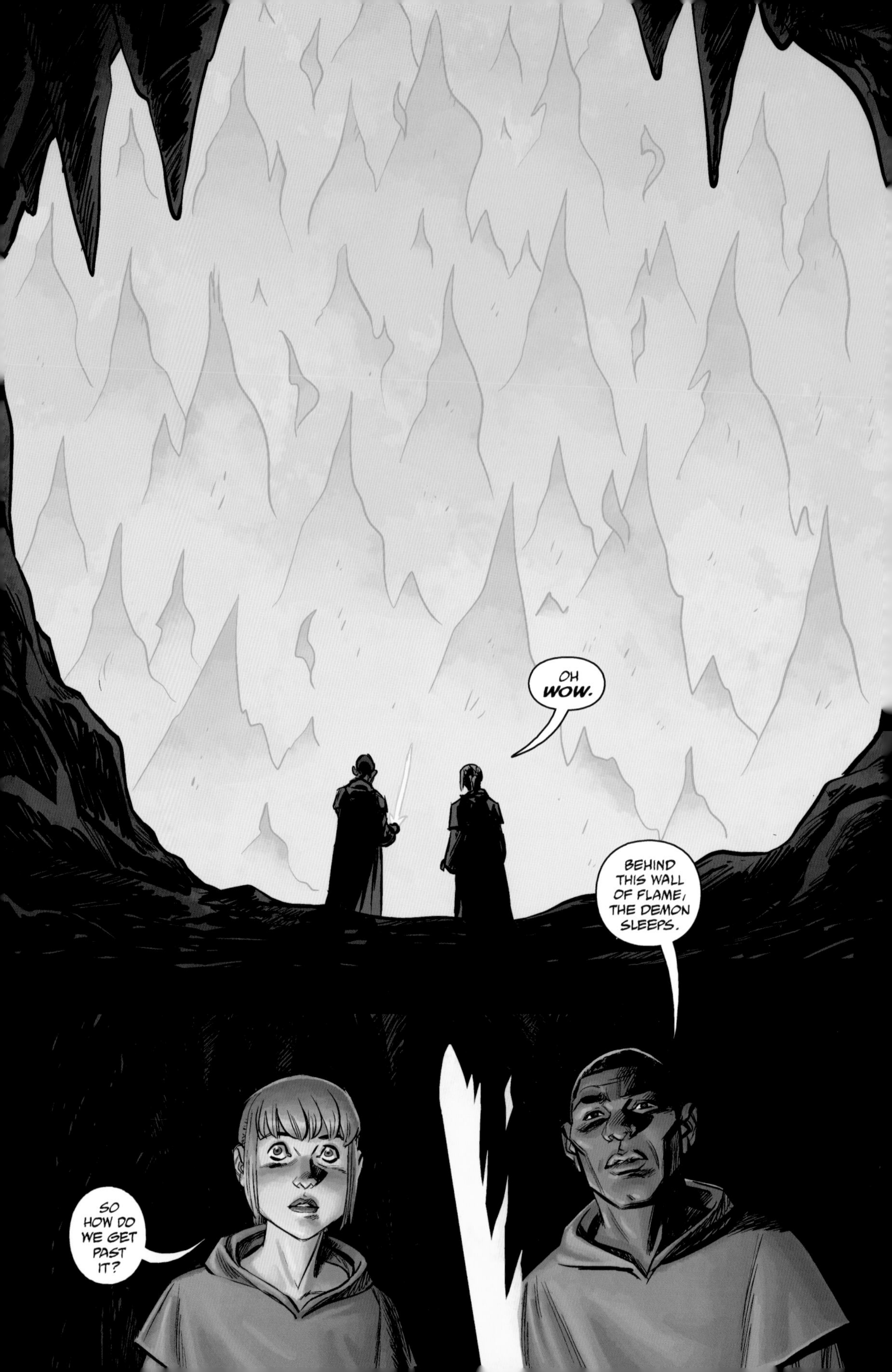
OH **WOW.**
BEHIND THIS WALL OF FLAME, THE DEMON SLEEPS.
SO HOW DO WE GET PAST IT?

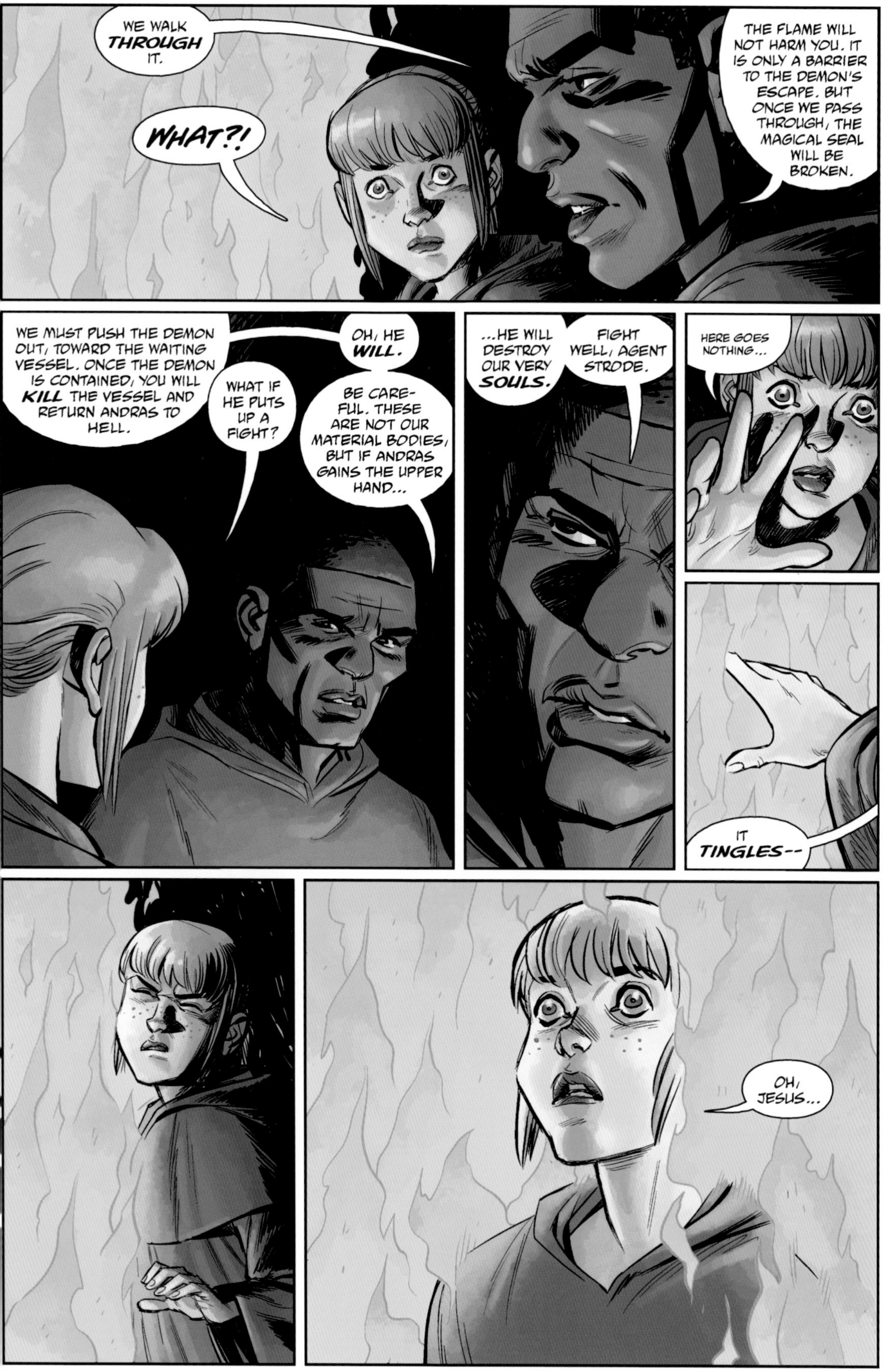
WE WALK THROUGH IT.
WHAT?!
THE FLAME WILL NOT HARM YOU. IT IS ONLY A BARRIER TO THE DEMON'S ESCAPE. BUT ONCE WE PASS THROUGH, THE MAGICAL SEAL WILL BE BROKEN.
WE MUST PUSH THE DEMON OUT, TOWARD THE WAITING VESSEL. ONCE THE DEMON IS CONTAINED, YOU WILL KILL THE VESSEL AND RETURN ANDRAS TO HELL.
WHAT IF HE PUTS UP A FIGHT?
OH, HE WILL.
BE CAREFUL. THESE ARE NOT OUR MATERIAL BODIES, BUT IF ANDRAS GAINS THE UPPER HAND...
...HE WILL DESTROY OUR VERY SOULS.
FIGHT WELL, AGENT STRODE.
HERE GOES NOTHING...
IT TINGLES--
OH, JESUS...

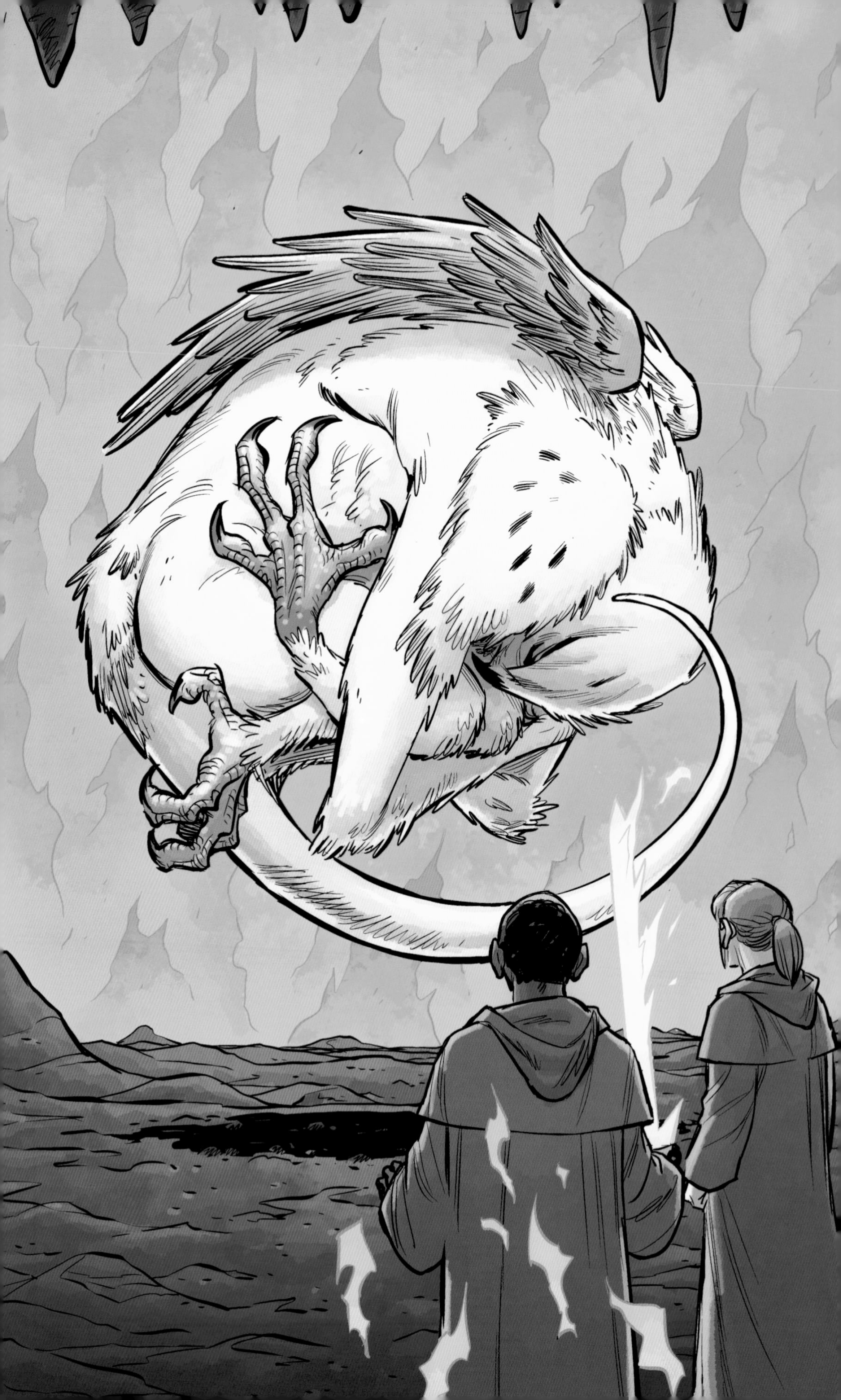

READY YOUR- SELF...

AWAKE, DEMON!

WE RELEASE YOU! THE DOORS OF YOUR PRISON ARE THROWN OPEN!

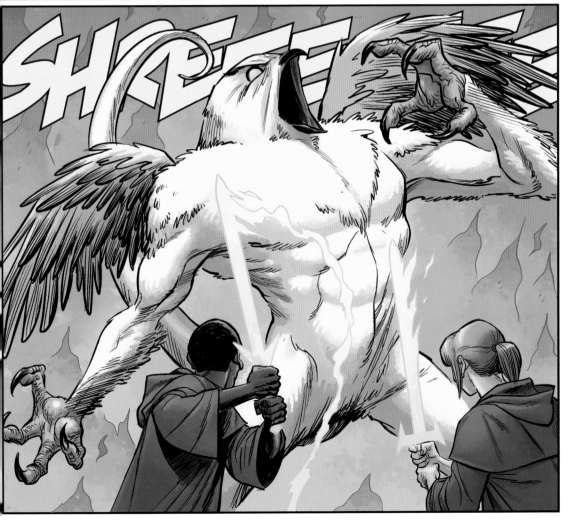

SHREEE

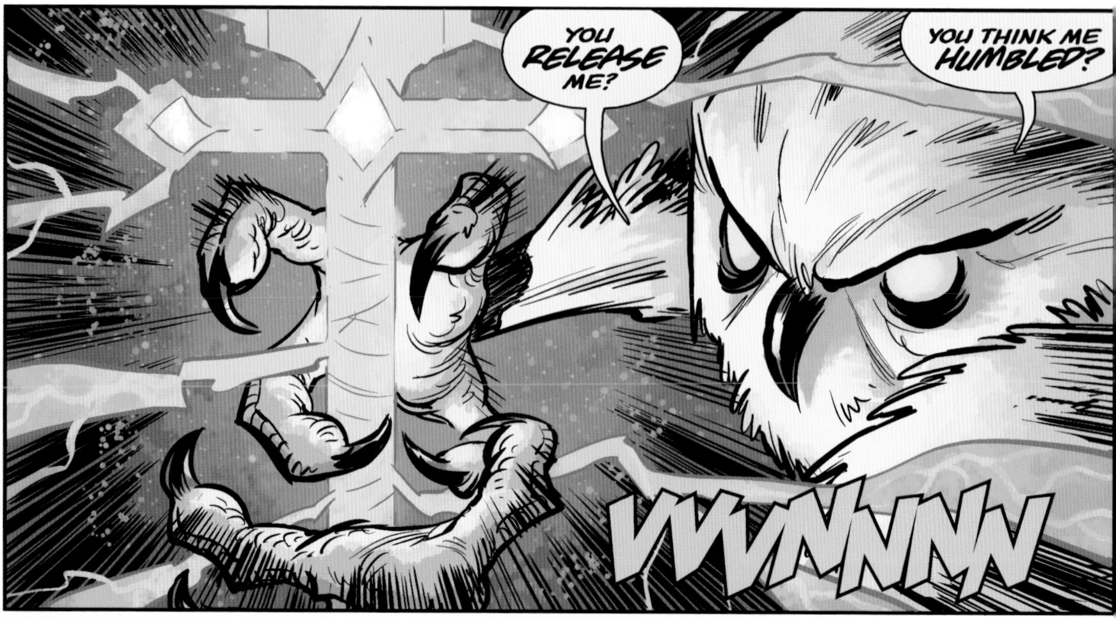
YOU RELEASE ME?
YOU THINK ME HUMBLED?
VVVNNNN

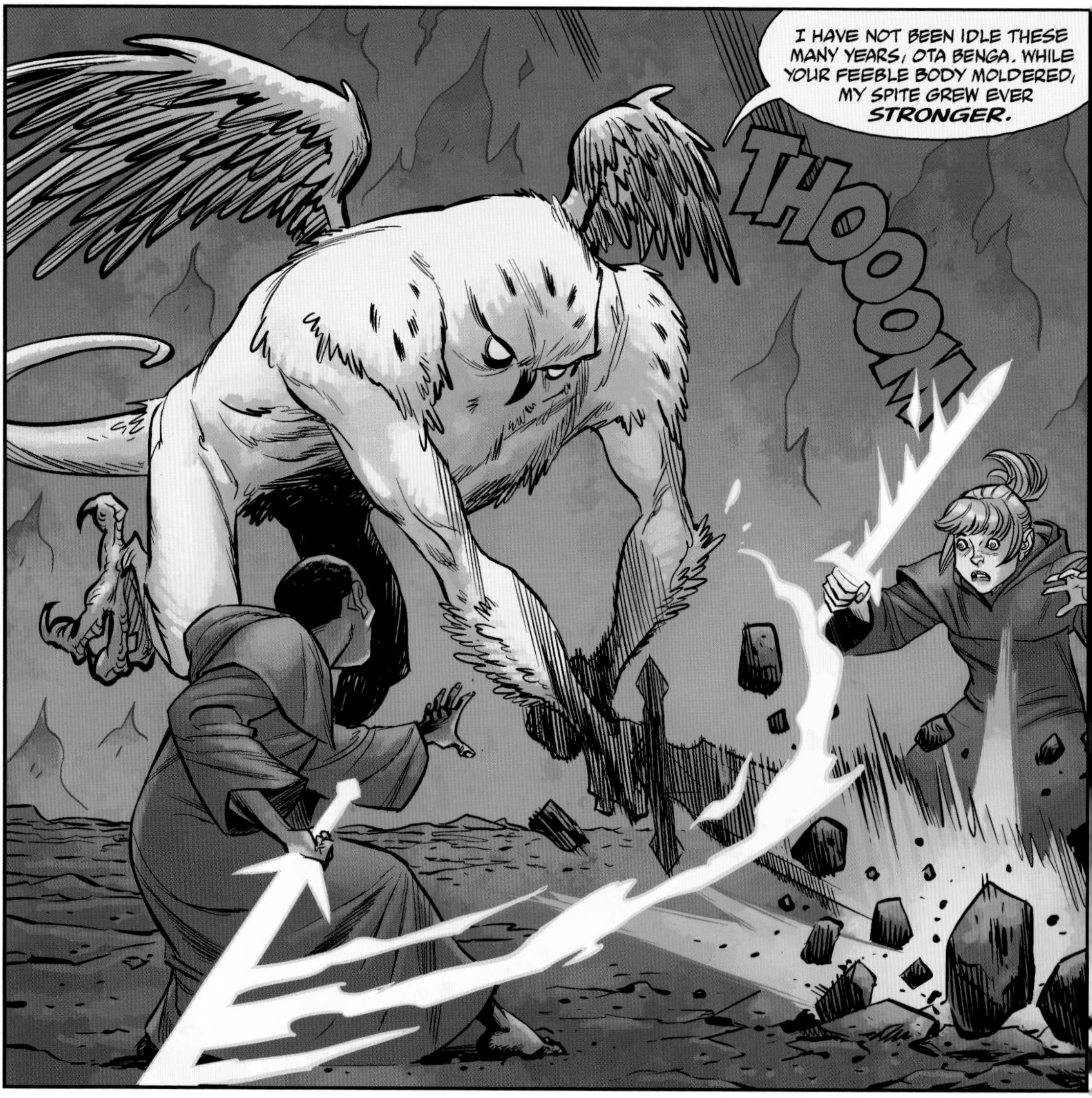
I HAVE NOT BEEN IDLE THESE MANY YEARS, OTA BENGA. WHILE YOUR FEEBLE BODY MOLDERED, MY SPITE GREW EVER STRONGER.
THOOOOK

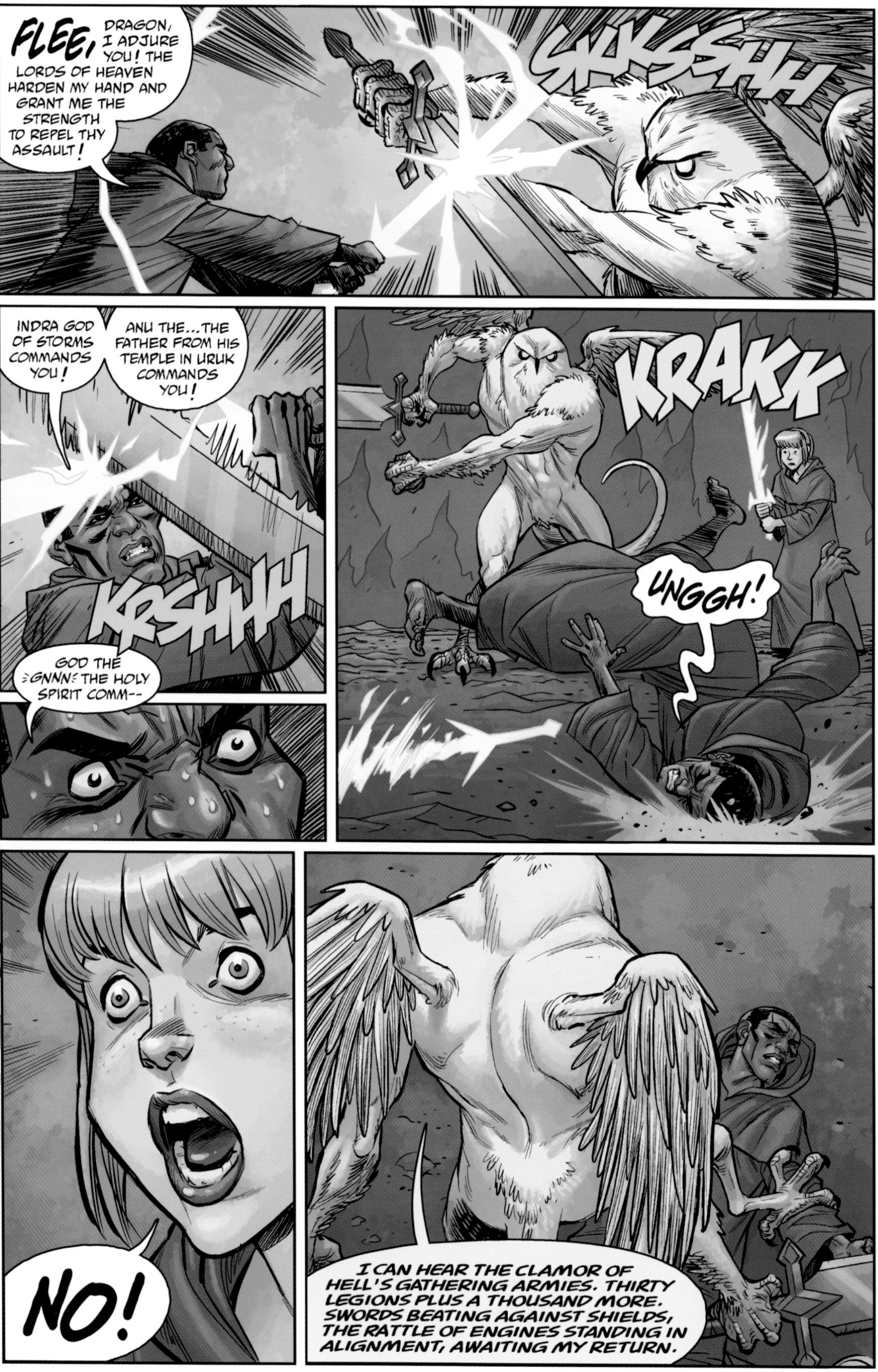
FLEE, DRAGON, I ADJURE YOU! THE LORDS OF HEAVEN HARDEN MY HAND AND GRANT ME THE STRENGTH TO REPEL THY ASSAULT!
SKKSSHH
INDRA GOD OF STORMS COMMANDS YOU!
ANU THE...THE FATHER FROM HIS TEMPLE IN URUK COMMANDS YOU!
KRSHHH
GOD THE GNNN THE HOLY SPIRIT COMM--
KRAKK
UNGGH!
NO!
I CAN HEAR THE CLAMOR OF HELL'S GATHERING ARMIES. THIRTY LEGIONS PLUS A THOUSAND MORE. SWORDS BEATING AGAINST SHIELDS, THE RATTLE OF ENGINES STANDING IN ALIGNMENT, AWAITING MY RETURN.

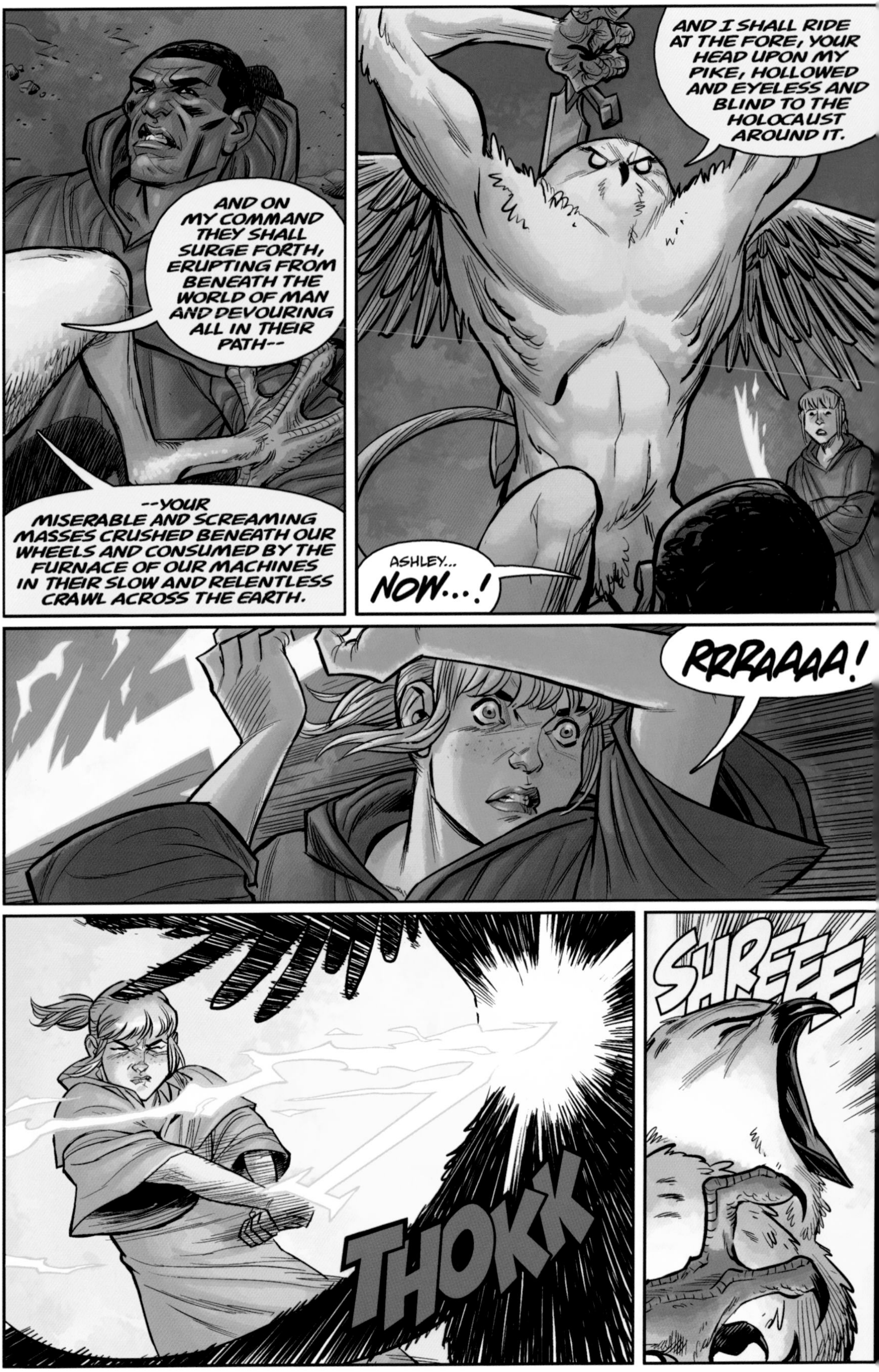
AND ON MY COMMAND THEY SHALL SURGE FORTH, ERUPTING FROM BENEATH THE WORLD OF MAN AND DEVOURING ALL IN THEIR PATH--
--YOUR MISERABLE AND SCREAMING MASSES CRUSHED BENEATH OUR WHEELS AND CONSUMED BY THE FURNACE OF OUR MACHINES IN THEIR SLOW AND RELENTLESS CRAWL ACROSS THE EARTH.
AND I SHALL RIDE AT THE FORE, YOUR HEAD UPON MY PIKE, HOLLOWED AND EYELESS AND BLIND TO THE HOLOCAUST AROUND IT.
ASHLEY... NOW...!
RRRAAAAA!
THOKK
SHREEE

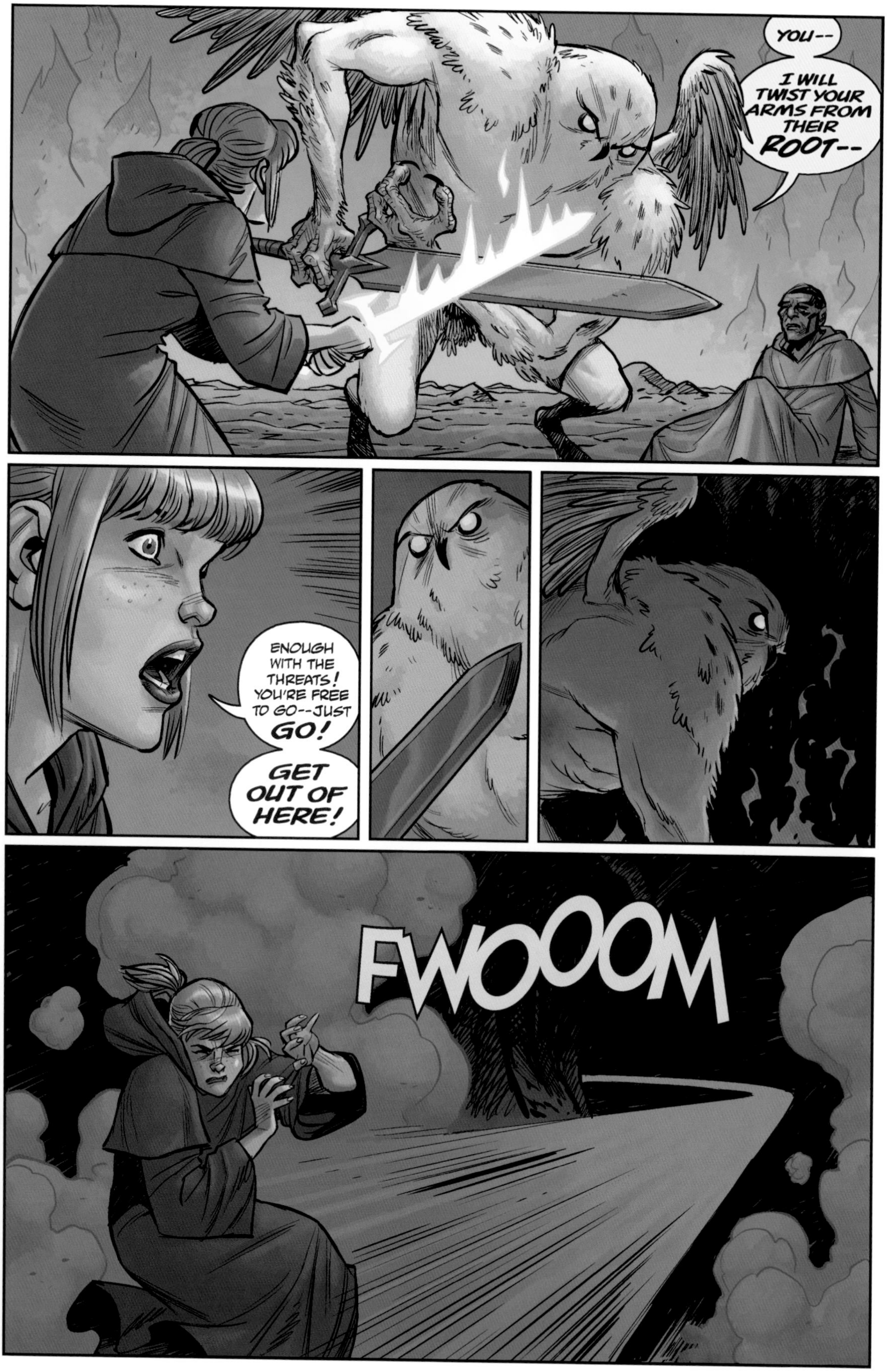
YOU--
I WILL TWIST YOUR ARMS FROM THEIR ROOT--
ENOUGH WITH THE THREATS! YOU'RE FREE TO GO--JUST GO!
GET OUT OF HERE!
FWOOOM

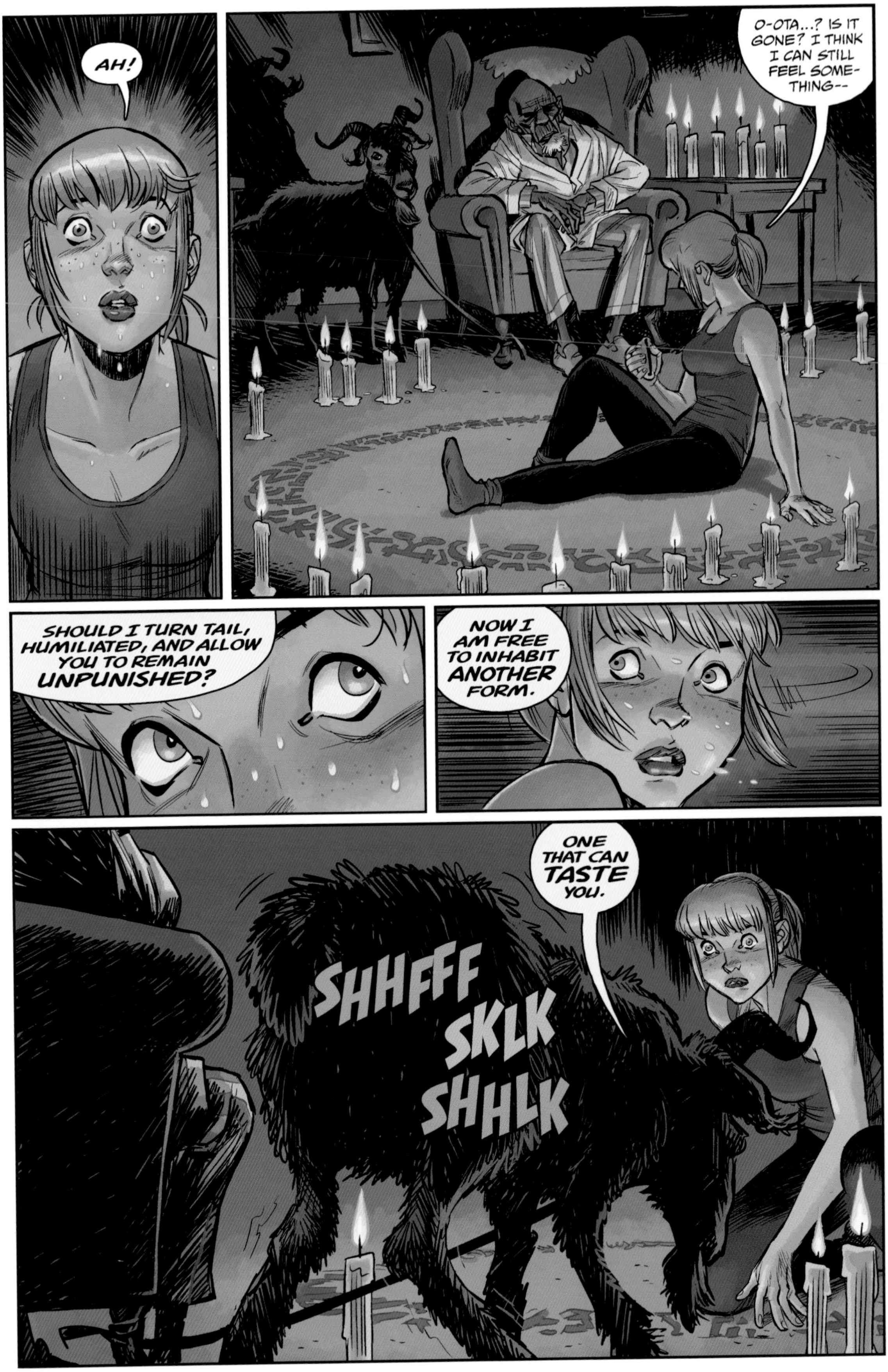
AH!
O-OTA...? IS IT GONE? I THINK I CAN STILL FEEL SOME-THING--
SHOULD I TURN TAIL, HUMILIATED, AND ALLOW YOU TO REMAIN UNPUNISHED?
NOW I AM FREE TO INHABIT ANOTHER FORM.
ONE THAT CAN TASTE YOU.
SHHFFF
SKLK
SHHLK

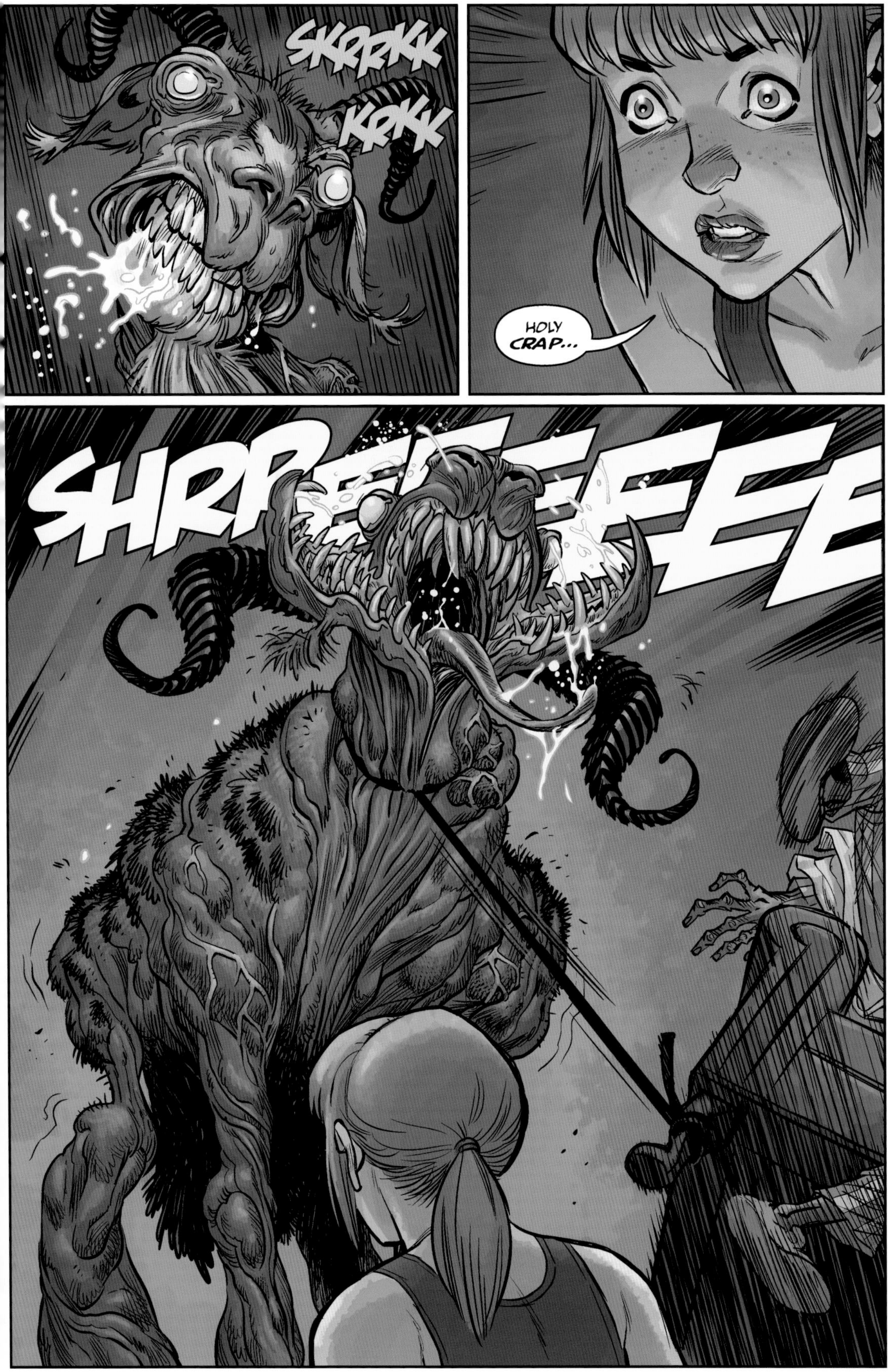
SKRRKK
KRKK
HOLY CRAP...
SHREEEEEE

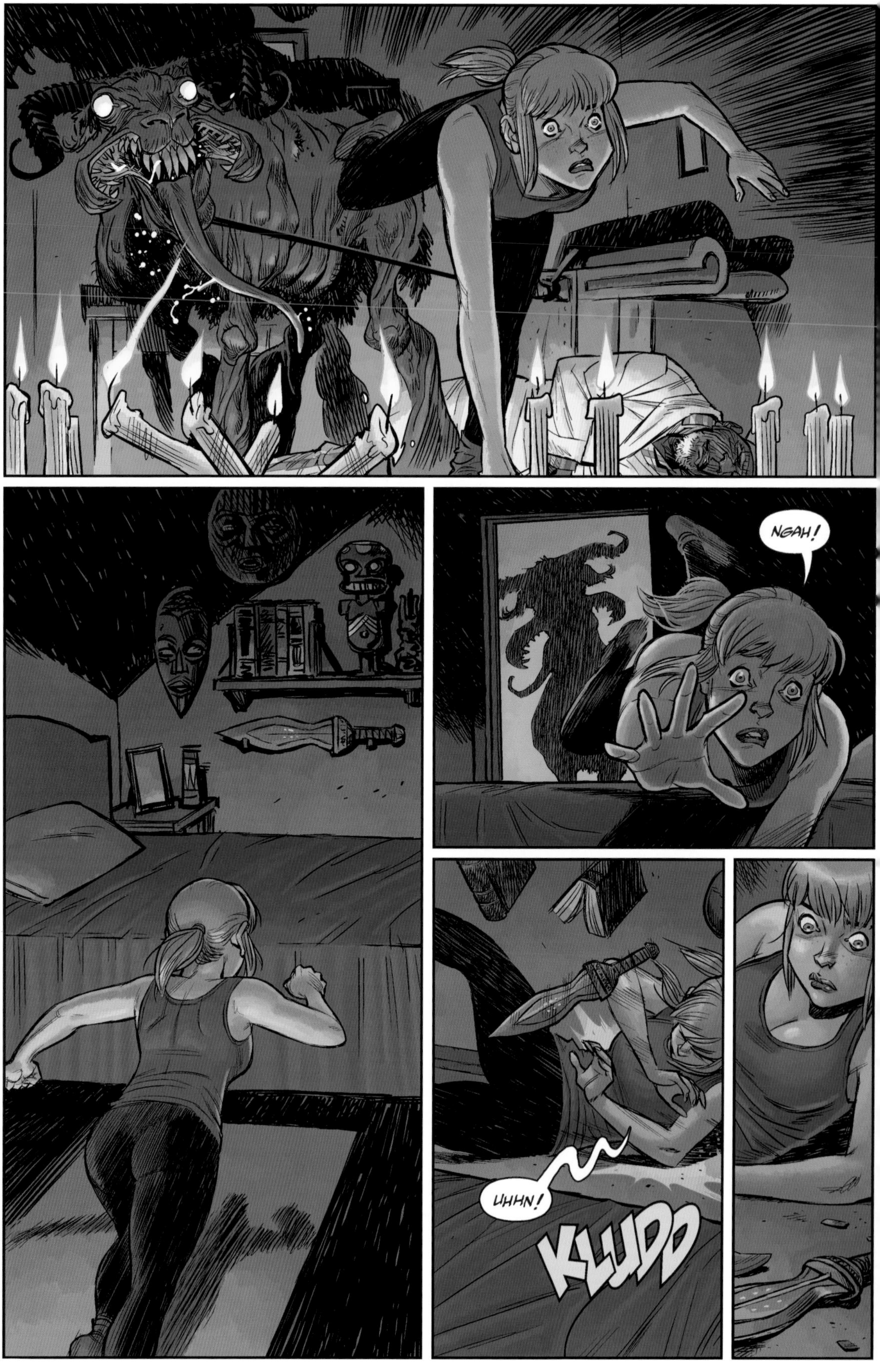
NGAH!
UHHN!
KLUDD

YOUR HAND **TREMBLES**, GIRL. IT **BETRAYS** YOUR **FEAR.**

WHERE IS YOUR **BRAVADO,** LITTLE ONE? NO **SURPRISE** ATTACKS?

KLONK

HRRRRK

GNNAAAH!

SKLRTCH

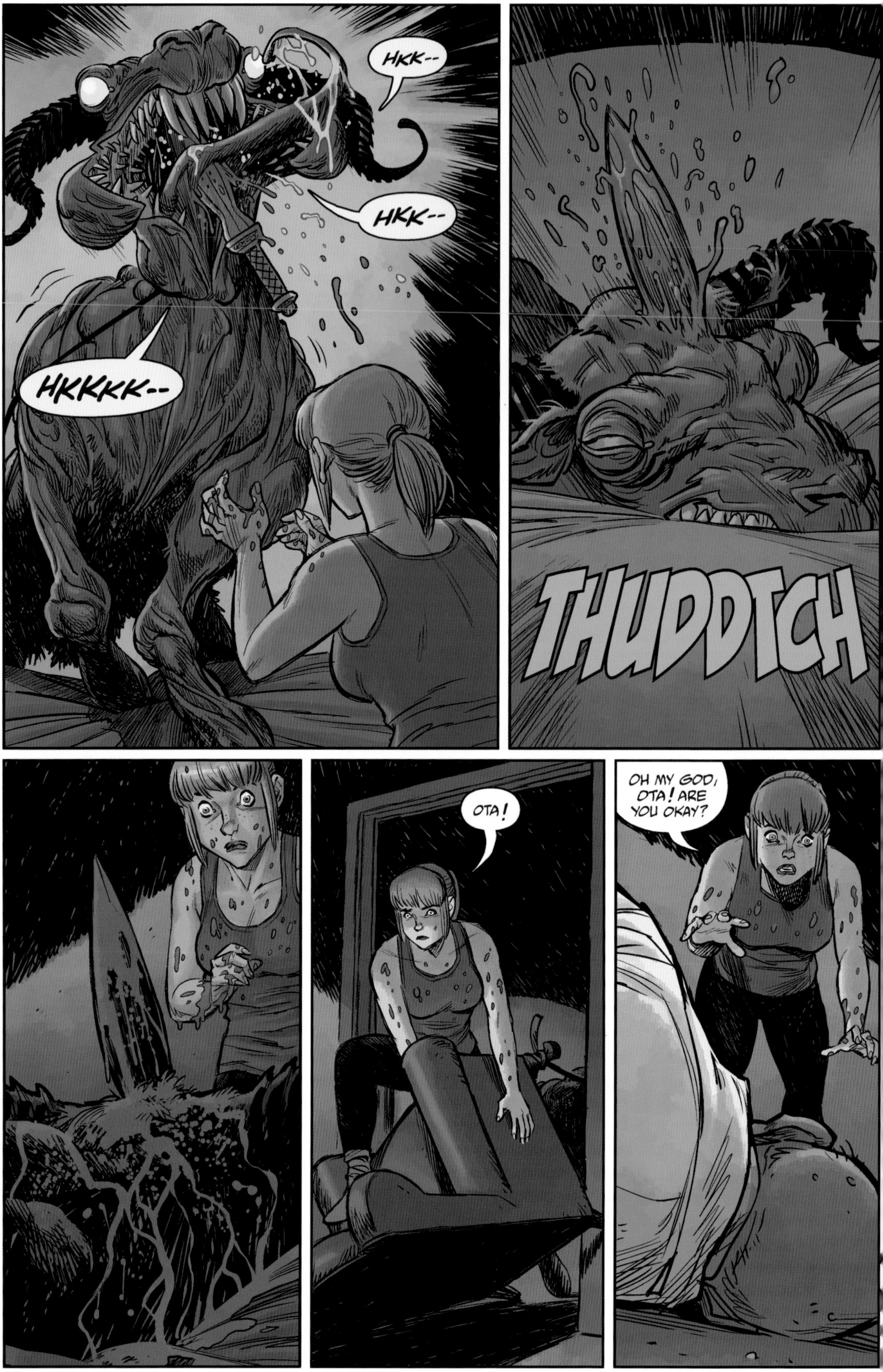
HKK--
HKK--
HKKKK--
THUDDTCH
OTA!
OH MY GOD, OTA! ARE YOU OKAY?

I...AM **DYING**, AGENT STRODE...

THE DEMON IS **GONE**, SENT BACK TO HELL WHEN YOU KILLED ITS HOST... I AM **DRAINED** OF THE ENERGY THAT SUSTAINED ME...

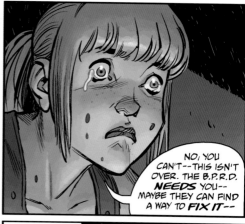

NO, YOU CAN'T--THIS ISN'T OVER. THE B.P.R.D. **NEEDS** YOU-- MAYBE THEY CAN FIND A WAY TO **FIX IT**--

I AM **TIRED**, AGENT STRODE, AND I SHOULD HAVE LAIN DOWN TO REST LONG AGO.

LEAVE ME...AND CARRY ON.

I--I CAN'T...I DON'T KNOW WHAT TO...

YES. YOU DO.

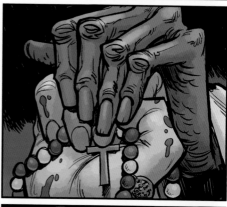

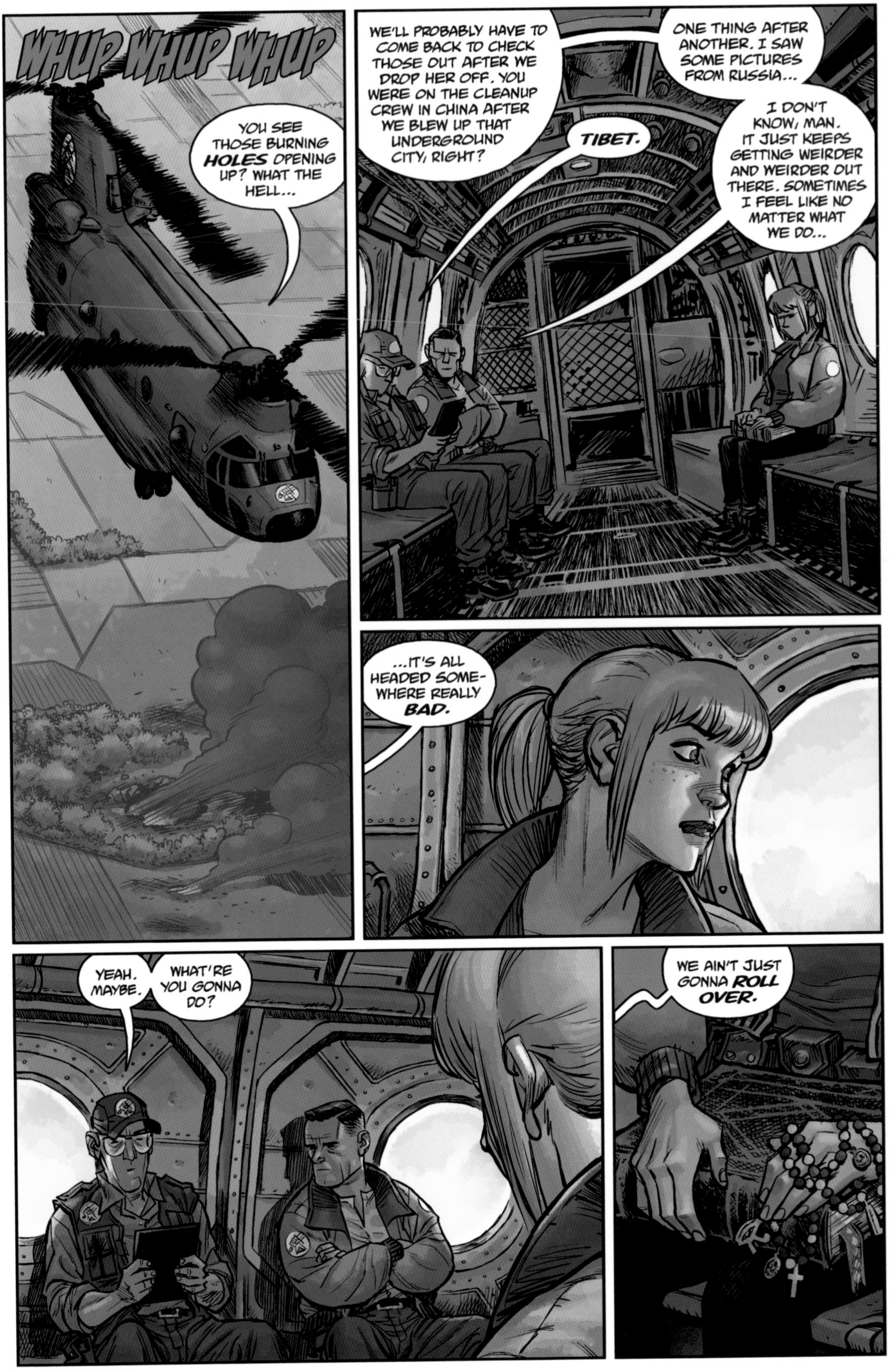
WHUP WHUP WHUP
YOU SEE THOSE BURNING HOLES OPENING UP? WHAT THE HELL...
WE'LL PROBABLY HAVE TO COME BACK TO CHECK THOSE OUT AFTER WE DROP HER OFF. YOU WERE ON THE CLEANUP CREW IN CHINA AFTER WE BLEW UP THAT UNDERGROUND CITY, RIGHT?
TIBET.
ONE THING AFTER ANOTHER. I SAW SOME PICTURES FROM RUSSIA...
I DON'T KNOW, MAN. IT JUST KEEPS GETTING WEIRDER AND WEIRDER OUT THERE. SOMETIMES I FEEL LIKE NO MATTER WHAT WE DO...
...IT'S ALL HEADED SOMEWHERE REALLY BAD.
YEAH. MAYBE.
WHAT'RE YOU GONNA DO?
WE AIN'T JUST GONNA ROLL OVER.

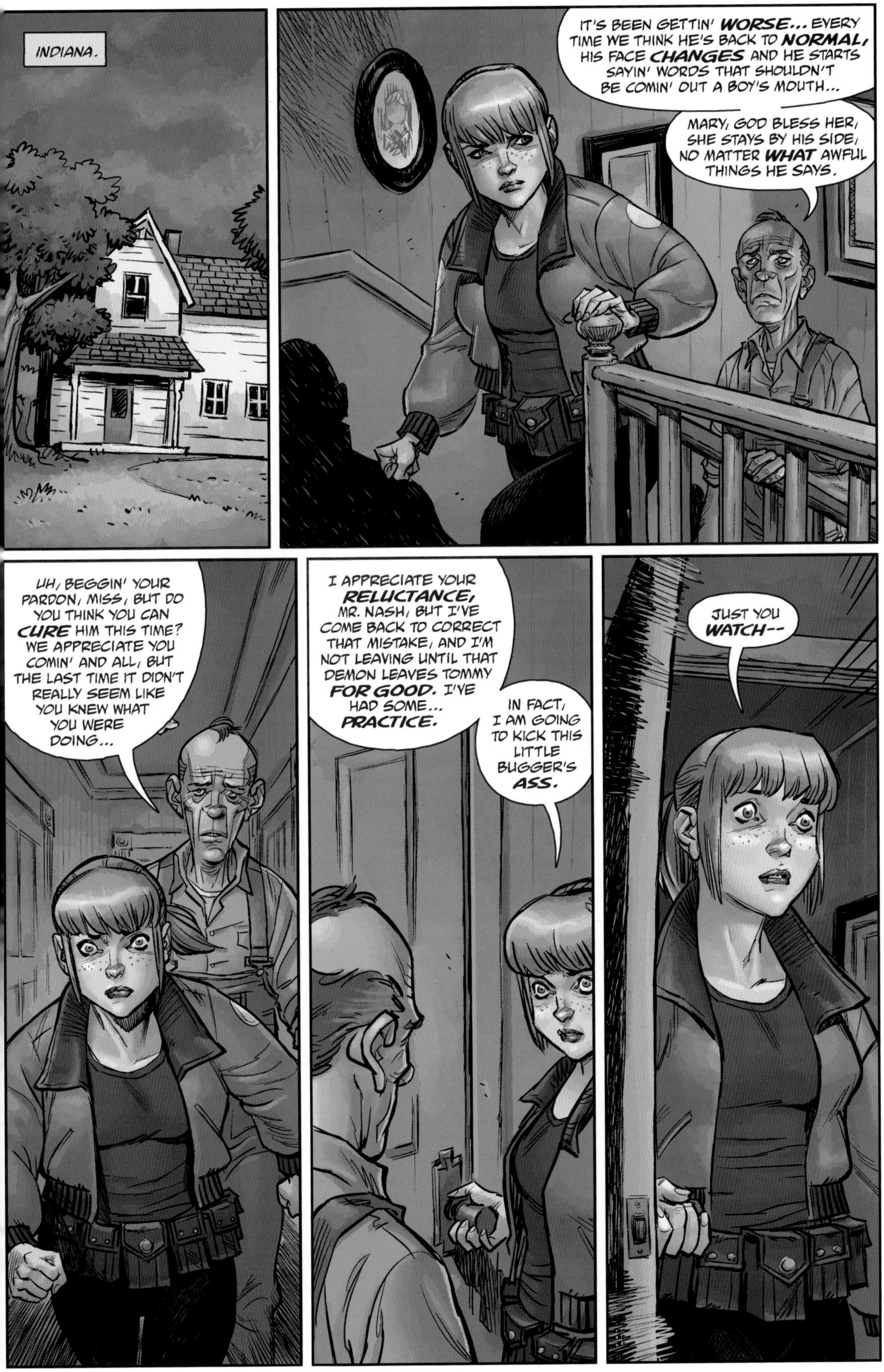
INDIANA.
IT'S BEEN GETTIN' WORSE... EVERY TIME WE THINK HE'S BACK TO NORMAL, HIS FACE CHANGES AND HE STARTS SAYIN' WORDS THAT SHOULDN'T BE COMIN' OUT A BOY'S MOUTH...
MARY, GOD BLESS HER, SHE STAYS BY HIS SIDE, NO MATTER WHAT AWFUL THINGS HE SAYS.
UH, BEGGIN' YOUR PARDON, MISS, BUT DO YOU THINK YOU CAN CURE HIM THIS TIME? WE APPRECIATE YOU COMIN' AND ALL, BUT THE LAST TIME IT DIDN'T REALLY SEEM LIKE YOU KNEW WHAT YOU WERE DOING...
I APPRECIATE YOUR RELUCTANCE, MR. NASH, BUT I'VE COME BACK TO CORRECT THAT MISTAKE, AND I'M NOT LEAVING UNTIL THAT DEMON LEAVES TOMMY FOR GOOD. I'VE HAD SOME... PRACTICE.
IN FACT, I AM GOING TO KICK THIS LITTLE BUGGER'S ASS.
JUST YOU WATCH--

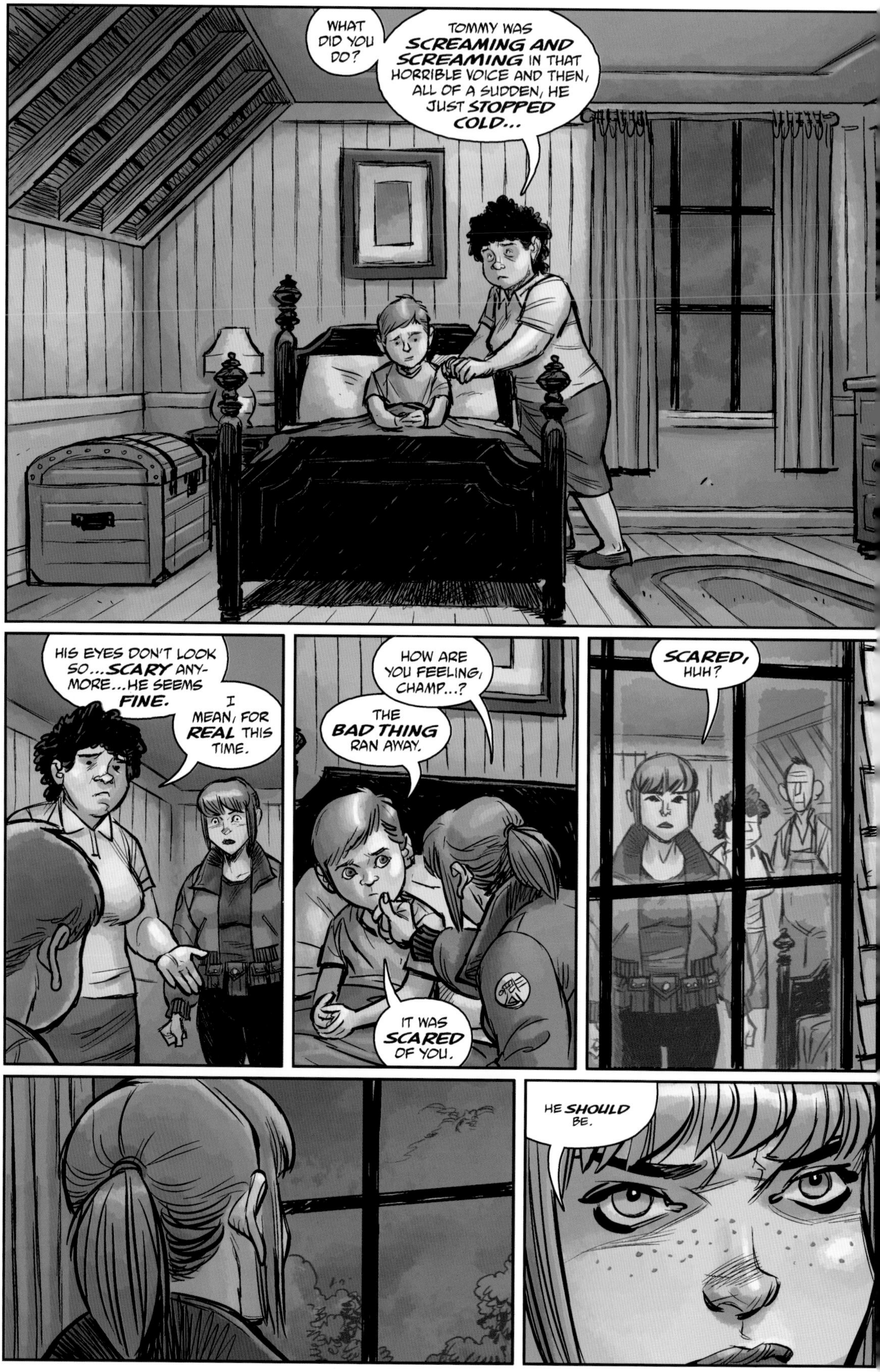

WHAT DID YOU DO?
TOMMY WAS SCREAMING AND SCREAMING IN THAT HORRIBLE VOICE AND THEN, ALL OF A SUDDEN, HE JUST STOPPED COLD...
HIS EYES DON'T LOOK SO...SCARY ANY-MORE...HE SEEMS FINE.
I MEAN, FOR REAL THIS TIME.
HOW ARE YOU FEELING, CHAMP...?
THE BAD THING RAN AWAY.
IT WAS SCARED OF YOU.
SCARED, HUH?
HE SHOULD BE.

THE END

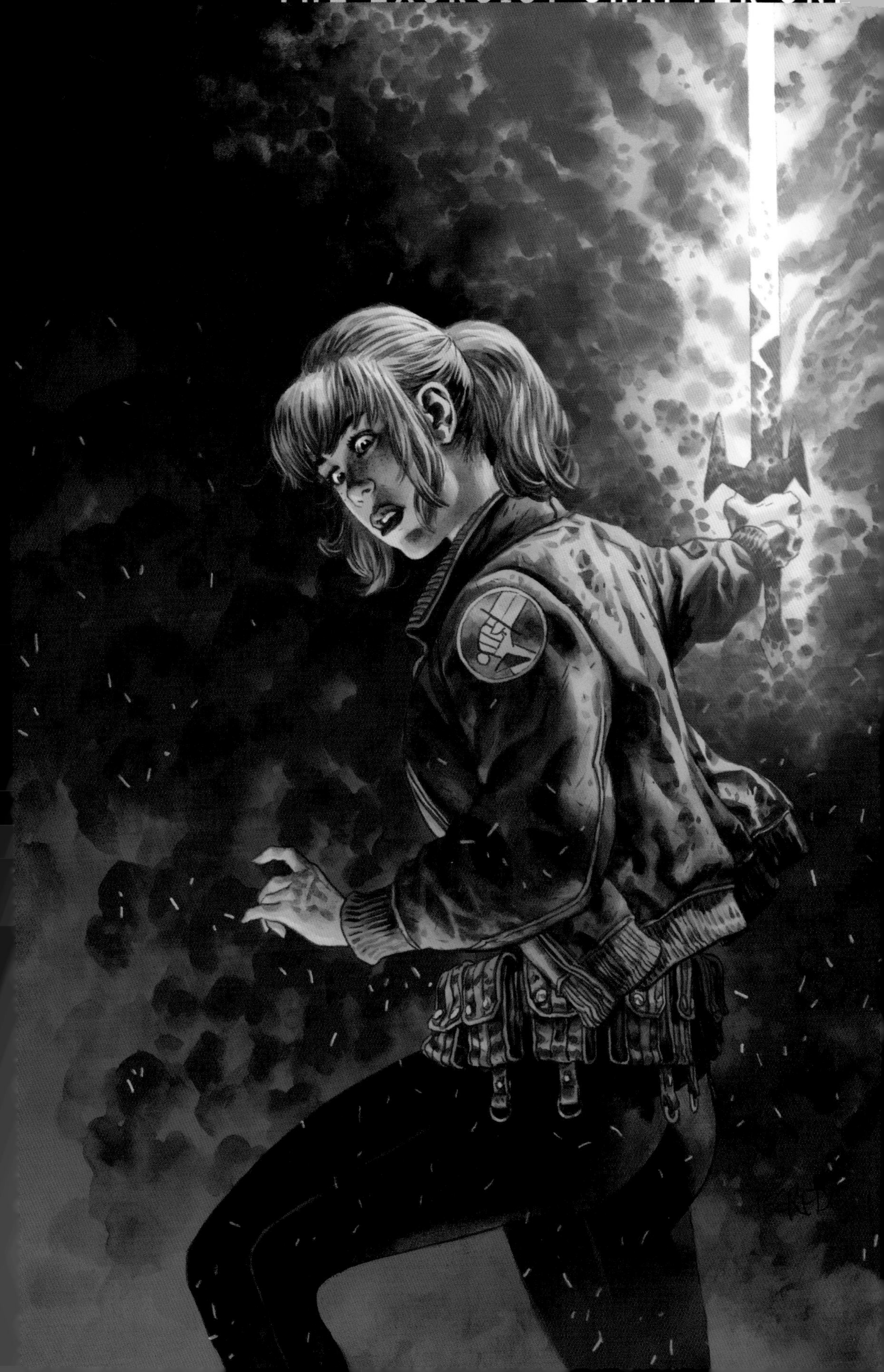

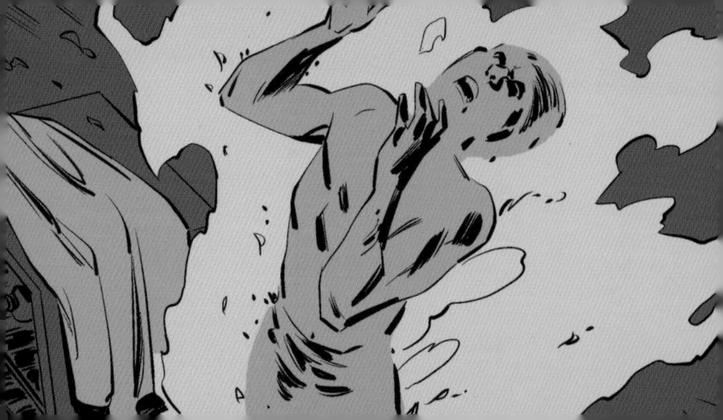

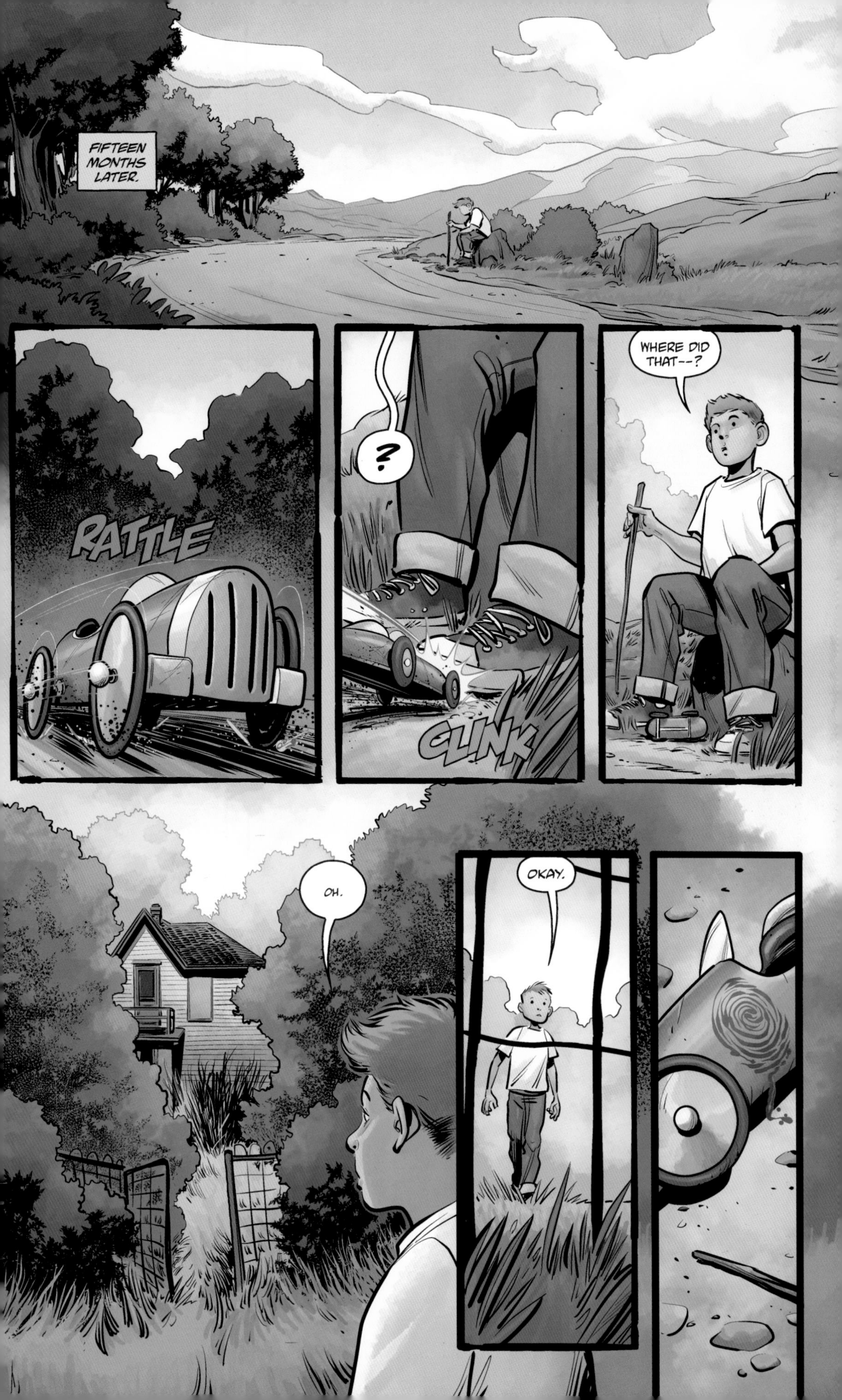
FIFTEEN MONTHS LATER.
RATTLE
?
CLINK
WHERE DID THAT--?
OH.
OKAY.

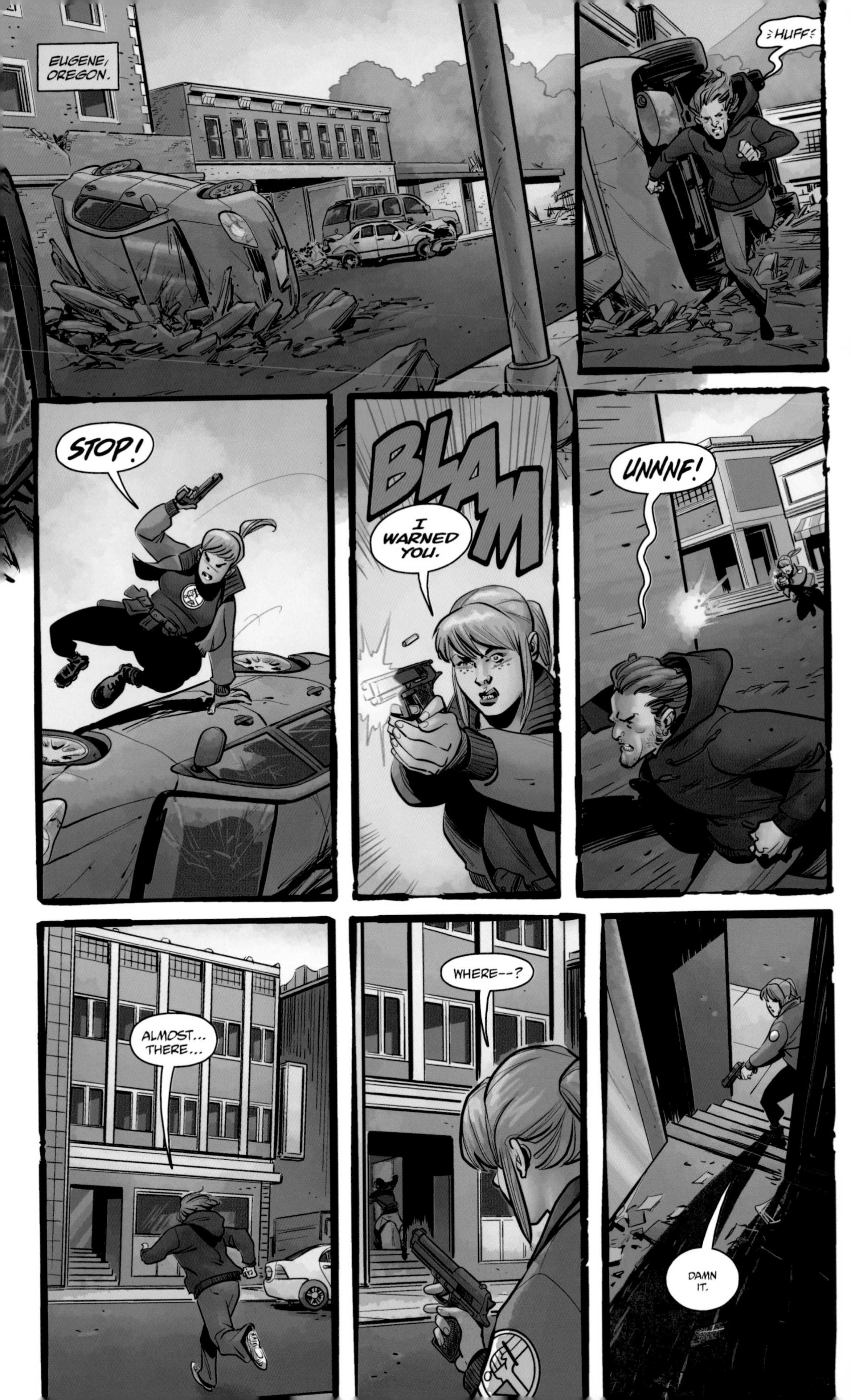
EUGENE, OREGON.
HUFF
STOP!
BLAM
I WARNED YOU.
UNNNF!
ALMOST... THERE...
WHERE--?
DAMN IT.

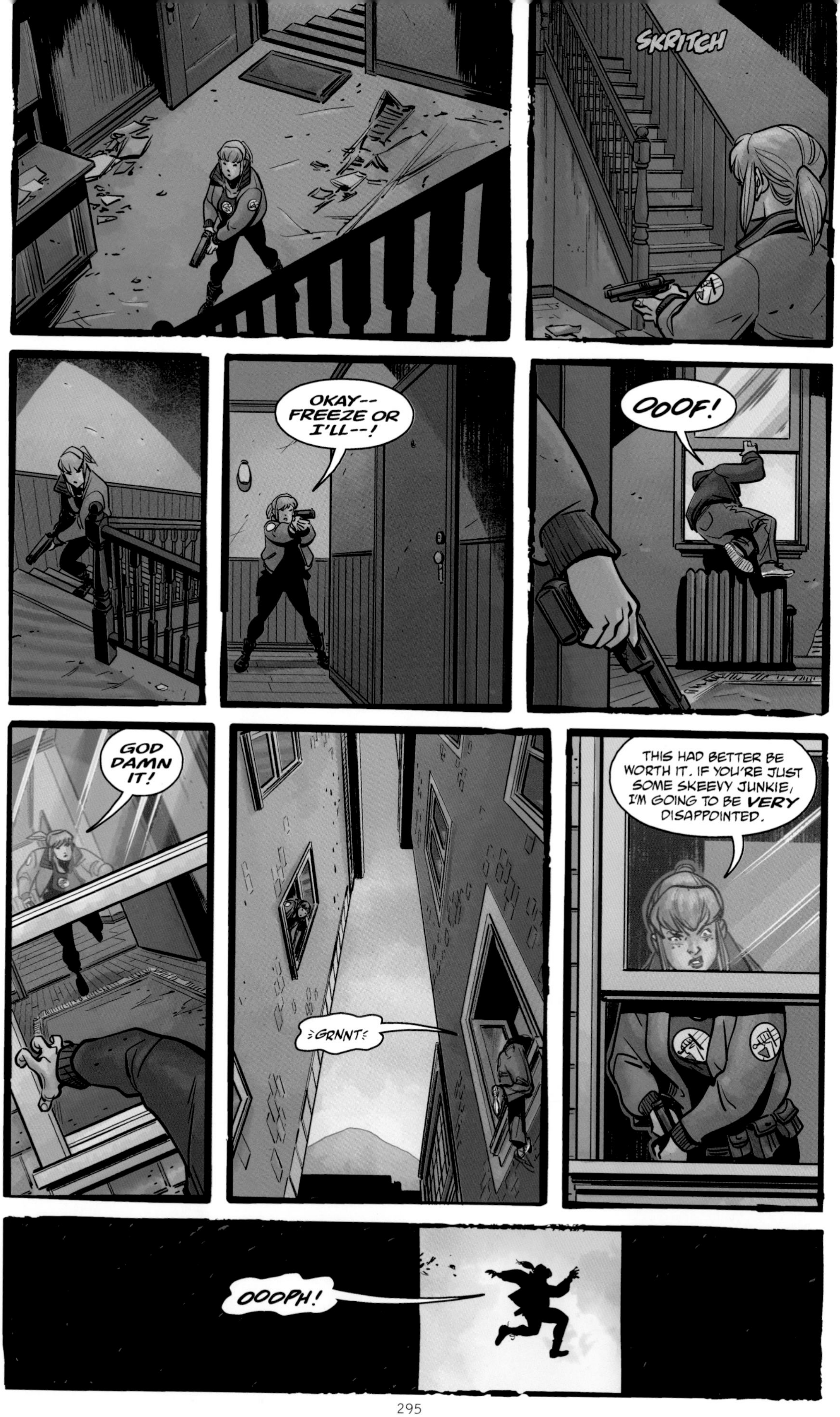
SKRITCH
OKAY-- FREEZE OR I'LL--!
OOOF!
GOD DAMN IT!
GRNNT
THIS HAD BETTER BE WORTH IT. IF YOU'RE JUST SOME SKEEVY JUNKIE, I'M GOING TO BE VERY DISAPPOINTED.
OOOPH!

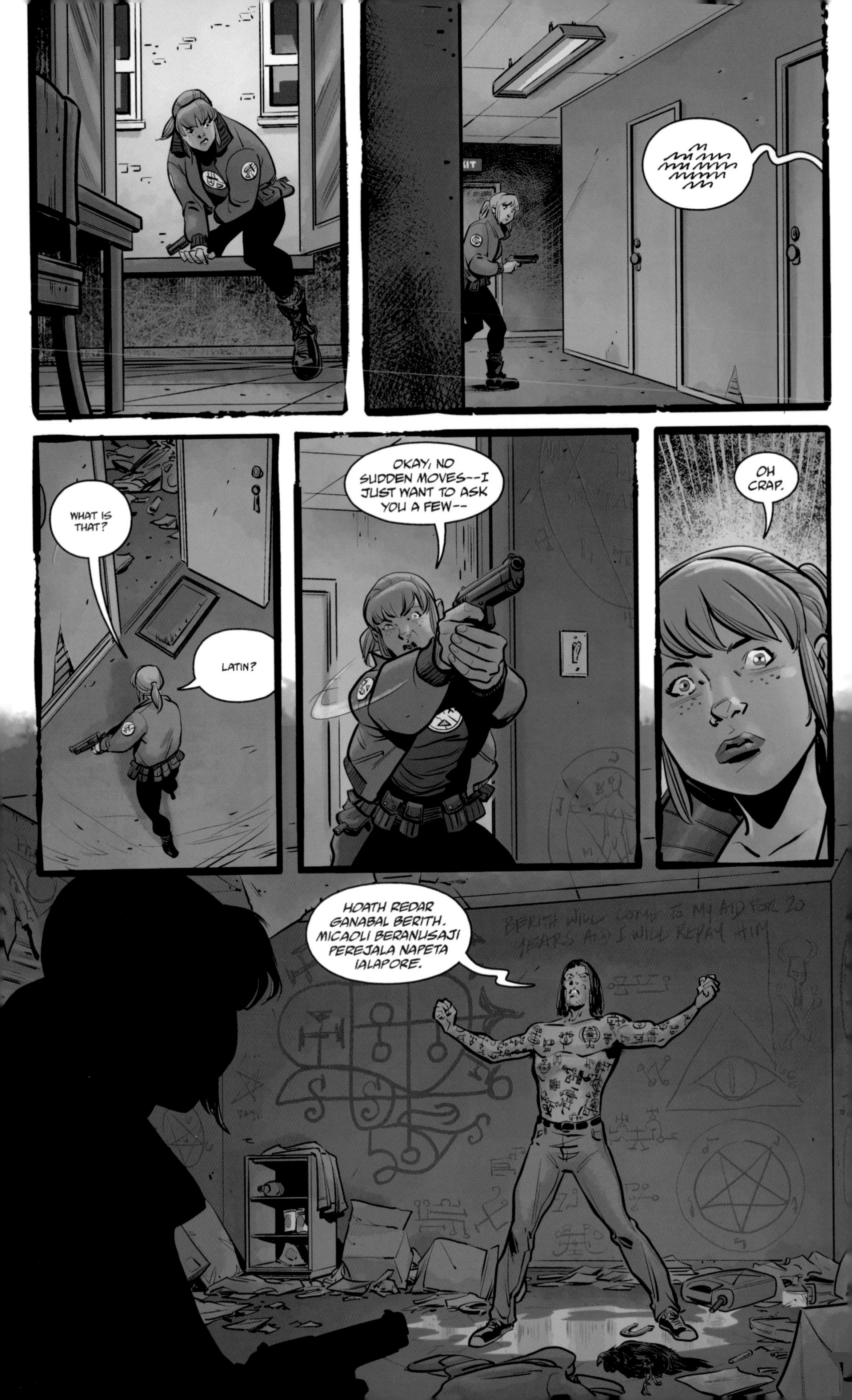

WHAT IS THAT?
LATIN?
OKAY, NO SUDDEN MOVES--I JUST WANT TO ASK YOU A FEW--
OH CRAP.
HOATH REDAR GANABAL BERITH. MICAOLI BERANUSAJI PEREJALA NAPETA IALAPORE.
BERITH WILL COME TO MY AID FOR 20 YEARS AND I WILL REPAY HIM

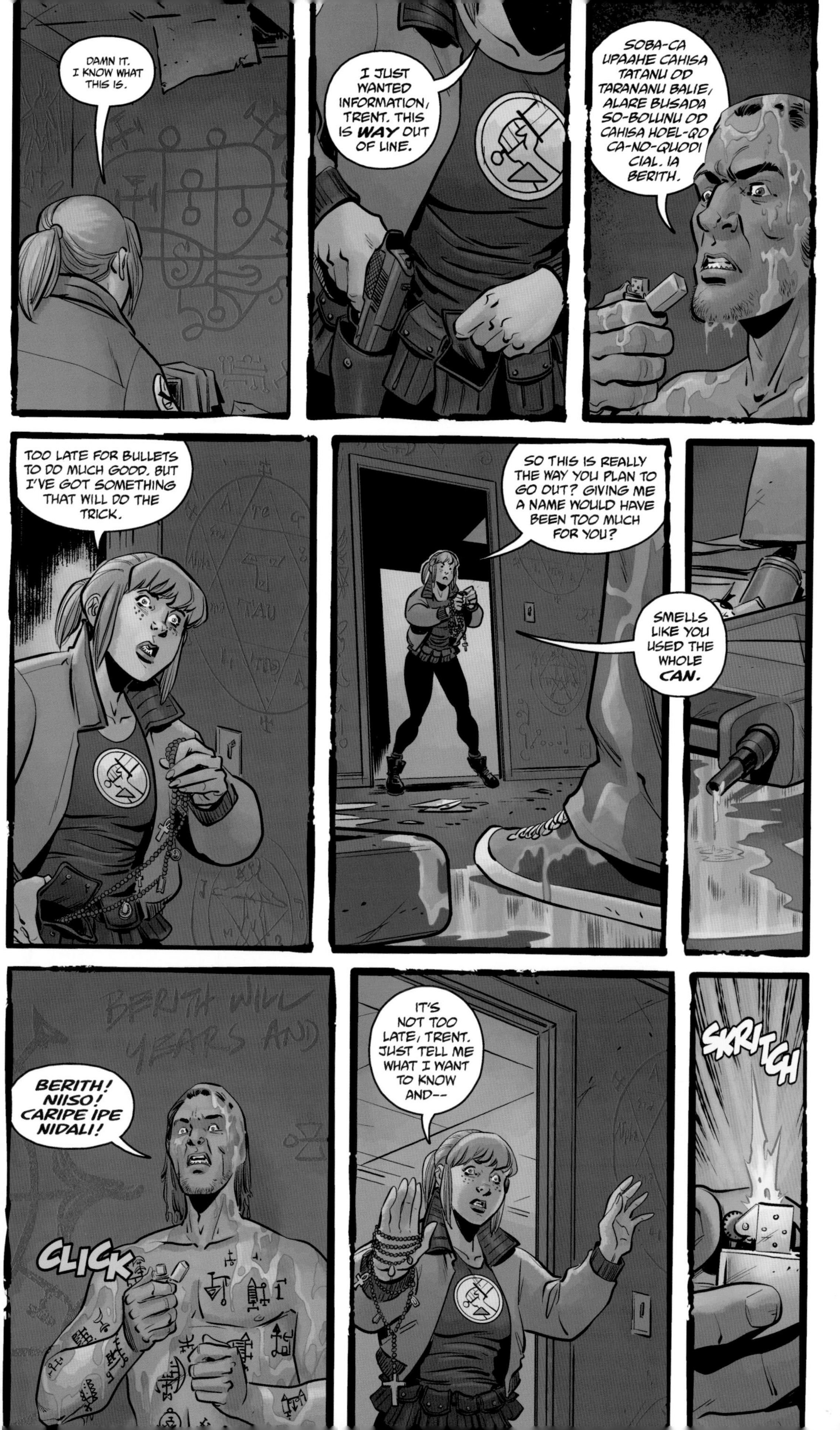
DAMN IT. I KNOW WHAT THIS IS.
I JUST WANTED INFORMATION, TRENT. THIS IS **WAY** OUT OF LINE.
SOBA-CA UPAAHE CAHISA TATANU OD TARANANU BALIE, ALARE BUSADA SO-BOLUNU OD CAHISA HOEL-QO CA-NO-QUODI CIAL. IA BERITH.
TOO LATE FOR BULLETS TO DO MUCH GOOD, BUT I'VE GOT SOMETHING THAT WILL DO THE TRICK.
SO THIS IS REALLY THE WAY YOU PLAN TO GO OUT? GIVING ME A NAME WOULD HAVE BEEN TOO MUCH FOR YOU?
SMELLS LIKE YOU USED THE WHOLE **CAN.**
BERITH WILL YEARS AND
BERITH! NIISO! CARIPE IPE NIDALI!
CLICK
IT'S NOT TOO LATE, TRENT. JUST TELL ME WHAT I WANT TO KNOW AND--
SKRITCH

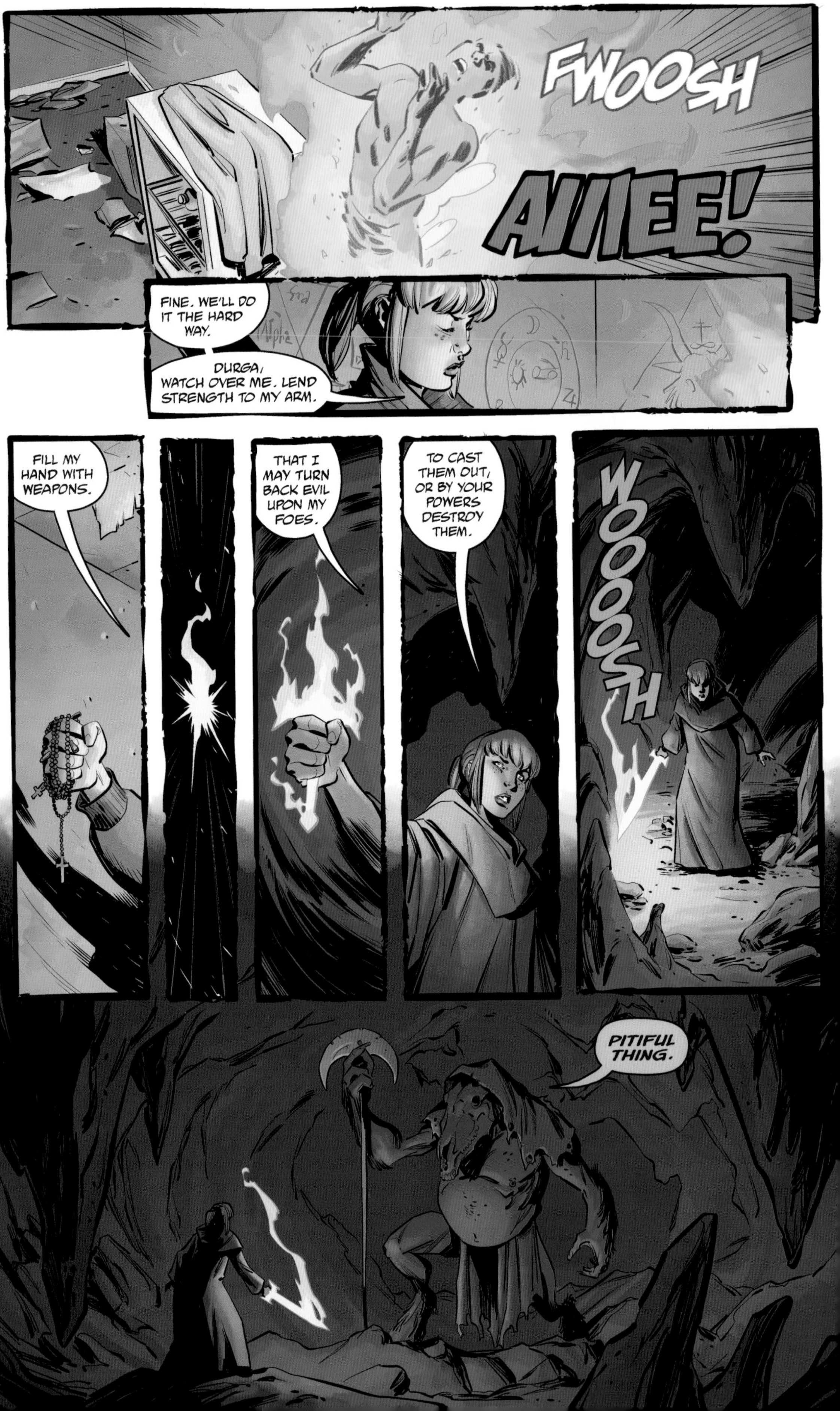
FWOOSH
AIIIEE!
FINE. WE'LL DO IT THE HARD WAY.
DURGA, WATCH OVER ME. LEND STRENGTH TO MY ARM.
FILL MY HAND WITH WEAPONS.
THAT I MAY TURN BACK EVIL UPON MY FOES.
TO CAST THEM OUT, OR BY YOUR POWERS DESTROY THEM.
WOOOOOSH
PITIFUL THING.

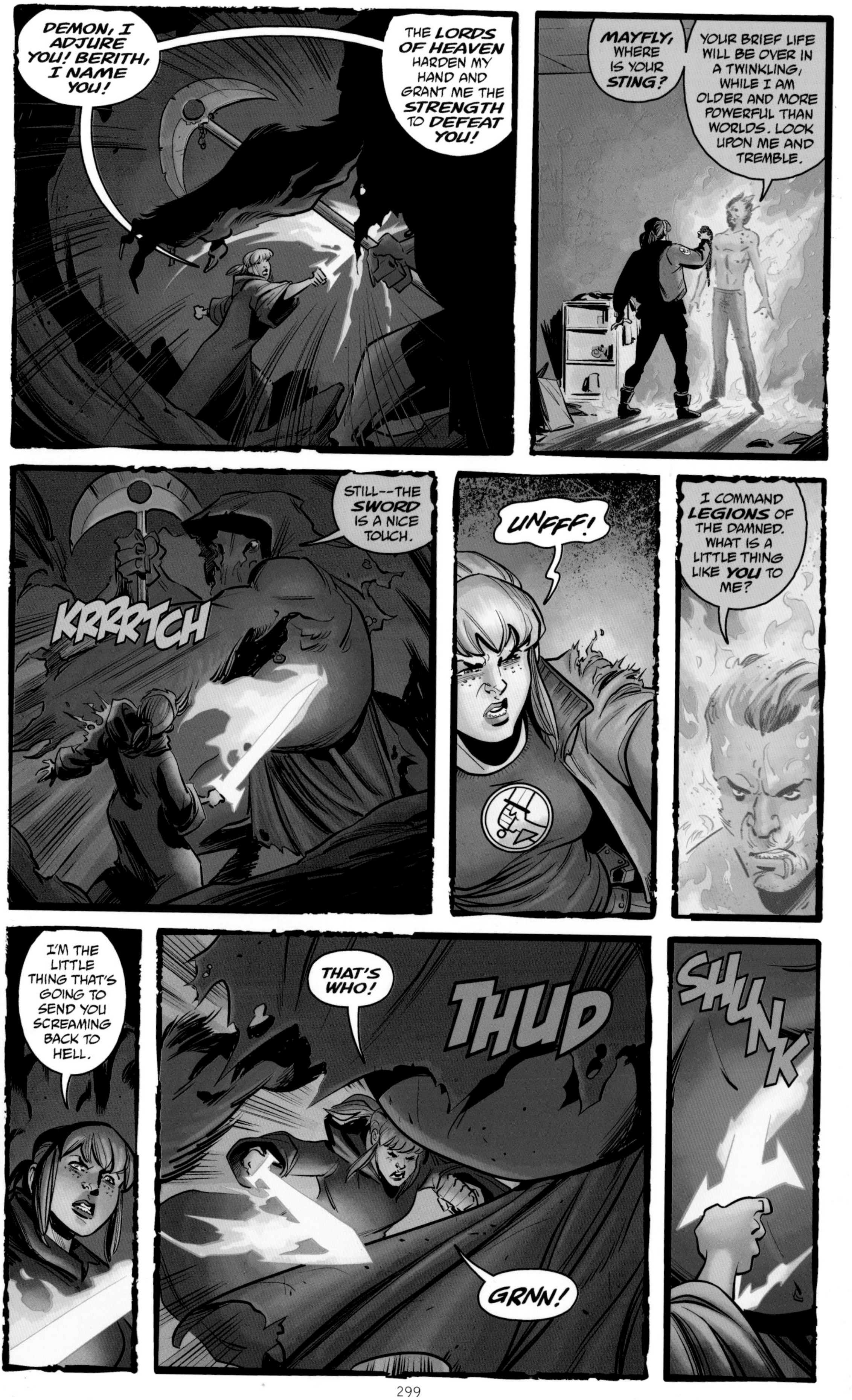
DEMON, I ADJURE YOU! BERITH, I NAME YOU!
THE LORDS OF HEAVEN HARDEN MY HAND AND GRANT ME THE STRENGTH TO DEFEAT YOU!
MAYFLY, WHERE IS YOUR STING?
YOUR BRIEF LIFE WILL BE OVER IN A TWINKLING, WHILE I AM OLDER AND MORE POWERFUL THAN WORLDS. LOOK UPON ME AND TREMBLE.
STILL--THE SWORD IS A NICE TOUCH.
KRRRTCH
UNFFF!
I COMMAND LEGIONS OF THE DAMNED. WHAT IS A LITTLE THING LIKE YOU TO ME?
I'M THE LITTLE THING THAT'S GOING TO SEND YOU SCREAMING BACK TO HELL.
THAT'S WHO!
THUD
GRNN!
SHUNK

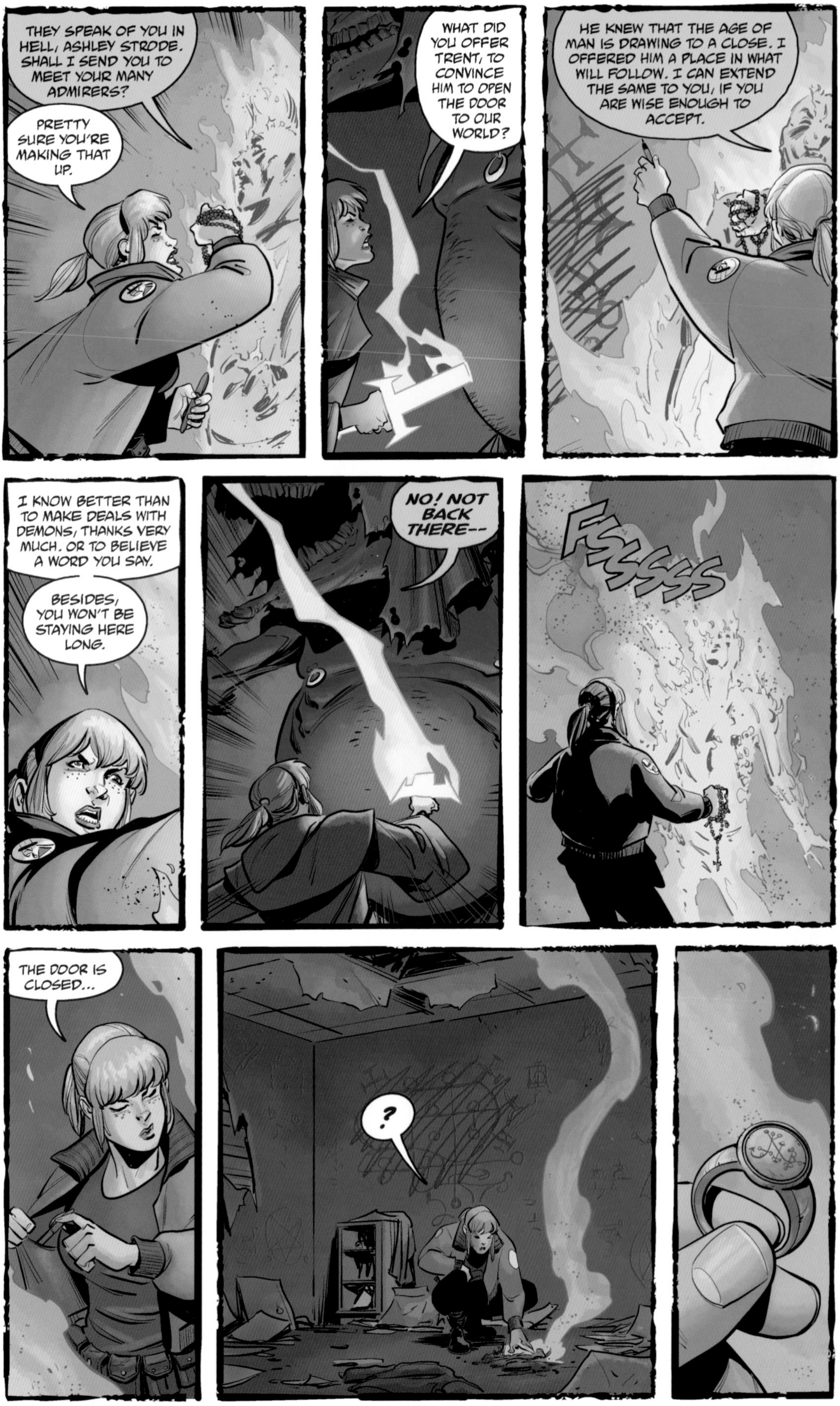
THEY SPEAK OF YOU IN HELL, ASHLEY STRODE. SHALL I SEND YOU TO MEET YOUR MANY ADMIRERS?
PRETTY SURE YOU'RE MAKING THAT UP.
WHAT DID YOU OFFER TRENT, TO CONVINCE HIM TO OPEN THE DOOR TO OUR WORLD?
HE KNEW THAT THE AGE OF MAN IS DRAWING TO A CLOSE. I OFFERED HIM A PLACE IN WHAT WILL FOLLOW. I CAN EXTEND THE SAME TO YOU, IF YOU ARE WISE ENOUGH TO ACCEPT.
I KNOW BETTER THAN TO MAKE DEALS WITH DEMONS, THANKS VERY MUCH. OR TO BELIEVE A WORD YOU SAY.
BESIDES, YOU WON'T BE STAYING HERE LONG.
NO! NOT BACK THERE--
FSSSSSS
THE DOOR IS CLOSED...
?

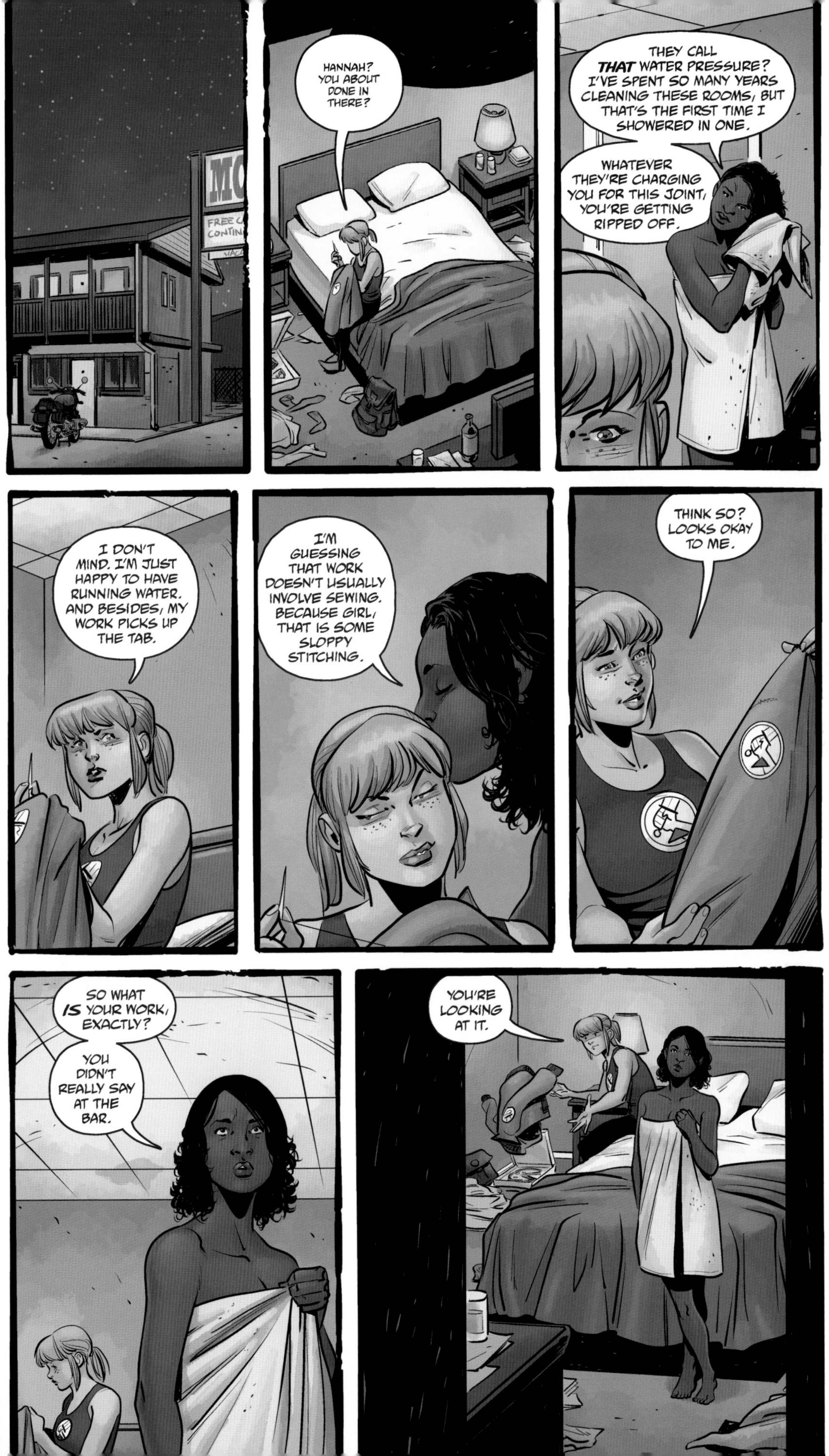

MO
FREE C
CONTIN
HANNAH? YOU ABOUT DONE IN THERE?
THEY CALL THAT WATER PRESSURE? I'VE SPENT SO MANY YEARS CLEANING THESE ROOMS, BUT THAT'S THE FIRST TIME I SHOWERED IN ONE.
WHATEVER THEY'RE CHARGING YOU FOR THIS JOINT, YOU'RE GETTING RIPPED OFF.
I DON'T MIND. I'M JUST HAPPY TO HAVE RUNNING WATER. AND BESIDES, MY WORK PICKS UP THE TAB.
I'M GUESSING THAT WORK DOESN'T USUALLY INVOLVE SEWING. BECAUSE GIRL, THAT IS SOME SLOPPY STITCHING.
THINK SO? LOOKS OKAY TO ME.
SO WHAT IS YOUR WORK, EXACTLY?
YOU DIDN'T REALLY SAY AT THE BAR.
YOU'RE LOOKING AT IT.

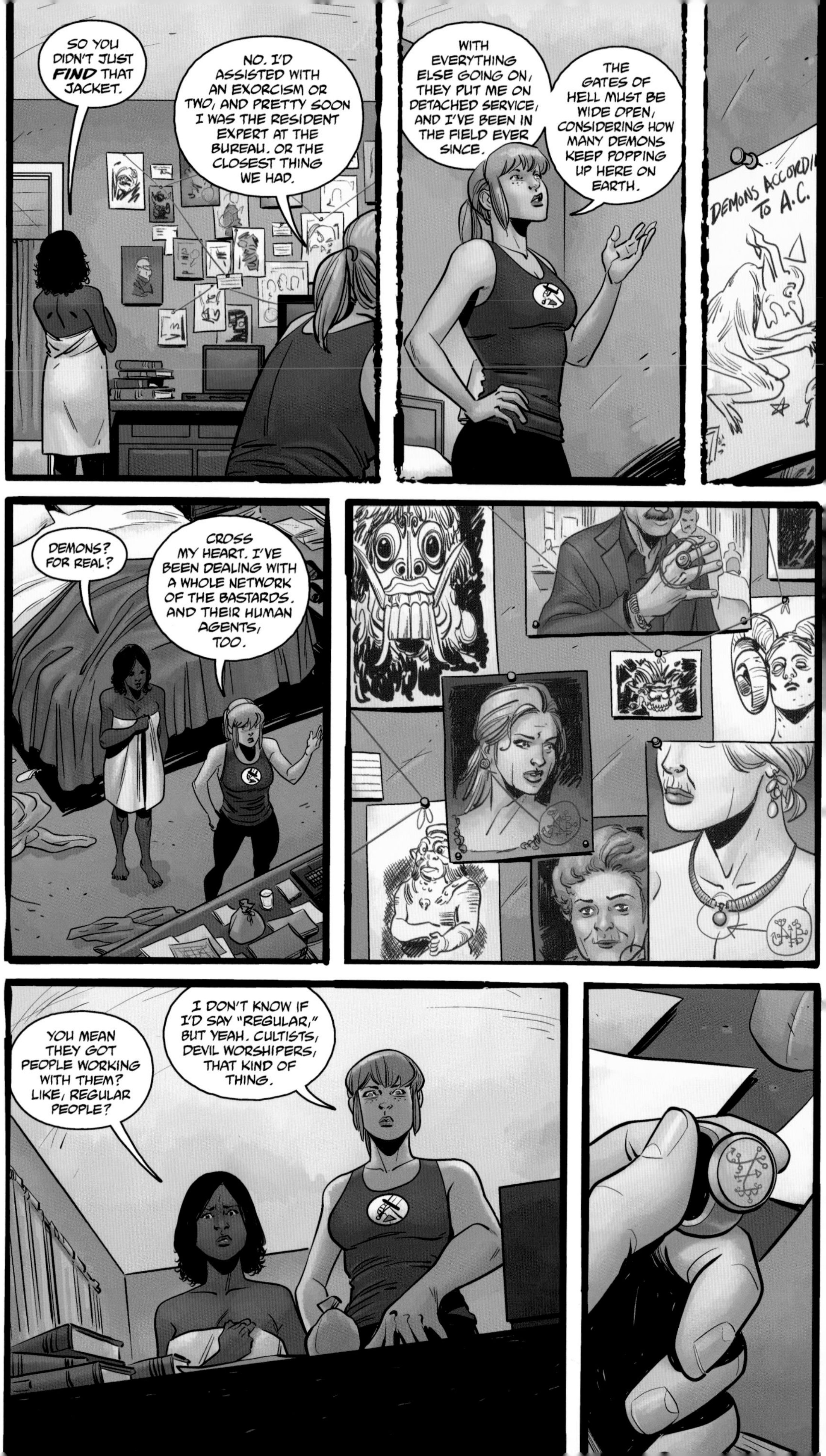

SO YOU DIDN'T JUST **FIND** THAT JACKET.
NO. I'D ASSISTED WITH AN EXORCISM OR TWO, AND PRETTY SOON I WAS THE RESIDENT EXPERT AT THE BUREAU. OR THE CLOSEST THING WE HAD.
WITH EVERYTHING ELSE GOING ON, THEY PUT ME ON DETACHED SERVICE, AND I'VE BEEN IN THE FIELD EVER SINCE.
THE GATES OF HELL MUST BE WIDE OPEN, CONSIDERING HOW MANY DEMONS KEEP POPPING UP HERE ON EARTH.
DEMONS ACCORDI
TO A.C.
DEMONS? FOR REAL?
CROSS MY HEART. I'VE BEEN DEALING WITH A WHOLE NETWORK OF THE BASTARDS. AND THEIR HUMAN AGENTS, TOO.
YOU MEAN THEY GOT PEOPLE WORKING WITH THEM? LIKE, REGULAR PEOPLE?
I DON'T KNOW IF I'D SAY "REGULAR," BUT YEAH. CULTISTS, DEVIL WORSHIPERS, THAT KIND OF THING.

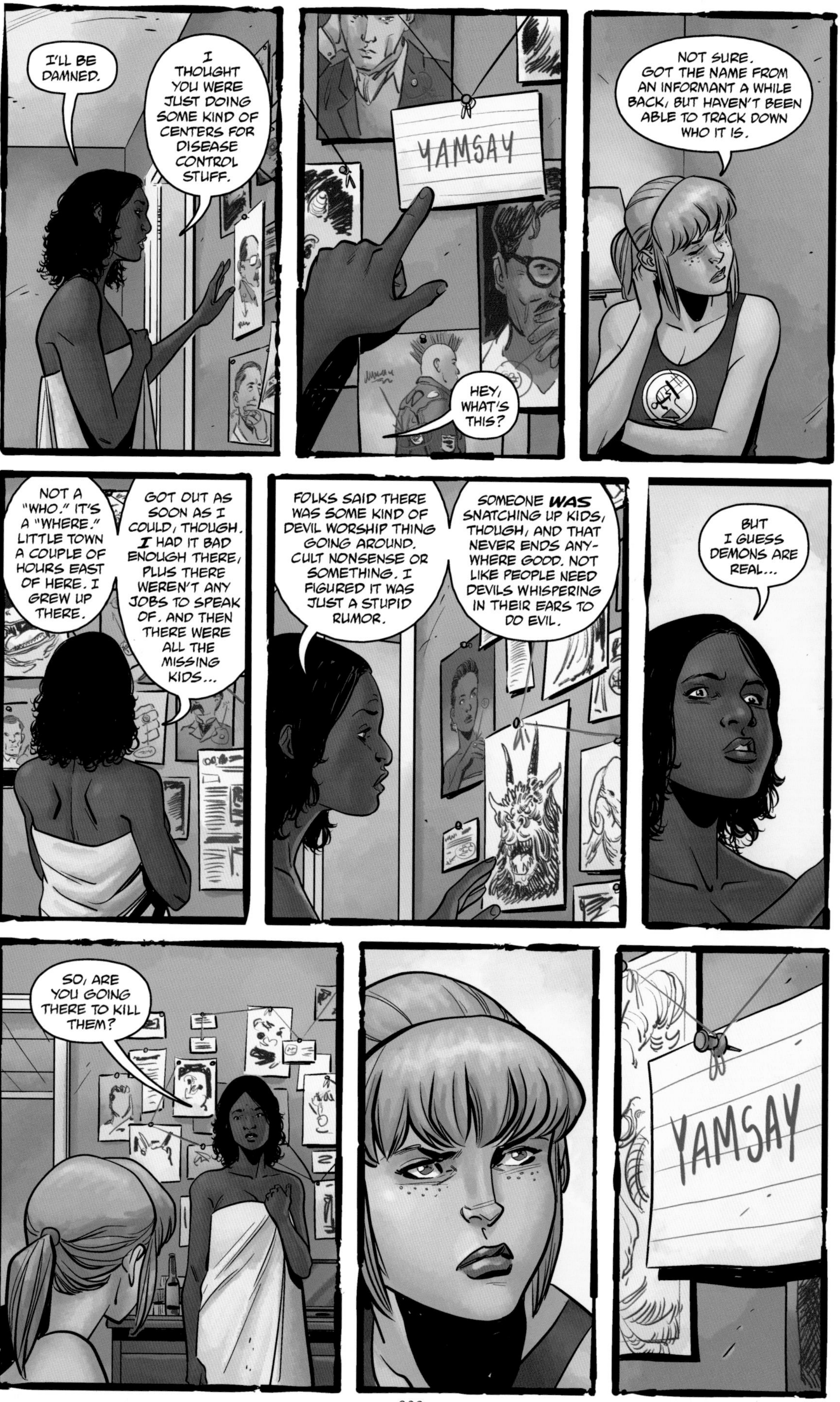
I'LL BE DAMNED.
I THOUGHT YOU WERE JUST DOING SOME KIND OF CENTERS FOR DISEASE CONTROL STUFF.
YAMSAY
HEY, WHAT'S THIS?
NOT SURE. GOT THE NAME FROM AN INFORMANT A WHILE BACK, BUT HAVEN'T BEEN ABLE TO TRACK DOWN WHO IT IS.
NOT A "WHO." IT'S A "WHERE." LITTLE TOWN A COUPLE OF HOURS EAST OF HERE. I GREW UP THERE.
GOT OUT AS SOON AS I COULD, THOUGH. I HAD IT BAD ENOUGH THERE, PLUS THERE WEREN'T ANY JOBS TO SPEAK OF. AND THEN THERE WERE ALL THE MISSING KIDS...
FOLKS SAID THERE WAS SOME KIND OF DEVIL WORSHIP THING GOING AROUND. CULT NONSENSE OR SOMETHING. I FIGURED IT WAS JUST A STUPID RUMOR.
SOMEONE WAS SNATCHING UP KIDS, THOUGH, AND THAT NEVER ENDS ANYWHERE GOOD. NOT LIKE PEOPLE NEED DEVILS WHISPERING IN THEIR EARS TO DO EVIL.
BUT I GUESS DEMONS ARE REAL...
SO, ARE YOU GOING THERE TO KILL THEM?
YAMSAY

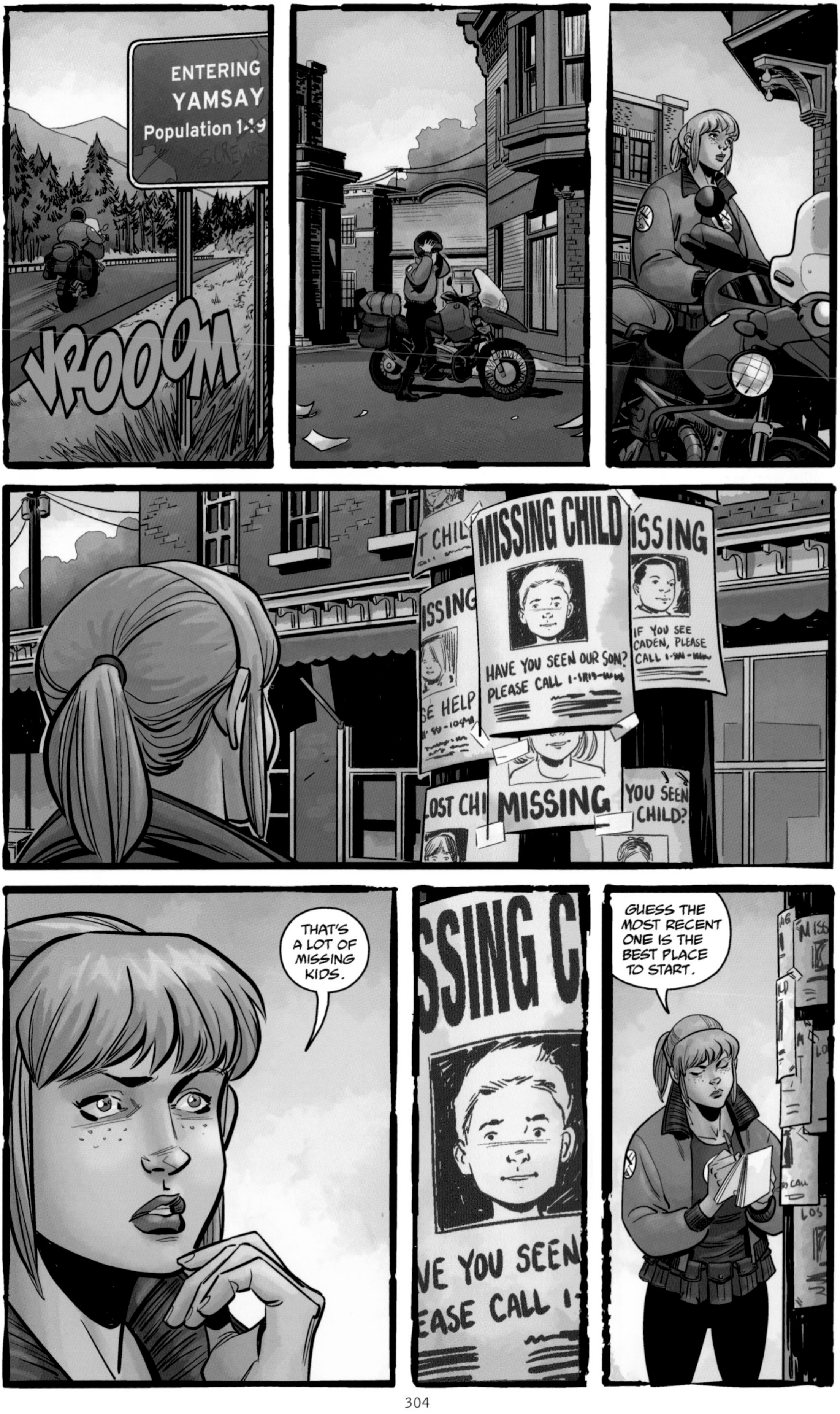
ENTERING
YAMSAY
Population 149
VROOOM
MISSING CHILD
HAVE YOU SEEN OUR SON? PLEASE CALL
ISSING
IF YOU SEE CADEN, PLEASE CALL
ISSING
SE HELP
T CHIL
MISSING
OST CHI
YOU SEEN CHILD?
THAT'S A LOT OF MISSING KIDS.
SSING C
VE YOU SEEN
EASE CALL
GUESS THE MOST RECENT ONE IS THE BEST PLACE TO START.

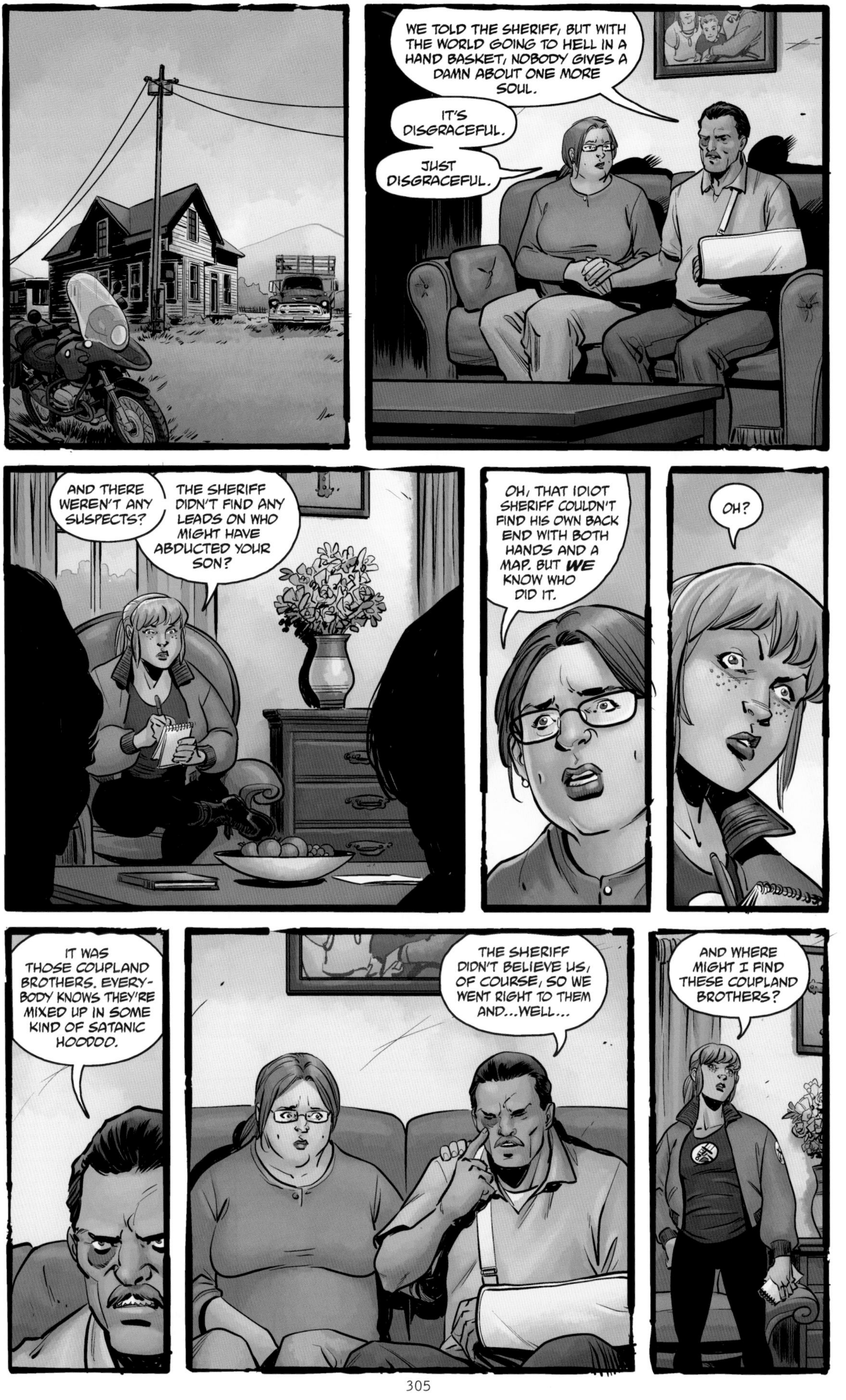
WE TOLD THE SHERIFF, BUT WITH THE WORLD GOING TO HELL IN A HAND BASKET, NOBODY GIVES A DAMN ABOUT ONE MORE SOUL.
IT'S DISGRACEFUL.
JUST DISGRACEFUL.
AND THERE WEREN'T ANY SUSPECTS?
THE SHERIFF DIDN'T FIND ANY LEADS ON WHO MIGHT HAVE ABDUCTED YOUR SON?
OH, THAT IDIOT SHERIFF COULDN'T FIND HIS OWN BACK END WITH BOTH HANDS AND A MAP. BUT WE KNOW WHO DID IT.
OH?
IT WAS THOSE COUPLAND BROTHERS. EVERY-BODY KNOWS THEY'RE MIXED UP IN SOME KIND OF SATANIC HOODOO.
THE SHERIFF DIDN'T BELIEVE US, OF COURSE, SO WE WENT RIGHT TO THEM AND...WELL...
AND WHERE MIGHT I FIND THESE COUPLAND BROTHERS?

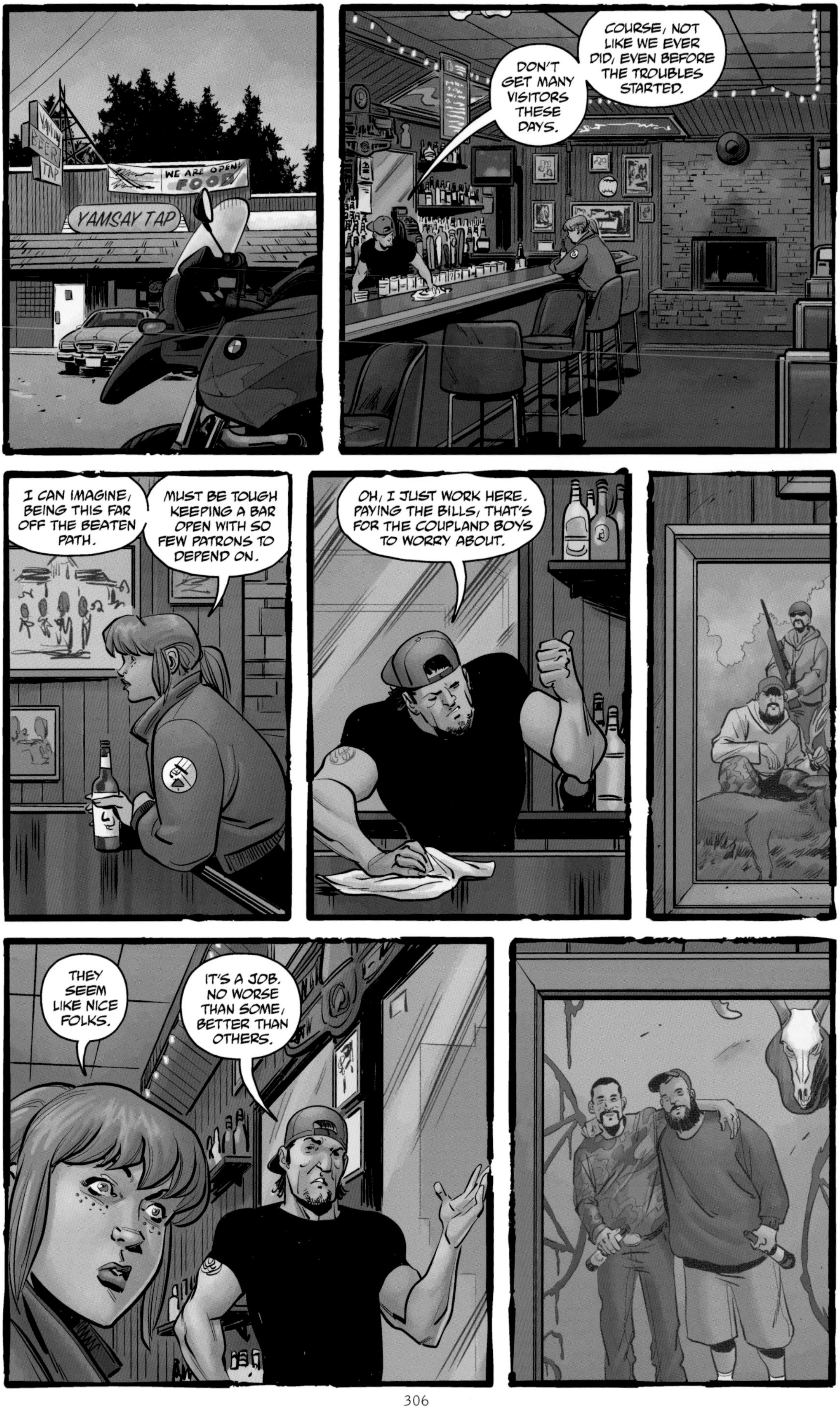
YAMSAY TAP
WE ARE OPEN! FOOD
DON'T GET MANY VISITORS THESE DAYS.
COURSE, NOT LIKE WE EVER DID, EVEN BEFORE THE TROUBLES STARTED.
I CAN IMAGINE, BEING THIS FAR OFF THE BEATEN PATH.
MUST BE TOUGH KEEPING A BAR OPEN WITH SO FEW PATRONS TO DEPEND ON.
OH, I JUST WORK HERE. PAYING THE BILLS, THAT'S FOR THE COUPLAND BOYS TO WORRY ABOUT.
THEY SEEM LIKE NICE FOLKS.
IT'S A JOB. NO WORSE THAN SOME, BETTER THAN OTHERS.

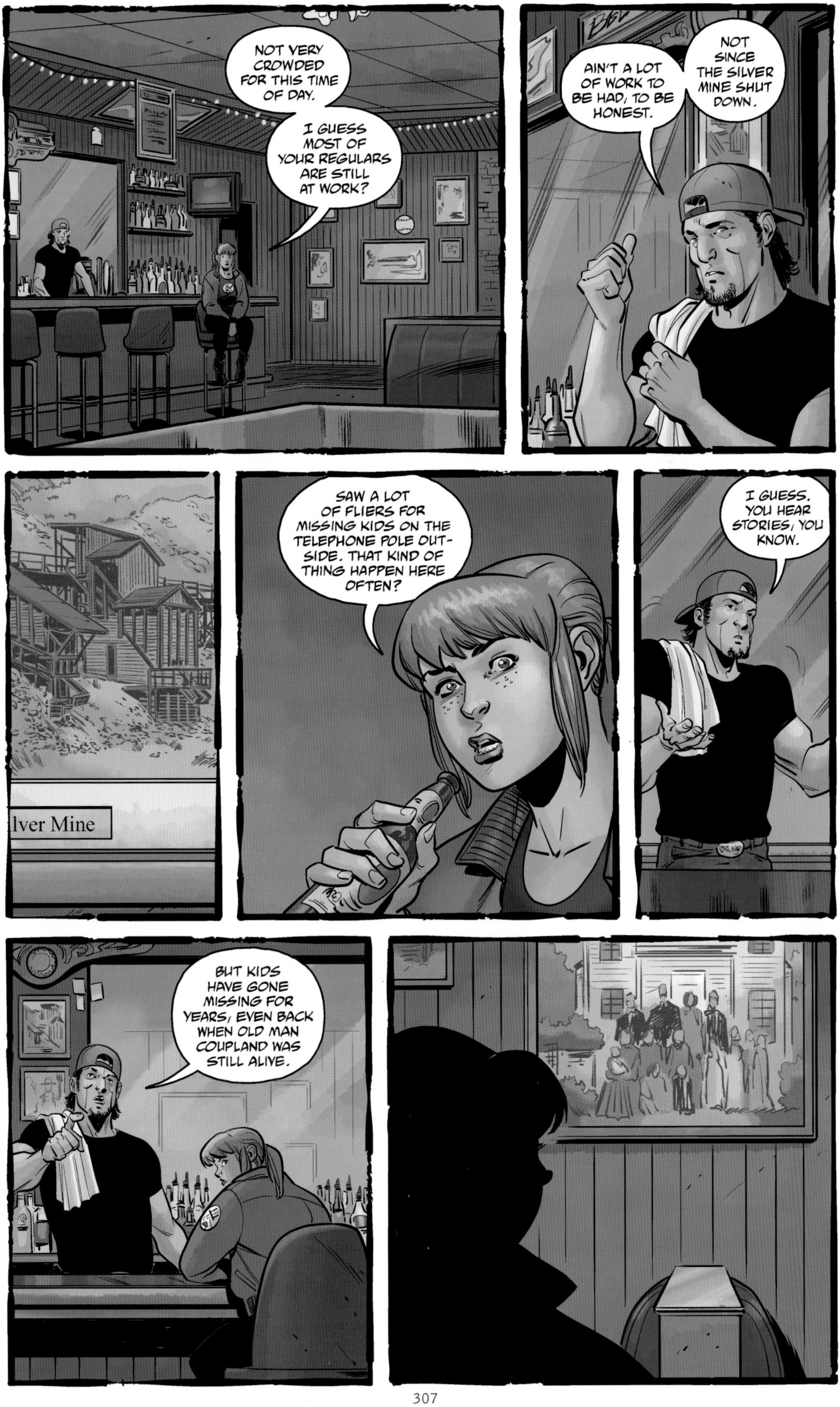
NOT VERY CROWDED FOR THIS TIME OF DAY.
I GUESS MOST OF YOUR REGULARS ARE STILL AT WORK?
AIN'T A LOT OF WORK TO BE HAD, TO BE HONEST.
NOT SINCE THE SILVER MINE SHUT DOWN.
lver Mine
SAW A LOT OF FLIERS FOR MISSING KIDS ON THE TELEPHONE POLE OUT-SIDE. THAT KIND OF THING HAPPEN HERE OFTEN?
I GUESS. YOU HEAR STORIES, YOU KNOW.
BUT KIDS HAVE GONE MISSING FOR YEARS, EVEN BACK WHEN OLD MAN COUPLAND WAS STILL ALIVE.

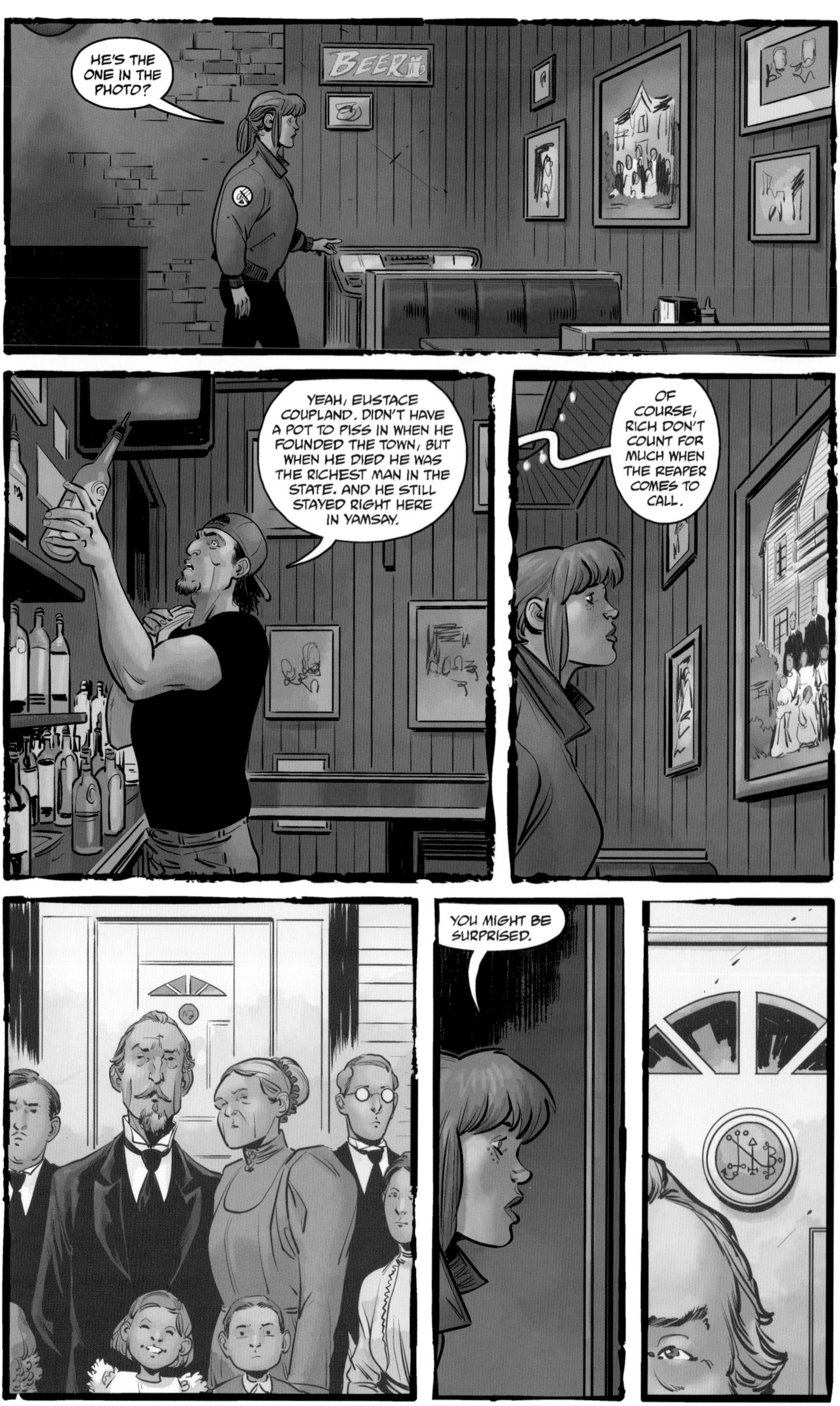

HE'S THE ONE IN THE PHOTO?
BEER
YEAH, EUSTACE COUPLAND. DIDN'T HAVE A POT TO PISS IN WHEN HE FOUNDED THE TOWN, BUT WHEN HE DIED HE WAS THE RICHEST MAN IN THE STATE. AND HE STILL STAYED RIGHT HERE IN YAMSAY.
OF COURSE, RICH DON'T COUNT FOR MUCH WHEN THE REAPER COMES TO CALL.
YOU MIGHT BE SURPRISED.

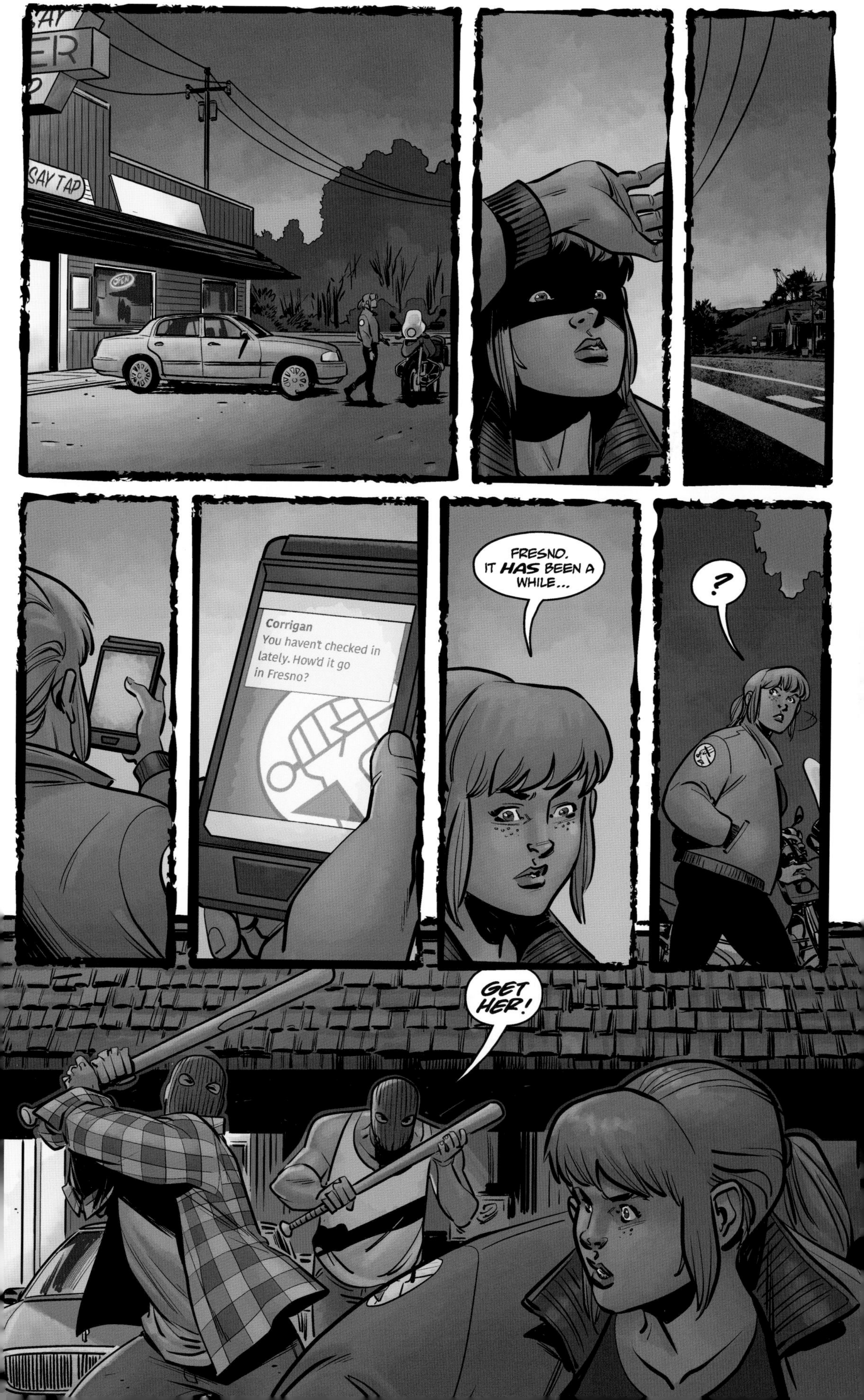
SAY TAP
OPEN
Corrigan
You haven't checked in lately. How'd it go in Fresno?
FRESNO. IT HAS BEEN A WHILE...
?
GET HER!

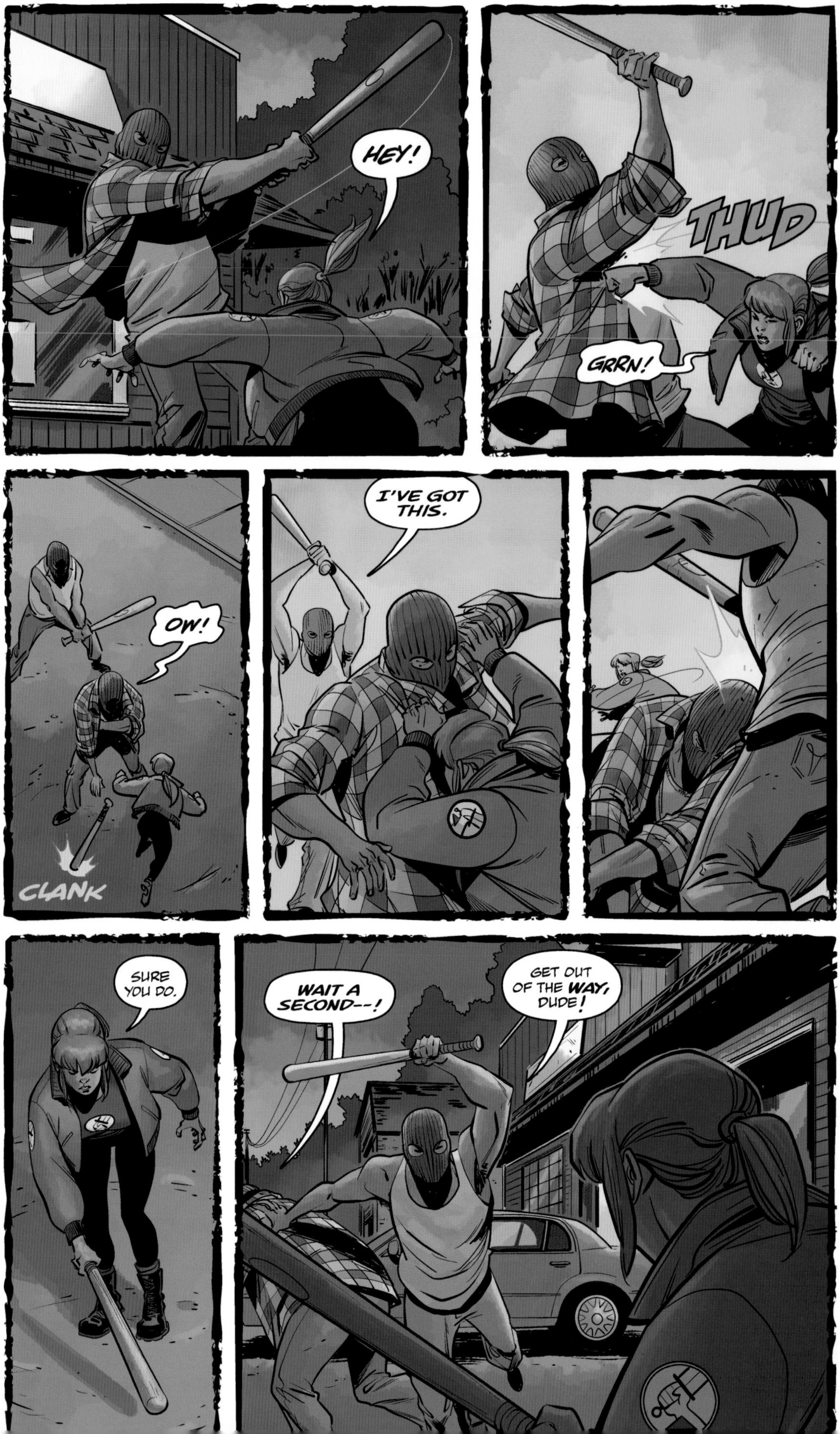
HEY!
THUD
GRRN!
OW!
CLANK
I'VE GOT THIS.
SURE YOU DO.
WAIT A SECOND--!
GET OUT OF THE WAY, DUDE!

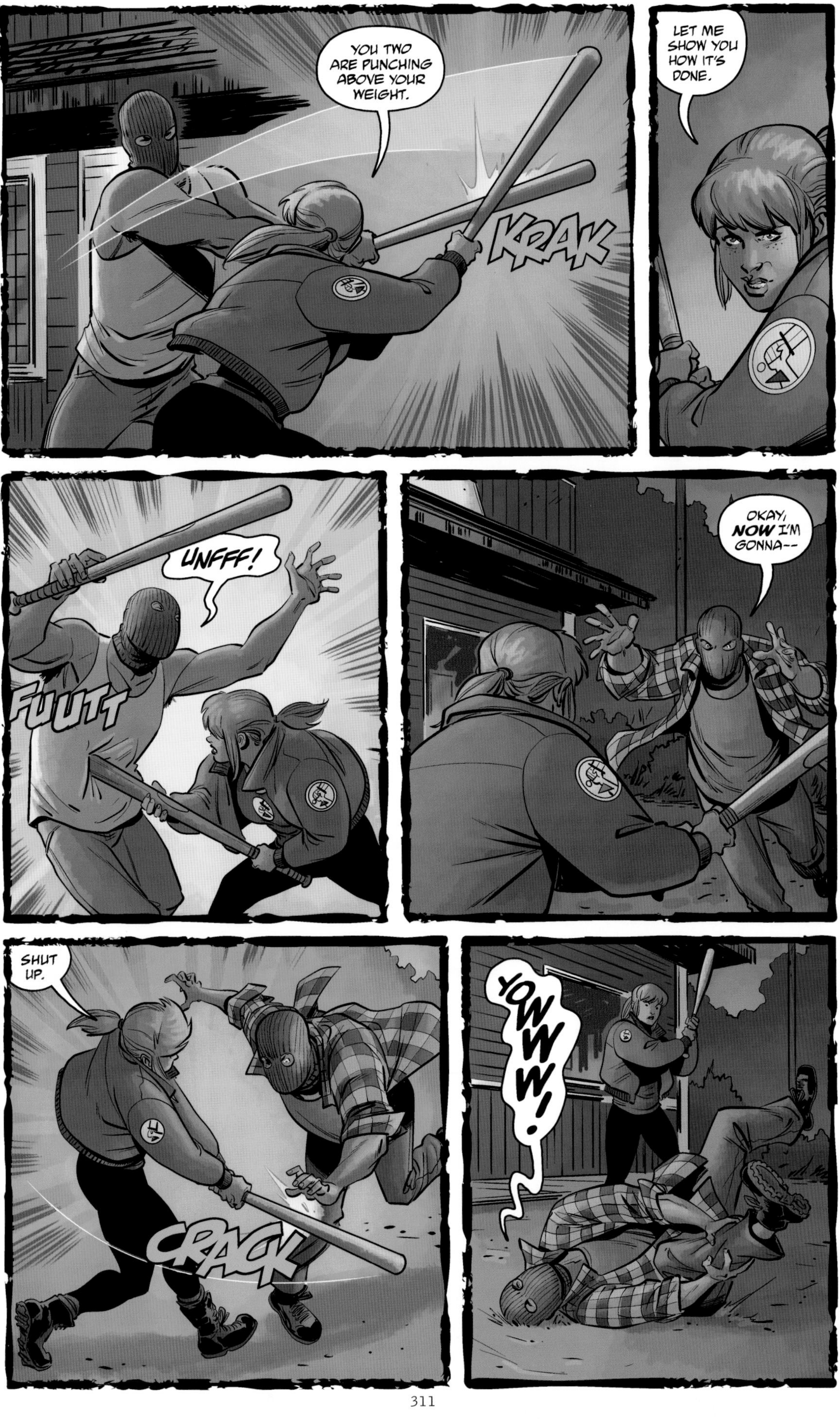
YOU TWO ARE PUNCHING ABOVE YOUR WEIGHT.
KRAK
LET ME SHOW YOU HOW IT'S DONE.
UNFFF!
FUUTT
OKAY, **NOW** I'M GONNA--
SHUT UP.
CRACK
YOWWW!

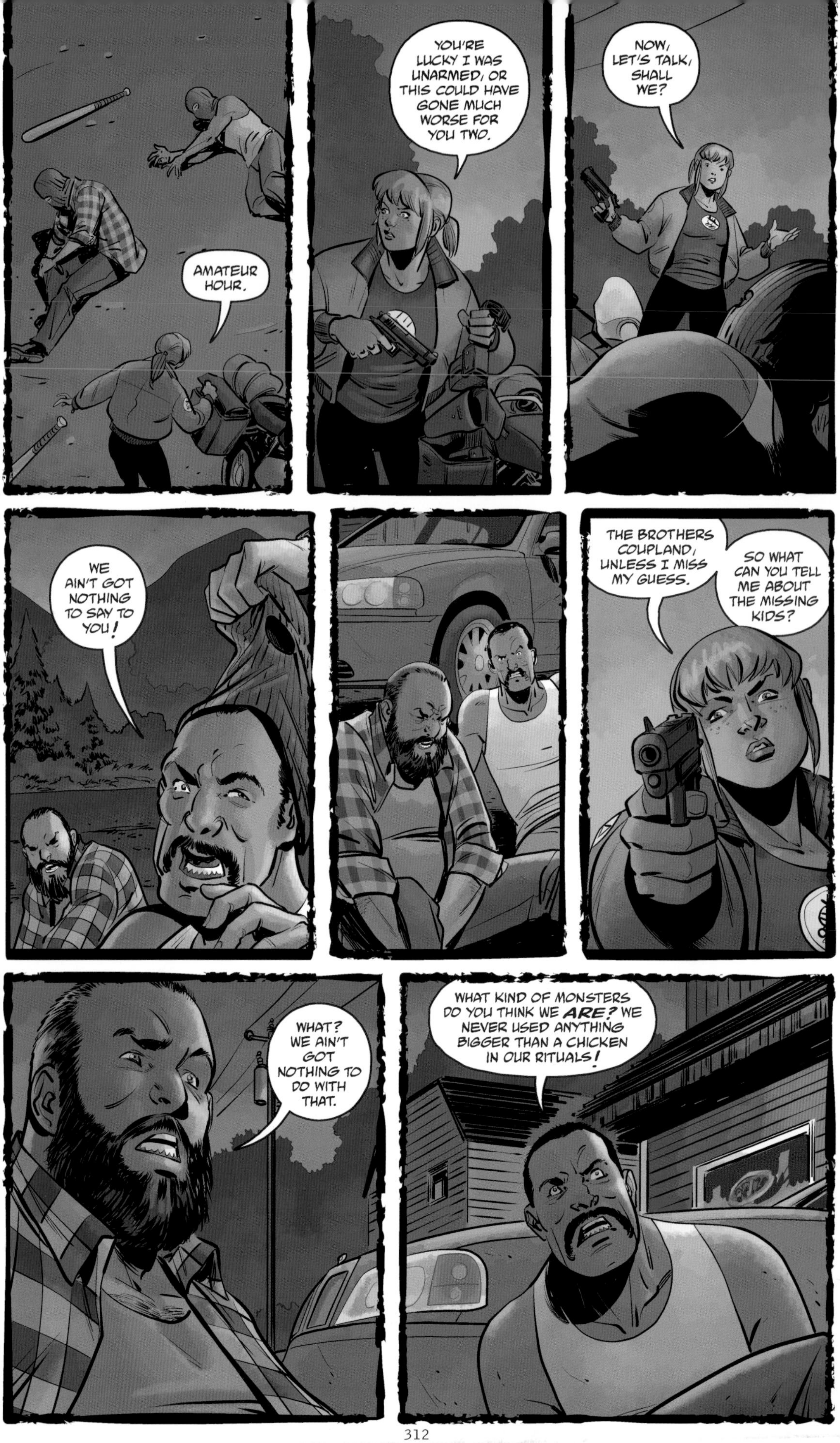

AMATEUR HOUR.
YOU'RE LUCKY I WAS UNARMED, OR THIS COULD HAVE GONE MUCH WORSE FOR YOU TWO.
NOW, LET'S TALK, SHALL WE?
WE AIN'T GOT NOTHING TO SAY TO YOU!
THE BROTHERS COUPLAND, UNLESS I MISS MY GUESS.
SO WHAT CAN YOU TELL ME ABOUT THE MISSING KIDS?
WHAT? WE AIN'T GOT NOTHING TO DO WITH THAT.
WHAT KIND OF MONSTERS DO YOU THINK WE ARE? WE NEVER USED ANYTHING BIGGER THAN A CHICKEN IN OUR RITUALS!

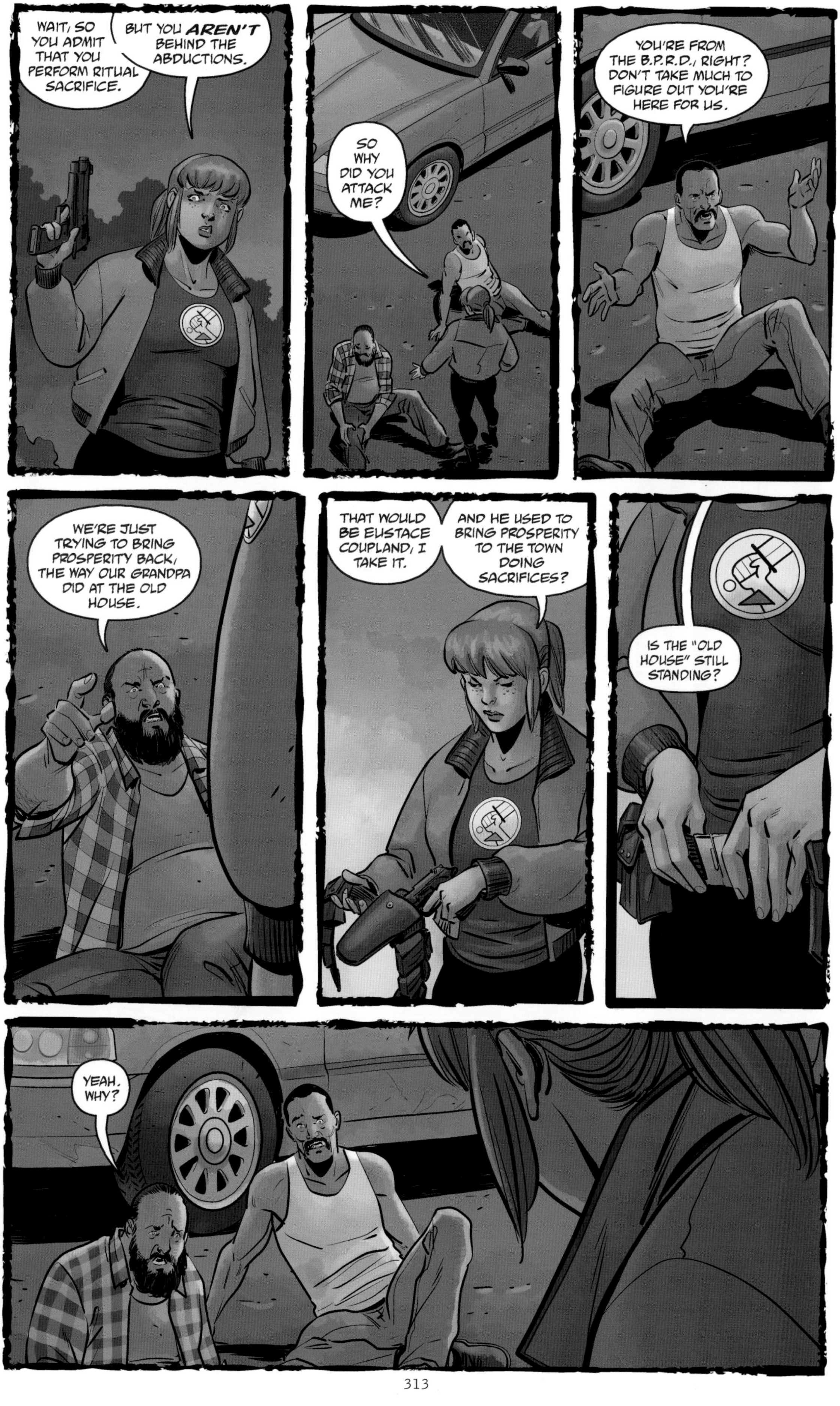

WAIT, SO YOU ADMIT THAT YOU PERFORM RITUAL SACRIFICE.
BUT YOU AREN'T BEHIND THE ABDUCTIONS.
SO WHY DID YOU ATTACK ME?
YOU'RE FROM THE B.P.R.D., RIGHT? DON'T TAKE MUCH TO FIGURE OUT YOU'RE HERE FOR US.
WE'RE JUST TRYING TO BRING PROSPERITY BACK, THE WAY OUR GRANDPA DID AT THE OLD HOUSE.
THAT WOULD BE EUSTACE COUPLAND, I TAKE IT.
AND HE USED TO BRING PROSPERITY TO THE TOWN DOING SACRIFICES?
IS THE "OLD HOUSE" STILL STANDING?
YEAH. WHY?

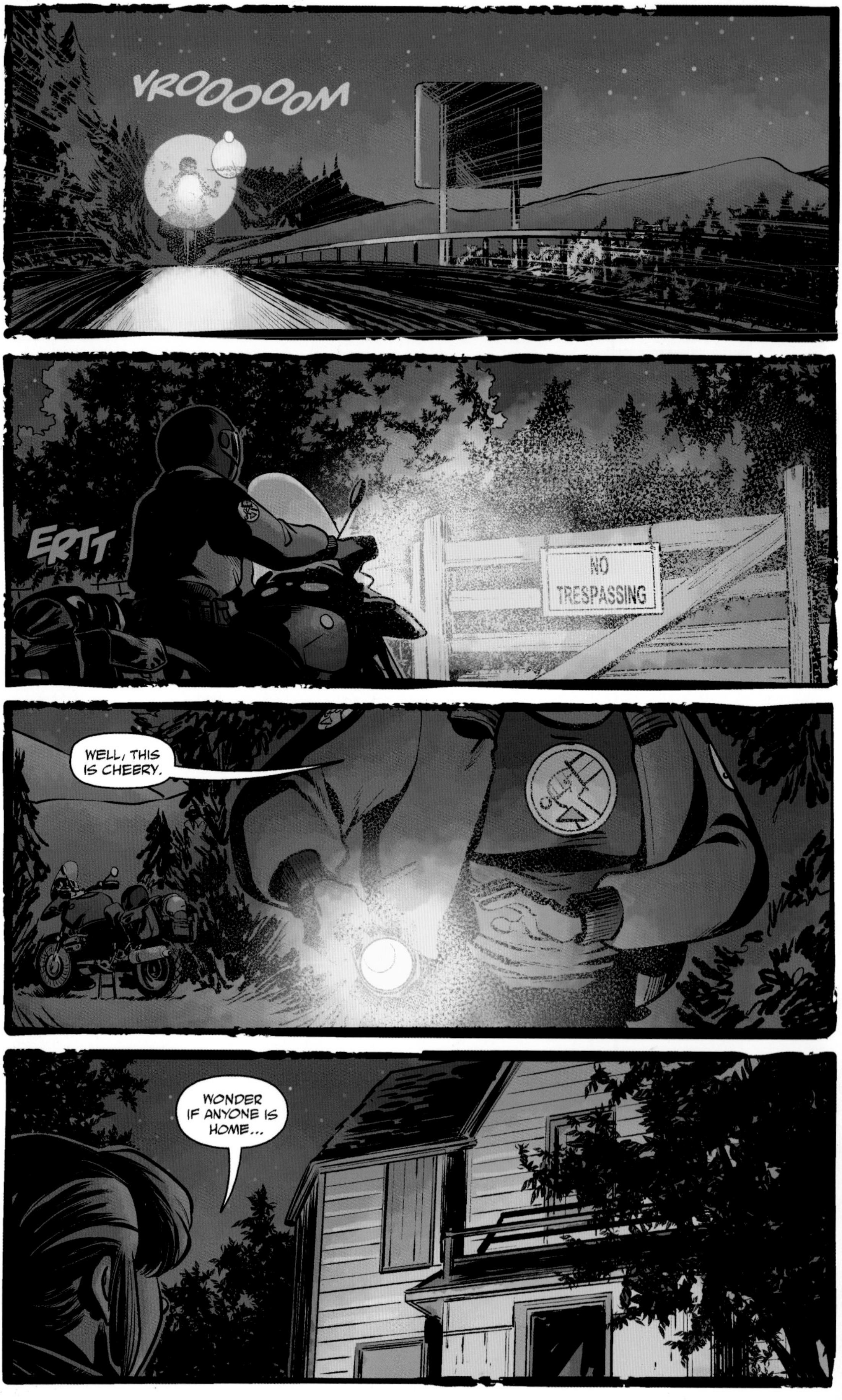

VROOOOOM
ERTT
NO TRESPASSING
WELL, THIS IS CHEERY.
WONDER IF ANYONE IS HOME...

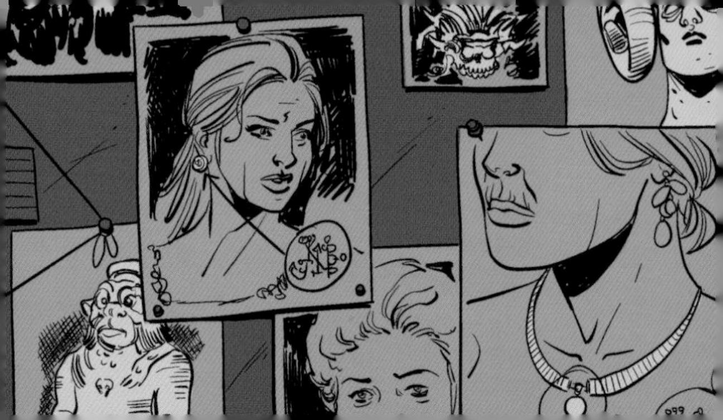

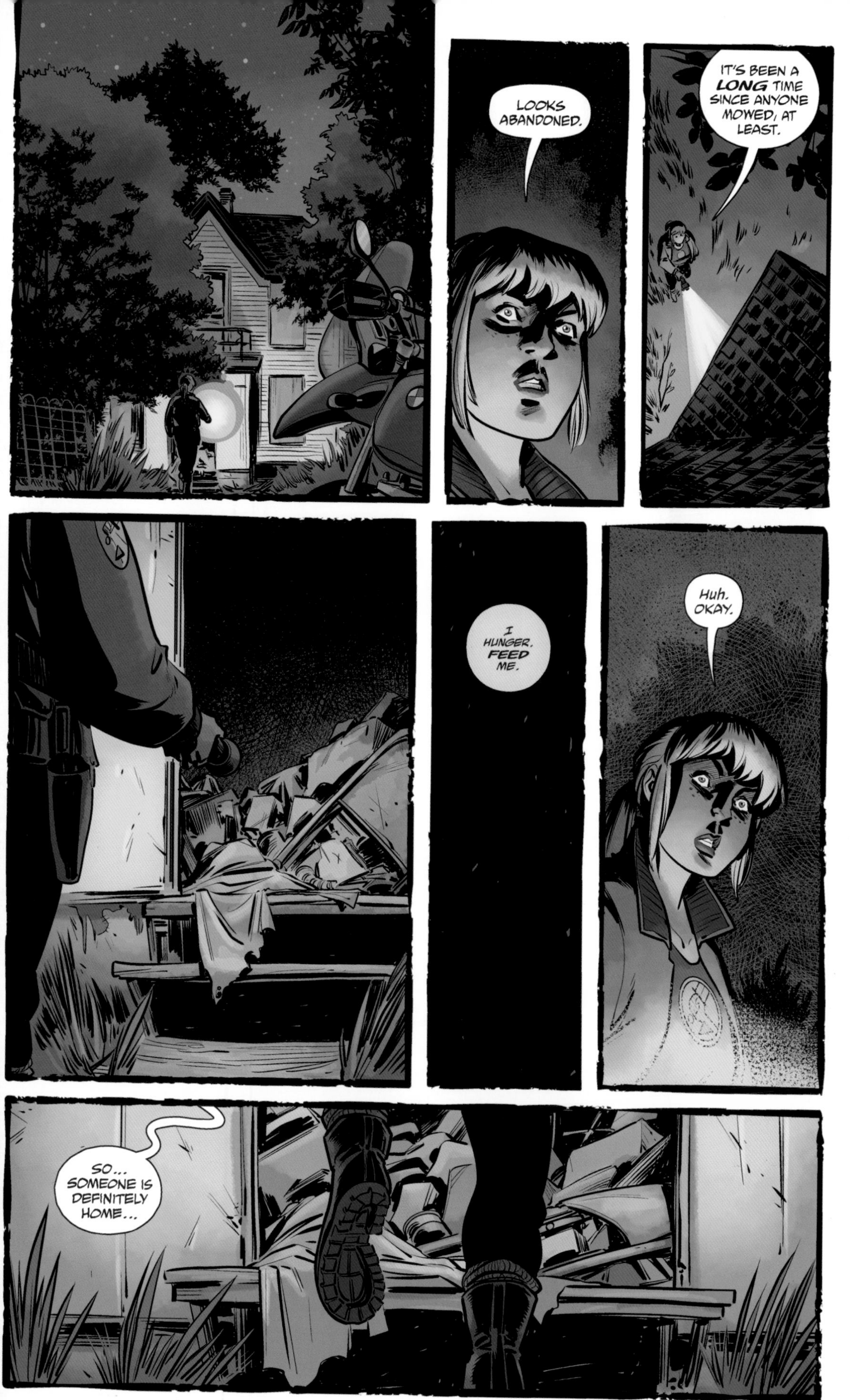
LOOKS ABANDONED.
IT'S BEEN A LONG TIME SINCE ANYONE MOWED, AT LEAST.
I HUNGER. FEED ME.
Huh. OKAY.
SO... SOMEONE IS DEFINITELY HOME...

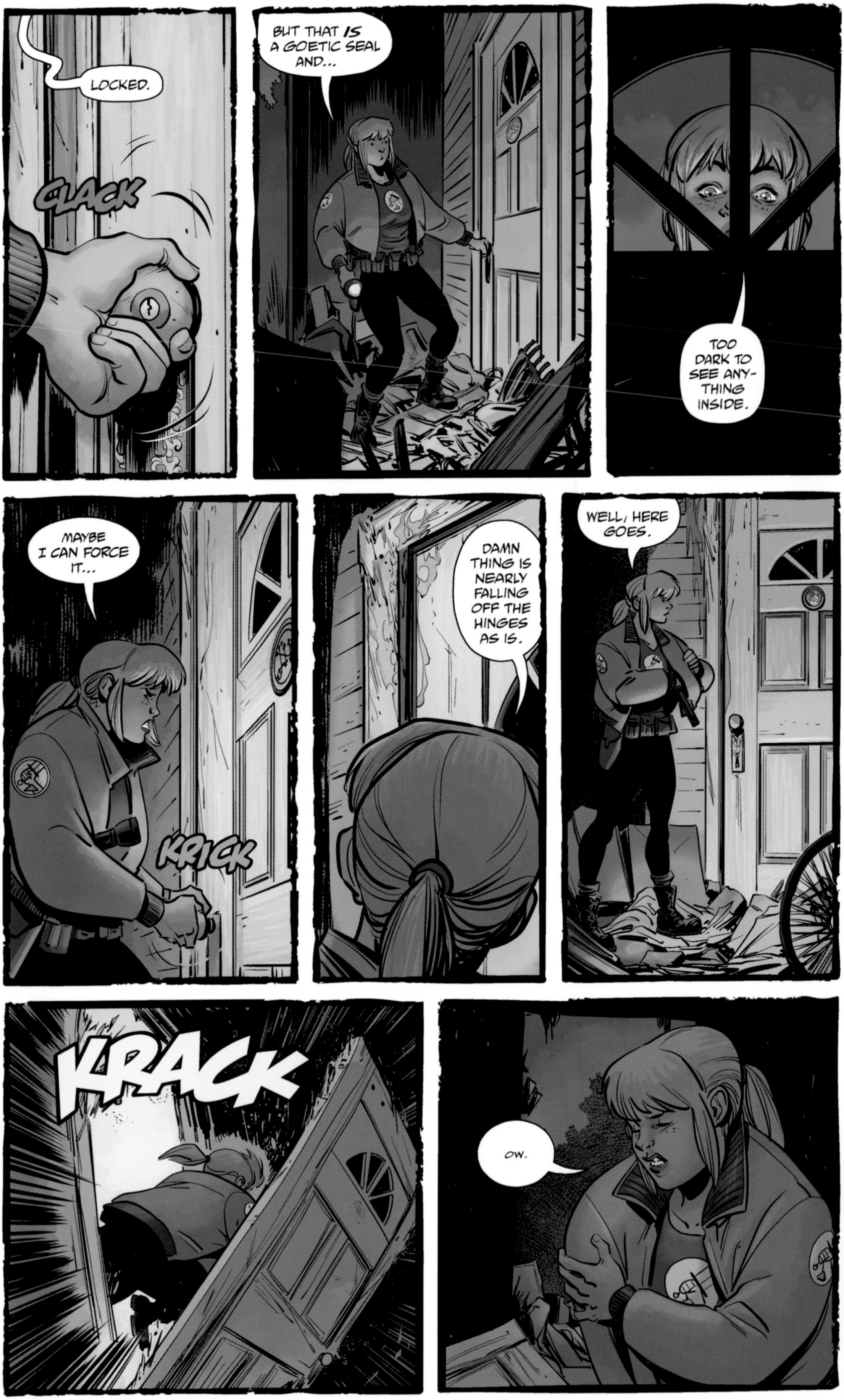
LOCKED.
CLACK
BUT THAT IS A GOETIC SEAL AND...
TOO DARK TO SEE ANY-THING INSIDE.
MAYBE I CAN FORCE IT...
KRICK
DAMN THING IS NEARLY FALLING OFF THE HINGES AS IS.
WELL, HERE GOES.
KRACK
OW.

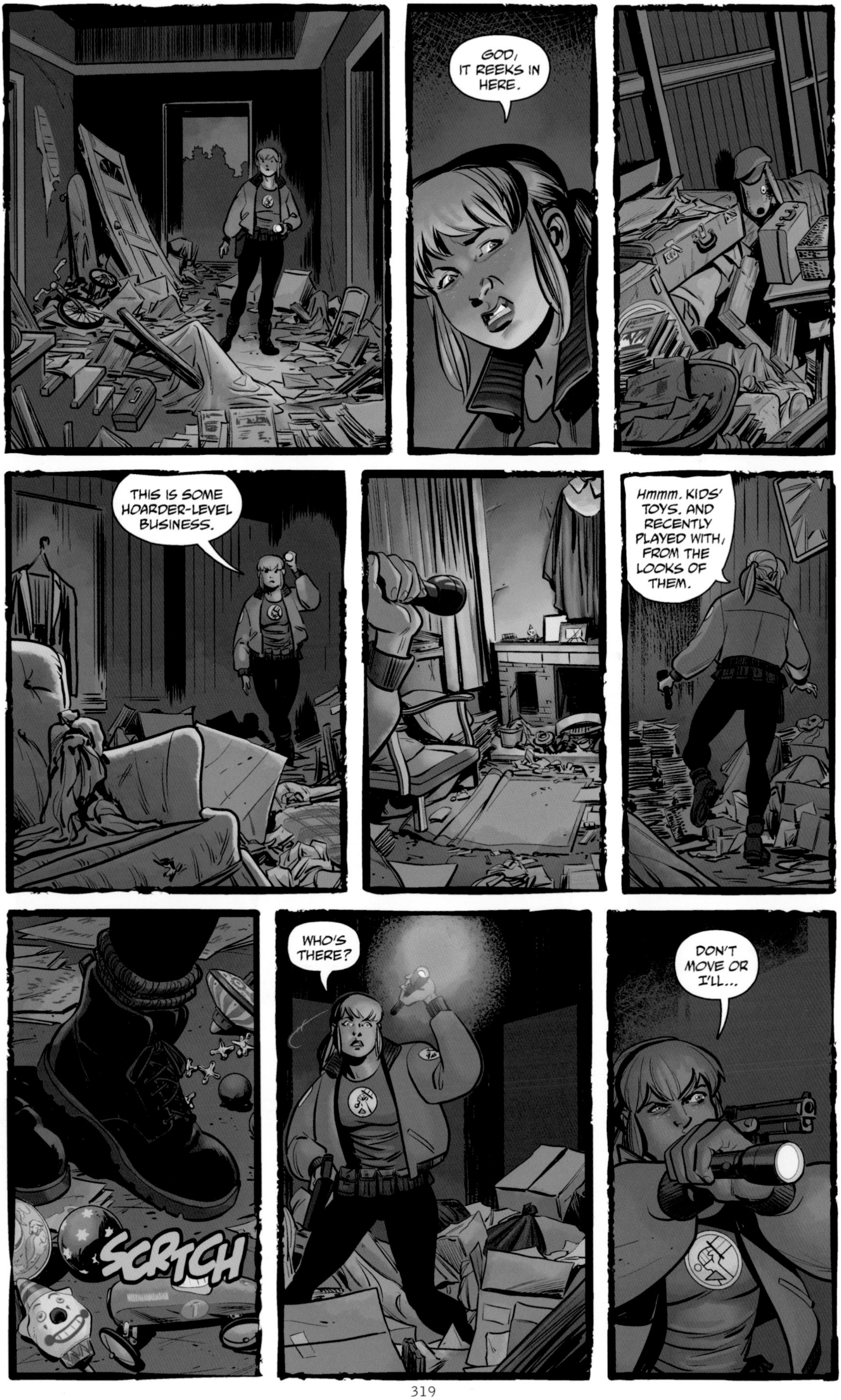
GOD, IT REEKS IN HERE.
THIS IS SOME HOARDER-LEVEL BUSINESS.
Hmmm. KIDS' TOYS. AND RECENTLY PLAYED WITH, FROM THE LOOKS OF THEM.
SCRTCH
WHO'S THERE?
DON'T MOVE OR I'LL...

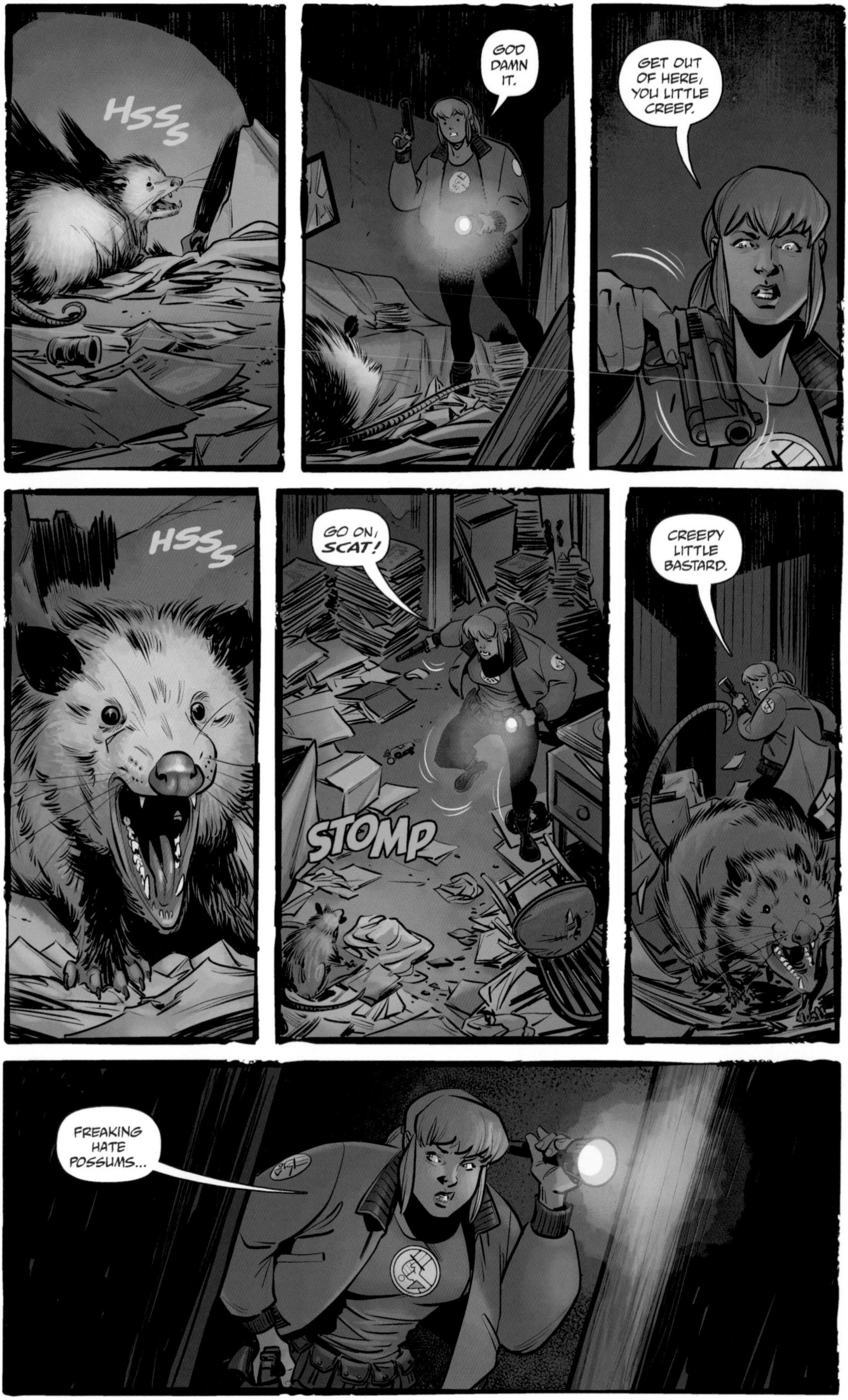
HSSS
GOD DAMN IT.
GET OUT OF HERE, YOU LITTLE CREEP.
HSSS
GO ON, SCAT!
STOMP
CREEPY LITTLE BASTARD.
FREAKING HATE POSSUMS...

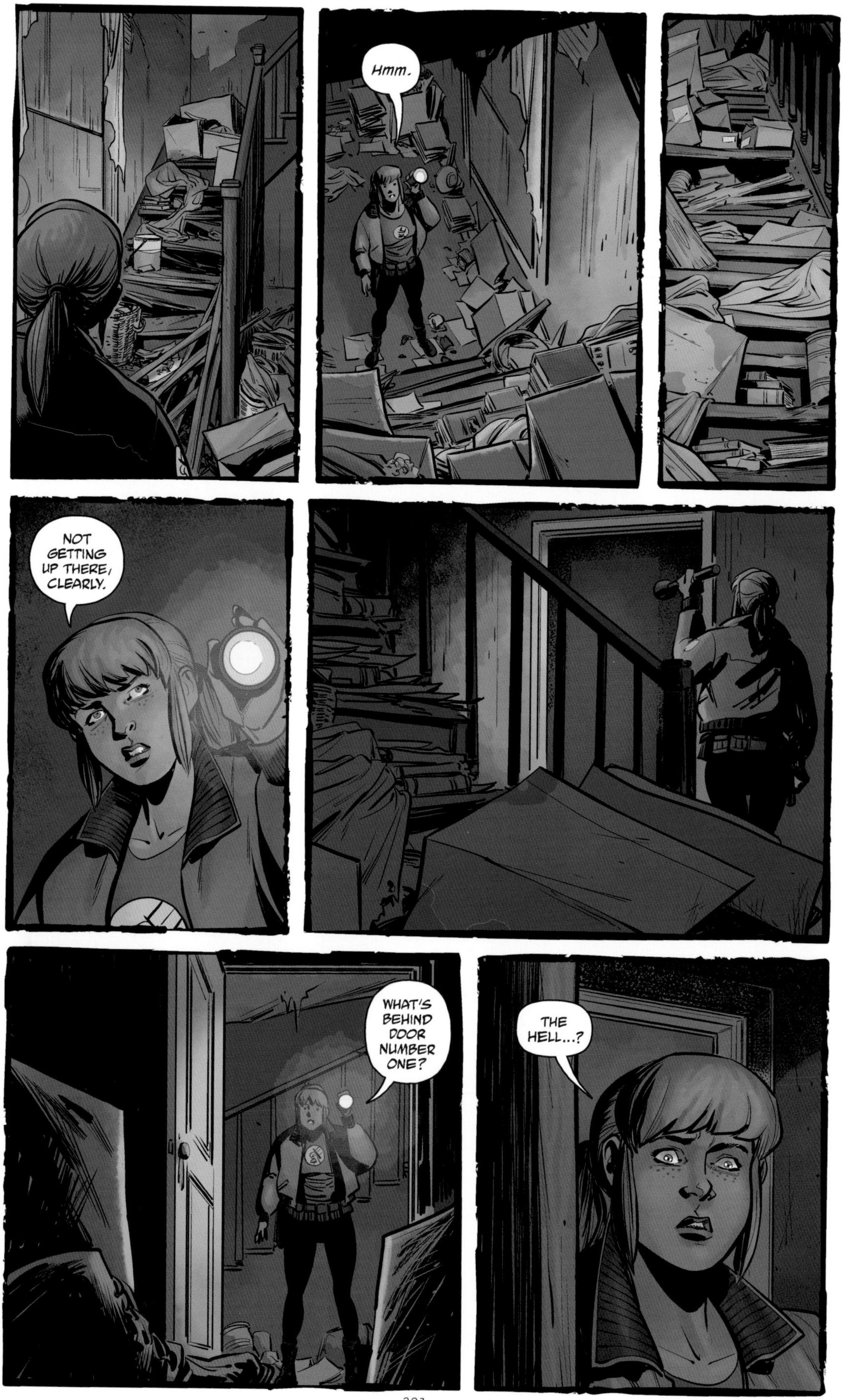

Hmm.
NOT GETTING UP THERE, CLEARLY.
WHAT'S BEHIND DOOR NUMBER ONE?
THE HELL...?

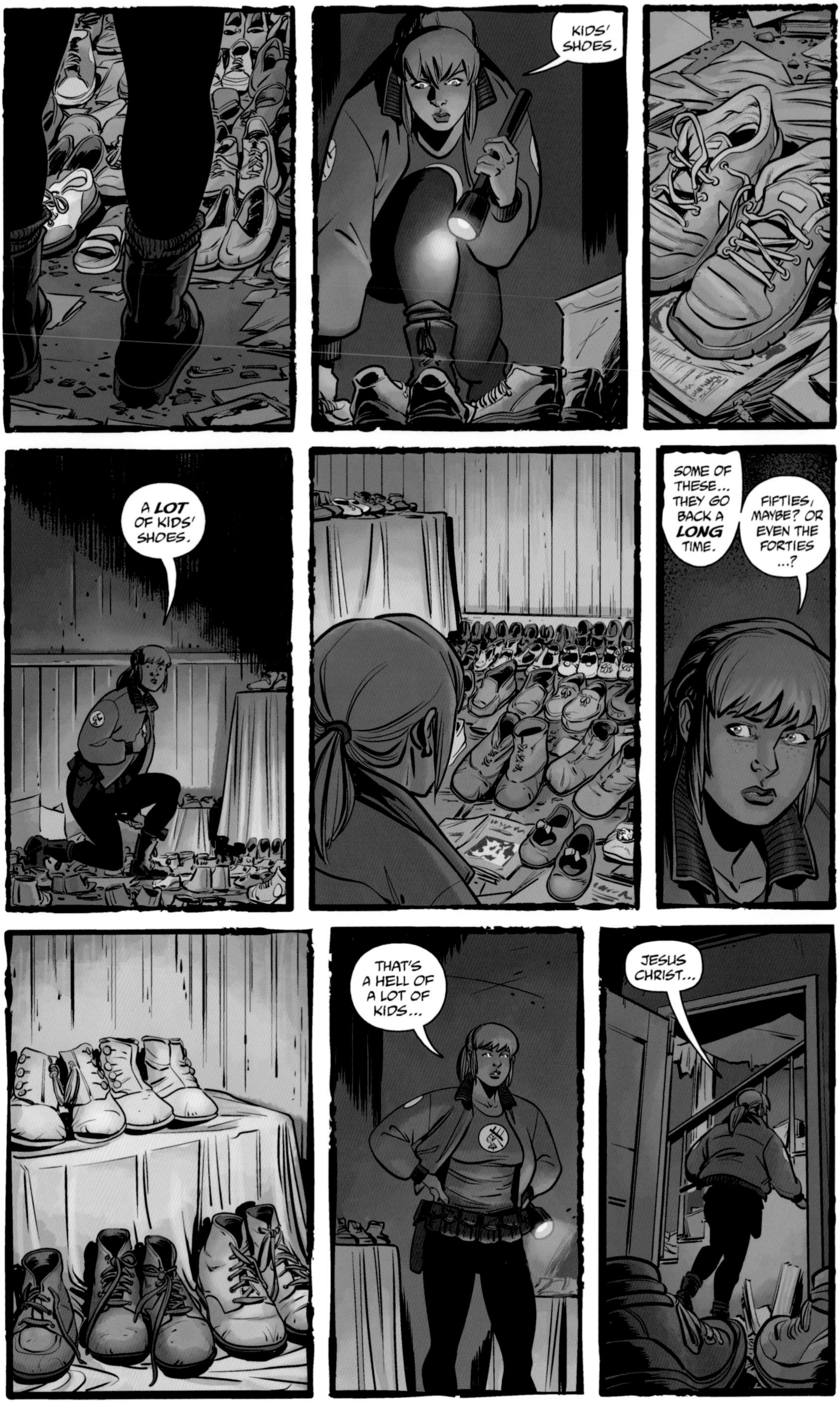
KIDS' SHOES.
A LOT OF KIDS' SHOES.
SOME OF THESE... THEY GO BACK A LONG TIME.
FIFTIES, MAYBE? OR EVEN THE FORTIES ...?
THAT'S A HELL OF A LOT OF KIDS...
JESUS CHRIST...

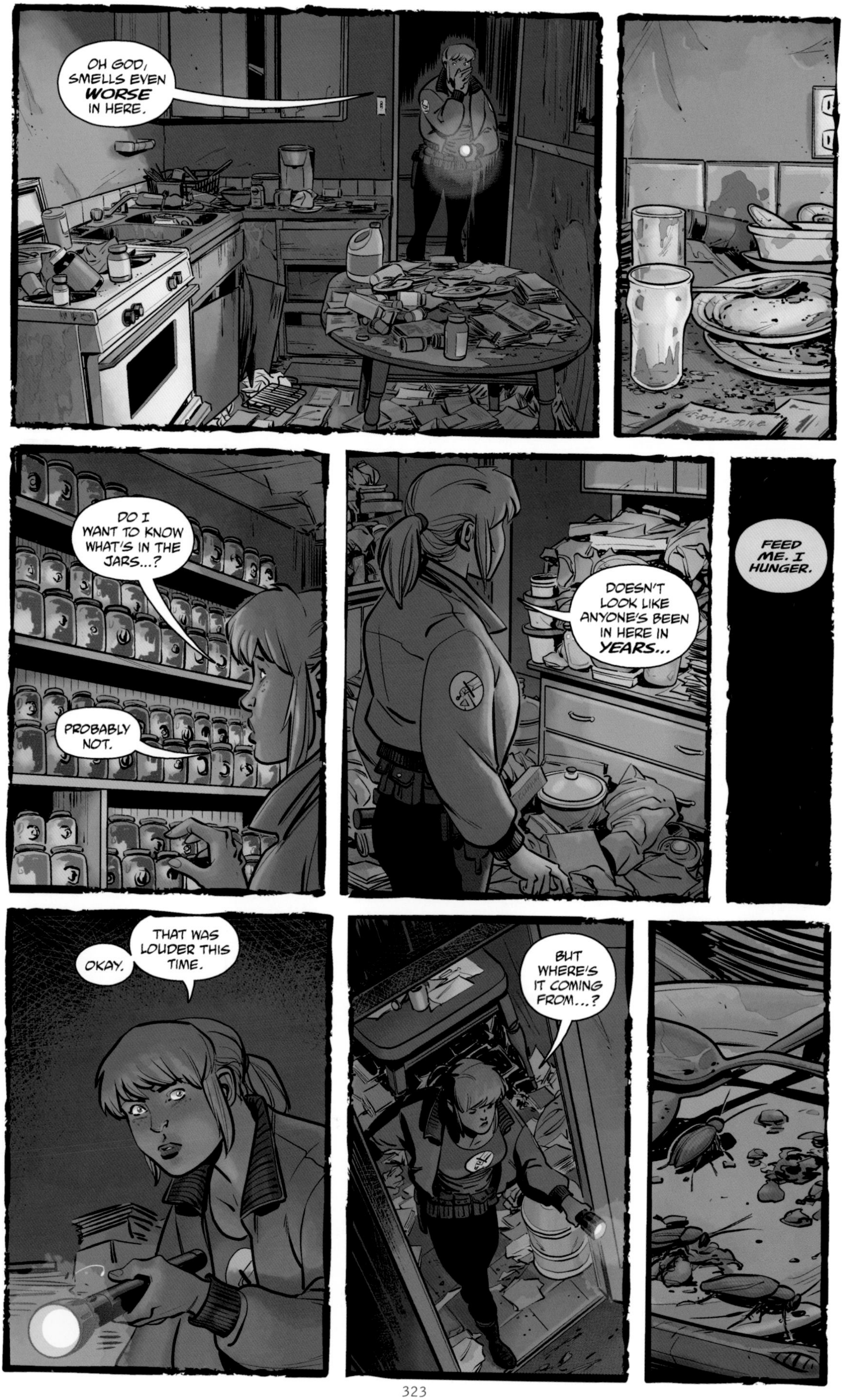
OH GOD, SMELLS EVEN WORSE IN HERE.
DO I WANT TO KNOW WHAT'S IN THE JARS...?
PROBABLY NOT.
DOESN'T LOOK LIKE ANYONE'S BEEN IN HERE IN YEARS...
FEED ME. I HUNGER.
OKAY.
THAT WAS LOUDER THIS TIME.
BUT WHERE'S IT COMING FROM...?

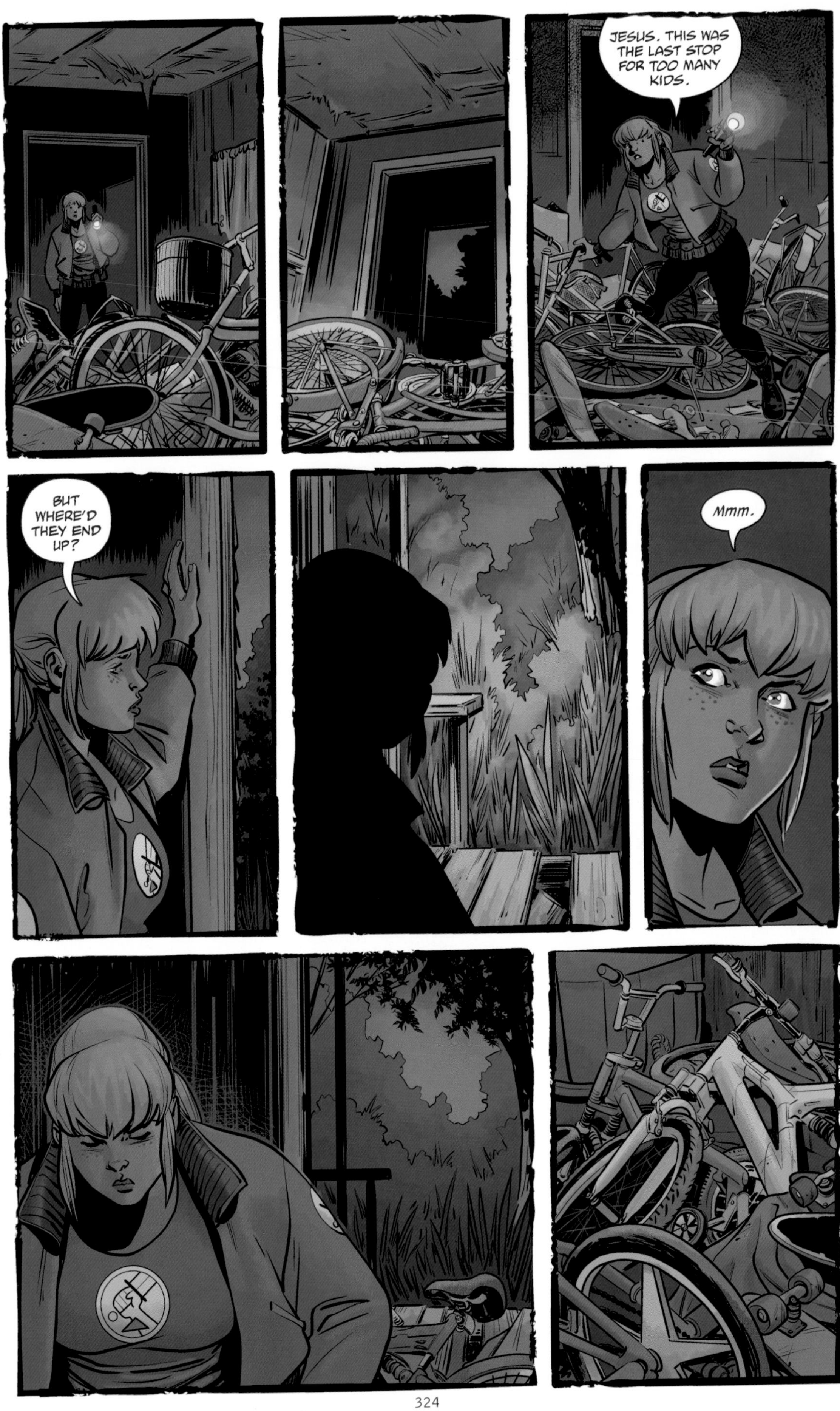
JESUS. THIS WAS THE LAST STOP FOR TOO MANY KIDS.
BUT WHERE'D THEY END UP?
Mmm.

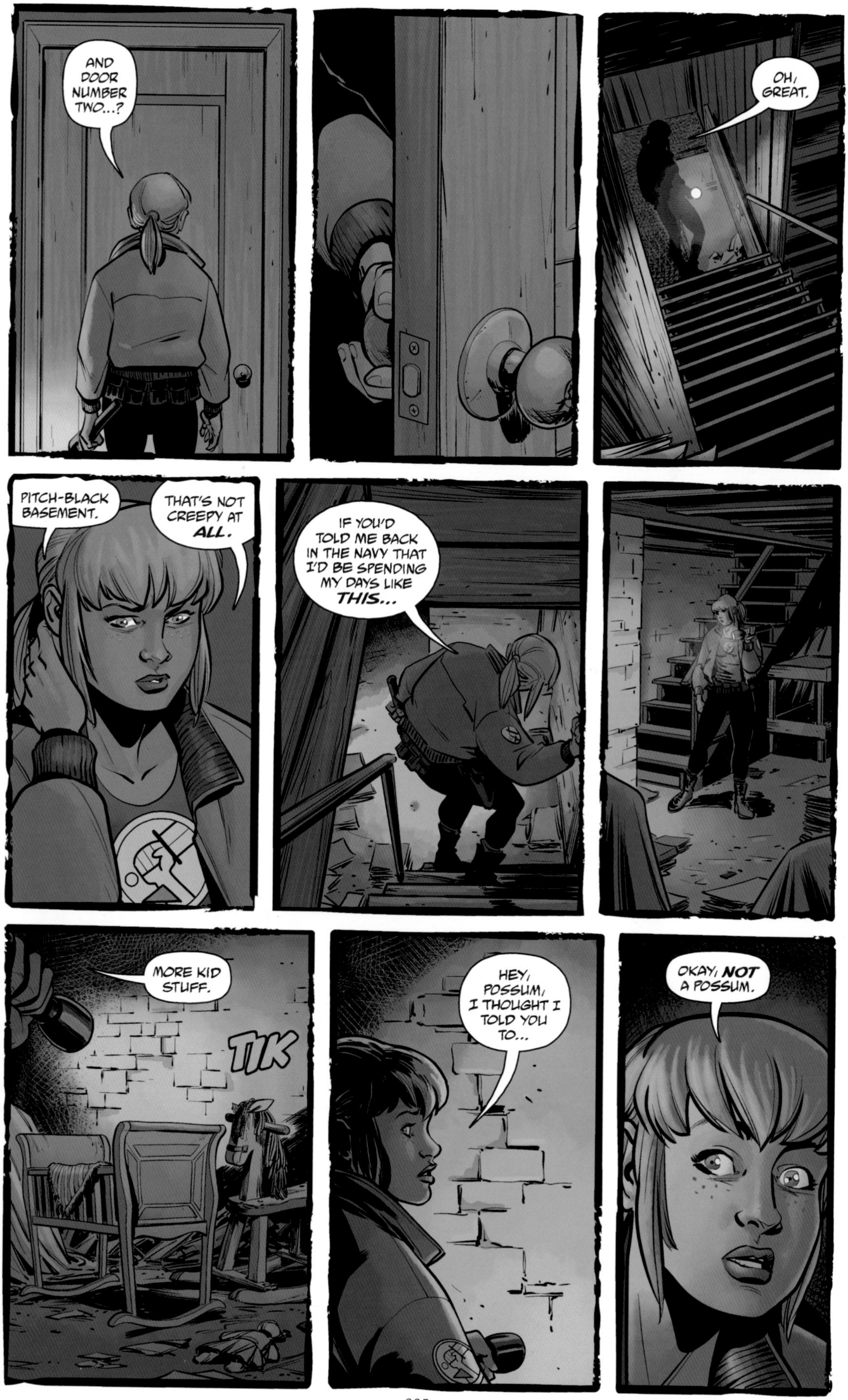
AND DOOR NUMBER TWO...?
OH, GREAT.
PITCH-BLACK BASEMENT.
THAT'S NOT CREEPY AT ALL.
IF YOU'D TOLD ME BACK IN THE NAVY THAT I'D BE SPENDING MY DAYS LIKE THIS...
MORE KID STUFF.
TIK
HEY, POSSUM, I THOUGHT I TOLD YOU TO...
OKAY, NOT A POSSUM.

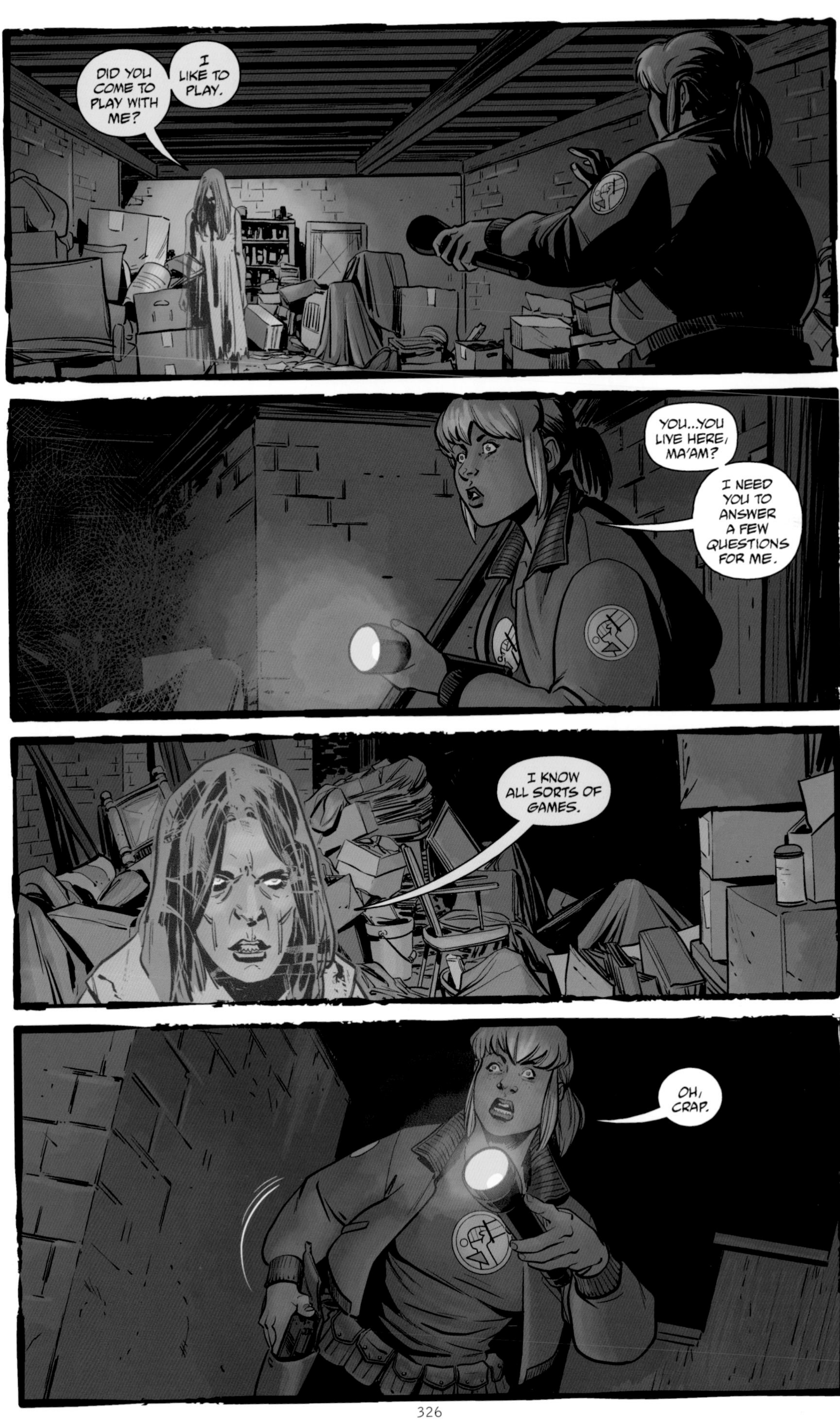
DID YOU COME TO PLAY WITH ME?
I LIKE TO PLAY.
YOU...YOU LIVE HERE, MA'AM?
I NEED YOU TO ANSWER A FEW QUESTIONS FOR ME.
I KNOW ALL SORTS OF GAMES.
OH, CRAP.

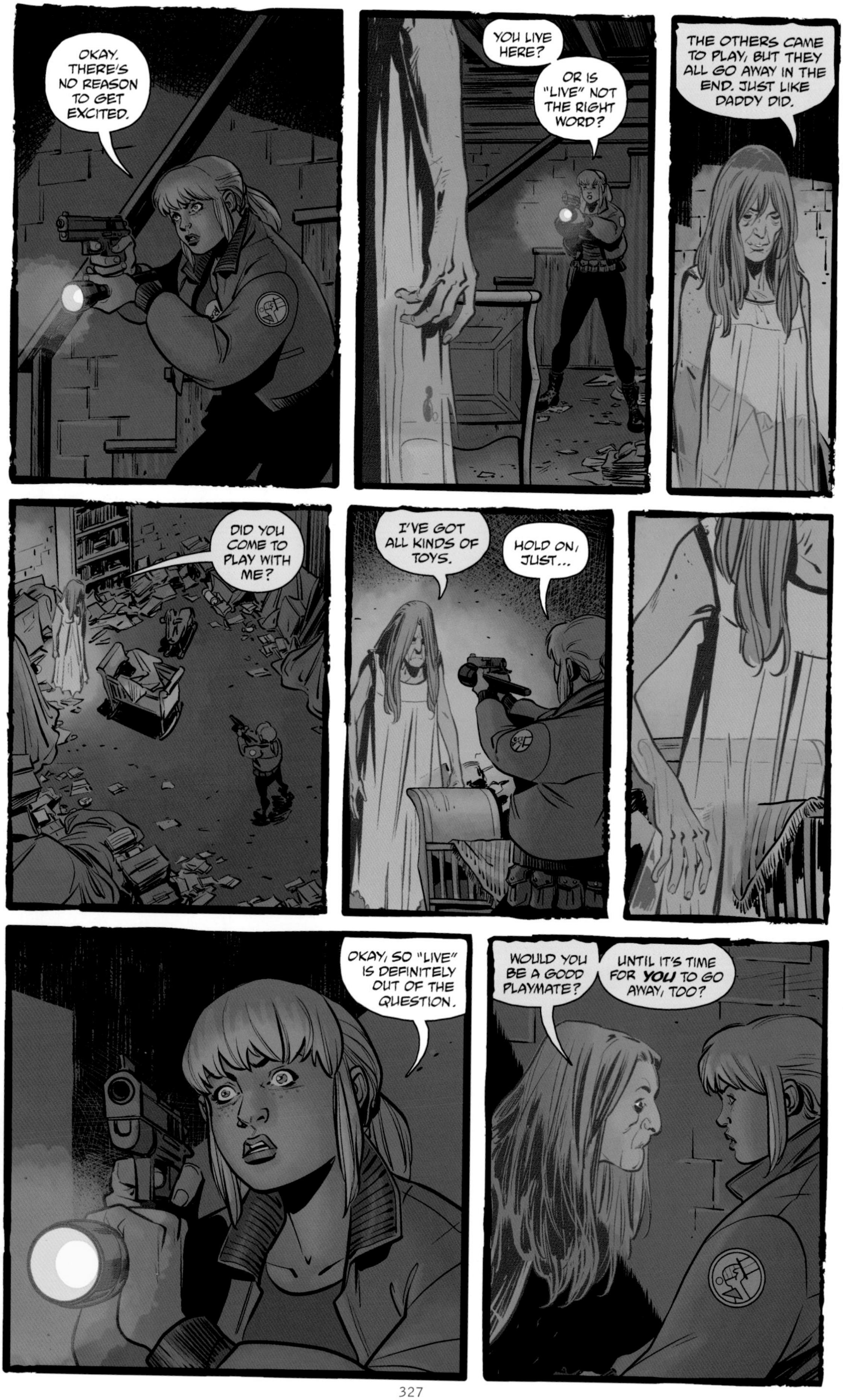
OKAY. THERE'S NO REASON TO GET EXCITED.
YOU LIVE HERE?
OR IS "LIVE" NOT THE RIGHT WORD?
THE OTHERS CAME TO PLAY, BUT THEY ALL GO AWAY IN THE END. JUST LIKE DADDY DID.
DID YOU COME TO PLAY WITH ME?
I'VE GOT ALL KINDS OF TOYS.
HOLD ON, JUST...
OKAY, SO "LIVE" IS DEFINITELY OUT OF THE QUESTION.
WOULD YOU BE A GOOD PLAYMATE?
UNTIL IT'S TIME FOR **YOU** TO GO AWAY, TOO?

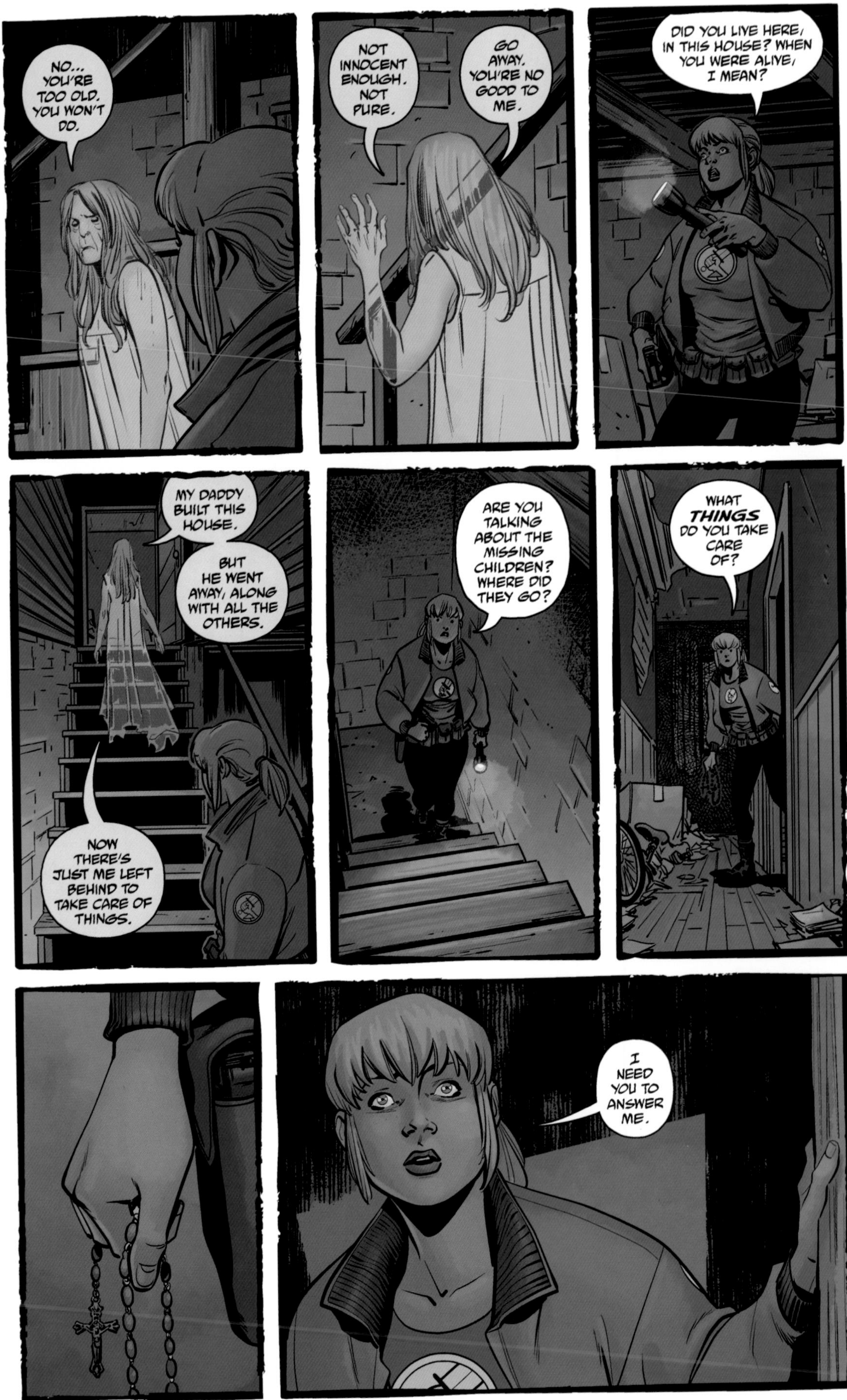
NO... YOU'RE TOO OLD. YOU WON'T DO.
NOT INNOCENT ENOUGH. NOT PURE.
GO AWAY. YOU'RE NO GOOD TO ME.
DID YOU LIVE HERE, IN THIS HOUSE? WHEN YOU WERE ALIVE, I MEAN?
MY DADDY BUILT THIS HOUSE.
BUT HE WENT AWAY, ALONG WITH ALL THE OTHERS.
NOW THERE'S JUST ME LEFT BEHIND TO TAKE CARE OF THINGS.
ARE YOU TALKING ABOUT THE MISSING CHILDREN? WHERE DID THEY GO?
WHAT ***THINGS*** DO YOU TAKE CARE OF?
I NEED YOU TO ANSWER ME.

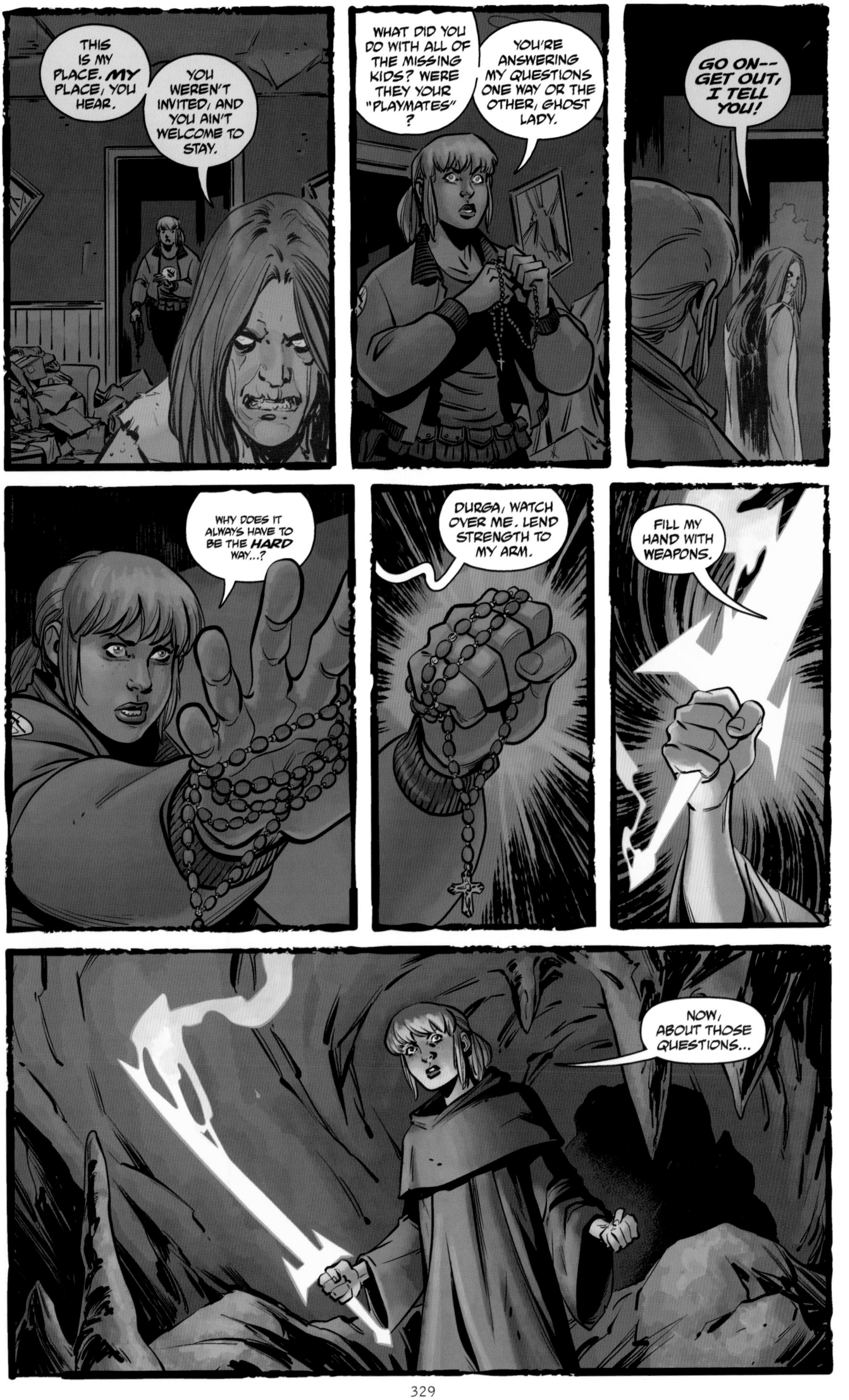

THIS IS MY PLACE. MY PLACE, YOU HEAR.
YOU WEREN'T INVITED, AND YOU AIN'T WELCOME TO STAY.
WHAT DID YOU DO WITH ALL OF THE MISSING KIDS? WERE THEY YOUR "PLAYMATES"?
YOU'RE ANSWERING MY QUESTIONS ONE WAY OR THE OTHER, GHOST LADY.
GO ON-- GET OUT, I TELL YOU!
WHY DOES IT ALWAYS HAVE TO BE THE HARD WAY...?
DURGA, WATCH OVER ME. LEND STRENGTH TO MY ARM.
FILL MY HAND WITH WEAPONS.
NOW, ABOUT THOSE QUESTIONS...

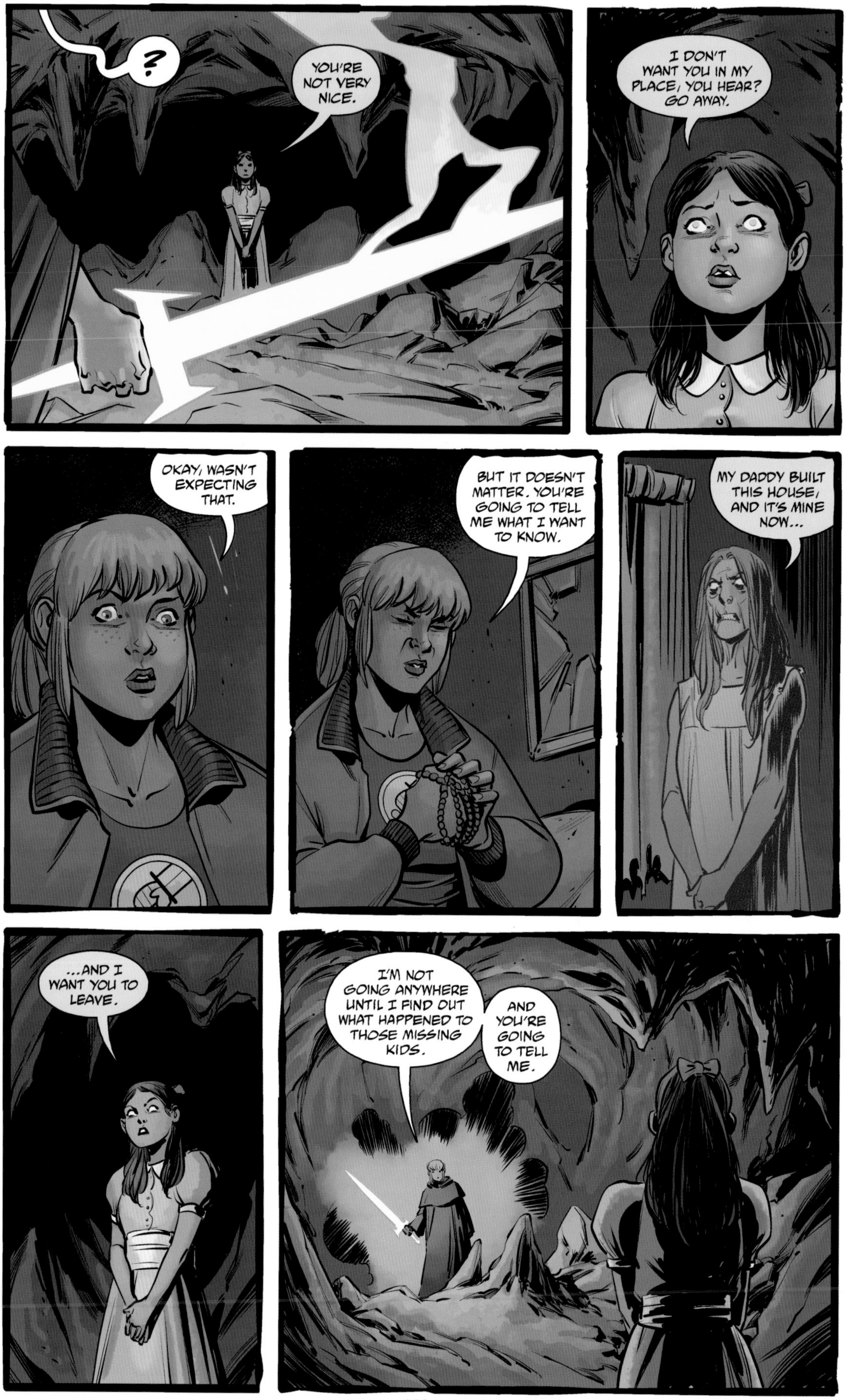
?
YOU'RE NOT VERY NICE.
I DON'T WANT YOU IN MY PLACE, YOU HEAR? GO AWAY.
OKAY, WASN'T EXPECTING THAT.
BUT IT DOESN'T MATTER. YOU'RE GOING TO TELL ME WHAT I WANT TO KNOW.
MY DADDY BUILT THIS HOUSE, AND IT'S MINE NOW...
...AND I WANT YOU TO LEAVE.
I'M NOT GOING ANYWHERE UNTIL I FIND OUT WHAT HAPPENED TO THOSE MISSING KIDS.
AND YOU'RE GOING TO TELL ME.

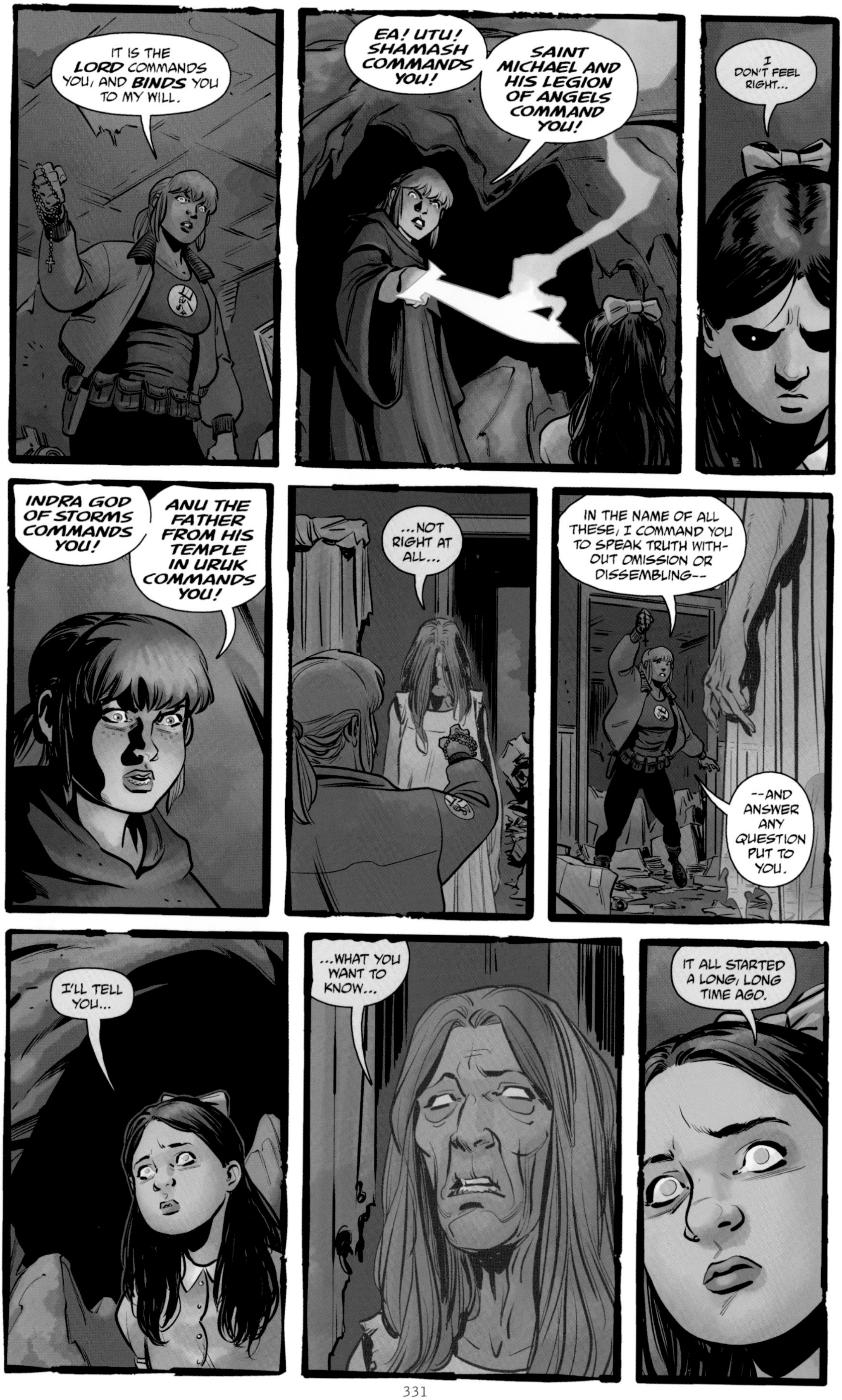
IT IS THE **LORD** COMMANDS YOU, AND **BINDS** YOU TO MY WILL.
EA! UTU! SHAMASH COMMANDS YOU!
SAINT MICHAEL AND HIS LEGION OF ANGELS COMMAND YOU!
I DON'T FEEL RIGHT...
INDRA GOD OF STORMS COMMANDS YOU!
ANU THE FATHER FROM HIS TEMPLE IN URUK COMMANDS YOU!
...NOT RIGHT AT ALL...
IN THE NAME OF ALL THESE, I COMMAND YOU TO SPEAK TRUTH WITH-OUT OMISSION OR DISSEMBLING--
--AND ANSWER ANY QUESTION PUT TO YOU.
I'LL TELL YOU...
...WHAT YOU WANT TO KNOW...
IT ALL STARTED A LONG, LONG TIME AGO.

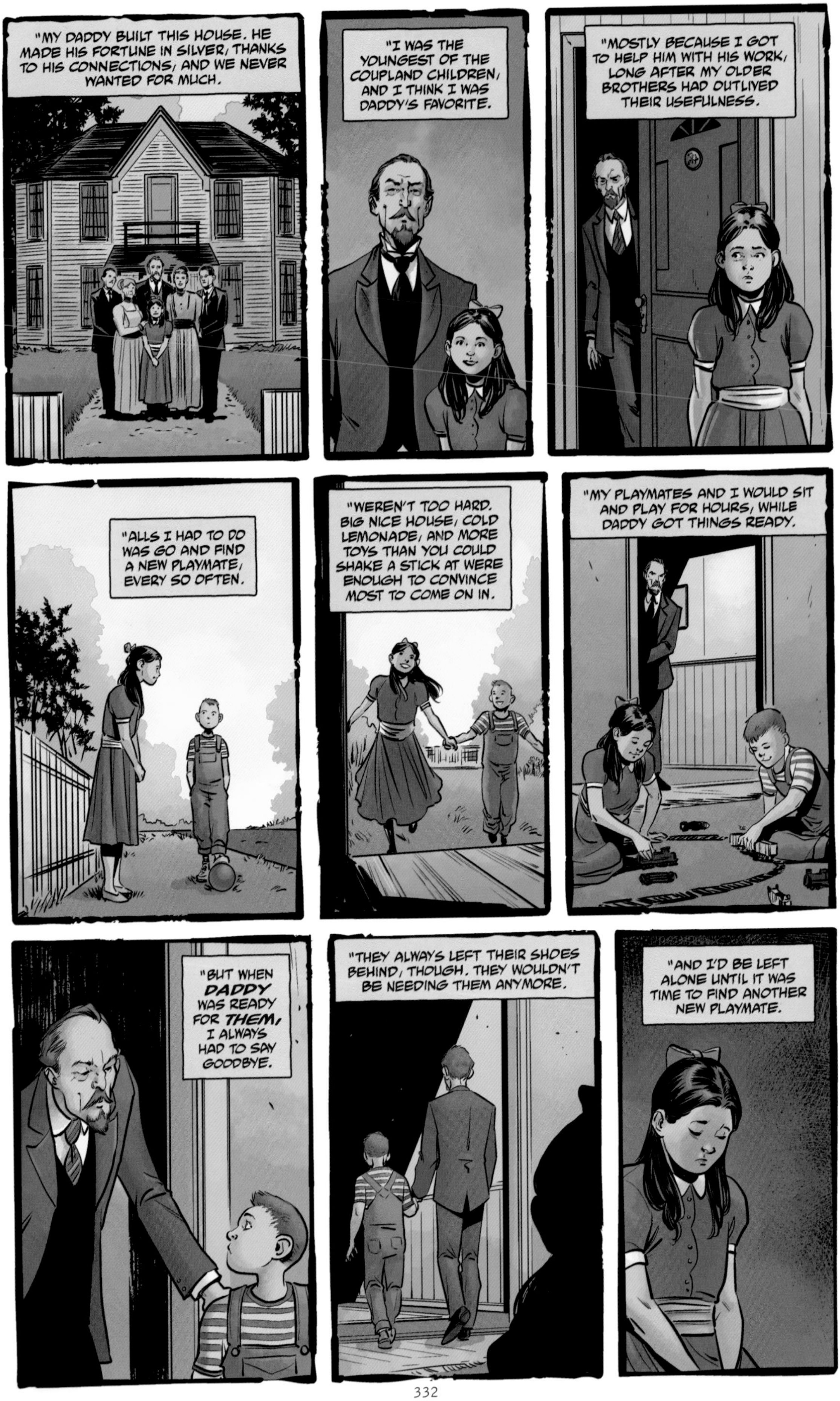
"MY DADDY BUILT THIS HOUSE. HE MADE HIS FORTUNE IN SILVER, THANKS TO HIS CONNECTIONS, AND WE NEVER WANTED FOR MUCH.
"I WAS THE YOUNGEST OF THE COUPLAND CHILDREN, AND I THINK I WAS DADDY'S FAVORITE.
"MOSTLY BECAUSE I GOT TO HELP HIM WITH HIS WORK, LONG AFTER MY OLDER BROTHERS HAD OUTLIVED THEIR USEFULNESS.
"ALLS I HAD TO DO WAS GO AND FIND A NEW PLAYMATE, EVERY SO OFTEN.
"WEREN'T TOO HARD. BIG NICE HOUSE, COLD LEMONADE, AND MORE TOYS THAN YOU COULD SHAKE A STICK AT WERE ENOUGH TO CONVINCE MOST TO COME ON IN.
"MY PLAYMATES AND I WOULD SIT AND PLAY FOR HOURS, WHILE DADDY GOT THINGS READY.
"BUT WHEN *DADDY* WAS READY FOR *THEM,* I ALWAYS HAD TO SAY GOODBYE.
"THEY ALWAYS LEFT THEIR SHOES BEHIND, THOUGH. THEY WOULDN'T BE NEEDING THEM ANYMORE.
"AND I'D BE LEFT ALONE UNTIL IT WAS TIME TO FIND ANOTHER NEW PLAYMATE.

"BUT THE TIME CAME THAT DADDY WAS CALLED HOME.

"THEN MY OLDER BROTHERS ALL MOVED OFF WITH FAMILIES OF THEIR OWN, AND I WAS THE LAST ONE LEFT.

"I GOT POWERFUL LONELY ALL ALONE IN THE HOUSE BY MYSELF.

"BUT I COULD STILL GO AND MEET NEW PLAYMATES FROM TIME TO TIME, WHEN I NEEDED TO.

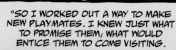

"THEY'D KEEP ME COMPANY A SPELL. UNTIL IT WAS THEIR TIME.

"NO ONE EVER CAME TO CALL...NO ONE EVER CAME TO VISIT. I JUST WENT TO BED ONE DAY AND NEVER WOKE UP.

"BUT I WAS STILL HERE, EVEN AFTER. AND GOT LONELIER STILL, WITH EACH PASSING YEAR.

"SO I WORKED OUT A WAY TO MAKE NEW PLAYMATES. I KNEW JUST WHAT TO PROMISE THEM, WHAT WOULD ENTICE THEM TO COME VISITING.

"AND THEY'D KEEP ME COMPANY FOR A SPELL, JUST LIKE ALL THE OTHERS BEFORE. NOT MANY, NOT TOO OFTEN...TILL LATELY..."

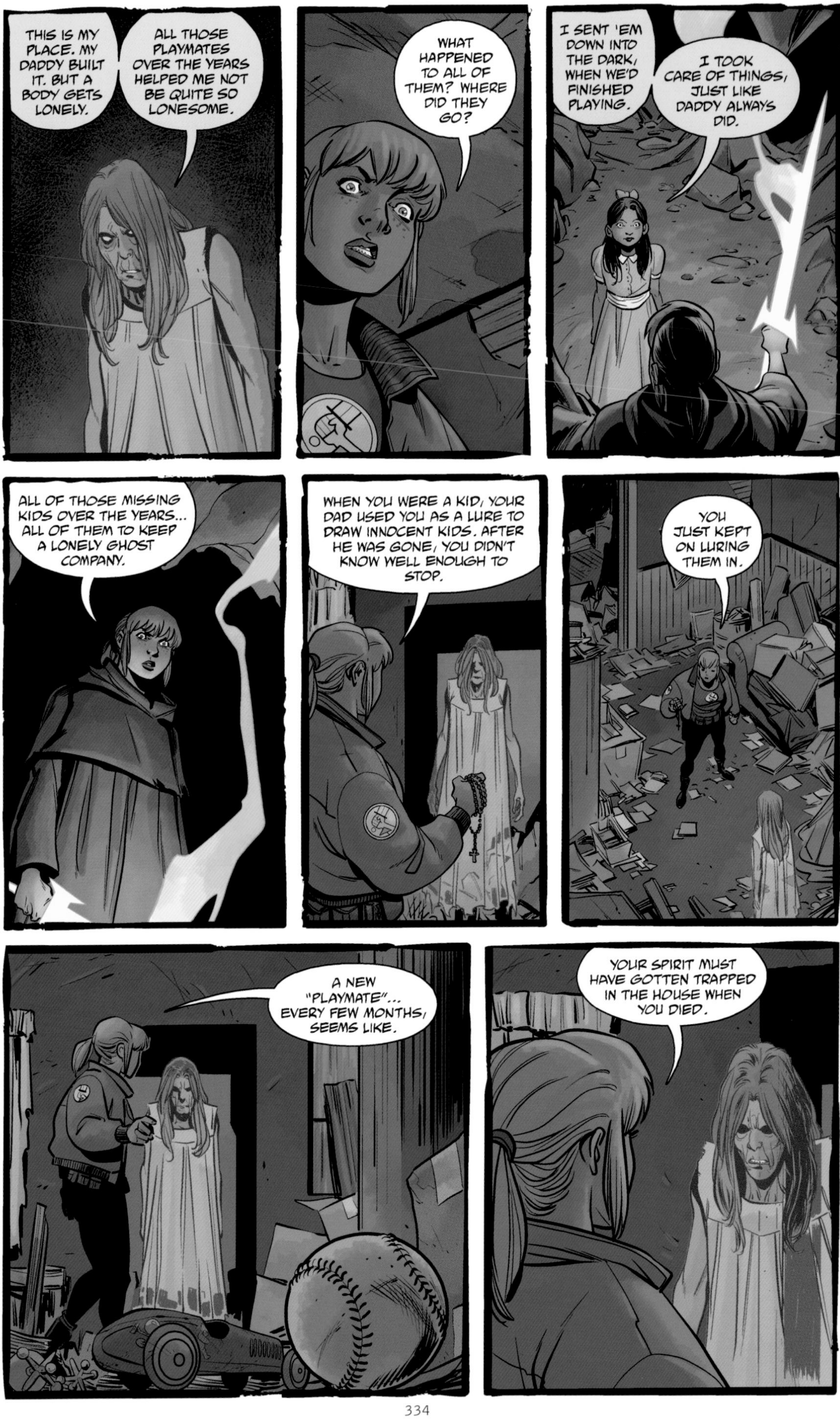
THIS IS MY PLACE. MY DADDY BUILT IT. BUT A BODY GETS LONELY.
ALL THOSE PLAYMATES OVER THE YEARS HELPED ME NOT BE QUITE SO LONESOME.
WHAT HAPPENED TO ALL OF THEM? WHERE DID THEY GO?
I SENT 'EM DOWN INTO THE DARK, WHEN WE'D FINISHED PLAYING.
I TOOK CARE OF THINGS, JUST LIKE DADDY ALWAYS DID.
ALL OF THOSE MISSING KIDS OVER THE YEARS... ALL OF THEM TO KEEP A LONELY GHOST COMPANY.
WHEN YOU WERE A KID, YOUR DAD USED YOU AS A LURE TO DRAW INNOCENT KIDS. AFTER HE WAS GONE, YOU DIDN'T KNOW WELL ENOUGH TO STOP.
YOU JUST KEPT ON LURING THEM IN.
A NEW "PLAYMATE"... EVERY FEW MONTHS, SEEMS LIKE.
YOUR SPIRIT MUST HAVE GOTTEN TRAPPED IN THE HOUSE WHEN YOU DIED.

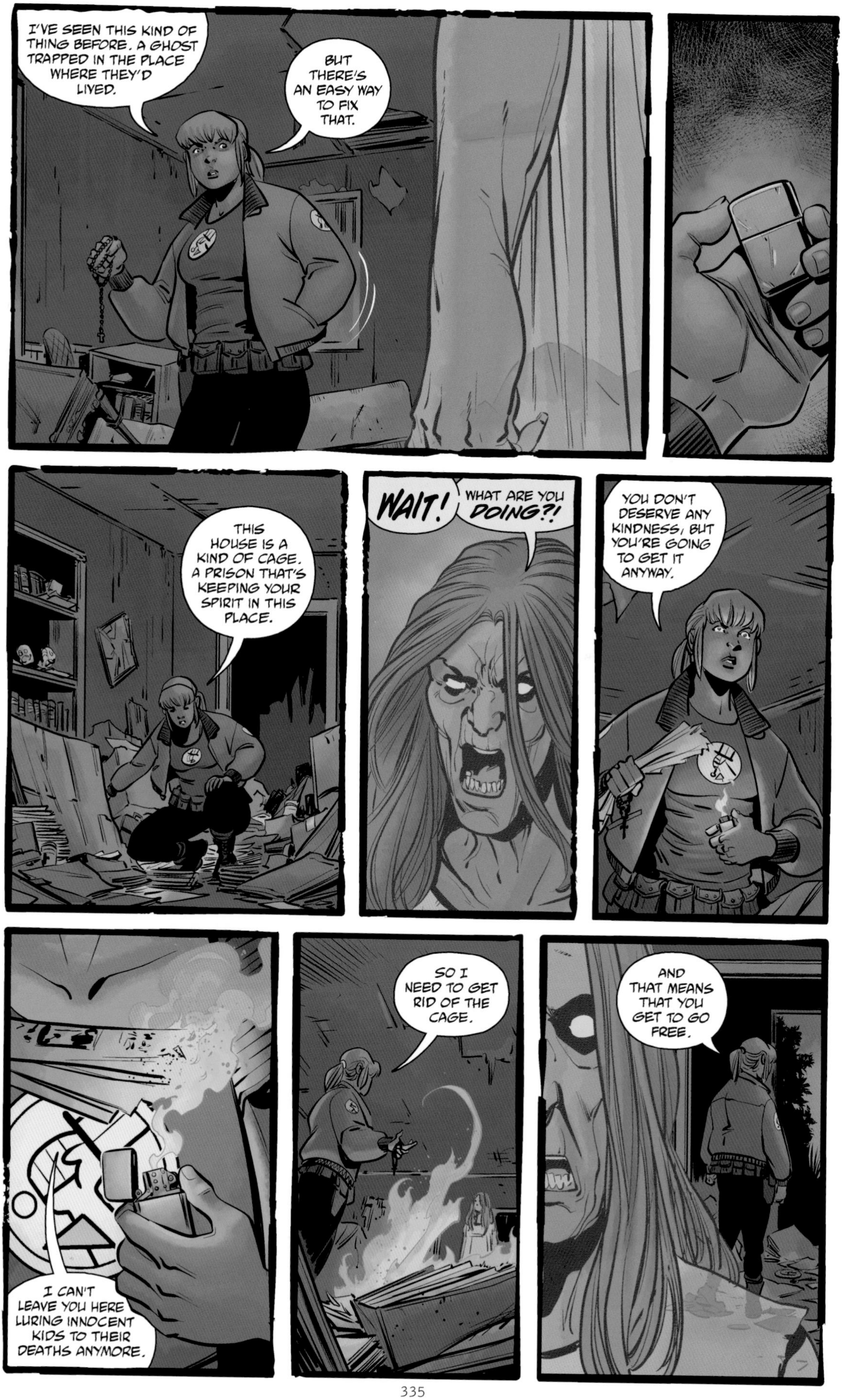
I'VE SEEN THIS KIND OF THING BEFORE. A GHOST TRAPPED IN THE PLACE WHERE THEY'D LIVED.
BUT THERE'S AN EASY WAY TO FIX THAT.
THIS HOUSE IS A KIND OF CAGE. A PRISON THAT'S KEEPING YOUR SPIRIT IN THIS PLACE.
WAIT!
WHAT ARE YOU DOING?!
YOU DON'T DESERVE ANY KINDNESS, BUT YOU'RE GOING TO GET IT ANYWAY.
I CAN'T LEAVE YOU HERE LURING INNOCENT KIDS TO THEIR DEATHS ANYMORE.
SO I NEED TO GET RID OF THE CAGE.
AND THAT MEANS THAT YOU GET TO GO FREE.

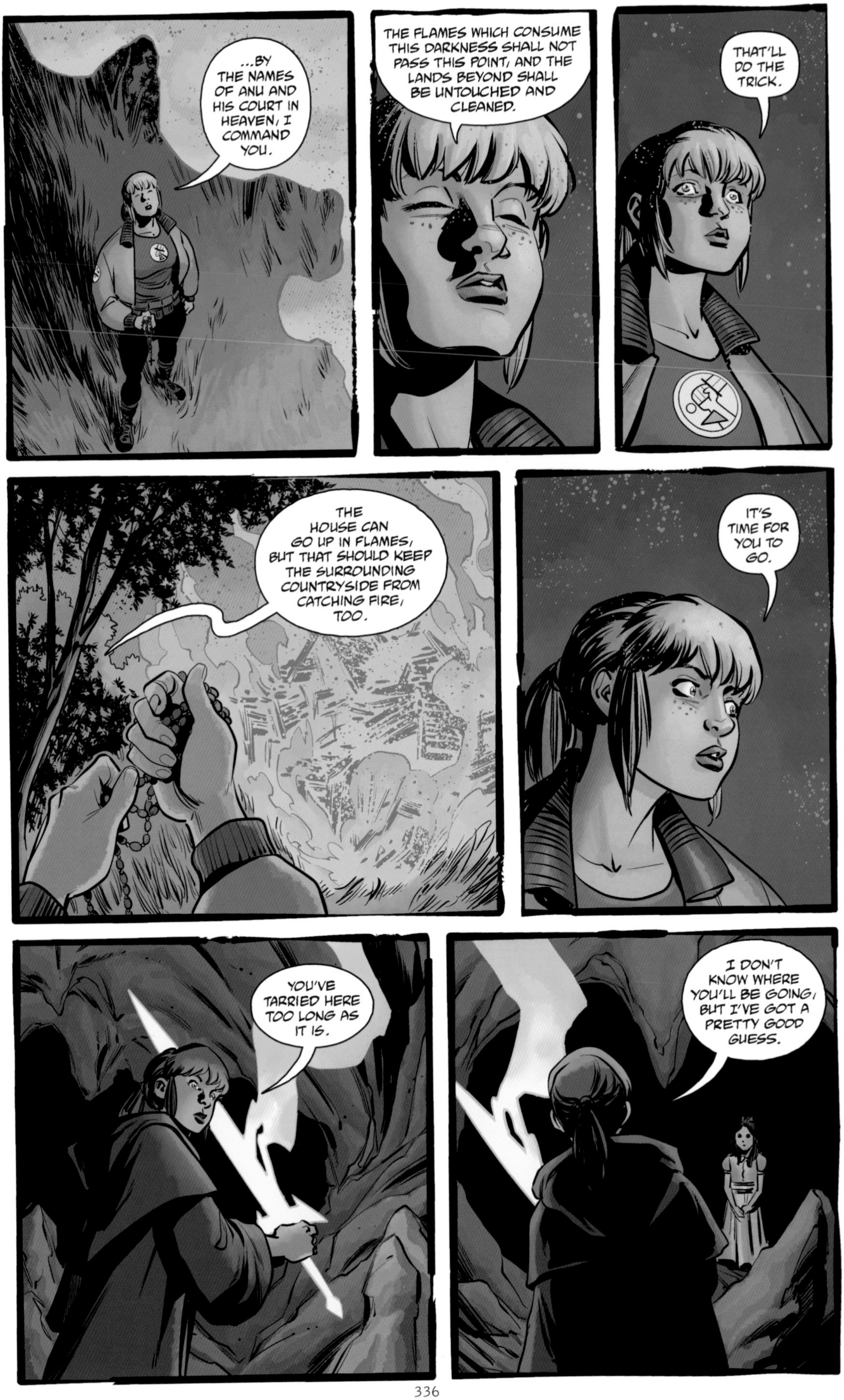
...BY THE NAMES OF ANU AND HIS COURT IN HEAVEN, I COMMAND YOU.
THE FLAMES WHICH CONSUME THIS DARKNESS SHALL NOT PASS THIS POINT, AND THE LANDS BEYOND SHALL BE UNTOUCHED AND CLEANED.
THAT'LL DO THE TRICK.
THE HOUSE CAN GO UP IN FLAMES, BUT THAT SHOULD KEEP THE SURROUNDING COUNTRYSIDE FROM CATCHING FIRE, TOO.
IT'S TIME FOR YOU TO GO.
YOU'VE TARRIED HERE TOO LONG AS IT IS.
I DON'T KNOW WHERE YOU'LL BE GOING, BUT I'VE GOT A PRETTY GOOD GUESS.

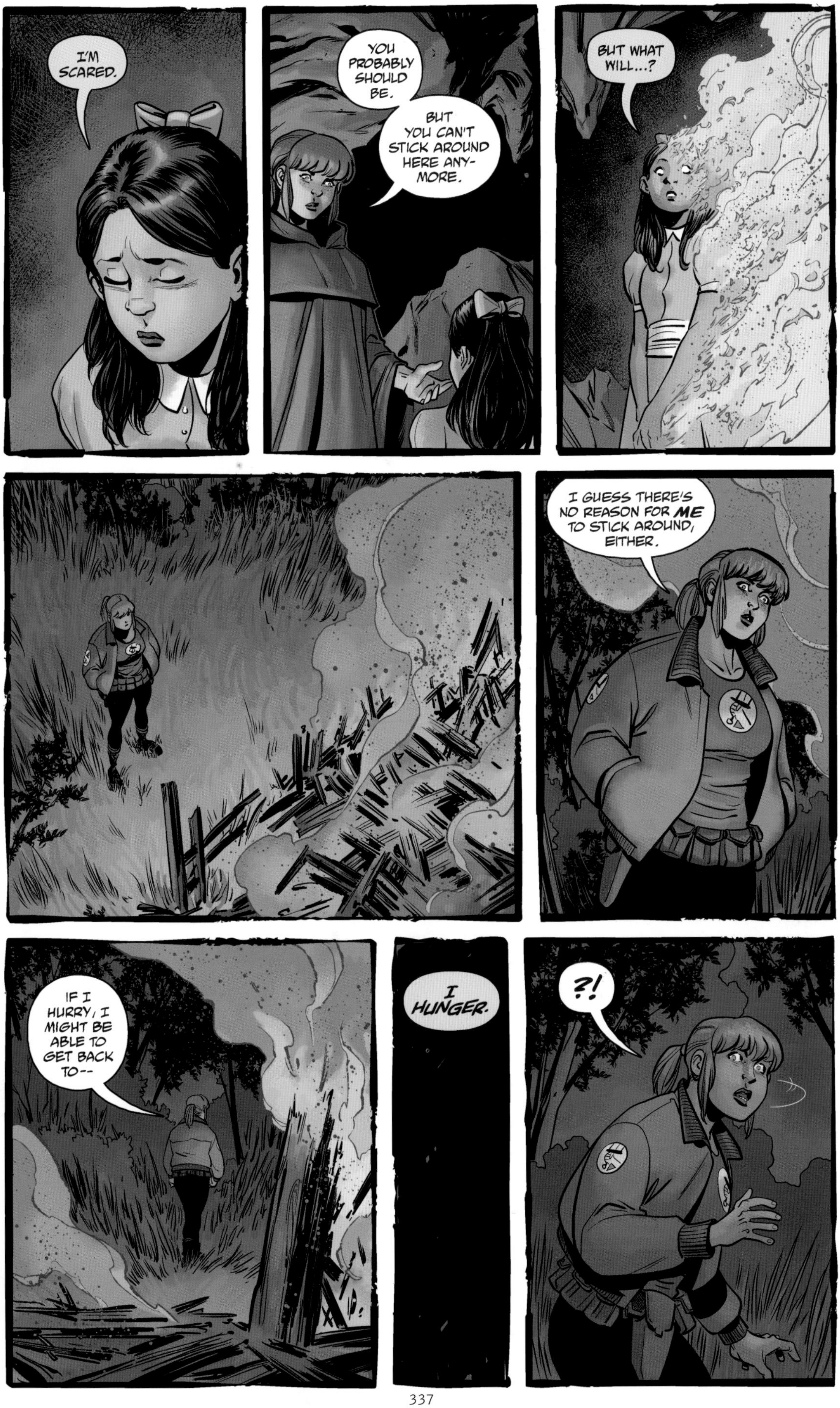
I'M SCARED.
YOU PROBABLY SHOULD BE.
BUT YOU CAN'T STICK AROUND HERE ANY-MORE.
BUT WHAT WILL...?
I GUESS THERE'S NO REASON FOR ME TO STICK AROUND, EITHER.
IF I HURRY, I MIGHT BE ABLE TO GET BACK TO--
I HUNGER.
?!

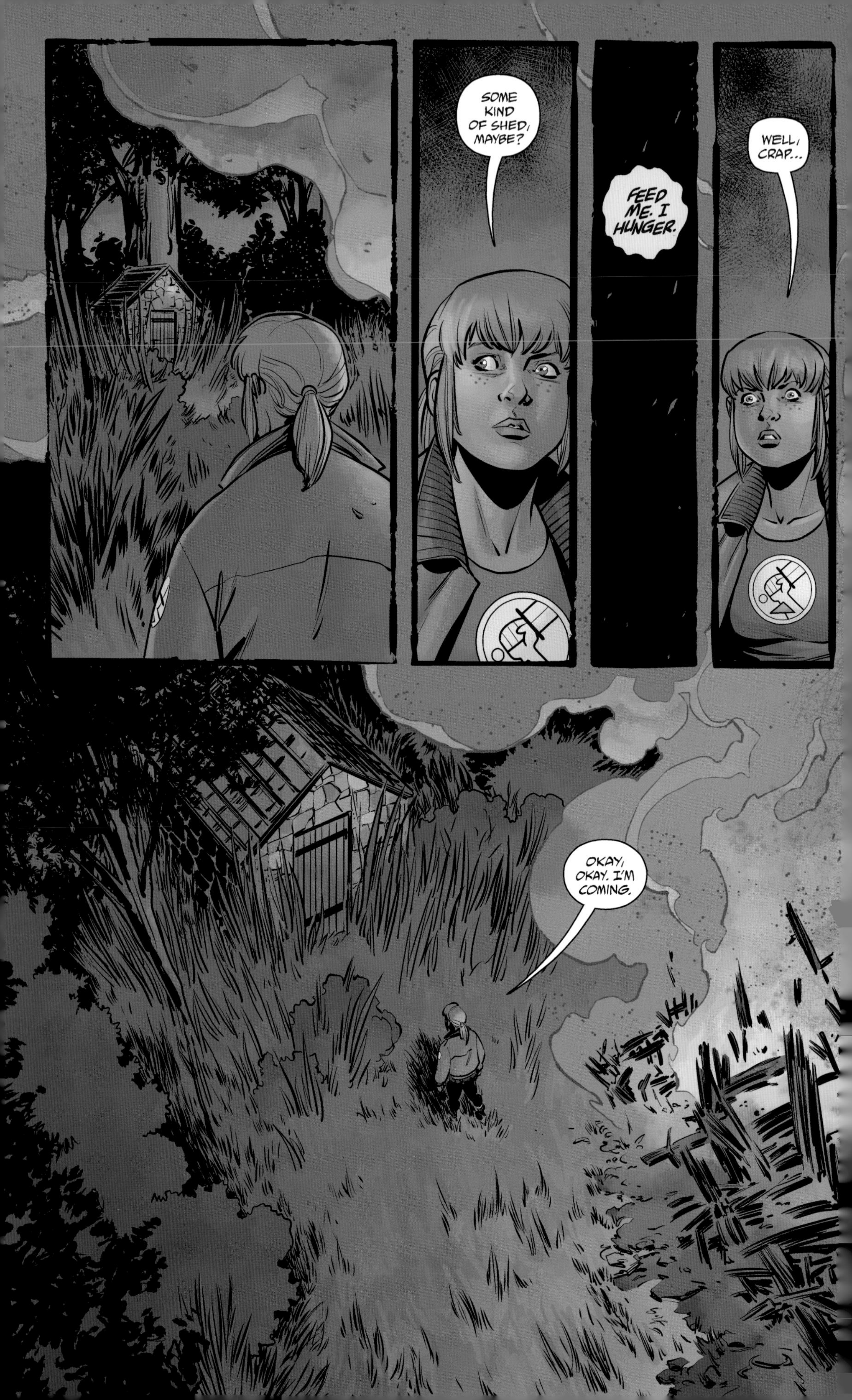
SOME KIND OF SHED, MAYBE?
FEED ME. I HUNGER.
WELL, CRAP...
OKAY, OKAY. I'M COMING.

THE EXORCIST CHAPTER THREE

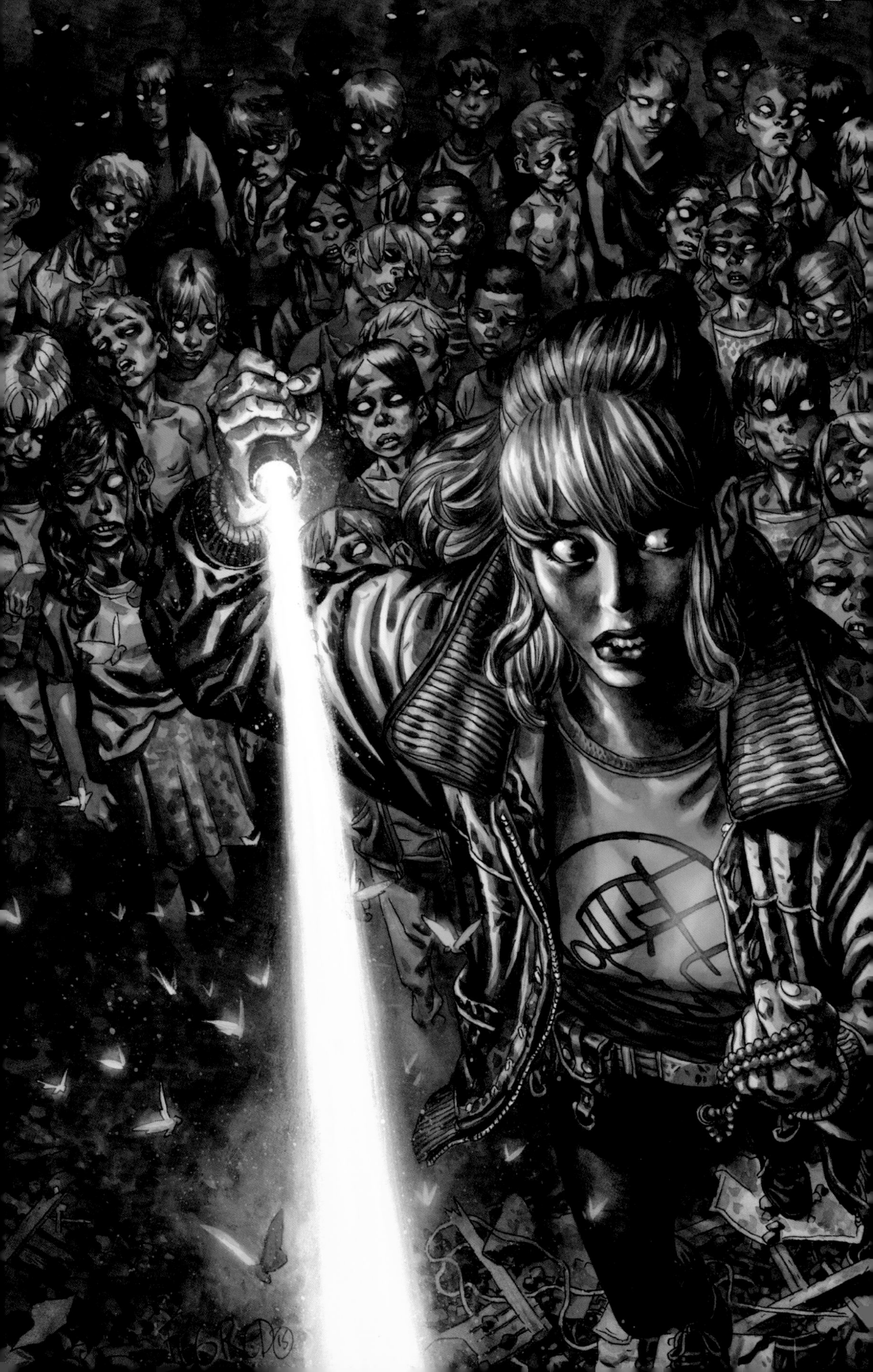

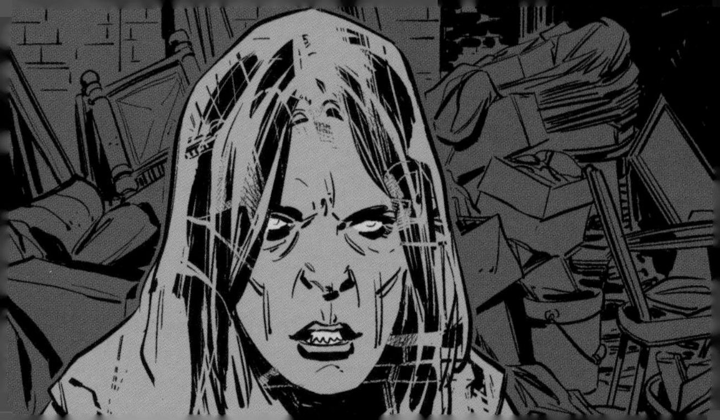

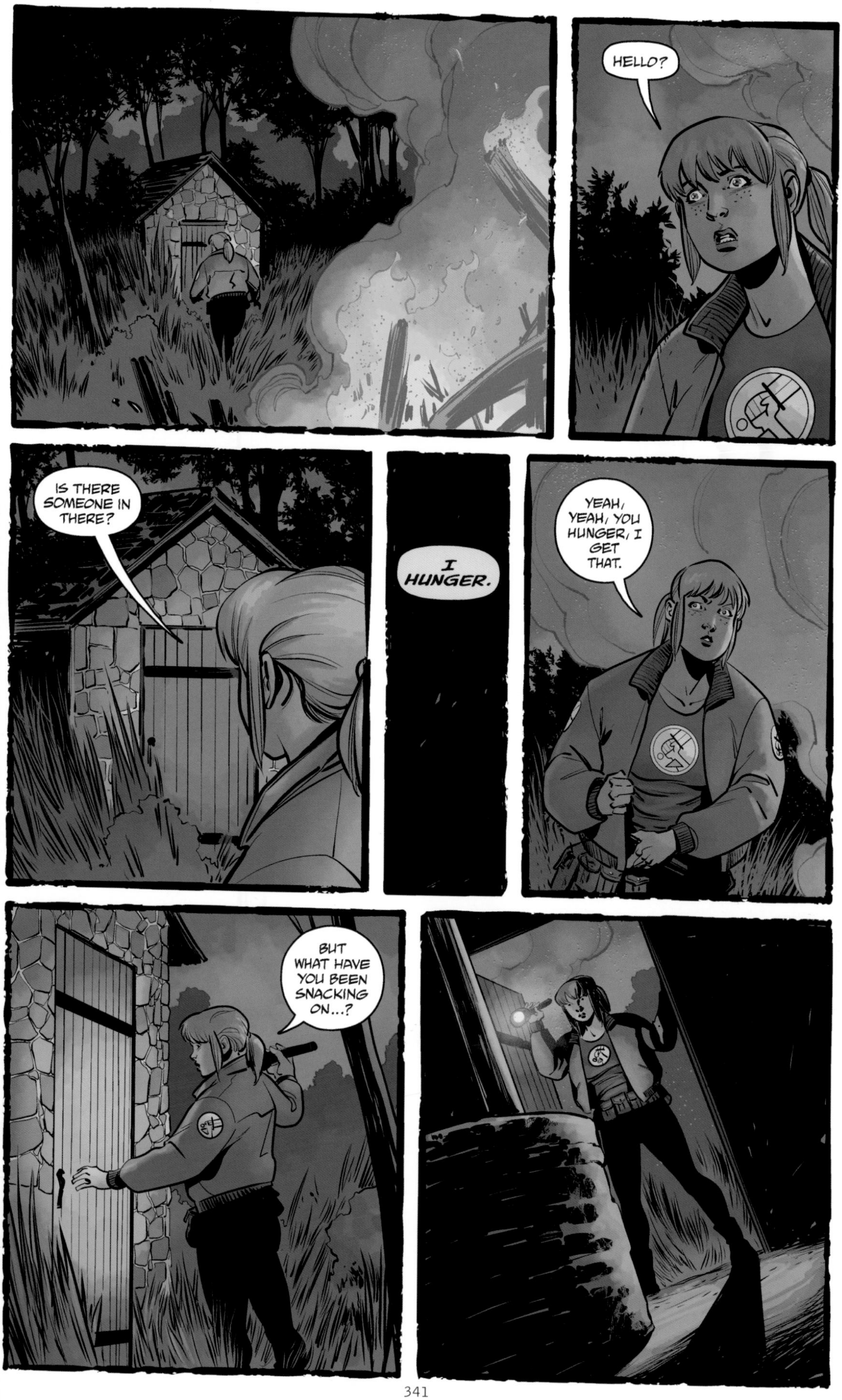
HELLO?
IS THERE SOMEONE IN THERE?
I HUNGER.
YEAH, YEAH, YOU HUNGER, I GET THAT.
BUT WHAT HAVE YOU BEEN SNACKING ON...?

OKAY, **NOT** A SHED.

IT'S A WELL HOUSE.

DOESN'T LOOK LIKE THE WELL'S BEEN USED FOR A **LONG** TIME, THOUGH.

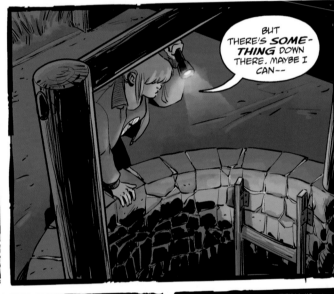

BUT THERE'S **SOMETHING** DOWN THERE. MAYBE I CAN--

OH, GREAT.

FZZZ!

≥SIGH≤...

WAP

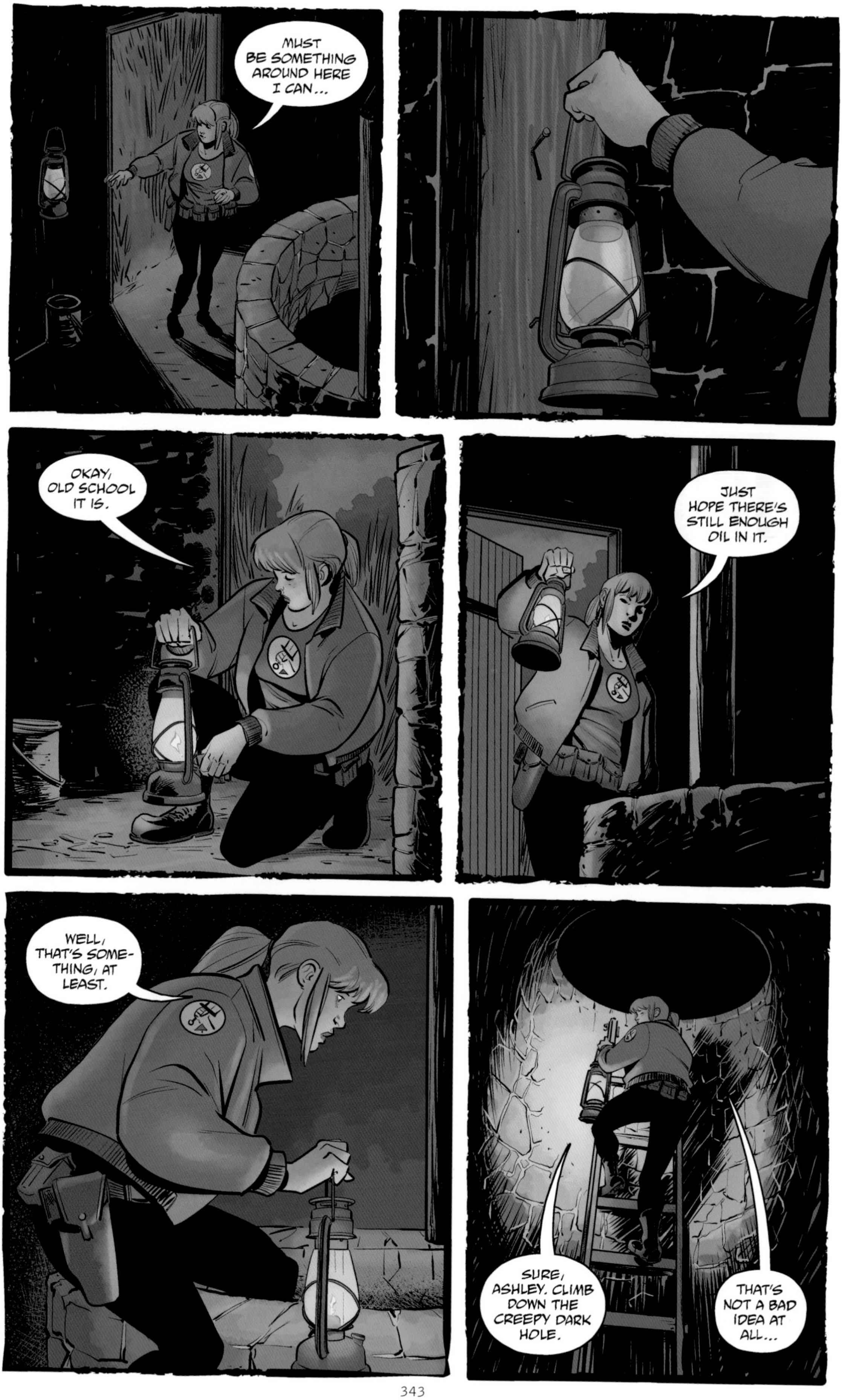
MUST BE SOMETHING AROUND HERE I CAN...
OKAY, OLD SCHOOL IT IS.
JUST HOPE THERE'S STILL ENOUGH OIL IN IT.
WELL, THAT'S SOME-THING, AT LEAST.
SURE, ASHLEY. CLIMB DOWN THE CREEPY DARK HOLE.
THAT'S NOT A BAD IDEA AT ALL...

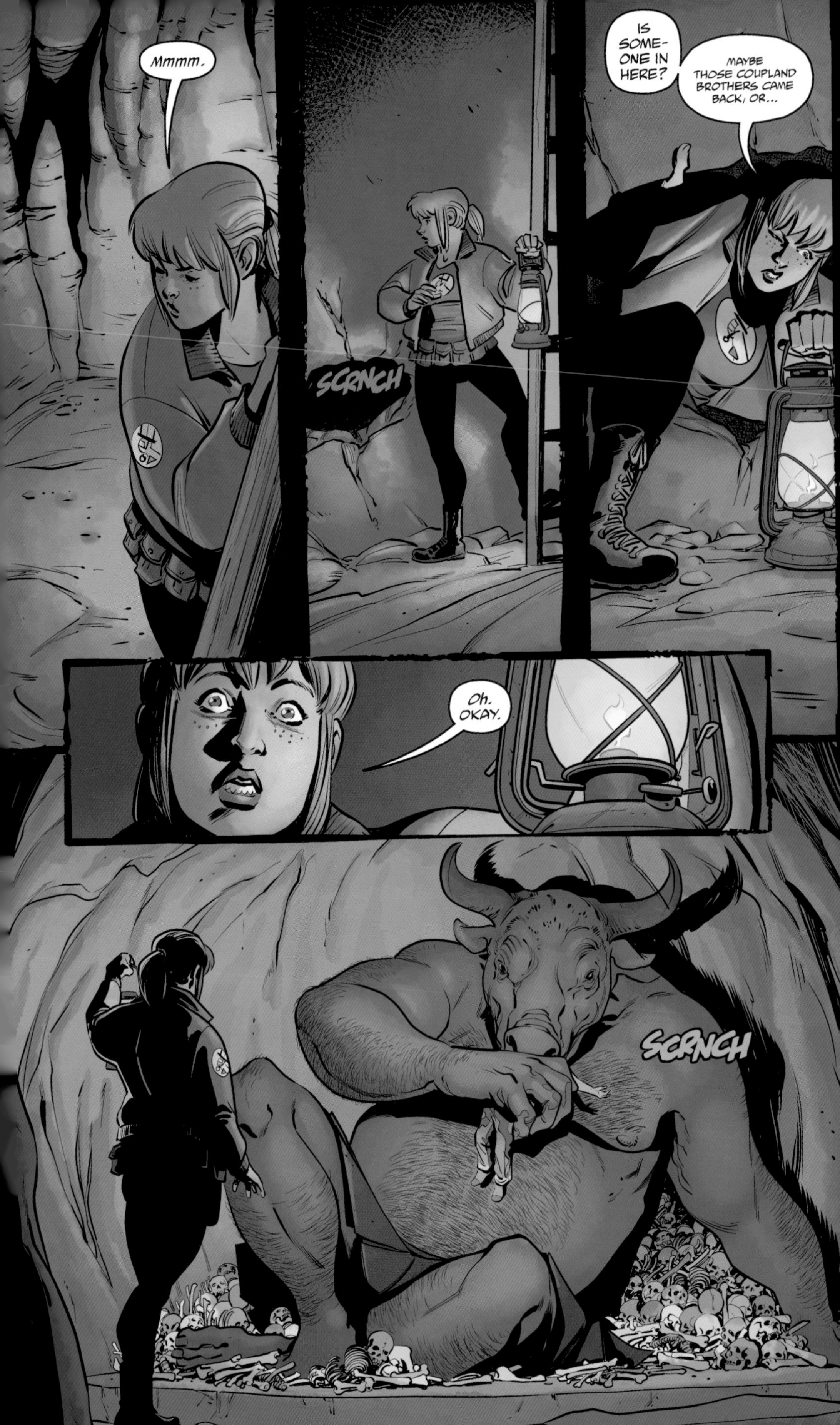
Mmmm.
SCRNCH
IS SOME-ONE IN HERE?
MAYBE THOSE COUPLAND BROTHERS CAME BACK, OR...
Oh. OKAY.
SCRNCH

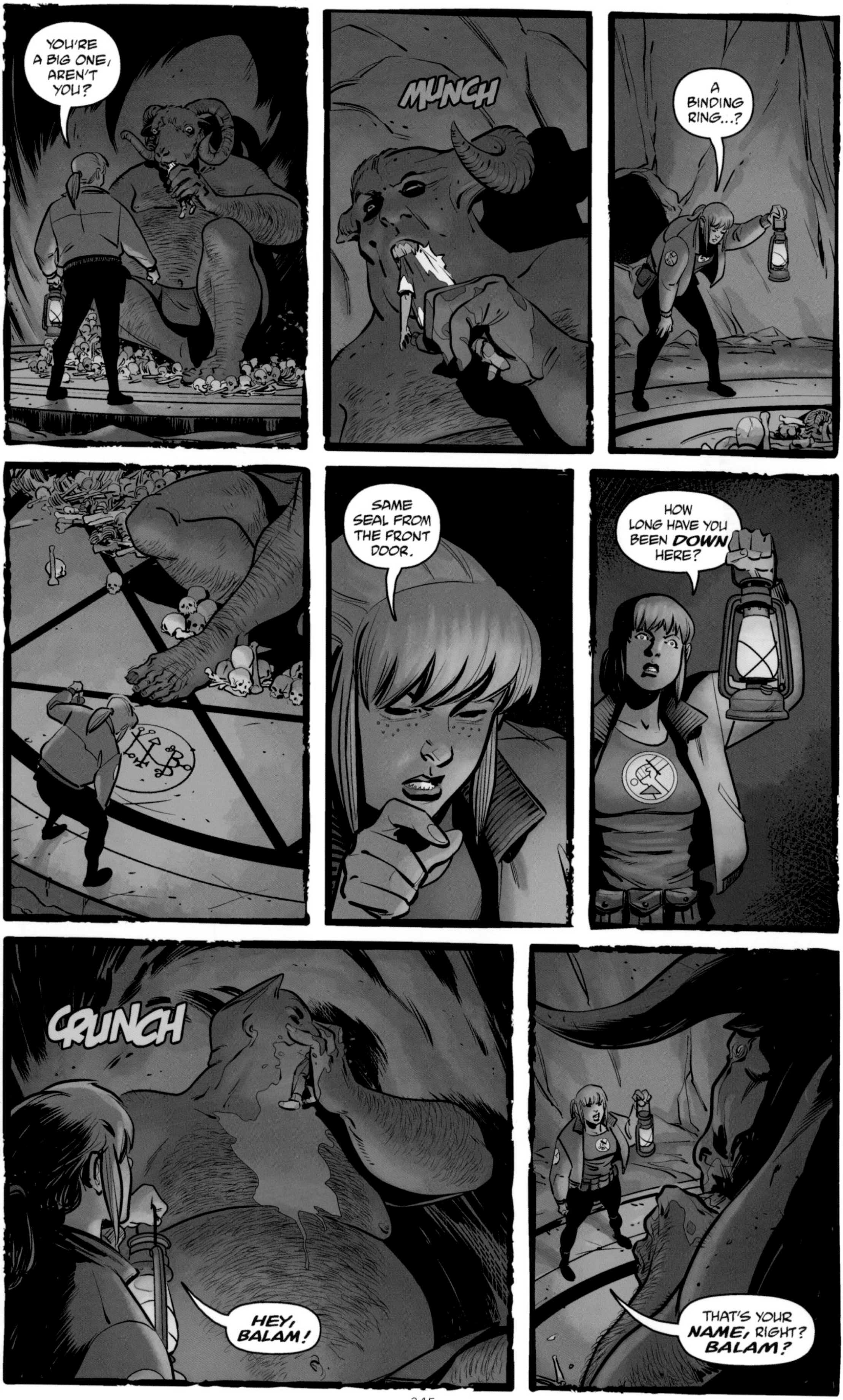

YOU'RE A BIG ONE, AREN'T YOU?
MUNCH
A BINDING RING...?
SAME SEAL FROM THE FRONT DOOR.
HOW LONG HAVE YOU BEEN DOWN HERE?
CRUNCH
HEY, BALAM!
THAT'S YOUR NAME, RIGHT? BALAM?

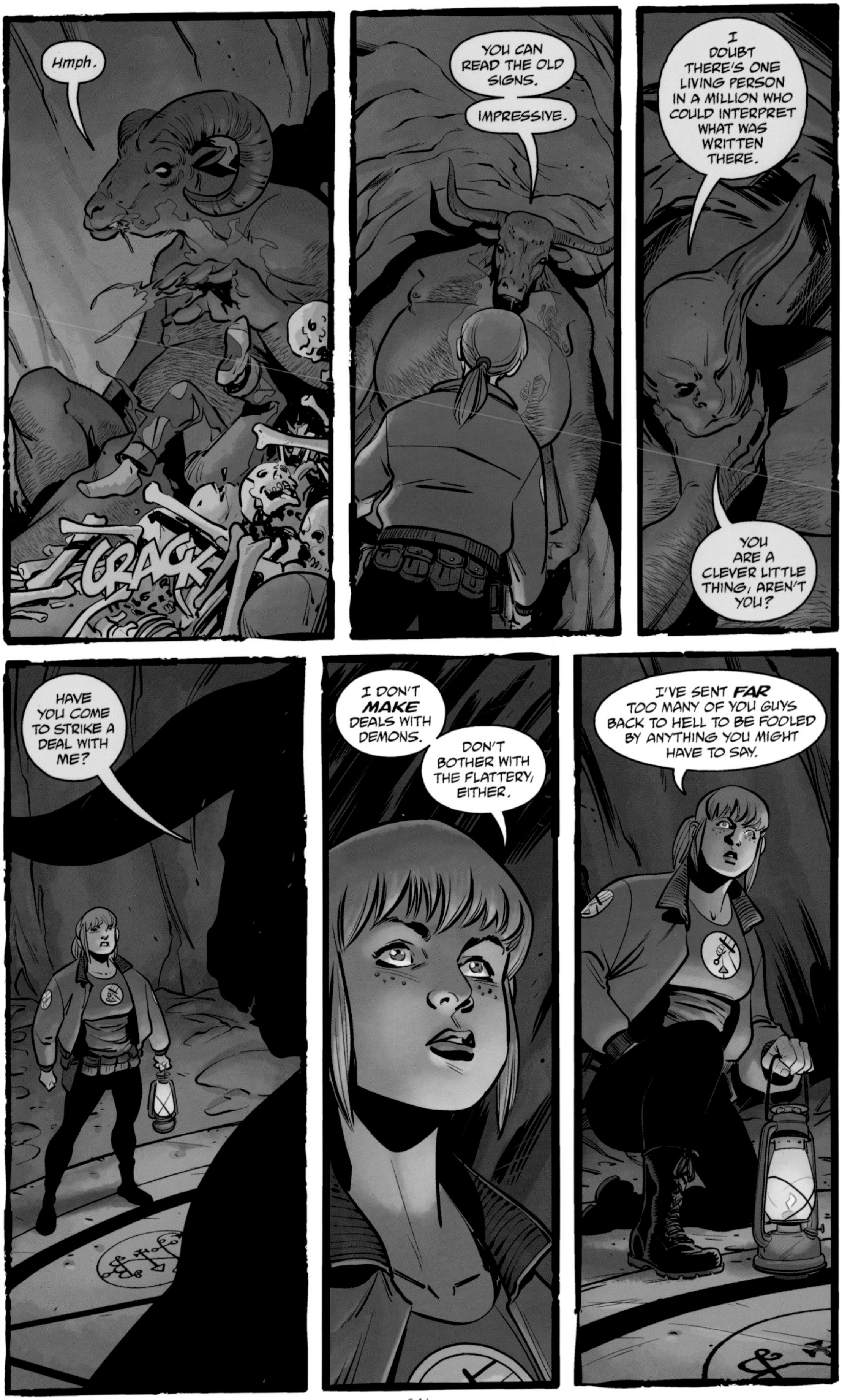
Hmph.
CRACK
YOU CAN READ THE OLD SIGNS.
IMPRESSIVE.
I DOUBT THERE'S ONE LIVING PERSON IN A MILLION WHO COULD INTERPRET WHAT WAS WRITTEN THERE.
YOU ARE A CLEVER LITTLE THING, AREN'T YOU?
HAVE YOU COME TO STRIKE A DEAL WITH ME?
I DON'T MAKE DEALS WITH DEMONS.
DON'T BOTHER WITH THE FLATTERY, EITHER.
I'VE SENT FAR TOO MANY OF YOU GUYS BACK TO HELL TO BE FOOLED BY ANYTHING YOU MIGHT HAVE TO SAY.

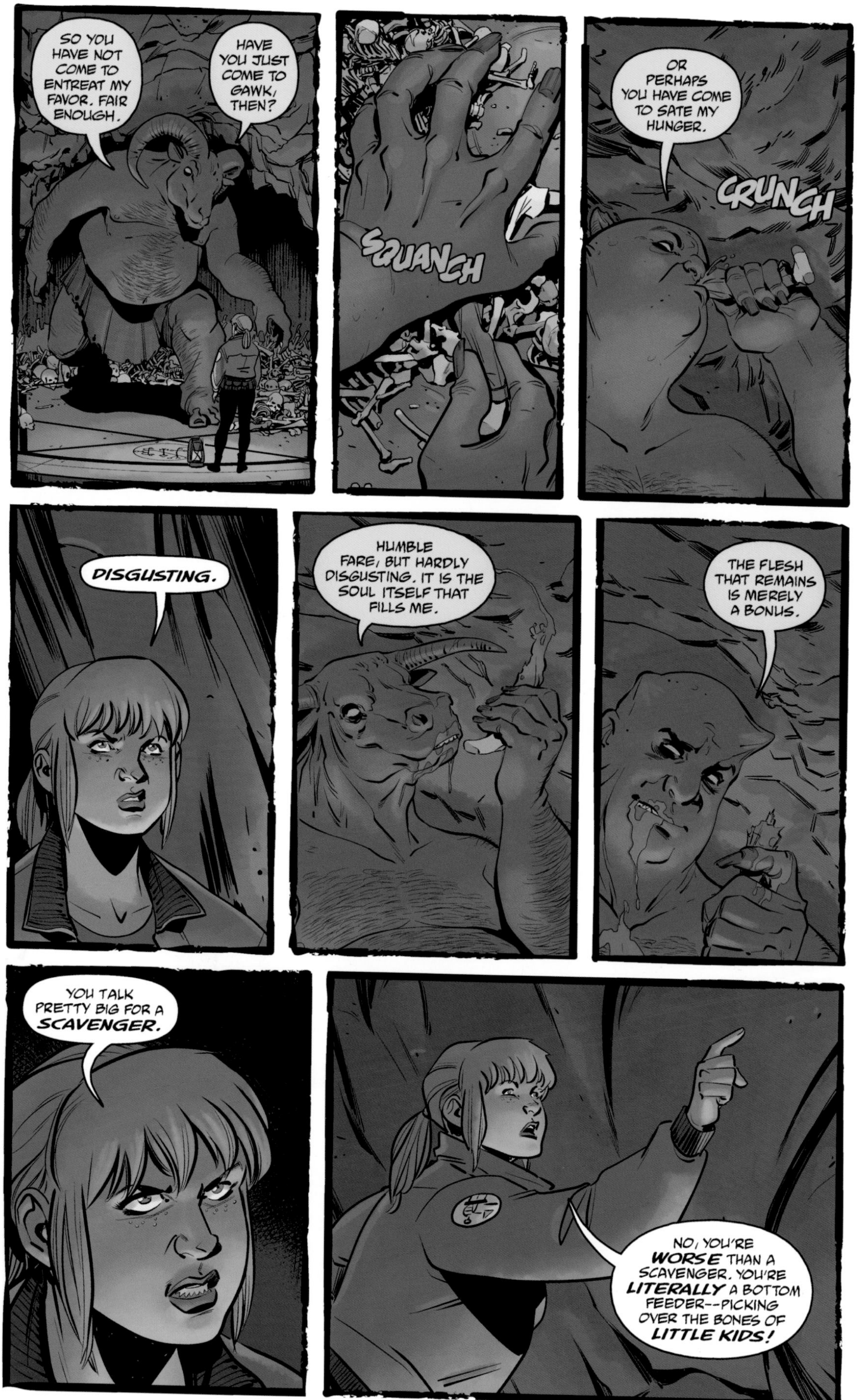
SO YOU HAVE NOT COME TO ENTREAT MY FAVOR. FAIR ENOUGH.
HAVE YOU JUST COME TO GAWK, THEN?
SQUANCH
OR PERHAPS YOU HAVE COME TO SATE MY HUNGER.
CRUNCH
DISGUSTING.
HUMBLE FARE, BUT HARDLY DISGUSTING. IT IS THE SOUL ITSELF THAT FILLS ME.
THE FLESH THAT REMAINS IS MERELY A BONUS.
YOU TALK PRETTY BIG FOR A SCAVENGER.
NO, YOU'RE WORSE THAN A SCAVENGER. YOU'RE LITERALLY A BOTTOM FEEDER--PICKING OVER THE BONES OF LITTLE KIDS!

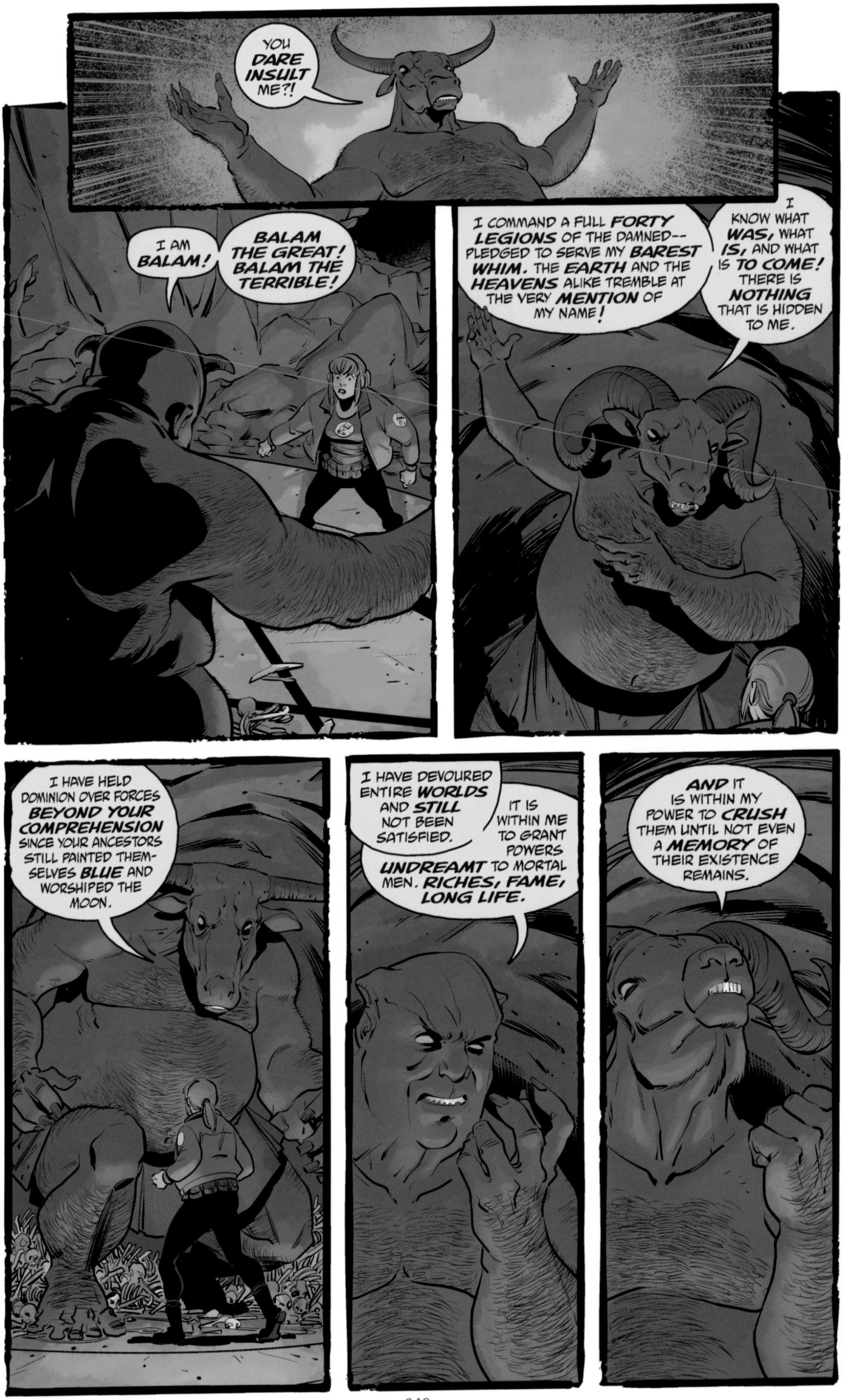
YOU DARE INSULT ME?!
I AM BALAM!
BALAM THE GREAT! BALAM THE TERRIBLE!
I COMMAND A FULL FORTY LEGIONS OF THE DAMNED-- PLEDGED TO SERVE MY BAREST WHIM. THE EARTH AND THE HEAVENS ALIKE TREMBLE AT THE VERY MENTION OF MY NAME!
I KNOW WHAT WAS, WHAT IS, AND WHAT IS TO COME! THERE IS NOTHING THAT IS HIDDEN TO ME.
I HAVE HELD DOMINION OVER FORCES BEYOND YOUR COMPREHENSION SINCE YOUR ANCESTORS STILL PAINTED THEM-SELVES BLUE AND WORSHIPED THE MOON.
I HAVE DEVOURED ENTIRE WORLDS AND STILL NOT BEEN SATISFIED.
IT IS WITHIN ME TO GRANT POWERS UNDREAMT TO MORTAL MEN. RICHES, FAME, LONG LIFE.
AND IT IS WITHIN MY POWER TO CRUSH THEM UNTIL NOT EVEN A MEMORY OF THEIR EXISTENCE REMAINS.

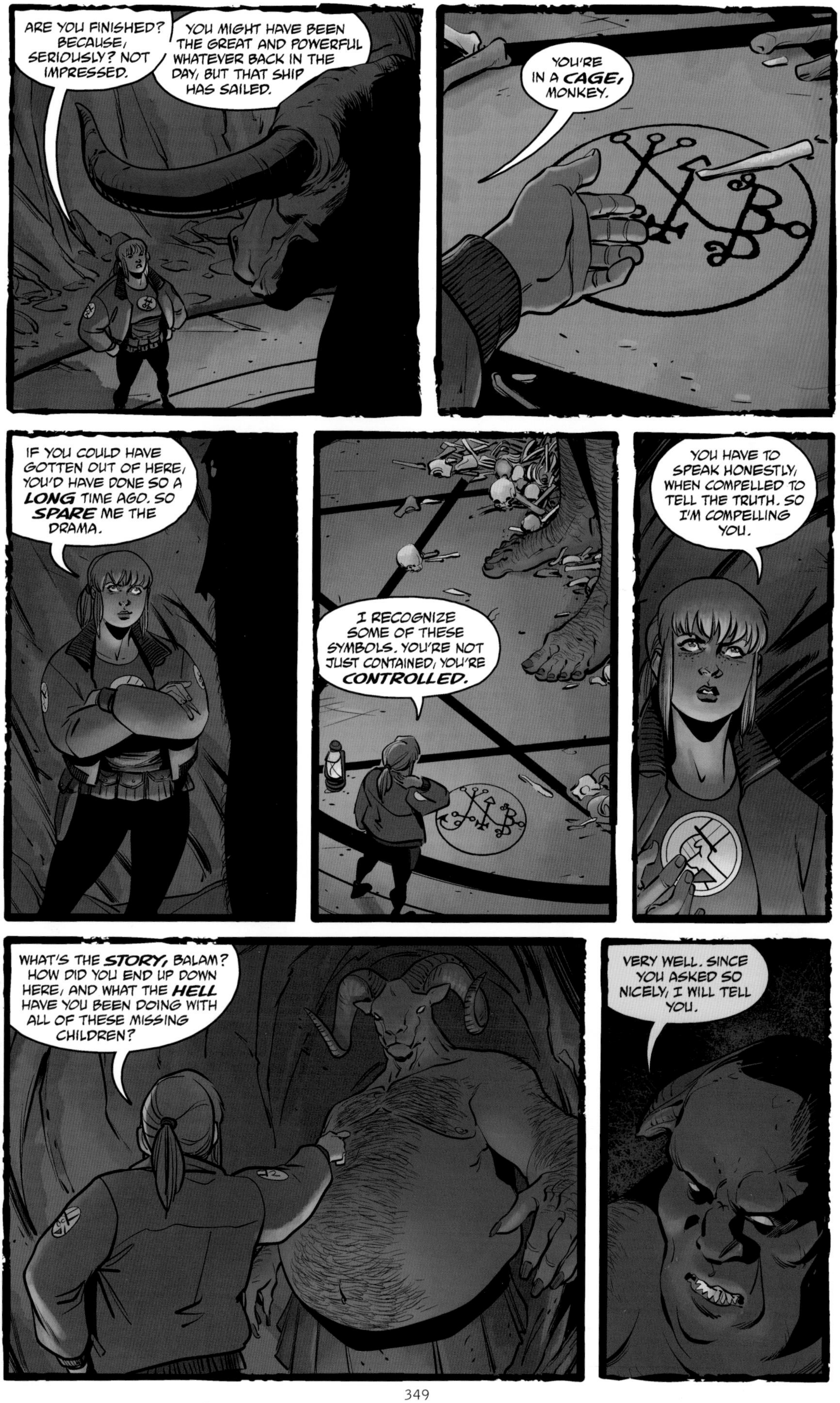
ARE YOU FINISHED? BECAUSE, SERIOUSLY? NOT IMPRESSED.
YOU MIGHT HAVE BEEN THE GREAT AND POWERFUL WHATEVER BACK IN THE DAY, BUT THAT SHIP HAS SAILED.
YOU'RE IN A CAGE, MONKEY.
IF YOU COULD HAVE GOTTEN OUT OF HERE, YOU'D HAVE DONE SO A LONG TIME AGO. SO SPARE ME THE DRAMA.
I RECOGNIZE SOME OF THESE SYMBOLS. YOU'RE NOT JUST CONTAINED, YOU'RE CONTROLLED.
YOU HAVE TO SPEAK HONESTLY, WHEN COMPELLED TO TELL THE TRUTH. SO I'M COMPELLING YOU.
WHAT'S THE STORY, BALAM? HOW DID YOU END UP DOWN HERE, AND WHAT THE HELL HAVE YOU BEEN DOING WITH ALL OF THESE MISSING CHILDREN?
VERY WELL. SINCE YOU ASKED SO NICELY, I WILL TELL YOU.

"YOUR MIND COULD NOT HOPE TO CONTAIN THE TERRIBLE MAJESTY OF THE GREAT CITY OF PANDEMONIUM, THE BEATING HEART OF HELL."

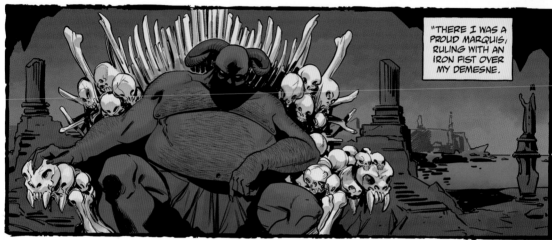

"THERE I WAS A PROUD MARQUIS, RULING WITH AN IRON FIST OVER MY DEMESNE.

"A KNIGHT IN THE ORDER OF THE FLY, I HAD A FULL FORTY LEGIONS UNDER MY DIRECT COMMAND.

"MORTALS WORSHIPED GROVELING AT MY FEET, CURRYING MY FAVOR, ENTREATING FOR POWER OR GLIMPSES OF THEIR FUTURES.

"BUT I GREW COCKY.

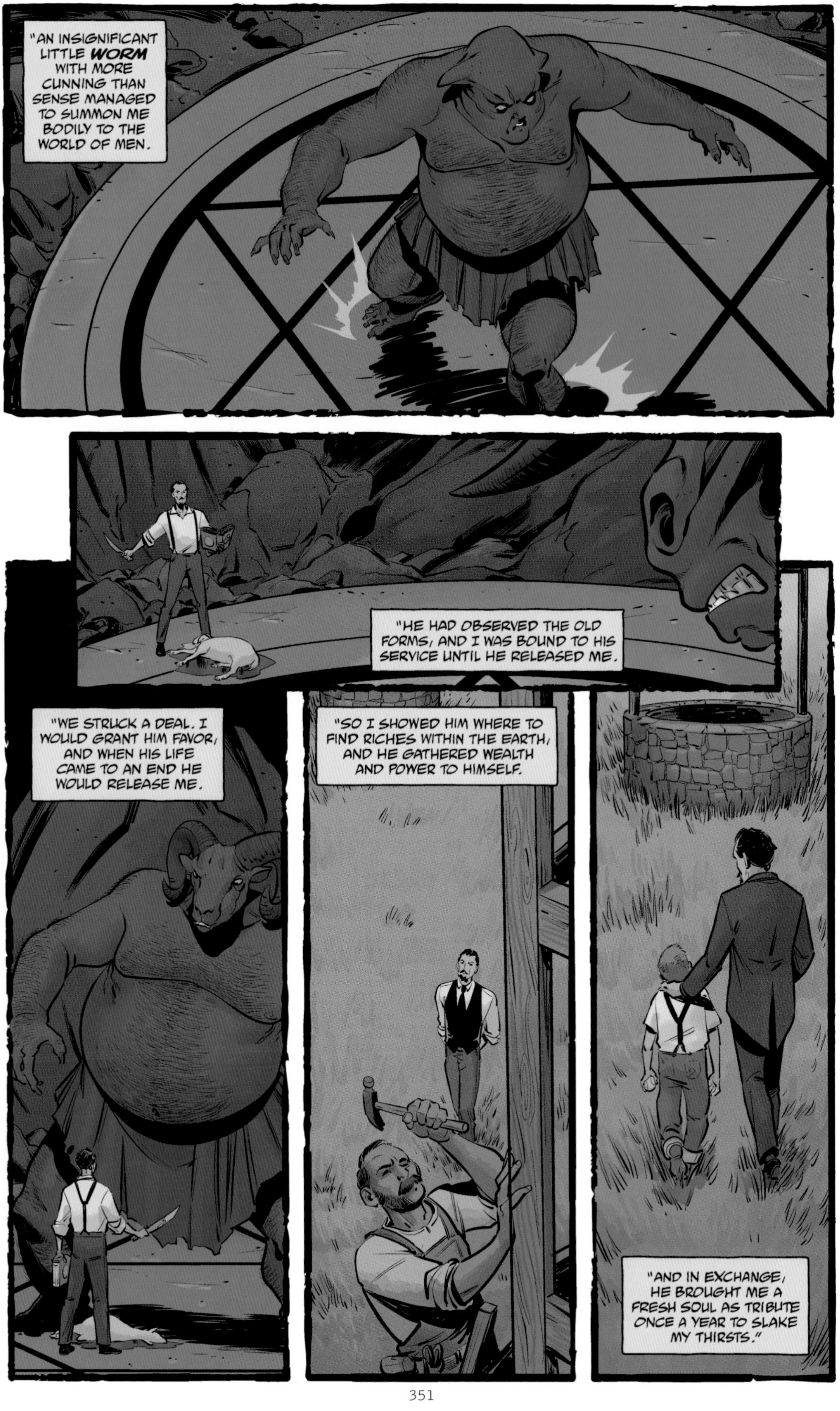
"AN INSIGNIFICANT LITTLE WORM WITH MORE CUNNING THAN SENSE MANAGED TO SUMMON ME BODILY TO THE WORLD OF MEN.
"HE HAD OBSERVED THE OLD FORMS, AND I WAS BOUND TO HIS SERVICE UNTIL HE RELEASED ME.
"WE STRUCK A DEAL. I WOULD GRANT HIM FAVOR, AND WHEN HIS LIFE CAME TO AN END HE WOULD RELEASE ME.
"SO I SHOWED HIM WHERE TO FIND RICHES WITHIN THE EARTH, AND HE GATHERED WEALTH AND POWER TO HIMSELF.
"AND IN EXCHANGE, HE BROUGHT ME A FRESH SOUL AS TRIBUTE ONCE A YEAR TO SLAKE MY THIRSTS."

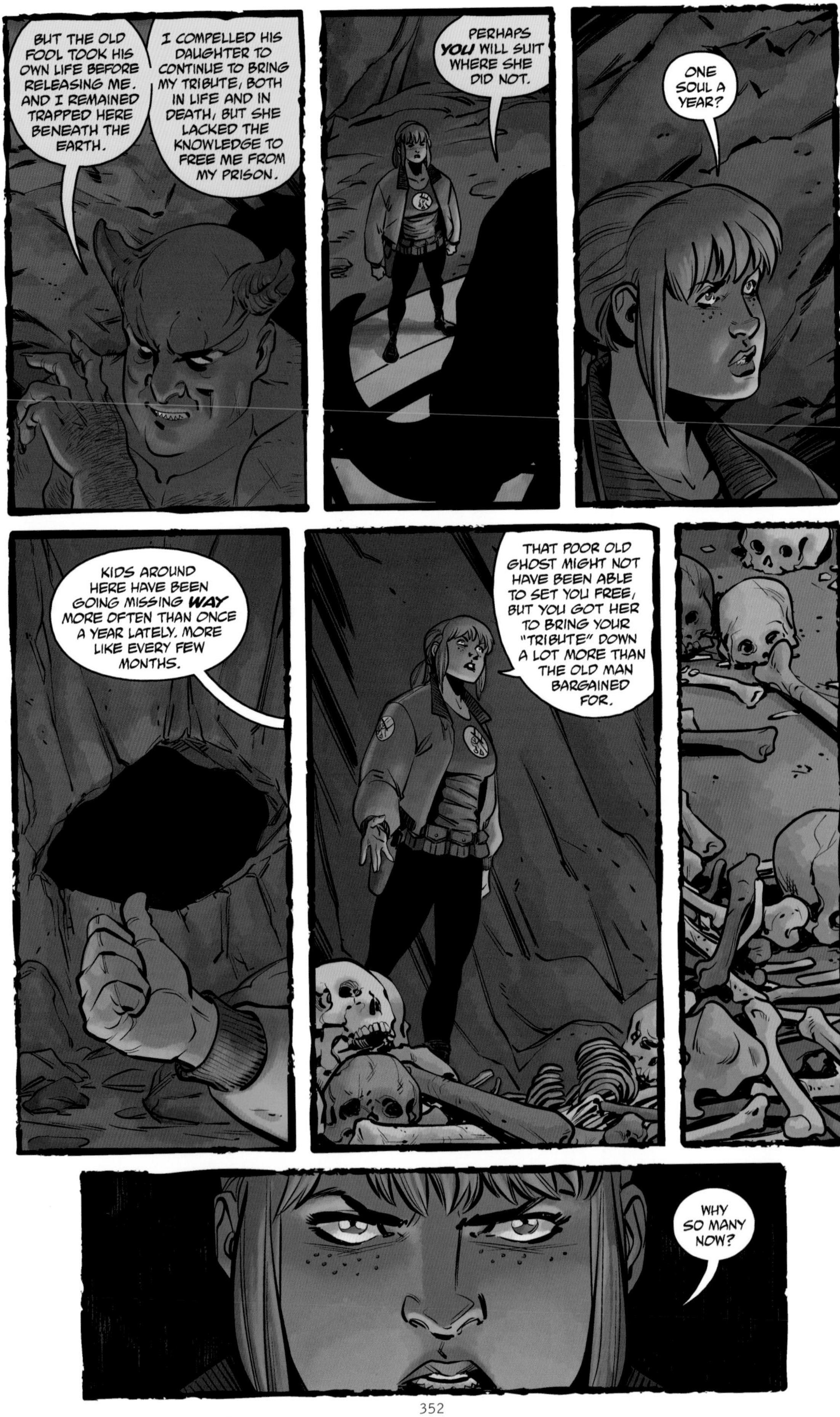

BUT THE OLD FOOL TOOK HIS OWN LIFE BEFORE RELEASING ME. AND I REMAINED TRAPPED HERE BENEATH THE EARTH.
I COMPELLED HIS DAUGHTER TO CONTINUE TO BRING MY TRIBUTE, BOTH IN LIFE AND IN DEATH, BUT SHE LACKED THE KNOWLEDGE TO FREE ME FROM MY PRISON.
PERHAPS YOU WILL SUIT WHERE SHE DID NOT.
ONE SOUL A YEAR?
KIDS AROUND HERE HAVE BEEN GOING MISSING WAY MORE OFTEN THAN ONCE A YEAR LATELY. MORE LIKE EVERY FEW MONTHS.
THAT POOR OLD GHOST MIGHT NOT HAVE BEEN ABLE TO SET YOU FREE, BUT YOU GOT HER TO BRING YOUR "TRIBUTE" DOWN A LOT MORE THAN THE OLD MAN BARGAINED FOR.
WHY SO MANY NOW?

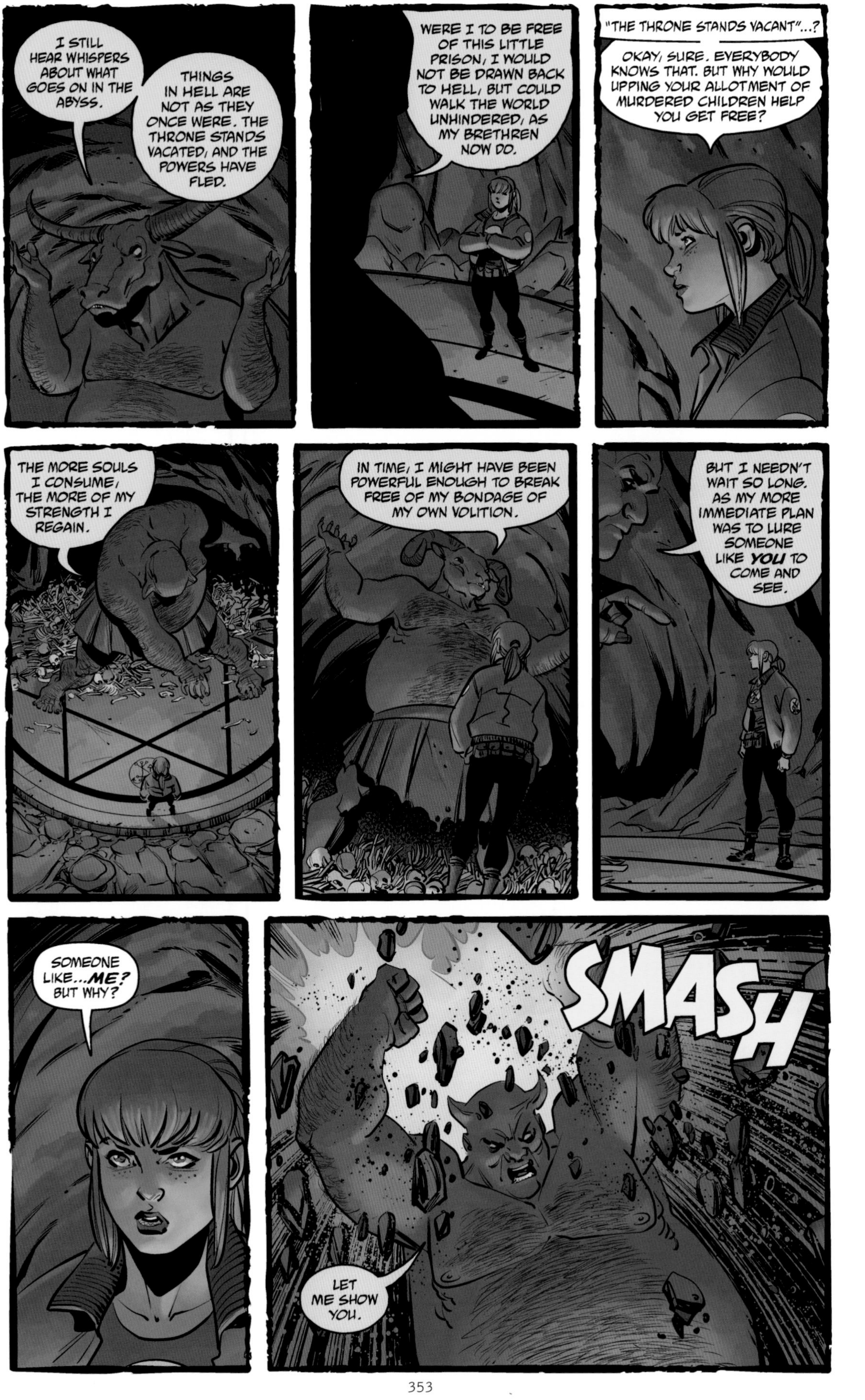
I STILL HEAR WHISPERS ABOUT WHAT GOES ON IN THE ABYSS.
THINGS IN HELL ARE NOT AS THEY ONCE WERE. THE THRONE STANDS VACATED, AND THE POWERS HAVE FLED.
WERE I TO BE FREE OF THIS LITTLE PRISON, I WOULD NOT BE DRAWN BACK TO HELL, BUT COULD WALK THE WORLD UNHINDERED, AS MY BRETHREN NOW DO.
"THE THRONE STANDS VACANT"...?
OKAY, SURE. EVERYBODY KNOWS THAT. BUT WHY WOULD UPPING YOUR ALLOTMENT OF MURDERED CHILDREN HELP YOU GET FREE?
THE MORE SOULS I CONSUME, THE MORE OF MY STRENGTH I REGAIN.
IN TIME, I MIGHT HAVE BEEN POWERFUL ENOUGH TO BREAK FREE OF MY BONDAGE OF MY OWN VOLITION.
BUT I NEEDN'T WAIT SO LONG. AS MY MORE IMMEDIATE PLAN WAS TO LURE SOMEONE LIKE **YOU** TO COME AND SEE.
SOMEONE LIKE...**ME?** BUT WHY?
SMASH
LET ME SHOW YOU.

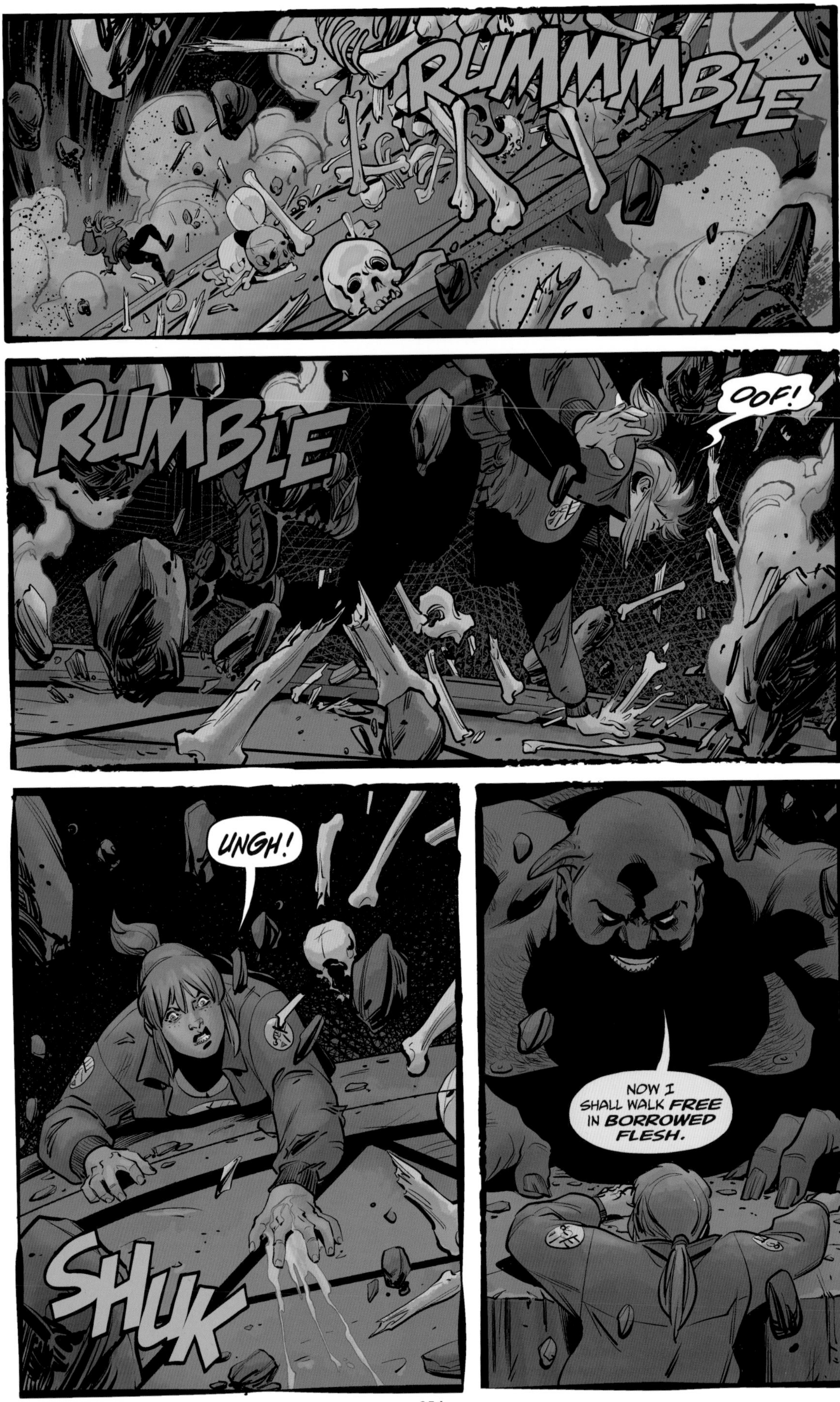
RUMMMBLE
RUMBLE
OOF!
UNGH!
SHUK
NOW I SHALL WALK FREE IN BORROWED FLESH.

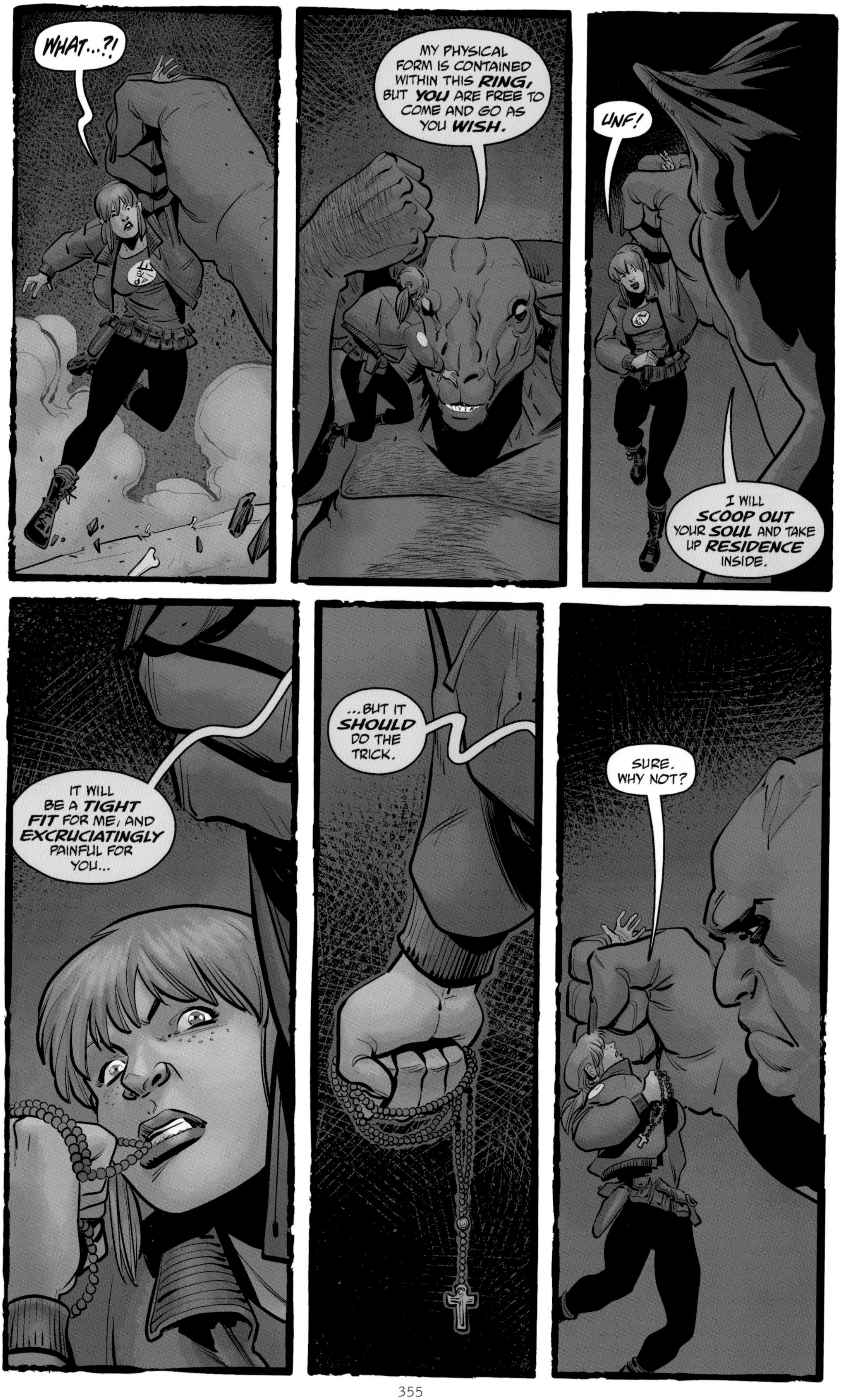
WHAT...?!
MY PHYSICAL FORM IS CONTAINED WITHIN THIS RING, BUT YOU ARE FREE TO COME AND GO AS YOU WISH.
UNF!
I WILL SCOOP OUT YOUR SOUL AND TAKE UP RESIDENCE INSIDE.
IT WILL BE A TIGHT FIT FOR ME, AND EXCRUCIATINGLY PAINFUL FOR YOU...
...BUT IT SHOULD DO THE TRICK.
SURE. WHY NOT?

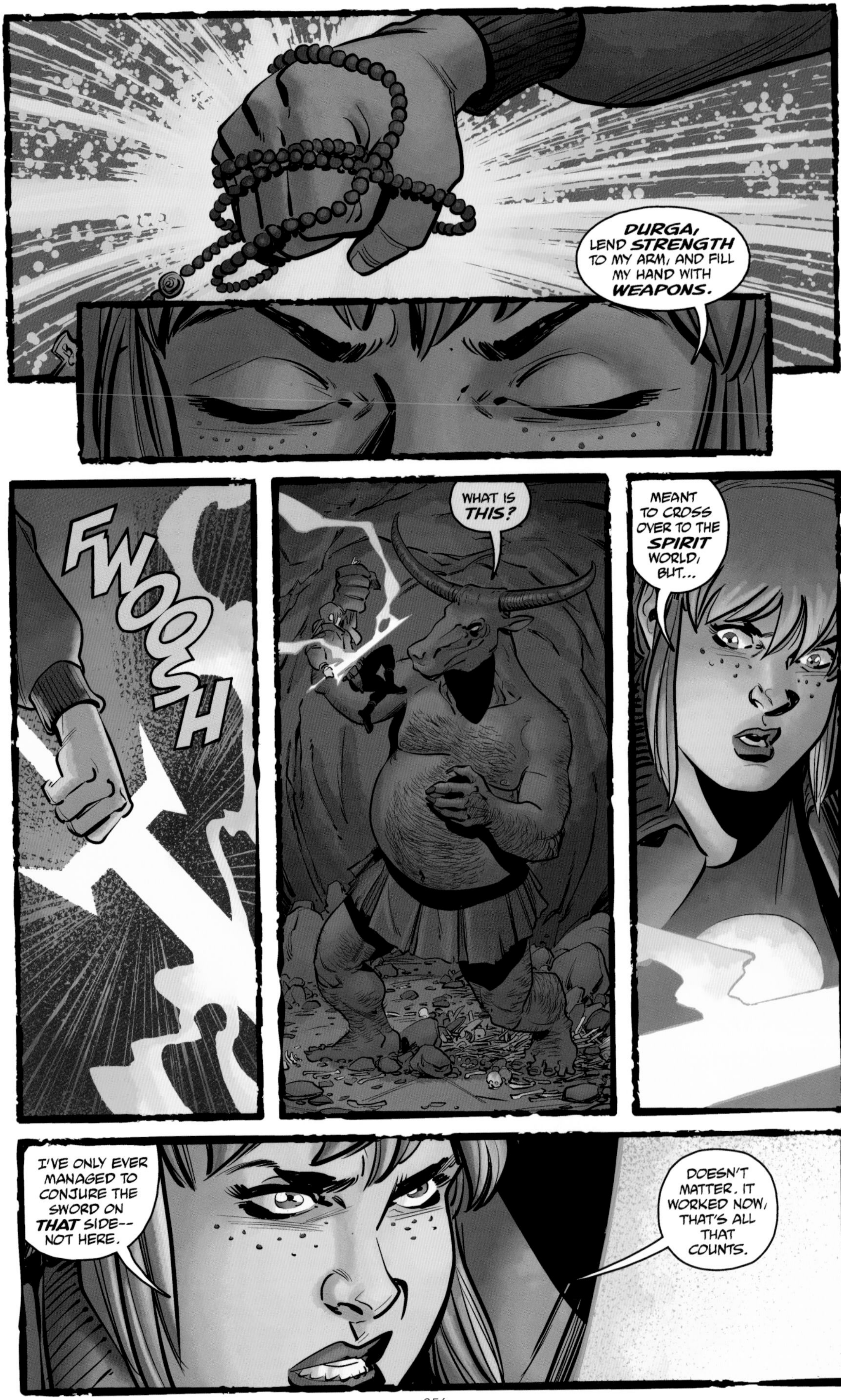
DURGA, LEND STRENGTH TO MY ARM, AND FILL MY HAND WITH WEAPONS.
FWOOSH
WHAT IS THIS?
MEANT TO CROSS OVER TO THE SPIRIT WORLD, BUT...
I'VE ONLY EVER MANAGED TO CONJURE THE SWORD ON THAT SIDE-- NOT HERE.
DOESN'T MATTER. IT WORKED NOW, THAT'S ALL THAT COUNTS.

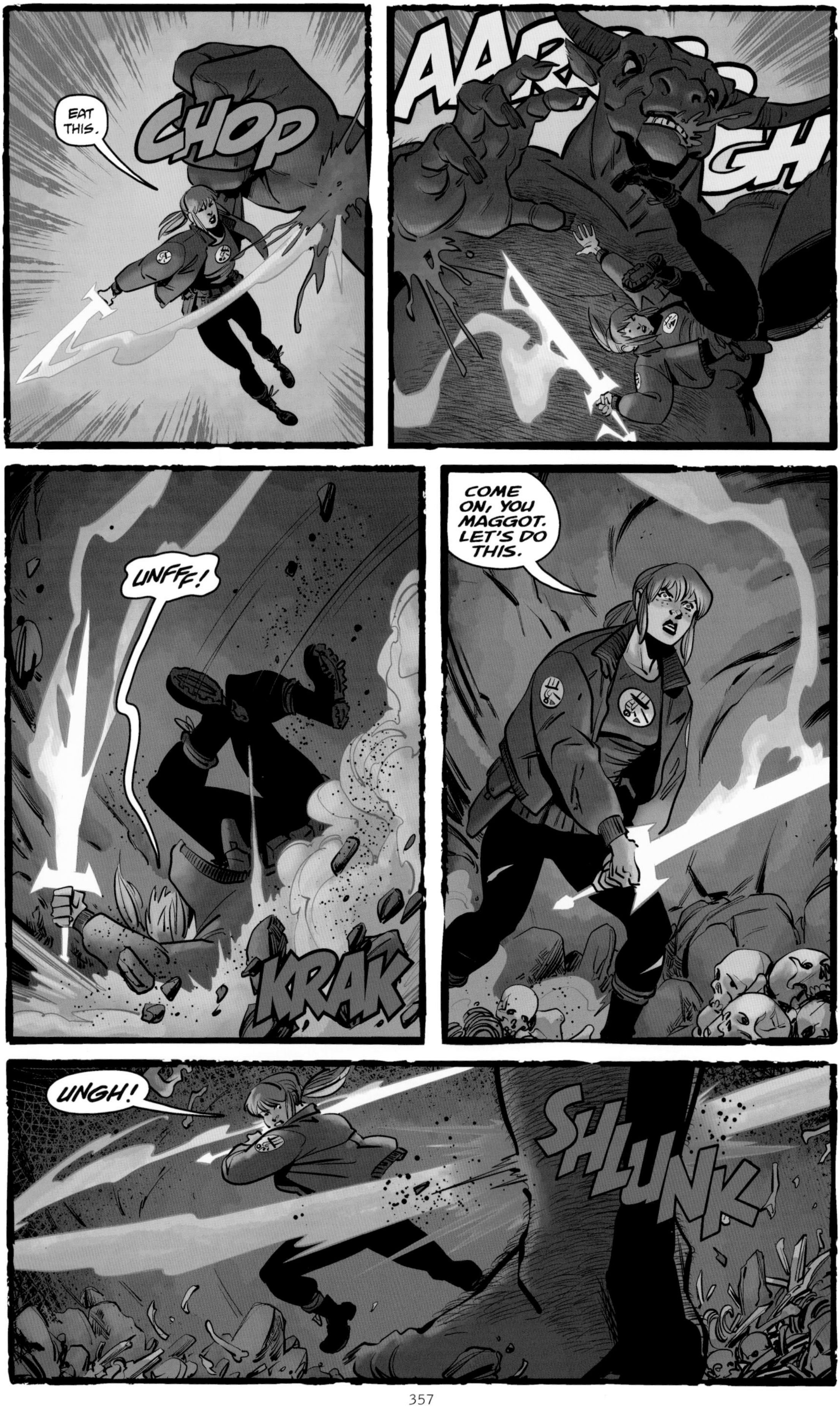
EAT THIS.
CHOP
UNFFF!
KRAK
COME ON, YOU MAGGOT. LET'S DO THIS.
UNGH!
SHLUNK

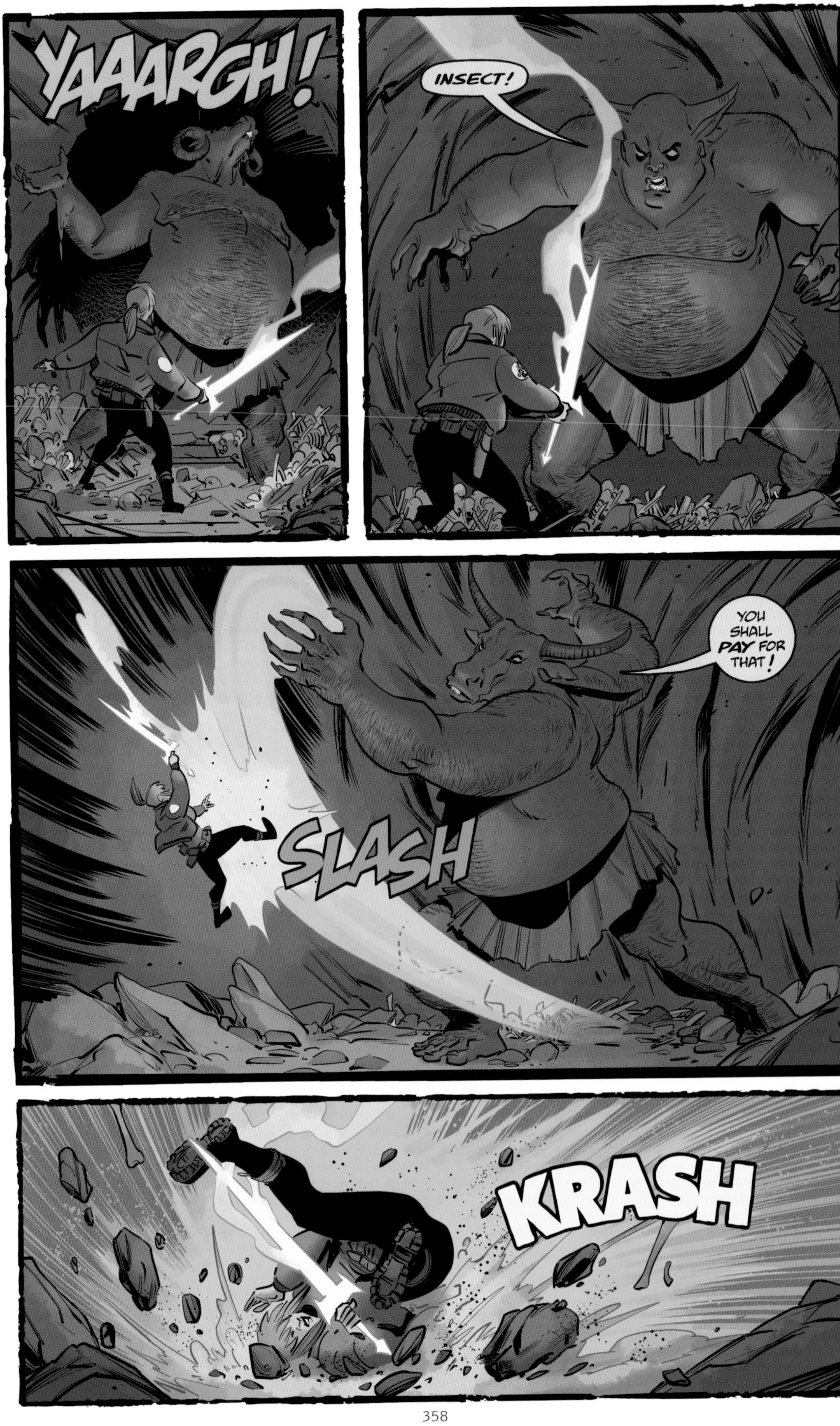
YAAARGH!
INSECT!
YOU SHALL PAY FOR THAT!
SLASH
KRASH

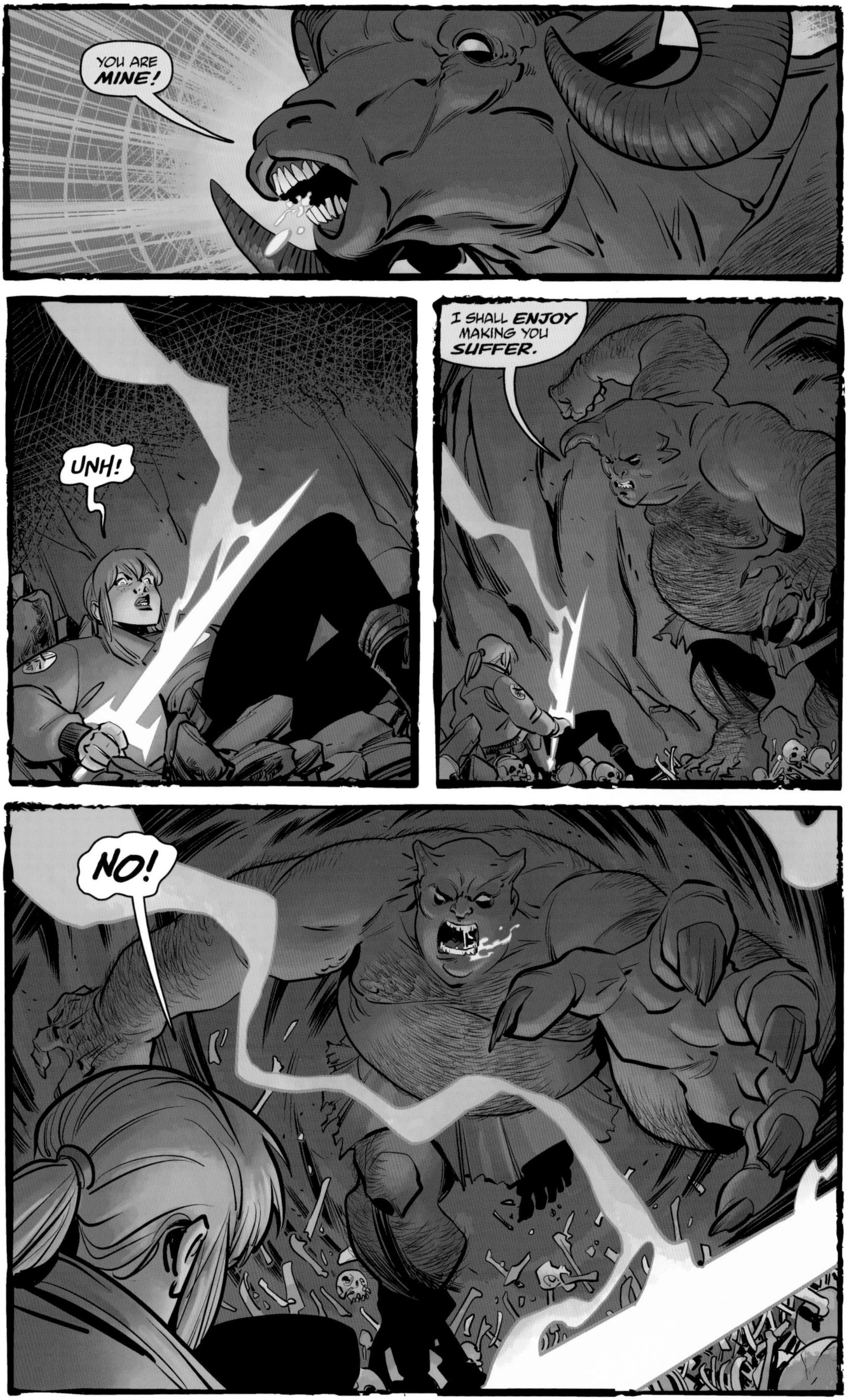

YOU ARE MINE!
UNH!
I SHALL ENJOY MAKING YOU SUFFER.
NO!

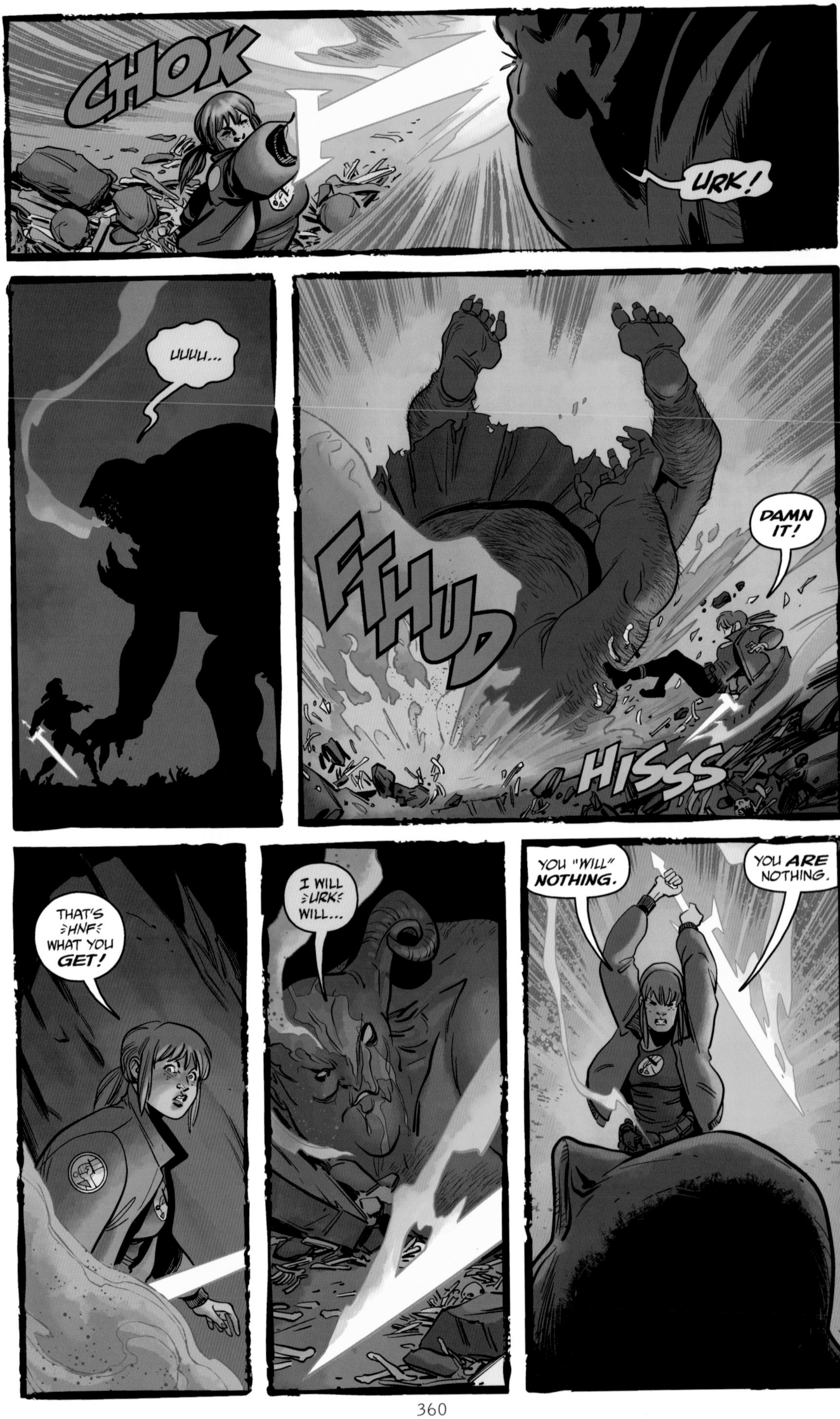
CHOK
URK!
UUUU...
FTHUD
DAMN IT!
HISSS
THAT'S HNF WHAT YOU GET!
I WILL URK WILL...
YOU "WILL" NOTHING.
YOU ARE NOTHING.

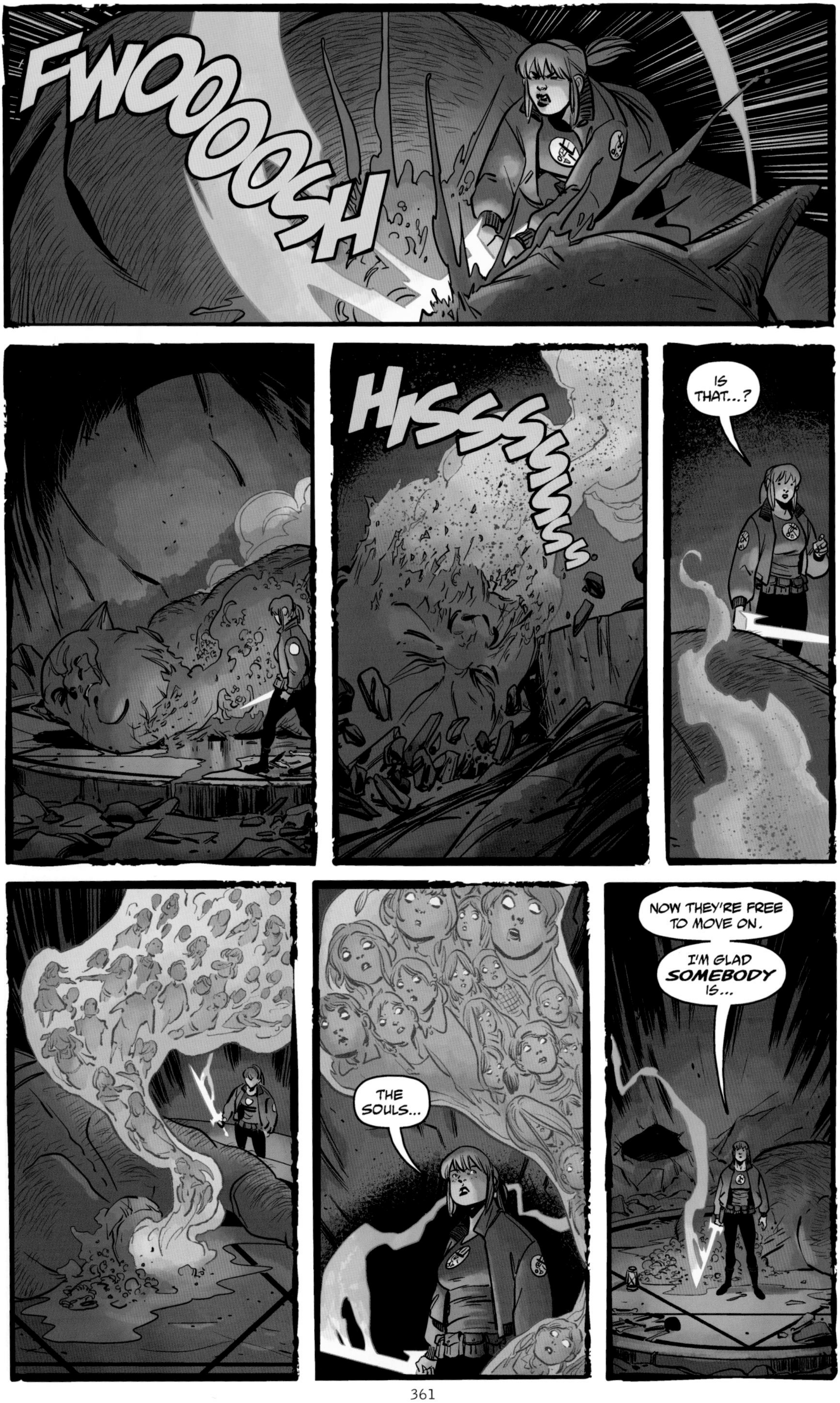

FWOOOOOSH
HISSSSSSS
IS THAT...?
THE SOULS...
NOW THEY'RE FREE TO MOVE ON.
I'M GLAD **SOMEBODY** IS...

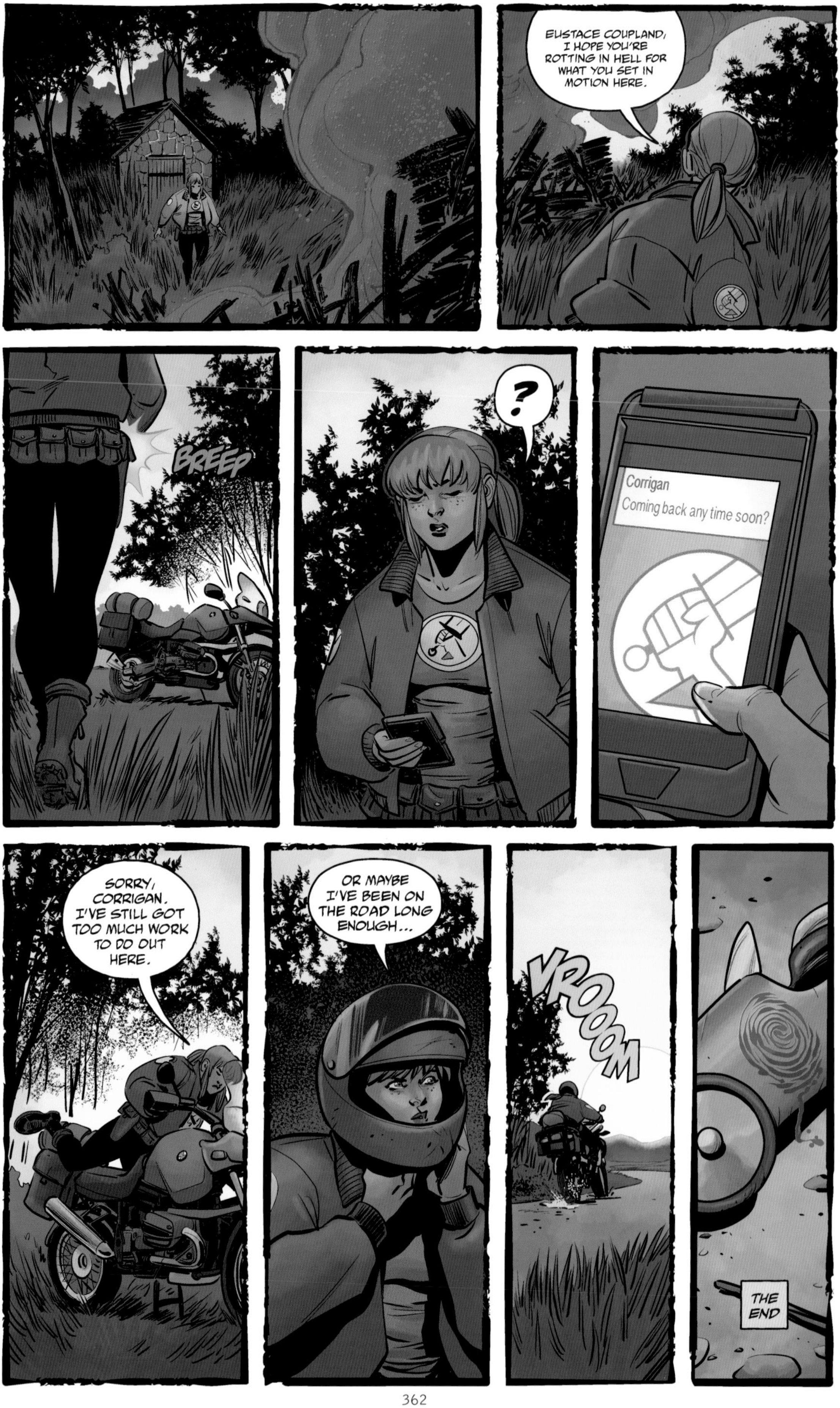
EUSTACE COUPLAND, I HOPE YOU'RE ROTTING IN HELL FOR WHAT YOU SET IN MOTION HERE.
BREEP
?
Corrigan
Coming back any time soon?
SORRY, CORRIGAN. I'VE STILL GOT TOO MUCH WORK TO DO OUT HERE.
OR MAYBE I'VE BEEN ON THE ROAD LONG ENOUGH...
VROOOM
THE END

B.P.R.D.™

SKETCHBOOK

Notes by the artists

THE BROKEN EQUATION

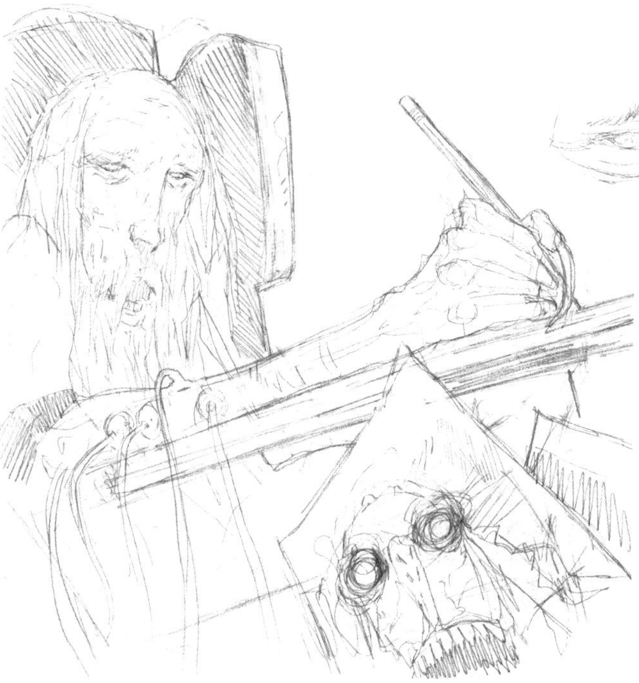

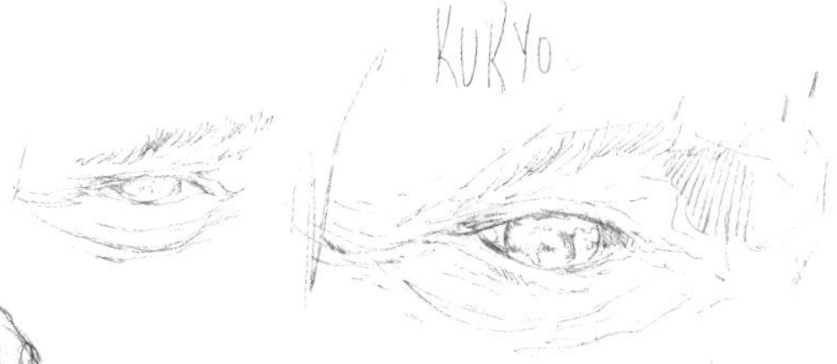
KUKYO

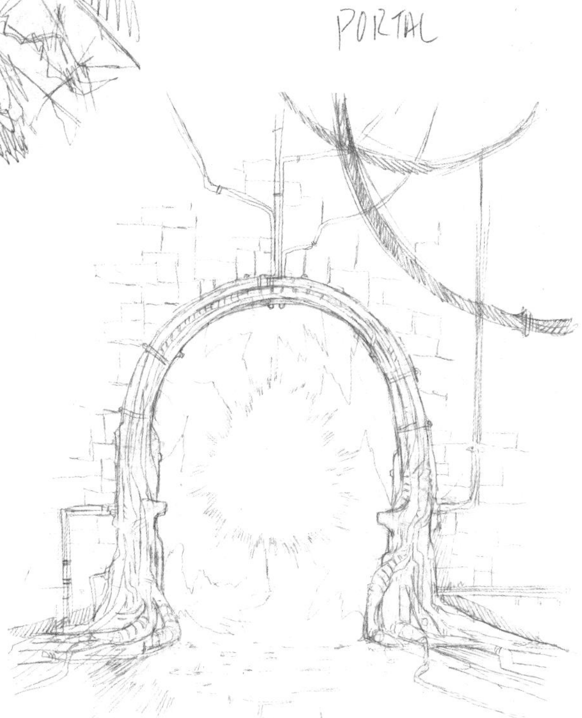
PORTAL

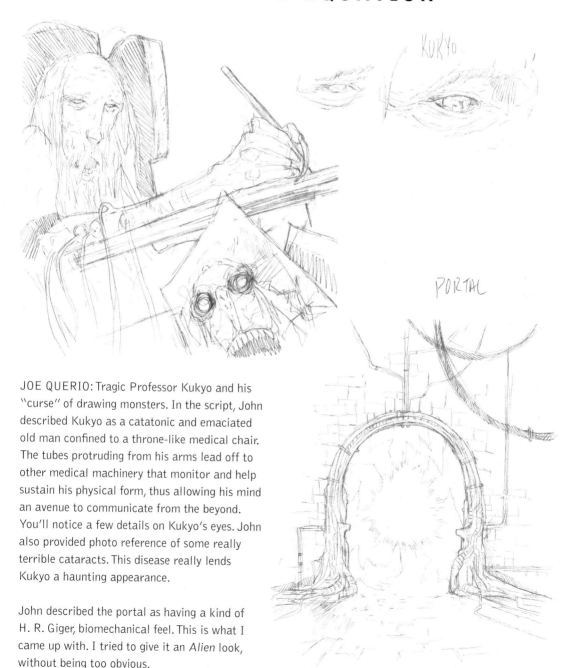

JOE QUERIO: Tragic Professor Kukyo and his "curse" of drawing monsters. In the script, John described Kukyo as a catatonic and emaciated old man confined to a throne-like medical chair. The tubes protruding from his arms lead off to other medical machinery that monitor and help sustain his physical form, thus allowing his mind an avenue to communicate from the beyond. You'll notice a few details on Kukyo's eyes. John also provided photo reference of some really terrible cataracts. This disease really lends Kukyo a haunting appearance.

John described the portal as having a kind of H. R. Giger, biomechanical feel. This is what I came up with. I tried to give it an *Alien* look, without being too obvious.

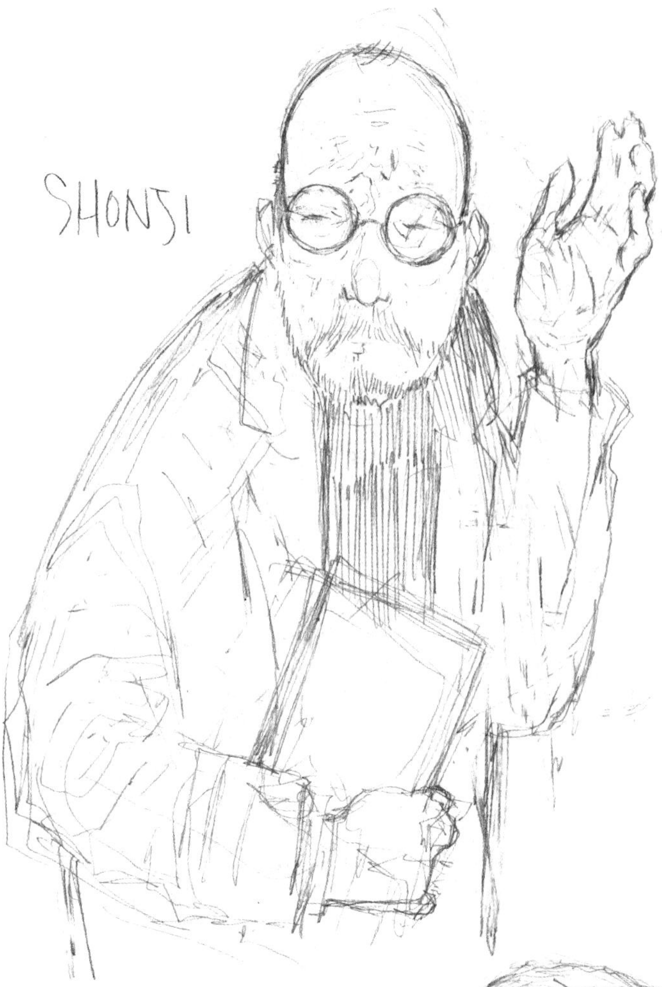
SHONJI

Some new characters here. Well, one, at least. I tried to make Shonji an innocent, unassuming doctor. Not much more to say than that. Sansom was described as being the weathered leader of the team (though I think Johann outranks him). I tried to give Sansom a kind of hard-ass but, at the same time, defeated look. Not too sure if it translates, but that's what I was going for.

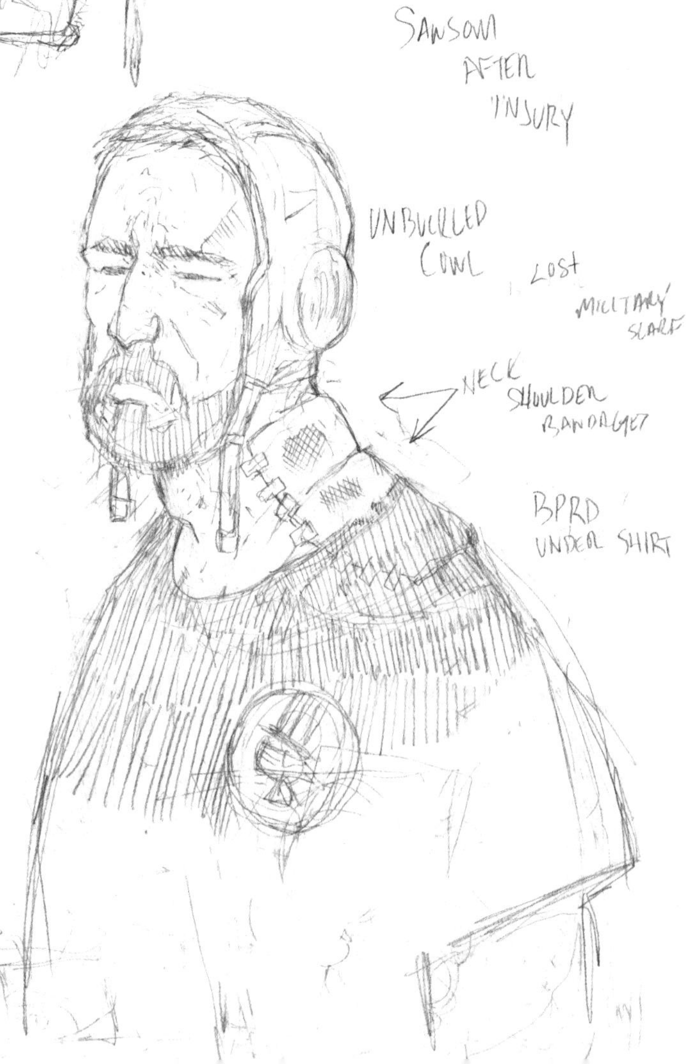
SANSOM
AFTER
INJURY
UNBUCKLED
COWL
LOST
MILITARY
SCARF
NECK
SHOULDER
BANDAGES
BPRD
UNDER SHIRT

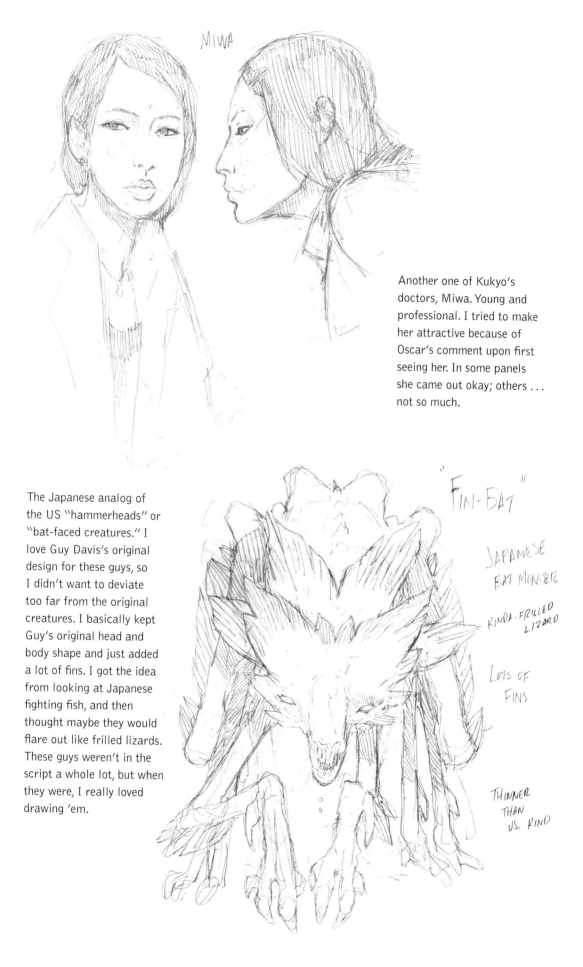

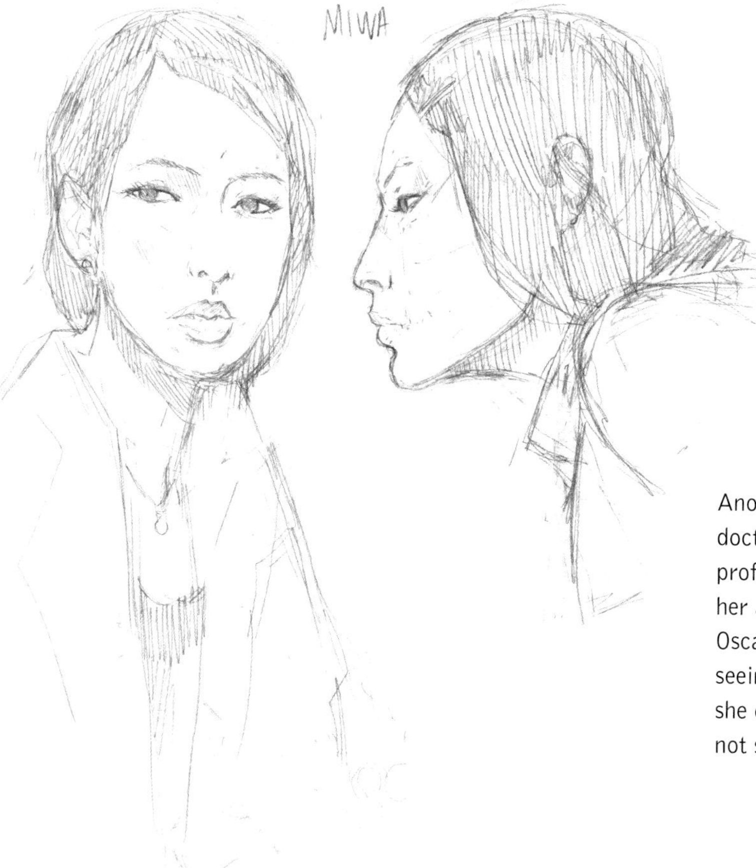
MIWA

Another one of Kukyo's doctors, Miwa. Young and professional. I tried to make her attractive because of Oscar's comment upon first seeing her. In some panels she came out okay; others . . . not so much.

The Japanese analog of the US "hammerheads" or "bat-faced creatures." I love Guy Davis's original design for these guys, so I didn't want to deviate too far from the original creatures. I basically kept Guy's original head and body shape and just added a lot of fins. I got the idea from looking at Japanese fighting fish, and then thought maybe they would flare out like frilled lizards. These guys weren't in the script a whole lot, but when they were, I really loved drawing 'em.

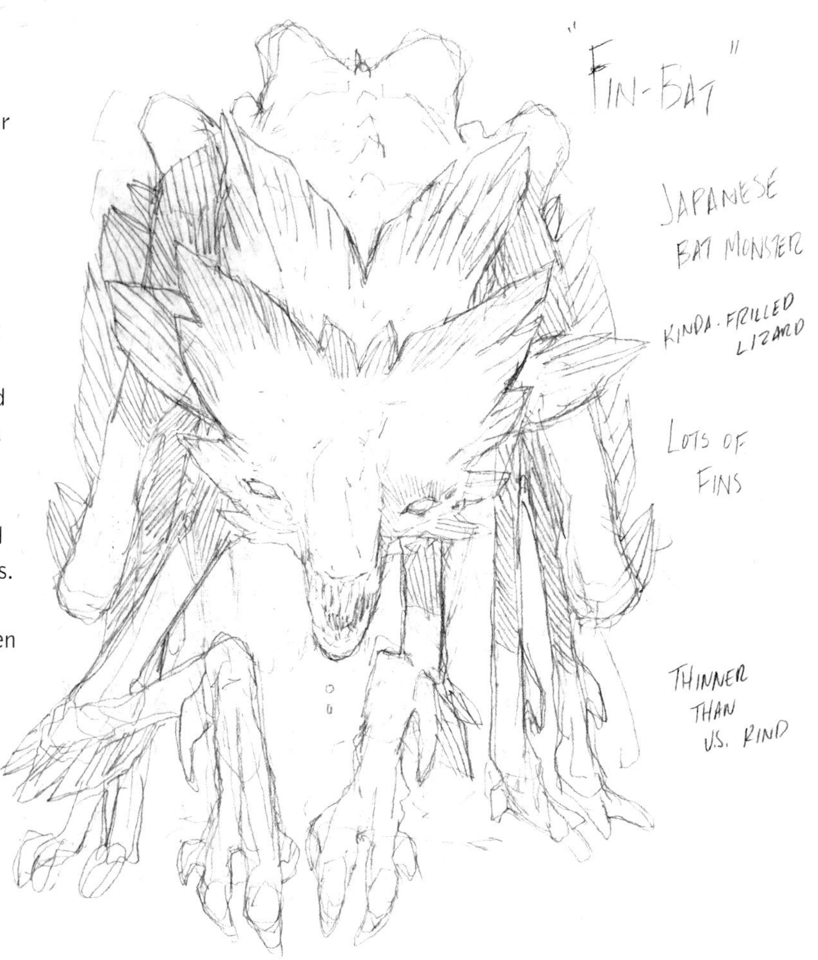
"FIN-BAT"
JAPANESE BAT MONSTER
KINDA-FRILLED LIZARD
LOTS OF FINS
THINNER THAN U.S. KIND

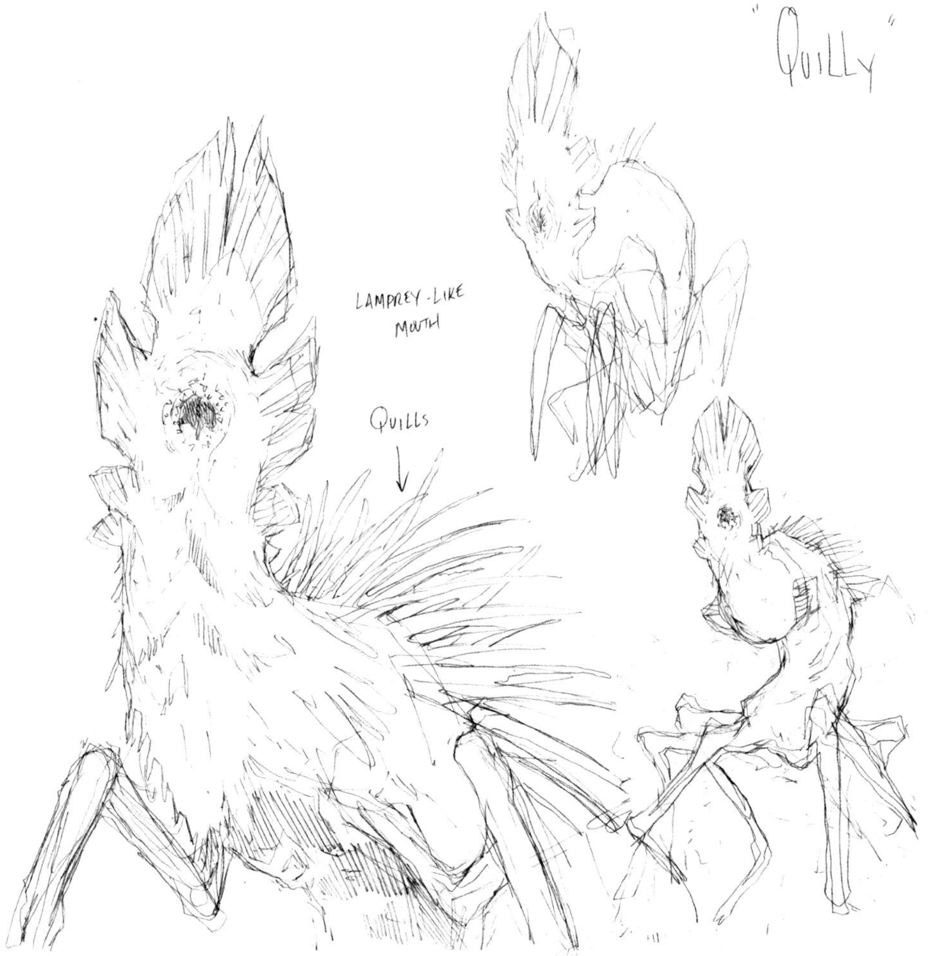
"Quilly"
LAMPREY-LIKE MOUTH
QUILLS

One of the Ogdru Hem. John's script basically said he just had to have quills somewhere. So I had a lot of freedom with him. "Quilly's" look was inspired by my favorite childhood show, Ultraman—though you really don't see that in the final design. I tried to give him a memorable head shape that would look menacing in silhouette. So I thought, more fins! The lower half of his body didn't really work, however. John said it looked too similar to "Brain," the other Ogdru Hem terrorizing Saitama. Mike then jumped in and redesigned its entire lower half. He seriously designed it in, like, fifteen to thirty minutes, and it was perfect!

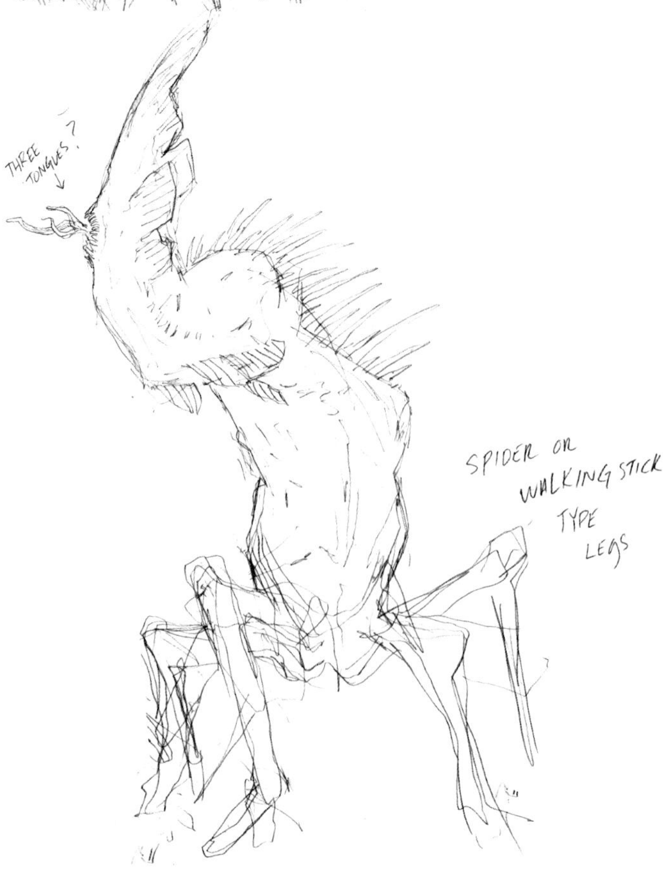
THREE TONGUES?
SPIDER OR WALKING STICK TYPE LEGS

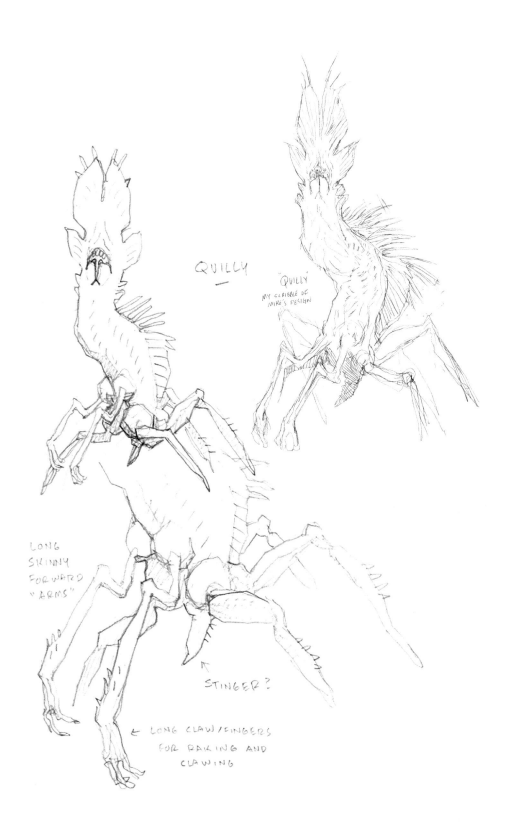

QUILLY

"QUILLY"
MY SCRIBBLE OF
MIKE'S DESIGN

LONG
SKINNY
FORWARD
"ARMS"

STINGER?

← LONG CLAW/FINGERS
FOR RAKING AND
CLAWING

Mike's take on Quilly.

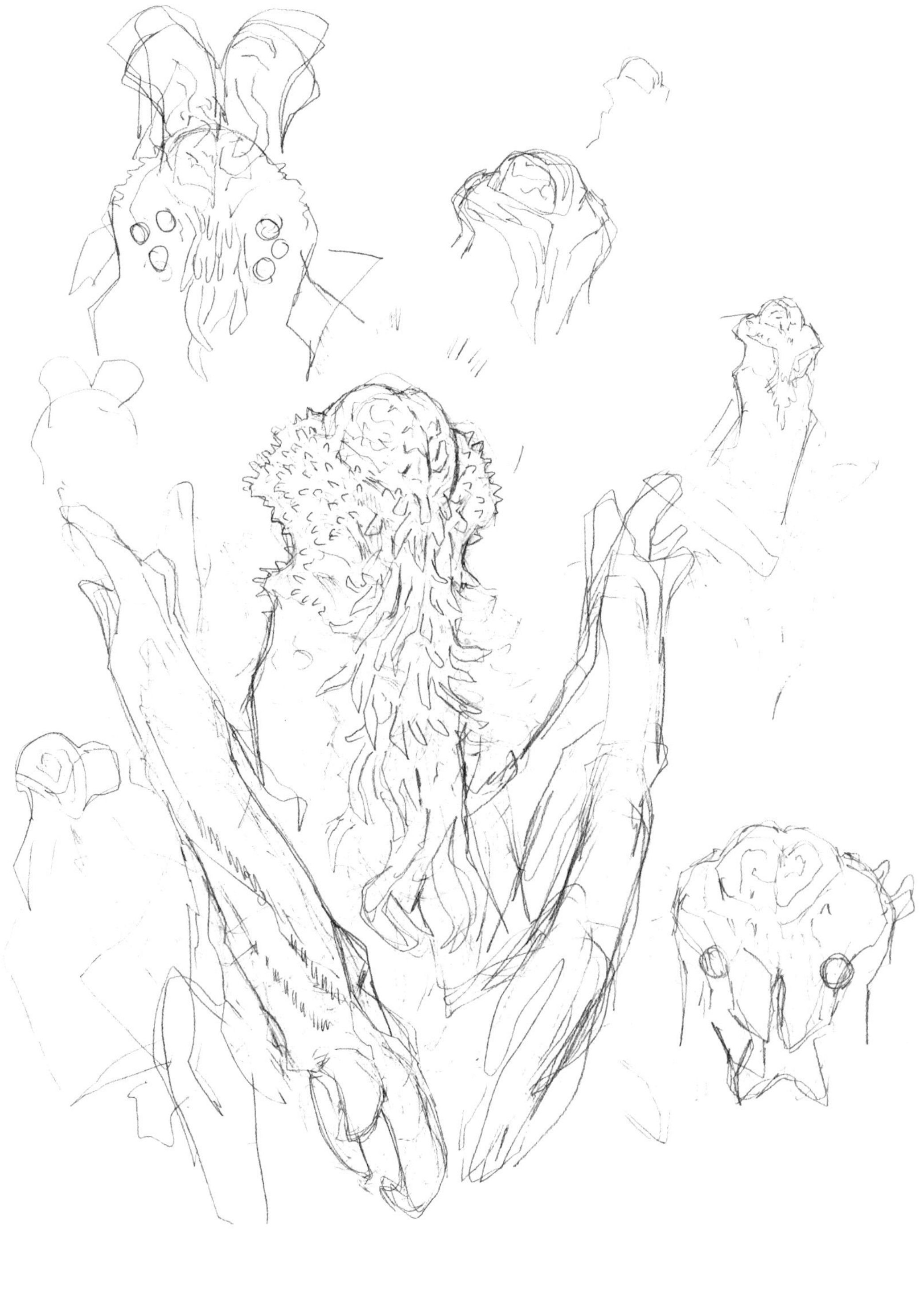

The other Ogdru Hem, "Brain." This one went through a lot of designs and changes. The next couple of pages show the variations. Another fun monster to design and draw.

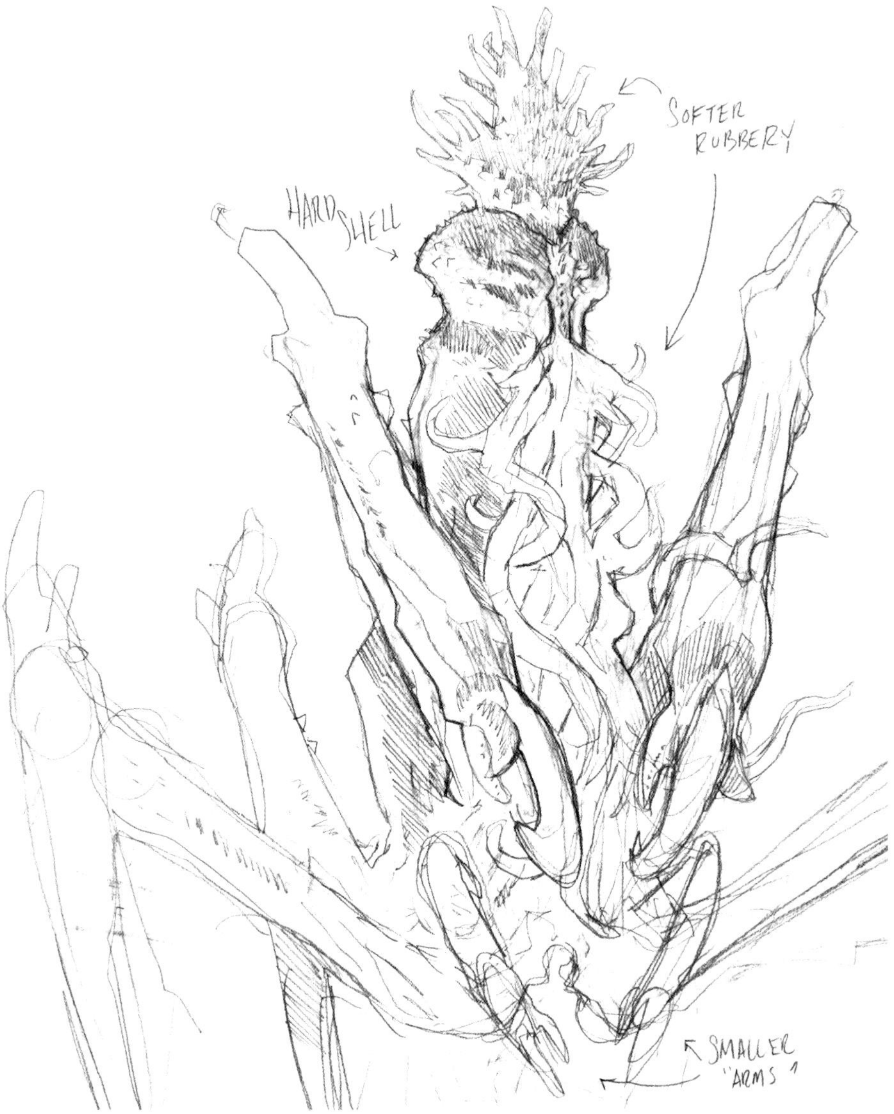
SOFTER
RUBBERY
HARD SHELL
SMALLER
"ARMS"

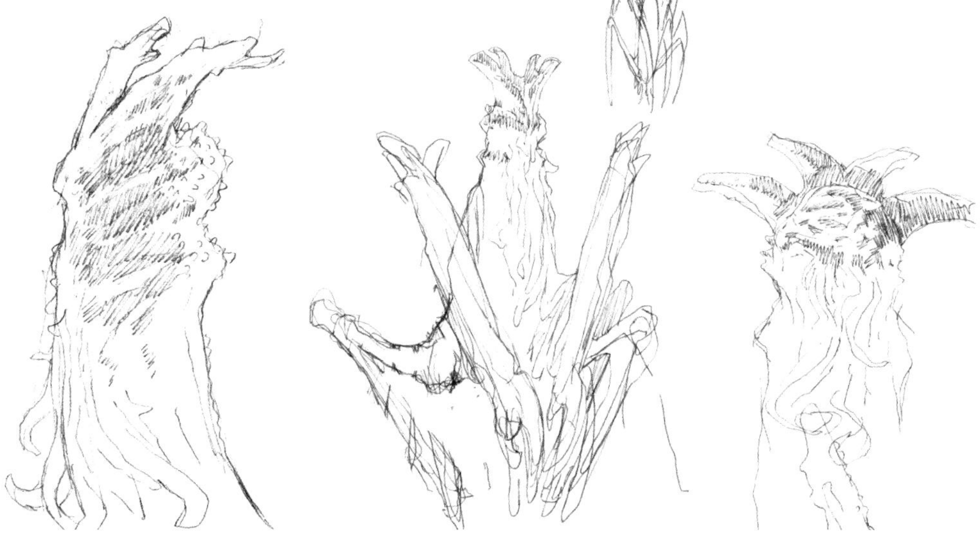

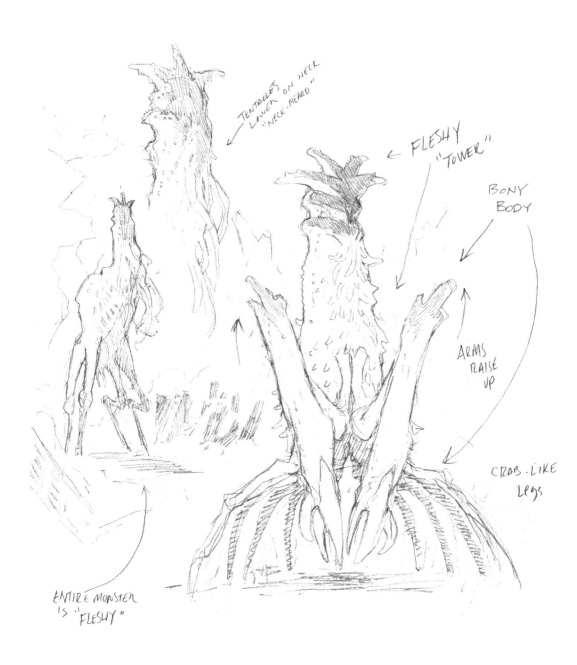

TENTACLES ON NECK
LOWER "NECK BEARD"

← FLESHY "TOWER"

BONY BODY

ARMS RAISE UP

CRAB-LIKE LEGS

ENTIRE MONSTER IS "FLESHY"

Facing: This guy is one of my favorites. Six astronauts smashed into one living organism. I was beaming with excitement when I read the pages with these hopeless "Challengers of the Unknown," as John described them. John wrote to me, "Just imagine an evil god using a bunch of bodies to make a big doll. He pulls off some pieces, smashes others together, and then there's this thing that can walk, and punch, and it can breathe because of the heads, but otherwise, it's just thrashing around." Seriously, who wouldn't be stoked about getting to design that!

Following page: Final design.

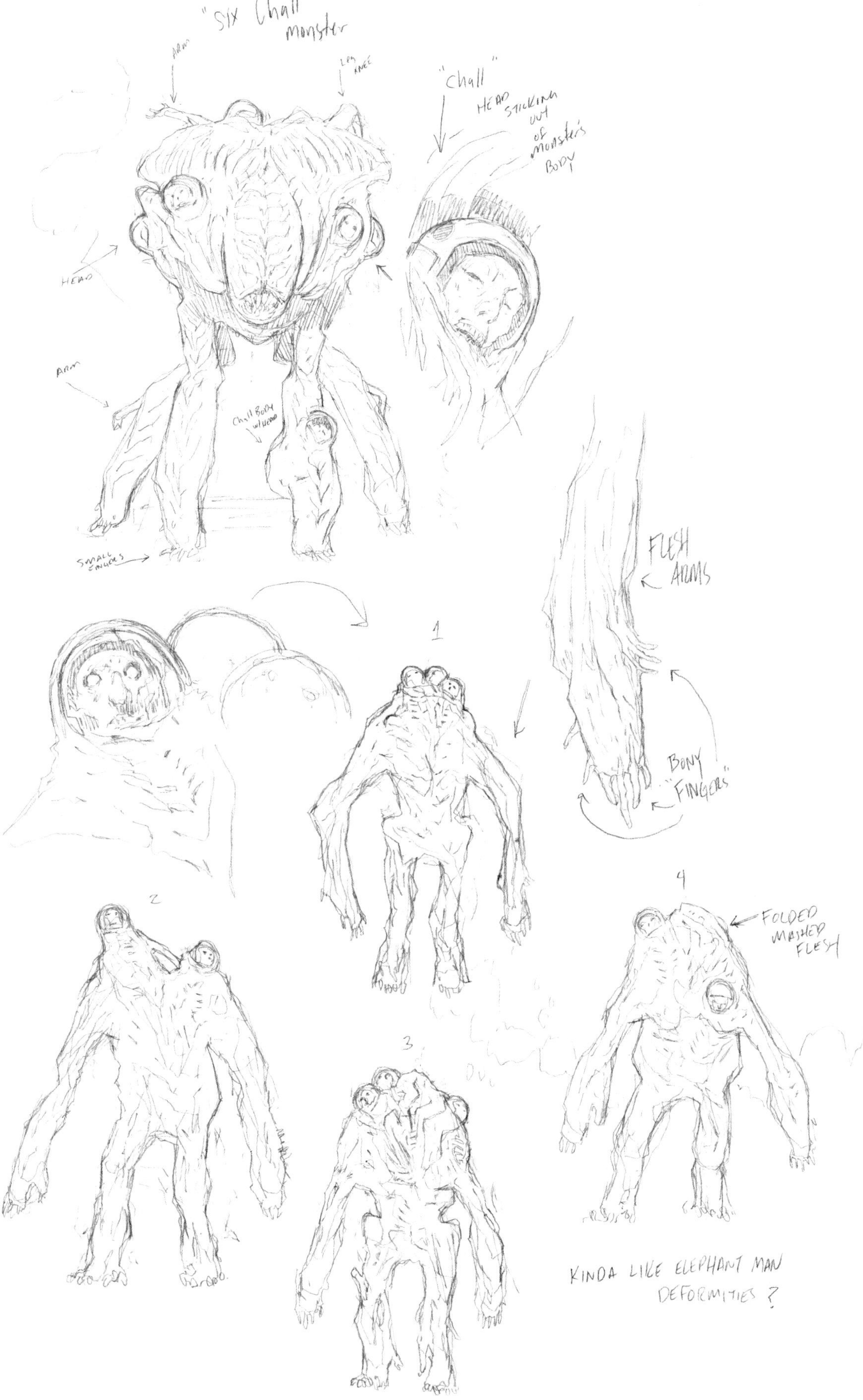
"Six Chall" monster
ARM
LEG KNEE
"Chall" HEAD STICKING OUT OF MONSTER'S BODY
HEAD
ARM
Chall Body w/ HEAD
SMALL FINGERS
FLESH ARMS
BONY "FINGERS"
1
2
3
4
FOLDED MASHED FLESH
KINDA LIKE ELEPHANT MAN DEFORMITIES?

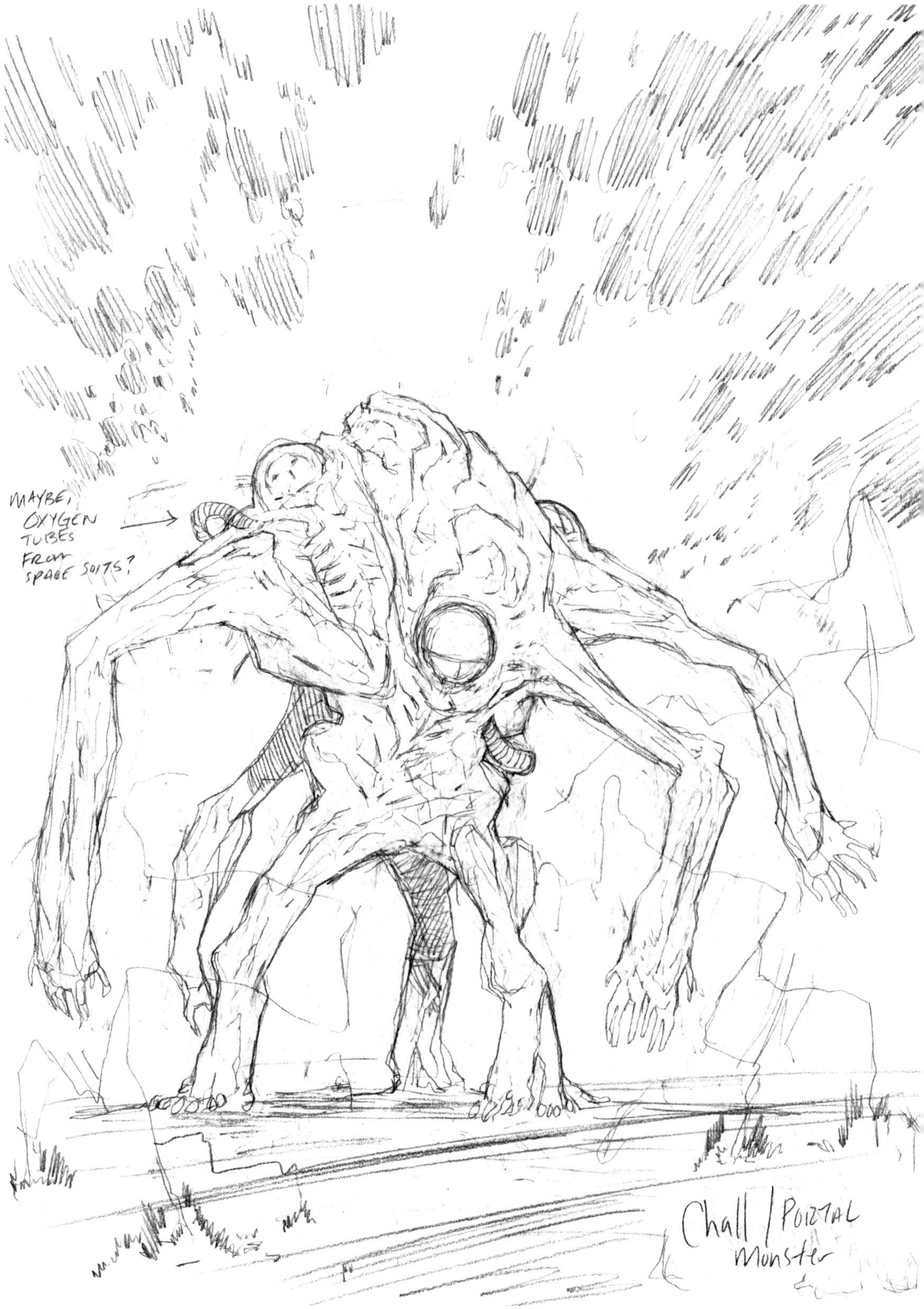
MAYBE, OXYGEN TUBES FROM SPACE SUITS?
Chall / PORTAL Monster

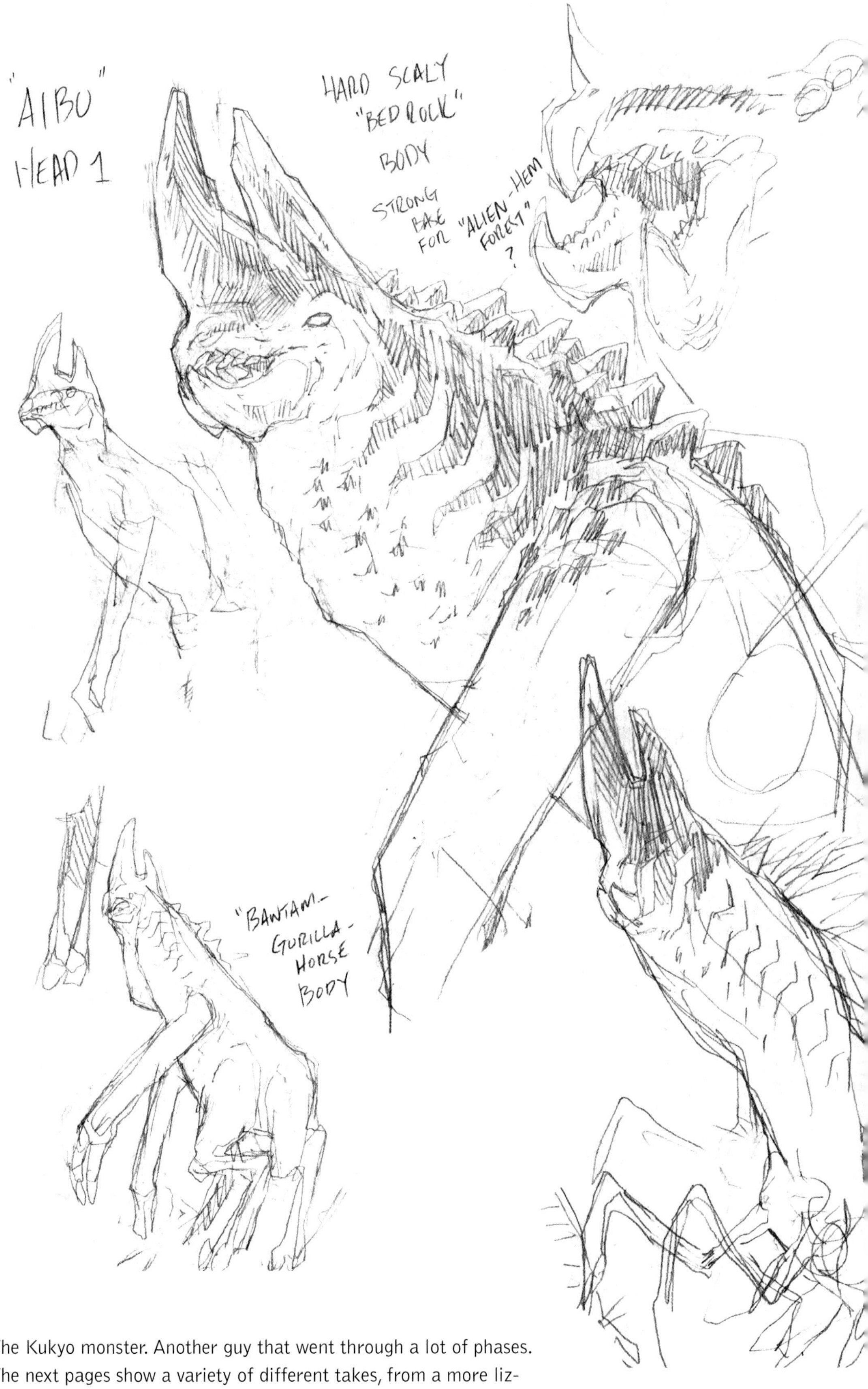
"AIBO"
HEAD 1
HARD SCALY
"BEDROCK"
BODY
STRONG
BASE
FOR "ALIEN-HEM
FOREST"
?
"BANTAM-
GORILLA-
HORSE
BODY

The Kukyo monster. Another guy that went through a lot of phases. The next pages show a variety of different takes, from a more lizard-like creature to a wild-eyed monkey. In the end, Scott had me combine different elements until "Aibo" got his final form.

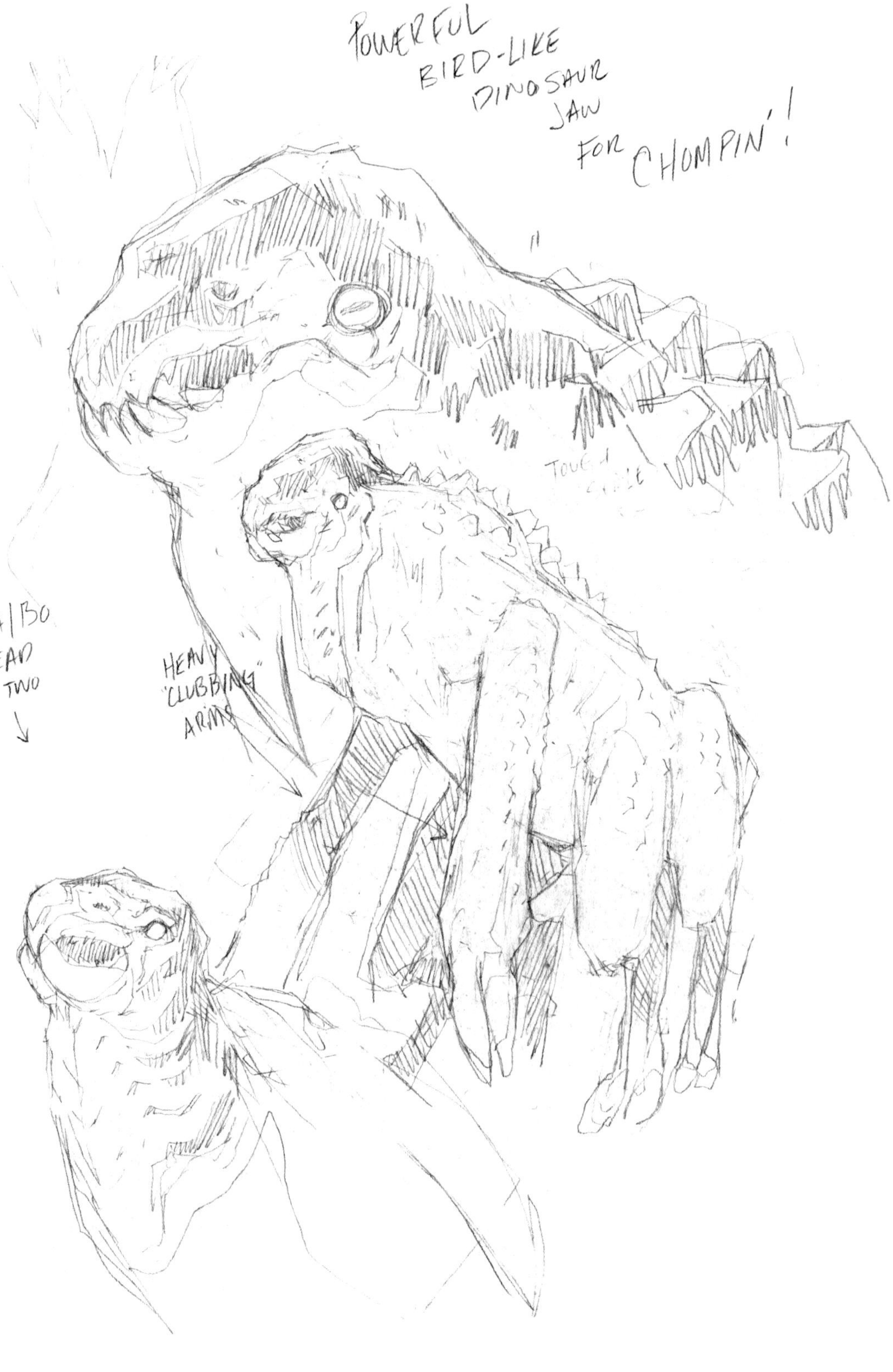
POWERFUL BIRD-LIKE DINOSAUR JAW FOR CHOMPIN'!
TOUGH
AIBO HEAD TWO
HEAVY "CLUBBING" ARMS

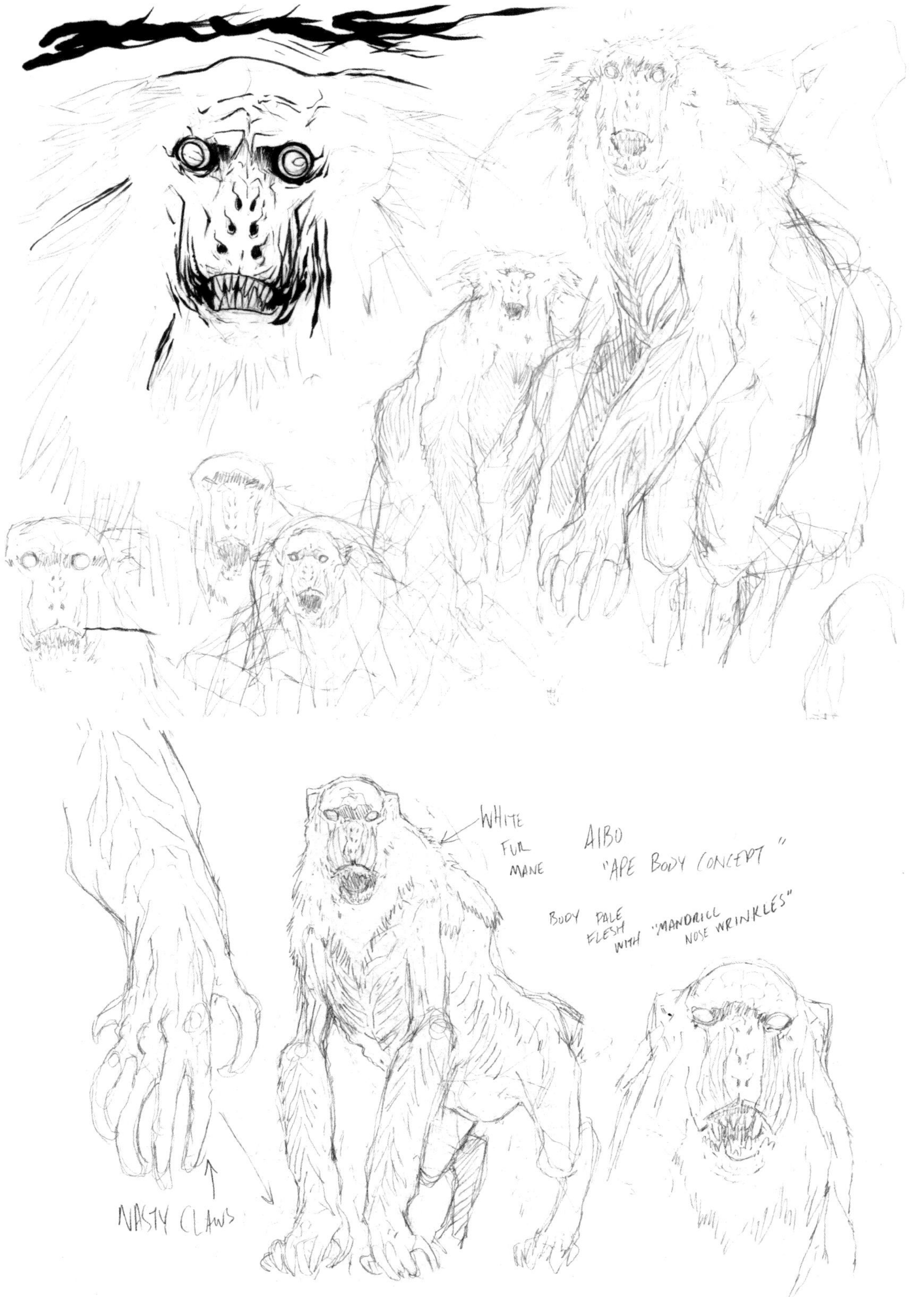
WHITE
FUR
MANE
AIBO
"APE BODY CONCEPT"
BODY PALE
FLESH
WITH "MANDRILL
NOSE WRINKLES"
NASTY CLAWS

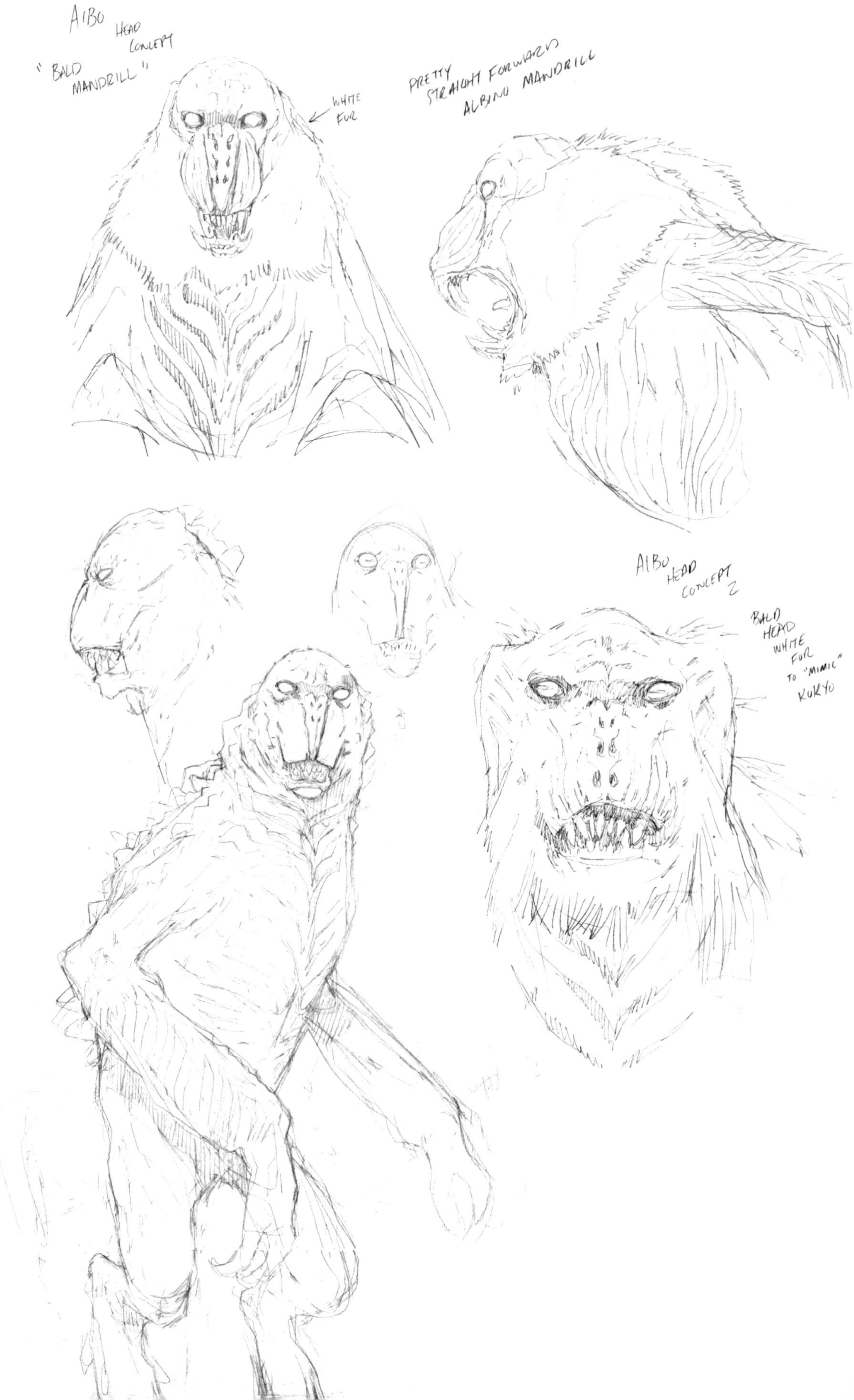
AIBO HEAD CONCEPT
"BALD MANDRILL"
WHITE FUR
PRETTY STRAIGHT FORWARD ALBINO MANDRILL
AIBO HEAD CONCEPT 2
BALD HEAD WHITE FUR TO "MIMIC" KUKYO

GRIND

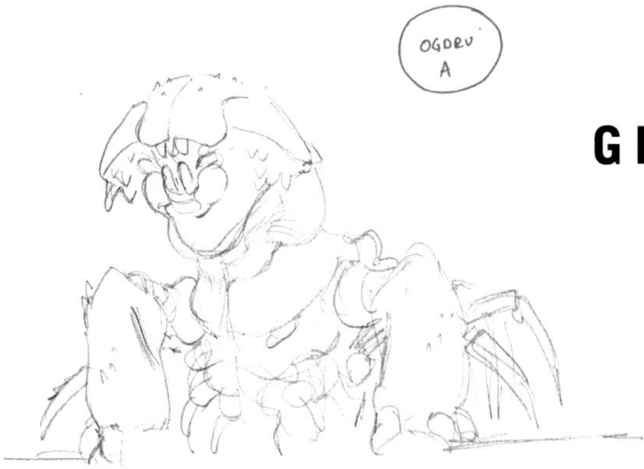
OGDRU A

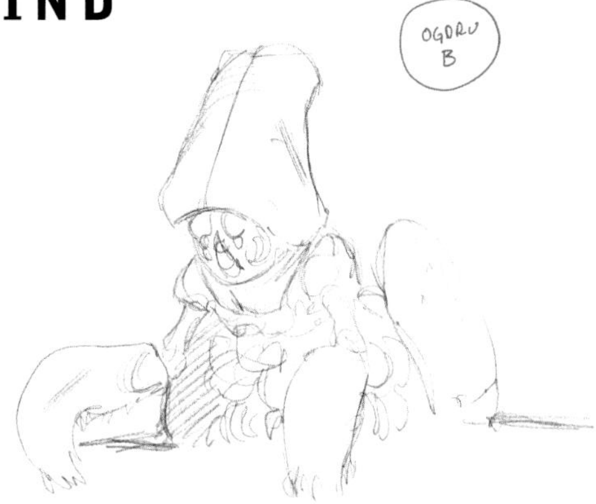
OGDRU B

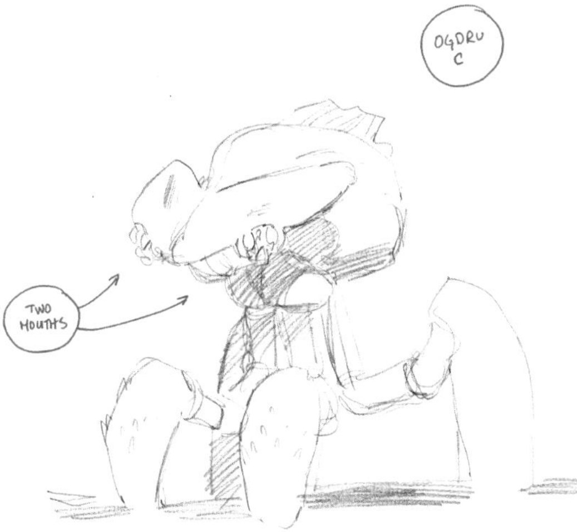
OGDRU C
TWO MOUTHS

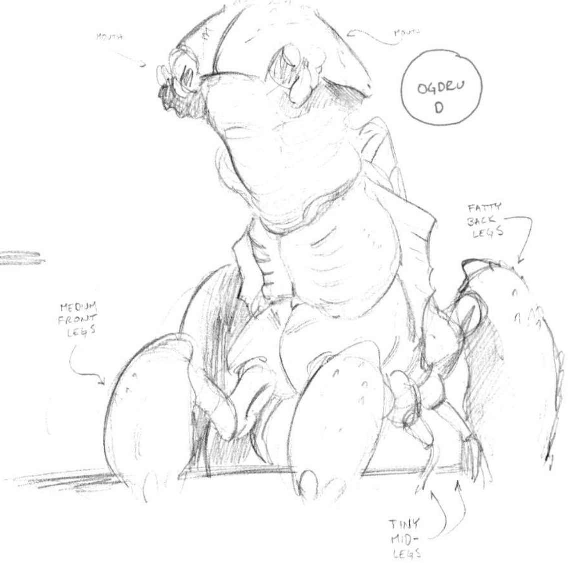
MOUTH
OGDRU D
FATTY BACK LEGS
MEDIUM FRONT LEGS
TINY MID-LEGS

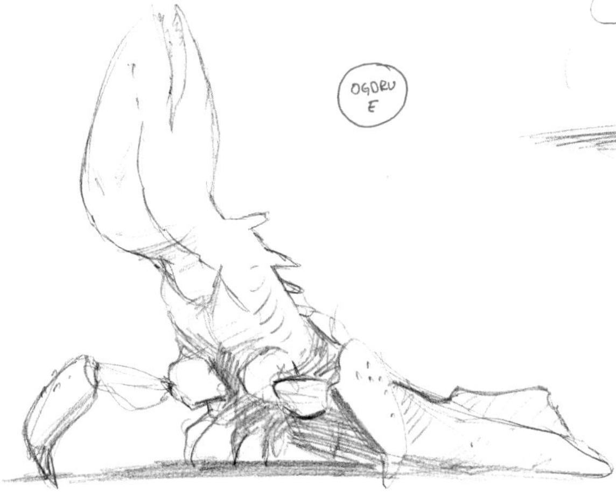
OGDRU E

TYLER CROOK: At this point it's getting harder and harder to come up with new and unique Ogdru designs that still look like they belong to the same family. There is a very specific aesthetic to these things, but that can kind of limit you at the end of the day.

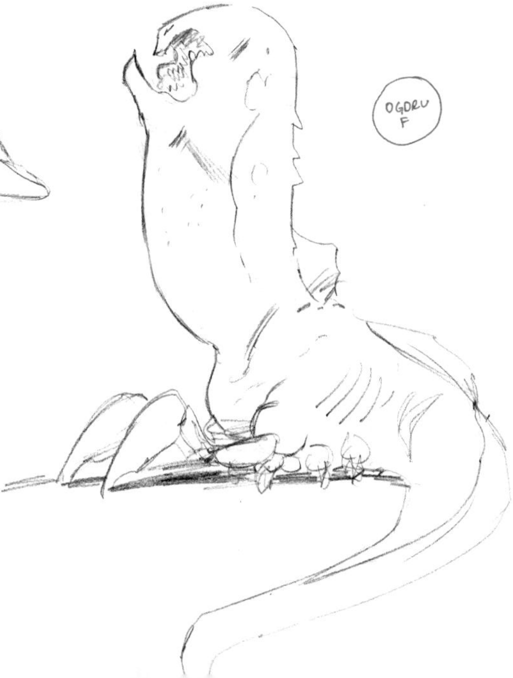
OGDRU F

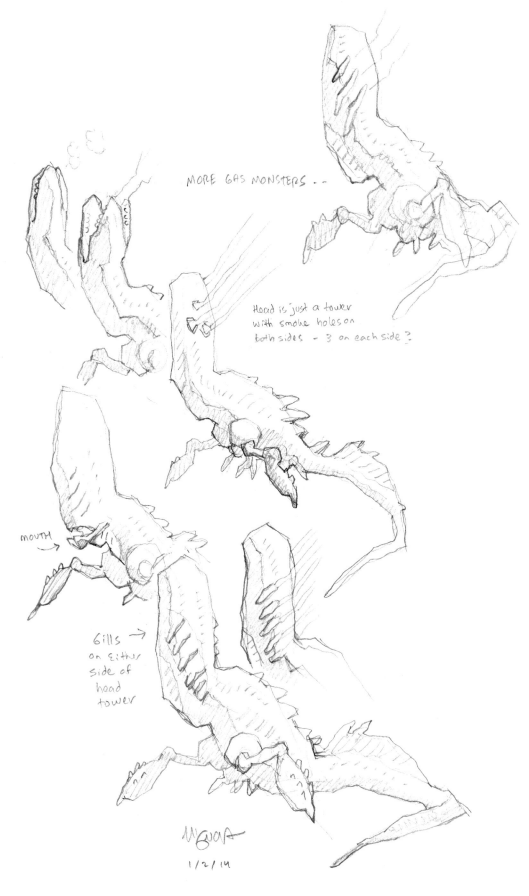

MORE GAS MONSTERS...

Head is just a tower
with smoke holes on
both sides – 3 on each side ?

MOUTH →

Gills →
on either
side of
head
tower

1/2/14

Mike's Ogdru Hem design.

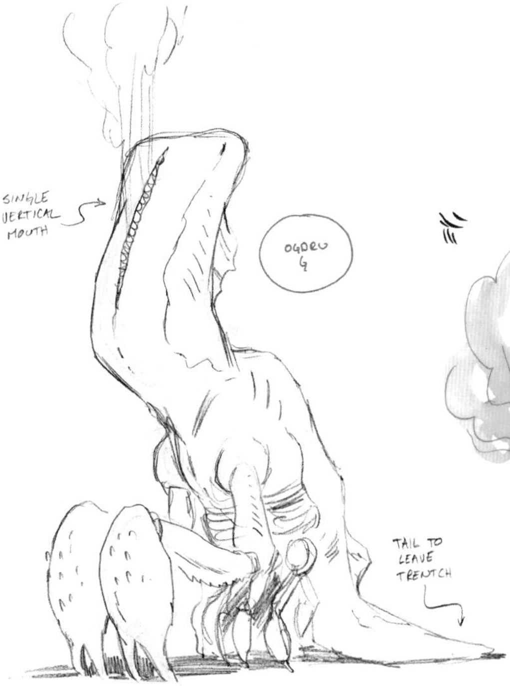
SINGLE VERTICAL MOUTH
OGDRU G
TAIL TO LEAVE TRENTCH

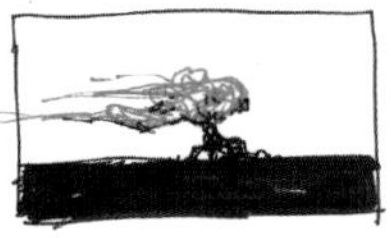

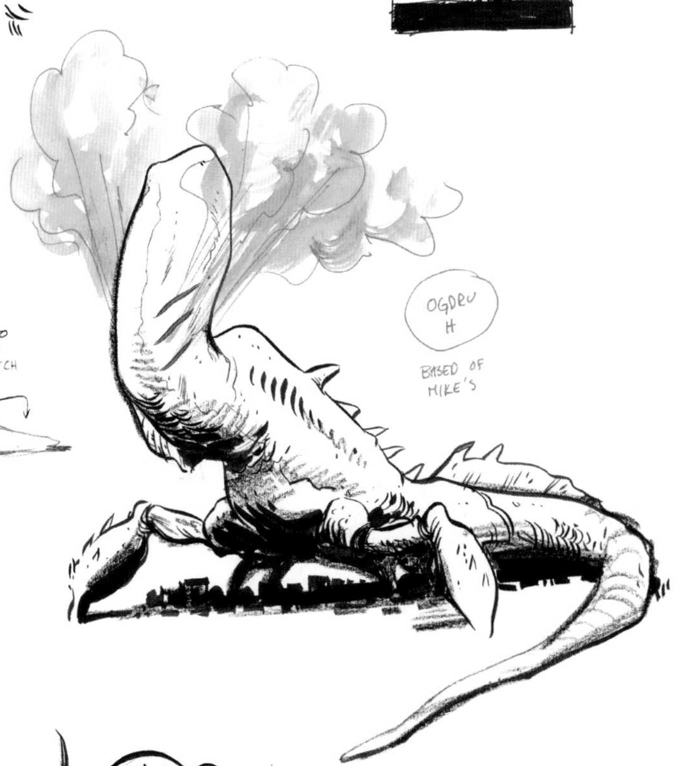
OGDRU H
BASED OF MIKE'S

We finally landed on the guy to the right. He needed to puff out that mutating gas, so we figured these gill things would get the job done. Mike did a pass, and then I did my version of Mike's pass.

This fungus/triffid thing is basically every kind of weird fungus I could find, crammed together.

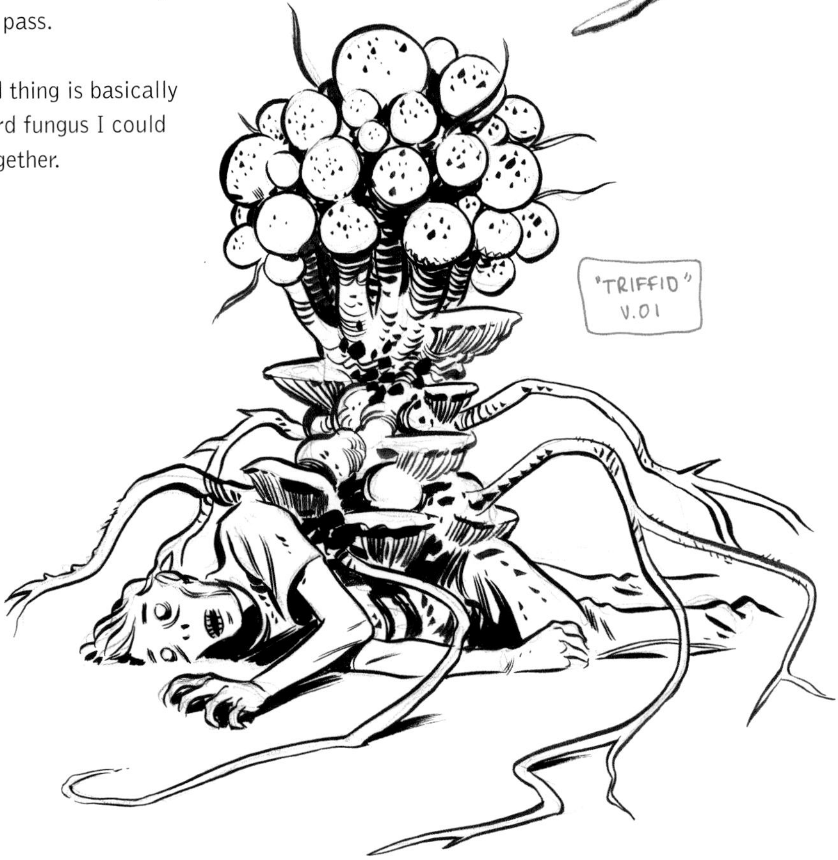
"TRIFFID"
V.01

THE DEVIL'S WINGS

LAURENCE CAMPBELL: *B.P.R.D.* #120–#121 cover roughs. Being asked to draw covers for *B.P.R.D.* was a great honor. These issues featured the first appearance of teenage Hellboy, so this was a baptism by fire. After reading the scripts I realized the two-parter featured two objects important to the arc—the dog tags and the wings badge. I came to the decision quickly to try to focus on these objects and use them as the connection between what was happening in the past and the present. #120 A and #121 A were my first ideas. It was then a case of just making sure all the design elements fit together after that.

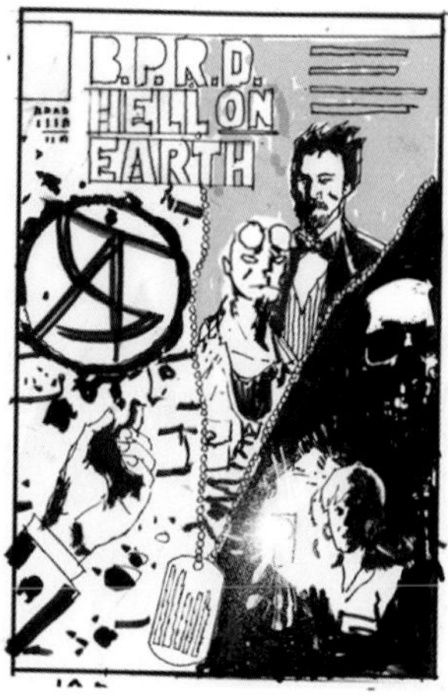

B.P.R.D.
HELL ON
EARTH

120 A

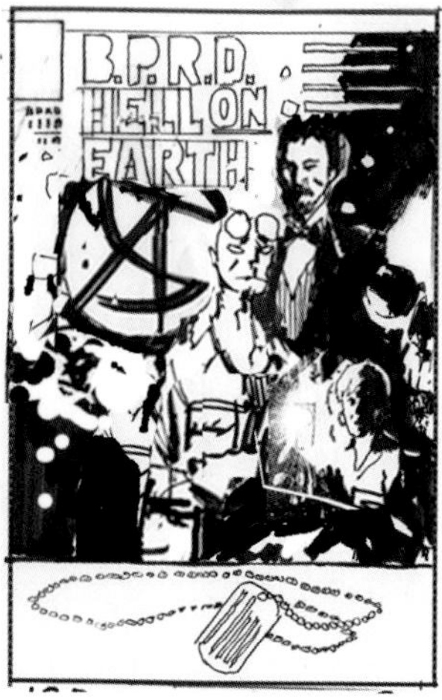

B.P.R.D.
HELL ON
EARTH

120 B

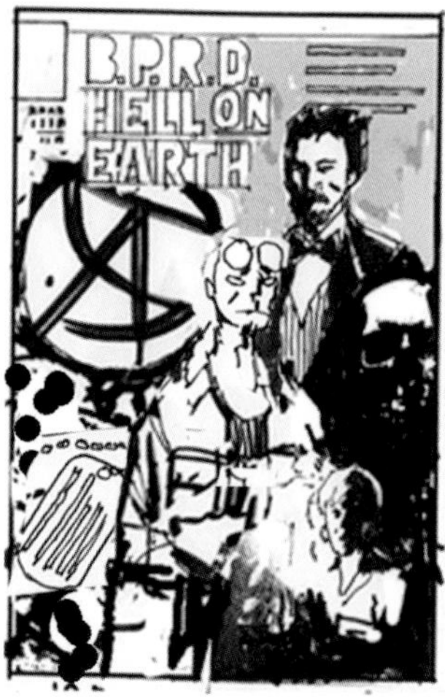

B.P.R.D.
HELL ON
EARTH

120 C

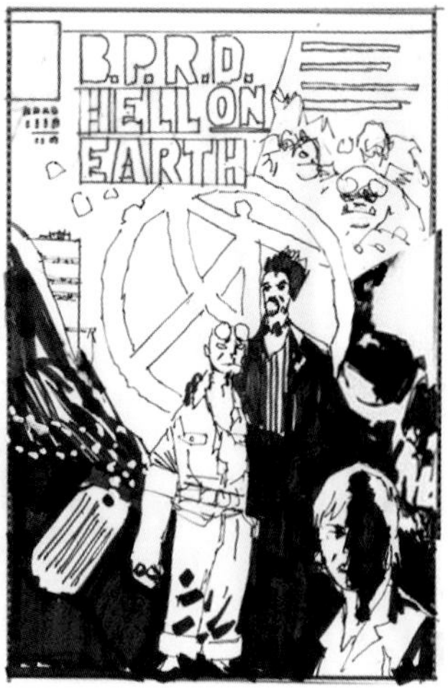

B.P.R.D.
HELL ON
EARTH

120 C

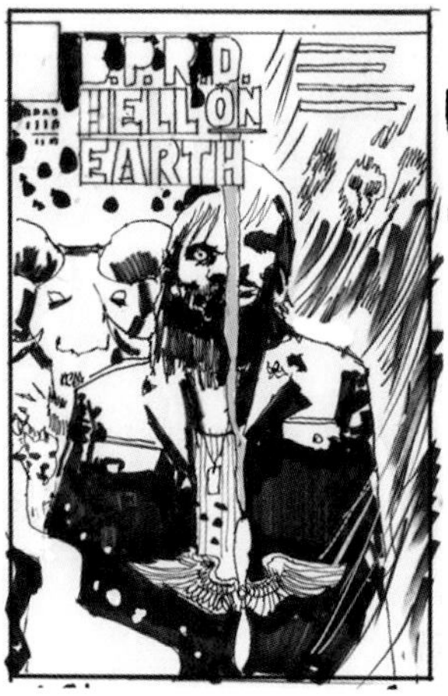

B.P.R.D.
HELL ON
EARTH

121 A

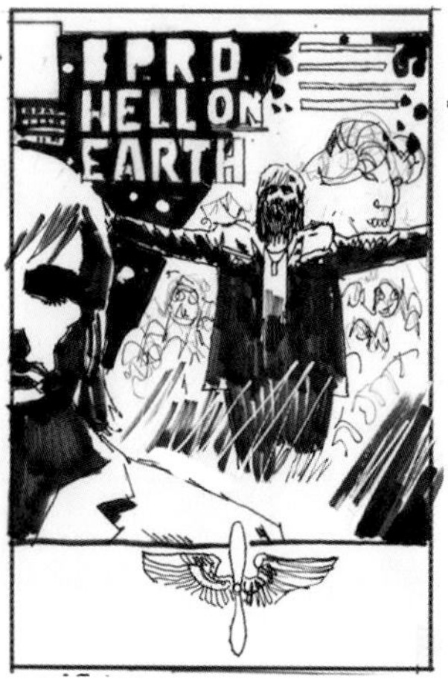

B.P.R.D.
HELL ON
EARTH

121 B

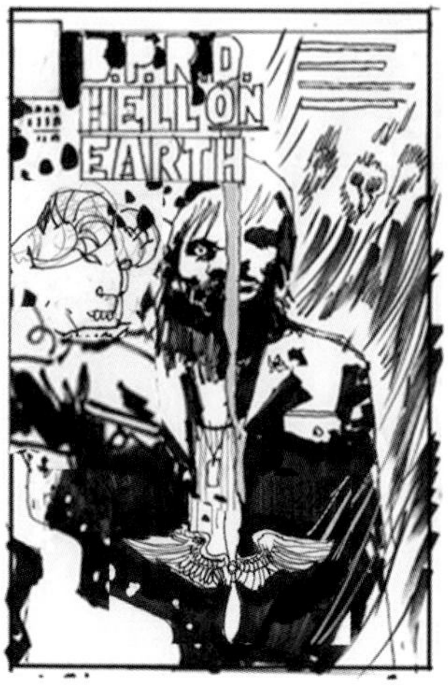

B.P.R.D.
HELL ON
EARTH

121 C

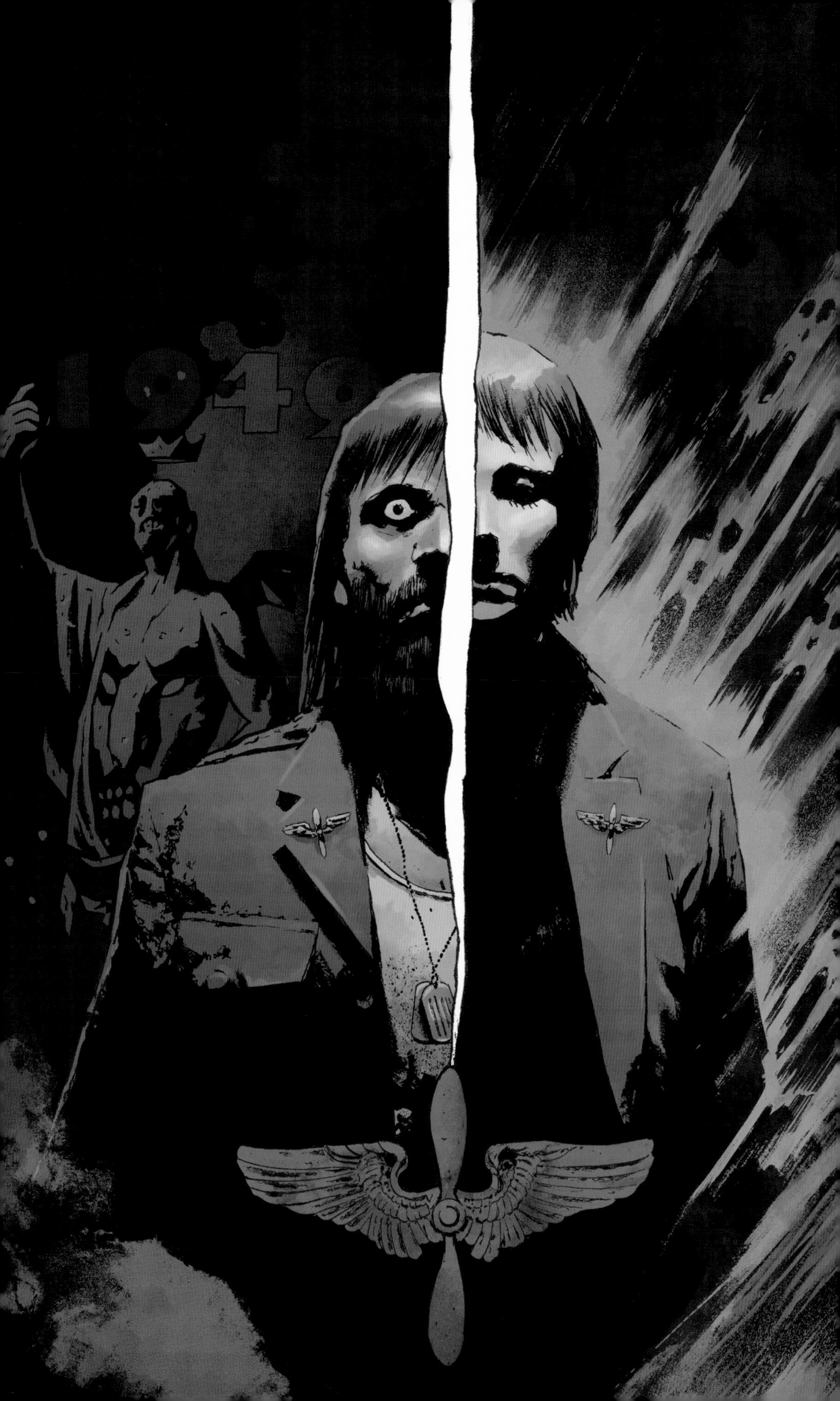
1949

B.P.R.D. #122–#123 cover roughs. The story is set in Japan. I wanted to capture this but in a subtle way. The thought of a red disk similar to what's used on the Japanese flag came pretty quickly; it's a great graphic image. John had given an excellent description of this old guy in a chair with drawings all around him and a gateway behind him. It took some time to connect the gateway to the shape of the red disk, but once I did it flowed very quickly from there. Add "Kirby Krackle" and I was happy.

With the cover for #123, I wanted to give a nod to Godzilla and *kaiju*. We were going to go with version D when Ryan Sook came up with an amazing image for the trade cover. Dark Horse went for another of Ryan's covers for the trade but thought this cover was too good not to use, so I worked with Ryan's rough—which was anything but. To be honest, Ryan did all the heavy lifting on this one.

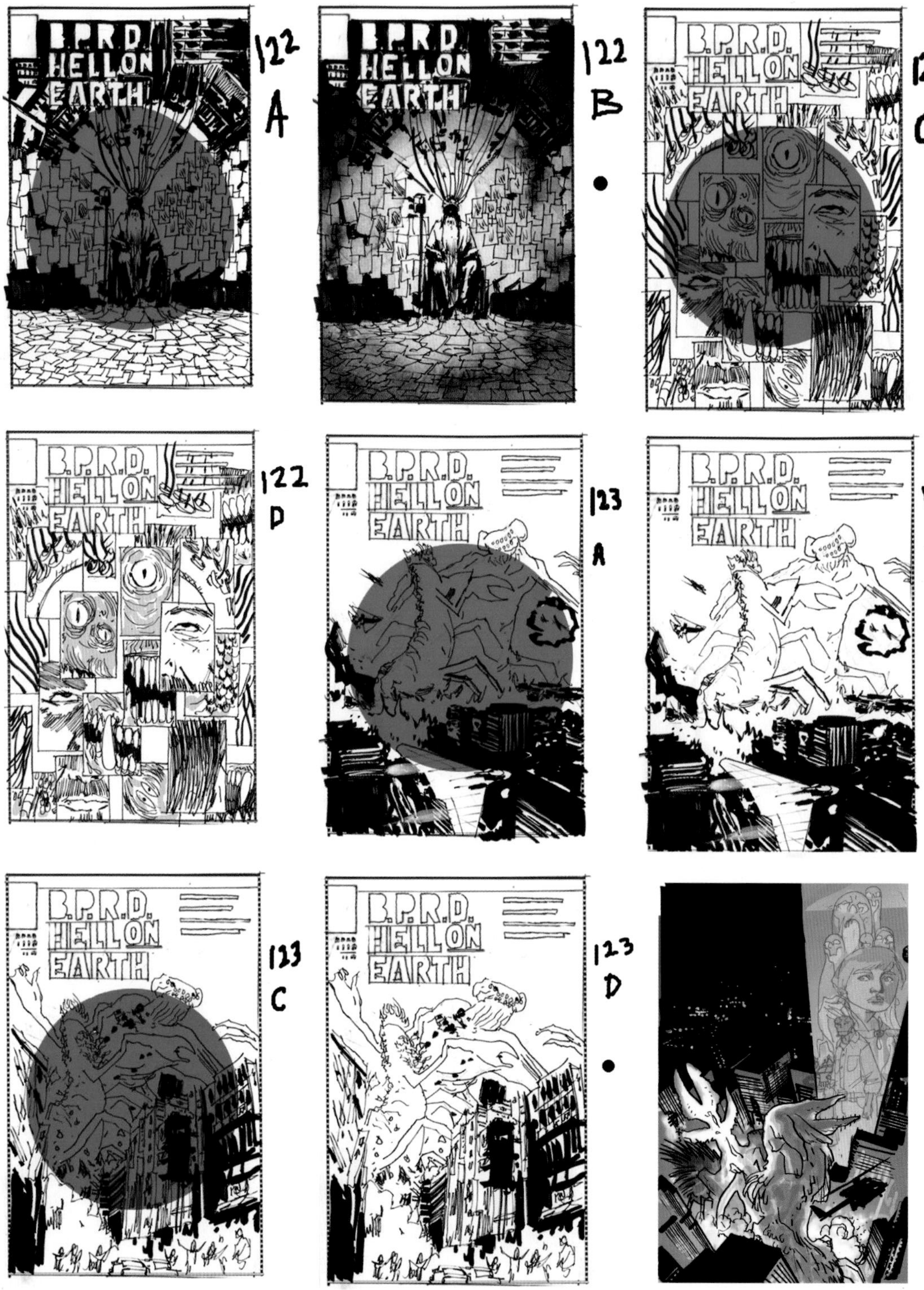

B.P.R.D. HELL ON EARTH
122 A
122 B
122 C
122 D
123 A
123 B
123 C
123 D

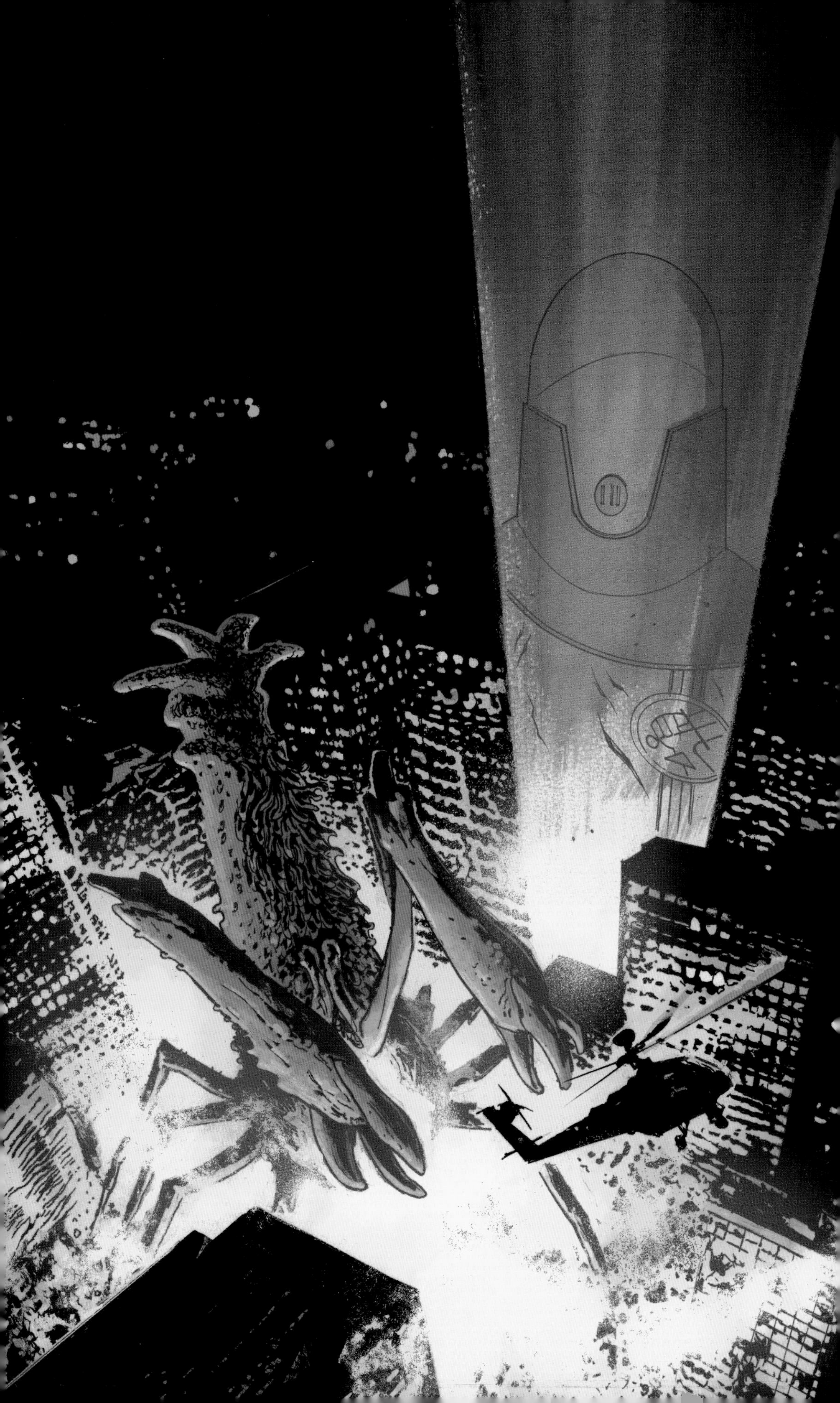

Cover to #124. After reading the script, the final image pretty much came into my head straightaway. Love the idea of two BPRD agents talking over coffee while outside all hell is happening. Probably the easiest cover I've done and probably one of my favorites so far. Wish it was like that all the time.

It also needs to be said that it's always a pleasure working with Dave Stewart on the covers. Frankly, he's the man who pulls it all together and makes it look good.

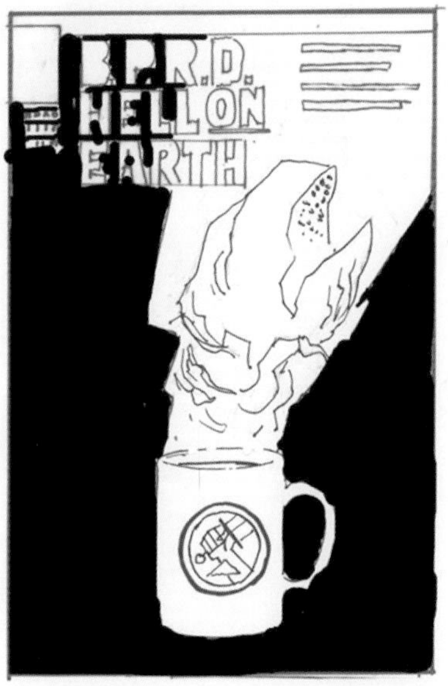
B.P.R.D.
HELL ON
EARTH

A

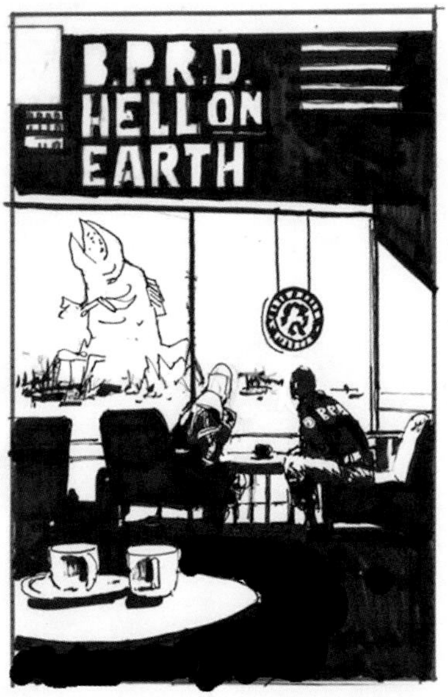
B.P.R.D.
HELL ON
EARTH

B

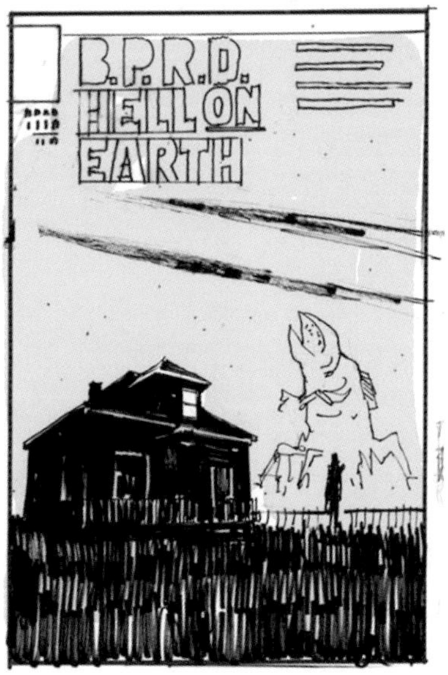
B.P.R.D.
HELL ON
EARTH

C

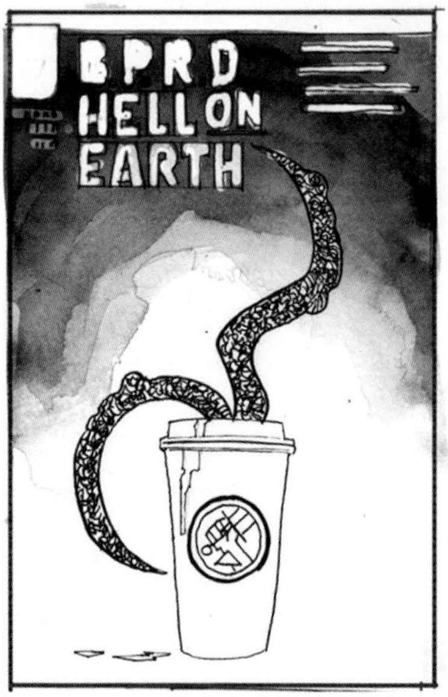
BPRD
HELL ON
EARTH

D

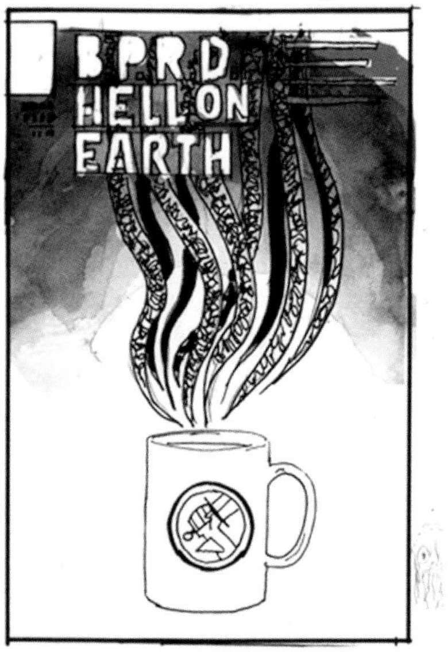
BPRD
HELL ON
EARTH

E

FLESH AND STONE

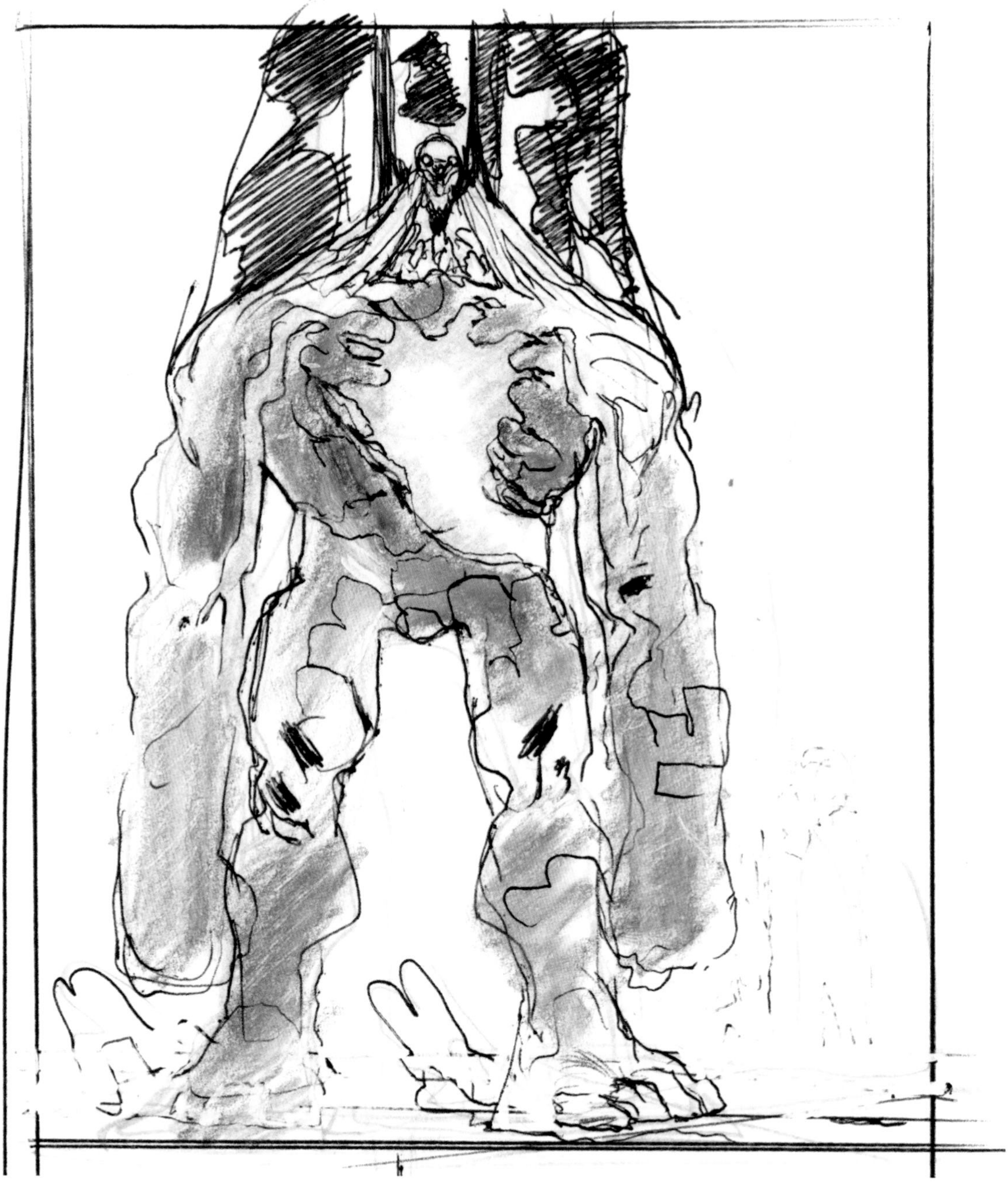

JAMES HARREN: The Black Flame returns! We last saw him blowing up a large portion of Manhattan—I wanted it to look like that took its toll on his body. Either that or there's a natural degradation of his human silhouette from being so gosh-darn evil. Regardless of the why, I wanted him to evolve and change as the series progressed.

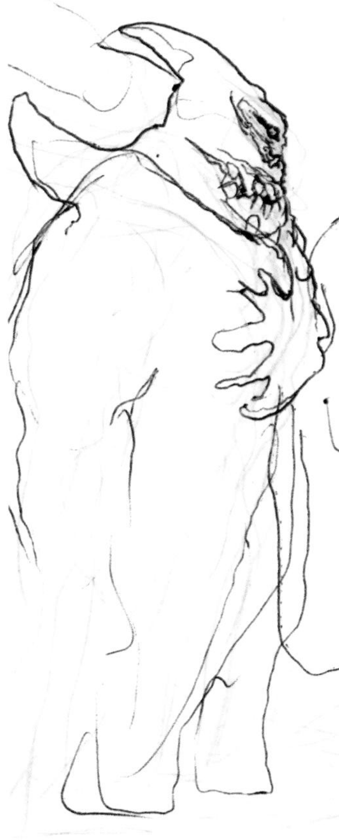
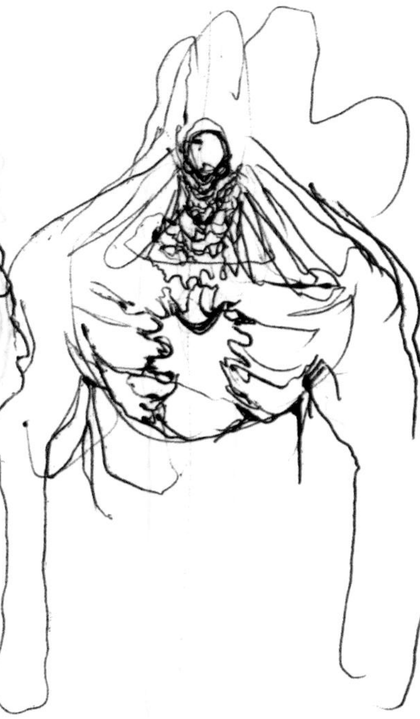
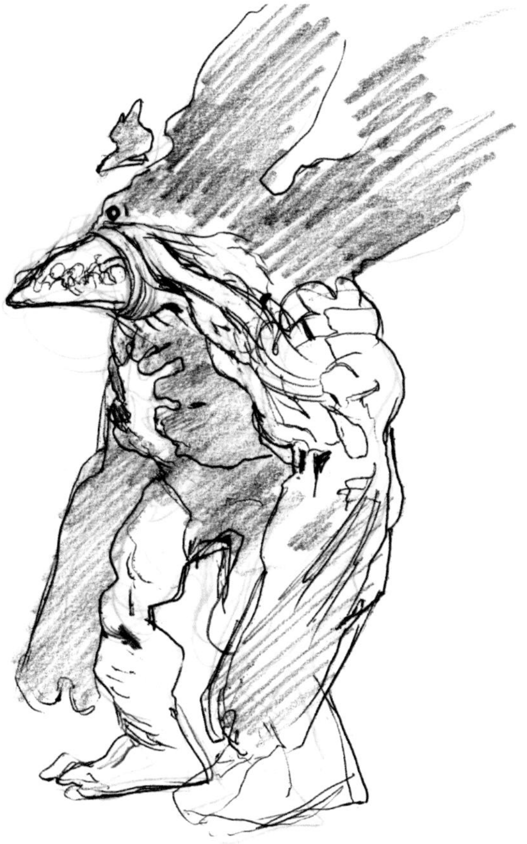
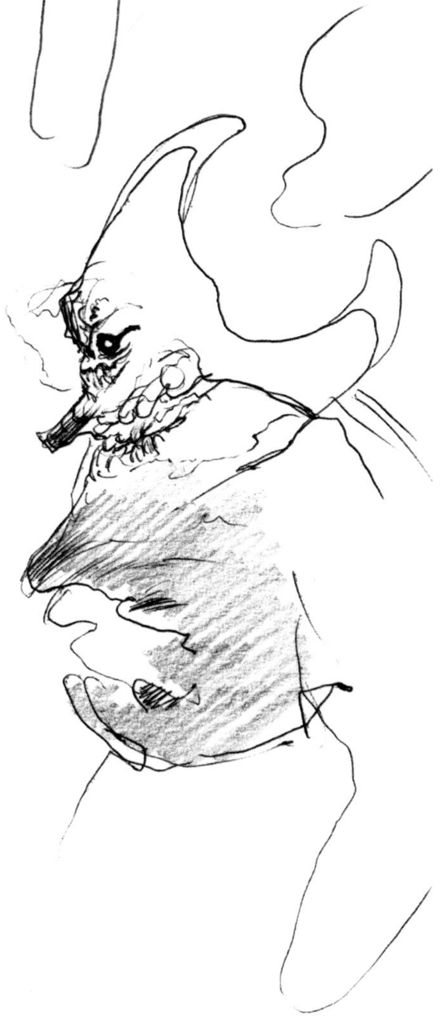

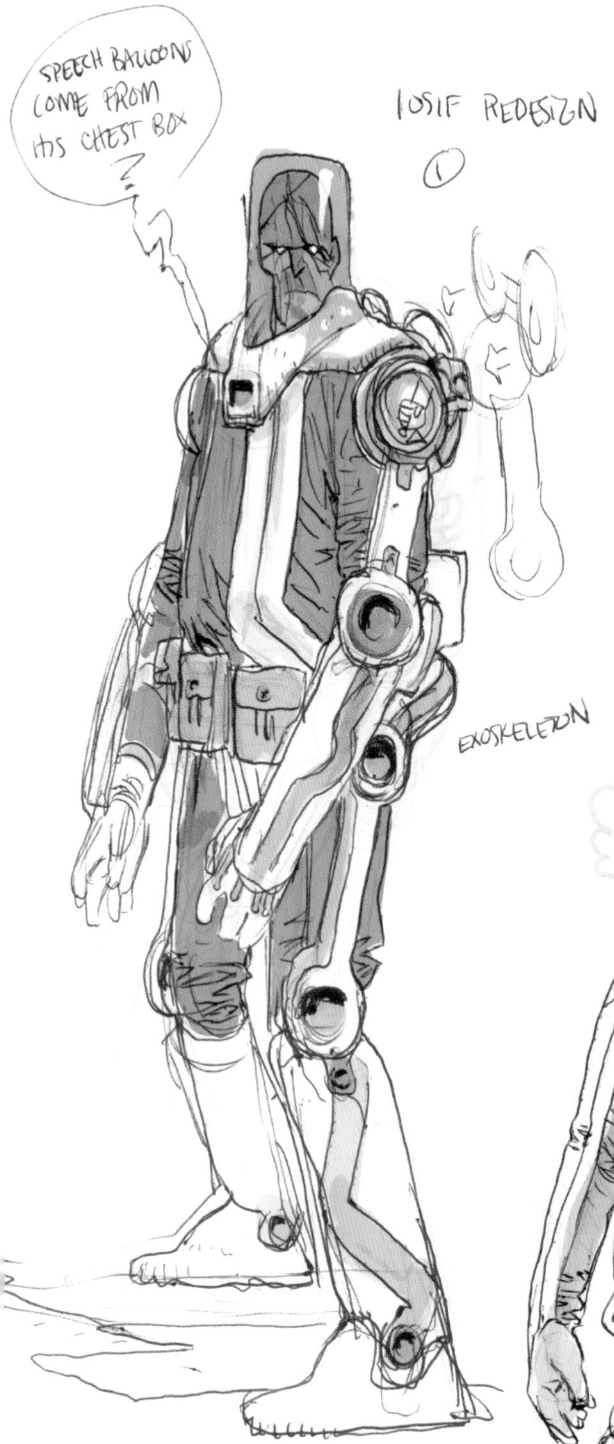
SPEECH BALLOONS COME FROM HIS CHEST BOX ?
IOSIF REDESIGN
1
EXOSKELETON

Iosifs! I tried to give Mike and John as many options as possible so we could pick the one that worked best with the character and the story. We wound up with clunky, early Iron Man/iron lung. I like that he looks cumbersome and as if he is trapped by this thing that's unnaturally extending his life.

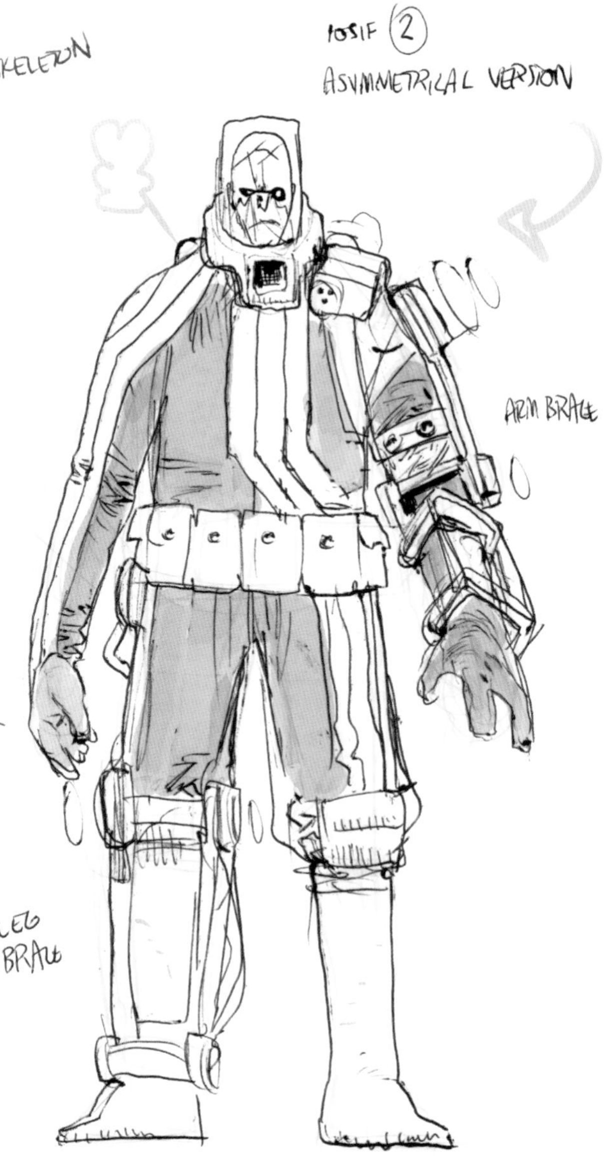
IOSIF 2
ASYMMETRICAL VERSION
ARM BRACE
LEG BRACE

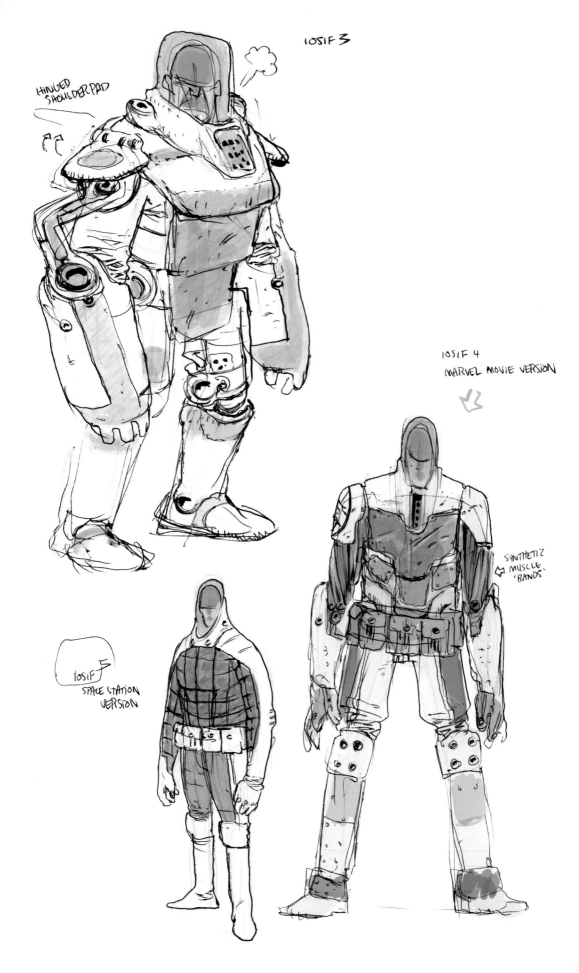

IOSIF 3

HINGED SHOULDER PAD

IOSIF 4
MARVEL MOVIE VERSION

SYNTHETIC MUSCLE 'BANDS'

IOSIF 5
SPACE STATION VERSION

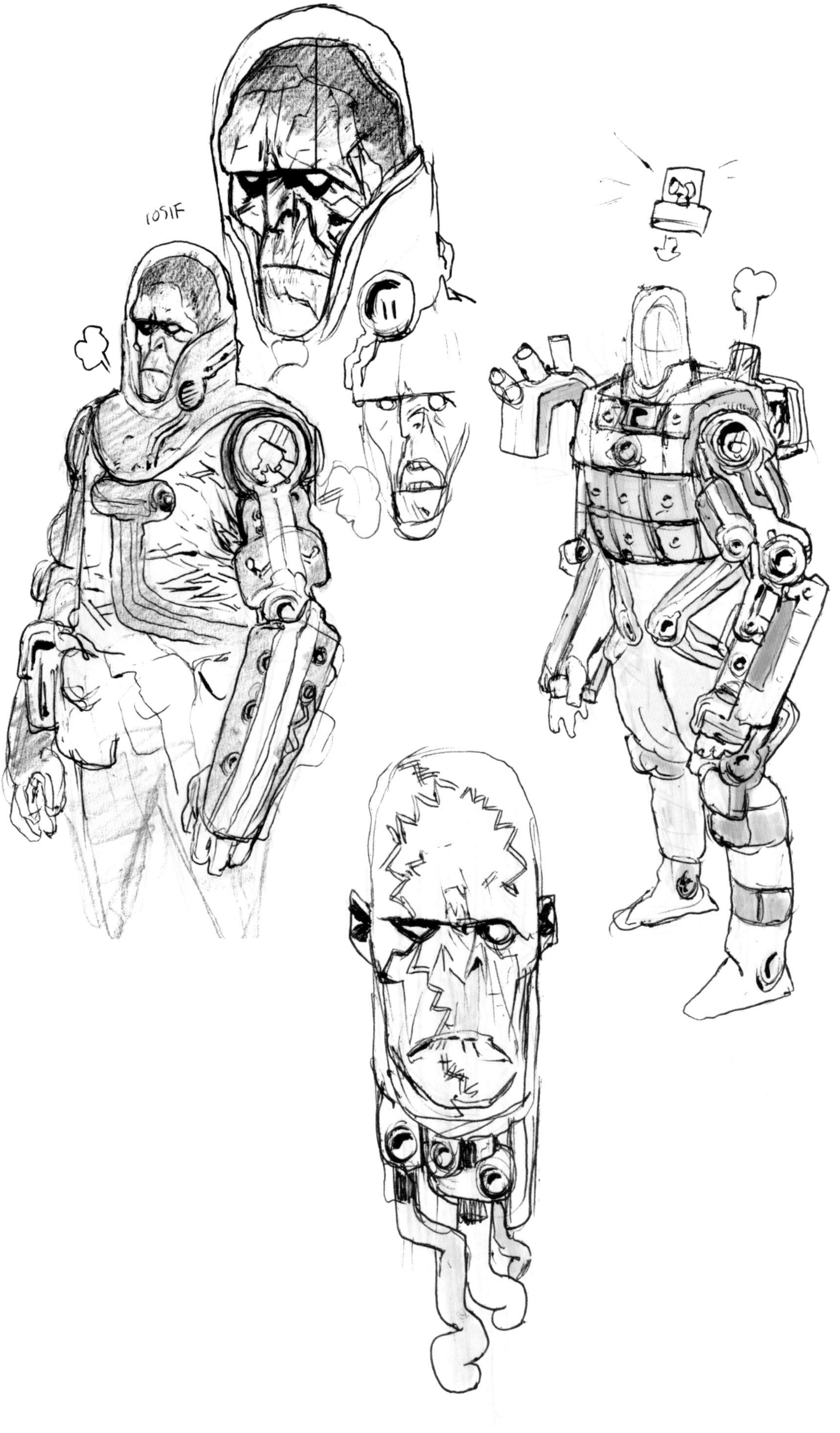
IOSIF

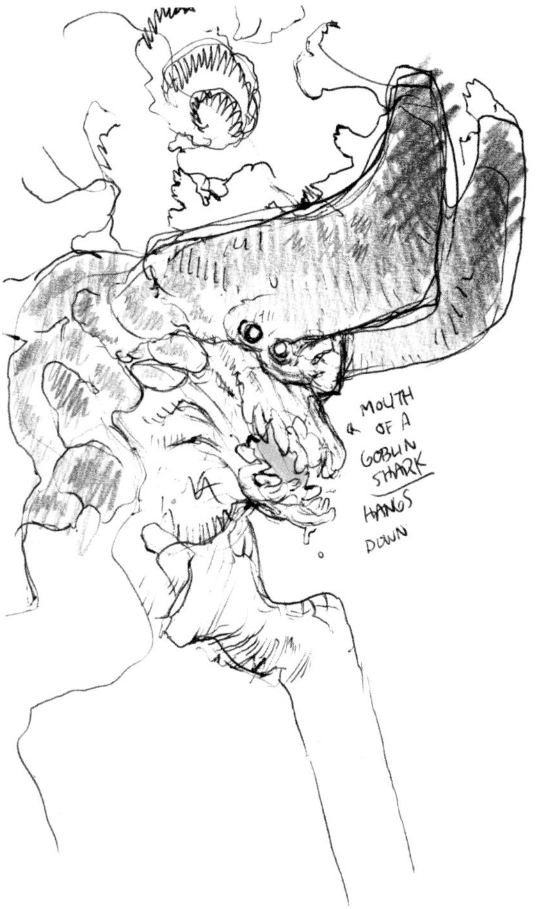
MOUTH OF A GOBLIN SHARK
HANGS DOWN

An unused monster design. This is what happens when you don't read the script properly. I designed the wrong monster! I forget how I managed to stray so far from what was actually needed. Probably drugs. I even got to the pencil and inking stage before someone tugged my coat, and I redesigned her to be the tubby tumor monster that we all know and love.

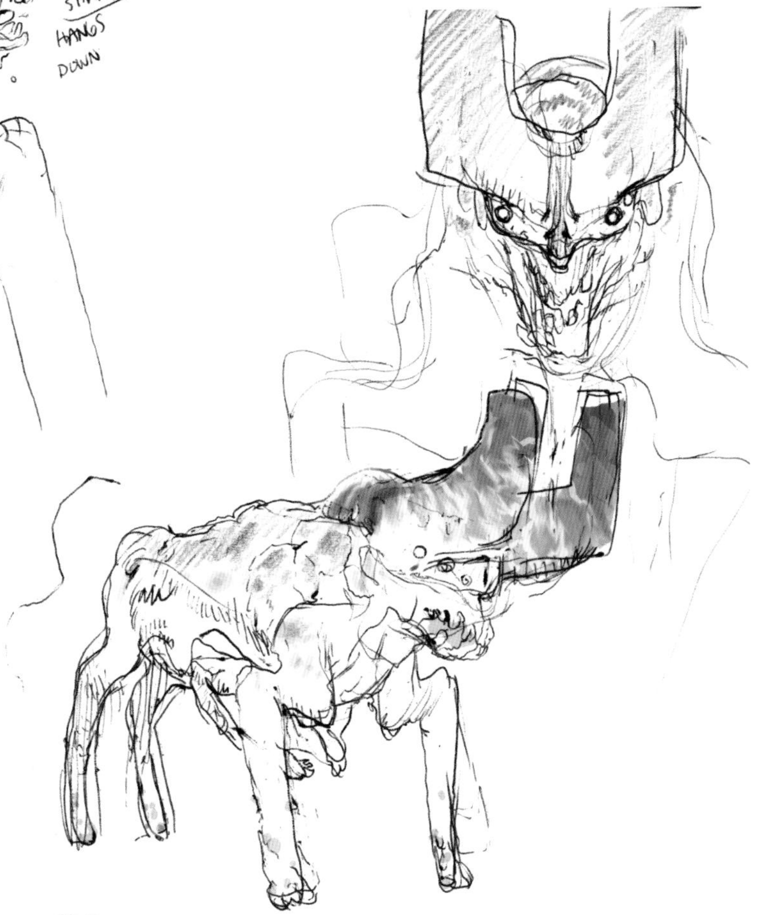

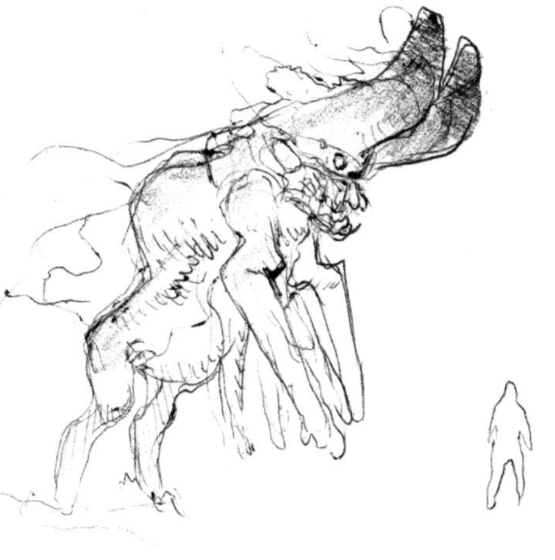

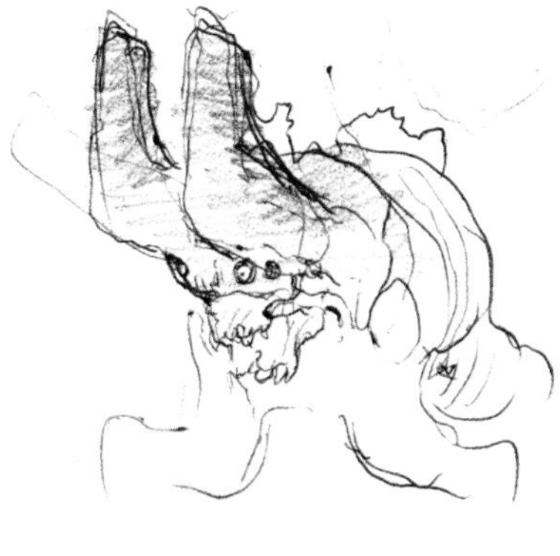

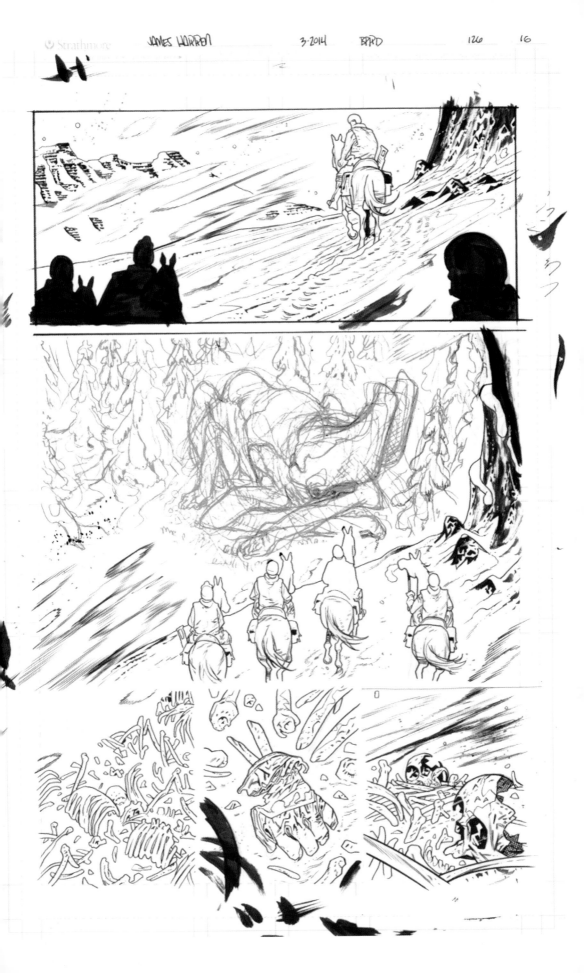

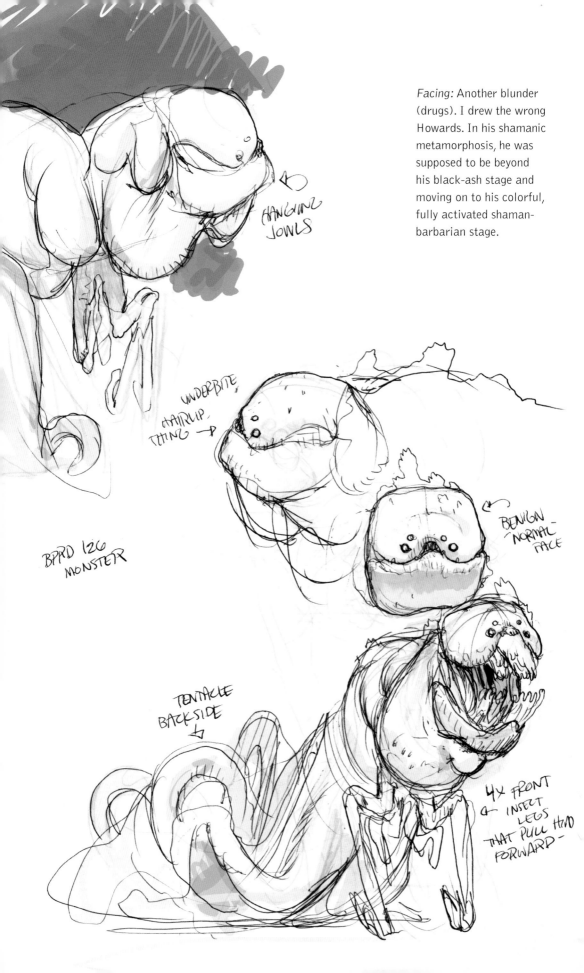

Facing: Another blunder (drugs). I drew the wrong Howards. In his shamanic metamorphosis, he was supposed to be beyond his black-ash stage and moving on to his colorful, fully activated shaman-barbarian stage.

HANGING JOWLS

UNDERBITE HAIRLIP THING →

BENIGN "NORMAL" FACE

BPRD 126 MONSTER

TENTACLE BACKSIDE

4X FRONT INSECT LEGS THAT PULL HIM FORWARD —

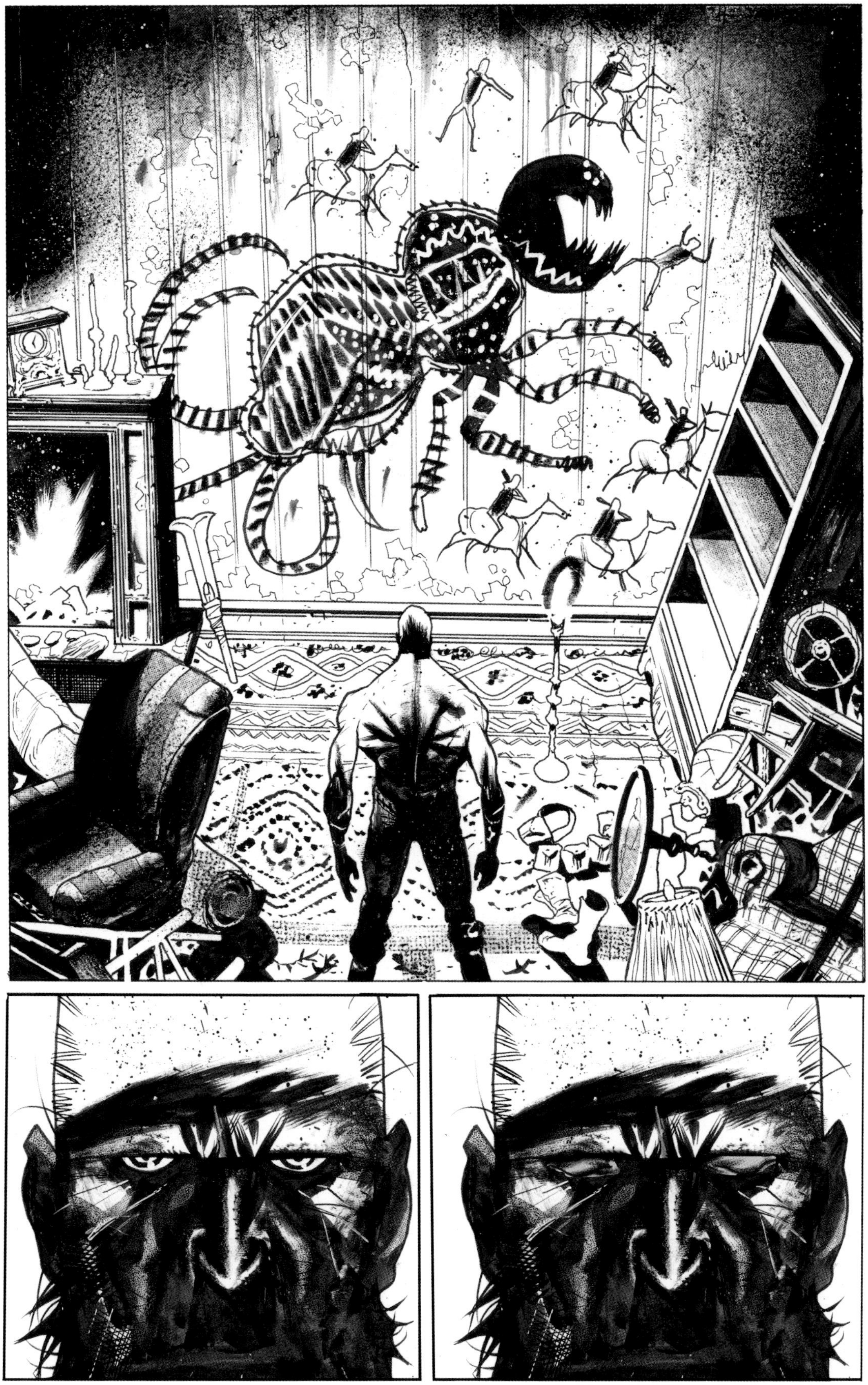

I don't remember having too much trouble with the fungal monster. John's description conjured a pretty specific image. I think we were all in love with the cordyceps mushrooms that take over ants' brains and later grow out of their heads like horns. What's not to love!

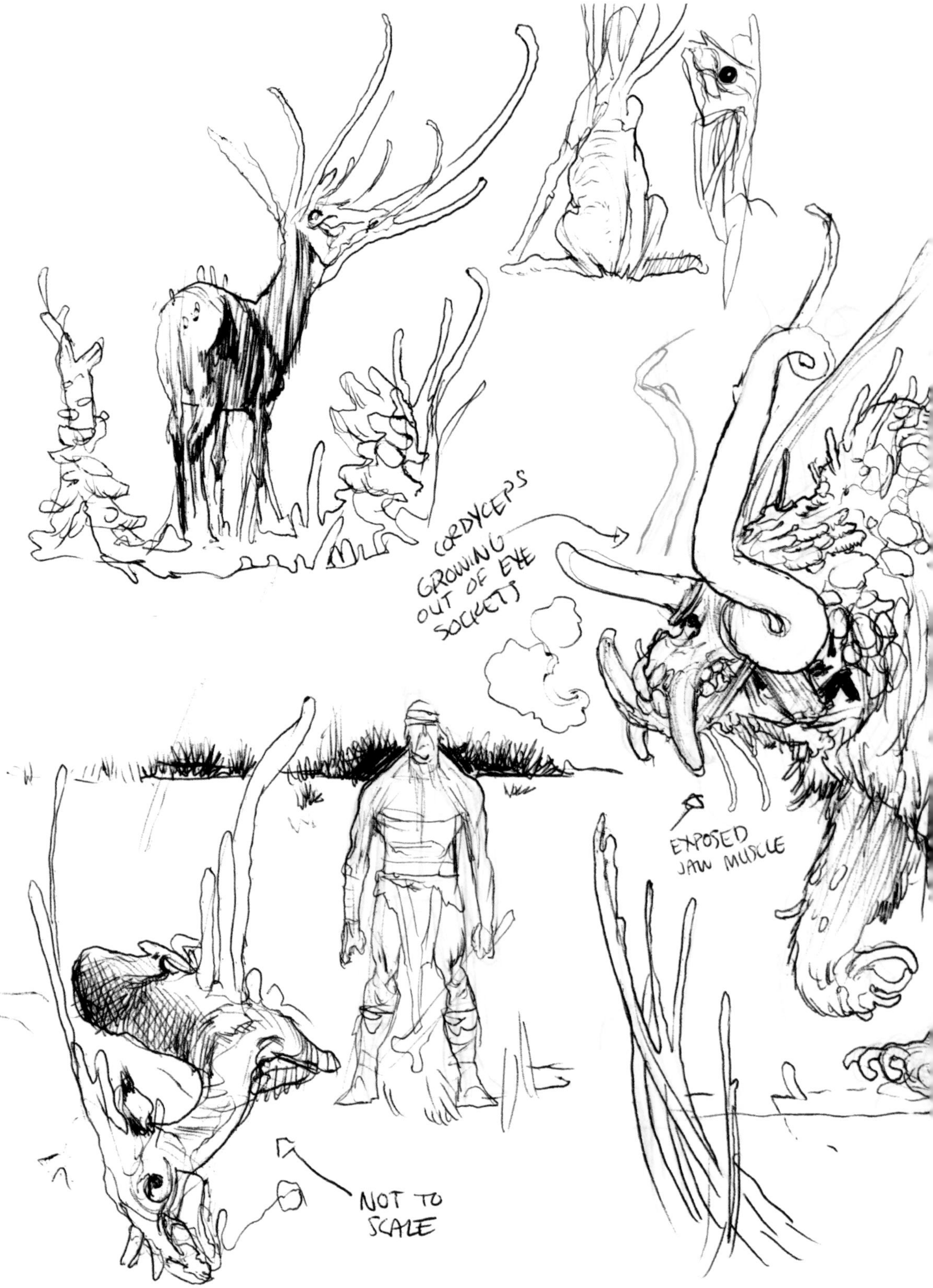

CORDYCEPS GROWING OUT OF EYE SOCKETS
EXPOSED JAW MUSCLE
NOT TO SCALE

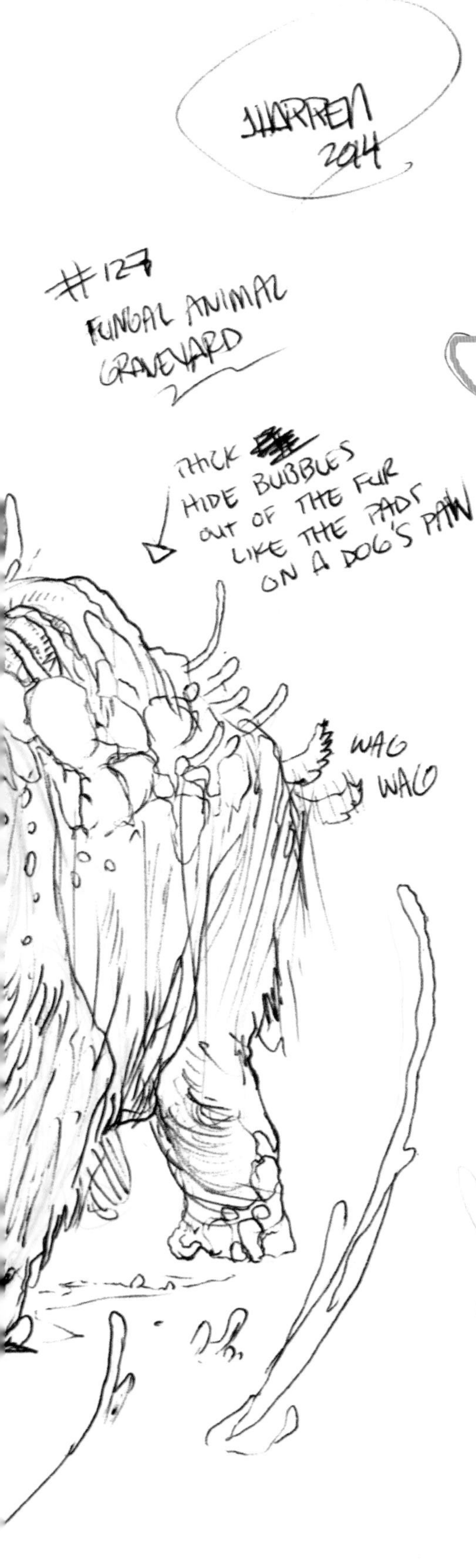
J.HARREN
2014
#127
FUNGAL ANIMAL
GRAVEYARD
THICK HIDE BUBBLES
OUT OF THE FUR
LIKE THE PADS
ON A DOG'S PAW
WAG
WAG

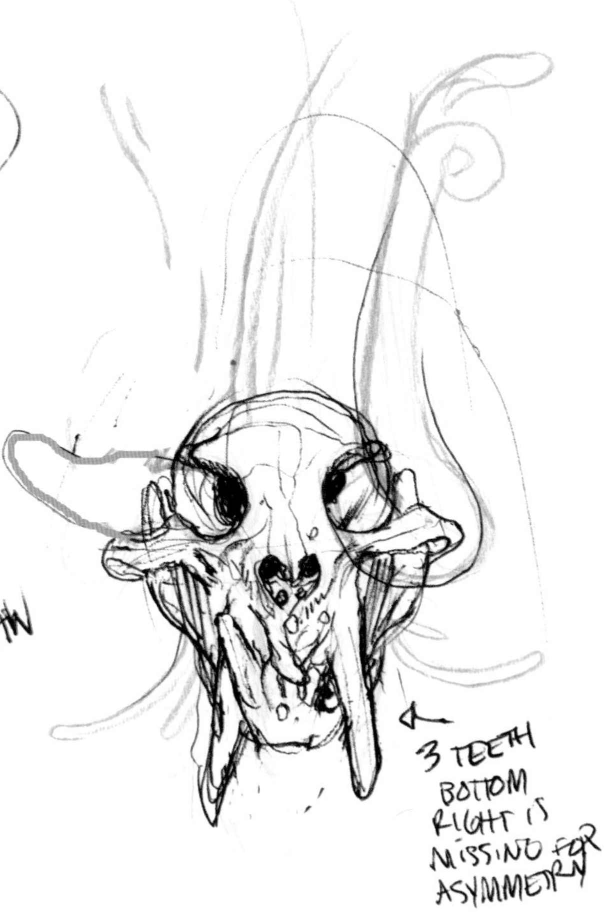
3 TEETH
BOTTOM
RIGHT IS
MISSING FOR
ASYMMETRY

A diagram of the fungal horns for Laurence to work off for his *amazing* cover series.

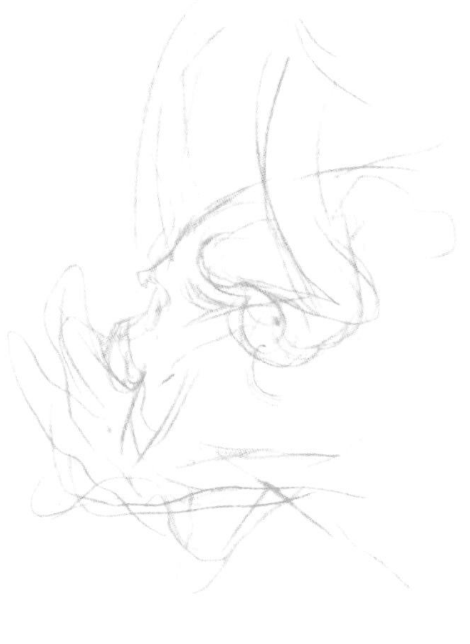

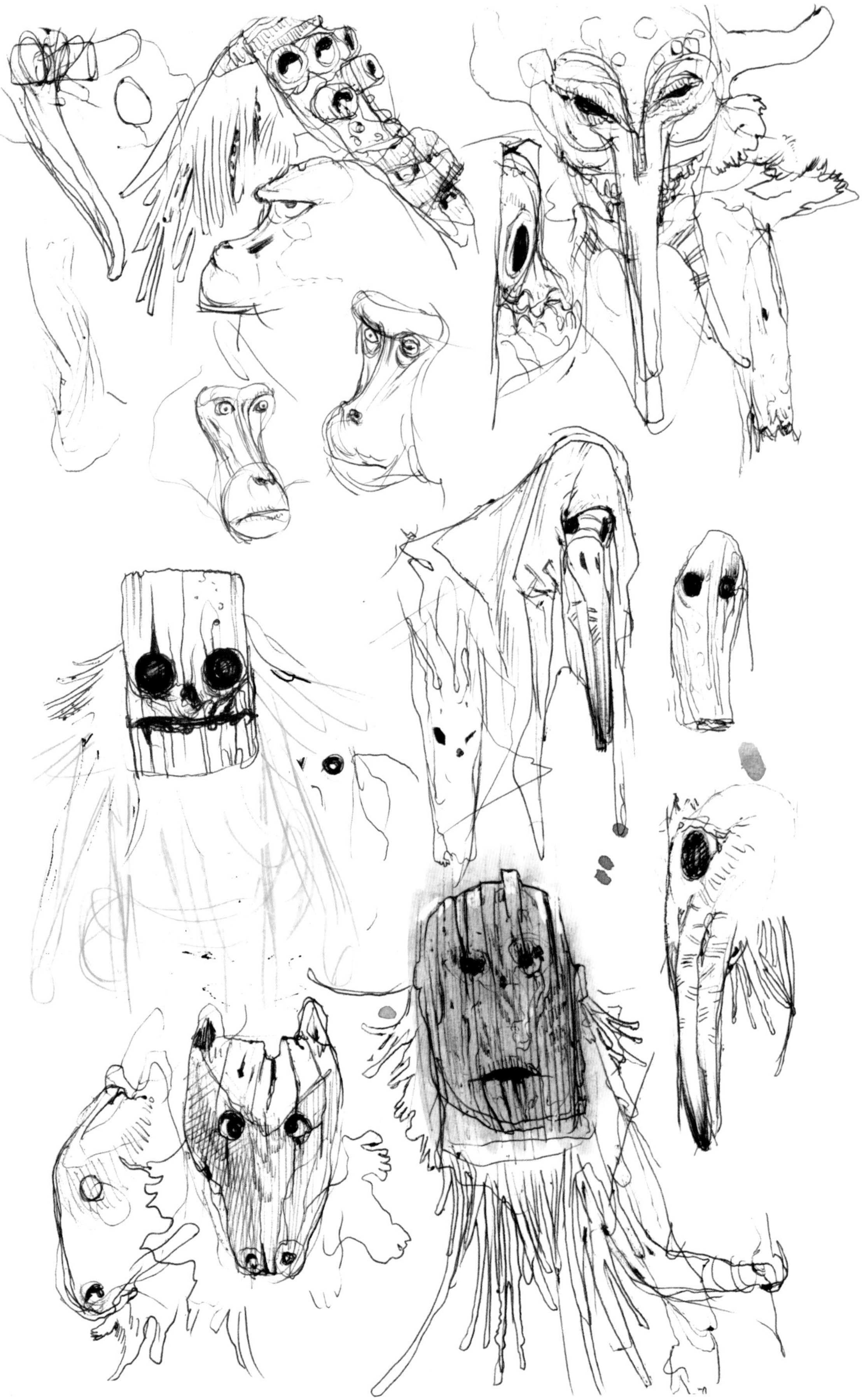

Looking for a sticky-mask idea for our evil fungus shaman. I was playing around with something that looked like a seventeenth-century plague doctor mask. That would've been neat.

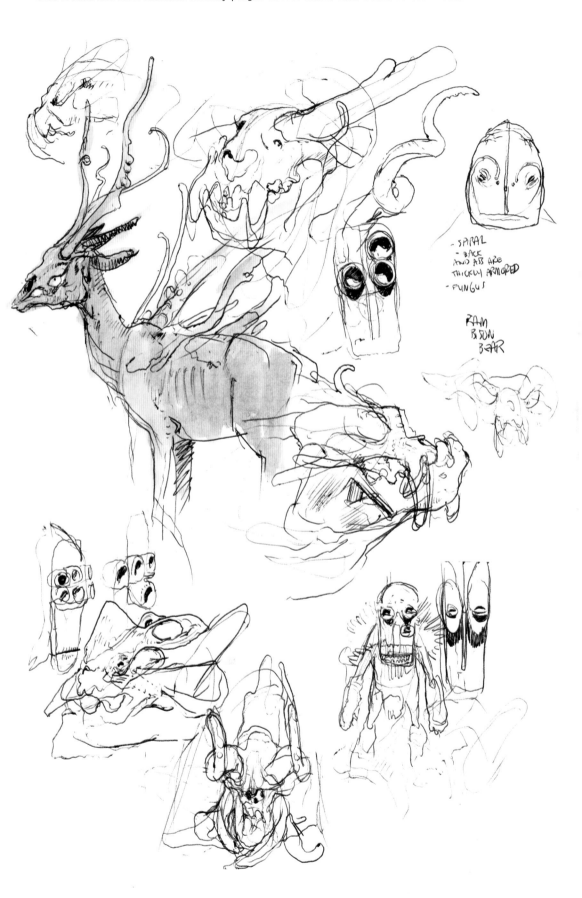

- SPIRAL
- BACK AND ASS ARE THICKLY ARMORED
- FUNGUS

RAM
BISON
BEAR

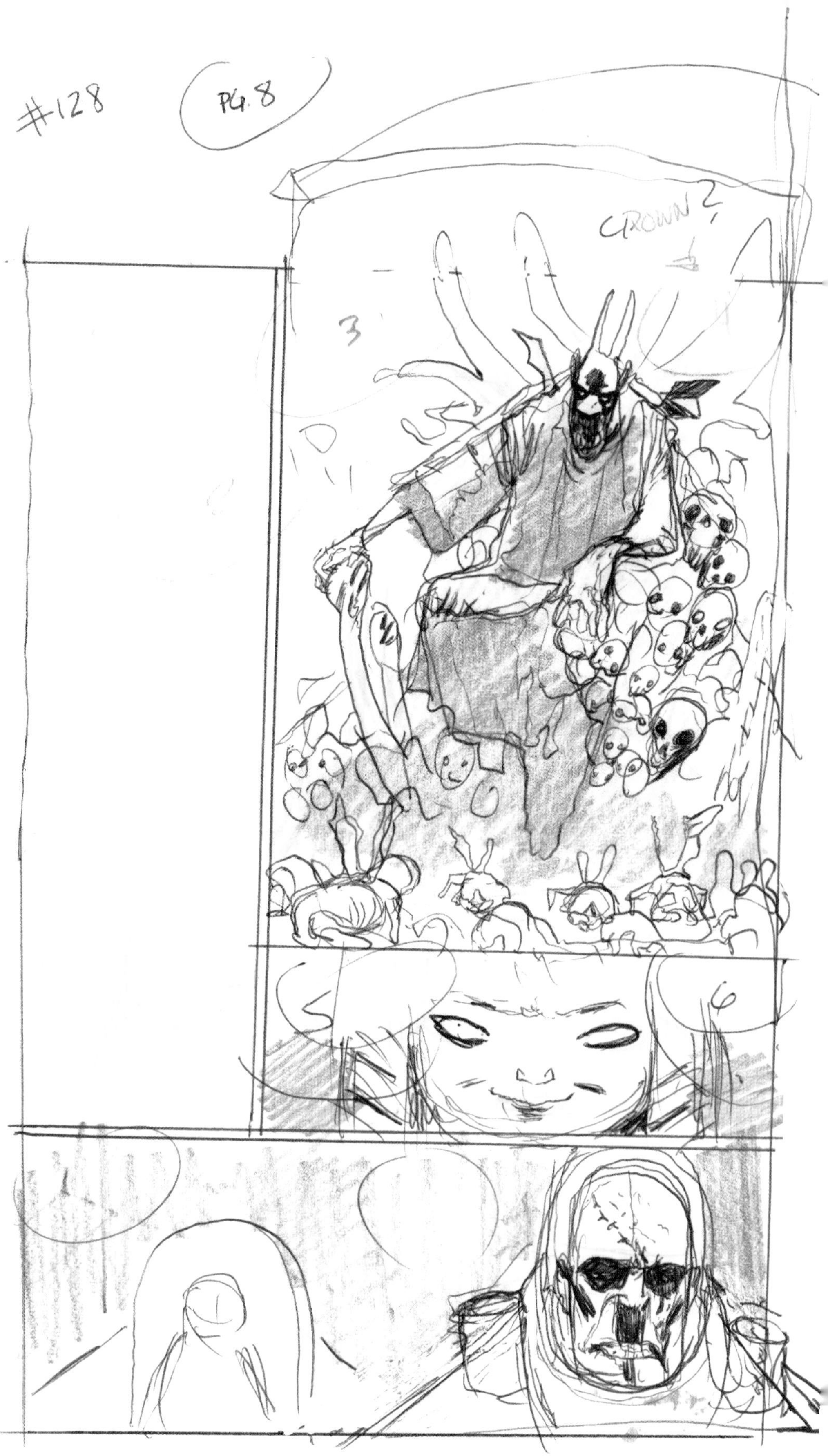
#128
PG. 8
CROWN?
3
4
6

Sketches and studies to try to get Mike's version of Hell right.

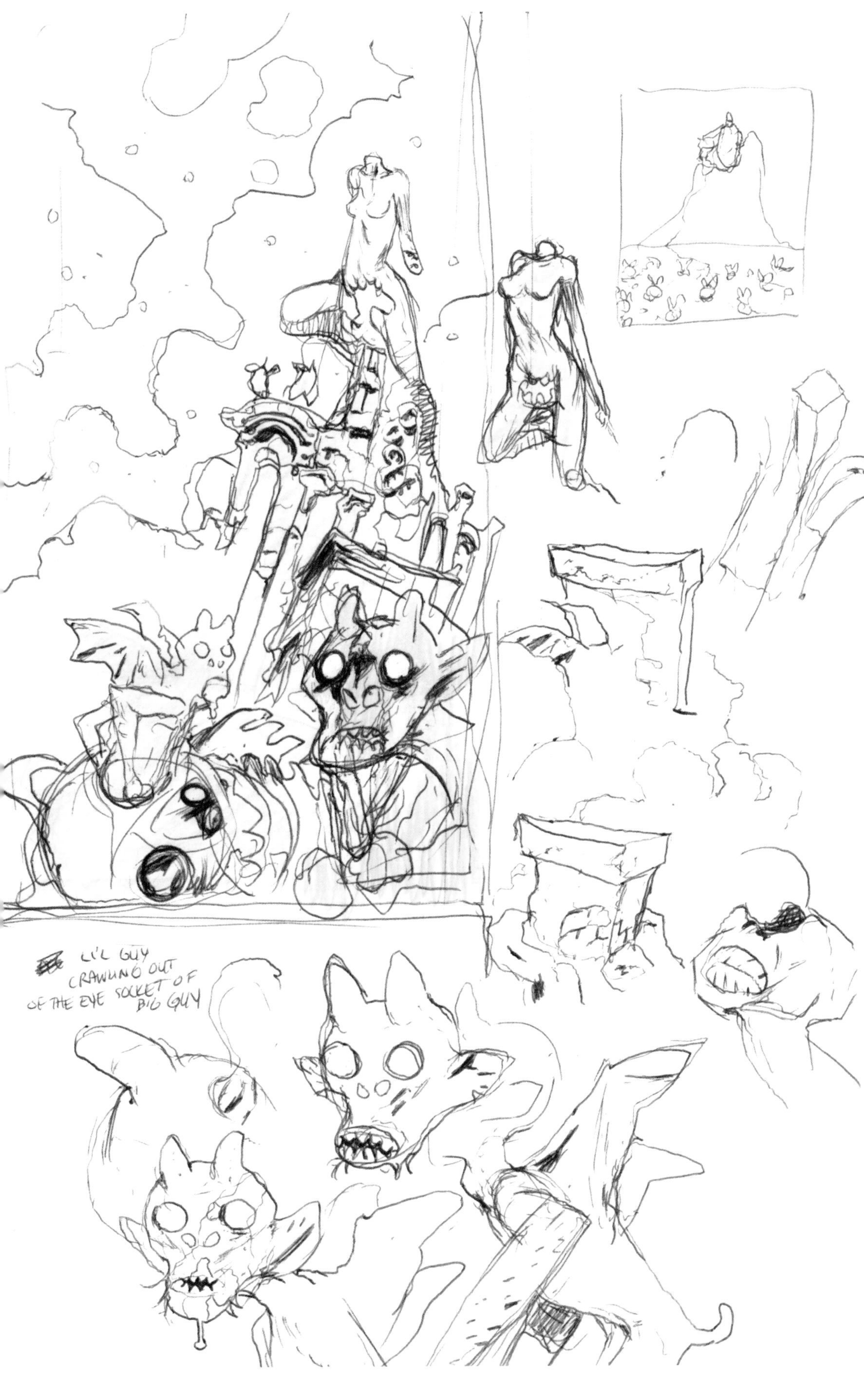
L'L GUY CRAWLING OUT OF THE EYE SOCKET OF BIG GUY

It was Laurence's idea to do the five covers of the original series as a single piece. Dark Horse produced a free print given away at New York Comic Con in 2014.

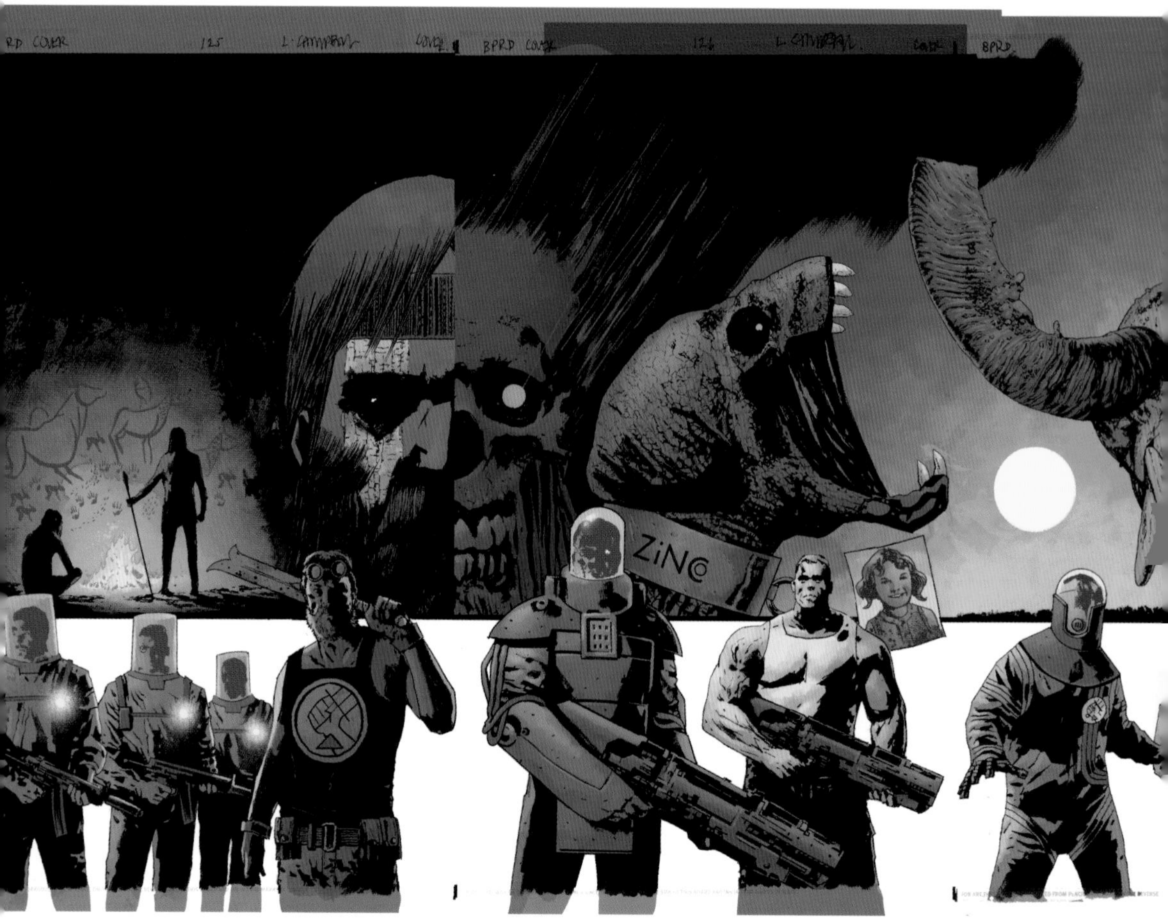
ZiNC

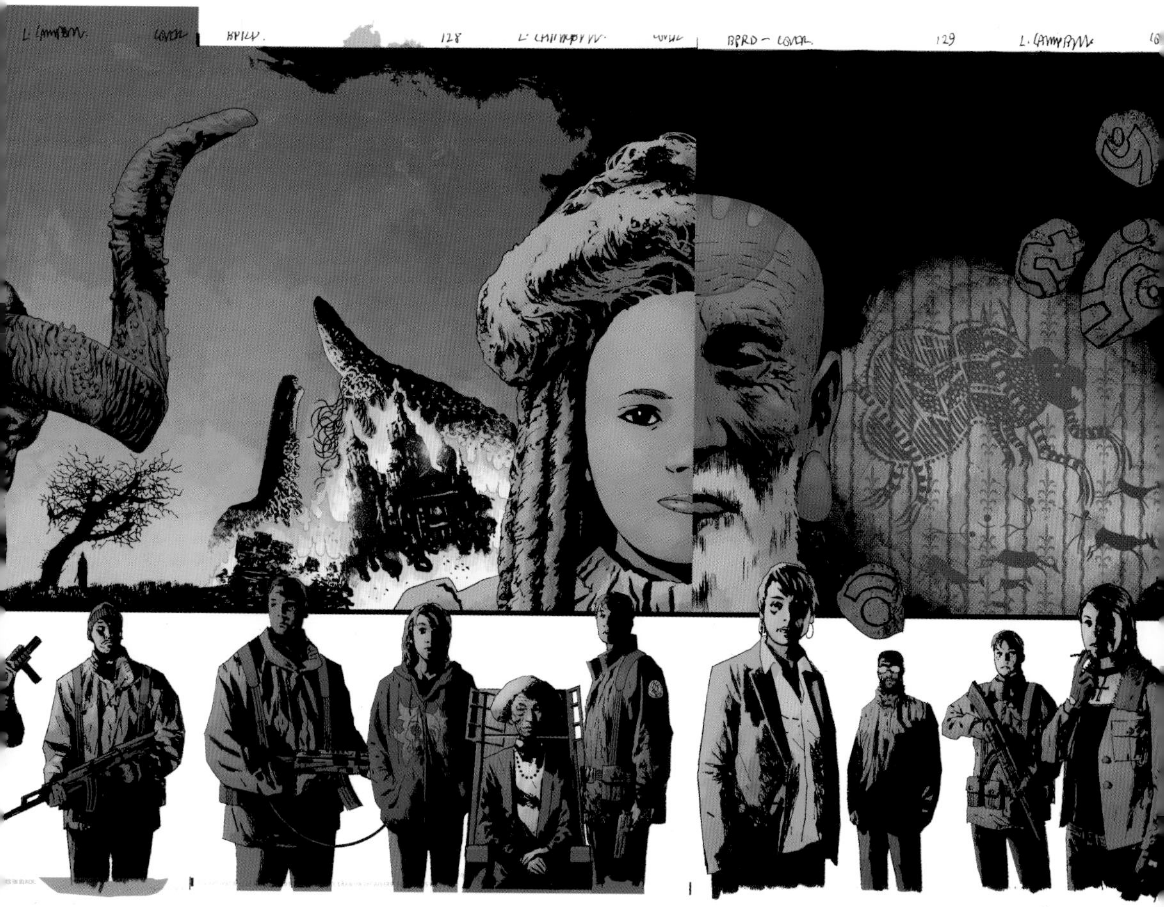

L. Campbell
128
BPRD – COVER
129

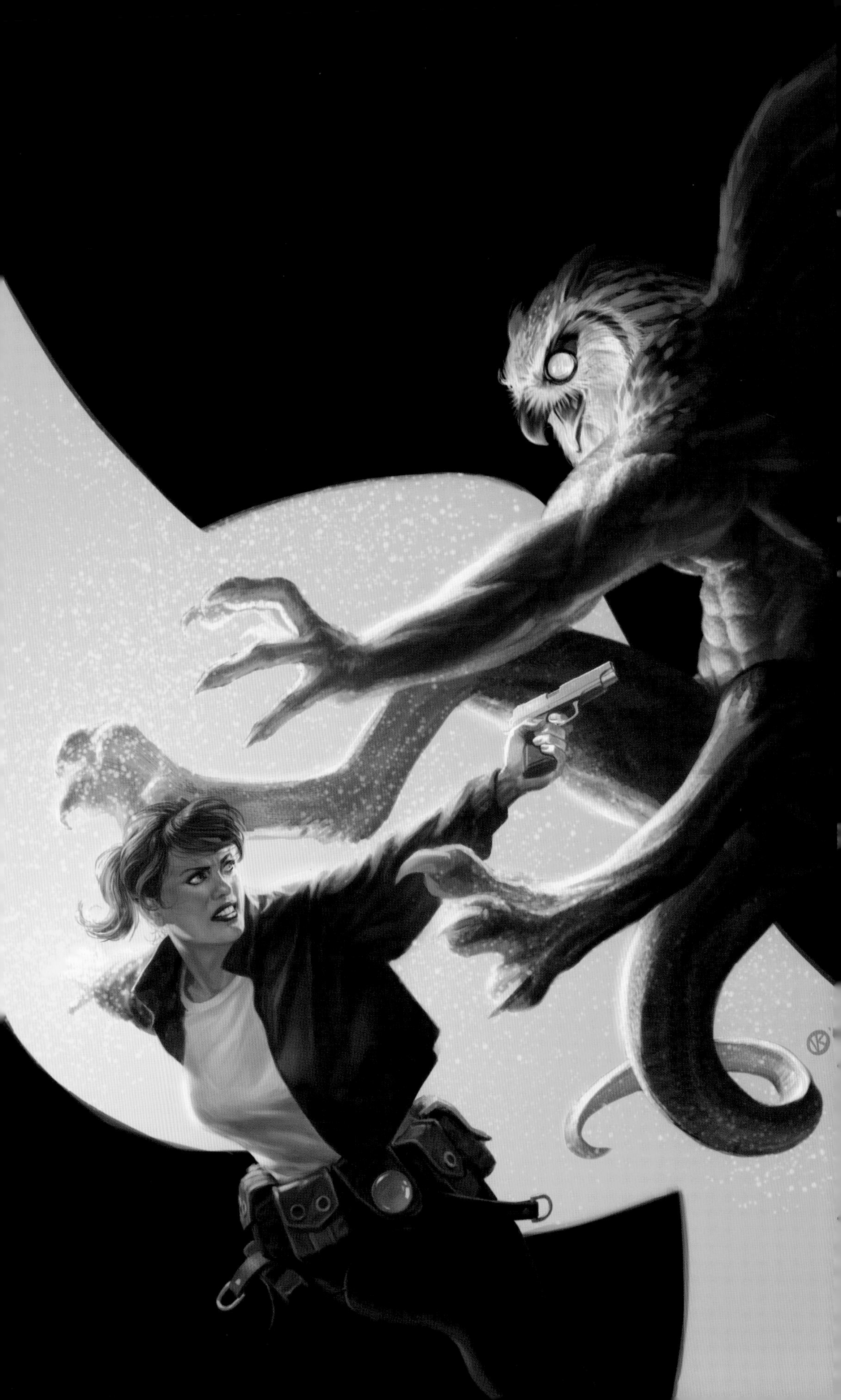

EXORCISM

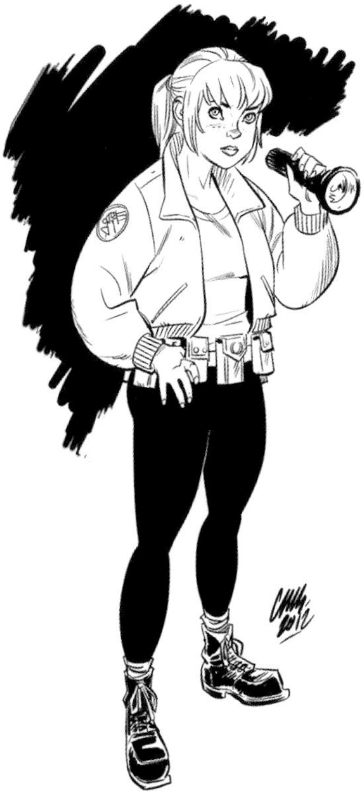

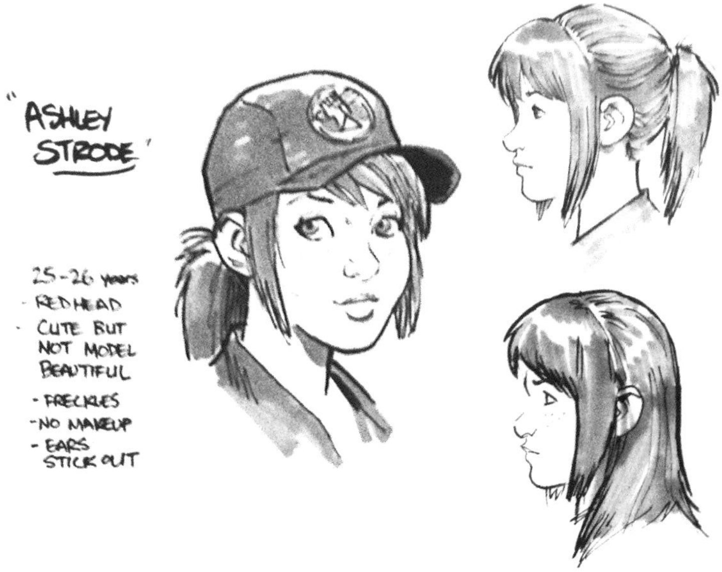
"ASHLEY STRODE"
25-26 years
- REDHEAD
- CUTE BUT NOT MODEL BEAUTIFUL
- FRECKLES
- NO MAKEUP
- EARS STICK OUT

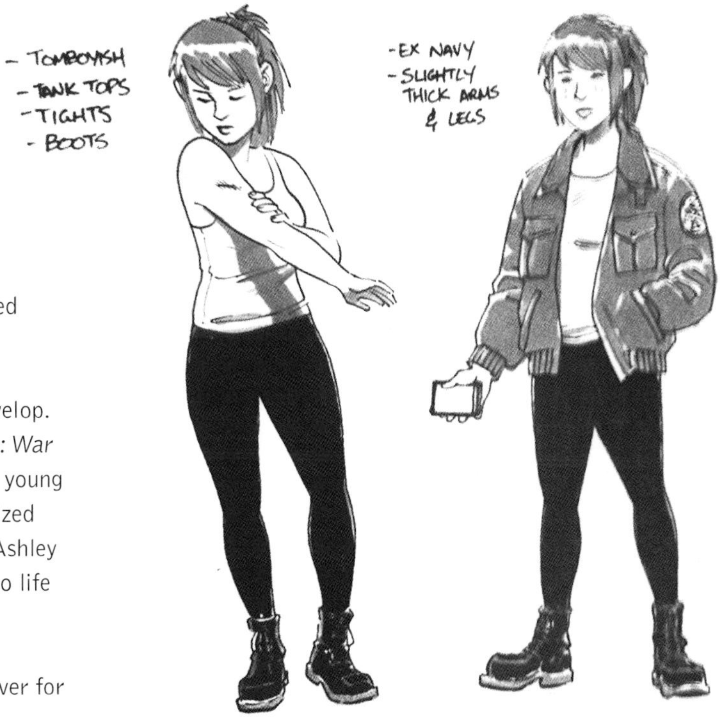
- TOMBOYISH
- TANK TOPS
- TIGHTS
- BOOTS
- EX NAVY
- SLIGHTLY THICK ARMS & LEGS

SCOTT ALLIE: When we asked Cameron Stewart to pitch a *B.P.R.D.* story, he asked for a female character he could develop. We pointed him to a *B.P.R.D.: War on Frogs* one-shot featuring a young agent named Ashley who idolized Liz Sherman. Cameron gave Ashley a last name and brought her to life in the two-part *Exorcism*.

Facing: Victor Kalvachev's cover for *Exorcism* #2.

Cameron worked out the plot for *Exorcism* with Mike and me, explaining what he wanted to do with the character while we fleshed out how that would work with the *Hellboy* mythology. We pointed Cameron to Andras, a demon from *The Lesser Key of Solomon*, who he designed for the book. Cameron created Sybacco, and Mike adjusted the design to fit his vision of Hell and demons.

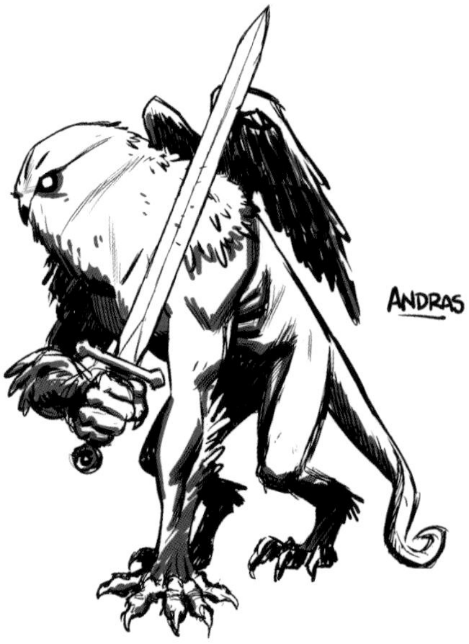
ANDRAS

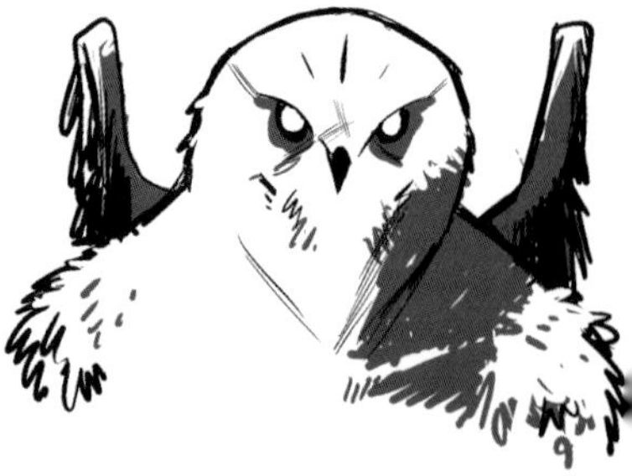

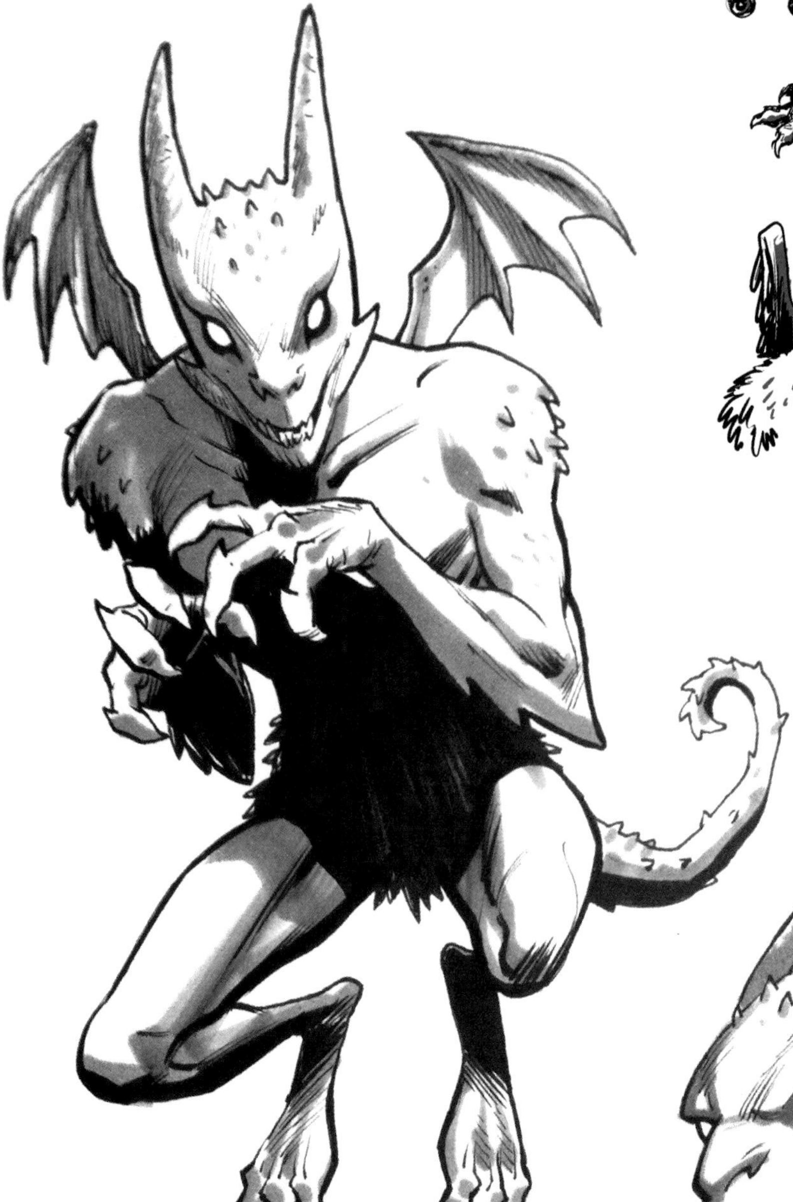

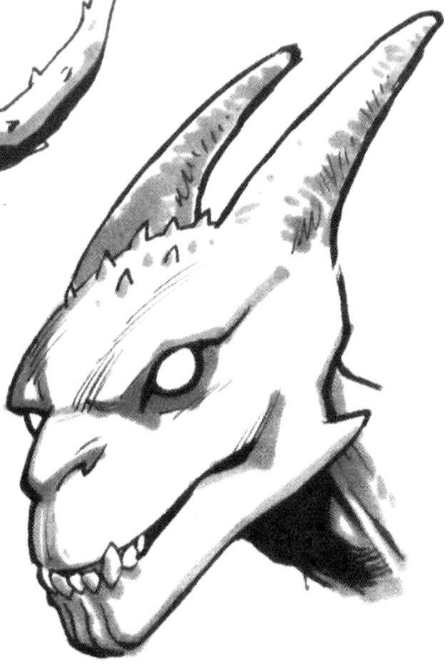
"SYBACCO"

SYBACCO -

I Like this guy!

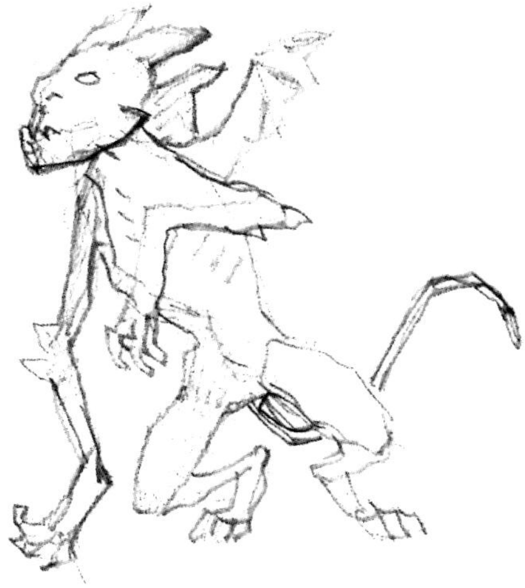

Just a couple suggestions -

(A) Maybe lose his shoulders and, in general, cut down on the anatomy -- to get away from the "man in a suit" look.

(B) Maybe lengthen his hands - so they are a little more like his feet - More like a chimp.

(C)

odd, but maybe creepy, idea: Maybe his neck can occasionally lengthen so his head can swing forward around - like a vulture neck.

Just a thought.

M

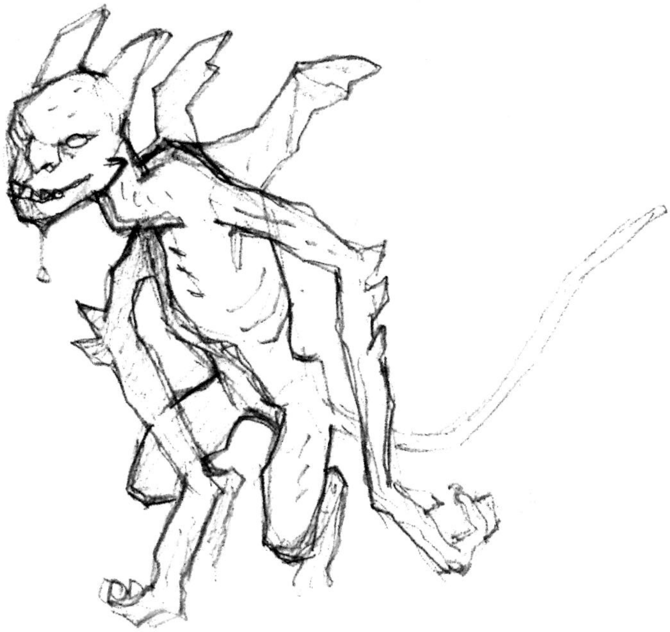

The house in *The Exorcist*, the second part of this book, is based on a house in central Oregon. A number of comics professionals have been out there, but it was Cameron who worked it into a comic first. He plotted the story of Ashley coming into her own as an exorcist in the house, but when his work on *Fight Club 2* went long, he turned the plot over to Chris Roberson and Mike Norton, neither of whom had been to the house (although Mike shares a studio and a series, *Revival*, with repeat visitor Tim Seeley, *below*, holding a 1960s newspaper found in the house). When the property was cleared out in 2014 we realized there was a second structure behind the main house, inspiring the climax of this story.

Facing: Mike Norton whipped up this pinup for the announcement that he'd be drawing the story instead of Cameron.

A couple of pages of his pencils appear following the pinup.

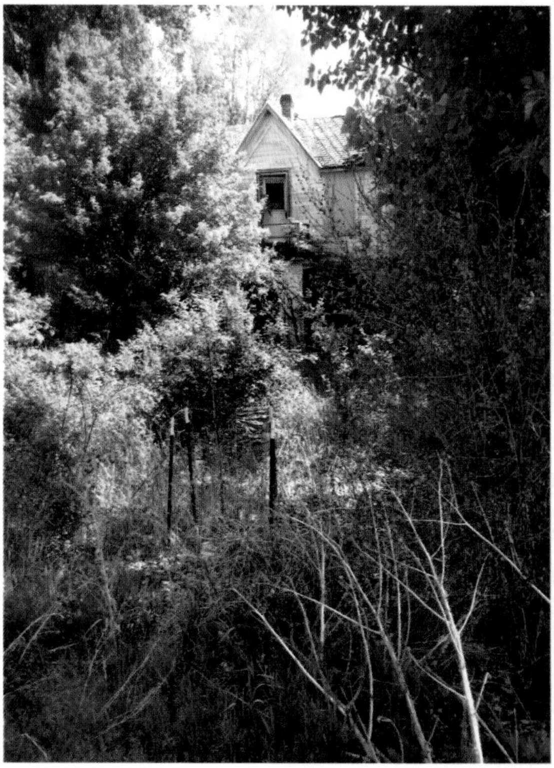

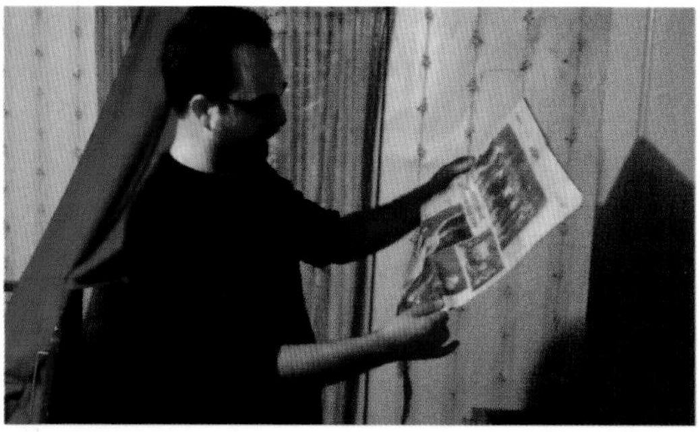

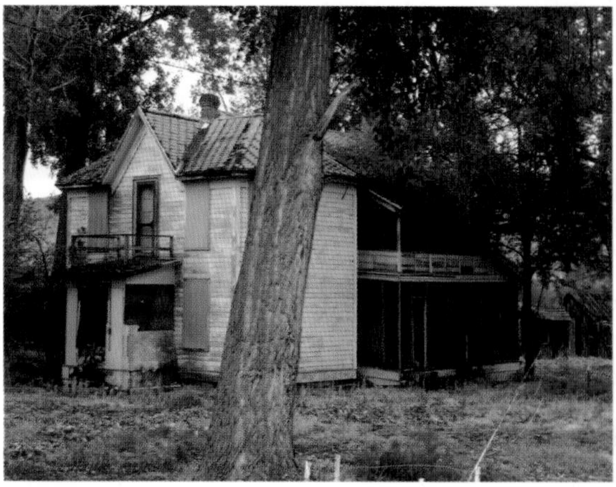

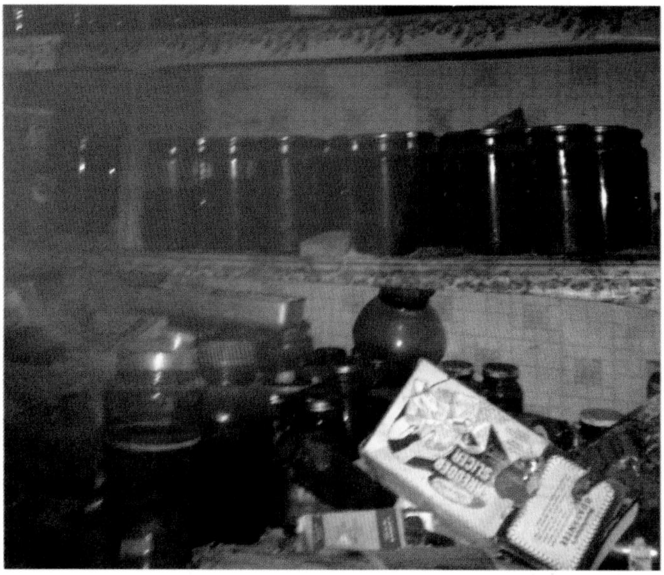

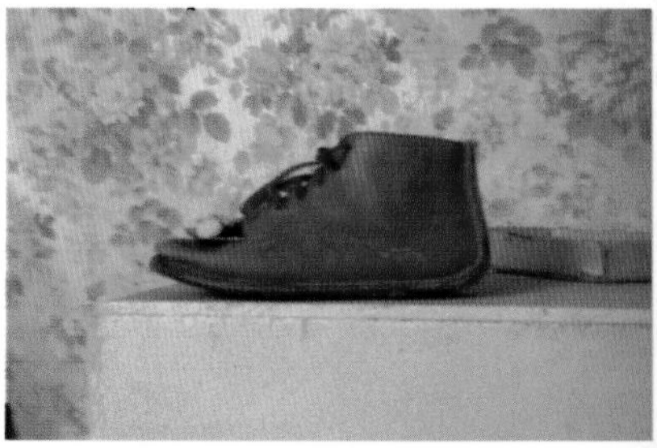

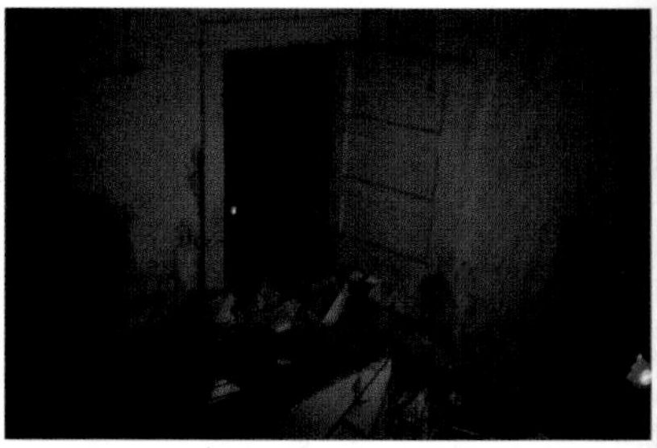

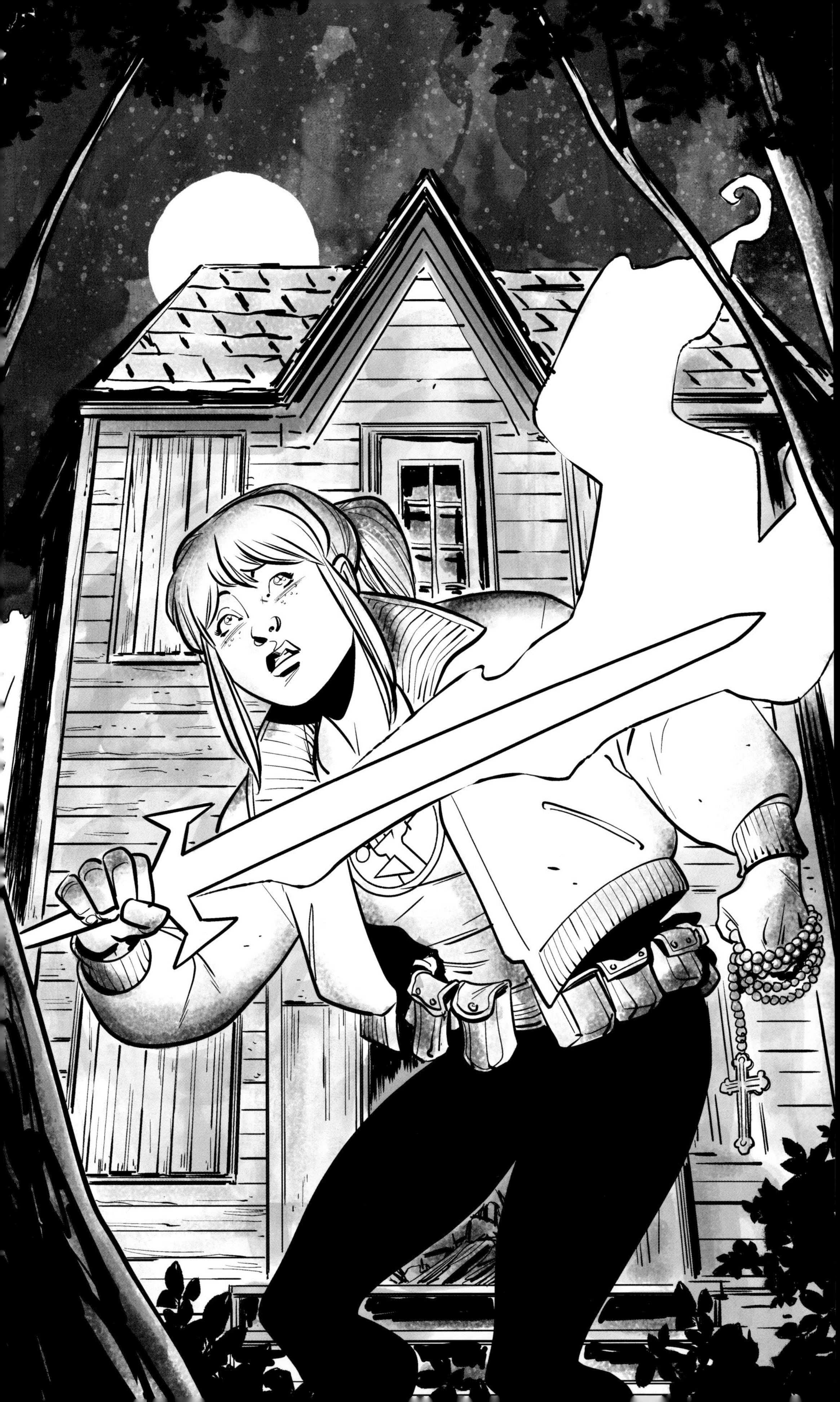

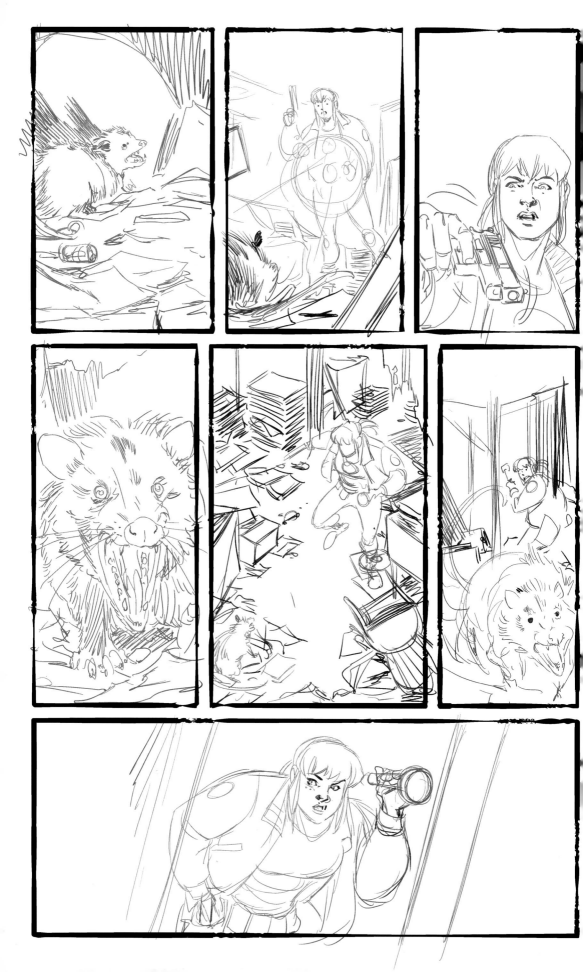

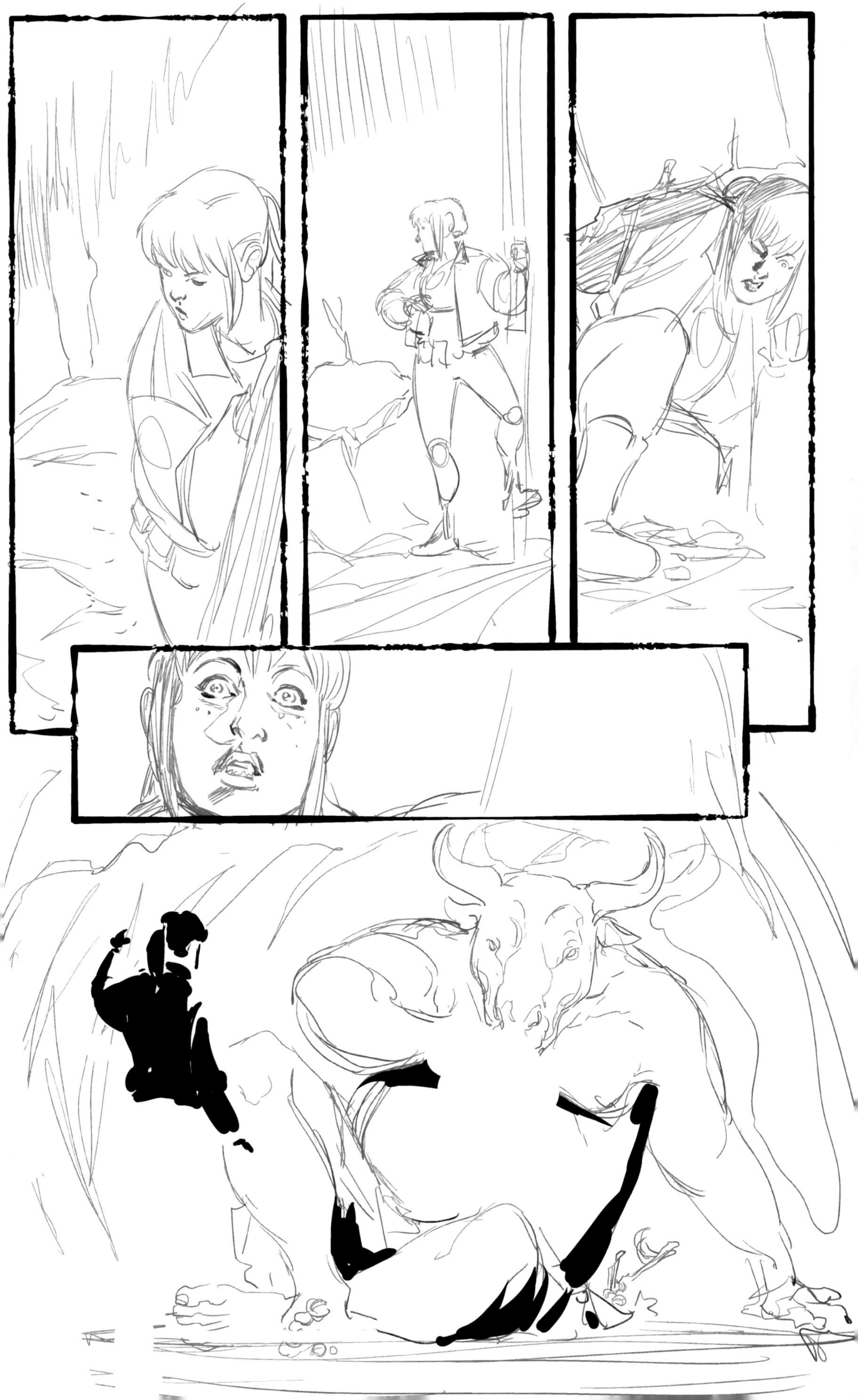

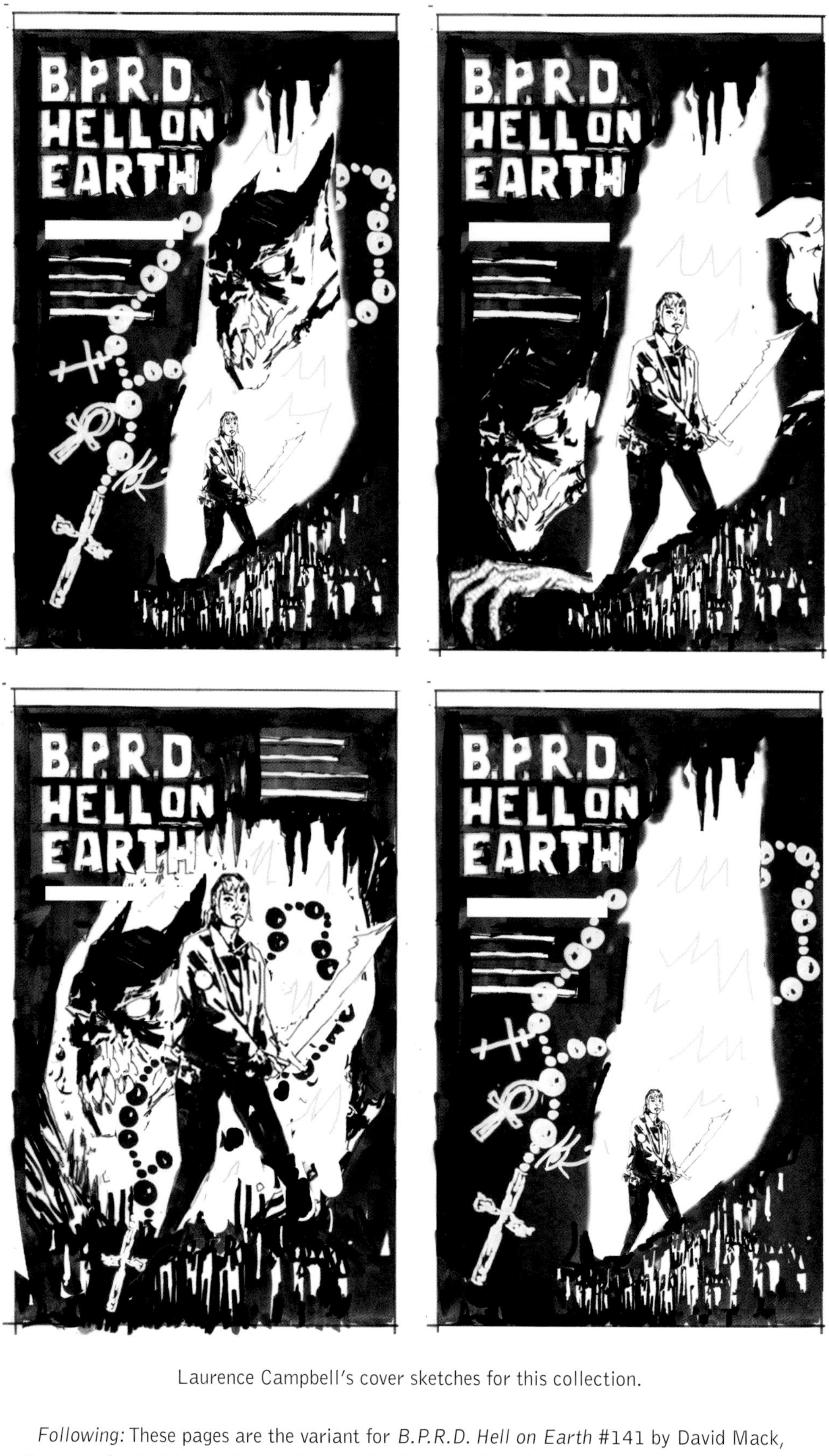
B.P.R.D.
HELL ON
EARTH
B.P.R.D.
HELL ON
EARTH
B.P.R.D.
HELL ON
EARTH
B.P.R.D.
HELL ON
EARTH

Laurence Campbell's cover sketches for this collection.

Following: These pages are the variant for *B.P.R.D. Hell on Earth* #141 by David Mack, the cover for trade paperback volume 10 by Ryan Sook, and the covers for trade paperback volumes 11 and 14 by Laurence Campbell with Dave Stewart.

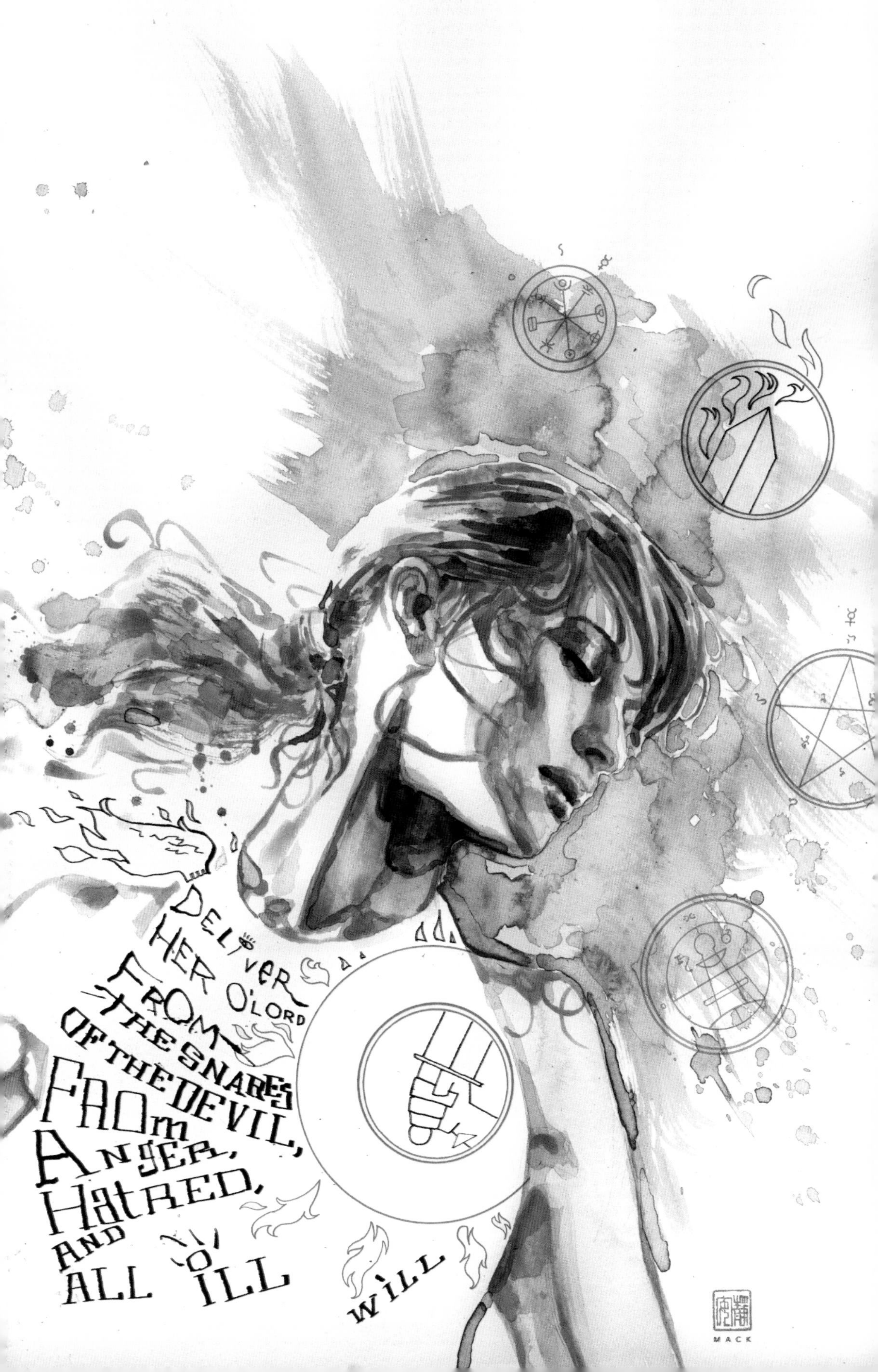

DELIVER
HER O'LORD
FROM
THE SNARES
OF THE DEVIL,
FROM
ANGER,
HATRED,
AND
ALL ILL
WILL
MACK

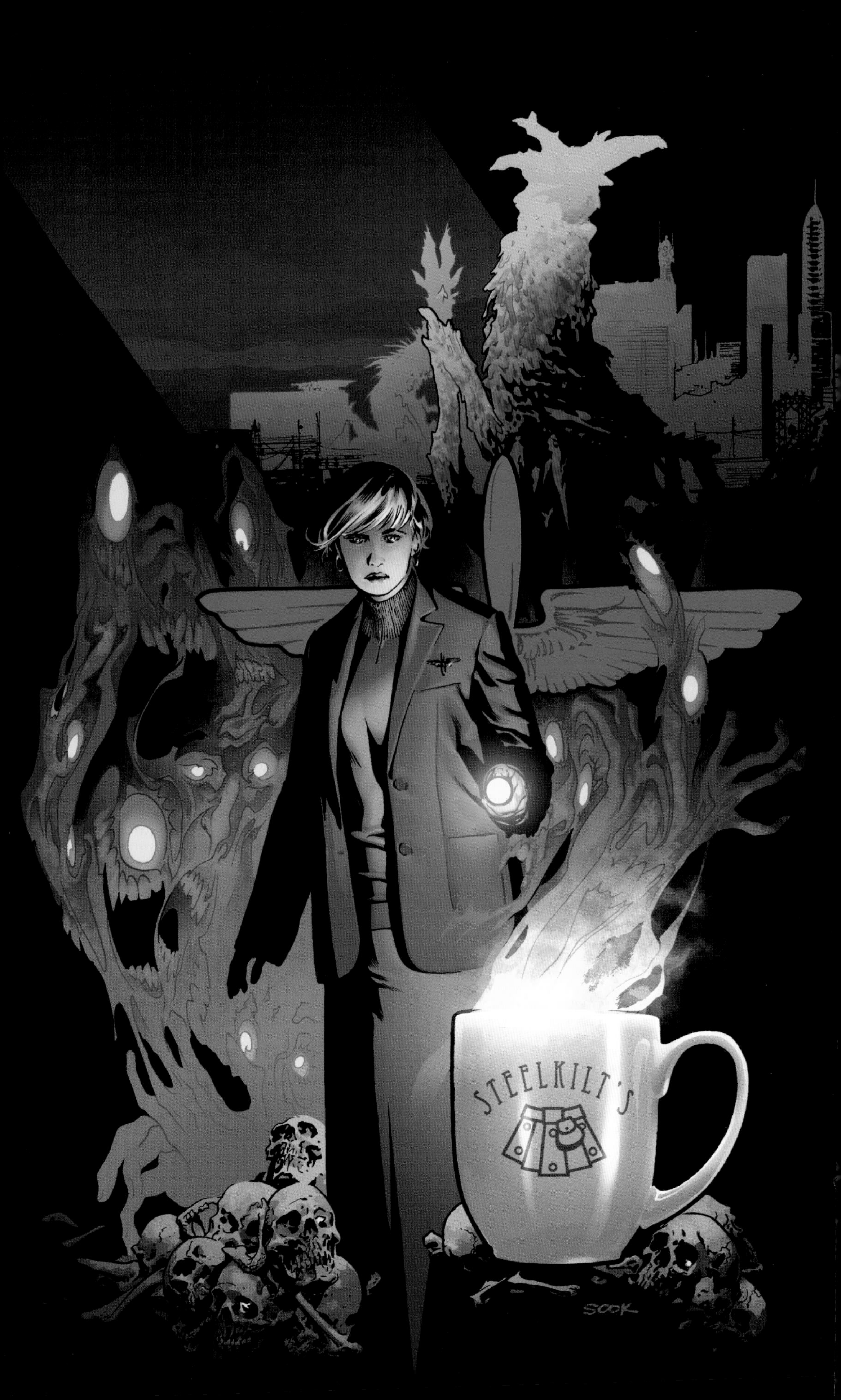
STEELKILT'S
SOOK

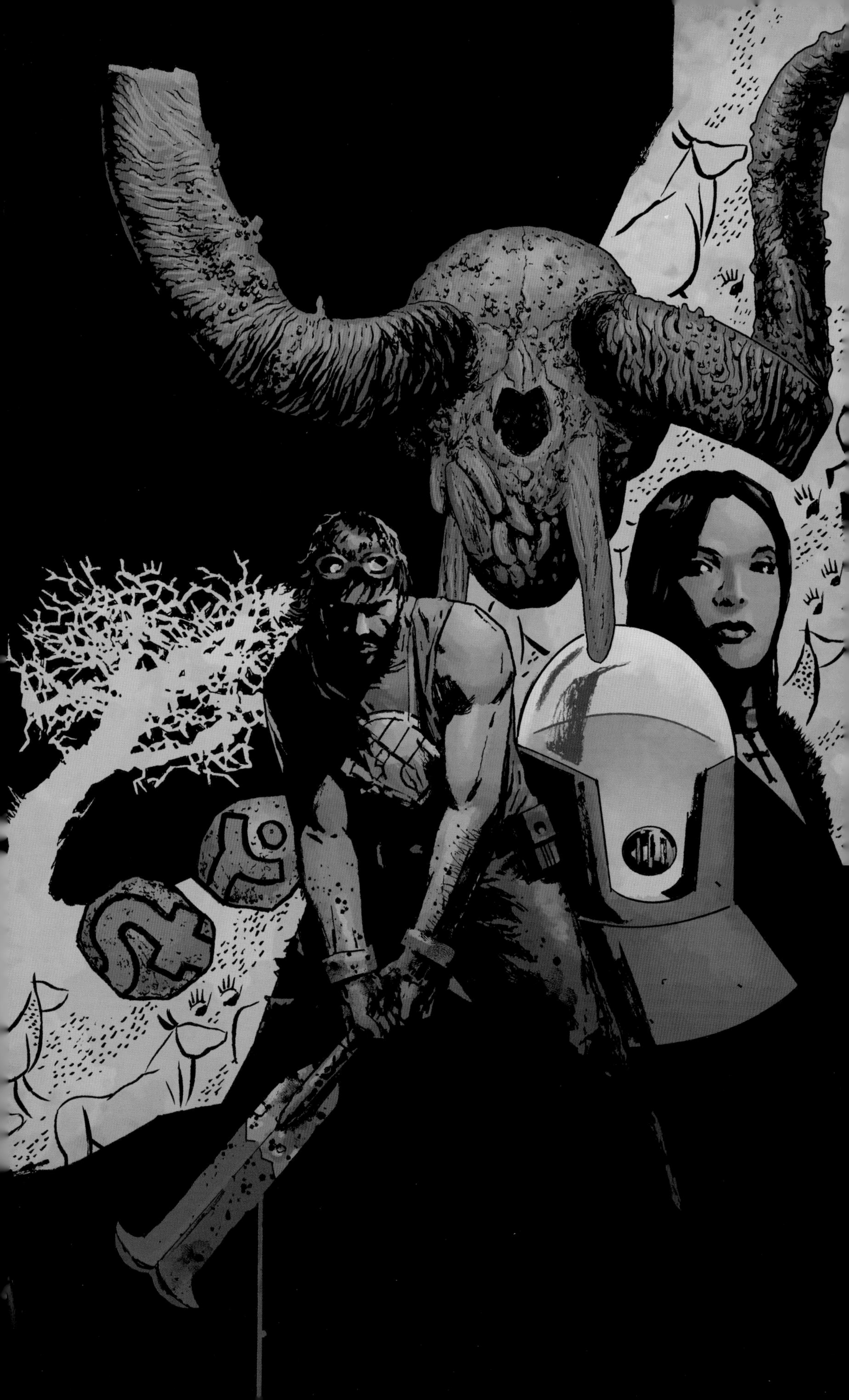

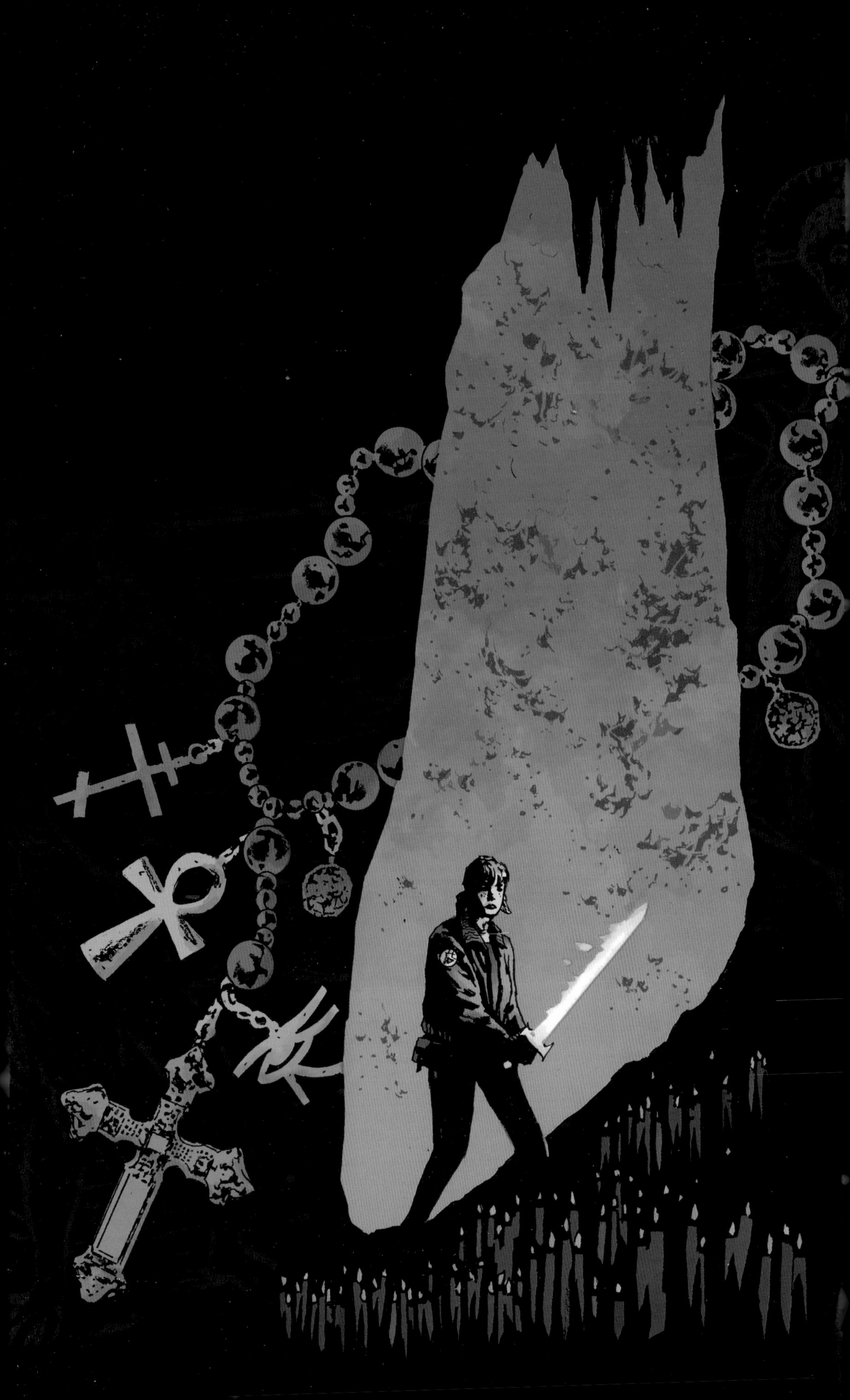